T0367467

LEGACY OF THE WAYFARERS

Rogues

By Charlton Clayes and
C. Malcolm Trowbridge, PhD.

iUniverse, Inc.
Bloomington

Legacy of the Wayfarers
Rogues

iUniverse books may be ordered through booksellers or by contacting:

iUniverse
1663 Liberty Drive
Bloomington, IN 47403
www.iuniverse.com
1-800-Authors (1-800-288-4677)

ISBN: 978-1-4620-7341-2 (sc)
ISBN: 978-1-4620-7342-9 (e)

Printed in the United States of America

iUniverse rev. date: 1/16/2012

CONTENTS

PROLOGUE

▼

...After they had set down the precepts which would govern the newly-created Central Spiral Collective, the Aldebaranians were not content to rest on their laurels or to leave anything to chance. The member worlds were, of course, free to select their own representatives to the Grand Assembly; and those representatives were free to name their own officers and, through many "suggestions" by the host race, to create and staff the commissions by which the Collective would rule. There was one exception, however, to all this "freedom," and that occurred within the Commission for Law Enforcement.

The late War of the Eight Suns had taken such a heavy toll of lives and property that many of the participants were left in a state of near-collapse. Had not the Aldebaranians stepped in and utilized the "power dampener" to immobilize all of the machines of war, that conflict might have continued until all of the worlds in the central spiral were utterly ruined. Yet, the antagonisms which had led to the Great War in the first place still existed afterward, and the Aldebaranians could not "dampen" those. Therefore, the Constabulary was formed to patrol Deep Space and to rid the space lanes of pirates, claim-jumpers, smugglers, free-booters, and anyone else who thought to earn a living by preying on others. More importantly, however, they kept a sharp eye out for remnants of the late War which refused to give up their arms and assimilate into the New Order. It was long and arduous work, and the agency was not always successful in its efforts (and it suffered not a few casualties). Thus, it had to maintain a constant vigil...

...The Fourth Murchison had little idea of what he was getting himself into when he accepted the post of the first Chief Constable. Otherwise, he might have refused the Aldebaranians and lived out his life as a "soldier of fortune"... It is perhaps fortunate for all concerned that he did not refuse. A strong military force required a strong-willed leader, and Murchison was nothing if not strong-willed. Even with the influence of the host race ever in the back of his mind, he almost singlehandedly molded the Constabulary into a well-oiled machine of efficiency and perseverance to suit both its purposes and his (and some have said that those dual purposes were really one and the same)...

Yet, ever mindful that old antagonisms could re-erupt at any time and plunge the central spiral into a fresh round of slaughter and destruction, the Aldebaranians required an additional, independent force — under their strict control — to serve as a counterbalance to the impulses toward lawlessness and warfare. Therefore, they created a body of law-enforcement officers as an adjunct to the CSC Constabulary to execute the laws passed by the Assembly rigorously but equitably. This independent – and unimpeachable – force was the Warden Service...

C. Malcolm Trowbridge, *The History of the Amazonian Federation*, vol. III, ch. 8, University of New Nairobi Press, 181 A.R.

CHAPTER ONE

▼

A NEW MISSION

Space folded in upon itself.

Then unfolded.

From the fold, a ship was spat out.

Constabulary Patrol Vessel #36 – christened *Steadfast* – was once again a part of reality.

* * *

If he lived to be a thousand years old, Warden (L1) Lixu Rodriguez would never get used to the physiological distress produced by the operation of a Murchison Oscillating Matrix Engine. He understood the mechanics of an MOME (barely), because such knowledge had been required at the Warden Academy, and he knew what to expect when a human being was engulfed by the tremendous forces which created a "shortcut" in Deep Space. But theory was one thing, and practical experience was another entirely.

When Captain Halvarson announced the switch from impulse-engine mode to MOME mode, the Warden had gone straight to his quarters and strapped himself into his bunk. Some of the crew – particularly the Captain, who had descended from a long line of seafarers – were able to take the transition standing up. Not Rodriguez! He preferred to be flat on his back when the MOME came on line. Even so, during the transition, he moaned and groaned incessantly. Fortunately, he had not yet taken a meal this day, or he would have lost that meal instantly. As it happened, he experienced only the "dry heaves" (a point which was no consolation at all!).

When the *Steadfast*'s chimes sounded the "all clear," Rodriguez continued to lie in his bunk until a modicum of normal bodily functions returned. Normally, he would have lain there for half a kilosecond.[1] This time, he "splurged" and stretched it out to a *full* kilosecond. All the while, he tried not to think about how sick he was – and failed.

Presently, the vidscreen in his quarters blinked on to reveal the image of the Duty Officer, Jr. Lt. H'rum, an Okath (though she didn't look any different from the parent race, the Ekath). Lt. H'rum was yellow-skinned with some slight black mottling about the neck. Her moon-like face was partially covered by the breathing mask all of her race wore in order to survive in an oxygen atmosphere. Reluctantly, Rodriguez sat up. A wave of dizziness washed over him immediately, and he slumped back, not daring to move a muscle.

"Lt. Rodriguez, bees you ill?" H'rum spoke in Standard.[2] Her voice had a squeaking quality, the result of the helium she was breathing. "Shall I dispatch a medical team?"

"No, no, I'm OK."

"'OK'? Ah, a human expression, meaning you bees well."

The related languages of the Ekath and the Okath were completely devoid of idioms, and both sounded as if a computer had designed them. Other races were forced to speak as precisely and as concisely in their presence in order to avoid misunderstanding.

"Correct. What do you want?"

"I wants nothing."

"Then why are you call – uh, communicating with me?"

---

1   The old units of time and calendar reckoning had been quickly discovered to be inefficient and meaningless for interstellar commerce and travel. Once the CSC had been established, the Grand Assembly tackled the problem head-on and adopted the Burruss metric clock-calendar which had been invented centuries before on Dunia. It expressed time in seconds, kiloseconds, megaseconds, and gigaseconds and utilized a simple shorthand easily understood by anyone regardless of his local system of measurement. The Grand Assembly established the zero-point at the moment the Convention of Aldebaran had been ratified by all of the former adversaries [the present narrative takes place on 1 Gs, 103 Ms, 790 Ks (give or take a few Ks's), Age of the Convention, or 1.103.790 AC – CC.] – CMT.

2   Because the Constabulary had been designed to be a multi-species organization, representative of all the member worlds of the Central Spiral Collective, it was necessary to develop a common language for ease of communication. All Constabulary personnel – from the Chief Constable down to the lowly private – learned to speak this polyglot language fluently before they were assigned to any duty station. As to the *nature* of Standard, it may be construed as a "pidgin" of Aldebaranian, one more example of that enigmatic race's hands-on approach to the Constabulary – CMT.

"I bears a message from the Captain for you. You must report to the Bridge at 04.50."

Rodriguez glanced at his chronometer. It read 04.30.

"I will report. Thank you, Leftenant."

The vidscreen darkened. Rodriguez sighed heavily and wondered what the Old Man wanted this time. He sat up again and noted with satisfaction that the Galaxy had stopped spinning around him. Cautiously, he slid his legs off the bunk and placed his feet on the deck. So far, so good. The real test was ahead. He stood up and experienced only a tiny wave of dizziness. He remained motionless until the wave passed.

As quarters went, his was neither cramped nor luxurious. A bunk, a wardrobe, some shelving for books and personal bric-a-brac, a writing desk with a straight-back chair (both bolted to the deck), a computer terminal with an ergonomic chair (likewise bolted), and an adjoining bathroom – standard issue for junior officers. Enough space so that he didn't bang his elbows when he turned around, but not enough to entertain large numbers of guests. Junior officers were not allowed to entertain in their quarters.

He padded into the bathroom, turned on the faucet of the sink, and splashed some cold water in his face. After toweling off, he looked at the face in the mirror in a manner suggesting he had never seen it before. In point of fact, he went through this same routine each and every time the ship transited through the MOME field. Why he did so was a mystery, even to him. Perhaps he wanted to re-assure himself that the wrenching sensation had not altered his appearance.

Lixu Rodriguez had been told by his grandfather that he could claim descent from Incan royalty on Dunia. And when your grandfather happened to be Dr. Spencer Rodriguez, Dunia's greatest diplomat and the very first Speaker of the Grand Assembly of the Central Spiral Collective, you tended to believe him. As a child, Lixu did believe, because it made him feel important. As he grew older, however, he began to harbor doubts about the royalty part; surely, Grandpapa had been exaggerating a bit in order to impress a very impressionable little boy.

Certainly, he had descended from the long-vanished Incans. The bronzed skin, the narrow face, the high cheekbones – all were typical of the indigenous peoples of that region once known as "Peru" and now part of Administrative District #17 of the United Dunian Government. At 180 centimeters, he might have stood head and shoulders above his ancestors, but no one would have mistaken him for any other ethnic heritage. The one outstanding difference between him and his forebears was his eyes; the epicanthic fold over them was the legacy from his Chinese mother, a pianist of renown on several worlds.

The face which peered back at him seemed to be the same as the one he remembered before the transition, and he was satisfied. He returned to the main area of his quarters, opened the wardrobe, and removed a fresh uniform.

His uniform consisted of a jet-black tunic, matching trousers, boots, and garrison cap, and a gold sash about the waist. A golden comet – the symbol of the Warden Service — adorned the tunic and the cap; and, above the comet, a single red dot denoted his official rank. He slipped on the uniform as easily as stepping into a comfortable pair of slippers and exited his quarters.

The corridor into which he stepped was one of eight which radiated from the center of this level of the ship. Each level had a similar lay-out, with one exception; whereas the corridors on all the other levels intersected to form a large central "plaza," those on this level, the central one, ended at the circular Bridge. The corridors were ten meters wide and five high, sufficient to accommodate the amount and type of traffic normally seen aboard a patrol vessel. The lighting was subdued so as not to discomfit light-sensitive races. On the bulkheads were directional arrows with captions in Standard, color-coded according to the ship's functions. The color on this level was red, designating the Command level.

Because of his role on board the *Steadfast*, Warden Rodriguez's quarters were relatively close to the Bridge. Had they been further away, he might have summoned up one of the ubiquitous electric, balloon-tired shuttle-cars which transported the crew from one point to another on the city-sized ship. Instead, he chose to walk and stretch his legs. The Bridge was only fifty meters away, and the exercise would do him good after his recent experience. He silently recited the mantra for tranquility that the Aldebaranians had taught him at the Academy and set off at a brisk but measured pace.

The *Steadfast* was a beehive of activity just now. It usually was after coming out of an MOME field. And the greater the transition period, the more hectic the activity. As a patrol vessel, the ship had to be ready for any eventuality at a moment's notice. Even thirty-five years since the formation of the Central Spiral Collective and the Constabulary, there were plenty of troublemakers in Deep Space to make life interesting for the unwary. In the early days, an unwary crew was likely to be blasted out of existence by a well-placed missile; the Constabulary had had its losses in this fashion by assuming that random re-appearances in "normal" space would protect its ships from attack. It had not taken into account the well-established fact that what one sentient being could make, another could un-make.

Most of the traffic here was on its way from the upper levels – mostly crew's quarters, plus commissary, infirmary, and recreational areas – to the lower levels where the support functions were located – armory, maintenance/repair shops, computer mainframe, and the like. Rodriguez seemed to be the only one walking. The shuttle-cars whizzed by him in a steady stream. As they passed by, he nodded curtly to their occupants, and the occupants returned the nod; if one of the occupants happened to be a senior officer, he touched his forehead in a perfunctory salute, and the senior officer did likewise.

All regarded him warily, however, because of his particular function on board ship. He was quite aware of this attitude toward him by the rest of the crew; but, since there was little he could do to alter their perceptions, he had learned to take them in stride. And, if truth be told, he preferred those perceptions as they often helped him in the performance of his duties.

The standard uniform of the Constabulary, though similar to his, was cobalt blue in color. His was the only black uniform on the *Steadfast*. Lixu Rodriguez held a unique position within the organization; he was a Warden who alone had the power of arrest and was assigned to a patrol vessel to exercise that power whenever the need arose. In point of fact, his rank as "lieutenant" was purely a fiction. Wardens had no rank *per se*, and the assignment of one to any of them was for payroll purposes.

When the enigmatic Aldebaranians created the Constabulary, they had in mind two distinct divisions: the Patrol and the Wardens. The Patrol in their ships traveled Deep Space and enforced the laws of the CSC, much like the police force anywhere in the Universe. The Wardens investigated criminal acts and supervised Monitoring Teams. The Aldebaranians had insisted that only Wardens should have the power of arrest in order to deter the possibility of misuse of that power by lesser members of the Constabulary; and they had also insisted that they should train the Wardens-to-be in a specially designed Academy in order to instill in the cadets the values they wished to impart to all the occupants of the central spiral.

It was this close connection to the host race which placed most sentient beings in awe – and not a little fear – of the Warden class. The Aldebaranians were as reclusive as they were powerful, and few had any extensive dealings with them; the "Community," as they preferred to call themselves, usually acted through intermediaries, such as the Chief Constable and the Speaker of the Grand Assembly – and the Wardens. Those selected to Wardenship were sworn to secrecy concerning the identities of their trainers and the nature of the training itself, a fact which contributed to the attitude towards them by the general populace.

Part of the awe – and fear – of Wardens stemmed from the persistent rumor that the black-clad officers could read minds and that, if one lied to them, they could detect the lie instantly and take drastic steps to punish the liars. Whether or not Wardens could read minds was moot since no one outside their organization was privy to the criteria for selection to their Academy. Nevertheless, the rumor was a useful tool as it fostered complete candor and/or co-operation on the part of those under interrogation. As a consequence, Wardens had few acquaintances outside their group. Mostly, they traveled alone and spoke to others only when necessary.

As he strolled down the corridor, Rodriguez was assured that his stroll would be undisturbed by anyone. He had only his own thoughts for company.

Presently, he came to the end of the corridor and crossed an invisible boundary which separated it from the circular space of the Bridge. Beyond, twenty meters in diameter, lay the heart and mind of the *Steadfast*. On a patrol vessel, the Bridge did not in any fashion resemble the bridge of an ordinary MOME-powered ship. Here, all bridge functions were set around a railing which circled a large empty space; here, all of the ship's senior crew monitored the workings of this behemoth and remained in constant communication with the support crew below who actually pushed the buttons and flicked the switches. Each area was color-coded according to its purpose. Rodriguez sauntered toward Gold Zone.

Gold Zone – "Ship's Command" – consisted of two monitors and two chairs. Currently, both chairs were occupied, and both officers were studying their monitors intently. The Captain and his Executive Officer were conducting an evaluation of the *Steadfast*'s status, required after each emergence from an MOME field. The energies generated to produce the field were enormous and capable of creating havoc at any point of production. An overload could crush the ship like an eggshell, and it behooved the Captain to learn immediately if his vessel was still running smoothly.

The Warden gazed blandly at the monitors as a flood of reports from all stations succeeded one another in rapid fashion. The data were meaningless to him, and he wouldn't have traded places with the man sitting before him for all the platinum in the Galaxy. Abruptly, the monitors went dark, and the two senior officers relaxed and leaned back in their chairs, apparently satisfied that they still had an operational ship. Rodriguez coughed politely. The Captain and the XO swiveled about to peer at him haughtily.

Captain Olaf Halvarson was a huge man, standing just under two meters and weighing 120 kilograms. His face was craggy and angular; his eyes – a deep blue – peered out from under thick brow ridges and bushy eyebrows. His hair was sandy and close-cropped. In the manner of his Nordic ancestors, he wore a long, thick beard, also sandy but with streaks of gray. Halvarson was a New Swiss,[3] and he was literally born and bred to be a Ship's Captain in the Constabulary. The Aldebaranians had recognized at once the sort of

---

3   New Switzerland [*Tau Ceti 2 on Dunian star charts – CC*] is the capital world of the Central Spiral Collective, and Constabulary Headquarters is located just outside its chief city, New Geneva – CMT.

humans who colonized New Switzerland – politically neutral, highly skilled in technical and scientific matters, and industrious to a fault – and they had endeavored to form the Constabulary around such a people. While the New Swiss did not dominate the Collective, their influence was considerable. And, thanks to the host race's insistence, the position of Ship's Captain was reserved exclusively to them. An inhabitant of another world might rise to the exalted rank of Executive Officer, but no further; that position was the end of the promotion list for any non-New Swiss.

The Captain's uniform contrasted sharply from that of Rodriguez: a cobalt-blue tunic with yellow epaulets and a yellow sunburst over the left breast, matching trousers with a yellow stripe down each leg, black boots, a black belt with platinum buckle, and a blue barracks cap with a yellow starburst. The epaulets sported a single platinum starburst, a Captain's rank. Halvarson wore his uniform with the confidence that he had won the right to wear it.

He smiled broadly but mirthlessly at the Warden.

"Ah, Leftenant," he spoke in a deep, rumbling baritone which exuded the power of his rank, "how good of you to be so prompt."

Rodriguez smiled back, not so broadly but equally as mirthlessly.

"You sent for me, Captain?"

"Yes, there's an…incoming message for you."

He swiveled again and gestured at the bulkhead to his right and the niche which was imbedded there. The niche contained a clear glass bowl filled with salt water; inside the bowl was a lumpy, grayish mass the size of a human brain, floating serenely. A rapidly pulsating, pinkish glow surrounded it. Rodriguez grimaced. This was the one drawback to being a Warden in his humble opinion, but it was a necessary evil.

"How long has it been in this state?"

"Since before we warped out. Naturally, we had no time to inform you then."

"Naturally. It looks to be an urgent message, judging from the frequency of the pulsations."

"You would know best," the Captain acknowledged dryly.

The Warden stepped over to the niche, his face a mask of grim determination. He opened an adjacent panel, removed a set of electroencephalographic sensors and a black box the size of a cigarette pack, and untangled the EEG cables. He pressed the sensors against various points on his skull and jacked the cables into the box. He drew a deep breath and released it slowly, then plunged his hand into the bowl of water and lightly touched the gray lump.

Instantly, his body stiffened as a sensation akin to an electric shock coursed through his entire nervous system, and the color drained from his face. Captain Halvarson had seen this scenario many times before, but he still winced at the sight. Beside him, the XO, Commander Tomiko Krishnamurthy, a diminutive, graying Romulan, had not; she had recently been promoted to her present position, and this was her first major encounter with a Warden. She watched in horror as Rodriguez was gripped by a force she would never know or understand.

* * *

— *Greetings, fellow sentient. We are the* aaxyboxr. *How may we assist?*

— *Greetings to the* aaxyboxr. *I am sentient Rodriguez. Do you have a message for me?*

— *Searching. [Pause] Yes, we have one lengthy message. Reading. "To Warden (L1) Rodriguez aboard the Patrol Vessel* Steadfast *from Lt. Commander Ruba at Constabulary Headquarters. New orders for the* Steadfast, *as follows. You are hereby ordered to locate, arrest, and detain a cell of the terrorist organization known as the "Reman Army of Liberation," whose last whereabouts was Planetoid 48 in your sector. A member of this cell is one Dr. Mubutu Weyerhauser, wanted for questioning on charges of assassination, attempted assassination, sabotage, and possession of contraband weapons. You will first rendezvous with Patrol Vessel* Faithful – *present co-ordinates: -2.805, 74.335, 0.4995 (Galactic) – in order to receive a special operative who can verify the identity of Dr. Weyerhauser." End of message.*

— *Thank you. I will send the standard acknowledgement to Lt. Commander Ruba.*

— *It is done.*

— *The peace of Kum'halla be with the* aaxyboxr.

— *The peace of Kum'halla be with sentient Rodriguez.*

* * *

The sensation which had gripped Rodriguez ceased as abruptly as it had begun, and he was able to pull his hand away from the gray lump. He relaxed visibly and stood still while the color returned to his face. Presently, he removed the EEG sensors from his skull and unjacked them from the black box. He took a deep breath, released it slowly, and faced Captain Halvarson.

"Here are you new orders, Captain," he stated flatly and handed over the black box.

"I can't recall how many times I've seen this...procedure, but it still amazes me how this gadget can record brain waves, then transmit them into words and images on a computer screen."

"Our brain waves are no different than ordinary radio signals. They carry the same types of data. This simple device is merely the medium by which the data can be read."

"'Simple'? Huh! Nothing the Aldebaranians have ever come up with can be classified as 'simple.' They're at least a thousand years ahead of us."

"The Community is an old and wise race, and they have many such 'gadgets' at their command. Even I don't understand them all." He smiled mirthlessly again. "I'll return to my quarters now, Captain."

He pivoted and strode away. Halvarson and Krishnamurthy stared at his retreating figure with feelings of resentment by one and awe by the other.

"Just between me and you, Commander, I've never met a Warden yet who didn't come off as an arrogant bastard. Lt. Rodriguez is a pup compared to you and me, but he talks and acts like he's as old as the hills."

"Aye, sir," the Romulan murmured, "I agree completely. But, you have to admit that the Wardens are usually right."

"That's what makes them so damned arrogant. Well, let's take a look at our new orders."

He returned to his station, inserted the black box into a special slot on his console, and pressed the gray button next to the slot. A kaleidoscope of colored shapes filled the monitor, then coalesced into a bright white. Words began to form on the screen, the same words which had been relayed into the brain of Warden Rodriguez. In addition, the image of a face appeared beneath the words, a representation of the fugitive, Dr. Mubutu Weyerhauser. The representation was not a very good one; the face looked lifeless as if the wearer had been caught in a bad moment.

"Dr. Weyerhauser doesn't look like your average terrorist, does he?" the XO remarked. "But, then, what Reemie does? Those ground-grabbers are so unfashy."

"Do I detect a bit of bigotry, Tomiko?"

"Sorry, sir. Cultural habits and all that. I'll mome back to the green zone."

"And just where did you pick up spacer's slang?"

Krishnamurthy smiled wickedly.

"You don't want to know."

"Hmmm. Well, we're to proceed to Planetoid 48 to find the good doctor. Planetoid 48. I consider myself well-traveled, but I'm not familiar with that world."

He pressed the red button in a row of multi-colored buttons which connected him to all of the support Zones. The image of a brown-skinned human appeared on his vidscreen.

"Sensors. Lt. Commander Tuva 'ere, sir."

"Bring up the Display, Commander."

"Aye, sir."

The lighting on the Bridge dimmed. Simultaneously, a pinpoint of white light appeared in the exact center of the empty space within the railing. Other, multi-colored lights began to surround it, like the layers of an onion, until the entire space was filled with a holographic array.

It was no ordinary hologram. It was, in essence, a planetarium generated by the ship's computer and projected onto the Bridge through hundreds of tiny lenses imbedded in the surrounding bulkheads. Each point of light represented a body in space – stars, planets, moons, asteroids, comets, etc. – in relation to the *Steadfast*, represented by the white point in the center of the display. The ship's sensors gathered data second by second and continually updated the positions as the patrol vessel traveled through Deep Space. The images were assigned the colors they presented to the naked eye – the stars by their spectral type, the rest by their reflective properties – but no effort was made to assign relative masses. The present array located all spatial objects within a ten-light-year radius, but it could be expanded to a maximum of one hundred light-years. With fine tuning, the computer could focus on a particular region and magnify it for closer inspection. As a map of the Cosmos, the Display was unparalleled and formed the foundation of the ship's astrogation system.

Currently, the *Steadfast* was located at 2.810, 74.335, 0.4995 (Galactic), patrolling Deep Space some twenty light-hours from CSC member-world S'amhi'i. The central authority of that world had complained that pirates were operating in its star system and that several of its freighters had been reported missing. The *Steadfast* had been the nearest patrol vessel and so had been dispatched to investigate. The new orders reflected a newer, more urgent "clear-and-present danger" to the peace of the central spiral, one which superceded any pirate activity and required immediate action.

Captain Halvarson directed Commander Krishnamurthy to enter the co-ordinates of Planetoid 48 into the Display, and she did so with alacrity. In the array, a small green light at the perimeter at +15.65 degrees latitude, -75.80 degrees longitude (relative to the ship) blinked into existence, pulsating rapidly. The XO made some adjustments on her console, and the blinking light took center stage in the Display. On her vidscreen, the computer supplied her with all the known data about this world – and it was sketchy at best.

"A rogue world," she reported. "About 20,000 years ago, it was pulled out of its orbit around some unknown star by unknown means and has been wandering ever since. Whatever atmosphere it may have had has long since been dissipated. It may have been inhabited, but certainly it isn't now. CSC has not gotten around to sending an exploration team to gather more information."

"What in the world would any terrorists want with it? It doesn't appear to have any strategic value, and it wouldn't make a very good hide-out."

"I suppose we'll find out when we get there."

"Right."

Halvarson turned back to his vidscreen and pressed the blue button in the Zone section. The image of the astrogator-on-duty, a ruddy-faced Dunian, appeared. He was speaking to a junior officer when his vidscreen signaled for his attention.

"Ah, Astrogation . Sr. Lt. Colon here, sir."

"Lay in a course to the *Faithful*, if you please, Mr. Colon."

"Aye, aye, sir!"

The Captain then called up the Helmsman (Silver Zone). Lt. Commander Felicia von Lichtenburg, another New Swiss, smiled briefly, then assumed a neutral expression.

"Take us to the *Faithful*, Commander."

"Aye, aye, sir!" she cooed and engaged the *Steadfast*'s impulse engines.

"Now, we'll see what's what, Tomiko."

*   *   *

Warden Rodriguez had not told the Captain the complete truth, because the complete truth had not, in his estimation, been necessary. He did plan to return to his quarters to meditate, but first he was going to make a side trip to the Galley. Contact with the *aaxyboxr* was always a grueling experience. In the first place, it placed an enormous strain on the entire body – nerves, muscles, skeleton, internal organs – and the strain continued for up to a kilosecond after contact had ended; and, in the second place, it drained the contactee of a considerable amount of energy and left him/her ravenously hungry.

He wished there were a more user-friendly method of communication, but the physics of Deep Space precluded that possibility. Ordinary radio was effective only for short distances, a few light-hours at most; for astronomical distances, it was impractical. Needlessly to say, the lack of near-instantaneous communication was the greatest stumbling block in the central spiral. The Murchison Oscillating Matrix Engine had solved the problem of *traveling* over great distances, but no one had yet found the means of *talking* over great distances.

Not until the Aldebaranians came on the scene to put a halt to the steadily debilitating War of the Eight Suns.

The Aldebaranians introduced many new concepts and machines to the "lesser" races of the central spiral, some of which were welcomed by one and all, some of which were welcomed by only a few, and some of which were welcomed not at all by anyone. But the host race offered only a "package deal"; it was either that or a return to the bad old days. The "lesser" races yielded to the logic (painful though it might be) and accepted the package. Peace and prosperity reigned in the central spiral once more and would continue to do so until someone discovered a means to counteract the Community's power dampener.

One of the pieces of the package was offered only on a limited basis. This was the fantastic facility for instantaneous communication by the *aaxyboxr*. Where this species called home, the Aldebaranians had declined to say; they intended to maintain a monopoly on the use of these creatures. Long ago, they had discovered that the *aaxyboxr* possessed a hive-mind; no matter where in the Universe an individual unit might be, it was always in contact with every other individual of its species. How this was accomplished, the Aldebaranians had also declined to say; they saw the uses – and misuses – for the creatures, and they were determined to control absolutely those uses. Subsequently, when they had instituted the Constabulary, they placed one *aaxyboxr* on each patrol vessel, and only the Warden assigned to each ship was allowed to make contact with the creatures.

It may be fairly said that few sentient beings cared to come into contact with the *aaxyboxr* once the ramifications of contact were known. For, not only was there the physiological stress present, but also psychological stress against which anyone not trained to be a Warden had no defense. The creatures had the uncanny ability to read minds as if they were open books and therefore to understand the motives for contact. Those who bore no malice or selfish intent could bear such scrutiny, and the Aldebaranians screened their candidates for Wardenship very carefully for signs of an ability to pass this muster. Consequently, the rumor spread that the Wardens could also read minds; and, for that alleged reason, were they held in awe and fear.

At the moment, however, Warden (L1) Lixu Rodriguez did not care what others might think of him. Rather, he cared about satisfying the hunger pangs which were gripping him.

The ship's Galley – along with the other common areas – were located, by no means co-incidentally, on the level above that of the Bridge and also centrally located. When the Warden entered, he discovered that it was sparsely populated. The technical crew for the current shift was at its duty stations, and off-duty personnel were likely in their quarters or in one of several recreational areas. The combat crews were undoubtedly on alert for any signs of trouble after the *Steadfast* had emerged from the MOME field.

At his entrance into the Galley, he experienced the typical reaction to his kind from the handful of individuals already seated. They glanced up to eyeball the new arrival, recognized who (and what) he was, and quickly averted their eyes. Rodriguez ignored them all. He went through the serving line with two trays and filled both with everything which was edible by humans. He then retreated to the farthest corner and proceeded to wolf down the contents of both trays non-stop. Somewhat satisfied, he departed the Galley as deliberately as he had entered, aware that the stares followed him every step of the way.

He still felt no desire to return to his quarters just yet, and he wanted to walk off his huge meal. He proceeded to the ramp which would take him level by level to the uppermost one where the Observation Deck was situated. The jaunt was not without incident, however. Halfway through the upper levels, he narrowly avoided colliding with a group of Capellans who were on a dead run and not stopping for anyone or anything. The one in the rear was barking at the rest relentlessly in Alkono. Rodriguez smiled at the sight in spite of himself. Sergeant Utumi seemed to be in an especially good mood this day; ordinarily, he would have had his squad running *twice* as fast.

That a group of Alkon warriors was serving on board a Constabulary patrol vessel might have been cause for alarm amongst the uninformed. Capella had been a member of the Alliance for Free Space during the War of the Eight Suns, and it had supplied the only resource it possessed – a horde of mercenaries – as its part of the war effort. Not all of Capella had been in favor of war, however; some few had been of a visionary bent, and they had wished to broaden their – and their world's – horizons in a more peaceful manner. After the Aldebaranians terminated the War and formed the Collective, these few leaped at the opportunity for wider contact with other races. Along with the far-seeing segments of other alien worlds, they took positions in the CSC bureaucracy and added their expertise to the whole. Subsequently, they were able to persuade the Constabulary to incorporate Alkon warriors into ship's crews. Naturally, there was a great deal of resistance at first, given the reputation – real or imagined – Alkon warriors had acquired in the late War. But, because the Aldebaranians had insisted upon representation of all races in all aspects of the Collective, a compromise was agreed to; a small complement of warriors would serve on each ship, acting as scouts (at which they excelled) and training separately from other troops. In time, it was hoped, old antagonisms would be buried and the Capellans could be fully integrated into the combat/rescue missions.

As he watched the Capellans fade into the distance, Rodriguez marveled (again) at what the Community had been able to accomplish in so short a time. Members of the former Alliance for Free Space working along side members of the Amazonian Federation instead of slaughtering each other out of hand was a minor miracle in itself. A central government with a representative legislature where individual member worlds could iron out their differences peaceably had been a masterpiece of social engineering; the central spiral was now so much a bustle of commercial ventures, cultural exchanges, and scientific and technological development that no one could imagine an end to it all. True, there were pockets of resistance and disorder – the reason why he and his kind were necessary – but, with the assistance of the Community, the CSC would achieve perfection in due time.

And, had not the Community done what it had done in the first place, his own life would have taken a substantially different course. Growing up under the tutelage of his famous grandfather (and, to a lesser degree, his diplomat father), young Lixu Rodriguez had been expected to pursue a diplomatic career himself. He had been sent to the right schools to study political science, the art and history of diplomacy, and interstellar relations, and he had been placed upon graduation in the right bureaucracy where he would be noticed by the right people. Young Lixu had taken it all in stride and never questioned his fate. To him, it seemed like the grandest adventure of all.

Fate had other plans for him, however, in the person of the Aldebaranians. The host race was in the habit of reviewing the scholastic records of all sentient beings who had successfully navigated the academic shoals and undercurrents, and they had found a rare anomaly – in other races, that is, but common in their own. They discovered that some brains were wired (to use a computer term) differently from those of the general population; this difference would allow the possessors to interact with the *aaxyboxr* without suffering undue stress.

Young Lixu Rodriguez was one of that rare breed who applied thought processes not normally used by his contemporaries to solving difficult problems. He was then contacted by the Aldebaranians and invited to participate in a special examination – for which they provided an innocuous rationale – to determine his precise mental abilities. Flattered to the core that he had attracted the attention of this advanced race, he quickly and eagerly submitted himself to their care. The written and oral parts of the examination were strictly perfunctory; the host race wanted to learn which of the candidates could actually survive contact with the *aaxyboxr*. Lixu survived, although the experience wrenched his mind as it had never been wrenched before, and recovered his mental equipoise after an acceptable period. More importantly, the *aaxyboxr* had performed their own examination, studying his mind point by point, and pronouncing him to be a true sentient being.

Lixu was then offered the position of Warden Cadet, to be specially trained at an academy on the host race's home world. After much deliberation and consultation with friends and family – especially with his grandfather (who approved) – he accepted, and his life took a radically different course. And, though he hadn't been a Warden for very long, he knew he wouldn't refuse the opportunity again if he had it all to do over.

No system of corridors existed on the Observation Deck, just an elevator which linked it to the level below. The elevator deposited its passengers in the exact center of the Deck so that the observers had an unobstructed, one-hundred-degree view of Deep Space. The viewing area was actually a hemisphere of glass tiles ringed with lounge chairs; the observer could seat himself in one spot for a time, get up, walk around the circumference, and sit down to view the Cosmos at a new angle. Many of the crew, including the Warden, availed themselves of the opportunity.

Rodriguez took a seat completely at random and relaxed. From his vantage point, the brightest object in space was S'amh'i [*Eta Carinae on Dunian star charts – CC*] itself. The second brightest was a gas-giant world in this star system, the fourth from its primary. The one habitable world – the second one called "Sam'h'i'e" by the locals – could not be seen as it was currently on the far side of the star. Other, more faraway stars peppered the cosmic ocean like flotsam. The immensity of the panorama filled the observer with an excitement second only to the one he had experienced upon being admitted to the Warden's Academy. Given a preference, he would sit here during his entire tour of duty. Unfortunately, duty came first, and he had to take his moments of relaxation when he could.

A slight rustling sound behind him stirred him out of his reverie. He turned in his seat and spied Lt. H'rum approaching the circumference of the Deck. He made eye contact and smiled at her. Okath (and Ekath) did not smile with their mouths. Even if they could smile with their mouths, no one would know since their mouths were usually covered by the breathing apparatus they were obliged to wear when off their home worlds. Instead, they bobbed their heads to show friendliness. Lt. H'rum was bobbing enthusiastically.

The paradox of the Okath and the Ekath was the subject of many a debate in medical and social-science circles. The two races were genetically identical but politically opposite to each other. The Okath had been victims of political oppression on Eka-xan and had fled *en masse* to settle on Oka-xan, located in the same system as New Switzerland. Whereas the Ekath had despised humankind because of perceived arrogance and aggressiveness, the Okath had welcomed it with open arms. And, during the Great War, the two took opposite sides of the conflict. It was a safe assumption that the Okath liked everything about humans, almost to the point of fawning over them. Certainly, no Ekath would be bobbing *his/her* head at a Warden!

Like all of her race, Lt. H'rum was short-statured and roly-poly in appearance. She had only four digits on her hands and feet; missing were the "pinkie" finger and the little toe of human extremities. Her skin color reminded one of a permanent case of jaundice which had given rise, after first contact, to a rash of derogatory humor which was quickly dispelled once the two races got to know one another. Attached to her belt was the ever-present and ever-needful helium tank.

"Greetings, Leftenant," the human said cheerfully. "Are you off duty now?"

"Salutations, Leftenant. Yes, I bees. You also?"

"Wardens are never off duty. I'm just relaxing until I'm needed again."

"I thinked not that Wardens relaxed. Your kind has a…certain reputation."

"Don't believe everything you hear about us. We're still flesh and blood like everyone else."

"Yet, the stories I haves heared…"

"Exaggerations, no doubt."

"Perhaps." There followed an awkward pause, then: "Ah, observes, Leftenant. The *Faithful* haves comed into view."

Rodriguez followed her gesturing hand. About five kilometers off the port bow, the Constabulary patrol vessel the *Steadfast* had been ordered to rendezvous with stood by waiting for contact from its sister ship. Its current mission was patrolling the adjacent sector of Deep Space; although that sector contained no habitable worlds, the Constabulary had had to change its policy concerning the coverage of every star system in the central spiral due to the Memgo Affair and the very real possibility of criminal activity anywhere.

Three hundred years ago, Dunians would not have conceived of a ship like the Constabulary patrol vessels. They had been nurtured on the concept of a needle-shaped craft to the exclusion of all other configurations, and they had believed that that design was the only efficient one. This misconception arose from the fact that needle-shaped craft were indeed efficient in an atmosphere, allowing them to travel at great velocities. There was no need for such a design in Deep Space, however, because there was no friction and therefore no drag. Spacecraft could have any design imaginable without sacrificing velocity. It had taken Dunians nearly a century to accept this truism and incorporate it into their thinking.

Constabulary ships, like all MOME-operated vessels, looked like nothing so much as a dumbbell floating in space. The two end spheres were not of equal size. The smaller one was a kilometer in diameter and contained the crew and their machines and habitats. Separated from it by a cylinder fifty meters in diameter and five hundred meters in length was the business end of the ship, a two-kilometer sphere with the apparatus to warp space and make interstellar travel practicable. Some crewmembers resided here as well, riding herd on the massive – and risky – MOME, a job not for the foolhardy. Ungainly-looking though they may be, these vessels had no equal for sheer power – until the Aldebaranians disabled them all in one fell swoop with their power-dampening device.

Rodriguez and H'rum watched with detachment as the two ships closed the gap between them. They were shaken out of their detachment by the beeping of the Warden's vidphone. He switched it on and peered at H'rum's relief in the Green (Communications) Zone, a female Dunian with a narrow face.

"Lt. Rodriguez," she intoned, "you are to report to Conference Room A."

"Thank you, Leftenant." He switched off and regarded the Okath. "Do you see – uh, do you understand now what I meant about duty, H'rum?"

"I envies not you, Leftenant. I bees content to be a simple soldier."

*   *   *

Conference Room A, adjacent to the Captain's quarters on the central level, hosted Command Staff meetings for everyone Lt. Commander and above. The "day" aboard a patrol vessel was seventy-five kiloseconds long (divided into five shifts of fifteen K's each), and Captain Halvarson usually assembled his senior officers every fifth day – unless an urgent matter arose. This day, such a matter had arisen.

The conference room was nondescript, since it hadn't been designed for anyone's comfort. It contained an oval table and the requisite number of chairs, all white molded polystyrene, and a one-meter-square vidscreen mounted on the bulkhead behind the Captain's chair. Already present when Rodriguez strolled in were the Captain, the XO, the Zone Commanders, the Commanders of the troop and fighter brigades, the Chief Medical Officer, and the Chief Engineer. None of them were pleased by the Warden's tardiness. Halvarson regarded him with a baleful eye.

"I thought you were going to your quarters, Leftenant," he grumbled.

"I decided to make a side trip to the Galley. The *aaxyboxr* take a lot out of me."

"I see. Well, take your seat. I'm about to contact the *Faithful*."

Rodriguez took the only seat available, at the opposite end of the table from the Captain. The officers nearest him shifted their own chairs slightly away from him. He studiously ignored the snub and gave his attention to the Captain.

The latter switched on the vidscreen, and the image of his counterpart on board the *Faithful*, Captain Frederick Kleindienst, appeared. Captain Kleindienst possessed a narrow, wolf-like face and beady eyes, and he seemed to be always casting nervous glances in all directions. He was seated in his own Conference Room A, but he was not surrounded by his senior officers; neither was he alone, however, for the presence of a slender arm to his right could be seen on the screen. He brightened suddenly upon spotting Halvarson.

"Olaf! Hello! You're looking well for an old man."

"Hello yourself, Freddy. And who are you calling 'old'?"

"Well, you *are* three years my senior. That makes you *old* in my book."

"Ha-ha. So, what do you know about this new mission I've been assigned?"

"No more than you do, pal. All HQ wanted me to do was to pick up a 'special operative' on Remus and deliver her to you."

"I assume she's with you now."

"Right." He turned his head toward the other person in the conference room. "Leftenant."

A slender young woman slid her chair closer to Kleindienst so that all on the *Steadfast* could see her. She would have passed for human if not for her pallid complexion. Otherwise, she had a full, sensuous face, twinkling ice-blue eyes, and long, nearly waist-length, silver-blue hair. She was also wearing nothing but a cobalt-blue bikini. Her rank, a single diamond, was imbedded in an epaulet hanging around her neck. She smiled at the officers of the *Steadfast* like a mischievous child.

"Oh, God!" Commander Krishnamurthy murmured. "A Pluj!"

Halvarson scowled at her. The few human males in the room straightened up and put on their best friendly faces. Rodriguez did likewise, but not for the reason the others did.

"Ladies and gentlemen," Kleindienst announced, "may I present Lt. Anafu Ralfo, lately the Second Science Officer of the *Reliable*?"

Lt. Ralfo cupped her hands before her face.

"To the officers of the *Steadfast*," she responded after the fashion of her kind in a feathery-light voice, "with you Our Lady be."

"Welcome to the *Steadfast*, Leftenant," Halvarson greeted her in a very friendly tone. "We will be pleased to have you aboard."

Now Krishnamurthy scowled and crossed her arms defiantly.

"You I thank, Captain Halvarson. And already a familiar face I see. With you Our Lady be, Lixu."

"The Lady be with you as well, Anafu," the Warden replied, cupping his own hands. "It's good to see you again."

"A Warden you are. Impressed I am."

"As soon as you're aboard, Leftenant," Halvarson interrupted, "please join us here to be debriefed."

"Aye, sir."

Lt. Ralfo saluted both Captains and moved out of the picture. Kleindienst grinned wickedly.

"Good luck, Olaf."

"Thanks, Freddy. I may need it." He switched off the vidscreen and turned to Rodriguez. "How long have you known Lt. Ralfo?"

"About fifteen gigs. As you may know, my father is Dunia's ambassador to Pluj. And Anafu's mother is the Chief Administratrix of the planet. We were frequent guests in each other's residences. Anafu and I practically grew up together."

"How splendid. Then you won't have any objection if I assign you responsibility for her good behavior while she's aboard?"

The Warden frowned. What was the Captain playing at? It was common knowledge that Constabulary officers did not care for the presence of a Warden aboard their ships because of the latter's reputation. For that reason, most Wardens tended to maintain a low profile until they were absolutely needed. Rodriguez understood that and accepted it. But why should his relationship to Anafu Ralfo put anybody into a snit? Jealousy? Potential rivalry? The notion was too ludicrous to entertain seriously.

"Do you expect trouble, Captain?"

"You of all people should know the effect the Pluj have on us. I just want to keep things on an even keel."

"Very well. I pledge her good behavior while she's on board. You'll excuse me now. I'll meet her at the Dock, show her her quarters, and escort her here."

"Begging the Captain's pardon," the XO said as soon as the Warden had departed, "I'd like permission to confine all human males to their quarters for the duration."

The human males in the conference room stared at her in disbelief. The Captain seemed amused by the suggestion.

"Does that include *me* as well, Commander?"

"Um, well, I – uh–"

"Never mind, Tomiko. Permission denied. Our young Warden has given us his pledge. We can all rely on that. And we can rely on him to keep himself in check. Aren't Wardens supposed to take a vow of chastity, or something like that?"

"I still think she's going to be trouble – sir."

The Captain and the XO sunk into a sullen silence. Neither trusted him/herself to speak his/her mind about the radical disruption in the routine of the ship. But both hoped and/or prayed that the disruption would be short-lived and that they could go back to the relatively benign business of keeping the peace in an unpredictable Universe.

CHAPTER TWO

▼

RE-UNION

STRICTLY SPEAKING, THE *STEADFAST* AND its sister ships were not warships *per se*. They had a limited defensive capability in the form of missile batteries; but, like the aircraft carriers in ancient days, they functioned principally as transport vessels. One might have thought that such vessels would be quite vulnerable to attack, and one would be correct – in theory. An MOME-equipped ship depended upon its physical components for its defense, but it also had a psychological weapon. It had been demonstrated rather dramatically in the early days of the Central Spiral Collective, when pirates, rogue elements from the military wings of both the Alliance for Free Space and the Amazonian Federation, and assorted other criminals that it was sheer folly to attack a Constabulary ship-of-the-line unless the attacker wished to commit suicide. Striking the command sphere posed no problem; but a careless shot which hit the MOME sphere usually meant instant annihilation for anyone or anything within five light-years. The energies created by Murchison's invention equaled several super-novas, giving even the most hardened criminal second thoughts when confronted by a patrol vessel.

The true warships were the attack fighters nestled inside the ship. The typical fighter brigade consisted of six squadrons of four attack fighters, two heavy-weapons vessels, and one support vessel each, plus eight troop carriers for the purposes of boarding enemy vessels and /or engaging in rescue operations. During stand-down, the troop carriers remained on the next-to-the-lowest level of the command sphere of a patrol vessel; each was parked in a ring which ran around the perimeter and entered/exited via its own hatch.

This area was popularly called the "Dock," and it actually contained ten parking berths; the extra two were reserved for visiting shuttlecraft.

Warden (L1) Lixu Rodriguez stood at the head of one of these reserved berths, awaiting the arrival of Lt. Anafu Ralfo. He cast several nervous glances all around frequently. He hadn't been in this part of the *Steadfast* since he first came aboard forty megaseconds ago, and he didn't care to be. Frankly, the place gave him the shivers. It was a cold and unfeeling area, devoid of anything remotely hospitable and comfortable. It was an area to enter and exit as quickly as it was humanly possible to do.

Others were present here at the moment, those who operated the hatches, monitored the incoming and outgoing traffic, and ran routine maintenance checks on all parked vessels. As they had their own affairs to conduct, they paid little heed to the stranger in their midst. Even if they hadn't been occupied, they still would have kept their distance from a Warden. Speak only when spoken to was the watchword down below.

Rodriguez recalled the admonition of his Aldebaranian mentor at the Academy so many megaseconds ago. Master Fresh-Bloom-in-the-Face-as-the-Day-Begins (a very rough translation of his actual name that a human tongue could never pronounce) had been reproving his "lack-wit of a pupil" for the seventh time that day for failing to understand the true nature of the role of a Warden in the larger society. "Master Fresh" (as the young cadet always addressed him) told him that a Warden must never be moved by the passions of those around him/her but must be guided only by the Five Principles of Enlightenment; therefore, the Warden must ever hold him/herself apart from the masses and walk a solitary path. "Know you, pupil," Master Fresh had said, while poking him on the chest with a stubby finger, "that they will hate you and revile you and think great evil of you. But in spite of that, you must remain steadfast in your duty. It is the essence of Enlightenment."

Enlightenment.

This was the code by which all Wardens conducted themselves in both their personal and professional lives. Enlightenment was the foundation of all morality; the laws of the masses were mere reflections of this code and were evil if they contradicted the code. Enlightenment contained only five statements, or Principles, which should never be violated for any reason. The First Principle was the Sanctity of All Life; a Warden may not take a sentient life under any circumstances (this was the reason a Warden was issued a tranquillizer gun instead of a lethal weapon). The Second Principle was Fidelity to the Truth; a Warden may not speak falsely or break his bond. The Third Principle was the Equity of Justice; a Warden may not engage in double standards. The Fourth Principle was Adherence to Duty; a Warden may not disregard his mission, no matter the circumstances. And the Fifth Principle was Purity of Mind and Body; a Warden may not allow him/herself to engage in dissolute behavior. Enlightenment had been drilled into the cadets from the day of their orientation to the day of their graduation. The recitation of the Five Principles began and ended each day, and each day contained a lesson plan around each of the Five, derived from the past experiences of the Masters. These lessons were taught as rigorously as the academic work and the physical training. No Warden was ever permitted to forget the Five; the consequences were too awful to contemplate.

Rodriguez endured the avoidance around him in the stoical manner he had been taught and contemplated his surroundings by way of diversion. He focused first on a circle of lights embedded in the bulkhead above the parking berths. These lights indicated the status of the berths – blue for "occupied," amber for "unoccupied." An incoming vessel was directed to the first available berth showing an amber light; once the docking procedure had been completed, the light turned blue. His attention was drawn next to the berths themselves. They were all nondescript, save for a pair of parallel magnetic rails which held the vessels fast. When the rails were powered, the vessels were drawn into the berths; when the power was off, the vessels slid out the hatch.

The Warden's reverie was interrupted by the sound of a klaxon, a soft hooting which heralded the arrival of an incoming vessel. In his mind's eye, he pictured the standard docking procedure: (1) the airlock de-pressurizes; (2) the outer hatch opens, and the vessel enters; (3) the outer hatch closes, and the airlock re-pressurizes; (4) the inner hatch opens, and the vessel is drawn into the berth.

The sounding of the klaxon initiated a new round of activity on the Dock. Technicians who had been performing other duties now hastened to their berthing stations. Two NCO's – one, a balding, stocky Dunian; the other, a hairless, rail-thin Uhaad – pushed by Rodriguez without looking at him directly; he had to step back quickly to avoid being knocked to the ground. The two techs checked their operating consoles, made a few notations on an electronic notebook, and turned to the vidscreen above them to monitor the vessel's arrival.

Rodriguez listened intently as a soft whine indicated the opening of the outer hatch, followed a centisecond later by another one as the hatch closed. Another centisecond passed, and the louder whine of the opening of the inner hatch filled his ears. The Dunian NCO now threw the switch which powered the magnetic rails, and the incoming vessel slid effortlessly onto its berth. The Uhaad closed the inner hatch and changed the status light.

The new arrival was a squat, beetle-shaped shuttlecraft which resembled nothing less than a scaled-down CID freighter. It was designed to carry up to four passengers in relative comfort; in a pinch, it could handle twice that number, though less comfortably. Every MOME-equipped ship carried one for just that purpose. As soon as it had docked, the techs rolled out a wheeled staircase, positioned it at the shuttlecraft's hatch, and waited expectantly. A moment later, the hatch slid open to reveal the pilot of the vessel, a Romulan junior lieutenant. She stepped out and descended the staircase with a practiced nonchalance; she smiled emotionlessly at the techs but frowned slightly when she spotted the Warden. Fast on her heels was her passenger.

Unlike the pilot, Lt. Ralfo flashed a big, warm smile at everyone she saw, regardless of their station in life. She practically bubbled over with good will. The Pluj were extroverts *par excellence*, and Anafu Ralfo was typically Pluj. She smiled even wider (if that was possible), and her eyes twinkled when she spied Rodriguez. Without qualms or embarrassment, she trotted over to him, threw her arms around his waist, and hugged him tightly. He hugged back, but not as enthusiastically.

"Lixu," she greeted him in Pluj, looking into his face with wide eyes and brushing his cheek lightly with her fingers, "I have not seen you in a long time."

"Nor I you, Anafu," he responded in kind. "You look as lovely as ever."

"And you also."

"*Ahem*," the pilot interrupted the re-union, "'Scuse me, ma'am, but I've got to return to the *Faithful*."

"Of course." Ralfo caught the eye of the Dunian tech, a senior sergeant with four orange stripes on his right sleeve. "Sergeant, only one bag I have. So kind to get it you would be?"

"Yes, ma'am!" the NCO replied rapturously and practically ran into the shuttlecraft to retrieve the bag. He re-appeared a few seconds later and trotted over to Ralfo. "Here y' are, ma'am. Where to?"

"I'll take that, Sergeant," Rodriguez interjected.

The tech looked at him – without actually making eye contact – with an air of resentment.

"Yes, *sir*," he grumbled and pushed the bag into the Warden's hands.

"I'll show you to your quarters, Anafu. Then you'll debrief Captain Halvarson."

"It will be wonderful to be working with you, dear Lixu," she gushed as they strolled out of the Dock. "Mother will be greatly surprised but pleased to hear this news."

"And how is your mother?"

"As busy as ever. The work of a Chief Administratrix is never done. And she always complains about Amazonian bureaucracy."

"She's not alone in that respect. And your father?"

"Pluj" was a catch-all nomenclature, because the sole inhabitants of that star system [*Alpha Eridani (Achernar) on Dunian star charts – CC*] had deemed it so. The name of the star – an orange, class K sun – the one inhabited planet (fifth from its primary), and the race of beings on it were all called "Pluj," and one differentiated between them from the context of the conversation. The mean temperature of the planet was minus five degrees Celsius – hence the lack of pigmentation in the skin of the inhabitants. No one could mistake a Pluj for any other race of beings.

No one could mistake a Pluj for another creature for another, very salient reason: the female of the species dominated the culture. Pluj society was matrilinear, matrilocal, and matriarchical and had been since Time immemorial. Other worlds, such as Dunia, had boasted of having a few matriarchical societies; but, properly speaking, those societies were only quasi-matriarchical. Females might have control over the transfer of property or the tracing of one's lineage, but males were still the dominant force in governance and warfare. On Pluj, however, there was a complete reversal of the gender roles; females ran the government, operated the businesses, administered the social institutions, and populated the military, police, and fire-fighting elements. Males kept up the homes and raised the children. Child-bearing was still a female function, however, and no Pluj had yet been able to reverse Biology.

As has been told elsewhere, the Pluj became fascinated with humans after first contact because (1) humans and Pluj were nearly identical genetically and (2) the human concept of the equality of the sexes was such a novel idea that the Pluj had wished to study it in depth. Humans and Pluj became allies in the War of the Eight Suns, and the female military proved to be the equal of its human counterpart. And, at the conclusion of hostilities, Pluj joined the Federation.

Psychologically, the Pluj behaved much like children. That is to say, they were completely guileless and spoke their minds on all occasions, much to the discomfit of other races. They could be as petulant as human children were wont to be, yet maintained a mature attitude toward all facets of existence. And has been intimated elsewhere, one aspect of Pluj psychology stood out: they were highly sexual creatures and could be quite aggressive in sexual situations when they put their minds to it – which was often. Intercourse with a Pluj could be very pleasurable and very enervating at the same time, because she made love with reckless abandon and was quite innovative in her techniques. Few males were ever quite the same afterwards once they had engaged in a sexual free-for-all with her.

This then was the sort of creature which had invaded the *Steadfast* and which had so worried its XO. Whether a Warden of the Constabulary could keep such a creature at arm's length so that a modicum of efficiency could be maintained while she was aboard was anybody's guess. No one – least of all in the upper echelons – was taking any bets.

There was one taboo imposed upon alien races, and that was never to inquire after a Pluj's *male* parent. The males of Pluj – collectively referred to as "i-Pluj," ("not Pluj") – were the invisible part of that society, and the politically correct individual did not mention them at all in public and only rarely in private. Yet, Lixu Rodriguez had grown up on Pluj, and his family had been on cordial terms with Lt. Ralfo's family; he had related as much to her father (whom he jokingly called "Uncle Ceptu") as to her mother. He felt he could inquire after him as if he had actually been a Pluj himself.

Ralfo smiled wryly. Far from resenting the question, she found it amusing.

"Your 'Uncle Ceptu' still grumbles about his 'burdensome' household chores. The old dear. He loves his work, but he will not admit it."

"I've missed all of you, you know."

"And we have also missed you." She glanced at him coyly. "I have thought about you many times."

*　　　*　　　*

The group which greeted the arrival of Lt. Ralfo – some expectantly, some not – was a decidedly grim group. Captain Halvarson was anxious to learn more about the mission to Planetoid 48 beyond the lone fact that he was supposed to apprehend a cell of the Reman terrorist organization, the JUR.[4] And, if the Captain was anxious, so were his senior officers; and they had shown it by avoiding eye contact with him and making small talk with each other. Commander Krishnamurthy's anxiety was tempered, however, by the resentment of having to be in the same room with a Pluj. Because all human males were mesmerized by that sensuous race, all human *females* felt threatened. And Tomiko Krishnamurthy was no exception to that rule.

The Warden remained a picture of stoicism as befitted his kind. Underneath he was bemused by the reactions he was perceiving around the table. For her part, Ralfo projected the image of a child about to open her birthday presents, and she could have sat there for many kiloseconds without changing her facial expression.

"We'll get right to the point," Halvarson intoned, "since time is of the essence. Lt. Ralfo, I presume you have a full understanding of this mission. Would you enlighten us, please?"

4　*Jeshi kwa Uhuru za Remus* in Amazonian (Army for the Liberation of Remus), i.e. Reman Army of Liberation – CMT.

"Certainly, Captain," she burbled. Her expression became more serious. "Of a new cell of terrorists operating in this sector, Office 18[5] has learned. You may have heard that, two megs ago, highjacked after departing Ru'uhaad the cruise ship *Astarte* was. Office 18 believes that responsible this cell was. What the purpose of the highjacking was not known is. But rumors there have been that interested in MOME technology the JUR is."

"And what part does this Dr. Weyerhauser play?"

"An astrophysicist by profession he is. Until two megs ago, at the University of New Nairobi he taught. Office 18 believes that a JUR mole he was. Now disappeared he has."

"Two megs ago, eh? At the same time the *Astarte* was highjacked. Rather an interesting co-incidence, wouldn't you say?"

"Aye, Captain. To apprehend him and his cell we are charged."

"And where do you fit in?"

"A student of Dr. Weyerhauser I was when, at the Academy, astrophysics he taught. Him positively to identify I can."

"I see. Lt. Rodriguez, can you corroborate any of this?"

The Warden stirred himself out of a mini-reverie during which he had been reflecting on memories of life on Pluj and fixed Halvarson with a piercing look. The latter grimaced and was determined not to be intimidated by the younger man. Rodriguez was somewhat annoyed over having been dragged into this conversation; he was present only because Constabulary regulations dictated that the assigned Warden on a patrol vessel attend all ship's briefings, whether or not (s)he had anything to contribute. And he felt that he had nothing to contribute at this time. Anafu had described the situation succinctly and accurately, and anything he might say would have been redundant. Personally, he'd rather have been back on the Observation Deck, contemplating the grandeur of the Cosmos and his place in it, as Master Fresh had drummed into him at every opportunity. Captain Halvarson, he believed, was being petulant over this sudden disruption in ship's routine and sought to take out his frustrations on the handiest target, i.e. the one person on the *Steadfast* he had no use for.

"We Wardens have our own intelligence network," he stated flatly, "via the *aaxyboxr*. What we have discerned corresponds almost exactly with the findings of Office18."

"'*Almost* exactly'?" The speaker was Commander Rux Arari, a Bitha, who commanded the troop brigade on the *Steadfast*, as reflected by the "crossed rifles" insignia on his uniform. He was a lean and wiry sort with skin the color

---

5   The official designation of the Constabulary intelligence unit. It generates as much fear and loathing as the Wardens, much for the same reasons – CMT.

of an orange; he had deep-sunken, jet-black eyes and a bright red crest which ran from the bridge of his nose to the nape of his neck over an otherwise short cropping of yellowish hair. "Mean you what, 'almost exactly'? Know you what that do not others?"

"We have known about this particular cell for about fifty megs, closely monitoring the movements of its members as best we could without tipping our own hand. We suspected they were behind the highjacking of the *Astarte* from the very beginning. Also we were aware of Dr. Weyerhauser's JUR sympathies."

"And why didn't you inform *us* of this intelligence?" the Captain asked through clenched teeth.

"To what purpose, Captain? Office 18 has done a credible job of assessing the situation. How would your understanding have been enhanced by what we knew?"

"Simple professional courtesy?"

"We Wardens tell you what you need to know," came the blunt response. "Anything else is superfluous."

Halvarson's jaw muscles worked furiously as he attempted to rein in sudden rising passions. On the one hand, he was angered by Rodriguez's cavalier attitude; he had, like most of his fellow officers, little love for Wardens, found them, to a man and woman, as arrogant, high-handed, unco-operative, overly demanding, and cold-blooded a lot as ever were born/hatched/cloned, and would not have missed any of them if they were all to disappear from the Universe. Even though the Warden he had to deal with was only a recent graduate, that one clearly had absorbed the persona in its entirety and exhibited it with no hint of embarrassment, instead reveling in it. On the other hand, he was required by Constabulary regulations to show the assigned Warden every courtesy, to keep him informed about the workings of the ship and its crew, and to co-operate completely during those rare times when the Warden actually performed his specified duties. It was a hard task even in the best of times, given that the Wardens never seemed obliged to reciprocate. Now, when a mission of crucial importance arose where the peace of the Central Spiral Collective was concerned, this lack of reciprocity was galling to the *n*th degree. The Captain's mind seethed with rage even as he struggled to maintain a mask of calm.

Commander Rux was not so reticent, however. He jumped to his feet even as his crest turned a dusty rose.

"'*Superfluous*'?" he roared, then muttered something in his native tongue. Is *no* information 'superfluous' if concerns it our mission. Cannot send I – *will* not send I – out my people if are they not *completely* informed of the dangers may face they."

"Commander Rux," Halvarson spoke in as even a tone as he could manage, "resume your seat. I'll not tolerate a breach of etiquette."

The Bitha glared menacingly at Rodriguez for a long moment (and the Warden returned the glare impassively). He bowed toward the Captain and sat down. The other officers shifted in their seats nervously.

"Very well, Leftenant, have it your way. But, I caution you, if this mission is compromised by anything you've neglected to tell us, I'll hold you personally responsible."

"Understood, Captain."

"Lt. Ralfo, is there anything else you can add to our understanding?"

All during the previous uproar, the Pluj sat in embarrassed silence. A naturally ebullient race, the Pluj discussed their problems amicably; they avoided acrimony and ill temper and harsh language like the plague and sought consensus. If ever acrimony, ill temper, or harsh language reared its ugly head, the Pluj would fall into a deep silence until such time as the angry party ran out of steam or became less angry (whichever came first). They would then launch into a bout of self-effacement in order to put the angry party into a more conciliatory mood. It was a wholly unorthodox ploy; but, more often than not, it worked. The Pluj were past masters at putting others off their guard and thus winning the argument.

There was no argument to win here, however, and Ralfo recognized a conflict of personalities when she saw it. And, since it did not have its roots in the current situation, she could do little to defuse it; she could only keep quiet and hope the storm would blow over quickly. When Halvarson addressed her again, she had been studying the scratch marks on the conference table and attempting to form a picture out of them.

"One more thing there is, sir," she replied, instantly assuming her normal cheerful self, "although a minor point it is. A...lady friend on Romulus Dr. Weyerhauser had; and, before his disappearance, her regularly he had visited."

"Do you think she was aware of his...'extra-curricular' activities?"

"Unknown. Worth investigating her it may or may not be."

"Well, that's not for us to say. We'll carry out our present orders until such time as we get new ones. Dismissed, ladies and gentlemen."

Halvarson leaned back in his chair and sighed deeply and noisily. The debriefing had not gone at all well, and he had been perilously close to losing his temper and saying several things he would live to regret. Out of the corner of his eye, he noted that not everyone had left the conference room. Krishnamurthy –good old faithful Krishnamurthy! – had remained behind and was eyeing him with no little concern. He gave her a tight little smile.

"Almost had a knock-down, dragged-out fight there, didn't we, Tomiko?"

"Yes, sir, and I was hard put to know who to soma[6] first."

The Captain chuckled.

"Next time, soma *me* first. Then I won't have to look at Rodriguez's smug little face."

"Yes, sir. I'll be sure to do that."

He looked at her in mock surprise at the cheerfulness in her voice.

"And, of course, you'll have to assume command of the ship."

"Yes, sir." She broke out into a toothy grin. "*Temporarily*, of course."

"Of course. Let's get back to the Bridge, shall we? The sooner we complete the business on Planetoid 48, the sooner we can go back to safer duty – like catching pirates!"

*   *   *

"*What troubles you, pupil?*"

"*Master Fresh, I wish to know how to deal with those who try to provoke me to anger.*"

"*Have you not already learned that lesson? Were you asleep when I taught it to you?*"

"*I was not asleep, Master, but the lesson was…unclear.*"

"'*Unclear'? How so?*"

Lixu Rodriguez, Warden (L1), remembers the stern expression on the face of Master Fresh-Bloom-in-the-Face-as-the-Day-Begins as the pupil attempts to explain to the teacher the elusiveness of what ought to be a clear-cut concept. As a Warden, he will encounter persons who will challenge his authority and seek to undermine it. He will encounter persons who will use semantics as a weapon in order to confuse, to obfuscate, to twist a meaning to its opposite, in order to make him look like a fool. Most significantly, he will encounter persons who, having lost the argument on the level of logic and reason, will resort to violence and lure him into regretful actions. Enlightenment has taught him the First Principle, the Sanctity of All Life, which prohibits him from committing acts of violence. Provocation to violence by ignorant persons is therefore also to be avoided. But how should one react to such provocations?

Master Fresh listens to this stuttering, tongue-tied human youth impassively, stoically. What he is thinking is a complete mystery, for no one except another member of the Community really understands one of his own. Under such

6   A reference to somazol, the tranquillizing drug used by the Constabulary to render difficult prisoners less difficult. It is also used by the Wardens in their sidearms – CMT.

scrutiny, Cadet Rodriguez is understandably nervous (and the reputation of this alien race only adds to his nervousness) and is sure he is making a fool of himself. Nevertheless, he perseveres because he must know the answer to his question, lest he fail in his duty as a Warden and bring disrepute to the Service.

"What I mean, Master, is that someone will try to make me lose my temper and cause me to lash out in anger."

"Is this all? For this, you take up valuable time?"

"Yes, Master. I beg your forgiveness, but the lesson must be…clarified."

"Must it, lack-wit? And why *must it?"*

"Because, Master, I – I am a lack-wit and would have your wisdom."

"Ah, and so you shall, pupil. Attend my words, then, and do not fall asleep!"

Lixu Rodriguez, Warden (L1), replays in his mind that memorable session wherein Master Fresh launches into a lengthy lecture, peppered with specific examples of acts of provocation (and he remembers thinking in the back of his mind that his mentor must have been using actual events as teaching tools), all the while jabbing the "lack-wit" on the chest with his finger. The pupil thanks his teacher for the valuable insight and hastens to his next appointment.

The young Warden compares what Master Fresh has taught him with his recent response to provocative behavior. He is not entirely satisfied that he has acted properly; yet, under the circumstances, i.e. adherence to the Fourth Principle, Steadfastness to Duty, he believes that he has done the best he could do. What would his mentor have said? He shudders to think of the response. The teacher is very wise, and the pupil is…just a lack-wit.

*   *   *

Three kiloseconds later, the ship's klaxon sounded a "red alert." The crew of the *Steadfast* scurried to their battle stations. Some thought it was simply another in an endless series of drills; nevertheless, they hurried to get to where they were supposed to be because a senior sergeant would be standing by ready to report any "slowpokes" to the Officer of the Deck.

Warden Rodriguez also hurried, not because tardiness on his part would be reported to the Officer of the Deck (he was responsible only to his superiors in the Warden's Service) but because Wardens were obliged to report to the Bridge in these situations in case they were needed to fulfill their prime function. He had been meditating in his quarters after returning Lt. Ralfo to hers (and politely refusing an invitation to stay with her "for a while") when the alert sounded, and he broke into a brisk trot as soon as he was in the corridor. All around him, crewmembers of all ranks and zones proceeded in all directions like panicked ants, barely avoiding collisions with each other.

He entered the Bridge just behind Commander Rux and a platoon of troopers. The latter quickly took up positions at strategic points around the ring. Their assignment was to protect the Bridge and its denizens from assault in the unlikely event of the *Steadfast*'s being boarded by enemy combatants. Each of the troopers carried a heavy-duty automatic rifle, a pistol, a thirty-centimeter bayonet, and enough ammunition for a kilosecond-and-a-half of sustained firing. They wore the standard camouflage uniform augmented by a visored helmet and bulletproof body armor. Their officer, an Ekath lieutenant, spoke to each briefly, then took up his own position at Gold Zone.

The Warden went straight to that sector himself but did not address Captain Halvarson immediately. Instead, he peered at the Display to assess the situation from his own perspective. Warden's training included a rigorous indoctrination into military tactics, on both the individual and the collective levels, excluding the use of deadly weapons as that would have compromised the First Principle. Because they were assigned principally to warships, they needed to know how militaries functioned in a given scenario, planet-side or in Deep Space; by the time that this phase of their training had been completed, they knew as much about tactics as any general or admiral. (Warden's training also included a rigorous indoctrination into the martial arts – some known on Dunia, some on Alko, others completely alien in nature – which could disable an enemy (without killing him) by any of several dozen methods.)

His trained eye and mind, then, took in the "scene" as it unfolded via the hologram before him. Ten light-seconds from the *Steadfast*'s position, a Bithan freighter (as represented by an aquamarine blip in the Display) had been intercepted by two vessels of unknown origin (two black blips in the Display). The Blue Zone officer-on-duty had spotted the three vessels as soon as they had entered the ship's sensor range and reported this fact immediately to the Captain. Halvarson recognized the scene for what it was – an act of piracy – and sounded the alert. Rodriguez tensed. If the pirates were apprehended, he would be pressed into duty.

Five seconds after Rodriguez, Commander Enrique Mbaku, a Romulan, who commanded the attack fighter brigade – his uniform sported a "wings" insignia – steamed onto the Bridge, half-dressed, and struggled to straighten out his uniform on the fly. He joined the Captain, the XO, and Commander Rux; he gave only a cursory glance at the Warden, then concentrated on the Display.

"Pirates, no doubt," he muttered.

"Indeed," Halvarson agreed. "They haven't spotted us yet, so we have a bit of an advantage."

Mbaku nodded and spoke into his personal vidcom.

"Squadrons One and Two, report!"

"Squadron One," a booming voice replied, "standing by."

"Squadron Two, standing by."

"HW One, report!"

"HW One, standing by."

"Prepare to launch on my mark." He glanced at the Captain, who merely nodded. "Launch!"

The launch bays for the attack fighters and the auxiliary vessels were located along the length of the cylinder which joined the spheres of an MOME-equipped ship. Three very practical reasons governed this positioning. One was the efficient use of space which otherwise would have been wasted; and the extra structural supports needed to hold the launching mechanisms mitigated against the most vulnerable part of the ship. Two, the need for a large number of war craft of various sizes required a large space, and the half-kilometer-long cylinder could accommodate all thirty vessels quite easily with enough room left over for extra supplies, equipment, and munitions. Three, the location avoided the venting of toxic exhaust gases near the more densely populated command sphere; from the cylinder, these gases were spewed harmlessly into space. The bays formed six rows along the length of the cylinder, spread equidistantly around its circumference; each row held one squadron, and alternate rows contained either a heavy-weapons or a support vessel.

The bay hatches were hinged affairs which opened like the petals of a flower before the Sun. The vessels were attached to the inner surfaces of the hatches electromagnetically; when the order to launch came, the hatches swung open, the electromagnets were switched off, and the CID fighters shot out under their own power. Under normal conditions, an attack force could be operational within sixty seconds.

For this particular operation, Commander Mbaku had assessed the threat level posed and deemed it sufficient to send out only two squadrons of fighters and one of the heavy-weapons cruisers. His judgment could have been overridden by the Captain and a different task force assembled. But Mbaku had had considerable experience in dealing with pirates, claim-jumpers, free-booters, smugglers, and the like (the medals on his dress uniform attested to that fact), and Captain Halvarson trusted his judgment implicitly. The order to launch this task force had been approved tacitly, and it now sped toward its target.

In the Display, nine new blips of the same color as all Constabulary ships appeared, moving away from the center of the hologram and toward the black blips. At first, the task force maintained its standard formation: the two squadrons in a diamond pattern with the cruiser in the middle. Midway between the *Steadfast* and the pirates, the squadrons began to fan out in an enveloping pattern. The task-force commanding officer in the cruiser directed the pilots, based on her radar read-outs. The idea was to take the pirates by surprise and prevent any possibility of escape by surrounding them.

The element of surprise almost worked. The task force had closed the gap by eighty per cent when it was apparently spotted. Someone on one of the pirate vessels had been more alert to external threats than to future rewards from his looting and had given a warning to his fellows. One of the vessels veered away from its intended victim and followed a course back towards Ru'uhaad, leaving its companion to an uncertain fate. The task-force CO barked out an order, and Squadron One broke formation to pursue the fleeing ship. Constabulary attack fighters possessed the most powerful engines in the Central Spiral Collective, and the pursuit was a foregone conclusion. The fighters soon caught up to the pirate and ordered it to surrender. The pirate captain ignored the order and tried a few evasive maneuvers. The ploy did not succeed. Attack Fighter One-A fired one of its missiles, equipped with an infra-red sensor and a proximity fuse; the missile detonated one hundred meters from the target. The explosion buckled the hull near the vessel's engine; the engine ruptured, and the vessel disappeared in a blue-white fireball.

Simultaneously, the second pirate, upon receiving the order to surrender, had also attempted to flee. But, Squadron Two had nearly enveloped it, cutting off any possible escape. And, when the first pirate was destroyed, the second's captain wisely powered down and waited to be boarded. Imprisonment on Xix[7] was not a desirable fate for any wrongdoer for any reason; but for some, it was preferable to instant death in Deep Space.

With the surrender of the second pirate, the task-force CO notified the *Steadfast*. Commander Rux issued orders that two troop carriers – one with a full complement, the other with only the pilot and co-pilot – be dispatched to the scene. The troopers would board the pirate, round up whomever they found, and secure half of the prisoners on each carrier under heavy guard. Warden Rodriguez hastened below and boarded one of the carriers in order to carry out his prime function and place the pirates officially under arrest.

When the carriers arrived, the Warden encountered a suddenly recalcitrant pirate crew. They would not open the airlock and threatened to kill anyone who attempted to breach the hatch. The pirate leader (who sounded very much like an Ekath) actually quoted various laws passed by the Grand Assembly which, presumably, gave a suspect certain rights before an arrest was made. Rodriguez countered that the particular law quoted applied only to planet-

7   Crimes against persons were punishable by imprisonment ranging from 500 megaseconds to life; crimes against property were punishable by imprisonment ranging from 100 to 500 megaseconds [cf. Article Five ("Law Enforcement"), Section Five ("Crimes and Punishments"), paragraphs two and three (respectively) of the Treaty of Aldebaran, as amended in AC 28] – CMT.

side offenses against Constabulary personnel and property and that crimes committed in Deep Space were covered by an entirely different set of rules. The pirate leader remained adamant and wished to negotiate. The Warden replied that negotiation in the present circumstances was unprecedented and that it would go well for him and his companions if they surrendered peaceably and threw themselves on the mercy of the courts. At that point, the pirate leader played his final card.

"I haves heared about a plot to use Planetoid 48 – which bees not far from our present location – as a weapon. Admittedly, my informant beed intoxicated when he speaked to me, but he provided me with enough information to give his story some credibility."

At the mention of Planetoid 48, red flags went up in Rodriguez's mind. Was this pirate somehow aware of the *Steadfast*'s new mission in this sector? Or was he simply grasping at straws, hoping to delay his inevitable fate?

"What sort of plot?" he asked cautiously.

"I possesses no details, but it involves the human terrorists knowed as the JUR."

"And why are you telling me all this?"

"In exchange for a more lenient sentence, I will speak the name of my informant who bees able to provide details of this plot. If you will grant this request, I shall surrender."

"I have no authority to grant that request."

"Who haves it then?"

"I'll have to speak with my superiors."

"Speaks to them then."

"It will consume some time."

"As you humans says, we bees not going anywhere."

Ordinarily, Rodriguez would not have given the pirate the time of day. Instead, he would have continued to talk until the troopers found a way to inject a somazol-gas grenade into the ship and waited until the pirates passed out before breaching the hatch. This was standard operating procedure for dealing with recalcitrants. The introduction of a new element in what would be a routine arrest had now changed matters considerably and put SOP on hold – at least for the time being. He would return to the *Steadfast*, contact HQ, and describe the situation. If HQ thought the pirates were attempting to sell a load of slag, SOP could go on as planned. If not…

The Reman Army of Liberation had been a pesky problem almost from the beginning of the Amazonian Federation. The Twins – Romulus and Remus in a shared orbit – had been at each other's throats even longer than that; but, in the early days, it had been strictly a war of words. As the years passed and Reman demands for political and economic reforms went unmet, the war of words became a war of weapons as the more violent faction of the reform party launched a campaign of sabotage and assassination. Their targets were mostly Romulans and Romulan enterprises, but they were not above "punishing" their own if they felt that their own were "collaborators" against and "traitors" to Remus's national integrity. They had sympathizers and apologists everywhere; and, it was rumored, some of these were Ekath, who would have liked nothing better than to see their rival, Romulus, thrown into ruin, a fitting revenge for having "imperial designs" on "free space."

So long as the Remans confined themselves to their own star system, the Constabulary had to remain neutral and not interfere in the internal affairs of member worlds. The Central Spiral Collective believed, however, that the JUR would someday be a threat to the whole of the Collective and formed contingency plans for dealing with it. Several resolutions had been introduced into the Grand Assembly to prepare the member worlds for that eventuality. Until then, the Constabulary held itself in abeyance, albeit prepared to strike at a moment's notice.

That eventuality finally arrived when the Reman terrorists took their first tentative steps to widen the scope of their operations. It began with the establishment of secret bases outside of Rhea Silvia's sphere of influence from which to attack Romulan shipping. At first, the attacks were blamed on pirates looking for valuable cargo to re-sell on the black market. The JUR did steal cargo and re-sell it in order to finance their more expensive operations, but their main thrust was to disrupt Romulus's economy in the only way they knew how. It was not until the Constabulary actually captured one of these "pirate" vessels and discovered an all-Reman crew did it realize the truth of the matter. Now that the terrorists had moved out into Deep Space, the Constabulary could act, and it immediately put its contingency plans to work.

The JUR hatched many plots to achieve their goals, but usually they were of the more mundane sort. Seldom did they involve exotic plans – until now. Now, a pirate – a *real* pirate – was suggesting that Reman terrorists were planning to use a runaway world as a weapon. What that entailed might fuel much speculation, but HQ needed to have this information and to make its own decision as to its worth.

Rodriguez informed the task-force CO of his intention to return to the *Steadfast* and requested transport. One of the attack fighters was assigned to the task. The flight back was not entirely uneventful; the pilot believed that his craft was acting "sluggishly" and put it through a series of maneuvers in order to pinpoint the problem. The Warden was certain that the pilot was doing this just to annoy him but said nothing; it wouldn't have done any good to complain, he concluded.

As soon as he returned to the patrol vessel, he made straight for the Bridge. His sudden appearance and obvious haste raised some eyebrows, but no one questioned him. A Warden did what a Warden was pleased to do. He bypassed Gold Zone altogether and pulled up before the niche which contained the *aaxyboxr*. He took a deep breath and made contact with the gray lump.

*   *   *

— *Greetings, fellow sentient. We are the* aaxyboxr. *How may we assist?*
— *Greetings to the* aaxyboxr. *I am sentient Rodriguez. I wish to send a message.*
— *State the message.*
— *"To Warden (L3) Worthington at Constabulary Headquarters from Warden (L1) Rodriguez aboard the* Steadfast. *I have in custody a pirate who claims to know a person who has additional information concerning the JUR cell on Planetoid 48. In exchange for a lenient sentence, he will provide the name of this informant. Please advise." End of message.*
— *It is sent.*
— *Thank you. The peace of Kum'halla be with the* aaxyboxr.
— *The peace of Kum'halla be with sentient Rodriguez.*

*   *   *

After breaking contact, Rodriguez took a seat in the nearest empty chair (which happened to be the XO's) and waited in deep silence for a response to his message. Captain Halvarson begrudged him for usurping Krishnamurthy's station but said nothing; it wouldn't have done any good to complain, he concluded.

Presently, Lt. Ralfo stepped onto the Bridge in the hopes of being updated on the current situation. When she spied the Warden, she grinned hugely and quickly went to his side. He returned her smile and got to his feet.

"Our Lady be with you, Lixu."

"The Lady be with you, Anafu."

"What has happened?"

The Warden gave a brief account of the capture of the pirates and of the deal their leader wanted to make.

"Do you trust him?"

"I never trust any criminal to speak honestly. Usually, they're stalling for time. Still, some decisions are not mine to make. I'm waiting for advice from HQ."

"When this affair is over, I would like you to request leave time and visit Pluj."

"I'd like that too. I've missed communing with your parents."

"Um, Leftenant," Halvarson interrupted, "you're being 'paged'."

The Captain gestured toward the *aaxyboxr*, now glowing pinkishly. Rodriguez nodded by way of acknowledgement. Ralfo stared at the thing in the bowl with fascination.

"Is that what I think it is?"

"Yes, an *aaxyboxr*."

"I have heard of them— mostly rumors. But I have never seen one of them."

The Warden went to the niche and made contact again. The electrical sensation coursed through his nervous system; his body stiffened, and the color left his face. The Pluj gasped in shock at the change in his appearance; he was as lifeless as a statue. In reaction, she gripped his forearm. It felt like touching a corpse in the final stages of *rigor mortis*. Worry lines – rare in her species – crept over her face. The contact seemed to go on forever, but it lasted only a few seconds. Rodriguez became animate once more, though his face was beaded with perspiration. Ralfo did not release her grip until she was sure he was still alive.

"The pirates want to make a deal," he finally reported to the master of the *Steadfast*, "and I've just received authorization to negotiate. Then I'll be on special assignment to pursue whatever leads are provided."

"Very well, Leftenant. I'll make the arrangements."

"Captain," Ralfo spoke up, "permission Lt. Rodriguez to accompany I request."

"Why?"

"If about Dr. Weyerhauser this informant knows, his information I can verify."

"I...see." In the back of his mind, the Captain welcomed the opportunity to rid himself – if only temporarily – of a real nemesis and a potential one at the same time, but he mustn't be seen to be too anxious about the prospect. "You may have a point there. Very well, permission granted. I'll make further arrangements."

The Warden and the Pluj departed the Bridge, the former off to his assigned transport and then to the pirate vessel, the latter to her quarters to pack a travel bag. Behind them, Captain Halvarson smiled broadly.

CHAPTER THREE

▼

TERRORISM STATED

THE INNER RING OF STONES formed a rough circle, approximately ten meters in diameter. They numbered sixteen in all, one at each of the primary, secondary, and tertiary points of an imaginary compass. All of the stones were indigo in color, and those at the primary points of the "compass" bore an additional crimson dot at their centers. The primary stones were approximately twenty-five centimeters wide and ten centimeters high; the secondary and tertiary stones were half as wide and tall. The stones exhibited a great deal of weathering, and much of the coloring had faded as well.

The outer ring of stones also described a circle, approximately fifteen meters in diameter. It consisted of only eight stones, set roughly equidistantly from each other. These stones were also twenty-five centimeters wide but fifteen centimeters high. And they were crimson-colored with blue dots in their centers. Weathering and fading were also in evidence in this ring.

In the center of the concentric rings stood a single pillar of stone, approximately six meters high and half a meter thick. It was slightly tapered toward the top. It possessed no coloring at all; in sharp contrast to the rest of the ring, it was a slate-gray. It too showed signs of weathering, and a five-centimeter piece had been gouged out of it near the base as if by a chisel. The piece itself lay near one of the primary stones in the inner ring. A similar monolith, even more damaged, occupied a point between the inner and outer rings near one of the tertiary stones opposite the one where the chiseled piece lay. And a third monolith whose top twenty centimeters had been knocked off as if by a hammer stood five meters beyond the outer ring in a line with another tertiary stone.

The surrounding landscape consisted of hard-packed soil, slightly reddish in color, with pebbles and small rocks scattered all about. No living thing – no grass, no trees, no shrubbery, no "weeds" – existed here; all of this world's vegetation had long since died out and decomposed back into the soil. Bereft of the warmth and light of a sun to trigger photosynthesis, this world had lost the ability to sustain Life.

Planetoid 48 was essentially a dead world.

This site – which on Dunia would have been labeled a "stone henge" occupied the edge of what once was a vast plain. In three directions, the barren land stretched to the horizon; foothills peppered with large boulders lay in the fourth direction. The henge (if that was what it was) seemed to be the only unnatural object for kilometers around. It was eerily silent as befitted a dead world. Above, the sky – eternally night – was filled with stars, cold dark eyes looking down upon the desolation.

Twenty millennia ago (according to the best estimate by astronomers of all races), Planetoid 48 had been somehow torn away from its parent body somewhere deeper in the central spiral and sent wandering toward an unknown destination. [8] Either it would pass out of the Galaxy altogether or it would be captured by another star or it would collide with another world with catastrophic consequences. The "henge" was proof that the runaway had once possessed intelligent life, a race of creatures still centuries away from industrialization. Thus, they had had no means by which to escape the death of their world; without a life-giving sun, their crops quickly failed, and they fell into oblivion.

The only known about this world was that it was currently plowing its way through the Central Spiral Collective with alarming recklessness. Astronomers on a dozen planets had concurred on this point, but none of them could assure that it posed no danger to life and property; given the potential of its being influenced by the stars and planets it passed by, altering its course at random, its status could change from benign to destructive within a quarter of a megasecond. The only thing anyone could do was to keep a sharp eye on it and report any noticeable changes in its behavior; contingency plans in the event of any changes were legion.

And now, it was learned, Planetoid 48 was inhabited once again – by a

8   Cf. Dr. Betty Ann Mao, "Possible Origins of Planetoid 48: A Survey," *Journal of the Amazonian Astronomical Society*, vol. 110, no. 8 (Ride 120 A.R.). This treatise is sketchy at best and makes too many assumptions, but no one else has come forth with any alternative theory – CMT.

cell of the dreaded Reman Army of Liberation, whose purpose there was open to considerable speculation.

One of these new "inhabitants" approached the stone henge, slowly and deliberately. He wore a heavy, fur-lined, hooded parka, thermal trousers, heavy gloves, and insulated boots. Because this world had long been torn away from its sun, it was bitterly cold on the surface; essentially, it was one vast tundra, not dissimilar to the Dunian region known as "Siberia." He also had a breathing mask; the long journey through the void had dissipated much of this world's atmosphere, and an external supply of air was required. The figure shone a flashlight before him to guide his way through the rubble. He halted at the outer ring and searched the ground with minute attention.

The glare of the flashlight – the first light this world had seen in twenty thousand years – picked up the glint of metal near one of the red-dotted stones. This individual had spotted the incongruous object quite by accident on a previous visit and would have examined it then and there but for the deadly cold penetrating even his heavy clothing. On this trip, he made his way unerringly to the mysterious object and hoped to return to his shelter in order to examine it closely before the cold made life miserable for him.

The artifact was a square piece of silvery metal, approximately five centimeters to a side and five millimeters thick. The only distinguishing marks on either side was a set of four hieroglyph-like symbols at the corners; the marks had not been crudely scratched as might have been the case of its being produced by a primitive race but appeared to have been engraved into the metal by a sophisticated tool. Whoever was responsible for the artifact had displayed great skill and thus presented the would-be explorer with a large enigma.

The explorer pocketed the square and searched the ground again. Perhaps he could find another artifact before the cold forced him inside. He had not taken more than a dozen slow paces when he heard his name being called. He reached into the parka's oversized pocket and withdrew his personal vidcom.

"Yes? What is it?"

"Dr. Woyer'auser, where the frag are ye?" a nasal twang issued from the device.

"I'm at that henge I told you about two days ago. I've just found the most amazing object."

"Gor! Ye're not 'ere to fraggin' soightsee. Ye 'ave a task to perform, and we'd loike ee to be doin' it."

"All right," the individual identified as "Dr. Weyerhauser" responded, not bothering to disguise the annoyance he felt over this interruption of his explorations. "I'll be there shortly."

"And, in the future, Doctor, dinna ye wander off wifoot tellin' sum'un."

Doctor Mubutu Weyerhauser mumbled something under his breath and popped his vidcom back into his pocket. He gave the henge one last look around, shook his head in frustration, and trudged off in the direction of the foothills. Out of habit, he cast his gaze into the eternal night sky and pondered the alien pattern of stars. The astrophysicist in him wondered what patterns the long-dead inhabitants of Planetoid 48 had viewed as they went about their evening routines, what color their sky might have been, and what astrophysical phenomena they had witnessed and created myths about. And what had passed through their minds when their world was wrenched rudely out of its orbit? When had they realized that they were adrift in the cosmic ocean, never to find safe harbor again and doomed to die a slow, agonizing death? What little anyone knew about this rogue had come from the enigmatic Aldebaranians, and then only grudgingly. It was a given that they knew much more than they were telling and that they were not going to tell any more unless something extraordinary occurred in either the political atmosphere of the CSC or the social milieu of the Aldebaranians themselves. Meanwhile, this world posed any number of unanswered and unanswerable questions, an intolerable situation for an astrophysicist.

Beyond the foothills was a mountain range. It would never challenge the Himalayas or the Alps on Dunia for sheer height and impassable valleys. They appeared to be weathered-down versions of their former selves. Yet, to the casual eye, they seemed formidable enough. The Doctor was not going to be on Planetoid 48 long enough to find out, and he immediately dismissed the idle thought.

As he strode up the nearest foothill, he marveled that the gravity of the runaway was similar to his native Remus. Why that should be was yet another mystery; the gravity on this world should have been less than it was. He should have been able to run up and down these foothills without breaking into a sweat. Breaking into a sweat in this chill atmosphere would have been disastrous; he would have suffered instant frostbite – or worse. For that reason, his pace was slow and deliberate.

Ahead, he spotted the entrance to a tunnel. Planetoid 48 was riddled with tunnels and caves which he and his party had discovered when they landed here twenty days ago. And, from the nature of the excavations, he had concluded that the whole network was created in a short span of time; the shapes and sizes of the tunnels were non-uniform, and the surfaces were not smooth. Moreover, they tended to zig-zag as if the excavators had not had a clear idea of where they were going. The caves were no less roughly hewn and inconsistent in shape and size. Haste, not perfection, had been the watchword here. Obviously, the original inhabitants had burrowed underground quickly in order to keep warm once they realized that they were moving away from their sun. And there they remained until they eventually starved to death.

In one respect, the presence of this network of tunnels and caves was a blessing in disguise for the newcomers, for it had saved them considerable labor in adapting this world for their own purposes. They had selected the current tunnel system quite at random and enlarged it in order to accommodate the equipment and supplies they needed. They had not been any less hasty in their work since they had no intention of setting up house permanently; two days of round-the-clock excavation served to provide them with a reasonably comfortable work environment.

Dr. Weyerhauser entered the tunnel mouth and approached the portable airlock which separated the tunnel system from the outside world. The airlock kept the cold out and kept an artificial supply of air in. He entered a code in the device's control panel; the outer hatch opened, and he stepped in. The same code closed the outer hatch and opened the inner one. He began a long, slow descent toward the base of operations for his group. He had to stoop in many places, because the tunnel's height could not accommodate him (giving an indication of the size of the original inhabitants); and, because of his unfamiliarity with his path, he kept banging his head against one projection of rock or another. Fortunately, his parka blunted the impacts; otherwise, he might have been a walking mass of cuts and bruises.

Eventually, he set foot in the cave where his fellow Remans were busy at their assigned tasks. He removed his cold-weather gear and hung it on hooks drilled into the rock near the entrance for that purpose. Other hooks extended for four meters along the cave wall and were all occupied. If not for his dark complexion inherited from his mother, he might have easily passed for the New Swiss his father was. His face was lean and raw-boned, and his physique large and muscular. He stood nearly two meters tall. His hair was sandy in color, and his eyes a deep blue. He had been the product of a brief liaison, and he was always self-conscious about that inconvenient fact. Growing up on Remus, where he stood out like Kolikov's ivy[9] in a flower garden, he tended to keep to himself. Nevertheless, he considered himself a loyal Reman and had joined as many anti-Romulan rallies as he could. These activities had brought him to the attention of the JUR – that, and the fact that he was a trained astrophysicist.

And now he found himself far from home, participating in God-knows-what sort of scheme his companions were hatching.

This cell, specially created for the unknown scheme, numbered thirty-six

---

9   Kolikov's ivy were purplish clinging vines, thick as ropes and tough as steel, found on the planet Amazon. They sense their prey by heat-sensing, seize it, and kill it by constriction. They were named for their first human victim – CMT.

(including the Doctor). Ordinarily, JUR units consisted of no more than a dozen individuals; terrorist groups needed to move quickly and unseen, and large numbers tended to slow down the unit and therefore compromise the mission. This unit, however, was engaged in a special project, and the labor involved required a greater number. Not all of the cell was in this particular cave; two dozen others were elsewhere, seeing to different facets of the mission. The dozen who were here scurried about as if they were attempting to meet a deadline. They wore the standard "uniform" of the JUR: gray coveralls trimmed in yellow with a representation of the Reman national flag – a yellow rectangle with a white star in the upper-left-hand corner – on the left breast, a red-and-green plaid scarf, black sandals, and a yellow tam o'shanter. None wore anything to suggest rank. They all had a rank; but, in the tradition of secret military operations, they did not display it.

If not for the unusual surroundings, the Remans might have been seen as ordinary technicians in a control center. The cave was a control center, but it was hardly ordinary. It was crammed with computers, sensor arrays, video monitors, communication devices, and radar screens, all set along the walls seemingly in no particular order. Overlooking the complex was a large electronic "map" similar to ones used by planetary port authorities; it depicted in real time the configuration of the region of Deep Space in which Planetoid 48 was traversing. All of the equipment was tied in to the master control board located roughly in the center of the cave. Space heaters had been placed in optimum spots in order to ward of the chill of the cave. Most of the Remans were busy testing their equipment and/or making adjustments, physically and electronically, in order to coax the maximum performance out of their charges. That some of them were unfamiliar with sophisticated gear was evident from repeated adjustments and expressions of frustration.

The leader of this cell sat at the master control board, studying it intently. As new information appeared on the monitor, he barked fresh orders at specific individuals and kept at them until he saw what he wanted to see. Like most of his kind, he was short-statured; his lean face, beady eyes, and wispy moustache gave him the appearance of a rat. And he wore a perpetual scowl as a result of long years of resentment against his lot in life. When he spotted Dr. Weyerhauser at the cave's entrance, he leaped to his feet, a look of annoyance written large across his face.

"It's aboot fraggin' toime!" he grumbled. "We requoire more readings."

"So soon?"

"Aye. Noo that we've entered CSC spyce, we'll be after needin' 'em four toimes a dy. And more frequently once we approach Rhea Silvia's system."

"I've already assured you that Planetoid 48 will pass within one light-year of Rhea Silvia and that there shouldn't be any significant astrophysical repercussions. What more do you want?"

"We're na tykin' anyfing for granted, Doctor. Even the sloightest deviaytion will frow a fraggin' spanner into oor plans."

"Ah, yes, 'our plans.'" The astrophysicist peered at the Reman in what he hoped was his best indignant expression. "You've not bothered to reveal to me what those plans are, Major Tshambe. I'd like to know what I've gotten myself into."

"Ye'll be told in good toime. Noo, the fraggin' readings, if ye please."

The two men stared each other down for the space of two heartbeats, and the Major won the contest. Dr. Weyerhauser knew as well as anyone here that the missions which came down from Central Command were expected to be carried out without question and that the mission leader was to be obeyed to the letter. He had heard tales of what happened to those who were not prepared to give 110% to the JUR; they met the same fate as persons deemed "traitors" to Remus and/or "collaborators" with the hated Romulans. He knew where his loyalties lay, but he hated to be kept in the dark.

The Doctor stalked off toward his own station, at the far end of the cave. This station consisted of a giant vidscreen, three meters by three, and a keyboard.

One of the first orders of business when the unit arrived at this world was to install a series of electronic telescopes at strategic points on the surface. The telescopes were connected to computers which translated the images into data bits and then transmitted those bits wirelessly to a central receiver; the receiver fed the bits into another computer connected to the vidscreen which restored the images. By this means, the operator could pinpoint to a thousandth of a degree where in Deep Space he was at any given moment. And Dr. Weyerhauser was considered the top expert in the Amazonian Federation for mapping Deep Space. No one was aware that he was also a Reman terrorist.

He sat down before the darkened vidscreen and activated his keyboard. Instantly, an image filled the screen. It was not an eye's view of the heavens such as one might see by looking directly into the night sky, but a computer-generated version. In this case, the image presented was a two-dimensional composite of Planetoid 48's current position. Forward and ten degrees to starboard, Ru'uhaad's sun [*Procyon on Dunian star charts – CC*], a green-tinged, class F5 star, revolved about a white dwarf. The combined stellar radiation served to bake the system's inner planet and create a desert world of the outer one. The Doctor pressed another key, and the image was replaced by another which derived from the telescope aimed along the path in which the runaway was traveling. His expert eye told him that that path had not deviated in the slightest from what he had seen on the previous sighting. Major

Tshambe, of course, would not be satisfied with his personal observations; he would demand hard evidence, as would the astrophysicist himself under other circumstances. He entered a command on the keyboard. A few seconds later, a print-out filled with numbers issued from a nearby printer.

Print-out in hand and smirk on face, he strode triumphantly to the Major's station and waited patiently until the latter was aware of his presence. Tshambe turned in his seat and looked at him with barely concealed contempt.

"Well?"

"Here you are, Major." He practically shoved the print-out in the other's face, a gesture which merited a baring of the teeth and a deeper scowl. "All is in order, as I've said."

"Ye needna be so smug aboot it. This is a delicate operytion, and we 'ave to do it boy the numbers."

"Roight ye are, guv," Dr. Weyerhauser responded, knuckling his forehead, a gesture which merited a flash of anger from his cell leader.

"Awy wif ee!" the Major growled. "And keep yersilf in readiness fum noo on!"

Dr. Weyerhauser wandered off and "inspected" his comrades' handiwork, his perplexity at the meaning of it all increasing by the nanosecond. His meanderings brought him around to the only two persons in this cell who had been the least bit civil to him and with whom he could carry on a decent conversation. Both men were calibrating one of the sensor devices. At his approach, they looked up and nodded in acknowledgement.

"How goes it, fellows?" he asked by way of making small talk.

"Foine, foine," both men murmured noncommittally, almost in unison.

The Remans glanced at each other nervously and shifted their weight from foot to foot. One of them, a slightly overweight sort, decided to take a bold stance.

"It's dyngerous, Doctor," he cautioned in a low voice, "to taunt the Myjor loike that. 'E's killed men for less reason."

"Cutty's roight," added the other man, a stocky sort with a scarred face. "As much as ye're needed 'ere, 'e wouldna 'esityte to do for ee if 'e fought ye was oot o' loine."

"Don't worry about me, Jingles. I may be a university professor, but I grew up in a tough neighborhood. I believe I can hold my own." He gestured at the device behind them. "What is all this about? Major Tshambe is being rather tight-lipped."

Cutty and Jingles exchanged more nervous looks. Every member of a JUR cell was under strict orders not to discuss their roles with anyone who was not in the know, even if that person were another JUR member. Whether that restriction also applied to members of the same cell who had not been briefed was debatable; but, for obvious reasons, neither man wished to tempt the Fates by being the first to answer the astrophysicist's question.

"Sorry, friend," Cutty said, "we canna tell ee. Orders, ye know."

"I'm sorry too. Well, you'd better get back to work. We mustn't upset the Major any further, must we?"

The Doctor grabbed his parka and drifted away toward the mouth of a tunnel opposite the one he had used to enter the cave. So far, the task force had merely scratched the surface in their explorations of the subterranean honeycomb. Not that they ever intended to in the first place – the mission (whatever it was) was following a timetable; and, once all of the components of the installation were in place, they would depart and monitor the runaway from a safe distance. At this point, they had set up shop in the largest cavern they had encountered and bypassed many smaller ones. From overheard scuttlebutt, he knew that three other caverns were being outfitted with machines of an unknown nature; individual work crews operated independently of each other, and any co-ordination was done by only Major Tshambe. Doctor Weyerhauser had been kept out of the loop entirely, but he had been occupying himself by exploring the surface of the planetoid. Now that activity was being restricted.

Therefore, he decided to go snooping *inside* this world to learn what he could about this mission. He doubted the Major would miss him for short periods; the man was quite wrapped up in his work. And, if the Doctor was discovered where he might not be welcome – well, what could the Major do to him? His expertise was still needed for the time being. And he intended to use the time he had in satisfying his curiosity.

The tunnel in which he now found himself had been strung with battery-powered lamps so that the work parties could travel without injuring themselves. Still, it was set in a sharp decline, and he had to watch his every step; otherwise, he'd be *rolling* down the tunnel. Presently, he came to a small cave off to one side. It was completely dark inside, the JUR having no use for it. He reached into the pocket of his parka, produced the flashlight, and switched it on. A powerful beam of white light split the darkness in two.

He ducked his head automatically and entered the cave cautiously, panning the flashlight's beam back and forth. At once, he discovered a disturbing sight: three skeletons, humanoid in design. The two larger skeletons were no more than a meter-and-a-half long and were clearly bipedal. The arms and legs were proportionately short but large-boned as if designed for hard, grueling labor. The rib cages were distended, suggesting a large lung capacity. The skulls were nearly spherical, and they were disproportionately large compared to the torsos. One of the large skeletons possessed a wider pelvis, indicating a female. The third, smaller skeleton was a miniature version of the other two – a child, apparently.

Dr. Weyerhauser swallowed compulsively. He had just discovered the remains of some of the original inhabitants of Planetoid 48, and the discovery left him breathless and not a little saddened. This...family had died where they lay, through either starvation or freezing. They had been there for thousands of years, and they would remain there for all eternity.

He swung the beam around to locate other skeletons which might be present but found none. Yet, the light illuminated in the outstretched hand (with only four digits) of the (male?) skeleton what could only be another artifact. It was also metallic, exactly the same size and shape as the one he had picked up at the henge. He was no anthropologist, but he had to guess that both artifacts held some religious significance – a talisman believed by the possessor to wield magical powers or to affirm his devotion to his god(s). Unfortunately, the object had not protected this family – or any others on this world – from an awful fate beyond their comprehension. Their god(s) had failed them utterly, and they bore mute testimony to the futility of relying on metaphysics for their comfort.

Dr. Weyerhauser now undertook to examine the new artifact more closely. This second square of metal contained only one symbol, and its appearance shocked him to the core. He'd seen this symbol once before, in the Galactic Museum of Natural History on New Switzerland, and he knew that the exo-anthropolgy people at the University – not to mention the bureaucrats of the Central Spiral Collective! – would love to get their hands on this piece. The symbol resembled an inverted "T" with a small circle attached to the right side of the vertical stem, halfway up.

It was the mark of the Wayfarers.

The Museum held roughly two dozen artifacts obtained from either CSC member worlds, associate-member worlds,[10] or uninhabited worlds (which may or may not have been inhabited once) scattered throughout the central spiral. The Museum displays ranged from coarsely-made paper to wooden, lacquered discs to stone slabs covered with vegetable-derived pigments to stylized sculptures carved from ivory (or its equivalent) or wood or hammered metal. On some of the pieces, other symbols were present, undecipherable – perhaps representing an ancient script; but, in none of them did the addenda detract from the central motif, the mark of the Wayfarers.

How these artifacts had come into the Museum's possession would fill a

___
10 Associate-member worlds are those classified as possessing Level 5 cultures, i.e. worlds which only recently engaged in Deep Space exploration and which are deemed by the CSC (with advice from the Aldebaranians, of course) to be capable of coping with the existence of alien races – CMT.

book. The methods of procuration were as varied as the material substances. For the most part, they had been donated, by amateur and professional exo-archaeologists, by the CSC Constabulary who had confiscated them from would-be looters, or by conscience-stricken looters who wished to make amends. In one notorious instance, the Museum personnel had asked no questions in their quest to add a most unique addition to their collection; and, it was no secret that they had quietly offered a bounty to anyone who came into possession of a likely specimen, a practice roundly condemned by the Galactic Institute of Exo-Archaeology on the grounds that it would open the door to looting (among other abuses). Whether or not the current collection was suitably provenienced, the Museum was keeping mum on the subject until such time as someone proved otherwise.

That the artifacts were, in fact, manifestations of the Wayfarers' having visited the worlds of origin was a given by professional and lay persons alike. There was, of course, no hard evidence for this acceptance – no "Kilroy-was-here" identifiers – the evidence (such as it was) was wholly anecdotal and circumstantial. The anecdotes derived from the folk legends of two-dozen or more cultures in the central spiral, all of which claimed that the ancient "gods" had worn this symbol about their persons and attached it to all of their great works. The circumstances were that there was no other rational explanation as to the true origin of the symbol; and, in that absence, Occam's razor prevailed – sort of. If it were true that all legends contained a grain of fact, then the case for the existence of a highly-evolved race of beings who had wandered through the Galaxy, performing "miracles," had a (albeit tenuous) foundation.

The astrophysicist turned the metal square over in his hand and mentally assigned it the role of "additional evidence" to bolster the foundation. Add Planetoid 48 to the list of worlds the Wayfarers had visited in the dim past and left their mark on the indigenous intelligent life-forms. Clearly (at least to his mind), the artifact and its symbol thus became part of a religious ritual by which the now-extinct intelligent life-forms worshipped their "gods." But it had not prevented their extinction, and so they were now no more than a statistic.

He pocketed the new artifact, made a mental note to requisition a vidcam in order to record the remains in this cave, and re-entered the tunnel. Presently, he came to a "fork in the road" which left him in a bit of a quandary. Which way to go? The fork to his left continued to decline, leading to a lower level; the right one seemed to have leveled off. He made his choice based solely on his preference not to go any lower than he had to and to opt for the easier path.

After he had gone approximately one hundred meters, he heard voices, those of another work party. One individual was arguing vehemently with another, but the voices were still too faint to determine the nature of the argument. Other voices – fainter still – provided a chorus for the main "performers." He advanced cautiously – no need to walk in on something before he knew what was taking place. He inched forward as stealthily as he could, not an easy task for someone of his height and weight. And the fact that the tunnel floor was littered with the rubble of the past and that of the present did not make the task any less hazardous; a misstep could turn an ankle or send rubble flying and clattering and defeating the purpose.

Eventually, he reached the mouth of a new cavern. The voices were more distinct now, and they were still in heated argument. What surprised – and dismayed – the Doctor was that the argument centered on the placement of a particular piece of equipment. One faction, lead by Major Tshambe's second-in-command, Lt. Mutanga, was for following the The Plan to the letter – no deviations allowed. The other faction (which seemed to include the majority of the team) countered with a common-sense approach; whoever was its chief spokesperson thought he had some technical knowledge the lieutenant did not and insisted that there was a more efficient method of positioning the equipment. If the two sides came to blows – and it seemed likely to, given the general temperament of the JUR – the entire operation could be thrown into an uproar. The astrophysicist saw himself being caught in the middle, a target for both sides.

In the end, Lt. Mutanga threatened to bring the Major in on the argument, and that dampened the ardor of the common-sense faction. Tshambe would also insist on following The Plan to the letter, and he would not hesitate to shoot anyone who he believed was an obstacle to the mission. Grumbling incoherently, the work crew returned to their individual duties.

Dr. Weyerhauser risked peeking into the cavern and instantly wished he hadn't. As he scanned the layout, he recognized every single piece of equipment here, knew exactly what its function was, and reluctantly agreed with the common-sense faction concerning the optimum efficiency of the placement. He had seen such an arrangement – a mock-up actually – during a field trip in his post-graduate days at the University. How the JUR had gotten its hands on this equipment was a secondary concern; what really mattered was what they planned to do with it. He did not like the implications it raised; it spelled danger in his book.

As stealthily as he had arrived, he retreated back down the tunnel. He felt perspiration running down his face, even though the environment was quite chilly.

*   *   *

"What is it like to touch the *aaxyboxr*, Lixu?"

Rodriguez and Ralfo were in the *Steadfast*'s shuttle, headed toward the Relay Station which orbited the Ru'uhaad system. The Warden had informed the pirate leader that his offer of information in exchange for a lenient sentence had been accepted by the Constabulary High Command and received the desired information. The pirates were on their way to New Switzerland to face justice, and the Warden's ultimate destination was Romulus in order to check out the lead.

He looked at his companion and marveled at the look of concern on her face. A Pluj seldom showed concern unless a matter of great moment was involved. And he didn't think one was. Clearly, Anafu was worried about his state of well-being.

"It's like grabbing an electric wire without any insulation, to be perfectly honest. The first time I made contact with one of the creatures, at the Academy, I broke off immediately. I thought I was going to be electrocuted." A small smile pursed his lips. "For that, I received *two* one-kilo lectures on the importance of establishing a rapport with the *aaxyboxr*, one from the instructor and the other from my personal mentor. Master Fresh was particularly caustic that day. He pointedly asked me if I wished to, quote, 'continue your education or to return to your former worthless existence,' unquote."

"And despite that, you stayed."

"Yes. I so wanted to be a Warden. I believed it to be the highest calling there was in the Galaxy, to be able to bring evil-doers to justice and to make the Galaxy safe for decent people." He chuckled. "I still think that way, but you won't hear me speaking so melodramatically again. Reality has a way of tempering one's enthusiasm."

"How 'tempered' were you?"

"*Humph!* My first assignment after graduation was monitor duty in the Memgoan system, right after the Constabulary decided to post a Warden in all planetary systems, inhabited or not, in order to prevent a recurrence of what had happened on Memgo 2."

"I have read about that. It was...distasteful."

"Quite. My tour there lasted fifty megs – fifty *boring* megs. Not my idea of bringing evil-doers to justice, I can tell you. I was happy when I was re-assigned to the *Steadfast*, although duty there has also been pretty much of a bore — until now."

"Yes, Lixu, now you are – what is the human expression? – 'in hot pursuit' of evil-doers."

She beamed grandly. And, because the smile of a Pluj is infectious, Rodriguez emulated her. She touched his cheek lightly.

"I am pleased to be working with you."

"And I with you, Anafu. I–"

"Excusing me, sir, ma'am," interrupted the pilot of the shuttle, a junior lieutenant of U'haadi origin, "we approaching the Relay Station."

A giant-sized MOME, specially designed to facilitate travel in Deep Space, the Relay Station resembled a small asteroid orbiting a star. Every star system which possessed planets had its own RS, and the RS became the outermost "planet" in the system, far enough away from the major natural bodies in order to prevent any astrophysical consequences due to the sudden gravity shift. The RS created a temporary, massive gravity well which brought two distant points closer together in accordance with relativity theory. These artificial worlds also served as bases of operation for Wardens on monitor duty.

"Thank you, Leftenant O-da. Contact the Station Manager, please."

The face which appeared on the shuttle's vidscreen belonged to a puffy, red-cheeked, completely bald human who exhibited the standard bureaucratic expression of annoyance at being interrupted in the middle of pressing duties. He stiffened appreciably when he spied the Warden's uniform, and a frown tugged at his mouth.

"Ah, Warden, Cn. Greathouse here. What can I do for you?"

"Warden (L1) Rodriguez requesting clearance to Rhea Silvia," the other replied formally.

"Certainly, certainly. I'll notify the Operations Officer right away."

"Thank you. May I speak with Warden Chork?"

"Of course. Anything else?"

"Thank you, no."

That went well, Rodriguez mused. Ordinarily, Amazonians want to know your business, right down to the last detail. And who's paying for the 'privilege' of using their RS. Cn. Greathouse must be a rarity in his bureau. Maybe that's why he's stuck out here at Ru'uhaad.

The next face which appeared on the vidscreen exhibited only the rudiments of humanoid features. It possessed two eye sockets inside of which red dots could be discerned, the barest hint of a nose, a slit for a mouth, and two nubs where ears should have been. It had all the marks of a sculpture begun, then abandoned. The skin color was akin to wet sand, and tufts of short black hairs dotted the skull and face. This creature was a S'am, the indigenous life-form from a planet deep inside the central spiral and the newest member of the Central Spiral Collective.

"L1 Rodriguez greets L1 Chork," the human said formally and steepled his fingers in the salute of the Warden Service.

"L1 Chork hreets L1 Rodri'ez," the S'am responded in a monotone and returned the salute, revealing hands with only three digits each. "How fare you, classmate?"

"I fare well, classmate. And you?"

"'Bored to tears,' I sink you Umans would say."

"I know what you mean. I too was on monitor duty until recently."

"Yes. We must be seasoned in our profession before hiven responsibility. What is your mission, classmate?"

Rodriguez gave a terse run-down of recent events which elicited a low-level hum from the S'am.

"Already, responsibility comes to you. I conhratulate you."

"Thank you, classmate. The peace of Kum'halla be with you."

"Se peace of Kum'halla to you also, classmate."

When Rodriguez broke contact, he noted that Ralfo was regarding him in a most pensive fashion. The Pluj were pensive only when they considered matters of state; to be pensive at any other time was a cause for wonder.

"*Chelzee ha* [what's wrong], Anafu?" he reverted to Pluj.

"*Da ha* [nothing]," she replied in kind. "I am just curious."

"About what?"

"Who or what is Kum'halla?"

He pondered the situation for a moment, then made a snap decision.

"What I'm about to tell you, Anafu, isn't well-known, and the Aldebaranians want to keep it that way for the time being. So, I'm asking you to keep this in strictest confidence." She nodded her assent, and he continued. "Kum'halla is the name of an ancient visitor to the Aldebaranian system. He may or may not have been one of the legendary Wayfarers; the Community is a bit mum on that point. Kum'halla found the forebears of the Community in a primitive state, and he undertook to educate them. The entire Aldebaranian culture is based upon his teachings; and, if they revere anybody in the Universe, it is he. When he departed their world, it is claimed, he took some of the Community with him to be his companions. 'The peace of Kum'halla' is their standard salutation and somewhat of a motto."

"I understand. Tell me more."

"Not now. We're nearing our warp-out point."

While the sole planet in the Ru'uhaad system orbited its double-star primary at a mean distance of fifty million kilometers (thus accounting for its global desert-like climate), Relay Station #37 was located a safe five hundred million kilometers away. The gravitational pull of the two stars tended to force its satellite into an irregularly-shaped orbit so that it described the same path only every forty cycles, after which it shifted into another path for another forty cycles, and so on. Consequently, the dominant species, the Uhaad, had a very complex calendar; an entire department of the local government existed in order to sort matters out. The builders of the RS had prevented any possibility of collision with the planet by placing it at the very fringe of the double star's gravitational field.

As the shuttle approached the giant MOME, the vidscreen lit up to reveal a bleary-eyed human, the Operations Officer-on-Duty.

"RS 37 sending to approaching Constabulary shuttle," he rasped.

The Warden observed that the Operations OD had not bothered to ask for the vessel's ID number, which was standard procedure. He smiled wryly. They wanted him out of their hair as quickly as possible.

"Constabulary shuttle sending to RS 37," Lt. O-da responded. "Standing by."

"Shuttle, you are green to RS25, RS14, RS7, and RS1. Do you copy?"

"We copying, RS37. Green to RS25, 11, 7, and 1."

"Shuttle, you are green for Passing Lane Alpha – repeat, Passing Lane Alpha."

"We copying, RS37. Green for Passing Lane Alpha."

The pilot dampened the flow of fuel in one thruster, then another, to maneuver his craft toward the designated point. The OD confirmed that he was on course, and he resumed full flow of fuel. A second signal indicated the ten-second delay until activation of the MOME.

At the mark, the shuttle departed Reality.

Like a flat stone skipping across a pond, so too did the shuttle "skip" across Deep Space by means of a "throw" from RS37. For the passengers, the rapid shifts in the background of stars was akin to watching a speeded-up slide show; no sooner had any of them focused on one scene than it was replaced by a completely different one. It had been reported in the early days of MOME-driven space travel that some passengers experienced disorientation and/or psychosis. "Skipping" across Deep Space twenty-five to fifty light-years at a time proved to be so unnerving that passengers were advised to view the passage at their own risk. As time wore on and humans (and aliens) became accustomed to the passage, the psychological effects diminished (but did not disappear completely).

Not so the *physical* effects.

The Murchison Oscillating Matrix Engine was an instrument of great power. It was also an instrument of great destruction, a fact which could have been attested to by any number of careless individuals – and others in their vicinity – had they survived to tell about it. Creating an artificial gravity well – or "twisting the fabric of space," to use a quaint ancient, and inaccurate, phrase – required a tremendous amount of energy to achieve. Such energies, by their very nature, were unstable at best and catastrophic at worst. Thomas Edison Murchison I (a.k.a. the First Murchison), who developed the MOME, blew apart his laboratory in what was then called "Australia"[11] during his initial experiments. Thereafter, he conducted his tests in the wide expanse of desert in the heart of the island where the risk to others (not to mention himself!) could be kept to a minimum. And, when he scaled up his tests to (relatively) full power, he had been obliged to work through others in orbit around Dunia.

The instability problem with the MOME (which still has yet to be overcome) was offset by operating it for only short periods of time. Of necessity, then, a spacecraft had to pass over the gravity well rapidly in order to avoid either (1) destruction when the well collapsed or (2) destruction when the well was sustained for too long a period. The subsequent rapid acceleration subjected the passengers to much physical stress. The stress could be ameliorated by cushioning and restraining equipment. Many humans (and aliens) learned to cope; those who could not sedated themselves before warping-out occurred.

The occupants of the shuttle had their own methods of coping: Rodriguez meditated as best he could, while Ralfo dozed off. Only the pilot remained alert, not only because he had to but also because it had been determined long ago that the Uhaad could endure the stress better than other races; therefore, they were generally tapped for pilot duty in non-combat situations.

When the shuttle re-entered Reality, RS1 loomed before it in orbit around Rhea Silvia at a distance of sixty thousand gigameters (where its effects would not disturb the natural order). Relay Stations were technically the property of the star systems of which they were the latest additions if those systems were inhabited by sentient beings engaged in space travel, and they were staffed (mostly) by the indigenous race; otherwise, the RS's were considered the trust territory of the CSC and staffed by selected individuals from the member worlds until such time (if ever) a qualified indigenous population appeared on the scene. Protocol demanded that all ships entering or leaving a star system identify themselves, state their business, and provide an approximate length of stay within the system. And nowhere in the Central Spiral Collective was this protocol more assiduously adhered to than in the Amazonian Federation and especially in the "home" system. Checking each and every vessel was the Federation's bread and butter; the lion's share of its revenues derived from fees and charges, fines and penalties, assessed against as many hapless ship's captains as it could.

"RS1 sending to Constabulary shuttle."

---

11 Now known as the United Dunian Government's Administrative District #10 (capital city: Sydney) – CMT.

"Constabulary shuttle sending to RS1," Lt. O-da responded nonchalantly.

"Shuttle, state your business."

"We pursuing leads concerning terrorist activity."

"Have you filed a request with the Bureau of Internal Security?"

"We unaware that we must. We on Constabulary business, RS1."

"Amazonian regulations require that all police matters be cleared with the proper authorities."

"Standing by, RS1." The Uhaad swiveled in his seat. "Warden Rodriguez?" The Warden remained immobile, lost in thought. O-da reached out and gently nudged him. "Sir? I needing your assistance."

Rodriguez's eyes snapped open, and he blinked once. He spotted the concern on the pilot's face and assumed an authoritarian demeanor.

"What is it, Leftenant?"

"Sir, the Amazonians not allowing us to pass. They saying we needing authorization."

"*Humph!* More bureaucratic mumbo-jumbo!"

The Warden unstrapped himself from his seat and took the empty co-pilot's chair ahead of him. He glared sternly at the Relay Station's duty officer who instantly blanched when he realized with whom he had to deal.

"What seems to be the problem, Officer?" Rodriguez intoned.

"Ah, Warden, ah, we require, ah, proper authorization for your visit – sir."

Rodriguez grimaced but said nothing. Instead, he reached inside his tunic and pulled out a golden disc five centimeters in diameter. It seemed to possess an inner light and glistened even in the dim illumination of the shuttle's interior. In its center was engraved the blazing comet of the Warden Service; superimposed over the symbol was the owner's last name and Service rank. Around the circumference of the disc, the motto of the Service was inscribed: "To safeguard the Galaxy." This, then, was a Warden's "badge," and Rodriguez held his up close to the vidscreen.

"*This* is all the authorization I need," he muttered ominously. "Kindly allow us to pass."

The duty officer swallowed a large lump in his throat and glanced to his left and right in the hopes that no one was noticing how uncomfortable he had suddenly become.

"Uh, aye, sir! At once, sir!"

The Warden smiled to himself and resumed his former seat. Ralfo, now awake, regarded him with no little awe. The shuttle's pilot went through the formalities, departed from the Relay Station, and charted a course toward Romulus.

CHAPTER FOUR

▼

INVESTIGATION BEGUN

MURCHISON SPACE CENTER IN NEW Nairobi was always a bee-hive of activity. The Romulans had desired it to be one, and they had worked assiduously to make it so. Other cities on Romulus had spaceports as well, but they were pale imitations of MSC. Anyone – human or alien – who had any business to conduct with the Amazonian Federation was obliged to make the journey to New Nairobi and its large complex of government buildings; the Romulans had seen that as a means of controlling tightly the commerce within the Federation's jurisdiction. Even those who came strictly for pleasure – whether it be to visit the museums, to "drop a bundle" in the legalized gaming parlors, or to seek out nominally illicit recreation – were channeled towards New Nairobi, again by design. Tourism was a huge industry, and the Romulans derived a large portion of its revenues from it.

To accommodate the thousands of daily visitors, then, required a suitable facility with which to greet them. And, once they had completed the construction of the core of New Town (in as meticulous a fashion as humanly possible), the City Fathers turned their attention to a new, improved spaceport to replace the makeshift one the original settlers had constructed. With a generous donation from the Second Murchison (who, of course, had an ulterior reason for his beneficence), they produced an edifice as grand and as splendid as any other structure in New Town.[12] In planned phases, they replaced old buildings with new until nothing of the old remained; state-

---

12 The dedication occurred in 51 A.R. – forty-six years before the Great War – and, according to many historians, contributed significantly to the imperialist ambitions of

of-the-art was the watchword, and no expense was spared. New docks, new repair shops, an innovative launching system, new computerized controls to co-ordinate all aspects of operation – everything essential (and a few things non-essential) for a facility worthy of the name found a place in the scheme of things.

The crown jewel in the Center was the reception area, that which the City Fathers had hoped to grab the attention of everyone who passed through it. The reception area was a mini-city in its own right, a deliberate move on the part of the designers. There were restaurants specializing in the cuisines of a dozen worlds, theaters to entertain all tastes, casinos offering various lures which promised instant wealth, dormitories available to lay-overs, a news bureau which posted the latest developments anywhere in the Central Spiral Collective in any language desired, a currency exchange, public restrooms suitable for all races, chapels dedicated to whatever god(s) one believed in, and much more. Incoming or outgoing passengers had little need to go into New Nairobi proper for their wants – they were all right here – but still they were encouraged to visit the city by visual and audio blandishments of all sorts and to partake of its charms.

Inasmuch as thousands of visitors passed through the gates of the Center, one might have supposed that illicit activities could be discovered there, and one would be correct. Large crowds always meant large sums of money in a dozen different currencies available to those who desired wealth without working for it; the criminal element was ever present in various guises, from prostitutes to pickpockets, from scam artists to "back alley" gamblers – and the beggars. They practiced their "trades" with caution and stealth, because the Center's security guards patrolled the concourses around the clock, and plain-clothes operatives worked to entrap the careless practitioners.

Because of the immense traffic at this, the heart of the Amazonian Federation, the scene took on kaleidoscopic qualities. Crowd composition – by race, by gender, by political allegiance, by tastes in fashion – shifted constantly, and no pattern ever repeated itself. It was, next to the facility on New Switzerland, the most cosmopolitan complex ever seen in the history of the Galaxy.

Into what might be described as "ordinary" sights walked what might be described as an extraordinary one: a Warden and his Pluj companion.

Pluj in and of themselves were not an unusual sight. They traveled the space ways nearly as much as any other race for as great a variety of purposes. And they tended to attract attention to themselves because of their well-

---

the Romulans. Cf. Dr. Tomas Bashaong's *A Brief History of the Amazonian Federation* (University of New Nairobi Press, 133 A.R.) – CMT.

deserved reputation as sexual gymnasts. Pluj (the planet) possessed a very chilly environment for most species, but its inhabitants had adapted. At home, they dressed comfortably while in public; in the privacy of their own homes, however, they went about *au naturel*. Elsewhere, they found most environments too hot for their comfort, and so they tended to wear as little clothing as local customs allowed (a mode which boosted their reputation). A Pluj could be spotted immediately, even at a distance, and she never failed to crane necks – especially those of human males.

A Warden, on the other hand, was a rare sight in these surroundings. Their function and their reputation (real and imagined) made it so. The former put them in the space ways, chasing pirates and claim-jumpers, not on planetary surfaces; the latter gave them supernatural powers which motivated "ordinary" people to avoid them at all costs. Therefore, when a Warden intruded him/herself into the world of "ordinary" people, (s)he was cause for concern.

And so it was in the present instance. And the fact that he had a Pluj in tow made their presence doubly distracting.

Warden (L1) Lixu Rodriguez was very much aware of the attention he and Anafu were attracting. He had heard the stories at the Academy about the reputation his kind were alleged to have; and, he had, in his short career, experienced first-hand the reactions of the "proles," the term used by Wardens to identify the rest of the sentients in the central spiral – except, of course, the Aldebaranians. He recalled having put the question to Master Fresh-Bloom-in-the-Face-as-the-Day-Begins about how to cope with the spectrum of emotions Wardens drew from the "proles." He also recalled, with a slight shudder, the expression on Master Fresh's face, an expression as full of revulsion as an Aldebaranian was capable of producing.

"'Proles'?" his mentor had asked in a too, too soft tone of voice. "That is a human slang word, is it not, lack-wit? Why do you use such words? Is your vocabulary so deficient that you must resort to crude expressions?"

"No, Master," the cadet had responded in a tremulous voice. "I – I merely repeat what others have said."

This response had provoked several pokes on his chest.

"Repeat not in the future. Describe a being as it is, *not* as you think it is. As to your question, you will serve a function that others do not fully comprehend. You must therefore concentrate on your function rather than on the lack of comprehension. Is this clear, lack-wit?"

Rodriguez strode down the concourse with even, deliberate steps, his body erect, his eyes barely glancing left or right, his face full of sternness. Inside, however, he was as much in awe of the onlookers as they were of him.

Sternness was not a quality which gripped his companion, however.

She ambled along, looking this way and that, drinking in the many sights (animate and inanimate) much like a school child on its first outing. Far from embracing the stoicism of her escort, she *ooh*ed and *ahh*ed at each new wonder, even if it were the most mundane thing in the Universe. Ralfo had been to Romulus before on several occasions, but the kaleidoscopic nature of the Murchison Space Center always elicited fresh reactions from a highly inquisitive race as the Pluj.

A more incongruous pair few were likely to see, but no one dared to point out that fact – at least in public.

This pair nearly made it out of the Center without incident. The Warden did not know how much longer he could maintain his stone face; he could feel his facial muscles tighten up, and he feared that they would become permanently frozen. Fifty meters from the main entrance, a plaintive cry behind him shattered his reserve. In Ekath/Okath-accented Romulan, he heard:

"Assists, please! I haves beed robbed!"

Rodriguez searched the crowd for the source of the plea. He did not have to search far, for the crowd was being forcibly pushed aside by two young humans who, one could safely assume, were the alleged robbers. One was tall and lean; the other was short and lean. Both wore tattered clothing, a mark of the hordes of unfortunate poor who populated Old Town. How they had managed to penetrate this far into the spaceport without attracting the attention of the security patrols was anybody's guess. Either Security was very lax this day or the culprits were very adept at stealth – up to a point.

"Do we intervene, Lixu?"

"We are law-enforcement officials, Anafu. We're obliged to assist, even though my heart isn't in it."

"*Khalee* [excellent]!" the Pluj exulted. "Action at last! I shall handle the one on the right."

It was doubtful that anyone present in the Center had ever seen a Pluj in combat mode. It was doubtful that anyone present would have believed that a Pluj could go into combat mode, given that race's reputation for pleasurable pursuits. Even Rodriguez, who had spent half his life amongst them, had never seen a Pluj in combat mode. Nevertheless, the Pluj dominated their military as they did everything else on their world, and they trained as rigorously as any male elsewhere. During the War of the Eight Suns, they had allied themselves with the Romulans and had fought alongside with militiamen. Their greatest victory came during a chance encounter with Capellan mercenaries during the Battle of Planetoid Delta. The Alkon warriors had never seen women in combat before; and, since their code of honor forbade them to kill a female (but encouraged them simply to *capture* and *enslave* the females from rival tribes), they became easy victims – the only time they were ever defeated in combat. After hostilities had ended, Pluj volunteers peppered the ranks of the Central Spiral Collective's police force.

With a grin, Ralfo bounded toward the oncoming pair. Ten meters from her chosen target, she let out a blood-curdling screech – the Pluj war-cry – which frightened and paralyzed all around her. The screech also served to slow down the would-be thieves as what they thought was a banshee came straight at them. Immediately, the "banshee" leaped into the air, timing her action so that she would descend squarely upon the Old Towner she had targeted. The young man attempted to avoid a collision by moving laterally, but Ralfo twisted in mid-air, lashed one leg forward, and struck her target on the side of his head, spinning him around. She landed gracefully, moved toward her prey, and delivered a quick punch to his solar plexus. He folded up and collapsed to the floor.

The second thief, either unaware of the fate of his companion or uncaring about it, continued to move toward the entrance of the Center. He soon came up against the Warden and tried to dodge him. Rodriguez pivoted on one foot, swung in a complete circle, and used his momentum to deliver a solid blow to the chest with his free foot. The Old Towner staggered backwards, slammed against a nearby pillar, and rebounded toward his assailant. He stared wildly at the latter.

"Down on your knees," the Warden said quietly, "and stay there if you know what's good for you."

The thief did not think twice about obeying the order.

"Aw right!" a gravelly voice intoned. "Move aside! Clear the way!"

A beefy, red-faced Romulan in the uniform of the Center's security force pushed his way through the crowd, came up behind Rodriguez, seized his shoulder, and spun him around.

"Aw right! What the frag is goin'…"

The guard's voice trailed off as he spied, first, the black uniform, secondly, the blazing comet of the Warden Service, and, finally, a pair of eyes gazing intently at him with all the force of twin laser-drills. He swallowed convulsively, took his hand away, and threw up a hasty and sloppy salute.

"Uh, sorry, sir," he sputtered. "I di'n't reckanize you. How may I assist you?"

"We've apprehended two criminals, Officer, and we're remanding them to your custody."

The guard blinked in confusion, then caught sight of the would-be thief on his knees. Rodriguez gestured toward Ralfo, who by this time was sitting on the chest of her "catch" and grinning hugely. The guard peered at her and blinked again.

"Uh, right, sir. I'll take charge of these two. You can count on me, sir."

"I'm sure I can. Let's go, Anafu. Our work here is done."

He and Ralfo moved toward the entrance. The crowd parted quickly to allow them an easy passage. Behind them, the guard heaved a heavy sigh of relief. Outside, Rodriguez pressed a button on a stanchion at the curb to summon a taxi, while Ralfo eyed him curiously.

"Lixu, you were reluctant to apprehend those criminals. Why?"

He peered at her sadly. Even though she was like a sister to him, he did not wish to use her as a sounding board. It was not the way of a Warden. A Warden ought to remain neutral at all times, lest (s)he crumble a delicate façade in the presence of an awed populace and risk losing the advantage they enjoyed because of that awe. Still, because she was his (temporary) partner on this mission, she was entitled to his thoughts.

"You saw how they were dressed. They were from Old Town, a place of broken dreams and faded hopes. Old Towners survive any way they can, and too often they resort to illicit methods. I saw similar people on Dunia before my father took up his diplomatic post on Pluj, and the sight left a huge impression on my youthful mind."

"You have sympathy for them?"

"Yes. But, for our unique circumstances, those two could have been you and me just as well. There's very little justice in this Universe, Anafu, especially economic justice. Unfortunately, we're policemen, and we have to enforce the law as it stands."

"Pluj do not worry about such matters."

"More's the pity, *takhichu* [soul-sister]."

Rodriguez shivered then, whether because of the weather or because of his mental state he was at a loss to say. To regain his stoicism, he changed the subject.

"It must be autumn here. There's a chill in the air."

"It may be a chill to you, *takhichu*,[13] but it is still uncomfortably warm for me. And though I enjoyed the exercise back there, I worked up a sweat."

Presently a taxi pulled up at the curb, its electric motor humming softly and its "For Hire" sign flashing rapidly. There was no sentient driver in the open-air ground shuttle; the vehicle was controlled by an onboard computer which contained an electronic map of New Nairobi. The map translated oral commands into binary language, and the latter plotted the necessary course. Imbedded in the frame of the taxi were sensors which received electrical

13 Since they are a matriarchal, matrilineal, and matrilocal race, the Pluj have no vocabulary denoting male-ness, e.g. "father," "son," or "brother." Instead, in the case of familial/special relationships, they use the common term, *takhichu*, as a sign of tenderness – CMT.

impulses from traffic signals at each intersection; the impulses relayed their co-ordinates to the electronic map which then checked them against the pre-programmed course. Since the development of this system, no taxi had ever gotten "lost," unless it was due to sentient interference with the computer. The same was true for the decrease in accidents, deaths, and injuries.

Rodriguez and Ralfo clambered aboard the taxi, and the Warden entered the destination on the shuttle's keyboard. The vehicle twittered musically in acknowledgement and hummed away from the spaceport.

The destination was the local Secretariat of the Central Spiral Collective, a monument which served as a constant reminder to the Romulans of their obligation to that part of the Galaxy beyond the Amazonian Federation. The Secretariat contained all of the local branches of the Commissions whose functions it was to enforce the laws passed by the Grand Assembly. Most Amazonians tended to take this presence in stride, but Romulans resented it almost to a man and woman. The building was a check on their ambitions to do as they pleased. For this reason – and many others – it was referred to as the "Dungheap" – as pejorative a term as anyone was likely to bestow upon it.

Wardens, when they made planet-fall anywhere there was a Secretariat, were obliged to report to the local Service office immediately. For the most part, they delivered, or received, special and/or last-second orders; occasionally, they picked up, or dropped off, special equipment. Always, they enjoyed the camaraderie of their own kind, away from the suspicions and resentments of the "proles." The local Service office also reported the on-world presence of each visiting Warden to local authorities in order to avoid any unpleasantness, even though Wardens expected full co-operation from the locals regardless of any announcements.

The traffic near the Murchison Space Center consisted mostly of commercial vehicles and other taxis ferrying goods and passengers to and from the spaceport. Occasionally, a private vehicle could be seen dropping off or picking up a person at the Center. Use of private vehicles was discouraged (but not forbidden) by the City of New Nairobi, which owned and operated the taxis and obtained a great deal of revenue from this monopoly, and the lack of public parking facilities was the chief means of discouragement.

The Center lay on the southern outskirts of New Nairobi, and south of it was Old Town, the original settlement established by Dunian colonization three-hundred-plus years earlier. West of both stood the local Secretariat of the Central Spiral Collective, a confederation of worlds possessing space-faring capability within a sphere two hundred light-years in diameter. A gap of a hundred meters separated the building from the city proper by design. The Romulans had wanted no part of it in their metropolis and had insisted on the separation without quite realizing that the CSC had already decided to construct outside the city on the grounds that the Collective was an entity in and of itself and that its property ought not to be swallowed up by any other entity.

The Secretariat was the tallest building on the planet (also by design), two stories taller than the Federation's vaunted Administration building. It had been constructed from slabs of black marble overlaying a titanium steel frame; the marble façade was polished so that it reflected all light. During the day, it glowed from the light of Rhea Silvia; at night, it was polka-dotted by the starry sky. As monuments went, it ranked second to none, built to demonstrate Authority in matters political, economic, and cultural; and though that Authority was often benign in nature, the statement it made to Everyman was unmistakable.

The taxi pulled up to the entrance of this formidable fortress defending Galactic Civilization and announced in a computer-generated female voice the fare due to the City of New Nairobi. The Warden retrieved his badge and placed it against the electronic reader in front of him. The badge contained a microchip (among others) which authorized the payment of any expense of a Warden from the Service's account in the Central Bank of New Switzerland. When the transaction had been completed, the taxi twittered in acknowledgement and spat out a receipt. Rodriguez and Ralfo climbed out, and the vehicle hummed off in search of new customers.

The lobby of the Secretariat was enormous as befitted the nature of the building. It had to be enormous in order to accommodate the huge amount of foot traffic which flowed back and forth seemingly endlessly. Here, as in the Murchison Space Center, one could observe all of the races of the Collective; here, two dozen of them conducted (or hoped to conduct) official business which would impact upon their individual societies and those of others. As a matter of course, the Secretariat provided suites for the embassies of these races where they could conduct any business they had in mind.

In the center of the lobby, a holographic representation of the building served as a directory to all of the Commissions, Bureaus, and offices in which one could entreat for redress of problems/grievances. Each level, each suite, each room was labeled on the image; at the press of a pressure plate, the labels could be read in any language one desired. The first level, beyond the lobby, contained a general information office, a communications center, a medical clinic, a security office, dining facilities, public toilets, a currency exchange, and a bank of elevators. The eight Commissions to which most of the Secretariat's business was addressed – Law Enforcement, Interstellar Trade, Primitive Cultures, Public Health, Cultural Affairs, Criminal Justice, Agriculture and Manufacturing, and Science and Technology – occupied the next eight levels. The three levels above those contained the embassies of the Collective's membership. And above those, on the topmost level, were the administrative offices of the Collective itself; here, matters involving community relations, personnel, maintenance, finance, and general services were handled. The presiding officer, the Regional Secretary, reported to the General Secretary on New Switzerland and, when called upon, to the Grand Assembly acting as a committee-of-the-whole.

Rodriguez and Ralfo made their way cautiously through the throng of bodies, scurrying about on their appointed rounds. Both took care not to make any overt contact with anyone they encountered; in some cultures, intimate contact by strangers was tantamount to assault and often provoked a vigorous response. Eventually, they arrived at the elevators, found one relatively empty, and rode it to the fifth level which the Commission for Law Enforcement occupied.

On the fifth level, the elevator opened onto another lobby. This one was not as large as that on the main level but spacious enough. It was well equipped with plush furniture, thick carpeting, potted plants (including many flowering plants) culled from all over the Collective, and wall decorations representing cultural artifacts from the member worlds. In the middle of this lavish array, a lone desk with the obligatory computer terminal squatted incongruously. Behind the desk sat a female sergeant of the Constabulary, either Ekath or Okath. Physically, the sole distinguishing difference between the two was the color of their teeth; Ekath teeth were amber-colored, whereas Okath teeth were pale orange. But, since both wore breathing masks most of the time, their teeth were seldom in view.

Rodriguez strolled up to the desk and flashed his best insincere smile. The non-com bobbed her head.

"Greetings, Warden, Leftenant. Welcome to Romulus Station."

"Greetings, and thank you," the Warden returned the courtesy.

"Your identity cards, please."

Rodriguez produced his badge and handed it over. Ralfo discreetly slipped her card from her bikini bottom and offered it. The sergeant passed both, one at a time, over a scanner built into the desk's surface and pressed a button on her console. The visitors were now duly registered. The non-com returned the badge and card.

"Thank you, sir and ma'am. You bees cleared to pass."

Rodriguez nodded his thanks, turned to his left, and began strolling down the long corridor which split this level into roughly two equal parts. Most of the level was taken up by the Constabulary proper, each mission of the Collective's police force having its own suite of offices. In addition, there were conference rooms, interrogation rooms, forensic laboratories, and a large room housing the mainframe where criminal records were stored. Two-thirds of the way down the corridor, a cross corridor appeared, and the Warden made another left turn. At the far end was another suite, the Warden Service's adjunct on Romulus. It had been placed deliberately out of the way because of Service preference; and, truth to tell, the remainder of the Constabulary had been only too happy to accommodate that preference.

The reception area here was smaller but still as spacious as any private-sector counterpart. Behind the desk sat a black-uniformed Bitha female with a reddish-brown crest. The single red dot on her tunic identified her as another L1.

Technically, there were no ranks *per se* in the Warden Service. Instead, the personnel were divided into five groups – L1 to L5. A Warden just out of the Academy began automatically as an L1. (S)he was evaluated every fifty megaseconds ; based upon this evaluation, the Service decided whether or not to advance him/her to the next level. Criteria for advancement included meritorious service, extraordinary performance of duty, and special skills. Advancement was necessarily a slow and arduous process, but no Warden was ever made to feel slighted if (s)he did not rise rapidly through the "ranks." It had been drummed into them as a matter of routine that they were an elite force and that an L1 had as much authority in a given situation as an L5.

Amongst themselves, Wardens addressed each other by their level and last name. Only when serving on a Constabulary ship or Relay Station were they ever addressed as "Leftenant"; the Constabulary insisted on ranking everybody, and "Leftenant" was good enough for a Warden, even if (s)he was an L5.

The Bitha gave Rodriguez a tight little smile and ignored Ralfo. He produced his badge, and the receptionist ran it across her scanner.

"Be the peace of Kum'halla with you, L1 Rodriguez."

"The peace of Kum'halla be with you, L1 Muz. I'm checking in as required."

Now the female Warden looked questioningly at the Pluj who stared back, wide-eyed, at the sight of a Bitha in black.

"This is Lt. Anafu Ralfo, lately of the *Faithful*," Rodriguez supplied. "She's been assigned to me temporarily on my current mission."

"Be the peace of Kum'halla with you, Lt. Ralfo," Muz intoned perfunctorily.

"Our Lady with you be, L1 Muz," Ralfo returned in her own fashion.

" Are you fortunate, L1 Rodriguez, that is Station Chief Crowder in." She pressed a button on her console. "Sir, is L1 Rodriguez reporting in."

"Excellent," a gruff voice issued from the desk's vidcom. "Send him in."

Muz nodded to Rodriguez, who nodded back in thanks. He started toward the office of the Station Chief. Ralfo moved in the same direction to the great surprise of the Bitha. The Dunian halted and faced his team-mate.

"Sorry, Anafu," he said in Standard. "Non-Wardens are not allowed past this point. Strictly speaking, you shouldn't even be in this suite at all."

"*Rakhee tenif* [how unfortunate]," she said, drawing her lips into a pout. "Nothing out here to do there is. Quite bored I will be."

"I won't be long. Talk to Muz, if you like, but try not to seduce her."

She scowled at him, then grimaced as she realized he was joking. Pluj did not seduce anyone without a proper introduction first. Rodriguez winked at her and continued toward the Station Chief's office.

By convention, Station Chiefs had to be L3's or L4's, the rationale being that, having paid one's dues on the front lines, one was entitled to a desk job. Moreover, the experience gained from front-line duty qualified a Warden for an executive position. Most Station Chiefs were L4's, and they also formed the Executive Committee of the Service which dictated policy; from their ranks came the L5's of which there were only two (also by convention) – a Special Consultant to the Speaker of the Grand Assembly and the prison chief on Xix, both of whom answered only to the Aldebaranians. The Station Chief on Romulus was the L4 with the longest service record because of the nature of the job; the Amazonian Federation required a watchful eye at all times, and the Service assigned its most experienced personnel to that Station.

The Warden who currently was Station Chief on Romulus was a burly Dunian with bulging muscles and a bull neck. He might have been more at home on a football field than in a Warden's uniform. He wore his dish-water-blond hair close-cropped and sported a thick handlebar moustache. He smiled hugely as Rodriguez entered and revealed several gold fillings in his teeth.

"The peace of Kum'halla be with you, L1 Rodriguez. Welcome to Romulus."

"The peace of Kum'halla be with you, Station Chief Crowder. And thank you."

"Have a seat." When the younger man was seated, the Station Chief leaned forward as if to share a confidence. "Would you rather speak Dunian than Standard?"

"Dunian, thank you, sir," came the reply in Dunian. "I haven't had much opportunity to speak it since I entered the Academy."

"Neither have I. It's always a pleasure to speak one's native language, don't you think? Standard is serviceable, but it doesn't leave much room for nuances."

"Quite right, sir." He paused for an appropriate length of time. "Have you been apprised of my mission?"

"Huh! I'd be a poor Station Chief if I didn't know everything that goes on in the Collective. I check the 'daily bulletin' twice a day, once when I come in to work and once when I go home."

Crowder gestured toward the corner of his office. Rodriguez followed the motion and spied a familiar sight: a niche in the wall containing the glass bowl with the *aaxyboxr* inside. He nodded knowingly.

"Perhaps I should cultivate that habit myself."

"I'd recommend it. You never know what little tidbits you might pick up." He regarded Rodriguez pensively. "Well, son, it appears you've been handed a mighty big assignment – after only fifty megs on the job."

"Yes, sir. A case of being in the right place at the right time."

"No doubt. What is your purpose on Romulus then? The 'bulletin' was a bit hazy on the details."

The younger man related the encounter with the pirates in the Ru'uhaad system and the deal worked out with their leader.

"Once I get the information I was promised, it's on to Planetoid 48. Then the real fun begins."

"Sounds like a wild goose chase to me."

"It may be, sir, but we can't be too careful where the JUR is involved."

"All too true." Crowder smiled wryly. "How do you like working with a Pluj? Oh, wait. I forgot – you grew up on Pluj."

"Yes, sir. With Lt. Ralfo's family, as it happens. So, it's not like I'm walking into anything new."

"Glad to hear it. I've taken the liberty of booking a suite for you at the Hotel Metro. It's small and not very luxurious, but it's quiet and out of the way; you won't attract the attention of any of the JUR agents hanging about in New Nairobi." He opened a drawer, took out a five-centimeter silver cube, and pushed it across the desk. "The suite has been 'de-bugged' as a matter of routine, but sweep it with this gadget all the same, just to be on the safe side."

"Yes, sir. Um, Lt Ralfo and I will need civilian clothes. Where I'm going, this uniform will stand out like a solar flare."

"I'll have a suitable wardrobe sent over in five kilos."

The Station Chief stood up, and Rodriguez jumped to his own feet. The two men shook hands.

"Good fortune, L1 Rodriguez. The peace of Kum'halla be with you."

"Thank you, sir. The peace of Kum'halla be with you."

The younger Warden departed, only to observe Ralfo and Muz holding hands and giggling like school girls. They broke contact at his approach, and the Bitha turned back to her terminal with a mock-somber expression on her face. Rodriguez gave the Pluj a quizzical look.

"Didn't I ask you not to seduce L1 Muz?" he asked her in Pluj.

"I was *not* seducing her," Ralfo replied indignantly. "I was providing tips on how to improve her sex life."

"Bithas have sex lives? I thought they were all cloned."[14]

"Surely your education is lacking, Lixu. We are finished here?"

"Yes. The next stop: the Hotel Metro."

*   *   *

The Hotel Metro was, as Station Chief Crowder had suggested, well off the beaten path. Visitors to Romulus who had money to burn – their own or someone else's – tended to patronize the top-of-the-line establishments downtown where they might indulge themselves in a wide variety of amenities. These places were near the civic center of New Nairobi, and their patrons could access both the government of Amazonia and the commercial district with equal ease. Those who had considerably less money to burn – the great majority of the influx – made do at lesser establishments further away from the hub.

Not that these lesser establishments were shabby flea-traps by any stretch of the imagination. The City Fathers would not have tolerated anything remotely resembling a crumbling ruin in the midst of their perfect city; they had very specific remedies to prevent any deterioration. All hotels in New Nairobi were inspected on an annual basis, and their inspection was most thorough. The inspectors made copious notes which formed the foundation of their final reports (and seldom did an inspector *not* write something down); the reports were then analyzed in detail and, from them, Notices of Deficiencies were issued to the owners of the targeted establishments. Owners had sixty days in which to correct the deficiencies; failure to do so incurred stiff daily fines until the corrections had been made. And, as an added incentive to action, the owners were not allowed to write off either the costs of the corrections or the fines accrued against their tax liabilities. By that means did the City Fathers enhance the city coffers.

The Hotel Metro, located halfway between the hub of New Nairobi and the western residential area, was a modest accommodation for visitors of modest means. A five-story affair, built from granite taken from a quarry on the far side of Romulus, it attempted to imitate old-line Dunian establishments with cornices on the main door, the facing windows, and the perimeter of the roof. An attempt had also been made to give the structure some color; the

---

14   Bi is the only member of the Collective to have legalized the cloning of sentient beings. But the procedure is limited to infertile couples who have exhausted all other avenues of reproduction, and a special license is required before any procedure is undertaken. The Bitha do not allow non-Bitha to apply for these licenses – CMT.

granite had been given a plaster overlay upon which various shades of green were daubed in intricate patterns. As appearances went, the Hotel Metro was neither a work of art nor an eyesore.

The interior of the hotel was much the same. Whereas the more luxurious establishments prided themselves on their plush carpeting, rich wall tapestries, elaborate chandeliers, and designer furniture in the lobby, here one found only moderately expensive furnishings, yet tastefully arranged. The lobby looked like somebody's living room, lived in but not worn out, and the owners had worked diligently to maintain that image. The décor had "Welcome" and "Enjoy your stay" written all over it.

If there was any flaw in the ambience of the Hotel Metro, it was the fact that the accommodations were suitable only for humans. On the other hand, there were establishments which catered only to non-humans, and no one bothered to level charges of "discrimination" against them. Only the large luxurious establishments could afford multi-ethnic accommodations.

Because of this trivial anomaly, the sight of a non-human sauntering through the main entrance and across the lobby to the front desk was sufficient to raise more than one pair of eyes. The sight of a Warden marching along the same path would have garnered the same reaction; it would not have occurred to either staff or patrons that even Wardens needed to sleep sometime. And so, the sight of a Warden in tandem with a non-human brought sharp gasps of surprise from a dozen throats, and a dozen pairs of eyes tracked their every step through the lobby.

Rodriguez, ever mindful of the effect that he and his kind had on civilians, plodded deliberately toward the front desk, looking neither left nor right. The sooner the mundane business of registering was completed, the sooner he and Anafu could get out of the limelight. For her part, Ralfo had never been in a humans-only environment (unlike many of her more well-traveled sorority), and her curiosity level increased the moment she stepped foot inside. She tried to take in everything at once, failed to assimilate anything, and gave up the effort. Instead, she focused on the desk clerk whose instant smile was not entirely professional.

The Warden stepped up to the front desk and fixed the mesmerized clerk with a steely glance. The latter's semi-professional smile turned immediately into a forced, wholly professional one.

"I believe you have a reservation for us," Rodriguez said quietly, "under the name 'Rodriguez.'"

The clerk consulted his terminal and brought up the "Reservations Pending" list. The list consisted of eleven items; the designated reservation was fourth in the queue. This one had been highlighted, indicating a high priority, and the next screen provided the details of the reservation. The names of the prospective guests were followed by their planet of origin, room assignment, and length of stay. The clerk nodded absentmindedly and turned to the new guests.

"Yes, sir, Mr. – ah, *Warden* Rodriguez, and, ah" – he peered at Ralfo's rank insignia and tried not to be too obvious in peering at other parts of her – "Lt. Ralfo. You'll be in Suite #16, one of our very best accommodations."

"Excellent. Do you have room service?"

"Yes, sir, around the clock."

"Fine. We'll be taking our meals in our rooms."

"Very good, sir. Would you please register now?"

He swiveled his terminal so that it faced Rodriguez. On the screen with the details of the reservation was a touch-pad area; when touched, the hotel's central computer scanned the guest's fingerprints and matched them to a previous scan made at the time the reservation had been made. In the case of government officials, the computer matched the fingerprints already on file in a given agency's database. In the present instance, the Hotel Metro contacted the central computer at the Secretariat. When the match was made, the words "Registration Completed" appeared on the screen.

"Your credit disc, please," the clerk asked.

The Warden retrieved his badge and handed it over. The clerk stared at it for a second as if it were a sacred object, then accepted it and slipped it into a slot at the base of the terminal. He waited the few seconds while the payment authorization was secured, removed the disc, and handed it back.

"Thank you, sir – and madam. The bellhop will show you to your suite."

Once, bellhops were young men (and, occasionally, young women) who ferried the luggage of a guest to and from his/her room, acted as a go-between for room service, and performed whatever errands the guest desired within the bounds of the civil law and the hotel's regulations. The bellhop's wages were minimal, and (s)he was expected to supplement them with monetary tips from guests for services rendered (and, by the same token, guests were expected to tip). By and large, bellhops endured this form of wage slavery and humiliating status for the sake of survival and looked to the day when they could better themselves, financially and socially. The position of bellhop, as one might guess, produced a great deal of turn-over, and a hotel manager could not determine from one day to the next what sort of service staff (s)he might have on hand. Hotels needed a service staff, of course, but a reliable and efficient one which did not cost too much. And so, this form of physical labor, like so many other forms before it, fell victim to automation.

The "bellhop" in the Hotel Metro (and others) was a slender cylinder, a meter in height and ten centimeters in diameter, attached to a one-half-by-two-meter platform for the guest's luggage, the whole on rubberized wheels. The mini-computer embedded in its upper end operated a tiny electric motor and contained an electronic "map" of the premises.

The desk clerk pressed a button on his console. Instantly, a panel in a nearby wall slid upwards to reveal several of the "bellhops" standing in a row waiting for activation. The clerk pressed two numerical keys, and one of the machines stirred into life, scooted forward, and halted before the desk. The clerk reached across the desk and inserted a key card into a slot in the machine's "head." A slight whirring sound issued from the "bellhop" as its computer digested the information keyed to the card.

"Guest assignment: Suite #16," it announced in a monotone. "Please place luggage on the platform."

The only luggage that either Rodriguez or Ralfo had were their travel kits. These the pair dropped unceremoniously onto the platform.

"Thank you," the machine intoned. "Please follow me."

The "bellhop" rolled away toward the bank of elevators on the other side of the lobby, selected one seemingly at random but actually according to a built-in rotation sequence in its memory bank and beeped a two-note command to "call" the elevator. When the car arrived, the machine rolled in, waited until it sensed the presence of warm bodies inside the car, and beeped another two-note command. The elevator door *whoosh*ed shut, and the car shot up to the second floor. The door opened again, and the "bellhop" exited, scooted unerringly down the corridor, and rolled to a stop before Suite #16. The key card in its slot popped out, and the Warden removed it. He swiped it across the card-reader adjacent to the door of the suite, and the lock disengaged. He and Ralfo removed their kits from the platform and entered the suite.

"Thank you. Enjoy your stay," the "bellhop" intoned and rolled away toward the elevator.

As suites went, #16 in the Hotel Metro would never match even the smallest units in any of the major establishments for sheer luxuriousness. It was meant to present the *image* of luxuriousness for those of modest means, so that they could boast of their "extravagance" to the folks back home. Nevertheless, the accommodation was well appointed: two spacious rooms, each with its own bathroom; a kitchenette and wet bar between the rooms; a dining nook in the larger of the two rooms; large walk-in closets; queen-sized beds; polarizing windows; the ubiquitous vidscreen/computer; and serviceable furnishings. It fairly shouted out "home-style comfort"; and, in fact, this attribute was one of the hotel's major selling points.

Ever the curious child, Lt. Ralfo began to explore these – to her – exotic surroundings. She was particularly intrigued by the queen-sized beds. Pluj did not use beds *per se*; rather, they slept and engaged in sex on what in another context would be called futons, i.e. large cushions set upon the floor. Ralfo jumped onto one of the beds and bounced up and down on it as if it were a trampoline, laughing like a giddy child all the while.

Meanwhile, the more serious Rodriguez made a security check with the silver-gray cube Station Chief Crowder had given him by pressing a small circular area in one of the cube's facets which was half a shade darker than the rest of the surface. The device hummed steadily as he swept it over the suite in long, slow arcs. Its purpose was to emit an electromagnetic pulse which, when interfacing with another electromagnetic device, would cause the cube to glow; by this means, the user could determine if a given area was "bugged" and, if so, pinpoint the "bug's" location. The Warden made a thorough search of the suite and did not neglect any part of it; even the bathrooms and the closets were scanned. At the end, the cube indicated a "clean" area.

The Warden Service was not being paranoid in this exercise. It was merely being cautious. Since it was a highly exclusive organization, it shared its information on a strict need-to-know basis and kept even that sharing to a bare minimum. For this reason (among many others), it was regarded with envy and suspicion, and other official agencies would have given their collective eyeteeth to gain all of its secrets – especially the Amazonian Federation, which detested it the most and would do whatever it could to unlock those secrets up to and including spying on a visiting Warden.

In the present instance, if word leaked out that a Warden was spending a few days in a local hotel for unknown purposes, the Federation's intelligence service would get to work immediately. Rodriguez's sweep of the suite was no guarantee that he and Ralfo were *not* being spied upon; it meant only that the Romulans hadn't gotten wind of their presence yet and so had had no chance to plant "bugs" beforehand. Standard operating procedure dictated that the Warden scan the suite each and every time he returned to the hotel, just to be on the safe side.

"Are we safe from eavesdroppers, Lixu?" the Pluj inquired when the scanning had been completed.

"For now. But the day is still young." He glanced at the vidscreen. "I'm starved. I haven't eaten anything since leaving the *Steadfast*. I'm going to put room service to the test."

"*Khalee.* I am going to get more comfortable. It is very stifling here."

She grabbed her kit and tripped away toward the adjoining bedroom. Rodriguez shook his head at her remark about the environment. The suite was set at an automatic temperature of twenty-two degrees Celsius, the comfort level for most humans but not for any Pluj. He activated the vidscreen and selected "Room Service" from the list of options; he then highlighted "Meals," which brought up the hotel's menu offerings, and studied the listings long and hard for something suitable. For one thing, although Pluj metabolism was nearly similar to that of humans, it was just different enough that a Pluj could not digest all human foodstuffs. For another, his stint at the Academy – feeling the influence of the Aldebaranians – had inured him to a specific diet. In the end, he settled on a vegetable salad for Ralfo and a pasta salad for himself and placed the order.

A light movement behind him signaled the return of his partner. He turned – and immediately frowned. In order to "get comfortable," Anafu Ralfo had followed normal Pluj behavior; she had shed her uniform and was now wearing only a smile.

CHAPTER FIVE

▼

TERRORISM DEFINED

DOCTOR MUBUTU WEYERHAUSER, LATE OF the University of New Nairobi, was worrying himself into a mental break-down. For the past four kiloseconds, he had alternated between being convinced that he had seen what he had seen and being convinced that he was delusional. He couldn't possibly have seen what he had seen. It was too unthinkable under the circumstances.

What he had seen – or thought he had seen – was the re-assembling of a Murchison Oscillating Matrix Engine in a cave on Planetoid 48. He was no quantum physicist or engineer, but he knew an MOME when he saw one. An MOME consisted of a spherical casing whose diameter varied according to the workload demanded of it, an outer framework of supportive beams, a mini-cyclotron which would generate gamma rays, and an electromagnetic-field generator. The field generator created an energy matrix inside the sphere; and, while the polarity of the matrix was being rapidly alternated, i.e. "oscillated," the mini-cyclotron bombarded it with gamma rays. The resultant forces created an artificial and temporary gravity well across the event horizon of which a vessel could traverse and shorten its journey by several magnitudes. That was the theory. The practical application was decidedly more complex.

The inventor of this marvelous machine, Thomas Edison Murchison I (a.k.a. the "First Murchison"), had blown up four different laboratories before arriving at a relatively controllable process. Yet, it was inherently unstable; one misstep spelled utter disaster. The official records of two dozen worlds bore witness to the terrible destructive power of an MOME. Those who constructed/operated/serviced the device earned the equivalent of three doctorates – structural engineering, quantum physics, and radionics – in the course of their training, but they labored under a tremendous burden. All the knowledge in the Universe could not compensate for a single act of carelessness. An MOME, de-stabilized, was a runaway train of colossal proportions, and those who de-stabilized paid the price by being reduced instantly to their constituent atoms.

Doctor Weyerhauser had a passing acquaintance with the official reports of MOME-related accidents, but the *unofficial* stories he had heard during his undergraduate days were enough to send chills up and down his spine whenever he chanced to recall them. And he was recalling all of them at the moment. The more he thought about what he thought he had seen in the deep cave, the more anxiety-ridden he became.

As he contemplated the situation, he wondered what his options were. In the end, he realized that he had no options. He was a virtual prisoner on Planetoid 48, subject to the whims of Major Tshambe; he could go nowhere off-planet without the Major's explicit authorization, and the Major did not strike him as the sort who would freely dispense authorization simply because someone in his command was having an anxiety attack.

The questions which kept running through his head and provided the fuel for the anxiety attack were (1) how had the JUR gotten their hands on an MOME, (2) why were they re-assembling it inside a planetoid, and (3) how were they planning to use it. None of it made sense.

In the first place, MOME's were designed to function outside a world's natural gravity field, i.e. Deep Space. The First Murchison had discovered the necessity for this the hard way, with the destruction of his laboratories; it was not until he had performed his experiments on the Mir Space Station that he achieved any success. Creating an artificial gravity well inside a large natural gravity well tended to produce shearing forces which destroyed a good deal of real estate. Murchison's initial experiments had been on a small scale; hence the damage was minor. Had he been working with an MOME the size of one which motivated, say, a Constabulary patrol vessel, very likely Dunia might have become another asteroid belt.[15]

In the second place, even if the shearing forces could be neutralized,

---

15 For this reason, the United Dunian Government in 154 ENO enacted the Huang Protocol (named after the Minister of Science who proposed it) which (among other things) outlawed the operation of an MOME inside another gravity field and made any violation a capital crime. When humankind spread out into the central spiral and established new colonies, it thoughtfully brought the Protocol with it. In due time, the alien races whom it encountered also adopted the Protocol out of self-interest. Since its passage, the Protocol has been invoked only once; all other violations have resulted in the destruction of the perpetrator, a fact which serves as the real deterrent to misuse – CMT.

enclosing an MOME inside a structure, natural or artificial, decreased its efficiency considerably. The larger the structure, the greater the decrease, because the surrounding materials tended to constrict the gravity well. Ideally, an MOME should be a free-floating construct in Deep Space; but that created other problems, not the least of which was the unintentional scattering of gamma rays into space and creating hazardous conditions for both animate and inanimate objects. The MOME's attached to a ship or orbiting a star system inside a beryllium sphere had been a necessary compromise. Sticking one in a cave deep inside a planetoid posed unknown dangers, creating great anxiety for some of the planetoid's occupants, however temporary.

Since his shocking discovery, Doctor Weyerhauser had avoided returning to the control center until he could sort things out in his mind. He knew he couldn't stay where he was at present for very long, as the Major would, sooner or later, request another set of readings from him. These readings posed another part of the puzzle. What were they for? He now dreaded taking them, because they seemed to be part of some sinister purpose.

Currently, the astrophysicist was hunkered down in the cave in which resided the skeletons of the family of unknown creatures who had once inhabited Planetoid 48, the cave which was now their tomb. It seemed to be the only peaceful place left on this world. He contemplated the remains of the male, the female, and the child. How had they died? Had they run out of fuel and frozen to death? Had they run out of food and starved to death? What had been their last thoughts? He was no anthropologist; he could not detect any signs on the remains which would provide any clues as to the manner of death. Perhaps it was just as well that he did not know. Their fate could not have been any more horrendous than that which awaited those who rode an MOME as if it were a simple shuttlecraft.

Eventually, he'd have to confront Major Tshambe with what he knew and insist that he be fully informed about this mission which required his specific scientific expertise and nothing else. What was worse – riding an MOME or risking the Major's ire? He'd rather navigate through the Wall without a computer than pick the lesser of those evils. How would the JUR leader react to his new knowledge? He had already been told that he was on a need-to-know basis and that he would be fully briefed "in due time." But, "in due time" was not good enough; he wanted information *now*.

On the other hand, even if the Major were forthcoming and told him everything, what good would it do him? He was trapped here. If he attempted to escape, how could he accomplish it? He hadn't the skills to pilot a spacecraft, even if he could access one. And, certainly, if he tried such a stunt, Tshambe would have him shot on the spot. For all he knew, the Major might execute him anyway, once the mission had been completed, on the grounds that he was a security risk.

He regarded the doomed family again.

You three had it easy. You knew exactly what was in store for you. The future was not a question mark.

"Doctor Woyer'auser!" his vidcom squawked. "Report, if ye please!"

"Time for another reading, Major?" the Doctor replied wearily.

"Aye. And, p'r'aps we willna be needin' too many more fum ee."

"That's welcome news. I'll be there shortly."

He started to exit the cave, halted abruptly, and reached into his parka's pocket. He withdrew the metal plaque with the symbol of the Wayfarers etched on it, gazed at it solemnly, and placed it next to the male where he had found it.

This belongs to you, my friend. Your god may have deserted you in your time of need, but I won't deprive you of the one comfort you possessed in life.

When the astrophysicist returned to the control center, he was surprised to see many of the team lounging about, smoking, or chatting idly. Most of them gave him only a perfunctory glance, then turned away. The two who had been disposed to acknowledge his existence, Cutty and Jingles, did not seem anxious to admit they liked him and thus also gave him the briefest of looks. He nodded to only them and ignored the rest. At this moment, he didn't much care what anyone thought of him.

Major Tshambe was the sole active person in the cave. He was making one call after another to work crews still engaged in re-assembling the MOME; and, from the gist of the conversation, Doctor Weyerhauser concluded that even their work was nearly done. The Major's final call was to the Reman ship which had brought this unit to Planetoid 48 and was now orbiting the world as a sentry. Then he swung around and faced his "scientific consultant."

"Been soight-seein' agyn, 'ave ye, Doctor?" Tshambe grumbled. "Well, na matter. Tyke yer readings and be quick aboot it."

Silently, the astrophysicist took his seat at his vidscreen and activated it. The image on the monitor revealed the movement of the runaway since the last reading. Ru'uhaad was now ten degrees sternward and fifteen to starboard, and nothing but Deep Space lay ahead. Planetoid 48 was still on its original course. The Doctor printed the data out and passed them over to the Major. The latter smiled humorously as he peered at the sheet.

"Na deviaytions so far," he muttered. "Good. Noo we can begin physe free."

"'Phase *three*'?" Doctor Weyerhauser asked, alarmed. "What's that all about?"

"Oi syed ye'll be fraggin' told in due fraggin' toime. Noo, off wif ee!"

"You'll tell me now, Major!" the other yelled, jumping to his feet. "I've been kept in the dark too long. You've got a bloody MOME down there in the lower cavern. How did you come by it? And what are you going to do with it?"

The tension in the cave rose to a level which required a laser-drill to cut through it. All of the JUR personnel who had been standing idly about froze in their places and exchanged nervous glances, waiting for the expected fireworks. Only Major Tshambe remained unperturbed as he peered coolly at his would-be inquisitor. Now Doctor Weyerhauser instantly regretted his rash act. He had just put himself on perilous ground, and there was no escaping it. Perhaps the Major would tell him what he wanted to know before he killed him. Perhaps he would not.

"Mybe it is toime to tell ee after all – for all the good it'll do ee." He waved the newest print-out in the Doctor's direction. "Tell me, what do all o' these readings indicyte?"

The astrophysicist was momentarily caught off guard. One minute, he was expecting summary execution; the next, he was being asked for expertise again. What game was the Major playing?

"Why, they tell us that this runaway has been on a straight-line course for the past 20,000+ years, from the junction of the central spiral with the main body of the Galaxy toward the Gap.[16] But, you know that already."

"Aye. And, in yer hexpert opinion, what's the next in'abited system it'll pass?"

The Doctor pursed his lips and squinted his eyes in deep thought. Then:

"After skirting two stars without any planets, it will encounter Rhea Silvia's system, passing by slightly above the plane of the ecliptic. But you know that too. What are you getting at, Major?"

"Will this floy-boy cause any damage?"

"No, of course not. It won't come near any of Rhea Silvia's planets."

"S'pose, 'owever, that it did chynge course, sy, six degrees toward the plyne o' the ecliptic. What then?"

"That's hardly likely. It's just idle speculation."

"'Umor me, Doctor. Myke a projection."

The astrophysicist eyed the other suspiciously, but his own curiosity had just been piqued. He returned to his vidscreen, called up the real-time image of the region of Deep Space through which they were traveling, and studied

---

16 A common term, used by spacers and non-spacers alike, it denotes the wide region between the central spiral and the inner one. Spacers avoid that region like the plague, attributing to it all manner of evils. So far as anyone knows, no one has ever traveled into the Gap and returned to tell about it – CMT.

it for a moment. Next, he called up a computer-generated image of the same scene and entered a command to project the image forward in time. The computer charted the future path and confirmed the fact that Planetoid 48 would pass by Rhea Silvia's system six degrees above the plane of the ecliptic. He then reversed the projection to the point where the rogue approached the system and entered a course change of six degrees toward the plane of the ecliptic. As he watched the new path unfold, rising horror clutched at his chest, and he could scarcely breathe.

"My God!" he whispered. "This new course would put Planetoid 48 within a degree of – *Romulus!*"

He swung around in his chair, his face pale at the implications of such a fly-by, only to confront Major Tshambe's smirking at him.

"A close encounter like that would cause irreparable damage. Earthquakes. Tidal waves. Volcanic eruptions. And a lot more." His brow furrowed. "But, as I've already said, this is idle speculation. This world won't be changing course anytime soon."

"It willna? Can ye be so sure o' that, Doctor?"

"You'd need a tremendously powerful force to affect such a change. You'd need…" His voice trailed away as a sudden monstrous realization crept unbidden into his consciousness. The horror he had felt before upon spying the MOME down below paled in comparison to that which he experienced now. "*Oh, my God!* You can't be serious!"

"Noo that ye're in the proper mood, Doctor, Oi'll tell ee the 'ole story aboot this mission."

Calmly, as if he were simply telling a favorite story, Tshambe related the events leading up to the present time. The Executive Committee of the JUR had come up with a bold plan: divert a small body in space and aim it like a missile at Romulus. Even a close encounter would suffice to cause chaos. Using one of the asteroids in the Wall would not be feasible because of the frequent patrols by Romulan security forces; a body from outside the system was required. And such a body had been discovered – the runaway Planetoid 48, heading in the general direction of Rhea Silvia. The directional force would come from a purloined MOME installed on the runaway, employing short warp-outs so as not to tear the world apart. The cruise ship *Astarte* was bound for the Ru'uhaad system – the rogue's next "port of call" – and it was selected as the likely source of an MOME.

Major Tshambe and his unit attacked the *Astarte* and, with a well-placed ekathite-tipped missile, separated the sphere containing its MOME from the rest of the vessel. There had been considerable loss of life amongst the crew and the passengers, but the JUR counted it only as "collateral damage." The Remans attached magnetic grapples to their prize and proceeded toward

Planetoid 48. Once they had arrived, the Major had the sphere set down in a mountainous region which would be easy to defend should the need arise. The small remnant of the crew of the *Astarte* still alive were rounded up and confined to a lounge on a lower deck. While the unit prepared the tunnels and caves for the transfer of the MOME, Tshambe returned to Romulus to collect his "scientific consultant."

Dr. Mubutu Weyerhauser had joined the political arm of the JUR while a graduate student at the University of New Nairobi and participated in any number of rallies advocating greater autonomy for Remus within the Amazonian Federation. Though he had heard rumors about acts of sabotage, thievery, and assassination, he ascribed them to Romulan propaganda. In the years he was a member, he had never engaged in "field work" – until Major Tshambe came knocking at his door one night and called upon his expertise in astrophysics. The work, he was told, required him to take a leave of absence from the University for an indefinite period. On the one hand, Doctor Weyerhauser was reluctant to take the assignment because he was nearing tenure and because he was in a relationship with a public librarian; on the other hand, he saw an opportunity to demonstrate his loyalty to The Cause and to promote its aspirations. Now, he was having misgivings about his decision.

As the Major droned on and on in his casual manner, his captive audience was close to fainting from the sheer horror the tale was creating in him. In one fell swoop, he realized that all of the rumors he had heard about the JUR's activities were not rumors at all, but cold, hard fact. He also realized that he was now a part of this monstrous criminal organization and that he would be punished as severely as any of his "team-mates" should the authorities get their hands on him. He could turn himself in and attempt to plea-bargain on the grounds that he had been deceived; but, first he had to escape these madmen, and escape was impossible.

The Doctor stared off in the direction of the lower cave where the pilfered MOME resided. Perspiration dotted his forehead, and his heart beat like a trip hammer. Slowly, he faced the Major and found his tongue again.

"You're *insane!*" he whispered hoarsely. "All of you – *totally stark raving mad!*"

The Major's smirk never left his face. If anything, it became more pronounced. He leaned back in his chair with an air of nonchalance.

"Yer hopinion is noted, Doctor. And we're still after proceedin' to physe free. The fraggin' Rommie barstards will soon py for their evil wys."

"You're condemning millions of innocent people to death."

"Na one of 'em is fraggin' innocent in oor book. Thy accepted the fraggin'

Rommie loifestoyle, and thy're just as guilty." He picked up his vidcom and activated it. "Lt. Mutanga, report!"

"Lt. Mutanga 'ere, Myjor. All is in readiness."

"Foine, foine. We'll be after commencin' physe free then. Foire up the MOME."

"Aye, sir."

At first, there was no discernable change in the geophysical dynamics of the environment. An eerie silence blanketed the scene, and the JUR personnel held their collective breath in expectation – whether of success or of death was irrelevant.

Then the expected change began as a slight vibration in the walls, floor, and ceiling of the cave. The team could feel it through the soles of their boots. Below, the MOME was building up its energy field. The vibrations increased in strength and frequency, and now the men heard a sound which imitated the scratching of a chalkboard with one's fingernails. Gooseflesh appeared on their skin, and their teeth were set on edge. And still the vibrations increased. The cave now began to tremble. The men quickly sat down on the floor before they were knocked off their feet. It seemed that Planetoid 48 was on the verge of tearing itself apart.

"We've got one quarter field strength!" Lt. Mutanga shouted through the vidcom.

"Copy that, Leftenant! Myntyn pooer!"

The tremors continued to build up. Then, without warning, a sharp wrenching motion was both felt and heard; and, though everyone in the cave had been sitting down, they were still thrown several meters in one direction or another. Those nearest the cave walls were slammed against them and held there as the MOME gripped the runaway with an iron fist. No one could move even if one had wanted to; the terrific g-forces were overpowering, and there were no acceleration chairs to provide a modicum of comfort.

"Lt. Mutanga!" Tshambe yelled. "Shut it doon!"

The tremors gradually died away, and the JUR personnel felt confident enough to regain their feet. One of them who had been slammed against the wall reported the possibility of cracked ribs. The Major ordered him to return to the Reman vessel in orbit.

"Are the rest o' ye in good workin' order?" The lack of negative responses was all the answer he needed. "Excellent. Noo, the proof o' the puddin', lads. Doctor Woyer'auser, we'll be after 'avin' some fresh readings."

The astrophysicist staggered over to his station. The activation of the MOME field had had a tremendous effect on his inner ear, and he was feeling a bit disoriented. At one point, he thought he was going to pitch forward on his face. Typically, no one offered to lend him a hand; the Major simply watched him contemptuously with arms crossed. Presently, he plopped into his chair and sat motionless until he found his bearings. He called up the image of the sector of Deep Space in which Planetoid 48 now occupied and gasped sharply as he examined it. Not willing to trust his befuddled brain, he re-issued the command. The image did not change. He turned slowly in his chair and peered at Tshambe.

"I can scarcely believe it. We've warped 10.5 light-years and changed course by 5.7 degrees."

This news elicited a round of cheers from the JUR personnel and a tiny smile from the Major. The Doctor shook his head at the implications of his findings.

"There won't be a collision of worlds, if that was what you were hoping for, Major. But, there will still be considerable damage and loss of life."

"Thank ee for yer confirmytion, Doctor. Ye've done a foine job for oor cause. Noo, ye're free to do some soightseein', if ye loike."

The astrophysicist took that as a dismissal and lurched out of his chair. He needed to find a peaceful place again and contemplate the awful plan of which he had become an unwitting agent.

*   *   *

The chime emanating from the vidscreen was quite insistent – too insistent in Captain Olaf Halvarson's opinion. At first, he tried to ignore it, but it refused to go away. He shifted in his bunk, carefully so as not to disturb the snoozing form beside him, and peered at the offending vidscreen with one bleary eye. He decided that the only way to shut the damned thing up was to answer whoever was calling him at this ungodly hour.

He swung his legs over the edge of the bunk and sat up, still not disturbing his bed partner. He yawned prodigiously, got to his feet, and padded over to the vidscreen, oblivious to the fact that he was stark naked. He jabbed at the "receive" button. The blank screen took form and revealed the anxious face of Lt. Commander G'lun, Chief of Blue Zone.

"Yes, Commander, what is it?" Halvarson mumbled.

"Sir, we haves…losed Planetoid 48," the Ekath replied in a tremulous voice.

"Excuse me?"

"Planetoid 48, sir. It haves…*disappeared*, sir"

The Captain stared at the yellow-skinned alien for the space of three seconds, wondering if he were dreaming all this. Then:

"How the devil do you lose a planet, Mr. G'lun?"

"I knows not, sir. When I began my shift, I maked a note of the position of the runaway, as per your orders. But, when I maked my five-kilosecond check, it beed not where it should haves beed. It beed not in the Display at all, sir."

"Did you check for malfunctions?"

"Aye, sir. That beed my very first action. There beed none. I also shutted the Display down and re-booted it. That helped not."

"Did you go to maximum range?"

"Aye, sir. Planetoid 48 bees not within 10 light-years of the *Steadfast*."

"All right, Commander. I'll be up in half a kilo. Halvarson out."

The Captain switched off the vidscreen and rubbed the sleep out of his eyes. He yawned again, padded to the head, and splashed some water in his face. While he slipped into his uniform, the body in his bunk shifted and revealed the placid face of Lt. Commander Felicia von Lichtenburg, Chief of Silver Zone. He gazed on her longingly.

Sorry to run out on you like this, Felicia. We'll have to continue your...debriefing another time.

Half a kilo later, Halvarson strode onto the Bridge like a man possessed. Those he passed elected not to show a pleasant face for fear of inviting a scathing one in return. He bypassed Command and headed straight for the Blue Zone. Lt. Commander G'lun jumped to his feet and nervously adjusted his breathing mask.

"All right, Commander," Halvarson grumbled without preamble, "show me the current view."

The Ekath sat down again and entered a command on his keyboard. In the Display, the computer-generated view of the local region of Deep Space coalesced into being. Slightly forward and to port lay Ru'uhaad. Other stars, planets, moons, and assorted space debris of appreciable size appeared in their proper, relative positions. The Captain strained to take it all in in a single glance.

"Now, show me where Planetoid 48 is supposed to be."

G'lun touched a new sequence of keys, and a green dot appeared in the Display, slightly aft and to starboard of the *Steadfast*.

"If Planetoid 48 bees on course," the Sensor officer offered an explanation, "this bees where it should bees, sir."

"That's a big 'if,' Mr. G'lun. Take me back to the view you logged when you began your shift."

The hologram changed minutely as G'lun brought up the positions of all astronomical bodies in the vicinity as they had been five kiloseconds ago. There, slightly aft and starboard of the ship, "lay" the rogue, moving away from the Ru'uhaad system. The Captain shook his head in disbelief. How could a whole world just disappear?

"Run another diagnostic, Commander. I want to be absolutely sure there's no malfunction."

"Aye, sir."

Halvarson returned to his Command station, sat down wearily, and called up the Ship's Log. While it was downloading, he mulled over what sort of entry he would make and what sort of reaction Constabulary High Command would have once they read it. If he were his superior officer, Commodore Vreeland of the Ninth Fleet's Task Force Two, he'd have to conclude that either the Commanding Officer of the *Steadfast* had been drinking too much or he had become unhinged. Yet, if Lt. Commander G'lun were correct – and there was no reason to believe he wasn't, because it wasn't in the nature of an Ekath/Okath to miss any details – then the impossible had just occurred, and HC had a huge problem staring it in the face.

On a hunch, he punched the button which connected him to the Green Zone and was greeted by a swarthy-faced Reman female.

"Communicytions. Lt. Tombu 'ere, sir."

Of all the worlds in the Central Spiral Collective which supplied personnel to its various agencies, none matched the enthusiasm for service in the larger entity than the Remans. This fact was a seeming paradox, given the additional fact that Remus also spawned the most obsessed, most single-minded, and most ruthless terrorist organization the Galaxy had ever witnessed. Even the ever-curious Capellans, who were utterly fascinated by the wider Universe, did not provide the numbers that Remus did. Remans worked diligently in whatever post they held if for no other reason than they despised Romulans and the Romulans despised the Collective. The ancient Dunian adage – "the enemy of my enemy is my friend" – never held sway more than it did in Deep Space. If Captain Halvarson had had anything to say about it, he would have staffed his ship entirely with Remans.

He did not have anything to say about it, of course, and neither did his superiors at HQ. Nor did the agency heads at any other CSC function. That decision had originally been made nearly thirty-five years earlier by the enigmatic Aldebaranians, the Galaxy's foremost pacifists who abhorred warfare so much that they took it upon themselves to prevent it wherever, whenever, and however they could. They were also the Galaxy's foremost cosmopolites and advocated absolute co-operation amongst the several species of intelligent life which inhabited the central spiral on the grounds that creatures who worked together were more able to understand each other better and hence able to avoid conflicts. To facilitate this mutual understanding, they decreed (although they termed it a "recommendation") that the CSC agencies would be staffed by equal numbers – or as equal as it was possible to get – from each member world. This decree/recommendation extended to the

Constabulary, and it often teamed individuals who had served, or were the offspring of those who had served, on opposite sides of the War of the Eight Suns, a situation which threatened at times to unravel the entire Aldebaranian weave. (One exception to this rule: each patrol vessel in the Constabulary was to include a complement of Alkon warriors who worked independently of other combat forces.)

"Is the *Faithful* still within communications range, Leftenant?"

The Reman checked her board.

"Just barely, sir. Anuvver free 'undred seconds, and thy'll be oot o' rynge."

"Signal them, if you please."

"Aye, sir."

Fifty seconds later, the face of Frederick Kleindienst, Captain of the *Faithful*, appeared on Halvarson's vidscreen. He looked bleary-eyed, disheveled, and none too pleased to have been aroused at an ungodly hour.

"Olaf, what the hell's the matter that you have to disturb my beauty sleep?"

"Sorry to wake you, Freddy, but I've got an emergency on my hands. Can you check your Display and locate Planetoid 48 for me?"

"I thought you were tracking it yourself."

"I was." He grimaced sheepishly. "I seem to have…*misplaced* it."

Captain Kleindienst goggled in amazement and suppressed the urge to laugh out loud.

"You did *what*? I don't believe this. You sound like a first-year cadet at the Academy."

"A first-year cadet wouldn't have had this problem. Would you please check for me?"

The screen blanked. An age passed before it lit up again. While he waited, Halvarson contemplated his upcoming court-martial for dereliction of duty, falsifying a Ship's Log, and malfeasance of office. He had had a great career until now; being cashiered from the Constabulary would not look good on any future resume.

"Olaf," Captain Kleindienst reported back, "my people can't find Planetoid 48 either. What the hell's going on?"

"I wish I knew. The damned thing just disappeared without warning. Worse, I can't report this to the Commodore, because my Warden is inconveniently on Romulus."

"You *are* in trouble, old buddy. I don't envy you at all. Wish there was some way I could help."

"You could be a character witness at my court-martial." He sighed. "Well, I'll just have to wait until my Warden returns. In the meantime—"

A crackling in the aural portion of the transmission and wavy lines in the video portion indicated that the *Faithful* was approaching the limits of communication range.

"You're breaking up, Freddy. I'll talk to you later."

"OK. Good [*crackle*] Olaf."

Halvarson stared at his dead vidscreen in stony silence. Why couldn't the First Murchison have invented a radio which did for communications what his oscillating-matrix engine did for transportation? If he had done so, no Ship's Captain would have to rely on the present clumsy arrangement. The "present clumsy arrangement" was, of course, the symbiotic relationship between a Warden and a unit of the *aaxyboxr*, but it was as close to instantaneous communication with any part of Deep Space as any sentient creature was likely to get.

Long ago, on Dunia, the science-fiction writers of the day filled their pages with fantastic devices for communication, transportation, labor, and easy living. None of them had gone into any great detail about how such devices worked but simply asked their readers to suspend their disbelief for the moment. Devices, such as "matter transmitters," "warp drives," "hyper-space radios," "androids," and "computer-controlled houses," were part and parcel of these stories; the heroes and heroines used these gadgets (which they seemed to know how to repair, should the occasion arise, without a complex technical manual and in quick order) to solve whatever dilemma beset them.

Sadly, the real world operated by different rules. An MOME, for instance, was not anything like a "warp drive"; it did reduce travel time to manageable proportions but did so based on scientific theory, not on imagination. A "hyper-space radio," on the other hand, was merely a pipe dream, and no amount of wishful thinking would change the laws of physics. Since radio waves could travel no faster than the speed of light, communications in Deep Space were limited to short distances, say, no more than a light-day, pragmatically speaking. Originally, Constabulary ships depended upon relaying messages from vessel to vessel across space — a slow, cumbersome method, but it was the only practical one.

Until the Aldebaranians interfered with the War of the Eight Suns, created the Central Spiral Collective, and introduced the *aaxyboxr* to the rest of sentient life.

Where they had found the hive-mind creatures, they declined to say. How the creatures could do what they did, they also declined to say. All they would say was that any unit of the *aaxyboxr* could communicate with another unit instantaneously no matter where in the Universe a unit might be. The age-old problem seemed to be finally solved. The catch was that the *aaxyboxr* operated through symbiotic contact with a sentient being capable of mind-to-mind communications, and those beings capable of it were Wardens. Therefore, only Constabulary ships with a resident Warden on board had also a resident unit of the *aaxyboxr*. The CSC thus had a distinct advantage over other entities, an additional reason for the latter to resent the former.

At the moment, Captain Olaf Halvarson of the Constabulary Patrol Vessel *Steadfast* was at a distinct *dis*advantage. He needed to contact his superiors immediately but had no way of doing so while Warden Rodriguez was on temporary re-assignment. He was, effectively, incommunicado, and he did not appreciate the fact one bit.

"I never thought I'd ever say this," he muttered to no one in particular, "but I need Rodriguez in the worst way."

"Sir?"

The Captain focused on his now lit vidscreen and peered at Lt. Commander G'lun.

"Yes?"

"Sir, I haves runned a fresh diagnostic." The Ekath paused and nervously adjusted his mask again. "There bees no change. The Display bees functioning normally."

"Thank you, Commander."

Halvarson now contacted the Helmsman on duty. A male Uhaad appeared on the screen.

"Helm. Lt. A-la here, sir."

"Mr. A-la, I want you to initiate a spiral course in two-degree increments. We will be conducting a search pattern in this region."

"Impulse engines only?"

"That's correct."

"Aye, sir. Initiating search pattern."

Some days, you have to do things the hard way, the Captain mused. *But, I'm going to find Planetoid 48 if it's the last thing I do.* He *humphed. And it may damned well be* the last thing I do *if I* don't *find it.*

CHAPTER SIX

▼

INVESTIGATION

"WHAT TROUBLES YOU NOW, PUPIL?"

Cadet Rodriguez stands before his mentor, nervously shifting his weight from one foot to the other. He has a question he needs an answer to, but he is quite embarrassed to ask it. Master Fresh-Bloom-in-the-Face-as-the-Day-Begins does not need to be the powerful mentalist that he is to know that his lack-wit of a charge is wrestling with himself – and losing.

"Master," the pupil stammers, "I am in need of guidance."

"Obviously. Why else are you here to disturb my meditations?"

"A thousand pardons, Master. I will withdraw and return later."

"You will not. You will have wasted your time and mine otherwise. This flies in the face of the Fourth Principle, does it not?"

"Yes, Master. You have taught that inefficiency leads to dereliction of duty."

"And so it does. Now, lack-wit, what guidance do you require?"

Cadet Rodriguez shifts nervously again.

*"It concerns – it concerns a matter of a – of a…*sexual *nature."*

"Does it indeed? Ah, you humans are so obsessed with sexuality. On the one hand, you crave new and varied – and frequent – experiences. But, on the other hand, your social conditioning teaches you that the sex act is evil and disgusting, not fit to be discussed in polite company. You will *discuss it, however, here and now."*

"What concerns me, Master, is the temptation to seek these…cravings. Our training has emphasized discipline of mind and body so that we may be steadfast in our duty. How then should we resist the temptation?"

"You should resist them in the same fashion that you resist all distractions. Have you learned nothing, lack-wit? I advise you to re-read Lesson Plan 7, section 10, sub-section 2. Focus on each word, each phrase, each sentence, and meditate upon what you have read."

"Thank you, Master," Cadet Rodriguez murmurs and beats a hasty retreat.

*　　*　　*

Warden (L1) Lixu Rodriguez was having a difficult time focusing on Lesson Plan 7, section 10, sub-section 2 at the present moment. The discipline it described might have worked well in the case of an ordinary, run-of-the-mill seductive human female, and it had worked for him on a couple of occasions. But no one – not even the super-intelligent Aldebaranians – could have foreseen the seductive power of the Pluj upon human males. Not only was Rodriguez in the company of such a creature, that creature was one with whom he had spent half his life and who was beyond the point of being merely pleased to see him again after a long absence. She was sending him a very specific message.

Humankind had encountered the Pluj a few years after it had encountered the Ekath. In point of fact, it was because of that previous encounter and the resultant enmity between humans and Ekath which sent the former further out into Deep Space to seek out allies against what they perceived to be an implacable foe. And allies they found – in the unlikeliest places. First, the Okath, who were ethnically related to the Ekath, but politically their opposites – then the Pluj.

Pluj was nearly one massive glacier with scattered pockets of fertile land. The first humans to visit it likened it to the far north or far south of their own home world and did not think it habitable or inhabited. They were wrong on both counts as their ship's sensors verified as soon as they were within range. Further verification followed almost immediately when a vessel from the planet intercepted them and signaled them to make a landing. A hasty language lesson ensued, and the visitors convinced the indigenous species that they were peaceful and wished to establish a trading mission.

The exploration team were literally astounded by what they discovered, having never seen the like anywhere else. Pluj society was unique, as their guides carefully explained to them. In prehistoric times, when men had ruled, a pandemic which was transmitted through testosterone and therefore effected only males nearly wiped out the male population. Left to their own devices, the females were forced to fill the vacuum; and, in doing so, they re-ordered the society to reflect their new superior position in it. Even after the pandemic had subsided and males began to increase in numbers, the females did not relinquish their high status but raised their male children to accept the new order.

Why the Pluj took to humans so readily and entered into an easy alliance with them has been the subject of great debate. One theory advanced was that the fact that Pluj were so biologically similar to humans, they may have been an offshoot in the distant past, however that had come about. Another theory said that the Pluj were intrigued by Dunia's gender equality (itself the result of the Six Weeks' War in pre-ENO times) and wanted to study it more closely. Whatever the reason, underneath the surface, Pluj and humans were still a mismatch.

In the first place, on Pluj, all positions of authority were occupied, and all authority was exercised, by females, a mirror image of human society wherein gender roles had been completely reversed for much of the planet's history. Females still bore the children – that much had not changed – but they decided when to have children and how many. In the second place, Pluj family lines were traced through the mother, and inheritances passed on to the daughters. When a male married, he took his wife's family name and moved into her house. Matronymics, not patronymics, were the accepted form of children's names. And, in the third place, the very concept of "Pluj" was a colossal religious conceit weighted in favor of the feminine principal. They worshiped a "mother-goddess" who had been the "Creatrix of All"; and they referred to this deity as "Our Goddess" or "Our Lady," because it was forbidden to speak her name aloud. The deity allegedly had elevated females to their superior status, and they followed her commandments faithfully. Most significantly, since the emphasis of any mother-goddess religion was on fertility and procreation, the Pluj engaged in uninhibited sex in all its varieties.

It was this latter characteristic which had a very profound effect on human males. Biologists long ago had determined that the female of any non-human mammalian species exuded biochemical substances called pheromones in order to attract mates for the purpose of procreation. While no one had yet discovered the same capability in *human* females, it was argued that, since humans had evolved from the "lower orders," there was no reason to believe that they did not have it, and finding human pheromones simply required more research. On the other hand, it was argued that, since human females were sexually receptive at all times, there wasn't any need for pheromones; the evolutionary process had shunted them off into the biochemical dustbin along with other disused body parts.

There was no question, however, that the Pluj exuded pheromones. The effect they had on sentient males was palpable, although the effect varied in strength from one species to the next, from near zero to extreme. Human males very definitely fell into the latter category; the presence of a Pluj in their midst quickly aroused them, physiologically and psychologically. For this reason, the Constabulary had decreed that any Pluj who served aboard its ships were either to be given assignments which limited their contact with males or to be assigned to all-Pluj crews (preferably the latter!).[17]

Warden (L1) Lixu Rodriguez had believed he could resist the "Pluj effect" by reason of his training by the Aldebaranians. All cadets went through a rigorous mental and physical regimen, the likes of which rivaled that which the average Alkon warrior underwent. (It was rumored throughout the Academy that the Capellans learned everything they knew from the Community; the latter neither confirmed nor denied the rumor, and the former dismissed it out of hand as an insult to their prowess.) Wardens were supposed to be stoical in the performance of their duties, and the training was designed to submerge personal feelings to a level which allowed the Five Principals of the Enlightenment to dominate one's thinking at all times. Wardens were not exactly unfeeling robots – though ordinary mortals were inclined to view them as such – but they were the next best thing. And, because Rodriguez had graduated in the upper one per cent of his class, he had every reason to believe he could withstand any temptations.

He was wrong.

Sr. Lt. Anafu Ralfo sat across the table from him delicately eating her salad. But she kept her eyes on him the whole time and smiled coyly. He tried to avoid eye contact altogether and to concentrate on his plate of spaghetti. It was difficult in the extreme. He could hear – or thought he could hear – his heart beating faster; he could feel – definitely – the flush of emotion warming his body; he could smell – literally – the odor of Ralfo's body as she pumped out pheromones by the kiloliter. He went through the mantra that Master Fresh had taught him, the mantra which served to focus one's mind in times of turmoil; he went through the mantra several times during one bite of pasta alone, and still his defenses were weakening. He wanted her, and he would not be satisfied until he had possessed her – or she him, depending on one's point of view. In the back of his mind, he realized that he should not have brought her along on this mission; only the fact that she might be able to verify anything his would-be informant would tell him overrode his better judgment.

When she had nibbled away the last of her salad, Ralfo rose and excused herself to the lavatory. But, before she left, she stretched languorously, as

---

17 In point of fact, there is only one such crew, aboard the Constabulary patrol vessel t *Reliable*, whose Captain is the lone exception to the New-Swiss-only rule – CMT.

a cat does, and gave him a generous view of her pubic area. He swallowed compulsively and forced himself to look away.

The respite from the pheromonic onslaught was brief, seemingly only seconds in duration. Ralfo sauntered back into his room and approached Rodriguez with great deliberation. Without warning, she sat down on his lap in a straddling position, wrapped her arms around his neck, and kissed him juicily, her tongue playing tag with his. Rodriguez did not – could not – resist and drank in the aroma of her body and the press of her flesh. In his mind, he cursed himself for being so weak-willed.

"Anafu, Anafu," he whispered when she came up for air, "why are you doing this to me? I'm a Warden, and I'm supposed to be on duty."

"Oh, *pafu* [nonsense]!" she murmured, covering his face with quick kisses. "You cannot be on duty *all* the time. It is time to relax and enjoy oneself."

"A Warden can't allow himself to be compromised like this."

"*Double* pafu! You still are the handsomest human I ever have met. Even before I became a woman, I thought so. Many times, I prayed to Our Goddess that She might quicken me so that I could experience the joys of sex with you." She gazed soulfully into his eyes. "Lixu, at the time of your last holiday from University, do you remember when you stayed overnight at our residence?"

Rodriguez let his mind drift back to that time. The University of New Nairobi had closed for Founders Days to observe the anniversary of the establishment of the human colonies on Romulus and Remus. As a native-born Dunian, he couldn't have cared less about such things, but he had appreciated the break from his studies. It was as good a time as any to visit his parents whom he hadn't seen in nearly a year, and he wanted to confirm their presence at his up-coming graduation.

The trip to Pluj had been uneventful, and he had snoozed most of the way. Upon arrival, he was met not only by his parents but also by the Chief Administratrix of Pluj, the planet's top official, and her daughter Anafu. The elder Ralfo was an old family friend, and it was not uncommon for her family and the Rodriguezes to exchange overnight visits. The Administratrix had a streak of gray in her hair – she always laughingly wrote it off as the "stress of my position brought on by too much arbitration" – but she was still a good-looking woman. And Anafu (who resembled her mother very much) had changed since he had last seen her; it was evident that she had passed through puberty and become a young woman.

To celebrate his "homecoming," the Administratrix insisted that he spend his holiday at her residence where he could catch her up on the latest gossip circulating throughout the central spiral. Naively, he had accepted.

The first night of his stay proved to be both eventful and embarrassing. He had had trouble falling asleep and decided to visit his hostess's private library and find something with which he could doze off. As he strolled down the corridor toward the stairs to the lower level, he encountered Anafu coming from the opposite direction. She was stark naked. He had known about the Pluj penchant for nudism in a private setting, but in the past the Ralfos had constrained themselves out of respect for their human guests' sensitivities concerning the practice. The encounter with Anafu therefore was the first time he had ever seen any of them *au naturel*.

And Anafu was a striking young woman. Like her mother, she was statuesque and buxom and affected some of the same mannerisms. The sight of her at that moment had an instant, and predictable, effect upon him; even if she hadn't been a Pluj, merely an attractive female, he would not have reacted any differently. But, she was a Pluj, and so she turned on her natural charms for his (her?) benefit. But he was a guest in the house, and he dare not repay his hostess's hospitality by having sex with her daughter – even if that was part of Pluj mores and if that was what the daughter wanted (and he was sure that she did). Attracted and embarrassed at the same time, he beat a hasty retreat back to his room and agonized until he fell into a fitful sleep.

Now he found himself in the same dilemma.

"Yes," he replied to her question. "It was an experience I'm not likely to forget. You intended to seduce me."

"I was hurt that you rejected me. I cried the whole night."

"I'm sorry about that, Anafu, but I couldn't take advantage of you in your mother's house. It wouldn't have been…right."

"That was the explanation that Mother gave when I discussed the incident with her."

"You told your mother?"

"Of course. Mothers always give guidance to their children. She said that humans have different mores and that I should have waited for the proper moment. But dearest Lixu, I so wanted you." She kissed him roundly again. "And still I do."

"You put me into a difficult position that night. I did want you as well, but… Do you know what I did when I returned to my room? I…abused myself."

Her eyes widened in surprise, and she glanced instinctively down at his groin. She placed her hand there and felt his erect member. He swallowed hard as a fresh wave of desire swept over him.

"You abused your *chuku*? Oh, my poor darling. You should have come to my room. I would have given such tender loving care to it." Impishness returned to her eyes. "I must remedy this."

Slowly, deliberately, she unbuttoned his trousers, reached in, and brought his manhood into full view. She squeezed it gently and was gratified to feel its throbbing. He did not resist but began breathing heavily as desire welled up in him; the pheromones that Pluj generated were taking their toll on him, breaking down the barriers he had set up through his training at the Academy. She fondled him briefly until he groaned; then she raised herself up, pushed his organ against hers, and wiggled slightly so that the head of his shaft was firmly inside her. Now she lowered herself and let the shaft slide deeper inside her. Both moaned softly as their desire intensified in parallel. She began to move up and down in rhythmic fashion, surrendering herself to her passion. He placed his hands on her breasts and massaged them slowly. All too soon, they climaxed at nearly the same moment. Neither of them moved, or wanted to move, for several moments but exchanged small, languorous kisses.

Finally, she raised herself again to release his organ, settled on his lap, and gazed soulfully into his eyes. He returned the expression.

"You were...wonderful, Anafu," he whispered. "I'm sorry I made you wait so long."

"For you, dearest Lixu, I would have waited all eternity. And now, I want to put that piece of furniture you humans call a 'bed' to good use."

*   *   *

They might have been mistaken for tourists, the man and the woman. The man had that look about him which fairly shouted "Dunian," a resident of the Home World who was venturing off-world for the first time, and which every Romulan had learned to recognize and take advantage of. The woman was unmistakably a Pluj, and she was obviously here to see the sights, judging from the way she craned her neck this way and that. The casual observer would have been wrong about the first assessment; the Warden had learned – reluctantly – how to put on a mask when in public. All would have been half-wrong about the second assessment; Ralfo, like all of her kind, always mixed business and pleasure.

They were wearing, allegedly, the latest fashion in tourist clothing. The man sported a chartreuse leisure suit, the trousers of which were hemmed at mid-calf and the jacket of which was collarless and buttonless. A white silk shirt and a pair of shiny, vinyl, brown, knee-high boots completed the picture. The woman wore very short, ruby-red shorts and a matching halter, plus similar knee-high boots. Few Romulans would have been caught dead wearing such outlandish clothing, and so it further marked the couple in the manner which they desired.

No one in the Hotel Metro would have pegged them as tourists, however, for the word had spread throughout the establishment, by guests and staff alike, that two Constabulary officers had checked in the evening before – and one of them was a Warden! As Rodriguez strode and Ralfo sauntered through the lobby, all eyes were upon them – surreptitiously, of course.

The Warden stared straight ahead, maintained his stoicism as best he could, and hoped that no one was paying any attention to his constant fidgeting. He hadn't worn civilian clothing since he entered the Academy, where all cadets were provided with long, flowing gray robes (similar to those worn by their Aldebaranian mentors) made from a coarse fiber which irritated the skin endlessly. And, after graduation, the gray robes had been traded in for the black uniform of the Warden Service. Now, after six years, he was wearing clothes he could swear were meant for a circus clown, and he silently cursed Station Chief Crowder for selecting such garb.

Ralfo, on the other hand, felt quite comfortable in her attire. It was no more and no less than what she was accustomed to wearing aboard ship, although she might have thought she was still over-dressed. Still, she was too caught up in her surroundings to pay much attention to the latest tourist fashions; she was too busy trying to absorb everything on Romulus. She would have been the Compleat Tourist, Constabulary officer or not.

Outside, Rodriguez hailed the next available taxi and instructed it to take them to the Murchison Space Center. Their eventual destination was Old Town, but they could not go there directly. New Town's taxi system operated only as far as the spaceport, just one more example of how New Nairobi's City Fathers had endeavored to isolate the seedier side of their metropolis and thus "protect" the image they wanted to project to the Universe. From the Center, the Constabulary officers would have to travel via the underground express which connected New Town to Old Town, the sole link between past and present (unless one wished to walk across ten kilometers of hard scrabble and scrub grass). There were taxis in Old Town, employing human drivers, but they were not allowed to operate further than the entrance to the underground express upon pain of imprisonment.

At the spaceport, Rodriguez and Ralfo traversed the promenade without examining the myriad of concessions that all tourists were expected to visit but headed directly to the underground express. Their passage was not unencumbered, however; they were solicited (illegally) at least eight times by enterprising individuals who offered "a fantastic opportunity in real estate"; "great deals" on jewelry, electronics, clothing, etc.; a chance to win an all-expenses-paid tour aboard the *Osiris*; and "sexual thrills beyond your wildest imagining" (the latter pitch was cut short when the pitchman realized he was talking to a Pluj). They were also solicited (legally) three times by persons representing authorized charities; Rodriguez dropped a five-carat note into each of the outstretched hands without noting to whom he was contributing and kept pushing forward.

At the far end of the promenade, the flow of traffic took on a decidedly different flavor. Few (if any) brightly attired tourists were to be seen in this area; few (if any) solicitors bothered to collar passersby and blandish them with fabulous offers. On the other hand, security guards were plentiful, and they maintained a highly visible presence. Here then was the New Town terminal of the underground express which transported Old Towners back and forth. The traffic flow consisted of those who were fortunate to find employment in the showcase city of Romulus and was steady around the clock as the laborers began or ended their work shifts. None stopped to sightsee lest (s)he arouse the suspicion of a security guard; being arrested for even the least offense cost a "loiterer" his/her job. The laborers moved quickly (and, for the most part, quietly), kilosecond by kilosecond, day by day, to their appointed destinations.

Facial expressions told the whole story of Old Town's relationship to New Town, and they were varied and malleable. In the course of one kilosecond, one might observe grimness, sullenness, despair, resignation, resentment, and weariness, often on the same face. If any of this miserable lot smiled, it was a humorless smile – one of the mouth but not of the eyes – aimed at a familiar face which disappeared as soon as the brief contact had broken off. Old Towners had little reason to be happy. While they earned better wages in New Town than in Old Town, they were still not able to lift themselves out of a subsistent existence and perhaps to find better accommodations in New Town.

To a man and a woman, the workers all wore the same garment: a gray coverall with a yellow-and-green armband. It was as much a uniform as military attire and set an entire segment of humanity off from the rest.[18] Employment in New Town was never guaranteed, of course; one could be hired or fired at will since the supply of cheap labor was always plentiful. Old Towners had learned long ago to take what they could get when and where they could because the alternative was too unpleasant to think about. This reality fueled their facial expressions as no other power could and set the stage for a potential tinderbox of rebellion.

Rodriguez and Ralfo eased themselves into the flow of traffic headed for the next outbound train. Their gaudy presence incurred few responses; Old Towners learned to stifle their curiosity so long as they were at the New Town end of the underground express and to mind their own business. Those few who did take notice of the strange pair examined them cursorily and then looked away to wallow in their own petty concerns. The Warden

---

18   This attire was mandated by law. Any worker caught not wearing it while engaged in employment in New Town faced arrest and a substantial fine and/or imprisonment – CMT.

warily glanced to and fro. Old Towners could be unpredictable at times, and it was prudent to stay alert. The Pluj, however, viewed the scene as yet another marvel to be absorbed, and so she continued to gawk.

The underground express consisted of two adjacent tunnels which ran the ten kilometers between New Town and Old Town. Each contained a train of five cylindrical cars riding on mag-lev rails and operating around the clock; the trains ran in opposite directions, passing each other at the mid-point in the tunnels. They were speedy; a one-way trip required only half a kilosecond. They were also free, a sop to a population which had precious few other amenities in life, and always crowded.

Rodriguez and Ralfo found themselves packed like sardines in a steady flow of humanity. They could not change directions, even if they had wanted to; it was either move with the crowd or be trampled by it. And only occasionally did they merit a brief glance of nascent curiosity. The Warden thought he detected a note of contempt in one man's eye, but the man averted his gaze before the suspicion could be confirmed.

Once aboard the outbound mag-lev train, the crowd engaged in its version of an ancient Dunian game called "musical chairs." One by one, individuals made for the nearest available seat, many times edging out their fellow travelers by mere fractions of a second. Long years of practice were at work here; a moment's hesitation meant a loss of opportunity and an extension of one's search. When the seats in the first car had filled up, the crowd surged into the next one and so on until all the cars were fully occupied. On this particular run, there were many people left standing in the central aisle. The Constabulary officers did not find a seat until the very last second before the train moved out of the terminal. That may have been a fortunate turn of affairs, however, for it meant that they would be among the first to get off at the other end.

The trip was happily uneventful. Most of the passengers kept to themselves. If, by chance, two or more of them in the same section happened to recognize each other, they held a sporadic conversation in barely audible tones. No one paid overt attention to the strangers in their midst, although the strangers were studying them.

Part of the training cadets received at the Warden Academy on the Aldebaranian home world was learning body language, the silent exchange of information every sentient creature "spoke" unconsciously. Rodriguez believed it was Master Walking-Briskly-Before-the-Rising-of-the-Sun who oversaw that part of the training. Master Walking drilled his students as relentlessly on this subject as any of the other instructors — and he was thorough! He said that each species – even his own – had its own body language and that he intended to instruct "you half-wits" in all of them so that, say, the rubbing of the nose by an Ekath/Okath would tell you one thing while the same action by a Forua would tell you something different entirely. It was a matter of personal pride for Rodriguez that he had learned these "languages" rather quickly, but he had not broadcast this fact lest he find himself standing before Master Fresh and enduring yet another lengthy lecture on humility.

For the duration of the trip, then, the Warden studied the body language of his fellow humans. He "heard" a cacophony of "sounds" from all sides. A facial tic. A shifting of the shoulders. A rubbing of the nose. A brushing back of the hair. A flexing of the fingers. A fluttering of the eyelids. A scratching of the leg. A licking of the lips. And a score or more of the inadvertent movement of body parts. All of them told him more about these pathetic creatures and their lives of misery than mere words ever could. It was not a pretty story, and he was happy he did not have to "read" it for very long.

When the mag-lev train pulled into the Old Town terminal, Rodriguez and Ralfo were quickly on their feet and marching toward the exit ahead of the other passengers. On the platform, they stepped to one side and allowed the crowd to pass by while they planned their next move. The terminal here was dingy and darkened – several overhead lamps had burned out or been broken and not replaced – and litter was everywhere, a sharp contrast to the New Town terminal. As soon as the crowd had thinned, they made for the stairs leading to the street level.

Outside, Rodriguez looked about for a taxi and saw one approaching the terminal. He signaled to it, and the cabbie pulled over to the curb in a nonchalant manner. The vehicle was as dilapidated as anything else in this neighborhood; it clanked and rattled and hissed and groaned, and it would not have surprised anyone if the thing fell apart on the instant. The driver was decrepit-looking and grimy; his eyes were rheumy, and his hair (what there was left of it) was stringy and unkempt. He wore shabby clothing and a bright red cap with a makeshift "taxi badge" pinned on one side.

The cabbie gave his potential fares a once-over, his eyes widening in surprise at the sight of freshly-scrubbed faces and clean clothes. He gave Ralfo a longer assessment. Surprise turned to pleasure, however, as the thought of gouging these obvious naifs percolated through his brain.

"Where to, Cn., Cns.?" he rasped.

"Vander Luten's," the Warden replied unhesitatingly.

The driver frowned. Vander Luten's was only two blocks away. He couldn't charge a large fare without being obvious about it. He shook his head in what he hoped was a sympathetic gesture.

"You don't wanna go there, friend. Vander Luten's got a bad rep. Lemme take you to a really *nice* place." *One where I can get a kick-back*, he added mentally.

"You're right," Rodriguez said smoothly. "I don't want to go there. But I have to. I've got business there."

The cabbie raised an eyebrow, shrugged his shoulders in resignation, and motioned them to get in. The interior of the taxi matched its exterior in dilapidation, with one extra "feature"; the seat sagged in all the wrong places, and a spring sprouted through the fabric when one sat near it. In addition, it was a hodge-podge of cigarette burns, food and beverage stains, and traces of bodily fluids of all sorts. Needless to say, an ill odor permeated the stale air and threatened to gag any unsuspecting passenger.

Rodriguez and Ralfo clambered in and sat down gingerly, half expecting to fall through the floorboards and onto the pavement at any second. The taxi chugged away, and the clanking and rattling and hissing and groaning increased in volume. Moments later, it pulled up in front of Vander Luten's Spacers Club. The cabbie turned to his fares and smiled wanly.

"Here ya are, friends. That'll be – um, K25."

The Warden smiled back, wryly. He could have walked from the terminal to this seedy dive of a "gentleman's club" and saved the expense. But strangers walking the streets of Old Town were prime targets for any number of predators whose needs varied with their circumstances; and, while he and Ralfo had been trained to deal with any exigency, he thought it prudent to avoid trouble and/or attention, even if he had to pay an exorbitant fare. He handed over three ten-carat notes and told the driver to keep the change. The latter nodded appreciatively. The Constabulary officers exited the vehicle hastily and unconsciously brushed themselves off.

Rodriguez regarded the self-serving sign on the building's façade and grimaced. This establishment was definitely the last place in the Galaxy he wanted to be; Vander Luten's was a hell-hole known throughout the central spiral as a place to avoid if one wished to retain his health and his money. A stroll down the streets of the capital city of Eka-xan would have been a cakewalk by comparison. Nevertheless, his business required him to be here. The pirate leader had provided him with the name, description, and location of his alleged informant concerning JUR activity, and there was no getting around it. How an Ekath would be so familiar with a tavern notorious for serving only humans (and their guests) was quite beyond his comprehension; but the pirate knew well the penalty for perjuring himself before a Constabulary official[19], and therefore he would have to be given the benefit of the doubt.

Briefly, he regretted again having allowed Anafu to accompany him. This

---

19 Article Five ("Law Enforcement"), section six ("Obstruction of Justice"), paragraph two of the Convention of Aldebaran states (in part) that "perjury before an officer of the law shall be considered an act of obstruction of justice and shall be punished as such...

dive was less of a place for a woman – even a Pluj – than it was for a man. And he couldn't very well leave her outside alone, because any woman – even a Pluj – was easy prey for the criminal element which lurked the streets of Old Town, day or night.

Inside, the potpourri of foul odors hit Rodriguez like a sledgehammer, and he quickly switched to breathing through his mouth. He wished now that he had been born an i-Pluj. Having evolved on a frigid world where a highly sensitive olfactory nerve would not have assisted in their survival (as opposed to hearing), Pluj tended not to notice odors (foul or otherwise) as much as other species. Still, he caught Ralfo wrinkling her nose in disgust – such was the cesspool in which they now found themselves.

The informant whom they sought was known simply as "the Professor." Whether he was or had been an academic was moot, but he was reputed to possess knowledge about many topics, academic or otherwise. And he peddled his knowledge as a merchant peddled products; whoever had the price received the information required. The Professor also bought knowledge if he believed it might be useful to someone else. And he bought and sold for cash principally; if cash was in short supply, he would settle for commodities (legal or otherwise) which he could convert into cash. Part of his reputation lay in the fact that the knowledge imparted was accurate; if accuracy was in doubt, he would preface his pitch with the words, "This is only a rumor, but…" Such was the Professor's ability to satisfy everyone's curiosity that Old Towners regarded him as "neutral turf" in their dealings (licit or otherwise). He may have been the only resident here who was so sacrosanct.

The pirate's description of the Professor had been quite specific: long, shaggy, graying hair; an owlish expression; a rumpled, thread-worn, blue business suit; black and maroon sandals. Rodriguez had no difficulty spotting his man, even though he was sitting in the far corner of the tavern. He sat alone, sipping a brandy and surveying the other denizens of this establishment.

The Constabulary officers attempted to negotiate the distance between them and their target as unobtrusively as possible, but it was far from possible given their appearance. All heads turned in their direction. Some of the patrons registered surprise and shock; others, anger and resentment. None seemed to be too happy about this intrusion of opulence into their world of misery. The Warden ignored them as he did most others and kept moving. He pulled up before the Professor's table and waited to be recognized.

The Professor registered his own surprise at this visitation. The gaudy pair was hardly his usual clientele. Besides, there was something about them which

Such offense will *double* any ultimate sentence against the accused [emphasis added]"
– CMT.

told him that they were not who they appeared to be. Still, he gave both a toothy smile. It never cost anyone to be courteous.

"Greetings, Cn.," he addressed Rodriguez in a soft tone of voice. Turning to Ralfo, he cupped his hands before his face and said: "The Lady be with you, my dear."

"Greetings, Cn.," the Warden responded in kind.

"With you also Our Lady be," the Pluj completed the ritual.

The Professor motioned them to be seated.

"What can I do for you, my friends?"

"We've been told you have information useful to our, uh, cause."

"And what cause might that be?"

"We're looking for an individual whose whereabouts we need to know."

"I'm sure you are, friend. Your kind always does."

"I beg your pardon?"

The Professor flashed another toothy grin.

"Do you take me for a fool? You two *look* like ordinary tourists, but ordinary tourists would not patronize a dump like Vander Luten's. Besides, I watched how you walked over here. I think you're policemen."

Rodriguez now grinned back.

"You're quite perceptive, Professor." He slipped his hand surreptitiously into his pocket and pulled out his badge carefully so as not to reveal it to anyone else in the room. "This *is* official business."

The Professor gazed at the symbol of the Warden Service with the briefest of awe and took a long sip of his brandy.

"What makes you think I'll tell *you* anything? I have a reputation to maintain. If it became known that I was a police informant, my life wouldn't be worth an Ekatha C-note."

"We'll pay your price for any useful information you might have."

"Indeed you will." Abruptly, he scanned the room. The other denizens were watching them closely, murmuring menacingly to each other and gesticulating in their direction. "But, I won't tell you a thing here. That bunch behind you is beginning to look uglier than they usually do. The longer you stay, the more likely they'll cause trouble."

"Care of ourselves we can take," Ralfo muttered.

"No doubt. But, I try to avoid trouble at all times."

"What do you suggest then?" the Warden asked.

"Return to the underground express – and quickly, judging by the mood of that bunch – and wait for me there."

Rodriguez nodded and started to his feet. The Professor held up his hand.

"Give me some money first. That might allay their suspicions."

The Warden reached into his pocket, extracted a twenty-carat note, and tossed it on the table. The Professor scooped it up and pocketed it with one smooth motion.

The Constabulary officers negotiated their way back to the entrance. They were tracked every step of the way by the increasingly hostile crowd; the murmuring became more menacing, and the gesticulations more animated. Rodriguez believed they might have to fight their way out of Vander Luten's after all. Happily, they did not have to and exited the building in one piece. The Warden paused only long enough to take a deep breath of fresh air, then told Ralfo to stay close to him.

Together, they quick-marched to the nearest street corner where a taxi was sitting idly. By no mean co-incidence, it was the same taxi in which they had arrived.

CHAPTER SEVEN

▼

FACT-FINDING

THE BRIGHTLY-COLORED DOTS SWIRLED AND pirouetted in a kaleidoscopic fashion. Unlike a real kaleidoscope, however, they did not re-form into new patterns but retained their original ones. Only their relative positions in space changed.

Captain Olaf Halvarson had been studying those shifting shapes in the Display intently for the past twenty kiloseconds, hoping against hope to spot a new dot in the familiar patterns which would signal the end of his search. The *Steadfast* was looping through this region of Deep Space near the Ru'uhaad star system in an ever-widening spiral while its on-duty crew – led by an increasingly frustrated captain – kept a collective blurry eye out for the rogue world, Planetoid 48. The tension on the Bridge was as thick as the fog on the planet Amazon. No one said a word – in any language – lest (s)he receive a baleful glare from Gold Zone

Commander Krishnamurthy also maintained a discreet silence as she sat next to her fuming superior. Her forbearance was uncharacteristic, since she was used to making comments of all sorts on any subject one cared to raise at the drop of a microchip. She and Halvarson had known each other since their days at CSC Flight Academy on New Switzerland and had graduated in the same class. There had been rumors that they were lovers, but both denied them. After graduation, they took separate assignments, she to Capella, he to Bi [*Omicron Orionis 5 on Dunian star charts – CC*], and rose through the ranks to their present ones. And, when the post of Executive Officer for the *Steadfast* came open, Tomiko Krishnamurthy was first in line to apply for it. Halvarson recommended her to the Chief of Operations, and the latter approved without question. They were a "team" once again.

Yet, the "team spirit" was definitely on hold at the moment, as the Captain gazed desperately into the Display for one lone point of light and saw nothing but "empty space." Krishnamurthy stole nervous glances at her friend-cum-commanding-officer and bit her tongue each time. Best to let him initiate any conversation even though he appeared to be in no mood for one. She sat rigidly in her seat and waited for the explosion she was sure would occur. Olaf had just so much patience.

Suddenly, the Captain started forward in his chair and thrust a finger toward the Display.

"What's that?" he shouted, his voice breaking. "Sensors, identify that signal!"

"Where, sir?" an Uhaad officer asked, a note of fear in her voice.

"There" – he picked up a laser-wand, aimed it at a dot of yellow at the fringe of the Display's field of view, and high-lighted it – "at, um, 70/13/+42, relative."[20]

"Regretting, sir, that a Dunian vessel. I calling up the traffic log?"

"No, no, never mind. Continue your search."

"Captain," the XO murmured, "if I may be so bold, I suggest you take a break. Go down to the gym and work off some of that nervous energy. I'll let you know if there are any new developments."

Halvarson peered at her in wonder, and she returned his gaze dispassionately. Then he displayed a lopsided grin.

"You always did know me better than I did, Tomiko. All right. If I stay here much longer, I'll have myself a nice little nervous break-down. But, I think I'll go down to the pool instead of the gym – cool off and all that."

"Very good, sir."

The Captain rose from his seat and would have walked away had not his vidscreen flashed into life, revealing the concerned face of the Green Zone officer, an orange-crested male Bitha. He immediately plopped back in his chair.

"Report."

"Sir, have we an incoming message from that Dunian vessel."

"Patch it through, Leftenant."

"Aye, sir."

The screen blanked for the space of a second, then revealed a very

---

20　Relative co-ordinates differ from Galactic co-ordinates in that the former measures from a ship's current position in Deep Space whereas the latter measures from the center of the Galaxy. Two ships could be in the same sector according to Galactic co-ordinates but have entirely different co-ordinates relative to each other – CMT.

frightened human face of Arabic origin. The man was actually perspiring and licking his lips repeatedly.

"I'm Halvarson of the CSC patrol vessel *Steadfast*. How may I help you, Captain?"

The Dunian swallowed a large lump in his throat and licked his lips again.

"Thank Allah you were nearby, Captain Halvarson. I am ibn-Walid, Captain of the DSS *Good Fortune* – although, if I may say so, we have had a stroke of *bad* fortune."

"Explain."

"We were on route from Capella to Ru'uhaad with a hold full of grain. About twenty light-years from our current position, a large object suddenly appeared in our path, and we were required to make an emergency course correction."

"A large object?" Halvarson's curiosity was now piqued. "How large?"

"Oh, very large, the size of Saturn's largest moon, Titan, I should judge."

"And it appeared suddenly?"

"Yes, sir, as if it had warped out from a distant point."

"Very interesting," Halvarson murmured, attempting as best he could to keep his growing excitement from manifesting itself openly. "Perhaps we should investigate. Might be a hazard to shipping, don't you know?"

"Quite hazardous, Captain," ibn-Walid agreed, licking his lips again, "if I may say so."

"Can you provide my astrogator with the co-ordinates of the encounter?"

"Most assuredly." The Dunian looked off to his left and barked an order in Arabic. "Thank you for handling this problem."

"All part of the service, Captain." To Red Zone (Astrogation), he asked: "Have you got those co-ordinates yet?"

"Coming frough noo, sir," replied a Reman officer.

Halvarson pressed a white button on his console, marked "MOME." Instantly, the lighting throughout the *Steadfast* began to pulse in a repeating pattern – three short, one long – which alerted the crew that the powerful engine was about to be engaged in one kilosecond. That was all the time they had to secure themselves and any loose objects in their vicinity. On the Bridge, the duty officers strapped themselves in.

"Sir," Astrogation reported, "the co-ordinytes 'ave been received, and a course relyed to the 'elm."

"Very good, Leftenant. Helm, proceed on my mark."

"Aye, sir!"

The Captain eyed his console chrono closely. It was moving too slowly to suit him, and he wished he could speed it up a little. Eventually, a kilosecond passed, and he pressed the white button again. Now, the ship's lighting dimmed to its lowest level. Anyone not secured would soon be in for a rough ride during the activation of the MOME.

"Helm, mark!"

The Helm officer pressed a red button on her console, then – along with the rest of the Bridge crew – braced himself for the ordeal to come.

At first, the *Steadfast* was filled with an eerie silence. Not a sound could be heard anywhere, from bow to stern. There was, however, activity, and it was occurring in the smaller of the two spheres which comprised an MOME-powered spacecraft. In this sphere, two simultaneous actions were taking place. The first involved the gamma-ray generator; it was stripping atoms of hydrogen of electrons and producing gamma rays in the process. Shortly, these rays would be channeled into the central chamber by means of an electromagnetic field. The second action involved the central chamber itself. The electromagnetic field was building up; and, at a pre-programmed moment, the field would start to change polarity, slowly at first, then more rapidly.

The eerie silence gave way to an imperceptible hum, more felt than heard, as the ship began to vibrate under the powerful forces being created. The humming intensified, and now it was clearly audible. Soon, it would become a screeching sound like fingernails on a chalkboard. At the pre-programmed moment, the oscillation of the electromagnetic field reached its maximum frequency. The two separate actions became one as the gamma rays were funneled into the chamber and interacted with the oscillating field. The most powerful force ever created by sentient beings was being unleashed, building in intensity second after awesome second. At a second pre-programmed moment, the MOME reached a level of strength which would allow the *Steadfast* to jump across Deep Space at a fraction of the time it took impulse velocities to cover the desired distance.

Space collapsed in upon itself, and the ship disappeared from this reality...

...and re-appeared approximately twenty light-years from where it had once been.

On the Bridge, the Helm officer pressed the red button again. In the smaller sphere, the gamma-ray generator ceased stripping hydrogen atoms of their electrons, and the magnetic field ceased oscillating. In a few moments, the eerie silence once more filled the ship. Captain Halvarson shuddered voluntarily in a symbolic gesture of shaking off the effects of the MOME. Beside him, Commander Krishnamurthy roused herself out of a yoga-induced trance she had learned to create for just this sort of occasion. The Captain pushed the white button a third time, and the ship's lighting returned to normal.

"Sensors!" he commanded, "give me the Display!"

Seconds later, the holographic image formed to reveal the particulars of the region of Deep Space into which the *Steadfast* had transited. Nowhere could the Ru'uhaad system be seen. Instead, the dominate feature was a red giant star around which two uninhabitable planets – and one Constabulary outpost – orbited, two-and-a-half light-years to starboard. At this point in time, both planets were on the opposite side of their parent, and the outpost itself was close to disappearing behind the red giant.

"I'll be damned!" Halvarson muttered. "That's Crenshaw's Star.[21] That Dunian didn't mention it at all."

"He *was* pretty rattled after all, sir," the XO said calmly. "Perhaps it just slipped his mind."

"Perhaps. Well, if that's Crenshaw's Star, then that outpost must be – let's see." He turned to his monitor and entered a command. The screen flashed into life and showed a list of celestial bodies for this sector. Halvarson scrolled down the list until he came to "Crenshaw's Star." He high-lighted the entry and punched "Enter"; the list was replaced by a description of the star, its planets and any other bodies in the vicinity – including the outpost. "Yes, that's Outpost #312, Lt. Commander Kaw commanding." He grinned. "Tomiko, our luck may be changing."

He pushed the green button on his console. A red-crested Bitha officer appeared on-screen.

"Communications. Lt. Tul, sir."

"Patch me through to the Outpost, Leftenant."

"Aye, sir."

Outpost #312 orbited Crenshaw's Star at a distance of twenty billion kilometers. Its orbit was five billion kilometers from the star's natural outer planet, and it had been positioned so that the orbit was inclined thirty degrees from the local ecliptic. This was standard operating procedure for the Constabulary. When the decision had been made by the CSC's Grand Assembly to place outposts around all star systems (inhabited or not) for the purpose of greater security, the Constabulary's High Command followed the recommendations of a specially formed panel of astronomers, astrophysicists, and planetologists who claimed the inclination would afford a better view of the system's contents and, not incidentally, avoidance of the chance of collision with those contents. The inclination varied from system to system;

---

21 Named for a Deep Space prospector who first explored the system around 120 A.R. in search of mineral wealth. He found it; but, before he could cash in on his discovery, he was murdered by pirates – CMT.

the criteria were the number of contents, their individual and collective dynamics, the potential for illegal activity, and the equal potential for the evolution of Life.

Outposts doubled as Relay Stations but measured only a kilometer in diameter. In this respect, they differed greatly from the huge Relay Stations which orbited inhabited systems; the lesser amount of traffic to an uninhabited system mitigated against a more powerful MOME. Otherwise, Constabulary personnel shared space with civilian crews; at no time did the former number more than twenty individuals and they rotated less frequently than the latter (a point which provoked no small amount of grumbling). Duty (and life) on an Outpost was a dreary affair, not only because its occupants were far from home but also because there was little to do in an uninhabited star system. The routine daily observations and the occasional cruise around the system via shuttlecraft engendered a certain sameness, and the personnel were hard put to devise barriers against the inevitable boredom and psychological stress. One had to be a tough-minded person to accept assignment on an Outpost, and not everyone volunteered.

The Command vidscreen lit up again, and Captain Halvarson peered at another male Bitha. This person sported a yellow crest which identified him as a member of one of Bi's racial minorities.[22] Lt. Commander Kaw Enteni actually smiled –a rarity in a race universally known for its humorlessness – and his jet-black eyes twinkled (literally). Halvarson's eyebrows arched at this uncharacteristic behavior.

"Ah, Captain Halvarson, wondered I when would return you my message. But, was necessary it to visit?"

"You sent me a message?"

"Yes, sir. Received you not it?"

The Captain turned to gaze at the niche wherein the *aaxyboxr* resided. He grimaced when he saw that the creature was pulsating rapidly. It was yet another unfortunate consequence of the absence of his Warden.

"Sorry, Commander, but the *Steadfast*'s Warden is on special assignment, and our communications capabilities are necessarily limited. What was your message about?"

"Reported a passing Dunian freighter that had it a near-collision with a celestial body. Said it that had appeared the body quite suddenly."

"Ah, yes. That was the DSS *Good Fortune*. Its captain contacted us as

---

22   There are four racial groupings on Bi. Red crests denote the dominant majority, while orange, yellow, and white (in descending order) form the minorities. Bithan society is caste-oriented, and there are specific rules pertaining to the interaction between each one – CMT.

well. That's why we're here. We're tracking that object with the co-ordinates the *Good Fortune* gave us."

"Have you any idea is what it?"

"A fairly good idea, actually. It's Planetoid 48, allegedly a base for a cell of the JUR. Somehow, it…disappeared from the Ru'uhaad system."

"'Disappeared'?" The Bitha's eyes went wide, and his crest bristled. "Is how this possible?"

"I don't know, but I intend to find out. Meanwhile, will you do me a favor?"

"Certainly, sir."

"Send a message to our Lt. Rodriguez. He's on Romulus at the moment. Just let him know about these new developments."

"Will do I at once."

"Thank you, Commander. Halvarson out."

He pressed the blue button, and the image of the Sensors duty officer appeared. Uhaad females were just as thin and hairless as the males.

"Sensors," she spoke in a whispery soft voice. "Lt. I-ta here, sir."

"Check for any anomalies in this sector and report any to me at once, Leftenant."

"Aye, sir."

The Captain then pressed the red button again.

"Lt. A-la, lay in the previous search pattern. We're going hunting again." He turned to his XO. "I've got a good feeling about this, Tomiko."

"Glad to hear it, Olaf. I thought I'd have to have Dr. Spura confine you to quarters for half a meg."

Halvarson gave her a mock scowl.

"You really want my command, don't you?"

Krishnamurthy simply smiled sweetly and leaned back in her chair.

*   *   *

"Master Fresh, is a visible presence always correct? Is there not a time for stealth?"

The Aldebaranian guru eyes his human pupil with his all-too-frequently baleful stare. It seems that this sprout has yet another daily question for him. This is a good sign; and he comes to believe that, if the sprout does not have a question, then one of two things must be occurring. The first is the need for medical attention to the sprout, and the second is the triumph of stupidity over wisdom. One does not become wise, Master Fresh has said time and again, if one stops asking questions and seeking answers. Even those of the Community have a need to ask a question now and then.

The cadet shifts his weight from foot to foot in that peculiar human ritual known as "nervousness." This particular cadet seems to be adept in this ritual; Master Fresh has not witnessed him standing still at any time he has come to him for private counsel.

"What do you mean by 'stealth,' lack-wit?"

"I mean, should we sometimes lay in wait, hidden from view, until the criminal approaches, and then take him by surprise?"

"Is this behavior not characteristic of the criminal himself, to lay in wait until his victim comes near?"

"Yes, Master, but—"

"And does not the Third Principle militate against such behavior whereby one apprehends one sort of criminal by open confrontation and another sort by stealth?"

"Yes, Master, but—"

"There is no 'but,' lack-wit. The power of the Warden lies in his visibility. By standing out, he provokes fear in the evil-doer and trust in the innocent. Hiding turns the Third Principle on its head."

The cadet thanks his mentor for his wise counsel and quickly departs. Master Fresh sighs deeply. He has high hopes for this one. This one may become a Warden yet.

*   *   *

Warden (L1) Lixu Rodriguez did not like hiding in the shadows. To him, it seemed like cowardice and fear, and he had had enough of that in his childhood. Growing up in the shadow of his grandfather, the legendary Spencer Rodriguez, the first Speaker of the Central Spiral Collective's Grand Assembly, and of his equally renowned diplomat father, he had learned to keep silent and not to disturb his betters. Only when he had enrolled in the University did he creep out of his shell and participate – on a limited basis – in the wider world. That sense of freedom was only temporary. When he had been admitted to the Warden Academy and come into contact with the enigmatic, awe-inspiring Aldebaranians, he had felt small again. Especially when he asked questions – lots and lots of questions – and the Masters seemed to begrudge him their valuable time. He had vowed that, should he become a Warden, he would be *so* visible as to instill as much awe in ordinary mortals as did the Community.

Now, however, he was as invisible as it was humanly possible to get in circumstances beyond his control.

Had he been merely passing through the terminal of the underground express on his way back to New Town, he would have walked boldly and unhesitatingly, regardless of the hostility he knew he would provoke amongst Romulans, whatever their station in life may be. For the moment, he had to remain in the shadows until the Professor arrived. If the Professor saw him standing in plain sight, he would abort the rendezvous and deny him any information he might have. This was unacceptable, and so the Warden hid himself away.

The terminal at this end of the transit system reflected what lay outside. There were concessions, automated and peopled, and the usual horde of solicitors who sought customers however they could. But the terminal was dingy, unkempt, and foul-smelling; it would have required a task equal to cleaning the Augean stables to sanitize the place. Its denizens were equally so, and they wore the habitual face of long-suffering and forbearance that all Old Towners did. Rodriguez and Ralfo with all their finery would have stood out like a Capellan in this crowd and would have been equally as welcome. No guards patrolled the premises; no amount of money would have enticed anyone to risk his/her life in this man-made jungle. The passers-through were on their own.

The Warden watched disinterestedly as a team of pickpockets worked the crowd. Old Towners preyed on one another as much as they did outsiders – a carat was a carat, after all, whatever its source. This attitude tended to re-enforce the suspicion and stand-offishness prominently displayed by one and all, especially by those who managed to have a few carats in their pockets. Rodriguez also counted at least six prostitutes hawking their "wares" and silently cursing those who rebuffed them. The whores were no more dressed up that the average Old Towner, and they were clearly not enjoying what they were doing; but, since they apparently had no other skills to speak of, they used their bodies in order to survive. And the beggars were present as well, of all ages and genders. One, a small boy dressed in rags, was doing a passable job of exhibiting a physical disability in order to gain sympathy; in another context, he might have succeeded without much effort. Or he might have robbed someone at knife-point. A carat was a carat, after all.

Rodriguez glanced at Ralfo. The Pluj was also studying the contents – human and otherwise – of the terminal, and she was as grim as any Pluj ever got. He doubted that she had ever seen this side of humankind before and wondered what thoughts were assaulting her naiveté. Later, he'd have to ask her. Pluj took most things in stride, but Old Town on Romulus had to be seen to be believed.

How long the Constabulary team waited for its informant to show himself was indeterminate. In a place where constant activity was the norm, one moment displaced another in rapid succession, and Time had a habit of losing all meaning. At least six inbound trains and as many outbound ones came and went, and the throngs changed their configurations with kaleidoscopic ease.

"Lixu," Ralfo murmured, laying a hand on his arm, "I see the Professor."

"Where?"

"There" – she gestured toward the entrance – "where an old woman is selling fruit."

He followed her gesture and spotted the vendor immediately. In the back of his mind, he noted Anafu's use of the human word "woman." The Pluj, having once encountered other species and quickly recognizing that they had specific attitudes – and vocabulary – for the various genders, learned to make such distinctions themselves whenever they were off-world for the betterment of interplanetary relations. Never would they have done so at home where males were an invisible caste.

Now he saw the Professor himself, picking over the vendor's wares and finally selecting what to his mind was the most edible of the lot. The informant handed over a few coins and strolled off, munching on his purchase nonchalantly. Occasionally, he would nod to a passerby whom he recognized and receive a similar salutation. The pickpockets, the prostitutes, and the beggars let him pass without interference, such was his reputation in Old Town.

As soon as the Romulan drew near, Rodriguez stepped halfway out of the shadows and signaled for his attention. The Professor, seemingly unfazed by the attention-getting gesture, walked by the Warden's position without turning his head. The latter frowned at the rebuff and would have signaled again; but, by this time, the informant was a few paces further on, and the Warden would have had to step out of the shadows completely, a prospect he did not particularly relish under the circumstances.

Abruptly, the Professor halted and began a search of his pockets. A worried look crossed his face as his search produced no results. He now gazed around the floor of the terminal, this way and that, and started to retrace his path. He stopped at the Warden's position, still searching the floor.

"You'll excuse the subterfuge," he murmured. "Can't be too careful in this business."

"Why take a risk at all?" Rodriguez inquired.

"Partly because I seldom refuse a commission – money is hard to come by, you know, even for someone with information to sell. And partly out of curiosity."

"Curiosity?"

The Professor now moved completely into the shadows and held the Warden's eyes.

"Yes. Why did you look me up? You aren't my usual run of clientele."

Tersely, Rodriguez spoke of his encounter with the pirates in the Ru'uhaad system and of the pirate chieftain's proposition.

"And you believed him?"

"He was facing life imprisonment on Xix. That's enough to make anyone truthful."

"So it is." The informant stroked his chin. "I seem to recall that... gentleman and some of our conversation. Why he thought I was in my cups, however, is beyond me. I was enjoying my first brandy of the day, as I recall."

"The Ekath think the worst of humans. Even one sip of alcohol makes you a drunkard in their eyes. What exactly did you tell him? And why?"

The Romulan rubbed his chin again and looked out of the shadows at the stream of humanity marching past in robotic fashion.

"The second question first. This pirate wanted to know what I knew about the disappearance of the *Astarte*; I got the idea that he was hoping to score some salvage. I told him what I knew – which wasn't much – from a conversation between two Remans I happened to overhear. When they saw me, they changed the subject. And, when our pirate 'friend' heard about *Remans* being involved, he left immediately."

"Does the name Mubutu Weyerhauser sound familiar?"

"Weyerhauser, Weyerhauser. Professor at the University of New Nairobi – teaches astrophysics, I believe. What about him?"

"Our pirate 'friend' seemed to think you could tell us about his connection to the JUR."

"Our pirate 'friend' is sadly mistaken on that point. I know Professor Weyerhauser only by reputation – his *professional* reputation, that is. I know nothing about his politics." He rubbed his chin a third time. "There may be someone in New Town who might know. I've heard that he has a lady friend."

"Do you know her name and where we can find her?"

"I think I'll need to see some money at this point. I've been rather forthcoming so far, and I'm not in the habit of dispensing free information."

The Warden smiled wryly and dug into his pocket. The Professor's eyes darted to the roll of bills which appeared in the other's hand, and his mouth twitched in anticipation. Rodriguez peeled off two yellow banknotes and handed them over. The informant took them without hesitation, and they immediately disappeared into a pocket.

"That's K100 for what you've already told us," the Warden explained, "and another K100 for the name and whereabouts of the lady friend."

"The person you're looking for is Petra Katanga. She works at the New Nairobi Public Library."

"Thank you, Professor."

"It's been a pleasure dealing with you, Warden. But, I wouldn't encourage any further contact, if you take my meaning. Good day, Cn., Cns."

The Romulan strode out of the shadows, patting one of his pockets and wearing a huge grin, and headed for the exit. Rodriguez turned to his partner.

"Well, Anafu, the investigation continues. Let's get out of here."

"I am ready. This place is so...unsavory."

The Warden regarded her with no little surprise. Her remark had been the most unkind thing he had ever heard her say. On the other hand, the Pluj were known to speak their minds on any subject, without regard to the nature of the reception of their opinions. Apparently, Anafu's sense of wonder was finally being eroded.

*   *   *

It is a known fact that institutions as much as living species evolve over the course of time. Despite all efforts to keep them as static as possible, they shift – physically, professionally, and environmentally – according to a number of variables. Many of these variables are external, but most are internal. External variables include change of mission, change of demographics, lack or abundance of funding (which, in turn, affect the services provided), and availability of trained personnel to oversee both mission and services. Internal variables include personnel attitudes toward the mission, adequacy of the marketing tools to promote the services, efficient use of the available funds, and client response to both the attitudes and the marketing. More often than not, a wide range of variables interact in a given situation, and never is the mix the same from one institution to another.

One of the hoariest of institutions in the history of any sentient species has been the Library. Second only to a centralized governing body for providing services to a community, the Library nevertheless has enjoyed a popularity down the millennia which a centralized governing body could not, because the services it provides are those of pleasure rather than those of necessity. And, yet, libraries also evolve, according to the attendant variables of the day.

On Dunia, in the century prior to the dawning of the Era of the New Order, the nature of the Library had been undergoing a rapid evolution. Our ancestors saw this institution as a source of printed books which could be accessed at little or no cost; the word "library" had derived from the ancient word for "book." They believed that the mission would always remain the same. They were quite wrong. The Library had to change in order to serve an ever-shifting demographic situation; it had to adapt new technologies and conduct new training methods in order to provide the services the new demographics demanded. Slowly but surely, the evolution from the printed word to the electronic word manifested itself; books *per se* were relegated to special collections in obscure corners of the Library while the lion's share of the available space was given over to the Age of Electronics.

The New Nairobi Public Library was no exception. In fact, the City Fathers had taken pains to ensure that an electronic library was the rule. Located at the fringe of the civic center, the edifice was a three-story monument of glass and steel shaped like an upside-down pyramid. There were no interior walls, only waist-high partitions which separated various sections from each other; anyone on the outside looking in had a view which stretched from one wall to another. The first story housed the administrative offices, a large multi-person reference desk, and the outreach area surrounding a central "plaza" in which a succession of brightly painted murals depicted the history of Romulus and the Amazonian Federation. Scattered throughout were relics and artifacts from those histories, rivaling anything in a conventional museum. The upper two stories consisted of row after row of cubicles with three-meter-high partitions for the privacy of the user; the computer terminals within the cubicles connected the user to any part of the Central Spiral Collective and provided him/her nearly instantaneously with whatever information or recreation (s)he desired. And it was a matter of pride on the part of the Library's Administration (not to mention the City Fathers) that very few of the cubicles went unused at any given time of the day or night. The use of the terminals were open to all species, whether residents of Romulus or not. True to form, however, the city of New Nairobi exacted a fee for any *assistance* in accessing information/recreation.

Into this marvel of architecture and of the logical extension of the Age of Electronics strode the Warden and his Pluj confederate. The former maintained his stoicism, while the latter reverted to her child's-eye curiosity. They made straight to the reception desk where a typical haughty-looking Romulan civil servant sat. The receptionist was thin with hawk-like facial features, graying hair, and eyes which mentally dissected a patron's mind in order to second-guess him/her. She wore the standard green-and-yellow uniform, but not well; it kept slipping and sliding across her lean frame, and she continuously re-arranged it. Upon seeing the visitors, her eyes narrowed to slits as she studied them as a biologist would his specimen.

"Good day, Cn., Cns," she said in her best professional voice which, when she uttered the appellation "Cns.," would have chilled an Uhaad to the bone. "How may I assist you?"

By way of response, Rodriguez pulled his badge out of his pocket and held it out for the receptionist's examination. Her eyes went wide with surprise, and her breath caught in her throat. Nervously, she attempted to straighten out her uniform again.

"I would like to speak to the Administrator, please."

"I believe the Administrator is in a conference at the moment, sir."

The Warden pushed his badge closer to her face. The movement caused the disc to glitter in the building's lighting. The receptionist blinked several times and swallowed compulsively.

"Interrupt him," Rodriguez intoned with all of the authoritativeness at his command. "I'm conducting an official investigation, and I require his co-operation."

The receptionist swallowed again, rose from her chair quickly, and retreated to the far end of the floor. The Warden smiled to himself. Score another one for the reputation of the Warden Service!

Presently, the receptionist returned with a pudgy, red-faced, and perspiring little man in tow. If her uniform was too loose on her, his was too tight, and his bulk was placing an undue burden on the seams in several places. He whipped out a large synthetic-silk handkerchief, mopped his face, and carelessly replaced the cloth in a back pocket. Rodriguez held up his badge again for the benefit of the Administrator. The latter blinked several times and began perspiring once more.

"Ah, Warden," he croaked, "what can we do for you?"

"Do you have a Petra Katanga in your employ?"

"Why, yes. She's in charge of, um, section 3-A upstairs. Is – is she in some sort of trouble?"

"Not that we can determine at this time. We merely wish to question her about an acquaintance of hers. Is she available?"

The Administrator turned to his receptionist and raised an eyebrow. The latter sat down before her terminal and tapped several keys. The monitor lit up to reveal the image of a young human male with wavy blond hair and an engaging smile.

"Yes, Administrator?"

"Harry, have you seen Petra?"

"No, sir. She hasn't reported for work for the past three days. I've had to fill in for her."

"I see. Thank you." The monitor went dark. "That's damned strange. Petra's never missed a day's work since she's been here. Warden, are you sure she's not in some sort of trouble?"

Rodriguez frowned. Where the JUR was involved, anything was possible. The Reman terrorists were as ruthless as Alkon warriors, and they were capable of any atrocity known to sentient beings, from assassination to torture, from kidnapping to sabotage. Nothing was above them in their relentless drive to free themselves from Romulan "tyranny" and the Amazonian Federation, and they carried out their mission as efficiently and as murderously as they could. In the present instance, Dr. Mubutu Weyerhauser was a known sympathizer; whether he was also a foot soldier could be determined only when the Constabulary apprehended and interrogated him. It may very well have been that he was being coerced by the JUR, but that was for someone else to establish.

How Petra Katanga fit into the picture was also anybody's guess. Despite her being a Romulan, was she a sympathizer as well?[23] Was she a member of the JUR who had seduced Dr. Weyerhauser into co-operating in whatever mad scheme they had in mind? Or had she been kidnapped in order to secure his co-operation? Was she in fact still alive, or had she been murdered because she knew too much about her lover's clandestine activities? So many questions, and no answers – the sooner the matter of her disappearance was solved, the sooner Rodriguez and Ralfo could return to their original mission on Planetoid 48.

"Hard to say, Administrator. We intend to find out, however. We'll start at her residence, if you'll provide us with an address."

In the foyer of the Library, Rodriguez extracted his vidcom and keyed in a coded sequence. Presently, the face of Station Chief Crowder appeared on the tiny screen. The latter smiled broadly.

"Rodriguez!" he boomed. "Glad to see you're still in one piece. What have you to report?"

The Warden tersely updated the situation which elicited a frown from Crowder.

"This is getting damned complex," he grumbled.

"Yes, sir. I recommend a Level Three bulletin to local law enforcement. Meanwhile, Ralfo and I are going to the Katanga residence to see what – if anything – we can learn from her."

"Right. Good luck."

"We'll need some sort of luck for sure, Anafu."

"You fear the worse, Lixu?"

---

23   There was, and still is, a semi-formal, non-political organization on Romulus which calls itself the "Friends of Remus." They advocate complete autonomy for their "brothers and sisters" who "labor under the heavy hand of faceless Romulan bureaucrats." They are considered to be misguided but harmless idealists by their peers – CMT.

"Master Fresh always instructed us to expect anything – even the unexpected. By doing so, we would never be taken by surprise."

"That was good advice."

Rodriguez nodded in agreement, even as his eyes took on a faraway look.

CHAPTER EIGHT

▼

MOUNTING TENSIONS

THE YOUNG SHAMAN STANDS BEFORE his congregation, now dwindled in numbers, and examines their faces. Those faces are filled with fear and anxiety, despair and hopelessness.

The shaman does not blame them for their feelings. He himself has been filled with foreboding ever since the old shaman died. The old shaman, before joining his ancestors, had given him a bundle of scrolls upon which had been written in a cribbed hand pronouncements by the old shaman's predecessors and admonished him to find what wisdom he could in them. Soon after the graybeard was sent off on his final journey to the spirit world, his young successor had endeavored to interpret the scrolls.

The memory of that first reading sends a shiver up his spine, to add to the shivers produced by the growing cold. He moves to place another log from the diminishing pile on the meager fire around which he and the congregation stands. Soon, there will be no more logs and no more fire. Soon, the people will freeze and be no more.

The young shaman is obliged to speak before the congregation on this particular day. Ironically, it is the Day of First Planting in his people's calendar, and he must perform certain rituals and say certain magic formulae. His heart is not in the effort, for there have been no first plantings of any kind for many long cycles and there will be none for the foreseeable future. The world has grown cold and dark since the gods took away the Sun and left the people without the means to grow food.

He looks at the fearful, anxious, despairing, and hopeless faces again. Some of the adults are weeping – weeping for themselves, for the few children who are left, for the way of life they have lost. The children also weep because they do not know why their parents weep, and it frightens them. The shaman comes to a hard decision and prays that the gods – the same gods who have deserted his world – will forgive him and allow him to join his own ancestors in the spirit world.

He raises his eyes and his arms to the dark, star-filled sky – the sky full of strange stars – and gives the opening prayer of the Day of First Planting, more out of habit than anything else.

"In the beginning, there was Kit'nito the Creator, and He created the world and the heavens and all that is therein. He created the Kit'a – we who are called the 'children of Heaven' – from the flesh of His own body and set them on the world which is called Kit'a'tanda, the 'blessing of Kit'nito.' The Lord Kit'nito provided for us our every need so that we might live and prosper. He taught us right behavior so that we might find favor in His eyes. And He promised us that He would keep and protect us until the Last Day.

"We give thanks" – here, the young shaman's voice catches in his throat – " for the blessings of Kit'nito. We give thanks for His bounty and His wisdom and His protection and pray that He will keep us forever. Rojom!"

The congregation mumbles "Rojom!" in unison, more out of habit than anything else, for their hearts are not in this ritual either.

"My children," the young shaman declares, "this day is supposed to be the Day of First Planting, according to our tradition. I need not tell you that our tradition no longer applies in these present conditions. Therefore, I have decided to abandon the rest of the ritual and to speak to you on another matter."

This pronouncement scarcely raises a stir in the congregation. They are too cold and too hungry to protest a deviation from tradition. They stare at the young shaman expectantly.

"I have here," he continues, "a memoir of the predecessors of my predecessor, the wise Jemaki, whom some of you may remember. In it, they give their views on why the gods took the Sun away from us. I will read you a portion.

"'Tradition has it that there was a war in the heavens, when the gods quarreled amongst themselves over which of them would rule. They used frightful weapons, weapons which roared like thunder and lit the sky brighter than the Sun itself. The earth shook continuously, and the people hid themselves in the caves and prayed to Kit'nito that He would intercede and halt the squabbling between His fellow gods.

"'The war raged on for many cycles as none of the gods seemed able to harken to the wisdom of Kit'nito. Then, one day, all was quiet again, and peace reigned across the world. The people at first were distrustful that there was no more war. But, as the days passed, and one cycle led to another, and war did not resume, they began to believe. And they rejoiced.

"'It was about this time that the shaman of our tribe (whom I knew in my childhood) began to notice certain discrepancies in his observations of the stars. They were not in the same positions as they had been before the war between the gods took place. Neither was the Sun. In truth, he believed that the Sun had shrunk! As the cycles passed, these discrepancies increased until he could no longer dismiss the awful realization that, in the prosecution of their war, the gods had taken the Sun with them when they departed Kit'a'tanda.

"'All this did he confide in me, when I was chosen to apprentice myself to him as a future shaman, because he had seen in me a hunger for the truth. Yet, he bade me not to speak to anyone about what he told me, even to his fellow shamans from other tribes. "They would not believe you," he said, "since you are yet a youth and not fully wise in the ways of Kit'nito." But, I kept his words in my heart; and, as my own observations of the stars and the Sun verified his, I decided to set down these words in a permanent form so that my successors – whoever they may be – might profit from them.'

"My children, I found this memoir hidden behind a stone in the cave where old Jemaki took refuge when the Kit'a could no longer endure the cold on the surface. At first, I refused to believe his story. But, as I pondered the matter and noted the discrepancies in the stars for myself, I could no longer deny the facts."

The young shaman pauses and casts his eyes over the congregation again. He sees that they too are incredulous. Some shake their heads in disbelief; others cover their ears in order not to hear any more wild tales.

"It is a hard thing to accept, my children, that the gods have done this to us, that the Lord Kit'nito failed to protect us. Why they did so, only they know. We, their children, must accept the reality.

"But, now I bring you hope at last. Let me tell you of the vision I had two nights ago." He takes a deep breath. Having refused to believe the truth, will the congregation instead believe the lie? "As I lay in my bed, waiting for sleep to overtake me, a great darkness came over me. I could not even see my hand in front of me, and I thought I had gone blind. Then, as quickly as it had come, the darkness passed away, and I found myself, not in my bed, but in a pleasant place, a meadow covered with grass and flowering plants as far as the eye could see. I knew at once that I was in the spirit world.

"While I marveled at the wondrous sights, a stranger approached me. I became frightened as he had taken me unawares. A tall man he was, much taller than we are, and pale-skinned. His eyes were as black as the night sky; and yet, they sparkled like the stars themselves. His hair was the color of fire, and it glistened in the sunlight.

"'What is thy name, my son?' the stranger asked me.

"'I am called Horuko,' I replied. 'And thou art?'

"'I am He Who Was and Who Is and Who Ever Shall Be.'

"At once, I threw myself on the ground and buried my face in my hands. I was in the Presence of the Lord Kit'nito.

"'A thousand pardons for my presumption, Lord,' I cried out. 'What willst Thou of me?'

"'Thou art of the world known as Kit'a'tanda?'

"'Aye, Lord.'

"'Thou seekest succor for thy people?'

"'Aye, Lord. They suffer greatly.'

"'Thou and thy people have served me well and faithfully. I shall give them succor.'

"'Thank you, Lord.'

"'Rise.'

"I rose and quaked before the Presence. I dared not look at Him. He then took my face in His hands and lifted it up to meet His face. He smiled at me, and I knew that I was about to receive His blessing. He gestured with His hand thusly" – here the shaman imitated the gesture – "and a golden cup filled with a clear liquid appeared magically before me.

"'These are the tears which I have shed for the woes of my children. Place one drop on each tongue, and all will be brought here to dwell with me forever.'

"After the Lord Kit'nito spoke these words, the darkness came over me again, and I found myself back in my cave. The cup He had given me was in my hand. This cup, my children."

He withdraws a golden cup from beneath his robe and holds it up for all to see. The congregation stares at it in wonder. The shaman takes another deep breath.

"Our Lord summons us to him, my children. Who will not answer His call? Who wishes to remain here in misery?"

One by one, men, women, and children rise to their feet and file past him. One by one, he places a drop of the clear liquid on their tongues. When he has ministered to the last individual, he bids them to return to their caves to await their summoning. Soon, he is alone.

Tears run down his cheeks as he contemplates the awful thing he has done. The dregs of the slow-acting poison which remain in the cup he pours on the ground and flings the cup away in disgust. Now, he contemplates the pendant hanging about his neck. He removes it and drops it on the ground in a symbolic act of resigning his office; he has no more congregation over which to be the shaman and can no longer wear it.

The young man walks slowly toward his own cave. He will join his mate and his child there. He has already given them the "tears of Kit'nito." He will try to comfort them as they depart this world. His own death will not be so painless, however. He has committed a great sin, and he must punish himself harshly.

*   *   *

Doctor Mubutu Weyerhauser, former Adjunct Professor of Astrophysics at the University of New Nairobi, sat quietly in the cave in which the remains of the indigenous family resided. Outwardly, he was calm; inwardly, he was seething with conflicting thoughts. The organization to which he had dedicated himself half his adult life had turned out to be more than he expected and less than he desired. He had believed it was full of idealists given to civil disobedience in order to advance their cause. Now, he had learned that it was full of genocidists given to mayhem and destruction. They had used him – and his naiveté (he had to admit) – in their nefarious schemes, and no excuse he could think of would absolve him of his part in those schemes.

What would his former colleagues think of him, once the news was out? Terrorist, murderer, saboteur, *traitor* – that's what they would think. True, he had never committed any of those despicable acts; but he was a card-carrying member of an organization which had, and he was just as guilty by association as the real terrorists. His former colleagues would undoubtedly hasten to disavow him, to strip him of his titles, perquisites, and awards, and to relegate all of his printed works to the dustbin. They would not speak of him, except in private in hushed whispers. They would relegate him to a footnote in the annals of academe.

Worse, what would Petra think of him? He had been tutoring her in preparation of her entrance exams in the University. But lately, they had grown closer, and he had dared to express his feelings toward her. She hadn't wanted a full-fledged relationship just yet, but neither had she dashed his hopes. There was no chance of any sort of relationship once the news was out, professional or personal. When she learned what he had been involved in, she would condemn him as the others would – terrorist, murderer, saboteur, *traitor* – and her condemnation would be the bitterest blow of all. If he lost her love, he had little to live for.

And it was all my fault for rushing into something before ascertaining the facts.

Neither his colleagues nor Petra could condemn him as harshly or as thoroughly as he himself could. And there was no escape from self-condemnation.

Doctor Weyerhauser regarded the family in front of him – his "adopted" family – the only family he now had left to him at this point in his misbegotten life. They looked so peaceful, lying there, huddled together. What had been their last thoughts before Death came to claim them? Had they been thoughts of love and tenderness toward each other, thoughts of regret and sorrow that they would no longer have one another to comfort and be comforted? Or had they been thoughts of anger and outrage over the horror an uncaring Universe had visited upon them and their entire species? Had they died peacefully or in agony, with a prayer or a curse on their lips?

This family of an unknown – and now extinct – race of sentient beings was the lucky one. Their cares were over, and they now reposed quietly for all Eternity. He, Mubutu Weyerhauser, on the other hand, had to go on living.

He rose to his feet and began to pace back and forth. Sooner or later, Major Tshambe would summon him to obtain yet more readings of an astrophysical nature, and he needed a plan to extricate himself out of his predicament. On one of his circuits of the cave, he spied an object he hadn't noticed before. It was partially hidden under scraps of cloth surrounding the male (?) skeleton. He retrieved it, carefully so as not to touch the remains, and discovered that it was a piece of parchment (or the local equivalent) inscribed with indecipherable symbols in neat columns. There were twelve columns total, and each contained twenty-four to thirty-six symbols. They resembled Egyptian hieroglyphics, but he was no expert in such matters. One symbol he did recognize, however, and it was larger than all the others – an inverted "T" with a small circle on the right side of the vertical stem, halfway down. The Wayfarers' symbol!

The Central Spiral Collective's Commission for Primitive Cultures would undoubtedly love to get their hands on this artifact. In the first place, they would have the opportunity to add yet another sentient race to their Catalogue[24] – even though the race was extinct. In the second place, they would be able to correlate this language (if this parchment actually listed an alphabet) to all others, current and obsolete, translate the document, and gain some clue toward cultural attainments by this race. And, in the third place, they might find a clue to the identity and/or whereabouts of that mysterious race who had traveled through the Galaxy and left enigmatic signs of their passing on hundreds of worlds. The last alone would be worth a king's ransom.

The Commission was not likely to get their hands on this anthropological treasure trove, however. Planetoid 48 was a doomed world. Many thousands of years ago, it had been doomed environmentally when it was inexplicably wrenched out of its orbit and sent spinning into the cold and dark of Deep Space. Shortly, thanks to the mad scheme of the JUR in their thirst for vengeance against Romulus, it would be doomed geophysically as well. The altered course it had just obtained would cause it to pass close by Romulus and interface with that world's field of gravity. The shearing forces would produce,

---

24 The "Central Spiral Collective Catalogue of Sentient Beings, Ancient and Modern" is the definitive source of information for this field of research. It can be accessed only at the Galactic Museum of Natural History on New Switzerland – CMT.

at one end of the spectrum of destruction, volcanic eruptions, tidal waves, earthquakes, and massive shifts in land masses; at the other end, a shift in axial alignment and one in orbital dynamics was entirely possible.

The ancient Dunian philosopher, Emmanuel Velikovsky, had once claimed that such a near-collision had occurred in Dunia's distant past – not only once, but *twice*, he said – and that the resultant calamities which befell the planet formed the basis of many folk legends. Some of Velikovsly's disciples had even suggested that Dunia had been displaced from its original orbit near Sol to its present one. The intruder, they said, became the planet Venus; and Mars in its turn was displaced even further from Sol and led to the demise of an unknown civilization which had flourished there.

Ancient legends and fanciful explanations aside, Dr. Weyerhauser knew from his own studies in theoretical astrophysics that the fate of Planetoid 48 – and Romulus – would be all too real. And he was powerless to do anything about it. He would not be able to save the artifacts he had discovered nor the family he had "adopted"; the tragic story of this world would never be shared and held up as a warning to others who would tamper with the Laws of Nature.

His own fate was, on the other hand, quite uncertain. He had objected to the mad scheme once he had learned of it, and he had defied Major Tshambe in front of his own men. The Major would not hesitate to execute him if he were considered to be a "security risk." He may already have come to that conclusion and was at this moment dispatching a team to search for him. He shuddered involuntarily at the prospect.

This train of thought was suddenly interrupted by a change of perception. The change was detected not so much through the sense of hearing as through the sense of touch. The walls, ceiling, and floor of this cave was vibrating, minutely at first but increasing at a slow, steady rate. The astrophysicist recognized its nature immediately; he had experienced the sensations not long before when he was much closer to the epicenter. The Major had ordered another test of the MOME!

The fools! he thought in outrage. *The mad fools! They'll shake this world apart yet if they keep this up.*

But why order a second test? Wasn't the Major happy with the results of the first one?

Presently, the vibrations reached their crescendo in pitch and held it there for the space of two seconds. Then, as slowly as they had been created, they faded away.

The Doctor's next sensation was the beeping of his vidcom. He removed it from his pocket and stared at it, pondering whether or not to respond.

"Doctor Woyer'auser," Tshambe's voice came through loud and clear and filled with his customary menacing tone, "report to Control at once, if ye please."

He remained silent, reviewing his options and concluding that he hadn't any options at all.

"Dinna ye myke me come lookin' for ee, Doctor. It'll go bad for ee if ye do – very bad indeed."

Of that, he had no doubt. He thumbed the "send" button.

"Very well. I'll be there shortly."

He cast a forlorn gaze at his "adopted" family. Would this be the last time he'd see them? He trudged off slowly as a man on the way to the execution chamber.

*　　　*　　　*

"You've activated the MOME again, Major. Why?"

When Doctor Weyerhauser entered the Command Center, one could have heard the proverbial pin drop. All activity ceased as the JUR personnel fixed their attention on the astrophysicist, and a deathly silence permeated the cave. The two members with whom he was on any sort of speaking terms, Cutty and Jingles, regarded him sadly; the others wore frowns as they might in the presence of an outsider. Tshambe presented a neutral image which was his usual one until he began speaking.

In view of all the latent hostility, the Doctor knew that his worst fears had been realized and that these grim men no longer trusted him (if they ever had in the first place). Undoubtedly, they had decided to dispose of him as soon as feasible. Very well, if he was doomed, he might as well get some last licks in. They could kill him only once. He assumed his best stern glare as he faced the Major as if the latter were some ill-informed student who needed correcting. He did not feel stern *inside*, however; inside, he felt weak all over, and he hoped it didn't show.

"Noo that ye know what oor plan is," Tshambe replied, "there's na need to wif'old informytion fum ee." He smiled insincerely. "After all, ye're a trusted member of oor group, aye?"

"Save the sarcasm, Major, and answer my question."

"And Oi'll do just that – as soon as you tyke a foinal reading."

"You want my expertise again?" the astrophysicist asked incredulously. "Whyever for?"

"It's voital to the answers ye want." He waved a hand toward the Doctor's station. "If ye please."

Doctor Weyerhauser plodded over to his computer, keenly aware that all eyes were still fixed on him, sat down, and activated the machine. An image appeared on the monitor, an image he didn't immediately recognize. He entered a command on his keyboard; co-ordinates began to form on the screen and confirmed the fact that Planetoid 48's course had been altered again. The rogue was now half a million kilometers from its last known position, on a course five degrees displaced from the previous one. He entered another command. A hard copy slid out.

He rose, plodded back to the control station, and practically shoved the hard copy in the Major's face. The latter frowned briefly, then resumed his neutral expression.

"If I'm not badly mistaken, our new course should put this world on a course closer to Romulus."

"Aye, that it will. Instead o' passin' it boy 'undreds o' kilometers and causin' only minimal damage, this rock will pass boy just *tens* of kilometers and shyke Romulus to its core. Oideally, it'll knock the planet oot of its orbit and send it 'urtlin' toward Rhea Silvia."

"If I didn't think you were insane before, I'm thoroughly convinced now." Tshambe squinted menacingly. "Have you given any thought to the ripple effect?"

"What ripple effect?"

"Obviously, you haven't. Romulus and Remus share the same orbit, thanks to a quirk in the original creation of this star system. The two planets are stable, relative to each other, but any alteration in the dynamics of one will have a negative effect on the other. If Romulus is displaced in its orbit by even the slightest amount, there's little reason to believe that the same thing you've got in mind for it won't happen to Remus."

A general murmuring immediately arose from the JUR people. The Doctor noted expressions of fear and concern on some faces, of frowns and disbelief on others. He regarded them defiantly, challenging them to refute his statements. They responded only by appealing silently to their leader. The latter's squint grew more pronounced.

"That's na true," he muttered.

"Isn't it? You brought me along for my expertise. Well, now I'm giving it to you." He confronted the rank-and-file again. "You'll defeat the purpose for which you banded together by placing your own families at risk."

Trepidatiously, Jingles, stepped forward, his face paling by the second.

"'E could be roight, Myjor. 'E *is* the hexpert in these matters."

The Major glared at his subordinate.

"It's na but bloody speculytion!" He turned back to the Doctor. "'Divoide and conquer,' aye, Doctor? Dinna ye troy me pytience, or it'll go very bad wif ee."

"It's still not too late to alter course again. Send this world out of the Galaxy altogether where it won't harm anyone."

"Oi see that Oi'll 'ave to send *ee* awy before ye corrupt moy people." He signaled to Jingles and Cutty. "Tyke the good Doctor to the MOME sphere and myke 'im comfortable. Oi'll desoide lyter what to do wif 'im."

The two JUR men approached the astrophysicist who looked at them accusingly. They pleaded with him with their eyes for him to co-operate. He shrugged, sighed in resignation, and gave Tshambe one last stern look. Then he stiffly walked off in the direction Cutty indicated he should go.

*   *   *

"What d'ya mean, you can't find anything? Look again!"

Captain Halvarson was on the verge of apoplexy. His face had turned beet red, and he was half-sitting, half-standing at his station. Commander Krishnamurthy slumped in her seat and tried to make herself inconspicuous.

The *Steadfast* was outward bound from Crenshaw's Star in a familiar spiral pattern. The Captain was following what he had been led to believe was a solid clue to the whereabouts of Planetoid 48. But, as the search pattern widened, and the Display revealed no interstellar anomalies of any sort – least of all a runaway world – his mood began to darken, and he took to muttering to himself. Simultaneously, the discomfit of the Bridge crew increased in direct proportion, and nervous glances all around became the most frequent movement. The most discomfited and nervous member was, of course, Lt. I-ta, the Sensors officer whose unenviable task it was to locate the target. Halvarson had ordered her to report her findings every kilosecond; and, if she were one second late with her report, he was on the vidscreen, scowling.

"Olaf," the XO said softly, "now would be a good time for that dip in the pool. You need to cool off."

"Oh, I do, eh?" He turned to peer at her dispassionate face and noted the concern in her eyes. "Well, maybe I do. We can't have the Bridge crew mutinying, can we?"

"No, sir. It would look bad on our next evaluation. HQ sometimes frowns on such things."

"All too true. All right, Tomiko, I'll go soak my head." He leaned toward her. "But I want you to report to me *immediately* if that damned world is spotted."

"Aye, aye, sir!"

Krishnamurthy followed him off the Bridge with her eyes and heaved a sigh of relief as soon as he had disappeared down the corridor. Olaf Halvarson was definitely under a strain, and no wonder. This entire operation was taking its toll on everybody – including, she had to admit, herself. CSC patrol vessels were supposed to keep the peace in Deep Space – preventing piracy, apprehending fugitives from justice from any of the member worlds, seizing contraband goods, etc. – they were not supposed to chase rogue planets which had a nasty habit of disappearing and re-appearing seemingly at will. This mission should have been assigned to a special task force, not a frontline vessel. HQ was not doing the *Steadfast* and its crew any favors. They'd be lucky if only half of the personnel had to report to the psych-docs.

No use crying over spilled k'a *juice,* she told herself. *That'll only make things worse.*

She rose from her seat and sauntered around the perimeter of the Bridge. If anyone made eye contact, she nodded and gave that person a tight little smile by way of boosting morale. She hoped her own anxiety wasn't showing.

Her peregrinations eventually took her to the Blue Zone. To keep herself occupied more than anything else, she strolled over and looked past Lt. I-ta and into the Display. The myriad of colored lights told her nothing she did not already know; the ship was once again chasing after shadows, and more surprises were surely ahead.

The Sensors officer became aware of her presence and gazed at her expectantly. At least, Krishnamurthy thought it was expectancy. One could never be sure with the Uhaad; thanks to their having only half the number of facial muscles as humans did, they seemed as expressionless as a mannequin. The Commander knew of a religious cult on Dunia who shaved themselves bare, but the Uhaad were born that way. Hairlessness was a survival mechanism on a world where the mean temperature was fifty degrees Celsius in the shade (and there was precious little shade); having no hair prevented the indigenous population from overheating and shutting down all bodily functions. Nevertheless, the lack gave the XO the creeps to look at someone with no eyebrows.

"Ma'am?" I-ta inquired.

"You'll have to excuse the Captain, Leftenant. He's – *we've* all been under a strain lately."

"Yes, ma'am. There something I can doing for you?"

"As a matter of fact, there is. I'm sure the Captain would have requested this if he hadn't been…pre-occupied. I'd like some course projections on Planetoid 48."

"Specifically?"

"First, I want to see the original path of the rogue, in the vicinity of Ru'uhaad."

Lt. I-ta began typing on her keyboard. On her terminal appeared the words "Planetoid 48: Original Location." Next, she asked for the co-ordinates of the runaway from the computer's memory bank. When they flashed into view, she entered the command "Transfer to Display." The holographic image representing the target world blinked into existence, and its path through Deep Space appeared as a dotted white line.

"Excellent. Now extrapolate that path as far as you can."

I-ta keyed in a command to the astrophysics database. At once, the dotted white line started extending along a theoretical path; as it progressed, the Display altered to show successive sectors of Deep Space through which Planetoid 48 would have passed had it remained on its original course. Presently, the image of the sector in which Rhea Silvia was located was displayed. The white line passed through that star system on the sun side of the gas giant Numitor, the third planet from the primary.[25]

"Interesting," Krishnamurthy commented impassively. "Now, Leftenant, let's go back to Ru'uhaad." A new command was entered, and the white line retreated through successive images in reverse order. "All right. Place Planetoid 48 at the co-ordinates that Dunian captain gave us."

The image shifted to reveal the sector in which the *Steadfast* was currently located.

"Plot the new path," the XO directed. The dotted white line diverged from its previous course and veered toward Crenshaw's Star. "Extrapolate as before."

The white line moved inexorably through the previous series of images until it once again approached the Rhea Silvia system. This time, however, the projected path took the runaway closer to Romulus and Remus. Both Krishnamurthy and I-ta gasped in shock at the new revelation.

"Ma'am, the rogue will passing dangerously close to Romulus!"

"So it would seem. How great a divergence was there?"

The Uhaad tapped two keys, and the computer spat out its response two seconds later.

"Nearly a six-degree shift, ma'am."

"And, since we can't locate Planetoid 48 in this sector, it may have shifted again."

"But how?"

"The answer to that question, Leftenant, is too monstrous to think about. File this data in a temporary folder. I've got to find the Captain."

Krishnamurthy quick-marched off the Bridge and sought out her shuttle

---

25 Numitor, at a distance of 750 gigameters from Rhea Silvia, is nearly twice as large as Romulus or Remus but only half as large as the other gas giant in the system, Aeneas, the outermost planet. Numitor is a rich source of cesium which, among other things, powers all CID ships – CMT.

car. The Captain and the XO were the only crew members assigned a vehicle; everyone else had to obtain one wherever they could. To ensure that no one "borrowed" the assigned vehicles – even in an emergency – they were programmed to operate by a special code issued to the assignees. She found hers in its customary spot, climbed aboard, and zipped away to the Recreation Deck.

Recreational facilities were located one level above that of the galley, and the juxtaposition was not accidental. Constabulary psychologists had determined that eating and working out went hand-in-hand, that one generally led to the other, and that both were essential to optimum health. There were facilities to suit all tastes, from the purely physical to the purely cerebral. One could choose from the former category a complete gymnasium, a heated pool, a basketball court, an indoor track or a racquetball/handball/volleyball court. In the latter category, one had access to an audiobook library, videogames, 3D chess, a music library, and a videodisc library. The crew lacked for nothing to occupy their off-duty time, and no one had any reason to complain that (s)he had "nothing to do."

All of the facilities were partitioned off in order to provide, in some cases, privacy and, in others, safety. All areas were clearly marked, and directional signs on the bulkheads were omnipresent. The pool toward which Krishnamurthy was headed occupied, for no particular reason, the exact center of the deck. Olympic-sized, it had been elevated three-meters above the deck and constructed with one-meter-thick re-enforced walls (through which the heating elements ran). It was strictly for swimming, and high-diving was prohibited.

The XO pulled up at the entrance, dismounted, and strolled into the poolside area. Immediately, she heard the sound of intense splashing, punctuated by male laughter and female squealing. She smiled wryly. Obviously, the Captain had found his own means of relaxing.

She climbed the short ladder which accessed the pool deck at the forward end and walked carefully across the wet surface to the pool's edge. Halvarson and Lt. Commander von Lichtenburg were cavorting like small children. Both were stark naked. It was not long before one of them realized they had an audience. The Chief Helmsman gasped in shock and tried to cover herself up; agitatedly, she signaled the Captain and pointed in Krishnamurthy's direction. Halvarson swung about, saw the broad smile on his XO's face, and went through his own routine of shock and embarrassment.

"Tomiko!" he roared. "What the hell?"

"I need to speak to you, sir – in private."

"Is this urgent?"

"Very. I've learned something that may point to a cataclysmic event."

"'Cataclysmic'? It's not like you to wallow in hyperbole, Commander."

"Ordinarily, I wouldn't. But, if what I suspect is true, then even 'cataclysmic' won't cover it."

"All right. Wait for me in my office. I'll be there in less than a kilo."

"Yes, sir." She started to turn away, then halted. "Sorry to interrupt your swim, sir."

*　　*　　*

True to his word, Halvarson burst into his office in three-quarters of a kilosecond. Krishnamurthy was sitting quietly in a chair facing his desk; upon his entrance, she quickly stood up, only to be waved back down by a very chagrined Captain.

The office was half as large as any of the conference rooms on the command level. Here, the Ship's Captain could consult in private with up to three of his senior officers. The desk was divided into two sections; the first was an ordinary writing space littered with the usual accoutrements of a chief executive officer, while the second was a built-in vidscreen, a duplicate of the one in Gold Zone on the Bridge. Beyond the four chairs, there was no other furniture. One bulkhead was decorated with Halvarson's awards, commendations, and citations; another held two complete rows and a partial third row of photos of all previous Captains of the *Steadfast*; when the current Captain either retired or was transferred, his photo would join the rest.

Halvarson sat down and peered at his XO for a long moment, intently studying her face. She returned his scrutiny dispassionately.

All right, Tomiko," he said at last, "this had better be good. I don't like anybody interrupting my...swim."

"Yes, sir. What I have to say will rattle even an Aldebaranian. And I've got the data to back it up – if you'll just access the Sensors database."

He did so. Krishnamurthy indicated the temporary file she had had Lt. I-ta create. The Captain opened the file and studied the graphics it contained. The XO walked him through each representation. A look of disbelief formed on his face, deepening with every sentence she uttered. When she had finished, he continued to stare at the screen. Then:

"If you're suggesting what I think you're suggesting, then you were right to call this 'cataclysmic.'"

"I can see no other explanation. The JUR apparently highjacked the *Astarte* for the sole purpose of obtaining her MOME. Now, they're using that MOME to maneuver Planetoid 48 into a collision course with Romulus."

"Is that possible?"

"We've lost track of that rogue twice already. I'd say it's possible. And this might explain why Dr. Mubutu Weyerhauser is involved." Halvarson raised an eyebrow. "He's an astrophysicist. He must be providing the data needed for the course changes."

"Yes, that would make sense – if your theory is correct. How do you propose to prove it?"

"A good question, and one I don't have an answer to. We got lucky when that Dunian freighter provided us with some co-ordinates. We can't count on that happening again."

The Captain leaned back in his chair and stared at the overhead, deep in thought. Krishnamurthy chewed her lip nervously. She hadn't been in this situation since her first posting after graduating from the Academy, and that was due to the natural state of the jitters of a Junior Lieutenant in a real-time environment. Simulations had been one thing, but actuality had been another. In time, she had adjusted to duty in Deep Space and worked her way up the ladder to her present rank and posting. Promotion had not come easy, of course; much hard work and attention to tedious detail confronted her every step of the way. Eventually, she gained the trust of all of her co-workers, above and below her rank.

Now, she was up against a problem the Academy could not possibly have prepared her for, since it lay outside of the bounds of thinkability. Who in his/her right mind could believe that an extremist organization like the Reman Army of Liberation would have the desire, the will, and the means to highjack an interstellar cruise ship, strip it of its MOME, strap that MOME to a runaway world, and steer that world toward a specific destination? If anyone else had suggested such a thing, she would have dismissed the notion as sheer lunacy. As it stood, she had come to this conclusion only after discarding all other possibilities. The evidence, circumstantial though it was, forced her to believe the seemingly impossible. And she had no way of proving it to others!

Halvarson abruptly came out of his meditation and leaned forward in an air of confidentiality.

"Assuming you're right, Tomiko – and you've been right so many times before – we find ourselves in a difficult situation – not the least of which is our lack of communications with the rest of the Galaxy. I'll admit that I was happy to get our Warden off the ship, if only for a short while. But, who could have foreseen this event? Now that I need that damned upstart, he's a hundred light-years away!

"We're at the edge of our jurisdiction, and I can't continue our pursuit of Planetoid 48 without specific permission from Task Force Command. And, when I tell Commodore Drucker why I need his permission, he's going to recommend me for a complete psychiatric evaluation. Without proof, I can't move; and I can't get proof unless I can move."

"So what do we do, Olaf?"

"We contact Lt. Commander Kaw again and have him send an urgent message to Romulus, requesting that Lt. Rodriguez return to the *Steadfast* ASAP."

"How will that help?"

"If we can convince him of your theory, he can convince others. As much as I hate to admit it, people listen when Wardens speak." He sighed. "To think I've come to the point where I have to rely on an upstart like Lixu Rodriguez. I tell you, Tomiko, there's no justice in this Universe!"

CHAPTER NINE

▼

DEAD END

NEW NAIROBI (NEW TOWN) WAS a city of concentric rings and resembled nothing less than a spoked wheel. The truth of this statement could easily be confirmed by a fly-over; each ring was clearly defined according to the purposes of its occupants, and no ring had mixed purposes. Wide, six-laned boulevards separated each ring, allowing for easy access to all structures. Radiating from the hub at the cardinal and sub-cardinal points of the compass were equally wide avenues.

The city's lay-out was deliberate. When the builders of New Town had decided to construct an eye-appealing capital, they planned meticulously; detailed architectural drawings were drawn up, accepted/rejected, and re-drawn before a single stone was laid or a single kilogram of cement was poured. The task was necessarily slow and tedious because of the close scrutiny it was given, but the City Fathers did not care. They intended to create a monument to the human spirit, no matter how long it took or how much money it cost or how great were the sacrifices it engendered.

The center of the city – the hub – was, of course, its tallest structure, the Administration Building, which housed not only the municipal offices (five floors) but also the planetary offices (ten floors) and the Federation offices (the top fifteen floors). Immediately surrounding the hub was a park, landscaped, groomed, and manicured to the last blade of grass, the last leaf, and the last twig; stiff fines awaited anyone who was so careless in his habits as to cause disorder therein. The next two rings were occupied by the auxiliary government agencies, the nature and extent of whose activities required a separate structure, e.g. the Port Authority or the City Library. In front of each agency was a map of the entire civic center, showing its position in the whole lay-out, and a directory describing its contents to the concerned office seeker.

The next ring was taken up by financial institutions – banks (local and off-world), insurance companies, mortgage brokers, credit unions, and the like. The City Fathers had deemed it necessary to keep such organizations as close to Government as possible. In the first place, they would be easy to borrow from (should the need arise); in the second place, they would be easy to regulate. As long as the institutions dotted their "i's" and crossed their "t's," Government would be content to take its cut of the profits and allow them to operate as they pleased. In a mercantile society such as Romulus, a rogue element was not to be tolerated, even for a day. The same could be said for the occupants of the next three rings where the giant interstellar corporations and major local companies held sway and did business with either the Federation or its inhabitants. Here, location was everything, and the several business concerns jockeyed from the very beginning to get as close to the seat of power as it was physically able; as soon as bankruptcy or eviction or sell-out occurred, a new round of jockeying took place. It was a never-ending game of "musical buildings," one which profited New Nairobi immensely. Early in its history, the City Fathers learned that huge revenues could be realized by not allowing the business community to own outright the property it occupied as had been the case on Dunia; instead, the buildings were constructed at city expense and then leased at high rates. As a consequence, taxes on ordinary citizens tended to be minimal.

Beyond the mercantile core lay the residential areas. Again, the city constructed them ring by ring, but the rings tended to be amorphous; that is, they were not segregated altogether by class but were "mixed." Had New Nairobi grown haphazardly in the manner of Dunian cities, there certainly would have been a great deal of class consciousness and snobbery. In a planned community, however, this was not possible; each prospective home owner had as equal an opportunity to build his/her "dream house" as the next person, regardless of his/her status in the community. Needless to say, the City Fathers encouraged large residences, since they generated greater revenues; property taxes were based on the *amount* of property owned, not on its alleged worth (which had been the traditional method on Dunia). Rates were assessed by the square meter, and home owners built according to what they could afford to pay in taxes.

Not all of any residential ring was taken up by private dwellings. Space was reserved for apartment buildings for single persons,[26] small retail concerns, recreational/educational/cultural activities, and religious observances. Pragmatically speaking, each ring was a mini-city, and the residents over the years had tended to identify themselves by the ring in which they lived, e.g. "Fivers" or "Eighters." Intentionally or not, then, New Town had a class consciousness unique in the annals of human history, and most New Towners accepted it with equanimity.

Each ring adhered to a pattern established by the City Fathers. Groups of private dwellings were interspersed with apartment buildings. Two shopping centers were located on opposing cardinal points of the ring, while educational, recreational, religious/cultural, and communal facilities occupied the other two cardinal points. The only differences were the individual appearances of the private dwellings which tended to be inhabited by minor bureaucrats and retirees living out their autumnal years on generous pensions.

Street addresses on the Dunian model did not exist in New Nairobi. The city strived to be cosmopolitan in its outreach and so eschewed the over-use of human geographical designations in order not to offend visitors from other worlds. Buildings were therefore given numerical designations, beginning with the number of the ring in which they were located; at an arbitrary point, the numbering began with "001A" on the inside face, then reversed itself with "001B" on the outside face. Each structure generated its own signal for the benefit of the automated taxis and for inclusion on an electronic map of the city which could be called up through any directory location.

Building #11-015B was a "U"-shaped apartment complex with four floors. As apartment buildings went, it could be considered modest; other such complexes were taller, although none was permitted to be higher than ten floors. The exterior décor reflected the ancient Dunian architectural type known as "Georgian," though the present structure could better be described as "neo-Georgian." In the first place, the front steps were moderate in size with a proportional pediment topping the doorway; in the second place, the construction material was yellow stone quarried from elsewhere on Romulus; in the third place, flattened columns bracketed a paneled doorway; and, in the fourth place, the pediment reflected a motif, not from Dunian but from Romulan history – two opposing human figures holding in outstretched hands a scroll inscribed with the acronym "USU."[27] In front of Building #11-015B, an immaculately manicured lawn with colorful shrubbery planted in

---

26 Rents tended to be adjusted to the earning power of the prospective renter, the city's sop to egalitarianism – CMT.

27 *Uhuru, Shugkuli, Ugunduzi* – "Freedom, Enterprise, Discovery" – the official motto of the Amazonian Federation – CMT.

strategic locations covered the twenty meters between the complex and the street. The walkway from the street to the main entrance consisted of leftover stone in a checkerboard pattern.

A taxi pulled up at this address, and a human male and a Pluj disembarked. Warden Rodriguez and Lt. Ralfo, still in their civilian clothes, strolled up the walk and halted before the building's vidscreen-directory. The Warden activated the vidscreen, and the directory came into view instantly. Listed were all of the present tenants; two units were marked as "Vacant." He highlighted the listing designated as "Katanga, P. — #311" and pressed the signal button. There was no response. He waited twenty seconds and signaled again. Still no response. He and Ralfo exchanged concerned looks.

"I suppose there's a reasonable explanation for why she doesn't answer. Unfortunately, I don't have time for reasonable explanations."

"What will you do now, Lixu?"

"I'll call the manager."

He found "Manager" at the top of the listings, highlighted it, and pressed the button. Ten seconds later, the directory was replaced by the image of a human female of Polynesian derivation; she had a round face, twinkling jet-black eyes, and an easy smile. The latter enlarged when she spotted what she hoped were prospects for one or both of her vacancies.

"Good day, Cn. And Cns. How may I help you?"

Rodriguez did not waste time with pleasantries but held his badge up to the screen. Upon seeing it, the manager's eyes went wide with surprise, dissolved to fear and loathing, and ended with a cautious but professional expression.

"Ah, *Warden*, how may I help you?"

"I'm here on an official investigation. May I be admitted?"

"Of course. Right away."

A buzzer sounded. Rodriguez turned the handle on the front door and pushed it open with ease. He and Ralfo stepped into the entryway of the building. It was a short hallway which led to the central corridor running the length of the floor. On either side of this hallway were identical banks of mail boxes, each corresponding to a numbered unit. At the intersection of the hallway and the corridor (both plushly carpeted), a door boldly labeled "Manager" confronted both tenants and visitors; as an afterthought, the management had placed a "Welcome" sign underneath the name plaque.

The Warden tapped lightly on this door and pushed it open. The manager quickly rose from her desk with a nervous smile. A middle-aged woman, she was of slight stature – no taller than Ralfo – but carried herself proudly. She was wearing a traditional sarong, red embroidered with white flowers.

"How do you do?" she said politely. "I am Cns. Leleuluani."

"Greetings, Cns. Leleuluani. I'm Ll Rodriguez, and this is Lt. Anafu Ralfo of the Constabulary."

"With you Our Lady be, Cns," the Pluj added, cupping her hands.

"Please, be seated." The team took two deeply upholstered chairs and nearly sank in them. "I, uh, apologize for my initial reaction. You weren't in uniform and took me by surprise."

"No need to apologize, Cns. Your reaction was quite understandable. The nature of our investigation required that we blend in with the general population."

"Ah, yes, your investigation. How may I be of assistance?"

"We're trying to locate the whereabouts of Dr. Mubutu Weyerhauser, late of the University of New Nairobi. We've learned that one of your tenants is acquainted with him, and we're hoping she can provide us with some information."

"Um, that'll be Petra Katanga, unit 311. Dr. Weyerhauser has been a frequent visitor lately. Not that it's any of my business, but I suspect they're more than just friends."

"The nature of their relationship doesn't concern us. We just want to ask her some questions."

"Have you tried the Library, where she works?"

"We did. She hasn't reported for work for several days."

"That's odd. Ordinarily, she's a dedicated worker. She's been helping me re-program the building's computer, but I haven't seen her in several days myself. I just assumed she and the Doctor were spending more time together. Do you think they...eloped?"

"Lixu," Ralfo whispered, "I do not like this. I have a...foreboding."

"I'm uneasy about it as well, Anafu. Cns. Leleuluani, would you please let us into her apartment?"

Sudden alarm crossed the manager's face, and she licked dry lips.

"Is Petra is some sort of trouble, Warden?"

"She may be. If you would, please?"

"Yes, yes, of course." She opened a desk drawer and extracted a white keycard with a blue stripe at one end. "Come with me please."

They took the elevator adjacent to the Manager's office to the third floor. As it happened, unit #311 was directly above the office; a laundromat facility faced it on the other side of the corridor. Cns. Leleuluani pressed the door buzzer firmly, waited five seconds, and pressed again. When she received no response, she slid her keycard into a slot near the door. A sharp click told her that the lock had been disengaged. She turned the handle and cautiously pushed the door open. She stood aside and let the Constabulary officers precede her.

The apartment, a one-bedroom unit, was comfortably appointed. Upholstered sofas and chairs, end tables, and shelving adorned the living room. An opening on one wall led to a combination kitchenette and dining room which contained the necessary array of appliances and functional furniture; an opening on the opposite wall accessed a bathroom with all of the customary fixtures and a bedroom with a queen-sized bed, a large chest of drawers, and a bedside table. Plush carpeting covered all floor areas except in the kitchenette and bathroom where vinyl was used instead. All lighting emanated from overhead lamps. The unit also possessed its own vidscreen.

"Cns. Katanga," Rodriguez called out softly, "are you there?"

There was no answer.

"Petra," the manager added, "it's Sheila. Where are you?"

Still no response came.

"Anafu, check the bedroom. I'll look in the bathroom."

They went their separate ways. Rodriguez had no sooner stepped into the bathroom than he heard a short cry from his partner.

"Lixu! " Ralfo called out in Pluj. "Come quickly!"

He crossed the distance in several long strides while cautioning Cns. Leleuluani to stay where she was with a wave of his hand. He found Ralfo standing near the bed with a look of horror on her face. Petra Katanga lay on the bed, her head twisted at an impossible angle. The Warden bent over the victim and touched her softly.

"Rigor mortis is just setting in. I'd guess she's been dead a couple of days."

"By Our Lady, who could have done this?"

"Under the circumstances, the *modus operandi* smacks of the JUR. One of the witnesses in the Memgo Affair, a geologist named Slade, was found with his neck snapped – along with a local prostitute – before we could get his testimony."

"But why this woman?"

"Apparently, she saw something – or someone – she shouldn't have. The JUR doesn't like to leave witnesses behind."

"*Kolkhee* [monstrous]!" the Pluj muttered. "She must be avenged."

"She will be, Anafu – and all like her."

Rodriguez returned to the living room, informed Cns. Leleuluani what he had discovered, and directed her to call the local police. She stood rooted to the spot, reluctant to leave. He shook his head sadly and gently but firmly guided her to the door. She departed with tears streaming down her cheeks.

The Warden pulled out his vidcom and punched in the code for Station Chief Crowder. The mustachioed face of the L4 registered surprise.

"Rodriguez! I was just about to call you. I've received an urgent message from the *Steadfast*. They need you back on board ASAP."

"Did they say why it was urgent, sir?"

"Negative. But, here's a twist: the message originated from Crenshaw's Star. Aren't they supposed to be near Ru'uhaad?"

"Yes. Crenshaw's Star is thirty lights away. What in the name of Kum'halla are they doing there?"

"I'll tell your shuttle pilot to prepare for your return trip. How soon can you leave?"

"Sooner than I expected. We've got a situation here." He briefed Crowder on the murder of Petra Katanga. The Station Chief received the report with no little outrage. "As soon as the local law arrives, I'll head for Murchison Center. Five kilos minimum."

"Check. The peace of Kum'halla be with you, L1 Rodriguez."

"The peace of Kum'halla be with you, L4 Crowder."

He pocketed the vidcom and turned to his partner. Ralfo was still dazed by what she had seen.

"Are you all right, Anafu? Surely, you've seen dead bodies before."

"It was a senseless act," she murmured. "That woman posed no threat."

"The JUR aren't guided by logic – or by compassion, for that matter. They just sweep aside anybody who gets in their way."

"Our ancestresses were so very correct long ago when they relieved males of all authority. Pluj is a happier place for it." She noted Rodriguez's furled brow. "I am sorry, Lixu. I do not include you. There are some males who are trustworthy."

"I'm glad to hear it. I–"

He was interrupted by the opening of the door and the entrance of two plain-clothes Romulan police officers, both of whom eyed him suspiciously. Then they caught sight of Ralfo and pursed their lips in wonder. They were the usual beefy types, and one of them looked more muscular than the other.

"Greetings, Cn.," the more beefy one said. "You reported finding a body?"

"I did. The body's in the bedroom. Her neck was broken."

"Uh-huh. And what's your name? And what's your business here?"

The Warden grimaced, extracted his badge, and held it up for both officers to see. At the sight of the golden disc, they gasped sharply; their eyes widened in surprise, and their bodies stiffened.

"I'm Warden (L1) Rodriguez, and I'm conducting a special investigation. I had hoped to gain some vital information from the deceased, but I was too late."

"Right – sir. What sort of investigation?"

"That's irrelevant, since I didn't get what I came for. You'll excuse me now; I'm required elsewhere. Have your superiors contact me on the CSC patrol vessel *Steadfast*, and I'll provide a full statement."

He signaled to Ralfo, and the two left without another word, leaving the Romulan officers gnashing their teeth in frustration.

*   *   *

The trip back to the *Steadfast* was even less eventful than the inbound journey. Both Rodriguez and Ralfo were deep in thought. The former was especially grateful for the respite, as he had much on his mind and wanted time to sort things out.

He still had mixed feelings about having had sex with Anafu. On the one hand, he had found her quite desirable, and not only because she was a Pluj. He had been infatuated with her while growing up on her world and discovered that their long separation while he was at the University and the Warden Academy had not diminished his feelings for her. Now that they were re-united, if only temporarily, he had given in to those feelings and found immense pleasure in the act. Having sex with the average Pluj was an extraordinary adventure for most human males, but having sex with one with whom one had known intimately for a long time was a lifetime dream fulfilled. And it hadn't hurt that Anafu was of the same opinion where he was concerned.

On the other hand, he was, first and foremost, a Warden, a special breed of sentient being. Wardens possessed certain inherent abilities which, through rigorous training (physical and mental), the enigmatic Aldebaranians were able to develop for the purposes of keeping the peace throughout the Central Spiral Collective. Wardens were akin to a priesthood, a tight-knit band single-mindedly pursuing a goal. Their unity had no ecclesiastical underpinnings, to be sure – though that point was debatable in some circles – but they behaved as if they had taken holy vows to observe chastity of mind and of body. Still, as many high-ranking Wardens had pointed out in private, there was no such obligation to be chaste; there were the Five Principles of the Shining Path, but those had more to do with the performance of their duties and not with the conduct of their personal lives. Nevertheless, the public perception of a Warden – encouraged by the Service itself – made no distinction between the two spheres.

It was true that no Warden had ever taken a spouse or raised a family. The official explanation was that a Warden was too busy maintaining the peace to engage in mundane matters. But, the plain fact of the matter was that they had needs as much as any other sentient being and acted very, very discreetly in satisfying those needs in order to maintain the mystique their mere presence instilled in the general populace.

Lixu Rodriguez may or may not have acted discreetly, and that was what was bothering him. Absent any mitigating evidence to the contrary, a human male in the company of a Pluj was, in the popular perception, a prime candidate for endless speculation. Rodriguez and Ralfo had disguised themselves in civilian garb and gadded about New Nairobi posing as tourists; no one would have suspected their being Constabulary officials engaged in official business. At the time, the Warden had given the impression that he cared little for the opinions regarding his presence and/or his purpose – the typical attitude of the Service – but, deep down, he was concerned. His concern, however, focused on his self-perception.

Thus far, he had not received any sign that he had done anything wrong. If he had erred, he would have heard about it instantly from Master Fresh-Bloom-in-the-Face-as-the-Day-Begins! Cadet Rodriguez found this out the hard way in his first year during a field trip in a large wilderness area on the home world of the Aldebaranians which lay adjacent to the Academy grounds. It had been an exercise in survival technique, and he had secreted a compass on his person in case he failed to read directions from natural sources. And, as it happened, he did become lost and disoriented. But, before he could use the compass, the booming voice of Master Fresh reverberated in his head, asking him what he thought he was doing. After much hemming and hawing, Rodriguez confessed his error and received the appropriate long lecture on following procedure. And he never forgot that humiliating experience.

All cadets who had survived to the final stage of their training had been impressed with the warning that admonishment of error would not end with their graduation but would follow them throughout their careers via their personal mentors. It was not explained how the mentors would manage this feat, but the hint was dropped that Wardens should expect the unexpected at all times. Rodriguez knew how it was done, however, and he suspected that other Wardens knew too; and, once he realized he was being monitored constantly, he had made every effort to stay on his guard at all times to ensure that his previous experience would never be repeated.

So far, so good. Master Fresh had not seen fit to signal him again mentally. Still, Rodriguez felt he was betraying a trust by indulging in personal pleasure while on duty. He promised himself to be more discreet in the future.

He glanced at Ralfo. She was asleep – again. Did she always sleep through a travel event? He shrugged and meditated further.

As far as he was concerned, the journey to Romulus had been a complete waste of time. He hadn't gotten any useful information about the whereabouts of Doctor Mubutu Weyerhauser; the trail had come to a literal dead end. And the information broker known as the "Professor" had contradicted the alleged lead provided by the pirate leader; he was willing to believe the broker whose reputation depended upon delivering accurate information than the pirate who was only looking for more lenient treatment. (He made a mental note to contact HQ and recommend that the terms of the deal with the pirates be withdrawn and they be dealt with to the fullest extent of the law.)

Moreover, the *Steadfast* had re-located to Crenshaw's Star. He was certain that there was an interesting story behind that inexplicable maneuver, but he would rather have been on board at the time and watched the story unfold as it happened. Now, he would have to rely on Captain Halvarson's summary of the event, and the Captain was sure to omit anything he considered "trivial." (He made another mental note, this one to recommend to HQ that the pirates' sentence be *doubled*!)

"Sir," the shuttle's pilot announced, "we coming up on RS 1."

"Thank you, Leftenant. Request a routing to Crenshaw's Star."

"Crenshaw's Star? We not returning to the *Steadfast*?"

"I've been informed that the *Steadfast* is now at Crenshaw's Star. Carry on, Leftenant."

"Aye, aye, sir."

The shuttle received its assigned Passing Lane and zeroed in on it. Seconds later, space turned inside out (and so did his stomach, in Rodriguez's humble opinion). RS1 disappeared, to be replaced by complete, utter blackness. Nothing was visible – not one single pinpoint of light which would connect a traveler to Reality. Countless millions of sentient beings had transited through an event horizon since the MOME had been developed, and each of them had described his/her experience in virtually the exact same words. For some (like Rodriguez), the experience engendered physical discomfort; and, for a handful of others, psychological distress overcame them. But no one would ever describe it as boring.

In due time, the shuttle arrived at Outpost #312. The pilot informed the Warden.

"Thank you, Leftenant. Patch me through to the Warden on duty, then contact the *Steadfast*."

"Aye, aye, sir."

The face which appeared on the shuttle's vidscreen seemed to be as fresh as that of Rodriguez. Certainly, there was not a trace of the world-weariness that more experienced Wardens tended to acquire after witnessing too much sordid behavior and too many heinous acts. L1's, just out of the Academy, were routinely assigned to outposts orbiting uninhabited star systems as a means of "seasoning" them; only rarely (as in Rodriguez's case) were any graduates posted to an inhabited system or to a patrol vessel. "Seasoning" usually lasted a minimum of fifty megaseconds after which the L1's were assigned to whatever vacancies needed to be filled. The Warden at Outpost #312 was marking time until she could find a position she could sink her teeth into.

"Warden (L1) Arbogast here," the young blonde Dunian stated matter-of-factly. She had the same epicanthic eyelids as Rodriguez, the mark of Asian ancestry. "How may I assist you?"

"The peace of Kum'halla be with you, L1 Arbogast. L1 Rodriguez here."

"Lixu! The peace of Kum'halla be with you as well. It's good to see you again after – what? – over a hundred megs."

"How are you, Akiko? Still coin collecting?"

"Not out here, I want to tell you. All I do is watch those two damn planets chase each other around their star."

"Lucky you. My first assignment was monitoring the activities of primitive sentients. They hardly did more than eat, sleep, and – well you know."

"So, you're on the *Steadfast* now?"

"Yes. And that brings me to why I've contacted you. Why is the ship here?"

"You could have gotten that information from Lt. Commander Kaw."

"Kaw is regular Constabulary, and he might not open up to me completely. I need an unbiased source."

"Well, the scuttlebutt is that the *Steadfast* is chasing down a runaway, um, Planetoid 48. It seems they lost track of it."

"You're kidding!"

"Not at all, old chum. I have to tell you that there've been a lot of jokes centering on that little dust-up."

"I can imagine. Well, I'll look forward to hearing what Captain Halvarson has to say for himself. The peace of Kum'halla be with you, L1 Arbogast."

"The peace of Kum'halla be with you, L1 Rodriguez."

The Warden turned to the shuttle pilot.

"Let's go home, Leftenant."

*   *   *

Rodriguez stopped at his quarters just long enough to toss his kit onto the bunk, and then he was off to the Bridge. He covered the distance in his usual measured pace. All the while, his mind was abuzz with the questions he intended to put to Captain Halvarson. He paid little attention to the activity going on around him; those personnel whom he passed ignored him as well.

He strode onto the Bridge with an assumed air of owning the place, automatically cast his gaze toward the niche where the *aaxyboxr* resided, noted that it was pulsating rapidly (meaning an urgent message was awaiting him), and made his way to it. He passed by Gold Zone without so much as glancing in that direction. Both Halvarson and Krishnamurthy eyed him cautiously. The former had opened his mouth to speak to him, realized that he was not going to have an "audience" until the Warden was good and ready to give him one, shut his mouth just as quickly, and fumed. The latter merely took in the scene with a wry smile.

The Warden took a deep breath, then placed his hand on the pulsating gray lump. His body stiffened as contact was made.

*   *   *

— *Greetings, fellow sentient. We are the* aaxyboxr. *How may we assist?*

— *Greetings, fellow sentients. I am sentient Rodriguez. Do you have a message for me?*

— *Searching.* [Pause] *Yes, we have two messages, both brief. In which order do you wish to receive them?*

— *The older one first, please.*

— *Reading.* "To Lt. Rodriguez aboard the Steadfast *from Lt. Commander Ruba at Constabulary Headquarters. Please report your progress in the matter of searching for Dr. Mubutu Weyerhauser.*" End of first message. Second message. Reading. "To L1 Rodriguez aboard the Steadfast *from Romulus Station Chief Crowder. New Nairobi Police Department anxious to receive your deposition concerning recent homicide.*" End of second message.

— *Thank you. I will reply to the first message as follows.* "The lead given to me by the pirate leader proved to be useless. I suspect he was stalling for time. Recommend that our deal with him be abrogated." *End of first reply. I will reply to the second message as follows.* "Inform the New Nairobi Police Department that I will provide a deposition in ninety kilos." *End of second reply.*

— *The replies are sent.*

— *The peace of Kum'halla be with the* aaxyboxr.

— *The peace of Kum'halla be with sentient Rodriguez.*

*   *   *

Rodriguez released his grip on the slimy mass, shuddered, and took another deep breath. Then he turned to face Captain Halvarson and Commander Krishnamurthy, both of whom had been watching him steadily while he was in rapport with the *aaxyboxr*. He approached the pair in a casual manner and displayed a mirthless smile.

"Tell me, Captain," he said softly, "how you managed to lose Planetoid 48."

Shock and surprise lingered on the faces of the Captain and the XO for a brief moment, then gave way to resentment from the former and curiosity from the latter. Halvarson also ground his teeth for good measure. The Warden maintained his air of stoicism.

"How the hell did you find out about that? You've been out of touch for nearly a quarter of a meg."

"We Wardens are never 'out of touch.' We have our methods of gaining information – which are irrelevant at the moment. Are you going to answer my question?"

"Yes, but not here. Let's go to my office."

He heaved himself out of his chair and marched off the Bridge. Krishnamurthy gestured for Rodriguez to precede her, and she brought up the rear. None of them were aware that all eyes were on them; the Bridge crew had not heard any of what had been spoken, but they had caught all of the non-verbal communications and were instantly alarmed.

Once in his office, Halvarson waved the other two to seats and slumped into his own. He eyed the Warden for a second or two and tried to calm himself.

"In answer to your question," he said presently, "I'll defer to Commander Krishnamurthy. She has an …interesting theory on the subject. Tomiko?"

The Romulan swiveled toward Rodriguez and began to speak in clear, crisp tones. She reiterated almost word for word what she had told the Captain about her investigation of the disappearance – twice – of the runaway and the conclusions she had drawn, farfetched as they may have been. The Warden absorbed her recitation stone-faced. When she had finished, he stared at the overhead for a few moments in silence. The Constabulary officers fidgeted in their chairs.

"This *is* an interesting theory," Rodriguez murmured finally, "and one which is not likely to be proved until we re-locate Planetoid 48. You're suggesting, of course, that we will re-locate it if we head for Romulus."

"That's exactly what I'm suggesting, Warden," Krishnamurthy replied firmly.

"And do you concur with your second-in-command, Captain?"

"I've known Commander Krishnamurthy since our Academy days, and she's never once been given to flights of fancy. Her theory seems preposterous on the face of it; but, if she believes it, I'm willing to go along with it."

"Well, I've been on one wild *aa* chase already. What's another one? I'll have to contact HQ and request that the *Steadfast* be re-deployed. They're not going to be happy with the reason I give, but I'll tell them you have my backing."

Rodriguez returned to the *aaxyboxr*'s niche, linked up, and sent his message to Constabulary HQ. Then he sat down in a commandeered chair to wait for a reply, however long it would take. While he waited, he meditated on the events which had led up to this moment in time. In particular, in accordance with the precepts of Master Fresh, he examined his own actions and behavior, searching for any errors in judgment he might have made. With the possible exception of the impromptu tryst with Anafu, he could find none; he had done everything by the book, both the Constabulary's book and that of the Aldebaranians. His only regret was that none of his actions had produced any tangible results, a fact which served to temper any self-congratulations on his part. Master Fresh, if he were still monitoring his pupils' progress, would be pleased by this self-analysis – though, of course, he would never say so to said pupils.

The Warden's meditations did not require him to close his eyes. He had been taught to meditate with eyes wide open, a method which to the uninitiated presented a stone face and a hard, penetrating stare to the outer world. This image provoked not a few nervous glances his way by the Bridge crew who had seldom seen a Warden in full meditation mode. Had he been fully telepathic, he might have been shocked by some of the mental comments being made in reaction to his continued presence.

Presently, Lt. Ralfo entered the Bridge and, upon spying Rodriguez, quickly strode over to his position. Her entrance created a stir of a different sort, especially amongst the human members of the crew. Given the Pluj's guileless attitude toward everything and everyone, she represented an unknown quantity to those whose lives were dictated by military routine. Needlessly to say, Ralfo cared as little for the opinions of others as did Rodriguez, but for personal reasons. She realized that her human partner was pre-occupied and sat down on the deck, cross-legged, and performed her own meditations (albeit on quite different matters).

To the uninitiated, the pair was a most incongruous sight.

CHAPTER TEN

▼

"CRIMES AGAINST HUMANITY"

WHAT WAS LEFT OF THE *Astarte* lay wrecked on Planetoid 48.

It – and the nine other cruise ships in the fleet of Deep Space touring vessels operated by the Murchison Transport Corporation – normally resembled "beads" on a "string." There were twelve "beads" altogether; ten of them measured half a kilometer in diameter and were reserved for the paying customers. The eleventh, only a quarter of a kilometer in diameter, was the heart of the ship; the upper hemisphere contained the bridge and the crew's quarters, while the lower hemisphere housed a highly sophisticated computer and the other vital technology necessary for the smooth functioning of all the ship's systems. The twelfth "bead" was a full kilometer in diameter and contained the awesome Murchison Oscillating Matrix Engine which could whisk the passengers to all of their tour stops on a given cruise ship's itinerary in a matter of hours. Of course, no tour lasted only hours since no one would be willing to pay the high fares the MTC charged for just a short trip; the tours therefore lasted three megaseconds so that the passengers could get their money's worth of enjoyment.

The *Astarte*'s passengers had been enjoying themselves, having concluded a visit to the fourth port-of-call (out of a scheduled seven) on their particular itinerary. Abruptly, their vacation turned into a nightmare as the cruise ship was attacked without warning by an unmarked vessel firing quite possibly illegally-obtained missiles. The attackers targeted the command sphere first in order to prevent any communications to a Constabulary station/vessel; then they fired upon the passenger sphere nearest the MOME's sphere and explosively separated the latter from the rest of the cruise ship. As a consequence, there was great loss of life in the two damaged spheres, and the remaining passenger units were left drifting in space, their occupants facing an unknown future. The attackers then attached magnetic grapples to the MOME's sphere and sped away from the scene of destruction.

The highjacked wreckage was hauled to Planetoid 48 and deposited unceremoniously between two mountain peaks. The attackers then boarded the sphere and rounded up the crew members which remained on it. To the latter's horror, they discovered that they were now prisoners of the Reman Army of Liberation and that they were required to assist in the dismantling of the MOME if they wished to continue to live. They were never told what the JUR was planning to do with the purloined equipment. Had they known, they most certainly would have fallen into either a deep despair or suicidal tendencies. How long they would remain blissfully ignorant was dependent upon the whims of a madman.

The latest victim of the madman gazed in horror at the wreckage the *Astarte* had become. This was his first view of it since he had been "recruited" after the attack upon it. In his mind's eye, he conjured up images of missiles exploding, hulls buckling, bodies flying off into space; he shuddered convulsively as he contemplated the number of corpses which must still remain in the severed part of the doomed ship. Dr. Mubutu Weyerhauser was sick to his stomach. He had never willingly harmed another sentient being in his life. Now, he realized that he had been unwittingly a party to mass murder – with more murders to come – and the thought gnawed at his mind.

The JUR operative known as "Cutty" nudged his arm and nodded toward the *Astarte* as a reminder to keep moving. He, Cutty, and Jingles had wended their way through the maze of tunnels which riddled Planetoid 48 in complete silence; there hadn't been much to say in the first place. The two terrorists were just following orders and had no inclination to engage in small talk, least of all on matters of philosophy. And Dr. Weyerhauser was still too stunned by Major Tshambe's revelation concerning the fate of the runaway to think rationally. And so the trio approached the one access point to the cruise ship which remained intact.

The access point to the MOME's sphere had been rendered into a gaping hole in the hull, a result of a thermal grenade being attached to it. After steering it to the rogue, the Major's men had fashioned a rope ladder to gain access to the interior. Cutty clambered up the make-shift first, followed by the astrophysicist, then by Jingles. Once inside, the Doctor saw fresh evidence of the assault. The JUR had deployed thermal grenades quite liberally; there were gaping holes and scorched areas everywhere he looked. In addition, bullet holes in the bulkheads abounded, and blood stains smeared every surface.

He pictured the assault in his mind's eye and forced himself to stop when the imagined scenes became too gruesome. With every step he took through the debris, he died a little inside.

Their destination was the crew's lounge. Major Tshambe had determined that this compartment was the safest place to corral the survivors – safest in terms of available means to prevent any counter-assault the prisoners might envisage. Two JUR men lounged near the hatch, their weapons casually hanging at their sides. Both were pulling at liquor bottles "liberated" from the sphere's galley. As the trio approached, they set the bottles aside and took up a semi-professional stance.

"'Ello, Cutty, Jingles," one of them mumbled, slurring his words. "What 'ave we got 'ere?"

"A new detynee, courtesy of the Myjor," Cutty replied. "Treat 'im wif respect, aye?"

"Ayn't 'e the professor we brought along, the one wif the important informytion?"

"Roight. That's whoy ye treat 'im wif respect. 'E's still not to wander aboot, 'owever."

"Kid gloves, it is, then. Welcome to the guest room, Professor."

"Boy the wy, chum, dinna ye let Tshambe catch ee sloshin' the alky. 'E's loiable to send ee to Asteride City."

"'Ell, Oi ayn't worried. 'E ayn't been up 'ere since we arroived – too busy wif 'is new ty."

"Just be careful, anywy."

The inebriate touched a finger to his forehead.

"Roight ye are, guv."

Cutty and Jingles pivoted and departed the way they had come. The inebriate peered at Doctor Weyerhauser and smiled crookedly.

"Come wif me, Professor."

He stepped toward the hatch he and his companion had allegedly been guarding. An infrared sensor set in the jamb registered body heat and activated the mechanism which slid the hatch-plate upward. Cutty entered, and the Doctor followed.

The lounge might have been a comfortable and inviting place to relax during off-duty hours at one time. It possessed upholstered furniture, end and coffee tables, various reading materials, a large vidscreen, a kitchenette, a wet bar, and soft lighting. At the present time, however, it was neither comfortable nor inviting; like everywhere else in the sphere, it displayed the aftermath of, first, the initial assault on the *Astarte* and, later, the crash-landing on Planetoid 48. The furniture was in disarray; the prisoners had moved it around to suit their needs. The deck was littered with debris –broken glass and food scraps

– which no one had bothered to clean up. The vidscreen had been smashed, and the lighting flickered like a strobe light, creating alternately, a harsh glare and dimness.

As soon as his eyes had adjusted to the flickering light, the astrophysicist counted two dozen survivors of the crew. Their uniforms – the standard red-and-white of the Murchison empire – were disheveled, grime-covered, and, in a few instances, blood-soaked. When the hatch opened, the prisoners jumped to their feet in alarm, their faces registering various degrees of anger, anxiety, fear, apprehension, and wariness. Despite their defenselessness, the JUR people did not take any chances of a sudden desperate rush but entered with weapons at the ready.

"Ye 'ave a new guest, mytes," the inebriate intoned in grandiose fashion. "Myke 'im comfortable, aye?"

He and his companion laughed raucously, then backed out of the lounge. The crew regarded the newcomer with a mixture of curiosity, wariness, and suspicion. The astrophysicist tried to appear self-confident but didn't feel so.

"Who's the senior officer here?" he asked no one in particular.

One of the detainees, a Bitha, took two tentative steps forward. His red crest showed signs of yellowing, his kind's equivalent of graying hair. He wore the three strips of a second-echelon officer, either the executive officer or a department head. A deep gash ran across his right cheek, surrounded by pinkish dried blood.

"Am I Mr. Tas," he responded in halting Standard. "Am I the Executive Officer of the *Astarte*. Are you who?"

"I'm Dr. Mubutu Weyerhauser, late of the University of New Nairobi. I taught astrophysics there."

"Did say the terrorist that were you a 'new guest'? Am not I aware that survived any of the passengers."

"I wasn't a passenger – on this ship anyway." He took a deep breath. "I came with the...terrorists."

The reaction to this admission by the *Astarte* survivors was immediate and predictable. Commander Tas hissed sharply and took a step backward. All of the others began to murmur amongst themselves and to cast ominous glances toward the Doctor. Many of them clenched their fists. The "new guest" expected to be mobbed at any moment.

"He's one of *them!*" one crew member shouted.

"The fraggin' bastard!" another yelled. "What the frag is he doin' here?"

"Let's give him what for!" a third person roared.

The officer held up his hand for silence.

"Is true this?" he muttered. "Are you one of the terrorists?"

Dr. Weyerhauser swallowed hard. He had better talk fast if he wanted to leave with a whole skin.

"Please, let me explain. It's true: I was a member of the JUR, but I belonged to the *political* wing of the organization. I've never committed any acts of violence."

A human and another Bitha now stepped forward and stood at Tas's side. Both wore a single stripe on their uniforms.

"You don't call *this*" – the human gestured with a bloody hand in a general direction – "an act of violence? Who do you think you're kidding?"

"Please, you must understand. When they asked me to contribute my expertise in astrophysics, I had no idea what they were planning to do – until it was too late. Believe me, I'm just as horrified as you are over what happened to the *Astarte*."

"A likely story!" the human retorted with a distinctly Romulan accent. "Let's do for him what he did for us."

The general murmuring began again, in louder tones this time. Several of the crew moved toward the Doctor. He inched backwards toward the hatch, envisioning himself being pummeled to death by this angry mob. He didn't blame them for reacting as they did; he might have behaved in a similar manner had their positions been reversed. As matters stood now, he was about to pay for his political naiveté.

"Wait!" the XO exclaimed. "Have his words a ring of truth to them. Would come why he here and confess if were he a terrorist?"

"To escape punishment?" suggested the other Bitha. "Must have we more proof of his innocence."

"Is there proof. Remember, placed the others him in here with us. Said they that was he another 'guest.'"

"He's a bloody spy," the Romulan offered. "If we start plotting against them, he'll inform on us. We'll all be murdered on the spot."

"I'm not a spy," the astrophysicist protested. "I was recruited into the JUR under false pretenses, and I was shocked when I learned what their real plan was."

"Was which?" Mr. Tas pressed him.

The Doctor slowly and carefully described his discoveries of the past two days, leaving no detail out. His words were received by varying degrees of disbelief, horror, and rage by all, including the senior officer. When he had concluded, the compartment was shrouded in an eerie silence; everyone was either too shocked to speak or too mistrustful of their feelings to speak rationally. The passing seconds seemed like megaseconds.

"Is this...*insane!*" Tas whispered at last. "Say is not it true."

"I wish I could. Now I find myself as much a prisoner as you do."

The realization of their fate hit the *Astarte* crew like a sledgehammer. Some wept openly and uncontrollably. Some pounded their fists on the bulkheads to keep from weeping. One individual shut down his mind, fell to the deck, and lay there in a fetal position. Others, including the Romulan, shouted curses and resumed their advance toward Dr. Weyerhauser. Only the XO seemed rooted to the deck, trying to assimilate what he had just heard. The Doctor once again feared for his safety. He needed to defuse this situation as quickly as he could.

"Mr. Tas," he beseeched, "don't you have lifeboats in this module?"

"Of course," the Bitha responded as the nature of the query snapped him out of his reverie. "Are they on the lower-most deck."

"If you can get to the lifeboats, you could escape. I can practically guarantee that the JUR will be too busy to notice."

"Have thought we of that possibility already. But, are there two hoo-mans outside with weapons, and will not hesitate they to use those weapons."

"But, suppose they were distracted long enough for your people to overpower them?"

"Have what you in mind?"

"I'll engage the guards somehow. I…used to be one of them. They might not suspect I'm up to something. When their backs are turned, you and your people jump them."

"Is it a great risk."

"Perhaps. But, if you stay here, you'll surely die."

"True. Tell me, Professor, are willing you to do this for us?"

Dr. Weyerhauser stared off into the distance. He had never been in a position where his safety was in jeopardy, and he had hoped never to be. He didn't know how he would react if the occasion arose. But the Cosmos had a way of playing tricks on mere mortals, and they seldom had things all their own way. Today, it was his turn to be tricked, and he was obliged to cope with an unpleasant truth as best he could. He did not relish what he was about to do, but he knew he had to do it or forfeit everything.

"I've been a fool, and my foolishness has cost lives. Somehow, I have to pay for my part in what happened to the *Astarte*. I'll help you escape."

"Do you trust him, Mr. Tas?" the Romulan grumbled.

"Do I. And will you also, if want you to live."

"Very well, but I intend to keep a close eye on him. The first sign of treachery, and he's dead!"

"As wish you."

"Do you have any liquor left?" the Doctor asked.

"May be there some. Why?"

"Those two out there are half drunk already. I'm going to push them over the edge."

The XO wandered off in search of liquor. He poked about in every conceivable place where liquor might be found (and in a few inconceivable places!). All the while, he made contact with each of his crew and apprised them of the plan; whatever he told them provoked expressions of wonder and/ or incredulity, but most of them nodded in acquiescence. The sole exception was the individual in the fetal position, now hugging himself and rocking back and forth. The Bitha returned with three half-filled bottles and proffered them to the astrophysicist.

"Is this all that could find I."

"It'll have to do. Thank you, Mr. Tas. Organize your people and wait for my signal."

He walked slowly toward the hatch and felt his stomach tightening into knots. At the hatch, he paused, took a deep breath, released it quickly, and passed his hand over the sensor. The guards pivoted at the sound of the hatch-plate sliding open. Neither of them did so steadily, and one of them nearly lost his balance. Both peered owlishly at their erstwhile comrade, trying to focus on his face and having a difficult time of it. The mental fog lifted partially from one of them.

"What d'ye want, Doctor? Ye're na to be oot 'ere."

"I'm fearful for my life, if you must know. Those people nearly mobbed me when they found out I was with you."

"So, that's what that commotion was aboot. We canna 'elp ee though. We 'ave oor horders."

"Of course. We mustn't disobey the Major. But, look, I noticed that you were running low on…refreshments. Are ye needin' a refill?"

He held up the bottles for their inspection. They re-focused their attention, recognized the offerings for what they were, and grinned crookedly.

"Well, noo, ye're a foine fellow after all, Doctor. We'll tyke charge o' those."

Dr. Weyerhauser handed two of the bottles over and eased himself into the passageway.

"I'd be pleased to make a toast to the success of our mission."

"Would ye noo? That's a good lad."

"Thank you." He raised the bottle he had kept for himself. "Here's to the liberation of Remus and freedom for our people! And death to the Rommie bastards!"

"Aye, death to the Rommie barstards!" the JUR men shouted in unison. "Free Remus!"

The terrorists took long swigs from their bottles. It made no difference to them what they were drinking as long as it contained alcohol. The Doctor had been counting on that. While he put his bottle to his lips, he only pretended to drink; surreptitiously, he made a hand signal to the *Astarte* crew.

The prisoners needed no second invitation. They had suffered greatly in the past few days, having seen their ship destroyed, their passengers and co-workers murdered, and themselves captured and enslaved. They were full of pent-up rage and desire for revenge but had had no means of purging themselves – until now. Now, they had a release valve – thanks to a most unlikely source – and they seized it without hesitation. Upon seeing the hand signal from the turncoat, Tas waved forward all those who were still physically and emotionally capable of acting. Not surprisingly, the Romulan and the Bitha junior officers were in the forefront.

Quickly, the prisoners rushed the hatch. They did not bother to be quiet about it but whooped like madmen. It was debatable whether the terrorists could have resisted the assault even had they been sober; since desperate people do desperate things, the assault was motivated by single-minded revenge and therefore took on the quality of an irresistible force. Since they were not sober, their befuddled minds and dull reflexes made the assault all the easier. At the whooping, they slowly turned around and froze in place when they spotted the mob. At the last second, they attempted to raise their weapons.

It was all over in a matter of seconds. The *Astarte* crew swarmed over both guards and pummeled them relentlessly and savagely with fists or objects they had grabbed in the rush. Dr. Weyerhauser had to leap out of the way to avoid being struck himself. He watched in horror at the violence he had instigated. When the crew had completely vented their rage, the JUR members lay still on the deck, covered in their own blood. Some of the blood smeared the crew's clothing.

The Romulan picked up the dropped weapons, an assault rifle of the sort used by the Constabulary,[28] and handed one to his Bitha comrade. He examined the weapon minutely, turning it slowly in his hands. Then he held it up high and regarded his co-workers grimly

"Well, men, we've got two of the fraggin' bastards. And now, we've got the means to get some more of 'em."

This elicited a hearty cheer from all except two. The two were the Doctor, who was alarmed by the potential for further violence, and the XO, who – though he was a Bitha – was also alarmed by the sudden change in attitude by

---

28   Generally, the combat brigades of the Constabulary employ the model RO-127 (the calendar year in Romulan reckoning) which is manufactured on Romulus. It is capable of firing magazines of 200 rounds each. The cartridges are designed to punch holes through solid steel, a plus when boarding enemy ships is necessary – CMT.

his subordinates. They were both worried that this newly-freed group might actually rush off and do something foolish.

"Wait!" the astrophysicist cautioned when the cheering had died down. "There are too many terrorists for you to deal with. I should know. And they're all armed. How they came by these particular weapons, I don't care to think about. But, they won't hesitate to use them, as you well know. You'll never take them as easily as you did these two. They'll cut you down in no time."

"We'll take them one by one," the Romulan countered, "and we'll gain more weapons."

"No, no," Tas disagreed. "Were not trained we as soldiers. Is the professor correct. Would die we all."

"So, what do you suggest?"

"Make we our way to the lifeboats and escape. Seek we then a Constabulary outpost and report has happened what. Will know they to do what. Is not this correct, Professor?"

"Absolutely. I've already caused enough deaths. I don't want to see any more of you die."

The Romulan regarded his comrades quizzically.

"How about the rest of you? You want to take revenge now that you're able? Or do you want to run away?"

"Have forgotten you the chain of command, Leftenant?" Tas grumbled. "Am I the senior officer here, and will do you as say I. And say I that leave we."

"Commander Tas is right," the lone female in the group put in, "and so's the Professor. We'd stand a better chance if we had the Constabulary with us. That's what they're trained to do."

A murmur of agreement rippled through the crew.

"All right," the Romulan conceded. "We'll do it your way, *but* we keep the weapons – just in case."

"Is it agreeable. Do concur you, Professor?"

"I do. The sooner we leave the *Astarte*, the safer we'll be."

"Then follow me to the lifeboats. Bring those are incapacitated who."

*   *   *

The pupil stands before his mentor and tries to control his nervousness. He is not succeeding.

It is the end of the first year of training at the Warden Academy, and all "Firsters" are to be evaluated. The evaluation will determine whether or not the pupil will be permitted to continue his/her training or be rejected. Eighty per cent of all candidates to the Academy are eventually rejected, most of them in the first year. While to the outside world it is no great dishonor to be rejected, given the rigorous standards set down by the Aldebaranians, the rejected candidates spend the rest of their lives in search of worthiness. Some even re-apply to the Academy, pleading for a second chance; only a handful is given that chance.

Cadet Lixu Rodriguez is fully prepared to hear the worst. During his first year, he has made a nuisance of himself, asking one hypothetical question after another and creating much exasperation in his instructors and especially in his mentor. He does not know it yet, but he has earned a reputation throughout the faculty and the administration as the "Grand Inquisitor." If he had known, his nervousness might well have assumed monumental proportions.

Master Fresh-Bloom-in-the-Face-as-the-Day-Begins is busy sifting through the reports he has received from all of the faculty and administrators concerning those whom he is mentoring. These reports are often long and detailed, and mentors will make their final decisions based upon what they read. The reports concerning Cadet Rodriguez are longer and more detailed than normally, and Master Fresh shakes his head frequently as he plows through them – which brings perspiration to the brow of the pupil. Master Fresh's reactions do not bode well for his chances of continuation, he believes, and he wonders what he will tell his parents when he returns home in disgrace. Grandfather Rodriguez will be especially displeased, as he had such high hopes of having a Warden in the family.

At last, Master Fresh sets the reports aside and regards his pupil balefully for several long moments. The silence is deafening, and Cadet Rodriguez desperately resists the urge to wipe his perspiration-soaked face.

"Tell me, pupil," his mentor breaks his silence abruptly, "what you want to do."

"Pardon me, Master?"

"Are you deaf, lack-wit? What do you want to do?"

"In which respect, Master?"

"That should be fairly obvious. Do you want to continue at the Academy? Think carefully before you answer."

Cadet Rodriguez does not have to think carefully. He knows what he wants to do. Ever since he received the invitation to attend the Warden Academy, he has known exactly what he wanted to do.

"Yes, Master," he replies firmly. "More than anything else."

"Do you see these reports before me? They all say essentially the same thing. All of your instructors are of one mind insofar as your abilities are concerned. I have not seen the like in my ninety [years] of mentoring."

He touches a report.

"Keen mind."

Another report.

"Great attention to detail."

A third.

"Ability to grasp complex concepts."

"One after another, my colleagues marvel at your thought processes. And I will tell you that I also marvel. But, do not let this praise go to your head, pupil, lest you lose your way in the end."

"Yes, Master."

"It is therefore recommended that you be allowed to continue your training – if that is what you truly want."

"It is my greatest desire, Master."

"Humph! Desire has a way of confounding the unwary, lack-wit. Nevertheless, I judge that you are fit to continue."

"Thank you, Master."

"Do not thank me just yet. As you humans are fond of saying, 'you ain't seen nothin' yet.' You are dismissed, Cadet Rodriguez. The peace of Kum'halla be with you."

*　　　*　　　*

As Master Fresh had predicted, young Lixu Rodriguez hadn't seen anything yet. As the memory of that encounter wafted through the Warden's mind, he wondered what his old mentor would make of his current situation, i.e. sitting on the deck of a Constabulary patrol vessel, next to a Pluj, waiting for a message from HQ, and drawing embarrassed attention from his theoretical shipmates. Perhaps the Aldebaranian would conclude that *he* hadn't seen anything yet!

How long the Warden and the Pluj had been sitting there waiting for the message seemed like a megasecond but was closer to two kiloseconds. Fortunately, part of the training at the Academy had been the disciplining of mind and body to cope with forced inactivity. Similar to yoga, the techniques employed shut down all unnecessary mental and physical functions so that the subject could concentrate on placing him/herself into a semi-trance state, perfectly aware of what was transpiring around him/herself but apart from it as if (s)he were viewing a drama on a holovision set. Rodriguez had set a certain signal as the release from the trance state, and he would remain where he was until the signal manifested itself.

The Bridge crew passed by him cautiously, fearing to "wake" him and risk his ire for disturbing him. Once Commander Krishnamurthy came close to see if he were still breathing. She would have been quite surprised and/or shocked to learn what the Warden was thinking during this "inspection." The only physical reaction any of the crew received derived from Lt. Ralfo, who was not in a trance state but sat and fidgeted while guarding over her partner/lover; *her* reaction was generally a look of annoyance at those who were regarding her Lixu like they would an annoying insect.

Rodriguez felt the signal before he heard it. When an *aaxyboxr* received a message, it not only pulsated in a pinkish glow but also emitted a barely audible hum. The Warden sensed the vibration of the hum several nanoseconds before he heard its sound waves. Instantly, all of his brain and body functions were restored to normal, and he was on his feet in a few seconds, startling both his companion and the entire Bridge crew. He stood before the *aaxyboxr*, took a deep breath, and grasped the pulsating mass. He stiffened into immobility as the alien creature took control of his brain and nervous system.

*   *   *

— *Greetings, fellow sentient. We are the* aaxyboxr. *How may we assist?*

— *Greetings, fellow sentients. I am sentient Rodriguez. Do you have a message for me?*

— *Searching.* [Pause] *Yes, we have one short message. Reading.* "*To Lt. Rodriguez aboard the* Steadfast *from Lt. Commander Ruba at Constabulary HQ. New orders for the* Steadfast, *as follows. You are approved for re-deployment in search of the rogue world Planetoid 48 and the JUR cell. You will re-deploy as soon as the* Loyal *arrives to relieve you of your post.*" *End of message.*

— *Thank you. I will send the standard acknowledgement to Lt. Commander Ruba.*

— *It is done.*

— *The peace of Kum'halla be with the* aaxyboxr.

— *The peace of Kum'halla be with sentient Rodriguez.*

*   *   *

The scene in Conference Room A was the epitome of confusion.

After Warden Rodriguez had transmitted HQ's new orders to him, Captain Halvarson immediately called a meeting of his senior staff. The latter entered the conference room with no little apprehension; and, as soon as the Captain apprised them of the situation, apprehension turned to shock, skepticism, and outright denial. Only Commander Krishnamurthy and the Warden sat quietly, the former ready to back up her Captain, the latter content to observe the reactions to an extraordinary turn of events.

Once Halvarson had finished speaking, the room erupted into a Babel of questions, comments, and cries of dismay. Everyone wanted to be heard, and orderly procedure be damned! It took the Captain nearly two dekaseconds to restore order and, even after he had, some few still mumbled under their breaths.

"I realize what a shock this news comes," he soothed. "I had difficulty accepting it myself. But, the fact remains that what might have seemed impossible yesterday has become possible today. And we have to make the best of it."

Lt. Commander Tuva, Senior Sensors Officer, raised her hand tentatively and was recognized.

"Oi dinna doot the Commander's abilities, sir, but this still looks loike supposition to me. Is there any 'ard evidence to back it up?"

"The only shred we've got is that Dunian captain's statement that Planetoid 48 appeared suddenly in front of him and nearly collided with his ship. Everything else is just a shrewd guess. But, HQ is convinced there's something to it, and we've got a 'go' to investigate. And, one more thing, Mr. Tuva: our resident Warden is convinced too. Whatever else we might think about Wardens in general, they don't go chasing after the wind."

Rodriguez smiled to himself. It must have pained the New Swiss immensely to make that admission. The Captain was right, of course; Wardens examined all sides of a situation before they decided on a course of action. This point had been drummed into them from the first week at the Academy to the last. No matter what subject was being taught or who was doing the teaching, keen observation and keener analysis were a constant theme, and woe betide that cadet who failed to heed it. Many times, Master Fresh had reiterated the theme in private interviews; and, happily, Cadet Rodriguez had not given him cause to rebuke him for failing to heed it.

He had witnessed what happened to a cadet who did fail, and that experience was sufficient to instill in him greater effort (if that was possible). The unfortunate individual had made the mistake of missing a key element in a simulated situation in the field. The class was to "solve" a murder by examining the "body" and deducing the identity of the "murderer." The cadet overlooked a vital clue and, as a consequence, accused the wrong suspect as the culprit. When the error had been pointed out to him, the instructor proceeded to analyze *him* in no uncertain terms. Aldebaranians seemed to delight in public humiliation as a means of conditioning their pupils to proper behavior. They believed that, by making an example of one, all would profit. They were generally right. Rodriguez himself had taken an instant vow never to be at the center of this sort of attention.

In the present instance, he had to sympathize with Lt. Commander Tuva. There hadn't been much to go on concerning the whereabouts of Planetoid 48; but Commander Krishnamurthy had made a brilliant, if unorthodox, argument and had backed it up with meticulous extrapolation. In the absence of evidence to the contrary, her view seemed to be the only logical one at the moment. Time would tell soon enough if she were "chasing the wind."

"I thank you, Captain," he said somewhat sarcastically, "for your vote of confidence. If I were Tuva, I'd be skeptical too. But, we must act on the evidence, no matter how strange it appears to be."

"Oi still dinna loike it," the Green Zone commander murmured, rubbing her jaw.

"Your reservations are noted," the Captain said curtly. "Commander Rux, this operation will entail special tactics, including landing on Planetoid 48 and neutralizing all threats."

"Aye, sir. Will use my people the travel time to the runaway to best advantage. Can count you on us."

"Excellent. Commander Mbaku, you'll basically be performing picket duty, making sure that no terrorist escapes."

"Anyone who tries to run," the Romulan growled, "won't run far. My people will pick them off, one by one."

"Captain Halvarson," the Warden piped up. "I'd like to make a special request."

"Yes?"

"My original mission – to apprehend and place under arrest Dr. Mubutu Weyerhauser – hasn't changed. I'd like a platoon of Commander Rux's troops and one of the Alkon scouts placed at my disposal to assist me. And, of course, Lt. Ralfo should accompany me."

"Arari, can you spare a platoon?"

"Is it no problem, as say you hoo-mans."

"Thank you, Captain. You'll excuse me now. I must meditate."

Rodriguez exited the conference room and made straight for the gymnasium. The "meditation" he had in mind would consist of working out with the nautilus equipment. In fact, he planned to meditate in this fashion for the duration of the chasing down of Planetoid 48. He hadn't had a decent work-out in several megaseconds, and he needed to be in tip-top shape before attempting to scramble across the surface of the rogue. The Academy had placed equal emphasis on the discipline of body and mind, and he had been neglecting the former. Master Fresh would be highly displeased and use the negligence to launch into a lengthy lecture concerning the importance of physical exercise in the general scheme of things. He, Rodriguez, had had his fill of lengthy lectures, and it behooved him to avoid another one by taking the proper steps.

Besides, he actually enjoyed working out with the nautilus equipment.

CHAPTER ELEVEN

▼

RE-DEPLOYMENT

THE FOREST IS DARK AND dank, full of shadows. The trees are densely packed and difficult to see through. The Enemy could be standing next to you, and you would never know — until it was too late.

The Soldier moves cautiously, working his way from one tree to the next. His eyes are busy, now peering left and now right, hoping to spot a tell-tale movement which will betray the Enemy's location. And he must also watch the ground in order to spy a booby-trap cleverly placed to maim or to kill an unwary militiaman.

The Soldier has seen too many of his comrades fall victim to either ambush or booby-trap. His best buddy, Howie, with whom he had grown up on Romulus and with whom he had gone through Basic and Advanced Training in the Romulan Home Guard, had been one of the first victims in the present campaign. Howie had not been watching where he was going and tripped a wire, releasing a spring with a sharpened stake. The image of Howie lying on the ground with a stake penetrating his brain through the eye socket continues to haunt the Soldier day and night.

And Howie had not been alone. Others in the unit had met similar, or worse, fates as the campaign ground on, meter by bloody meter. The Soldier is amazed that he has made it this far, and he is ever aware that a single misstep on his part will spell the end of his good fortune, permanently.

He doesn't mind dying — as long as his death has meaning — but, of course, he'd rather live. Being here, in this treacherous forest, is not conducive to long life, however. And the Enemy has the reputation of being the most ferocious, the most skillful, and the most deadly fighter in the Galaxy.

The Soldier remembers his briefing prior to his deployment on this world. The High Command had informed his brigade that a large contingent of Alkon warriors was present on Planetoid Delta, a small body which lay on the boundary between the space controlled by the Amazonian Federation and that by the Alliance for Free Space. Planetoid Delta was a strategic target, the High Command had claimed, because it was centrally located in the central spiral and whoever occupied it could launch multiple strikes against the foe's home worlds. Therefore, it had been impressed upon all combat forces that seizing and holding Planetoid Delta was crucial to winning the war.

Easier said than done, the Soldier had soon learned.

The Enemy asked no quarter and gave none. The campaign to seize and to hold this allegedly strategic world had quickly devolved into a struggle just to survive, and survival was a fleeting thing thus far. The Capellan mercenaries picked the militiamen off one by one, using a variety of weapons and tactics. Not once had they engaged in a frontal assault which would have made them easy targets. How could you fight an enemy if you couldn't see him?

The Soldier halts abruptly and peers at the ground. Is that a trip wire he sees? It appears too straight to be a natural *object. He kneels down slowly and carefully extends his hand. With his fingertips, he touches the suspect object ever so lightly. He is right. The object is artificial – it is, in fact, a length of cord – and he will wager a month's pay that it is connected to some devilish device which will kill him outright or make him wish it had.*

He must neutralize this booby-trap lest it work its horror against one of his comrades who may not be as observant as he. He must do so slowly, since he does not know exactly how it operates; if he is standing in the wrong place when he yanks the cord, he might well become the thing's victim after all.

With deliberate slowness, he rises to his feet. Even the slightest movement of air may trigger the device. He looks left and right again. The cord seems to stretch between two trees. Now he edges toward the nearest tree, one eye on his surroundings, the other on the tripwire. When he reaches the tree, he crouches down and examines its base. Sure enough, the cord is attached to the base, serving as an anchor for whatever is at the other end.

The Soldier suddenly realizes that he has been holding his breath all this while. And he has been perspiring heavily. This densely-packed forest keeps most of the heat of Planetoid Delta's sun out. Yet, he is not sweating because he is overheated but because he is overwrought. He closes his eyes and tries to control his breathing – a tall order when Death lurks behind every tree and bush and in every shadow. When his breathing returns to normal, he re-focuses on the task at hand.

In order to neutralize this device, he must position himself so that he is in the opposite direction of the cord. He does so while still in a crouch. It is a difficult maneuver. In the first place, he is carrying a full load of combat gear which, if he is not careful, will throw him off-balance. In the second place, the ground near this tree is uneven, and he struggles to maintain his footing. And, in the third place, he must be ever watchful or else he will be an easy target for any mercenary who may be nearby.

After what seems like an age, he positions himself on the opposite side of the tree where – he hopes – he can safely trip the cord. Smoothly, he removes his bayonet from its scabbard. He presses against the tree, reaches around the bole, and stretches his arm forward as far as he can. Now he whispers a curse. Even with the added length of the bayonet, he is still about fifteen centimeters shy of the cord. He must therefore edge around the tree a fraction in order to close the gap. The maneuver is risky – possibly lethal – but it must be done.

He slides around the bole ever so slightly until he finds the point where he can touch the cord with the tip of his bayonet. All he needs to do now is to give the cord a sharp tug and that should do the trick. He braces himself, holds his breath in order to control his movement, and sets the point of the blade squarely against the cord.

It occurs to him then that he could put this booby-trap to good use and turn the tables against the Enemy. If, when he triggers the device, he fakes a cry of terror, he might be able to draw one of the Capellans into a reverse trap and kill him. This is also risky – and possibly lethal – but he would have the element of surprise on his side for a change. He just might survive this campaign after all.

With the impromptu plan firmly in his mind, the Soldier jiggles the cord with his bayonet. Instantly, there is a sharp snap as whatever is attached to the other end is released and set into motion. He now fakes a scream of mortal agony and hopes that it is convincing enough to lure the Enemy into the open.

His acting done, he examines the nature of the booby-trap, now dangling uselessly from the neighboring tree. It is a make-shift noose, made from the same material as the cord. Had he been caught off guard, that noose would surely have looped around his neck and swung him upwards, either breaking his neck quickly or strangling him slowly. He shakes his head in wonder. If nothing else, Capellans are devilishly clever.

The Soldier lowers himself to the ground and peeks around the tree. He sees nothing but the gloom of shadows –

Wait! Did one of those shadows just move?

He stares in the suspect direction and squints. All is still. He curses silently again. He is getting jumpy and letting his imagination run away with him. That could be fatal here.

He calms himself down as best he can and blinks away the sweat dripping from his forehead into his eyes. He –

There! That shadow did *move! It was not his imagination after all.*

And the shadow is moving in his direction. It is moving just as slowly and as deliberately as he had been previously. As the shadow advances ever closer to his position, it begins to take shape. There is no mistaking that particular shape either. Very tall and very lean – it is definitely an Alkon warrior. And he is coming to inspect the fruits of his handiwork.

The Soldier discovers that his heart rate has increased significantly. That is not surprising. Few of his comrades had ever seen a Capellan for more than a fleeting second; and, for far too many of them, it had been the last *thing they ever saw. He is getting the best view of a Capellan any human ever had, and the experience is too frightening for words.*

But he must not panic. Panicking would be fatal. He must take a deep breath and slow his heart down. He still has the element of surprise. He still has an even chance of getting out of this situation with a whole skin.

He observes the Enemy halting underneath the empty noose, looking upward and stroking his nose. The latter gesture is how Capellans register puzzlement. The Enemy bends down and fingers the now loose cord; then he peers off in the direction of the tree to which the cord was anchored, the tree behind which the Soldier is hiding. The Capellan straightens up, resumes his stealth mode, and advances toward the anchor-tree.

The Soldier tenses. Life and Death are now hanging in the balance. In the next few seconds, either he or the Enemy will be dead. Slowly, he raises his bayonet to eye level. He must wait until the last possible second before exposing himself to view and make a quick thrust of the bayonet into the Capellan's vitals.

The Enemy is now only three meters away. The Soldier can clearly see his copper-colored skin and the tattoo of an alien beast on his bare chest. More riveting, however, are the other's yellow eyes, gleaming malevolently in the gloom. They are enough to frighten even the most stalwart individual. But the Soldier must not give way to panic, or else all is undone.

The Capellan approaches the tree, stoops down, and gently tugs at the cord. He strokes his nose a second time and peers off into the distance. Now is the right moment, the Soldier thinks.

With his bayonet before him, he reveals himself to the Enemy. The Capellan jerks his head upward, even as he reaches for one of his razor-sharp stilettos in a forearm scabbard.

The Soldier smiles broadly and says:

"Too late, Sergeant. You're dead."

The Alkon warrior puckers his lips, his kind's equivalent of a smile. He says:

"Aye. So I to be."

*   *   *

Rodriguez and Sgt. Utumi removed their virtual-reality helmets and slumped in their chairs exhausted. The Warden was perspiring in reality almost as heavily as he had been in the VR program; in reality, however, the sweat was due more to the confining helmet than to the tenseness induced by the programming. The squad leader of the Capellan scout unit was not perspiring at all. Capellans had no sweat glands, and their skin remained dry at all times. Still, Nature had given them a different mechanism to dispel excess heat energy. Heat was radiated away through the skin in a form of osmosis; the process was visible as a flushing of the skin so that a "perspiring" Capellan's normal copper color became a burnished copper.

The VR helmet enclosed the head of the wearer much like a pressure helmet used in work in a vacuum or at ocean depths. The difference between the VR apparatus and the other kind was that the former had no faceplate; it was completely opaque so that the wearer would not be distracted by extraneous images. What the wearer "saw" were computer-generated images of pre-programmed virtual realities. The programs were as exact as the engineers who designed them could make them; sights, sounds, smells, and tactile sensations of actual locations had been translated into data bits, and the bits had been recorded on special discs. Insert a disc marked, say, "Sahara Desert," and the computer transferred the program to the helmet. On the interior surface of the helmet, an array of studs protruded, pressing against the wearer's skull at strategic points; the studs corresponded with those areas of the brain which processed sensory input. The data from the program channeled through the studs, and the wearer could believe he was actually in the Sahara Desert.

The VR programs were designed to train combat troops in the ability to fight in all types of terrain and situations. Every trooper – from the lowest rank to the commanding general – put the helmet on and experienced all sequences at least once a year in order to be updated on the latest programming. Those troopers going into actual combat were given a "refresher course" in the scenario (s)he was about to enter. The programs could be played solo or as part of a group exercise. Often, a trooper would challenge another in a war game in order to hone his/her combat skills.

Most of the programs were representation of actual places based upon detailed descriptions provided by visitors to the sites. The program concluded by Rodriguez and Utumi depicted the setting in the war zone on Planetoid Delta, the battle for which had been one of the major land conflicts between the forces of the fledging Amazonian Federation and those of the hastily-thrown-together Alliance for Free Space some forty-plus years earlier. The battle pitted a brigade of Romulan militiamen against a tribe of Alkon warriors and was, by all accounts, the fiercest and most brutal engagement during the entire War of the Eight Suns.[29] The program was no less rigorous (some said *too* rigorous by half) than the actual event, and the High Command set a disclaimer on it to the effect that it was recommended only for high-ranking officers and NCO's who had successfully weathered all other programs in the VR library.

This program was required study by all cadets at the Warden Academy, and the Aldebaranians used it as part of the weeding-out of those who were on the borderline between advancement and dismissal. Rodriguez had played the program five times during his own training; and, although he had not "won" any of the VR battles, he did demonstrate improved skills which allowed him to continue on until graduation. This previous experience was a major factor in his "win" over Sgt. Utumi.

Utumi Ka-rok approached the Warden in a deliberate fashion and fixed him with a steady gaze. Interestingly, his grandfather had served as a mercenary for the Alliance in the Great War and was one of the few casualties the Alkonu suffered on Planetoid Delta. Such ancestry had elevated his son and his grandson to a high status, and he had been encouraged to find his true calling in the ranks of the Constabulary. Like all Alkon warriors, he knew how to fight – and win – and defeat (even in virtual reality) was a stranger to him.

The Warden saluted him as a signal that he had been a worthy opponent. The sergeant returned the salute in the same spirit.

"Utumi-go, thank you for the match. It was…invigorating."

"It my pleasure did be, Rodri-go." He closed his left eye, a sign of embarrassment. "You the first Oo-man to be who an Alkon warrior have defeat."

"I was lucky."

"Nay. The skills you from the Urrju did receive all the difference did make. Your training the equal to ours did be."

"Thank you, Sergeant. Coming from you, that is a real compliment."

"A true warrior it to befit."

---

29 For a more complete account of the Great War, read Ichabod O. Morituma's *Render Unto Caesar: The True Account of the War of the Eight Suns* (Amazonian Independent Press, A.R. 21). Morituma (now deceased) was a reporter for the New Nairobi *Star*, whose editorial policies incurred a great deal of wrath from officialdom. He interviewed survivors on both sides of the conflict, and his conclusions refute the propaganda generated before, during, and after the War – CMT.

"By the way, you're the first Alkonu I've heard who hasn't used the word 'accursed' to describe the Community. It seems like an automatic addition in many circles."

Utumi cocked his head leftward, his kind's equivalent to a shrug.

"It a rare thing to be, but some Alkonu the Urrju not to hate. I one of these to be. I their many contributions to galactic peace have see."

"Including my organization?"

The Capellan repeated his previous gesture.

"Someone the rules must enforce."

Any further conversation was put on hold by the approach of Commander Rux. The Bithan seemed to have adopted the swagger affected by human military personnel; but, in his case, it was an exaggerated affect and prompted the casual observer to believe that Rux could fall down at any given moment. He pulled up before the former "combatants" and frowned (which expression he also borrowed from humans). Utumi came to attention and saluted. Rux returned the salute absentmindedly and focused on Rodriguez. The latter did not salute, however, because Wardens seldom saluted anyone but their own kind, a fact which added fuel to the rankling among ordinary Constabulary personnel.

"Yes, Commander?" the Warden asked in a bemused fashion.

"Is your troop detachment ready for review, Leftenant."

"Excellent. Lead the way."

The Bithan pivoted and quick-stepped out of the training area, Rodriguez trailing in his wake. Utumi, having some off-duty time left to him, decided to fall in beside the human as part of his new-found respect for him.

The training area and the troop quarters were in the lower hemisphere of the command sphere between the command level and the computer mainframe. Rux headed for the nearest ramp and ascended to the troop level. Unlike other levels on the *Steadfast*, this one was one gigantic open space from bow to stern. The space was filled with row after row of double-decked bunks. Each platoon had its own section which was clearly delineated on the deck by a gridwork of red lines and orange numbers, and each was responsible for the policing of its own area. Where, on other levels, a central passageway ran, here a wide space between the center-most rows served to mark an equivalent; the unwritten rule was that this space was "neutral territory." At the opposite ends of this quasi-passageway were located the showers and latrines (suitably configured for the various races who served aboard the ship). Few of the bunks were occupied; most of the troopers were either in a training exercise or on the recreation level or in the mess hall.

The sole exception to this state of affairs stood in the "neutral territory." Here, a platoon, selected by Commander Rux personally, assumed the position of parade rest. At the sight of the approaching party, the senior sergeant in charge barked an order, and the unit came to attention. The Bithan halted before the non-com, a Romulan, and received a smart salute.

"Sir, Sgt. Running Deer and Gamma Platoon of Delta Company reporting for duty!"

"Be at ease," Rux commanded, returning the salute.

"Platoon!" Sgt. Running Deer spat out. "Parade – *rest*!"

The troopers assumed their former position, and Rodriguez could not help but notice that they were not as co-ordinated as they should have been – in some cases, by half a second. He also could not help but notice that none of them wore a pressed uniform; their uniforms looked as if they had been slept in. He wondered how clean they were personally. If any cadet at the Academy had shown up for class or training session as disheveled as this lot, (s)he would have (1) received a mini-lecture on the spot by the lecturer/trainer, (2) sent back to his/her quarters for a fresh uniform, and (3) received another mini-lecture from his/her mentor at the end of the day. These troopers could have benefited greatly under the gentle tutelage of any of the Aldebaranians. Perhaps he ought to take them in hand at the earliest opportunity.

"Sergeant," Rux was saying, "is this Warden Rodriguez." The Romulan glanced briefly at Rodriguez, and an eye twitched slightly. "Will be assigned you and your platoon to him during our mission to Planetoid 48, effective immediately."

"Aye, sir," the non-com murmured, barely disguising his reaction to his new assignment.

Rodriguez quickly scanned the faces of this multi-racial group for other reactions to re-assignment. Half of the troopers remained stoical, but their eyes took on a faraway look which spoke volumes to a trained observer like a Warden. The other half shifted their bodies imperceptibly and/or grimaced. Rodriguez pursed his lips. He was going to have an interesting time with this rag-tag bunch, beginning with Sgt. Running Deer.

Rux turned to Rodriguez and smiled mirthlessly.

"Is your new command here, Leftenant. Will leave I now."

The Bithan pivoted and noticed Sgt. Utumi for the first time since leaving the training area. He peered at the Capellan quizzically, then marched off. The latter watched him go and stroked his left cheek with three of his six fingers, a sign of his growing contempt.

The Warden fixed Running Deer with his best penetrating glare, and the latter actually flinched under the scrutiny.

"Well, Sergeant, it looks like we're stuck with each other."

"Aye, sir. What are your orders, sir?"

"Have you been briefed on the mission?"

"We're to chase down a cell of Reemie terrorists who've holed up on Planetoid 48. That's all I know, sir."

"I see. I've got an errand to run at the moment. Assemble the platoon in Classroom #6 in one kilo after we warp-out. I'll brief you further then." He re-examined his new "command." "And Sergeant, fresh uniforms, if you please."

"Aye, sir," came the growled response. "Platoon – *ten-hut!*"

The troopers came to attention, and Running Deer saluted the Warden smartly. The latter smiled sweetly and walked away. Sgt. Utumi fell in beside him. The two strolled to the forward end of the level, where the barracks of the Capellan squad were located, but remained silent. When they had reached those barracks, Rodriguez faced his companion.

"You seem distressed, Utumi-go."

The warrior rubbed his cheek with four of his fingers.

"Commander Rux you the dregs of his brigade have give. I them have see. They warriors not to be."

"I'm well aware of the shortcomings of Gamma Platoon of Delta Company. And I'm not surprised it was assigned to me. Constabulary personnel don't like Wardens any more than Romulans like Alkonu."

"You to the Captain will not complain?"

"No. It would be futile. But, I intend to put Gamma Platoon through a few paces while we're on route to Planetoid 48."

The Capellan puckered his lips and held the facial expression for several seconds as a sign of high amusement.

"I that would like to see."

"You're welcome to join us." He gave the sergeant a brief salute. "The peace of Kum'halla be with you, Utumi-go."

"Your campfire warm and bright to be, Rodri-go," Utumi replied, returning the salute.

The Warden walked away and toward the ramps and ascended to the command level. Once there, he debated whether or not to return to his quarters or to check on the status of the ship. He chose the latter and headed for the Bridge. His entrance elicited the usual reaction from the crew which he ignored. He glanced in the direction of the niche which held the *aaxyboxr*, saw that the creature was dormant, and ambled over to Gold Zone.

Captain Halvarson and Commander Krishnamurthy were engaged in a systems check – a daily requirement for all Constabulary ships, large or small – and therefore paid no attention to the Warden. Rodriguez let them go about their business and divided his attention between the Display and the Captain's vidscreen. Systems check did not take that long (unless there was a serious malfunction), and he would soon have their attention. He could afford to be patient.

Patience had been an important part of the curriculum at the Academy. It had actually been taught to all cadets in the first term of their training; "refresher" classes were held every other term thereafter. In practice, however, the mentors "taught" patience every single day, and their teaching methods ranged from mini-lectures to brow-beating (which were usually one and the same). Cadets were advised against hasty speech and hastier actions; the one led to enmity, resentment, and ill will, while the other led to undesirable reactions, tensions, and avoidable violence. And both undermined a Warden's credibility, a state of affairs which rendered him/her ineffective; and an ineffective Warden was of no use to the Service. A habitual lack of patience was grounds for dismissal. Master Fresh-Bloom-in-the-Face-as-the-Day-Begins believed that humans were the most *impatient* species in all Creation. They were always in a hurry to be somewhere; they never seemed to slow down – least of all *stop* – for anything; and they expected everyone else to keep up with them. Master Fresh never tired of pointing this out to Cadet Rodriguez, whom he believed was typical of the species. Cadet Rodriguez asked one question after another – mostly trivial – and wanted instant answers. Cadet Rodriguez pushed Master Fresh's own patience to the limits and had no idea of the dangerous grounds upon which he was treading. Happily, Cadet Rodriguez did have the sense not to exceed the limits, and that was why (among other things) he was allowed to wear the uniform of the Warden Service.

A sudden change in the Display caught his eye, and he studied it intensely. The computer generating the holographic image had given it a cream color, the designation for a Constabulary vessel. That, he thought, would be the *Loyal*, come to relieve the *Steadfast* so that the latter could track down the whereabouts of Planetoid 48. The arrival pleased him, because it meant he could finally carry out his original mission. The sound of Lt. H'rum's voice confirmed the fact.

"Communications to the Captain."

"Halvarson here."

"Sir, the *Loyal* haves arrived."

"Excellent. Patch me through, Leftenant."

"Aye, sir."

The image on the Captain's vidscreen changed from a seemingly endless parade of statistics to the cheerful face of Captain Hiroshi Meinhoff of the CSS *Loyal*. A lean-faced New Swiss, he sported a long scar across his left cheek, the result (he claimed) of a duel fought to defend a lady's honor.

"Olaf," he rasped, "I'm here to save your ass."

"Hah! You're here because no one else wanted to be, Hiroshi."

"Too true, my friend. You get the plum assignments, and I get the boring ones."

"It's not all that boring. Why, just 200 kilos ago, we picked up a bunch of pirates. Maybe you'll get lucky too."

"One can dream, I suppose. So, you're going to chase after Planetoid 48. Good luck!"

"Thanks. I suspect I'm going to need some luck. Halvarson out."

The Captain now realized that the Warden was standing nearby, watching him intently. He found this close scrutiny of his every move nearly as galling as the other's arrogant attitude toward him and his crew. He stifled his natural reaction and slipped on a look of concern.

"Do you want to contact your counterpart on the *Loyal* before we leave?"

"Not necessary, Captain. She knows all she needs to."

"Very well." He punched the red button on his console. Sr. Lt. Colon appeared on the screen. "Leftenant, lay in a course plotted by Commander Krishnamurthy."

"Aye, sir."

Halvarson now pushed the white button. The lighting dimmed, warning the ship's crew that a warp-out was imminent.

Rodriguez departed the Bridge at a quick pace. When the moment of switching on the giant MOME and warping Space (and Time?) arrived, he wanted to be in his quarters and flat on his back. Lying down might not be an effective buffer against the wrenching of all his internal organs, but he had experienced the transition standing up only once before, and he never desired to repeat that experience again. Best to lie down and grit one's teeth for the duration.

As he started down the passageway, the usual hustle-and-bustle surrounded him, as the crew scurried toward their individual warp-out stations or their own quarters. He had never bothered to interrogate anyone else about their reactions to warping-out because (1) he didn't care and (2) he didn't want the crew to get the idea that he was just like them. Perhaps, some day, he would, if only to satisfy his curiosity. Meanwhile, he ignored the activity around him.

When he entered his quarters, he quickly discovered that they were not unoccupied. Lt. Ralfo was sitting on the bunk in eager expectation. She jumped to her feet like an excited child, rushed over to him, and threw her arms about him. He hugged her in return, reveling in the softness and warmth of her body.

"I thought that I would have to wait outside for you, Lixu. But you left your hatch unlocked."

"I never lock my door. I don't have to. No one enters a Warden's quarters uninvited for love or money. Everyone is afraid of what might happen to them if they do."

"For love, *I* would enter. It has been more than a quarter of a meg since we coupled. Pluj do not like to wait that long."

"I've ...been busy."

"You are not 'busy' now."

"No. But, after we warp out, then we can make love."

A mischievous twinkle came into her eye, and she began to undo the snaps of his tunic.

"Pluj like to experiment, dear Lixu. I have a wonderful idea. We will make love *during* warp-out."

"You're serious?"

"Pluj are always serious about sex," she murmured as she continued to work on the snaps.

She pulled off his tunic and cast it aside, then gently grasped his neck, leaned forward, and planted a juicy kiss on his mouth. He responded instinctively and pressed his lips against hers. While they kissed, her tongue sought his, found it, and massaged it languorously. After a few seconds, she slid her lips across his cheek and down his neck, planting small kisses along the way. His breathing started to become labored, and a tingle of excitement rippled through his body.

She continued the oral journey over his chest, stopping briefly to flick her tongue across his nipples. I-Pluj did not have nipples, because of a different evolutionary path, and so Pluj were intrigued by nipples on human males. They quickly discovered that those males had an erotic reaction to lingual massage and thus included the practice to their sexual "repertoire." He sighed heavily as she massaged first one nipple, then the other.

Expertly, she unbuckled his belt and pushed his trousers and briefs down around his ankles. His penis was already semi-erect. She knelt before him and gently kissed the head of the shaft, and it stiffened further. Now, she played her tongue across the head, and he became fully erect. For good measure, she ran her tongue the full length of his manhood to its base, then back to the head which she kissed again, this time more languidly. He shuddered as successive waves of pleasure washed over him.

She led him to the bunk, pushed him onto it, and removed his trousers and briefs. She deftly removed her bikini, clambered on top of him, and straddled his hips. She grasped his penis, pushed it against her slit, and rubbed herself with it. For him, it seemed as if his manhood had just contacted a furnace; for her, it seemed as if she had contacted a hot poker.

She lifted herself slightly, leaned forward until the head of his shaft was a quarter of the way between her lips. Then she thrust downward and swallowed up his manhood nearly to the base. He moaned loudly and began to massage her breasts. She began the rhythmic pumping, slowly at first, then more quickly as the pleasure waves flooded *her* body. For long moments, she rode him like a rodeo rider on a bucking bronco.

Whether it was pure co-incidence or precise timing on her part, he climaxed at the same instant that the *Steadfast* warped out of the Crenshaw's Star system. The vibrations produced by the powerful MOME kicking in added to the sensation of having his penis stimulated by a Pluj who knew exactly what to do. He climaxed violently, lifting her bodily. That action served to bring her to climax, and she moaned in chorus with him.

She disengaged his penis from her slit and lay flat across his now sweat-covered body. While he stroked her back and caressed her buttocks, she peppered his cheeks and lips with tiny kisses.

"I love you so much, Lixu," she whispered.

"I love you too, Anafu," he whispered back. She now regarded him bemusedly.

"Well?"

"Well what?"

"You survived through the warp-out?"

He stared at her in wonder for a second or two, then grunted.

"Oh, yes, I survived. That was the first time I've been through a warp-out and not been sick to my stomach." He kissed her on the nose. "If fucking you is the 'remedy' for preventing that misery, I'm all for it!"

"I am happy to hear that, and at all times I will endeavor to 'cure' you." She smiled broadly. "Ah, Lixu, something hard is pushing against my belly. What do you suppose it is?"

"I believe it's another 'patient' for you."

"Then I must 'examine' it."

*　　　*　　　*

"Be seated, ladies and gentlemen."

Gamma Platoon of Delta Company was already in Classroom #6 when Rodriguez and Ralfo arrived. Sgt. Running Deer, operating on the age-old military principle of "hurry up and wait," had had his troopers in the room and occupying the front row of chairs two kiloseconds prior to the appointed time. When the Warden entered, he called them to attention and brought himself to attention as well. The officers sat down on chairs at the head of the room. Rodriguez scanned the platoon quickly. They had put on fresh uniforms, as he had asked, but somehow they looked as scruffy as before.

The troop brigade aboard a Constabulary patrol vessel consisted of four companies, three combat companies and one support company. Each company was commanded by a Lt. Commander and subdivided into (officially) four platoons; each platoon, commanded by a Senior Lt., had a troop strength of twenty-three – one Senior Sgt., two Junior Sgts., four Corporals, eight Senior Pvts., and eight Junior Pvts.[30] That was the general rule. Gamma Platoon of Delta Company, however, was a clear exception. It had only the one sergeant, two corporals, and three-fourths of the requisite privates. As Sgt. Utumi had so disgustedly pointed out, Gamma Platoon was the collection point for any disciplinary problems in a patrol vessel's troop brigade; these individuals would remain in this unit until the ship completed its current tour of duty at which time they would be either re-assigned to other, less desirable duty stations or mustered out altogether. In the meantime, they performed menial tasks aboard ship, i.e. police calls, KP, latrine duty, and any other similar errands the brigade commander could think of. And they still had their training exercises to perform – which rendered them not only scruffy-looking but also surly to boot.

These were the troopers Warden (L1) Lixu Rodriguez had to work with but, happily, he wouldn't have to work with them for too long – only until such time as he had apprehended and placed under arrest one Dr. Mubutu Weyerhauser. After that, he would release them to whatever fate lay in store for them.

"You have already been informed," he began without preamble, "that the *Steadfast* is in pursuit of a JUR cell hiding on Planetoid 48. What you don't know is that I have a separate mission – the arrest of Dr. Mubutu Weyerhauser, who is wanted for questioning in connection with recent JUR activities and who, by some strange co-incidence, has been rumored to be accompanying the cell on Planetoid 48. The bulk of the trooper brigade will be engaged in rooting out the cell wherever they're hiding. You, on the other hand, will be attached to me and run interference in my search for the suspect. Do you have any questions concerning the mission?"

Sgt. Running Deer was on his feet instantly. His face was as implacable as it was humanly possible to be.

"Sir, will we be permitted to defend ourselves? We know you Wardens have a thing about takin' life."

"As far as I know," the Warden replied, smiling oily, "the rules of engagement haven't been canceled in the last half meg. Yes, Sergeant, if

---

30 A support company, consisting of operators of heavy weapons (rocket launchers, flame throwers, 26-mm Gatling guns, etc.), were mostly sergeants and corporals who had had advanced training. These personnel tended to be elitist due to their (perceived) skills — CMT.

someone shoots at you, you are authorized to shoot back. As much as I – or any other Warden – would like otherwise, my mandate is not your mandate."

A hand shot up, and Rodriguez recognized the lone female in the bunch, a Dunian of Eurasian extraction by the looks of her.

"Will *she* be joinin' us – sir?" the trooper asked, inclining her head in Ralfo's direction.

"She will be, Corporal. She's the only one here who can positively identify Dr. Weyerhauser." He looked at the woman sternly. "And, since she is an officer, she'll be second-in-command of this task force. Do you have a problem with that?"

The question provoked some murmuring amongst the platoon. Running Deer was on his feet again.

"Bort the fraggin' high throttle, you fraggers!" he barked in spacer's slang. "I'll cinter every fraggin' one o' you unfashes!"

The murmuring died down, but looks of resentment remained on most faces, especially on the corporal. The sergeant regarded the Warden apologetically.

"Beggin' yer pardon, sir, but none of us have ever taken orders from a Pluj. It'll take gettin' used to."

"I understand, Sergeant. Hopefully, Lt. Ralfo will not be put in a position to issue orders, but she will if necessary. Any other questions?"

Dead silence filled the classroom.

"Before I forget it, I should point out that I've requested one of the Capellan scouts to be assigned to me as well." That remark inspired more murmuring which Running Deer cut short with a menacing glare. "To assuage your sensibilities concerning Capellans, whoever I get will not be working with you, but with me alone." He smiled briefly. "Just pretend he isn't there. Now, I'm scheduling a special training session in three kilos – full combat gear. Dismissed."

The sergeant called the platoon to attention, saluted the Warden, and marched the troopers out of the room in double-time. Rodriguez leaned back in his chair and sighed heavily.

"Do you expect trouble from them, Lixu?" Ralfo asked softly.

"Possibly. Officers always expect disgruntlement from the ranks under ordinary circumstances. And these are *not* ordinary circumstances. No one likes Wardens, and especially no one likes to take orders from one."

"But no one questioned you. They did *me*!"

"They didn't dare question me directly." He grimaced. "We Wardens have a reputation for ruthlessness, you know – undeserved, of course, but impossible to eradicate from the popular consensus. They'll question me *indirectly* through you. Sgt. Running Deer sent me as subtle a message as he was capable of."

"And if they give you trouble?"

"They'll live to regret it, assuming, of course, their actions don't get them killed first. The JUR aren't as forgiving as Wardens are." He chuckled quietly at his little joke. "Now, let's go see about our Capellan scout."

CHAPTER TWELVE

▼

COUNTER-REVOLUTION

DR. MUBUTU WEYERHAUSER AND HIS new allies found the journey to the escape pods rough going. There was scarcely any part of the MOME sphere which had not suffered any damage, and many parts had been utterly ruined in the effort to extract the MOME. The party had to twist and turn almost every meter of the way; and, more than once, they had been forced to take a detour around wreckage and down an alternate passageway. The Doctor's only consolation was that Mr. Tas knew where he was going; and the detours, while frustrating, were short ones, and they quickly got back on track.

The travel was further slowed down by the necessity of carrying the incapacitated members of the *Astarte* crew. In particular, the one who had had a nervous break-down when he learned what the JUR were planning to do with Planetoid 48 was causing a great deal of difficulty, not the least of which was his continuous moaning and groaning and periodical cries of "we're all going to *die*!" He was passed around to others when those who were carrying him had had enough of his whining.

At one point, on a companionway between the central deck and the one below it, a section of a bulkhead had torn loose and was lying in a heap before them, and there was no way around it. They solved that problem by getting down on hands and knees and crawling backwards across the metal plate. One of the party lost her footing and began sliding down out of control. Her cry of terror echoed and re-echoed throughout the companionway. She crashed into the crewman below her; both slid down and off the plate and tumbled a bit further than that, all the while screaming (her) and cursing (him). The two who were currently in charge of the traumatized man had their own problems, as the fellow refused to crawl but simply curled up into a ball, crying out that "we're all going to *die*!" He finally had to be dragged across the plate, causing one of the draggers to suggest that he be left behind. The Bithan commanding officer stifled that sentiment immediately.

Significantly, the party did encounter one of the JUR members. Why he was still in that location was left to speculation. He was just as surprised as they were; but, due to his training, his reaction was faster than theirs. He unslung his weapon and fired a few rounds, killing one of the crew instantly and wounding another. The Romulan officer now reacted and fired back, chortling with glee as he did so. The Reman collapsed in a bloody heap.

"Ha! Another of the bastards down!"

"Yes," agreed Tas, "but at great cost."

He hurried over to the wounded man. Blood was oozing out of his upper arm.

"Should have thought to bring I a first-aid kit."

"A make-shift tourniquet will do," Dr. Weyerhauser suggested. "A piece of cord, or a strip of cloth."

The Bithan hastily removed his uniform jacket. He firmly gripped the sleeve of his shirt, tore it off, and bound it tightly around the wounded man's arm. The blood stopped flowing.

"Should be first-aid kits in the lifeboats. Hope I that will do this tourniquet until get we there."

"Let's keep moving then."

The party resumed their slow pace but not before gazing solemnly – and in some cases touching gently – their dead co-worker.

Surprisingly, the remainder of the route was free of incident. The Doctor had thought that the gunfire might have attracted attention, but no one – especially the trigger-happy Romulan – spotted any more JUR people. Although no Remans were seen, one was *heard*. Two decks above that where the lifeboats were located, the astrophysicist's concentration on picking his way through twisted wreckage was interrupted by the familiar crackle of his personal vidcom. In the haste to escape, he had forgotten he still carried it. His heart sunk when he heard the measured voice of Major Tshambe. Was the Reman in hot pursuit after all? A feeling of panic began to form.

"Doctor Woyer'auser, where are ye?"

The Doctor debated whether he should reply. If he did, it was quite possible that some of the techs in the cell could triangulate the response and pinpoint his location, to the detriment of both himself and his party. If, on the other hand, he remained silent, the Major might believe that the vidcom had been abandoned, and he definitely would send out some of his people to search for him. It seemed like a no-win situation, unless the escapees could reach the lifeboats in time.

"Answer me, Doctor, and it moight go easier wif ee."

The astrophysicist really did not want to speak with Tshambe, despite the implied threat. He was about to toss the vidcom aside and push on.

"Dinna answer me then, *boyo*. Just listen. We've foond the guards ye murdered – two good men we needed to carry oot the mission. Oi willna toleryte this ootryge, even fum the loikes of ee. We'll 'unt ee doon and deal wife ee accordingly. That's a solemn promise, Doctor."

The panicky feeling intensified, and perspiration dotted the Doctor's forehead. The Major's reputation for ruthlessness was such that even the sound of his voice put fear into the hearts of those JUR members who knew him well. He did not make idle threats.

"Professor?" Tas murmured. "Will do he what promised he?"

"He will. There's no doubt in my mind. It's imperative then that we keep moving, and moving quickly. Our only advantage – I think – is that they don't know where we are."

"Agree I."

The party pushed on, but not as quickly as they would have liked. The damage to the MOME sphere simply mitigated against speed. And the fact that they had both physically and mentally wounded people in tow slowed them down further. Doctor Weyerhauser's feelings of panic continued unabated.

The lower decks, as the party soon discovered with no little dismay, had suffered the most damage, and their progress slowed to a snail's pace. The lower they went, the less head space there was; and, at the next to the lowest deck, the gap between deck and overhead would have given a dwarf claustrophobia. Fortunately, they didn't have to go that far as the lifeboats were on the *second* to the lowest deck. The Doctor peered down the passageway and frowned.

"What do you think, Mr. Tas? Can we access the lifeboats?"

"Will be it difficult, but possible." He pointed in the opposite direction to which the astrophysicist was looking. "Must go we this way."

The party set off in a crouch which after a while began to cramp up muscles. The crewmen now handling the traumatized man had the worst of it; their "passenger" clung to them, and his weight forced them into an even lower crouch. At one point, one of them was heard to mutter, "Can't we leave this nutter behind? He's slowing us down." No one paid him any attention.

It seemed like an age before they reached their destination, a semi-circular launch platform located directly below the point where the sphere was attached to the cylinder which connected it to the rest of the cruise ship. The launch platform contained fifty lifeboats, spherical pods three meters in diameter, arranged in five rows of ten pods each. In the event of an emergency, the pods were automatically activated; all an occupant had to do was to push the launch button, and his pod slid into the launch tube and ejected from the ship. Once the pod was launched, the distress beacon was automatically switched on and sent a continuous signal until its battery ran down – somewhere in the neighborhood of a standard year.[31]

Each pod was just large enough for one occupant. It contained rations, water, and air for two megaseconds. The theory was that, if all systems functioned properly, a rescue operation would not require two megaseconds to be implemented. And, in twenty-plus years, the theory had held up. In the present instance, the theory was going to be severely tested.

The launch platform had been "scrunched" along with everything else and, more often than not, the overhead was pushing against the hulls of the pods. Several members of the party moaned loudly when they assessed the situation (and the traumatized man was reduced to whimpering). Tas ordered the non-injured personnel to inspect all of the pods for actual physical damage. He located the platform's central control panel in order to assess the damage to the circuitry. Dr. Weyerhauser sat down on the deck and worried about their chances for survival.

One by one, the party re-grouped at the control panel. They reported that only twenty pods were free of any physical damage, e.g. cracks in the hull or being jammed between decks and therefore unable to move into the launch tubes. The Bithan added his piece of bad news; of those twenty, only seventeen had functional electronic circuits. The Romulan took it upon himself to state the obvious.

"Only seventeen useable pods, and there's twenty-three of us. That means six people have to stay behind." He regarded the astrophysicist with undisguised malice. "I'd like to 'nominate' one of those six."

Doctor Weyerhauser glared back at the man but did not rise to the challenge. Instead, he turned to the *Astarte* XO.

"Can't you squeeze two people into a pod? Someone will have to attend to the wounded" – he gestured at the whimpering man – "especially him."

"Wish I that were it so, but no, is it impossible. Regret to agree I that must stay six of us." He took a deep breath and let it out slowly. "As ranking officer, will be I one of the six."

The Doctor had once had little use for Bithans in general. Their society

---

31 By legislative decree of the CSC's Grand Assembly, a "standard year" was defined as the passage of fifty megaseconds. Most of the member worlds have accommodated themselves to this additional layer of time-keeping; the exceptions are Romulus and Remus (the former by choice, the latter by peer pressure) on the grounds that the convention is confusing and therefore inefficient – CMT.

was a bit too martial in nature to suit him. True, they made for excellent soldiers, and the ranks of the Constabulary were filled with them; on the other hand, they tended toward bluster and arrogance and empty threats and often spoke before thinking. While they might sacrifice themselves in battle if the situation called for it, few would countenance the concept of self-sacrifice as an ideal. Ideals were for philosophers, Bithans believed, not for soldiers who thought only in terms of accomplished missions.

Tas's statement, therefore, took the Doctor by surprise and caused him to wonder why the man had offered to stay behind and risk certain death at the hands of a vengeful Major Tshambe. Either he was wrong about Bithans in general or this Bithan was an exception to the rule. Whichever was the case, it provoked new respect.

It also provoked a re-thinking of his own position.

Up to this point, his major concern was to get as far away from his former comrades in the JUR as he could. If he could also get off Planetoid 48, so much the better. The so-called "mission" here was a lunatic one, and it was being led by a lunatic. Billions of innocent people – Romulans and Remans alike – would die horribly if Major Tshambe's group succeeded. Neither the Major nor his superiors back home had thought out the implications and consequences of their mad plan; but he, a trained astrophysicist, had grasped them almost immediately. The JUR, hoping for the total destruction of Romulus by which Remus could gain its independence, had not factored into their thinking the delicate balance between the two worlds. Romulus and Remus shared a common orbit; in effect, they were "wedded" to each other, and what befell the one would also befall the other. Destroy Romulus, and the balance would also be destroyed; Remus would become unstable and be either cast into Deep Space or thrown into Rhea Silvia. The JUR would have their "victory," but it would be a Pyrrhic one in the nth degree.

It was imperative, then, that he, Dr. Mubutu Weyerhauser warn the authorities about this mad scheme and assist them in any way possible, even if it meant a long prison term for him on Xix.

What had now changed his thinking was his awareness of survivors aboard what remained of the *Astarte*. If he escaped in one of the pods, he would deny another his/her chance of escape and leave that person to a horrible fate. And he already had more deaths on his head than he cared to think about; he did not want more if he could possibly help it.

And it really wasn't necessary for *him* to warn the authorities any more. If any of the *Astarte* crew managed to escape, they could do the job just as well. The Major might kill him – depending on his mood of the moment – but death was a fitting punishment for a mass murderer, wasn't it? He could atone for his crimes against sentient life by sacrificing himself for another.

"Mr. Tas!" the Bithan junior officer exclaimed. "Cannot be you serious!"

"Am I, Mr. Zam. Am I obliged."

"You'll be killed for sure," the Romulan added.

"Die I here or in Deep Space. Is what the difference?"

"Am I with you then," Lt. Zam declared. "O'Grady?"

The Romulan nodded in acquiescence.

"Aye. We've got guns – and we've got some scores to settle. We'll teach those fraggin' Reemies a thing or two!"

"Thank I you, gentlemen. Is half our problem solved."

"Make that *two-thirds* of your problem, Mr. Tas," Dr. Weyerhauser spoke up. "I'm staying as well."

"Is that very gracious of you, Professor. But why?"

"So that one more of your people can escape. I've got too much blood on my hands already."

"Is this some sort of trick?" O'Grady grumbled. "Are you settin' us up?"

"Hardly. The Major is more likely to shoot me than he will you."

"Please, Mr. O'Grady. Accept the Professor's offer. Has he knowledge of the terrorists, and will help he us to avoid them."

"Do you trust him?"

"Do I."

"All right." The Romulan squinted at the astrophysicist. "You're with us, *Professor*. But you make one funny move, and I'll put a bullet in your head."

The Doctor simply shrugged, then regarded the commanding officer.

"We need two more 'volunteers.'"

"Not so. Is it an unpleasant decision, but must keep I Mr. Corbo with me." He gestured at the traumatized man, still curled up and whimpering. "Is not he fit to operate the lifeboat. As for the sixth person, will hold I a 'lottery.'"

The *Astarte*'s XO gathered up the name plates of all those remaining and placed them in his service cap. He stirred the plates around a bit, shut his eyes, and pulled one plate out of the cap. He then read the name aloud in a sad tone of voice. He had picked the lone female in the group, Stewardess Hernandez. She moaned softly, hugged the person next to her good-bye, and took her place next to Tas.

The Bithan ordered the others into the escape pods and gave them some last-minute instructions concerning their behavior once they were in space. He shook each individual's hand as they boarded the pods and wished them well after the fashion of his own kind. Zam and O'Grady added their own words of farewell. Once the escapees were inside their pods, Tas secured the hatches and stepped over to the control panel. On the panel, the lifeboats still operable were indicated by a blue light; underneath the lights were white buttons. Tas pushed each of those buttons in turn. Instantly, a hum issued from each pod as it powered up, and the first pod fully powered up began to move slowly along its track toward the launch tube. The others followed until all were lined up in the tube. The launch-bay door opened automatically, and the lifeboats disappeared one by one. Their occupants' fate was now left to chance alone.

The Bithan shut down the system and faced Dr. Weyerhauser.

"Do we what now, Professor?"

"We hide, I think. The Major is sure to look for us, and I don't advise standing around until he shows up."

"Personally," O'Grady muttered, "I'd like to wait until he does show up."

"No, you wouldn't. The JUR are trained killers." He grimaced. "I should know. You wouldn't stand a chance against them. Best we keep out of sight until the Constabulary shows up."

"Can hide we here," Tas observed. "Have we enough rations to hold out for three megaseconds?"

"Right," the Romulan opined. "And, if the Reemies have as much trouble accessin' this area as we did, we could pick 'em off, one by one."

The astrophysicist shook his head in dismay. O'Grady seemed to have watched entirely too many tri-D action films[32] to think rationally. What had started out as a simple plan to avoid detection was deteriorating into a siege-mentality plot to protect one's territory against a marauding horde. The JUR in general, and people like Major Tshambe in particular, were not a marauding horde one could decimate with a bit of determination; while the JUR were every bit the homicidal maniacs most sentient beings believed them to be, they preferred to work in the shadows and to strike guerrilla-style. Against such tactics, it would be difficult, if not impossible, for a defensive force to survive.

The present scheme was definitely a case in point. To the casual observer, seizing control of a medium-sized body in space and sending it careening into another body might seem utterly fantastic – a plot out of a sci-fi tri-D film – but the notion fit well into the methodology of the JUR. In the first

---

32   The lion's share of these popular films – popular especially among humans who had no first-hand knowledge of the actual events – concerned highly romanticized depictions of battles during the War of the Eight Suns. Usually, the plots revolved around a heroic group of humans fending off attacks by the Alliance forces (which included wholly unrealistic suicidal attacks by Capellans). The reality, however, was that few of these encounters possessed the happy endings the tri-D writers and producers had incorporated into their films – CMT.

place, the scheme was so unorthodox as to be dismissed out of hand by most rational beings. That gave the terrorists an enhanced element of surprise; since no one expected this sort of attack, it would create the maximum amount of terror and devastation. In the second place, operating obliquely added to the prospect of catching the target off guard. Highjacking a cruise ship full of rich passengers would, by normal thinking, be the prelude to multiple demands for ransom, both for the ship and for the passengers, followed by the standard response to a hostage situation. If, however, ransom were not the objective – not even a consideration, for that matter – then all concerned would waste their time and resources engaging in fruitless actions while the terrorists carried out their real plan of attack.

Despite his threat to hunt down the escapees and deal with them accordingly, Major Tshambe was a good soldier in the JUR and thus had no intention of wasting his time and resources on meaningless activities. The *Astarte*, and all aboard her, had been expendable from the start; whether passengers and crew died during the initial attack or later on was of no concern to him. While he might have wanted to get his hands on his wayward ex-member and punish *him* for causing mischief, the mission came first. The escapees would die soon enough – when Planetoid 48 smashed into Romulus.

Dr. Weyerhauser could picture in his mind's eye O'Grady and Zam setting up an ambush which would never happen. What would they do if, after kiloseconds of waiting, the expected pursuit never materialized? Take the fight to the enemy, despite any advice against such action? The Doctor had already expressed his reservations about the Romulan's increasing belligerence. If the armed pair wanted to commit suicide, he wasn't going to prevent them. He intended to hide until the Constabulary answered any distress call and came to the rescue.

He was about to ask Tas where the best hiding place was when the voice of Major Tshambe issued from his vidcom (which he still hadn't bothered to throw away).

"Doctor, are ye still wif us? If ye are, listen up, *boyo*. Oi've just received word fum our ship that some o' the loifeboats 'ave been launched. Troyin' to escype, are ye? Well, it willna do ee na good. Oi'm aboot to order me people to shoot 'em. If ye're aboard one of 'em, Doctor, then it's good-boy to ee."

The astrophysicist jabbed the "send" button.

"Major!" he rasped. "Haven't you killed enough people already? It's *me* you really want. Let those people go, and I'll – I'll surrender myself to you."

Dead silence answered him.

"Major Tshambe, respond, please!"

Still there was no response. The Doctor shook his head sadly. This was his fault, if he cared to look at the situation objectively. He was the one who had recommended the surviving crew escape their imprisonment. He was the one who had inquired about the lifeboats. He was the one who had offered to distract the guards so that they could be overpowered. Now he had more blood on his hands.

The other escapees had been watching him carefully as he attempted to reason with the JUR leader, and their reactions were decidedly different. Tas and Hernandez displayed extreme alarm, while O'Grady and Zam gnashed their teeth in rage. The traumatized man resumed his litany of "we're all going to *die!*"

"That murdering bastard!" the Romulan spat out. "That sinks it. I'm not goin' to wait around while that fragger looks for us. I'm goin' to look for *him* and make him pay." He turned to his companion. "You with me, Zam?" The other nodded. "Ok, we're off."

"Don't be a fool, man!" the astrophysicist argued. "You won't last ten seconds against that bunch."

"Zam, O'Grady," Tas pleaded, "listen you to the Professor. Are committing you suicide."

"Then we'll take as many of 'em as we can. Sorry, Mr. Tas, but I can't stand around and do nothing" – he raised his weapon – "not while I've got this. Let's go, Zam."

The armed pair disappeared down the passageway which had brought them to the launch bay. The other escapees watched them helplessly.

"Shall do we what now, Professor?"

"We hide, as we planned. That's all we can do."

"Very well. Know I the perfect place. Follow you me."

*　　*　　*

The Soldier approaches the cross-passageway cautiously, hugging the bulkhead. A half meter from the intersection, she halts, cranes her neck, and peeps around the corner.

The cross-passageway is empty in both directions. At the far end, however, she thinks she spots a shadow on the bulkhead. It passes quickly, and she is unable to determine whether it was the Enemy lying in wait or simply a trick of the lighting. She remembers her sergeant's admonishment: "Don't get cocky! Stay alert! Assume that danger is all around you!"

She signals her comrades behind her to advance to her position. Even as they do so, she slips around the corner and begins to ease her way toward the far end where she thought she saw a shadow.

The mission has been rather straightforward so far. The Constabulary, alerted to pirate activity in this sector of Deep Space, has tracked down the suspected vessel and boarded it. One company of troopers has been dispatched forward and a second aft. Strangely, the pirates have offered no resistance, but neither have they surrendered. Their ship is wholly quiescent. There is nothing to do but search it meter by meter and be alert to ambushes from every nook and cranny.

The Soldier, a corporal in the platoon in the aft section of the vessel, has taken the point. Once or twice, she has heard gunfire issuing from the forward end and wondered about the situation there. Quickly, she has put the thought out of her head; she does not need to be distracted from her own mission. The Enemy could be right next to her for all she knows.

Slowly, she creeps along. Suddenly, one of the hatches she had just passed slides open with a whoosh. Instinctively, she drops to the deck and twists herself around. Thankfully, she has reacted in time. A hail of bullets passes through the space she had just vacated. She could swear she has heard each bullet as it whizzed by her.

Now, she spots the shooter. He is a nondescript humanoid of indeterminate origin, a brutish hulk wearing dirty and wrinkled clothing. He has piggish eyes which fairly radiate hatred. He grits his teeth in feral fashion as he swings his weapon toward his foe to fire again.

The Soldier brings her assault rifle to bear and lets loose a burst of fire of her own. The bullets strike the Enemy full in the chest. He grunts in pain, staggers backward through the hatch, and collapses to the deck as pinkish blood oozes from half a dozen wounds. The Soldier jumps to her feet and advances toward the hatch.

Another burst of gunfire forces her aside. How many are in this compartment is unknown, but she has little time to take a tally. She gropes for a thermal grenade attached to her equipment belt, presses the activating stud, counts to three, and tosses it into the compartment. The grenade, filled with magmatite,[33] explodes in a blinding flash of light. She can feel its tremendous heat even through her combat armor. She hears two distinct screams of terror as the magmatite incinerates the compartment's contents.

All is silent again. The Soldier doubts that anyone is left alive in the compartment to trouble her. She signals to her unit to advance and continues her slow, methodic pace down the passageway.

She rounds the corner at the end of the passageway and is instantly greeted by a group of six of the Enemy. She fires her weapon in a sweeping motion but

---

33 Magmatite is yet another product from the chemical "factory" known as Eka-xan, the home world of the Ekath. They had been developing it for use in the War of the Eight Suns when that conflict was unexpectedly brought to a close by the Aldebaranians. The chemical compound is now used exclusively by the Constabulary, principally as a means to clear obstructions – CMT.

fails to drop any of them. Now she notices that they are wearing the same sort of armor she is. Silently, she curses her bad luck even as she ducks back around the corner, barely escaping a heavy fusillade of fire from the sextet. She retreats in the direction from which she came, all the while signaling her unit to retreat as well. When she reaches the hatch through which she had thrown the thermal grenade, she enters the burned-out compartment and hugs the bulkhead.

The Enemy passes by. The Soldier steps out into the passageway and tosses a concussion grenade at their feet. It explodes with a deafening roar, and the sextet topples like ten-pins. She leaves them for the rest of the unit to deal with and resumes her scouting mission.

She rounds the corner again and spies a single Enemy. She raises her assault rifle to fire, but the other ducks behind an air duct and tosses a grenade in her direction. She is momentarily confused by the sight of the grenade, and her hesitation costs her her life. The grenade explodes, and darkness falls.

*   *   *

"*Damn!*" Corporal Chen swore as she tore the VR helmet off her head. "Where the frag did that grenade come from? I've run this program a dozen times, and there wasn't no fraggin' grenade before."

"That's because I added it to the program before you began the exercise," Warden Rodriguez replied softly. He was sitting in a chair at the side of the training area and had just removed his own VR helmet. "I wanted an element of surprise in the mix."

The non-com rounded on the speaker and was about to give him her two carats' worth of suggestions as to what he could do with his "element of surprise" when she realized who was speaking. She immediately bit her tongue and came to attention.

"Aye, sir. Thank you, sir."

Rodriguez rose from the chair and walked slowly toward her. She tensed.

"We'll soon be dealing with the JUR, Corporal. They're tricky bastards, not predictable like your run-of-the-mill pirates. Therefore, you should always expect the unexpected." He turned toward Sgt. Running Deer, who had also been monitoring Corporal Chen's progress (or lack thereof). "I've created a special program for all of the platoon to run. It's chock full of surprises, and I don't expect any of you to survive past the first five minutes. But it should give you an idea of what you'll be up against once we reach Planetoid 48."

"Aye, sir," the sergeant murmured. "I'll get my people hooked up right away."

The Warden returned to his chair and watched bemusedly as Gamma

Platoon slipped on their VR helmets amidst a smattering of grumbling and imprecations. He didn't care what they thought of him personally or professionally, of course, so long as they did what he wanted them to do. The program he had created was intended to weed out the slackers from the real soldiers. And, although this unit consisted of misfits, some were perhaps less so than others; this program would tell him who they were and if they could be of use to him.

On an impulse, he smiled to himself. How pleasant it was to be on the other end of the "chain of command." At the Academy, he and his fellow cadets had been constantly challenged to improve their performances; the mentors had been relentless in drilling them, day in and day out, and weeding out the chaff from the straw, so to speak. They looked continuously for the ones who had what it took to be a Warden, a keeper of the peace; every exercise, every lesson plan and lecture, and every admonition (private and public) had been designed to serve that purpose, and the mentors were experts in the weeding process. His own class had started out with seventy-five applicants. Only twenty had graduated, some (like himself) with special honors.

He remembered with pride – although Master Fresh would have provided him with a half a kilosecond's worth of sharp commentary on pride if he recognized it in a cadet – a meeting he had had with his mentor during his final year. He had braced himself mentally for the expected lecture on whatever it was Master Fresh was finding fault with and had gone through a litany of issues which might be the subject matter. Imagine his surprise, then, when he found himself being praised!

"Pupil," Master Fresh had said to him, not in his usual scolding manner but in a gentle voice which he had seldom heard during his time at the Academy, "it has come to my attention that you have done a wonderful thing."

"I have? Explain, Master."

"You have taken aside one of your fellow pupils and corrected his behavior. At last, you are showing some initiative."

Rodriguez had had to wrack his brain to remember the incident his mentor was referring to, but there had been many times when he gave advice to younger cadets on how to solve a problem or improve his/her techniques. And it wouldn't do to tell his mentor that he had "shown initiative" more than once. In the first place, boasting was as much discouraged as any other rude behavior; and, in the second place, no one argued with/contradicted an Aldebaranian and came away with a whole skin.

"Thank you, Master. I always endeavor to emulate your example. But, lack-wit that I am, I do not recall the incident to which you refer."

"Do you not? It was only yesterday. You instructed Cadet Klackamorg on his appearance while in class."

"Ah, now I remember. But, Master, that was such a trivial matter. I could hardly have been seen to show initiative. Initiative involves hard decisions, does it not?"

"Not so, pupil. Initiative involves *all* decisions, large and small. And, when you make the correct decision, according to the circumstances, you have shown initiative."

"I...see. Thank you for pointing this out to me, Master."

And now the pupil was the master. He would whip this rag-tag bunch into a reasonable facsimile of a fighting unit even if it killed them. For, if they didn't learn to act as a cohesive force, they surely would die, each and every one of them.

And so he watched intently as Gamma Platoon ran his special program through the VR helmets. Especially, he noted the facial expressions they registered as they encountered his "surprises"; for the most part, these expressions reflected agony, distress, and shock as unimaginable images filled and paralyzed their minds. On a piece of paper containing the names of the members of the platoon, he recorded how long it took before each individual either was "killed" or, more likely, ripped off his/her helmet in utter horror. The average end time was just under a hundred and fifty seconds, and one person never made it past fifty seconds. Three – including Sgt. Running Deer – lasted between one hundred and fifty and two hundred seconds, and one – Corporal Chen, who seemed to have taken his advice to heart – managed to hold out for two hundred and twenty-five seconds. He had no intention of informing any of them by how much they had failed — no use in depressing them any further than they already were. Rather, he'd simply have them run the program again. Practice made perfect, as the ancient Dunian saying went.

After he had instructed them to reflect on what they had experienced and to repeat the exercise, he became cognizant of Sgt. Utumi's presence. The Capellan showed mild annoyance, not at him, however, but at his "command."

"Yes, Sergeant?"

"Commander Rux me to you have order to report."

"I asked him to provide me with an Alkonu scout – the best man."

"*I* the 'best man' to be," the warrior declared indignantly. "I the sergeant to be, aye?"

"So you are. If the choice had been left to me, I would have chosen you myself. But, how did you convince the Commander to choose you?"

The Capellan puckered his lips.

"I my squad for this duty did order to volunteer. Commander Rux so much eagerness pleased did not be to see. Thus, he the one did choose who no eagerness did show, and I that one did be."

"Ha-ha. Reverse psychology. Very good, Sergeant, and welcome to my 'command.' Now, if you wouldn't mind, I'd like you to join the others in running the program I've created."

Utumi complied and cocked his head in surprise as the program commenced. He quickly recovered and settled in with a grim look on his face. Significantly, he lasted nearly three hundred seconds, such was the quality of his Alkon training. Upon removing his helmet, he peered at the Warden and puckered slightly.

"You several Alkon tactics have study, Rodri-go. I them immediately did recognize. Other tactics I did not."

"Some of those tactics derive from an ancient Dunian warrior's cult which called itself the 'Ninja.' A few of the Ninjas are still around, but they exist as little more than a gentleman's club. Other tactics I learned from the Urrju, and only Kum'halla knows where *they* picked them up."

"The program…most rigorous to be. An excellent one to have, Rodri-go. I my squad with it will test."

"I'd like to join you, if I may."

You most welcome will be. Now, I the program again will run."

Rodriguez left the training area and headed to the Bridge in order to check on the *Steadfast*'s position. Upon arriving, he spotted Commander Krishnamurthy in the command chair. Captain Halvarson was nowhere to be seen. This fact did not provoke any curiosity on the Warden's part; while it was standard procedure for the Ship's Master to be on the Bridge during any transition activity, that individual could be attending to any of several dozen matters while the MOME was re-energizing.

MOME's required a great deal of energy in order to produce their space-warping capabilities. How much energy depended upon the distance to be transited; ideally, an MOME could move its vessel 100 light-years per warp-out, but more often than not, it was in the 60-70 light-year range. But, regardless of the distance, all of the built-up energy was discharged at once, and the MOME had to be re-energized to achieve additional warp-outs. Most re-energizing required ten kiloseconds. In the meantime, the ship's crew marked time by checking and re-checking all functions for maximum efficiency.

The Warden strode over to the Display and studied the image. He noted with some wryness that the *Steadfast* was only thirty light-years from Aldebaran. What was Master Fresh doing at this particular moment? Was he brow-beating some hapless cadet?

May Kum'halla guide you, brother/sister, he whispered.

From this position in Deep Space, he estimated that two more warp-outs would be required before they arrived at the Rhea Silvia system. He hoped they would be in time to prevent the JUR from putting their cataclysmic scheme into action. Given the head-start the terrorists had plus the delays occasioned by trying to locate them, it might be a near thing to intercept Planetoid 48. What the *Steadfast* could do once the runaway was intercepted remained in the realm of speculation. His mission was still the simpler one: apprehend Dr. Mubutu Weyerhauser and hold him for interrogation. Captain Halvarson had the unenviable task of dealing with Weyerhauser's confederates and preventing calamity. The sooner he sounded out the Captain about their mutual problem, the better.

As if on cue, Halvarson strolled onto the Bridge. Krishnamurthy quickly vacated the command chair and took her own seat. The Captain sat down and conferred with her. Only when he had been updated did he deign to acknowledge Rodriguez's presence.

"Are you here for a reason, Leftenant?" he murmured. "Or are you just sightseeing?"

"A little of both, actually. I'm checking on our position, first of all. Then, I'm requesting a conference with you and the senior staff."

"Concerning?"

"Concerning the strategy we'll need to stop Planetoid 48 in its tracks."

"And I suppose you have some ideas on that subject?"

"It may surprise you, Captain, but, no, I don't. If I had, I wouldn't need to call a conference. I'd simply lay out my plan to you directly."

"I see. Thank you for your consideration, Leftenant. After our next warp-out then?"

Rodriguez nodded in agreement and ignored the other's sarcasm. After this mission had been concluded, he might consider a transfer to another ship. He saw no reason why he should take the New Swiss's abuse any longer than necessary.

When Halvarson signaled the count-down to warp-out, the Warden departed the Bridge immediately. He hoped Anafu was in her quarters.

CHAPTER THIRTEEN

▼

FIELD OF BATTLE

THE FIRST HUMANS TO VISIT the Rhea Silvia system recognized its uniqueness immediately. And the more they saw, the more unique they realized it was.

Fortunately for humankind, it was also hospitable.

The first point of uniqueness was an asteroid belt which encircled the entire system like a stone wall. Old Sol possessed an asteroid belt as well, but that feature served as a "partition" between the inner, warmer planets and the outer, colder ones. Rhea Silvia's asteroid field had the added quality – as later explorers were to discover, many to their peril — of being a gravitational minefield; the ebb and flow of gravitic forces pushed and pulled against each other (and against any unwary traveler who passed through it) and created an infinity of collisions. Those first explorers had bypassed the belt and so did not include a warning in their log to beware this part of the star system.

The second point of uniqueness was the presence of just four planets in the system – two warm inner ones and two cold outer ones. The inner planets were Dunian in nature while the outer ones were Jovian. Old Sol had never had such a perfect balance.

Old Sol never had the third point of uniqueness either: two planets which shared the same orbit. To say that the original explorers were amazed by the sight was to understate the matter by a factor of ten. By far the greater number of photographs taken were of this delicately balanced pair of near-identical worlds, and each member of the crew filled several pages of his/her personal log describing the wonder of it all. The lone astrophysicist in the team declared that, in his considered opinion, the "twins" had been created at the same time, "two gouts of fiery matter spewed out by their parent star at the same velocity and parked side by side (figuratively speaking) for all of Eternity." Further surprises awaited the humans.

The discovery of Rhea Silvia and her children by humankind might not have occurred – and the course of galactic history subsequently changed enormously – had it not been for an instance of serendipity. Following the conflict on Dunia which had rendered its northern hemisphere virtually uninhabitable and pushed the southern hemisphere to center stage, humans turned their eyes outward to locate new worlds on which to live and new sources of raw materials to exploit. The first explorers were mandated to search for G-class, i.e. yellow, suns which might have Dunian-type planets. They were not advised that such star systems were few and far between. Only desperation drove them on, and frustration was their major reward.

The *DSS Armstrong* actually did discover such a sun in the region of Canopus [*Alpha Carinae on Dunian star charts – CC*]. But the single planet which orbited it was a virtual house of horrors; a global rain-forest, it destroyed at will, and several of the crew suffered horrible deaths before the exploration was called off.[34] Dejectedly, the crew began the long trip home. Then the serendipitous moment occurred. One of the team, in an attempt to stave off boredom on his watch, sought to create new "constellations" in the star field through which the *Armstrong* was passing. As he did so, he spotted an F8-class star far to port whose "wobbly" motion suggested a gravitational "tug-of-war," i.e. it possessed planets. He then activated the ship's electron telescope and spied a four-planet system, including two Dunian-sized worlds.

While an F-class star is generally hotter and white in color, F8's are at the "cool" end of the temperature range and thus exhibit a yellowish tinge. That was all that was needed to alter the *Armstrong*'s course to take a closer look. And, as their lone astrophysicist effectively argued, the two inner worlds occupied what the ancient Dunian biochemist Isaac Asimov termed an "ecosphere" – a zone in which a planet was neither too close to (too hot) nor too distant from (too cold) its parent, but just right for the pre-conditions for Life to exist – for an F8's temperature.

They established orbit first around the world which eventually became Romulus and began an extensive, detailed study of its properties. They sent robotic probes to sample the atmosphere and to collect soil from the surface. They measured radiation levels, the strength and density of the magnetic field, the geological stability of various terrains, the concentrations of toxic

---

34 The exobiologist, Dr. Horace Chan, produced a thoroughly detailed study of the planet we now call "Amazon," based on both official reports and private diaries, entitled (somewhat luridly) *Death Stalked the Jungle* (University of New Nairobi Press, 51 A.R.). While later works exist, they owe their existence to Dr. Chan's scholarship – CMT.

elements in the soil, air, and water, and the mineral content of selected sites. And, when they had collected enough raw data to fill a small library, they set about to analyze the data. What stood out was the fact that there was very little vegetation anywhere on the planet (which explained the paucity of animal life). The semi-arid nature of this world would have to be terraformed if humans hoped to live on it. On the other hand, they were astounded by the presence of a wide variety of minerals; it was a miner's paradise and an answer to the depleted resources of Dunia.

They then traveled to the "twin" planet – the future Remus – which was about 500 kilometers less in diameter. They soon discovered the one oddity of this world, its one contribution to the third point of uniqueness of the star system: a reverse axial rotation. The astrophysicist opined that, when the two masses of material were shot out of the star, they acted like two billiard balls being hit at the same time; that is to say, the impact of "birth" set them off in opposite directions with opposing spins, one "clockwise," the other "counter-clockwise." She concluded that, if humans were to inhabit this planet, they would have to adjust to the idea that their sun would rise and set in directions opposite to those they had been accustomed to on Dunia.

The explorers found plenty of reasons for humans to establish themselves on this world. Where the first world lacked sufficient vegetation to sustain Life, the second possessed a super-abundance of it. Lush meadows, spectacular forests, a host of species of flowers and shrubs and what biochemically appeared to be fruits, tubers, edible roots, berries, and nuts – samples of everything were collected from every part of the planet and thoroughly analyzed. Some of the team were moved to taste the alleged foodstuffs, and these unofficial tests produced a range of reactions, from outright distaste to extreme pleasure. What especially pleased the crew was the fact that seeds brought from the home world for the purpose of ascertaining the viability of the soil germinated very quickly and became mature plants in only half the time required on Dunia. In short, this world was a farmer's paradise.

The explorers would like to have landed on either planet to conduct a physical inspection. But reasons of fuel consumption prevented them, because they needed sufficient reserves to return home safely. And so, they departed with their glowing reports and left the physical exploration to others.

The rest, as the ancients had said time and again, was history.

Fast forward a hundred and fifty years (Dunian reckoning):

There were two significant differences between the Rhea Silvia system those long-ago explorers had set their eyes on and that of the time of the pursuit of Planetoid 48. The first was the five-kilometer-in-diameter MOME which circumnavigated the outer limits of the system – Relay Station #1, the very first machine emplaced to transport ships throughout Deep Space in a fraction of the time it might otherwise have taken, even at relativistic velocities. The second was the tremendous amount of vehicular traffic between Romulus and Remus and between the Twins and RS 1; the comings and goings between two dozen different inhabited worlds rivaled, and often surpassed, those which had occurred in the days of sailing ships on Dunia. From the vantage point of the outer limits, this traffic appeared only as moving blips on a vidscreen, but it was mind-boggling all the same. A century and a half of human desire had made all the difference.

Warden (L1) Lixu Rodriguez watched those blips on the vidscreen at the Sensors console. He could have peered over Captain Halvarson's shoulder and seen the same sight on the Command vidscreen, but he was all too cognizant that the New Swiss did not care to have anyone – especially a Warden – peering over his shoulder on the grounds that the act made him look unprofessional. Instead, Rodriguez had found a relatively friendly face in Sr. Lt. H'lun and peered over *her* shoulder.

The *Steadfast*, after its final warp-out, lay off the Rhea Silvia system at a distance of 100,000 kilometers from Romulus's north pole. To port blazed the star at a mean temperature of 6300 C; to starboard, and more distantly, hunkered frozen Aeneas and its three moons. The fourth planet of the system, Numitor (with a single satellite), was on the far side of Rhea Silvia. From this vantage point above the plane of the ecliptic, the Constabulary ship could monitor virtually all traffic coming from or going to Romulus/Remus. It was, of course, more interested in a certain type of "incoming traffic" which needed to be 're-routed."

The *Steadfast* had made good time and arrived at Rhea Silvia ahead of Planetoid 48. Romulus was still intact, and normal traffic had not been disrupted by a cataclysmic event. The Warden believed that the ship's more efficient crew had given them the edge over a band of rank amateurs in propulsive systems; the JUR had had to rely on shorter warp-outs in order to compensate for their lack of expertise. Still, the time differential could not be very great, and the Captain needed to put a defensive screen in place very shortly.

As Rodriguez was monitoring the Blue Zone vidscreen, he was startled to see the images he had been studying abruptly replaced by Halvarson's face.

"I'm calling a 'war council' in Conference Room A in two kilos," the Captain announced. "I'm sure you'll want to join us."

"Absolutely. Thank you, Captain."

Was it his imagination, or had Halvarson actually spoken to him with a modicum of respect? He had no time to ponder the question, however. He had first to report to Station Chief Crowder that the *Steadfast* was now awaiting the arrival of Planetoid 48. He entered a special coded sequence into the vidscreen's circuitry, secured the link to the Warden section in the Secretariat on Romulus, and followed through with the sequence to Crowder's direct line. This was standard operating procedure when using non-Service equipment; it prevented any "tattle-tale" from eavesdropping on the conversation.

Warden (L4) Crowder was his usual cheerful self when the connection was completed. Rodriguez marveled at his superior's equanimity, given that the post of Station Chief entailed a great many stressful situations (the current one, for example). Perhaps he had been born cheerful. Whatever the cause, it didn't seem natural, but he for one wasn't about to wish that the older man look a little less cheerful. Seeing a smiling face on a trustworthy individual tended to put him at ease.

"The peace of Kum'halla be with you, Station Chief Crowder," the L1 began formally.

"The peace of Kum'halla be with you, L1 Rodriguez," came the standard response. Then: "You seem full of yourself, Rodriguez. I suspect that Lt. Ralfo has been taking good care of you."

The younger man blushed. Was Crowder taking a stab in the dark concerning his relationship with Anafu? Or was he such an open book, through either his expression or his posture? And what business was it of the L4's anyway what sort of relationships he cultivated? Barring any dereliction of duty, there wasn't any specific regulation banning liaisons with whomever one chose. He hoped the Chief was not the gossipy type.

"Sorry, Lixu. I didn't mean to put you on the spot. You just seemed… different from the last time I saw you, and I thought — Ah, well, never mind what I thought. Report."

"Thank you, sir." Tersely, Rodriguez updated the other on the Planetoid 48 affair, giving special emphasis on Captain Halvarson's plan of attack. "One supposes," he added, "that the strategy is standard for dealing with ordinary threats."

"And you don't think this is an ordinary threat?"

"How could anyone think otherwise, sir? The JUR's objective is horrendous in the extreme. Besides, as you well know, dealing with the JUR is far from dealing with pirates and free-booters."

"What would you suggest as a proper strategy then?"

The question rocked the younger man back on his heels. L1's were rarely, if ever, asked such a question. It was not for junior staff to devise policy or to advise senior staff in either the Warden Service or the Constabulary High Command on matters of strategy. Only when a Warden achieved L3 status would (s)he be invited to participate in decision-making. So, why was Crowder bothering to get *his* opinion on the matter at hand? Rodriguez took a deep breath and let it out slowly.

"Begging your pardon, sir, it's not for me to say. I'm not in any position to give advice."

"Who is then?"

"Sir?"

The Station Chief fixed him with a steely glare. Gone was the bemusement of a while ago.

"You've said that this is no ordinary threat. I fully agree. Therefore, I think we can dispense with the usual protocol. I'm asking you for your opinion, L1 Rodriguez. You *do* have an opinion, don't you?"

"Yes, sir, I do."

"Fine. That's what you'll provide Halvarson – whether he asks for it or not. The reason we put Wardens on Constabulary ships in the first place is to make sure Ship's Masters co-operate in the discharging of a Warden's duty, no matter the situation. If you've forgotten that point, I suggest you re-read Article Five, Section Five, paragraph four of the Convention of Aldebaran.[35] Do I make myself clear?"

"Yes, sir," the younger man replied stiffly. "Would you like to know what my opinion is as well?"

"That goes without saying. But send it to me through the *aaxyboxr*. We want to keep this exchange 'in-house.'" Crowder broke out in another wide grin. "OK, son. I'm through haranguing you. You're doing a good job so far. Keep it up. The peace of Kum'halla be with you, L1 Rodriguez."

"Thank you, sir. The peace of Kum'halla be with you."

*   *   *

If the senior staff of the *Steadfast* could have been more on edge, they might have been able to move the ship without the use of the MOME. Each of them in his/her own fashion exhibited a high level of nervous energy as the Captain updated them on the current situation and asked for their evaluations of the ship's readiness. Commander Rux, perhaps the most volatile of the group, kept brushing his crest when he was not speaking (which was infrequent). Lt. Commander von Lichtenberg picked lint (imaginary or otherwise) from her uniform. Lt. Commander Tuva ground his teeth so much that his jaw began to ache. And Lt. Commander O-bu, the Uhaad chief of

---

35 This part of the Convention deals with the powers of the Warden Service and was perhaps the most contentious part the signatories had to accept. None of the member worlds wanted to give anyone such authority over them on the grounds that said authority would violate their planetary sovereignty. But the Aldebaranians held firm on this point, accepting only an amendment which would require a Warden to submit to a review board if any charges of misconduct were filed against him/her – CMT.

Red Zone, smacked her lips continuously, a habit which annoyed those on either side of her and added to their own nervousness.

Perhaps the only persons in the conference room who did not exhibit any nervous energy were Chief Engineer Quintus Ling (who seemed bored by the proceedings), Commander Krishnamurthy, and Warden Rodriguez. The XO sat perfectly still in her seat and stared straight ahead at nothing in particular. Some might have said that her posture was a sign of edginess in itself, that the Commander dared not to move a muscle lest she draw undue attention to herself and deprive Captain Halvarson of the attention he required to get through a difficult task. As for the Warden, he had learned long ago how to relax, mentally as well as physically, and he was now in a semi-meditative state. But only semi-meditative, for his mind was mulling over what he needed to say if and when Halvarson called on him for his input.

It was a human tendency often to keep one's thoughts to oneself, to hesitate to discuss one's doubts and fears, and to enter into a state of denial when pressed. This was the racial baggage that Lixu Rodriguez had dragged along with him to the Academy. And, under close examination by one or another of the Aldebaranians, he had had to discard this baggage, one ugly piece after another. It hadn't been easy either; a half million years of social conditioning was a thing not to be undone overnight. It may be fairly said that he was still not one hundred per cent free of his baggage – thus the constant need for meditation.

Master Fresh had lectured him once at length on this need to meditate on a daily basis. Since the Aldebaranians had uncannily deduced the human condition after only a few years of contact, they knew that the human mind required a rigorous program of disciplinary exercises until such time as it became second nature; without such a program, human Wardens would surely fall back into haphazard modes of thinking, going off on tangents, and not focusing fully on the matter at hand. Rodriguez could remember all of the times he had let his mind free-associate, only to be brought back to the here-and-now by a thump on the chest and Master Fresh's strident question, "Where are you now, lack-wit?"

And so he meditated and focused and meditated some more. It became easier as time passed, but not quite yet automatic. He still had some distance to go.

The reports from the senior staff droned on and on. And then there was silence – a long, inexplicable silence. The Warden opened his eyes, half-expecting to be the only person left in the conference room. What he saw caused him no little embarrassment: all eyes were on him. The Captain was regarding him with a deep frown, and the rest with varying degrees of bemusement or disgust. He attempted a broad smile.

"My turn?"

"If you wouldn't mind, Leftenant," Halvarson replied testily. "Afterwards, you may continue your…communing."

"Not at all, Captain. I've been thinking about putting an alternative plan on the table."

"An alternative plan? Alternative to what?"

"Alternative to nearly every aspect of the SOP which you employ in apprehending pirates. We are not dealing with ordinary criminals here but with a highly-organized, well-disciplined, tenacious foe."

"We're well aware of who we're dealing with, Leftenant. What do you suggest?"

"First of all, a frontal assault is counter-productive. We have to take the JUR by surprise; otherwise, they will take measures which will put their hostages at risk."

"Assuming they have hostages."

"We have to assume that they do. And that means–"

The Warden was cut off by a chime from the vidscreen behind the Captain's chair. Halvarson activated it and swiveled just as the image of Sr. Lt. H'lun appeared on it.

"Yes, Leftenant?"

"Sir, Planetoid 48 haves comed within sensor range."

This announcement elicited a few gasps from some of the staff and exchanged looks of concern from others.

"Do you have positive identification?"

"Aye, sir. We compared the characteristics of the newcomer with knowed data. It bees the rogue."

"Thank you, Leftenant." The Captain pressed the "general alert" button on his console. "All hands, this is the Captain. Planetoid 48 has been sighted. We are now on Level Four alert." He then pressed the red button. Sr. Lt. Colon's face appeared on the vidscreen. "Lt. Colon, plot a course that will take us within half a light-year of Planetoid 48 – and directly between it and Romulus."

"Aye, sir. Plotting now."

Halvarson eyed his senior officers carefully and noted the look of frustration on the Warden's face.

"Sorry, Leftenant. Whatever you had in mind will have to be put on hold for the time being. To your stations, people!"

Wardens had no stations, per se, since, technically, they were only attached to a given ship's crew. Therefore, they were free to wander about and busy themselves however they could until such time as they were required to perform their main functions, i.e. placing criminal suspects under arrest and transporting them to a judicial venue. No one interfered with a Warden in the performance of his/her duty; interference invited an additional arrest and a visit to Xix, the Central Spiral Collective's sole penal facility. Neither did anyone engage a Warden during his/her "free" time; such actions netted one, at best, a short but polite exchange of greetings and, at worst, a short and curious stare.

Having nowhere to go under the circumstances and not wanting to endure a warp-out in a vertical position, Rodriguez headed toward his quarters. He thought briefly of returning to Lt. Ralfo's quarters where he could ride out the warp-out in a very pleasant fashion. Undoubtedly, she would have accommodated him without hesitation. But, strangely, he was not in the mood for pleasant *tete-a-tetes* at the moment. He had other things on his mind, not the least of which was the expected frontal assault on Planetoid 48. He hoped that, after warp-out, he could have an opportunity to present his plan to Captain Halvarson and to have it given serious consideration, but he was not overly optimistic. The Captain, having lost the runaway twice already, was going to do whatever he thought necessary to seize it, once and for all.

And that way, in the Warden's humble opinion, would be disastrous for all concerned.

*   *   *

The first Chief Constable of the Central Spiral Collective Constabulary had been a very unlikely choice. And, if humans had had their way in the choosing, they would have chosen someone less...disreputable.

The first Chief was a Murchison, and he was in fact Thomas Edison Murchison IV, a.k.a. the "Fourth Murchison," and he had two immediate strikes against him. The first strike was that he was a Murchison, a fact which struck in the craws of both Romulans and Remans, who had suffered (they claimed) from the machinations of the Third Murchison. The Twins had been adamantly opposed to the appointment of the son of their hated tormentor; but, because they were opposed, the other sentient races in the central spiral favored the appointment, and so the humans' wishes were swept aside (which also stuck in their craws).

The second strike against the Fourth was the fact that he was the very epitome of what the Constabulary was supposed to combat, i.e. the criminal element operating in Deep Space. Although he had been born with a platinum spoon in his mouth, he became disenchanted with the business practices of his father, aunts and uncles, siblings and cousins, and various in-laws; and, shortly after his graduation from college, he began associating with the "rough crowd" and not tending to the family business. In time, he gravitated toward the "career" of soldier-of-fortune, cruising Deep Space in a specially built craft, the *Skylark*, with a hand-picked crew. Many considered him, at best, a mercenary and, at worst, a pirate, but no one could catch him to bring him to justice.[36]

When the War of the Eight Suns broke out, the Fourth found himself in a dilemma. Should he put aside his pride and support Dunia's efforts in the conflict, or should he work against his fellow humans whom he viewed as "imperialists"? In the end, he chose a third path: neutrality. Throughout the hostilities, he avoided the forces of both the Amazonian Federation and the Alliance for Free Space however he could and worked to bring needed aid to the unintentional victims of the war. This latter activity brought him to the attention of the ever-watchful Aldebaranians; his willingness to defy the odds of a debilitating war and risk his life over beings he had never met greatly impressed this thoroughly enigmatic race. According to him, they formed a "protective aura" about his ship which safeguarded him against all attack. When the Aldebaranians had had their fill of a stalemated conflict, they stepped in and took decisive action – which netted them few friends on either side of the divide but against which no one could counteract. They dictated the terms of the Treaty of Aldebaran, effectively ending the war, and the Convention of Aldebaran, creating (among other things) the Constabulary. And they foisted upon an unsuspecting spiral arm the Fourth Murchison as the first Chief Constable.

It may be fairly said that the Fourth himself believed he was unworthy of the office and attempted to decline the honor. But the Aldebaranians were persistent – and persuasive – and got their way in the end. To the amazement of himself and of others, he discovered that he had inherited the organizational skills of his father and grandfather and used those skills to form a highly efficient police force to safeguard CSC space. During his career, he had a pet saying which he uttered on almost every occasion: "Keep it simple, stupid." He claimed not to be the originator of this phrase but to have read it in a history book about pre-ENO Dunia. By it, he meant that one should avoid complex solutions to any problem which may arise since complexity tended to exacerbate the original problem.

And, since the Fourth as Chief Constable assisted in the formation of the Warden Service (at the invitation of the Aldebaranians), that philosophy was part and parcel of a Warden's standard operating procedure.

Warden (L1) Lixu Rodriguez was of the considered opinion that Captain Halvarson's plan of attack was *too* simple, that it lacked the necessary finesse

---

36 Cf. to *M4: A Memoir*, edited by Cletus Korbinoff (University of New Nairobi Press, 120 A.R.), which purports to be a record of the Fourth's career up to the time of his disappearance – CMT.

to guide it toward a successful conclusion. He intended to introduce finesse into the equation, even if he had to tie Halvarson to his chair in order to make him listen.

After warp-out had been completed, he returned to the Bridge and found only mid-level officers at their posts. He grimaced. The senior officers, presumably, were back in Conference Room A, fine-tuning their strategy, and they had conveniently forgotten to notify him. But, when he entered that area, he discovered it to be empty as well. A search of all the other conference rooms proved equally fruitless. His brow furrowed in frustration. Where could everyone have gone?

There was one possibility. If the Captain intended to follow established Constabulary procedure for engaging an enemy force, he would send out sufficient fighter craft in an attempt to surround the foe and prevent any escape. Such deployment would originate from Commander Enrique Mbaku's Operations Center, a smaller version of a planetside command post. Why would the Captain choose to direct his attack from the OC rather than from the Bridge? He had to have some ulterior motive to deviate from SOP; and what that motive was, he (Warden Rodriguez) was going to learn, because deviations from SOP not instigated by the exigencies of the circumstances put his own mission at risk. And Wardens did not tolerate risks to their missions at all.

He commandeered one of the little intra-ship shuttles – an easy task considering that the crew were at their assigned Level-Four Alert posts and the passageways were deserted – and zipped off at the vehicle's top velocity of one meter per second.

The fighter brigade's Operations Center was located in close proximity to where the fighters were docked, i.e. at the juncture of the command sphere and the cylinder which linked it to the MOME sphere. Its central feature was a smaller version of the Display on the Bridge by which the brigade commander could track the progress of his forces in minute detail; the *Steadfast's* radar system picked up identification signals from each craft and relayed them to the holographic array. Other areas of the OC consisted of small briefing rooms, a pilot's lounge (with concomitant facilities), and the Commander's office.

There was always some activity going on in Operations. The brigade consisted of six squadrons – five combat and one support – and they trained as frequently as the troop brigade, employing basically the same methods. The fighter pilots donned the VR helmets and went through a series of simulated missions in order to hone their skills and/or to avoid whatever pitfalls the command staff cared to throw at them. The support squadron had their own scenarios to deal with, and often the Commander scheduled joint sessions where pilots and support crew rebounded against each other. Since the training sessions were quite grueling (on the assumption that, in Deep Space, the least little mishap always resulted in fatalities), they were limited to one every seventy-five kiloseconds (a standard "day" aboard a cruiser).

Additionally, one fighter squadron on a rotational basis was always on stand-by alert, ready to launch at a moment's notice. Therefore, the pilots haunted the lounge in full combat gear and relieved their boredom – and their anxiety – however they could. At this point in time, Squadron Four was on stand-by, and most of the pilots were glued to the giant vidscreen watching Planetoid 48 come into full view. When Rodriguez walked in, no one paid him any attention – which suited him entirely. He strolled over to the Operations desk and fixed the junior lieutenant on duty (a Dunian) with a steely glare. The latter winced visibly.

"I'm looking for Commander Mbaku," the Warden uttered in an ominous tone.

"Um, he's, um, in Training Room Two – sir," the officer stammered. He gestured to his left. "That way."

"Thank you, Leftenant." He smiled mirthlessly. "Carry on."

At Training Room Two, he heard several voices within, all of which he recognized. His suspicions were confirmed. He opened the door and entered nonchalantly as if it were the commonest thing to do. At his entrance, all heads turned, and all faces registered complete surprise upon seeing him. Captain Halvarson's surprised expression was tempered with chagrin which he could not hide entirely. Only Commander Krishnamurthy settled into bemusement, and she actually winked at him, a reaction which provoked a raised eyebrow, followed by a reciprocal wink, from him.

"Sorry I'm late, ladies and gentlemen," he announced disingenuously. "I, uh, took a wrong turn on Level Two-A."

"No need to apologize, Leftenant," the Captain murmured just as disingenuously. "We hadn't gotten around to discussing your part in the assault on Planetoid 48 yet. Take a seat."

Rodriguez sat down in the back row and sprawled out. Before him and behind Halvarson, a small vidscreen presented the same scene its larger version had. The runaway loomed like a leering face in some devilish nightmare; if it had had arms, those arms might undoubtedly reach out to snatch up the viewer and pop him/her into a gigantic maw of a mouth. The Warden grimaced. All hell was about to break loose unless he acted quickly and decisively.

He recalled his class on hostage situations at the Academy. It was the only class which was *not* conducted by an Aldebaranian. That race had never had any experience with hostage-taking, because the action had never before been encountered. The very concept of hostage-taking was, amazingly, strictly a human one; no other species in the spiral arm had ever engaged in capturing innocents and holding them for ransom. Prisoners were always taken, of course, in times of war and subsequently exchanged at a negotiated time and place, but the idea of taking prisoners for personal gain was – quite literally – *alien*. Thus, that particular class was taught by a human who was expected to know a thing or two about the topic.

Interestingly, Cadet Rodriguez had some small acquaintance with the instructor of the class. She was, when not instructing Wardens-to-be on the fine points of hostage situations, a full professor in history at the University of New Nairobi, and her field of expertise was the War of the Eight Suns. She also had a degree in criminal psychology and could quote chapter and verse concerning the major criminal acts in Dunia's past, including those of terrorist organizations which did snatch innocents for the purpose of ransom. Young Rodriguez had originally planned on going into the diplomatic corps, and her class on the Treaty of Aldebaran was a required course. At the Academy, he learned more than he cared to about hostage-taking.

Afterwards, he had put the question to Master Fresh concerning the proper approach to dealing with such situations. The professor had concerned herself with specifics and offered different approaches to different scenarios. In response to the question, his mentor had regarded him as much as a cow would an annoying fly.

"Think you that there is one all-inclusive approach, lack-wit?" he had said finally. "Think you that one course of action will resolve all situations?"

"Isn't there, Master? I…lack understanding."

"Indeed you do. Tell me, pupil, what is the First Principle?"

"Why, that is the Sanctity of Life, Master."

And what does it mean to you?"

"It means that whatever we do as Wardens, we should not put living beings in harm's way."

"Only what we *do*?"

Rodriguez remembered that he had frowned then, because he had had no idea of what his mentor was getting at.

"If you mean that, if we fail to do something and that failure results in harm to a living being, then I suppose acts of *o*mission should be avoided as much as acts of *com*mission."

"Does that not then lead to different approaches to different situations?"

"I…begin to understand, Master. We must analyze the situation, then select the proper response – whether it be action or inaction – in order to resolve the situation with the least loss of life."

"Very good, pupil. Now, leave me. It is time for my meditation."

Cadet Rodriguez had had much success thereafter with simulated situations, examining a problem from all angles and choosing the appropriate response. Occasionally, he had confounded his instructors by choosing a response not necessarily dictated by the Aldebaranians' world-view but which, on analysis, represented a unique twist on it. And, although the instructors were loathe to praise him for his innovation and ingenuity for fear of swelling his ego, they did encourage him to find fresh approaches to the standard wisdom.

Simulated exercises were not real-life situations, however, and computer programs could not contain all of the variables available to a sentient mind. Warden Rodriguez was now facing his first real test of what it meant to be a Warden in the first place, and his future career very much depended on how he handled the problem of Planetoid 48.

"What strategy have you planned, Captain?" he said quietly when Halvarson regarded him expectantly.

"The book calls for encirclement, followed by surgical strikes, then boarding. But we're dealing with a world here, not a ship, and the book may not apply. You said before that a different strategy was needed. What did you have in mind?"

"I agree that the book does not apply here. One, we have *potential* hostages to think about. Two, negotiations may or may not prove effective; the JUR are not known for negotiating if they think they've got the upper hand. And, three and most important, they do have the upper hand because, as Commander Krishnamurthy has so ably pointed out, they have a functioning MOME and therefore can play hide-and-seek with us until the end of Time."

"Which means?"

"Which means, we must reconnoiter the JUR's position and find a weakness we can exploit. I propose sending a scouting party to Planetoid 48 to do just that."

"But won't the Remans just warp-out when they see the scouting party approaching?"

"Not if you provide a diversion which will distract their attention away from a small vessel."

"What sort of diversion?"

"I'll leave that in your capable hands, Captain. Do you accept my proposal?"

Halvarson looked about at his senior officers and saw a variety of expressions. Krishnamurthy was smiling broadly and, when she made eye contact with him, nodded in agreement. Commanders Rux and Mbaku were engaged in a contest to see who could frown the deepest; the former merely shrugged, and the latter waved his hand in acquiescence. Everyone else appeared worried/thoughtful/disgusted/hopeful/blank and gave him no help whatsoever. He grimaced and wrinkled his nose at the same time.

"Very well, we'll play it your way. If you fail, then we'll go by the book."

"Agreed. Thank you, Captain."

"Who did you have in mind for the scouting party?"

"I've already been assigned a team. I'll take them."

The Captain's jaw unhinged. The nature of Rodriguez's "team" had not been lost on him, and it was all he could do to keep from laughing out loud.

"You can't be serious!"

"I'm well aware of why Commander Rux assigned those people to me" – he fixed the troop brigade commanding officer with accusing eyes, and the latter stroked his crest in the Bithan manner of exhibiting embarrassment – "but that is neither here nor there. I'm stuck with them, and they'll have to do." He smiled sweetly. "I doubt any of you will miss them – or me."

Captain Halvarson dismissed the accusatory atmosphere by contacting Sensors for an update on the status of the rogue. Upon receiving word that it was still on course toward the Rhea Silvia system, he returned his officers to their alert stations. Rodriguez headed for the troop barracks in order to pick up his "command."

Here was another first. Ordinarily, Wardens acted either alone or in concert with other Wardens. An elite group, they preferred it that way; outsiders tended to be less than fully co-operative and therefore to compromise the mission. On occasion, Wardens would take on "consultants," persons with special knowledge – as Rodriguez had done with Lt. Ralfo – but those arrangements were strictly temporary. If it had been suggested to any Warden that someday (s)he would be placed in charge of a Constabulary troop unit, (s)he would have shaken his/her head in disbelief. And Rodriguez himself would have dismissed the idea out of hand – under ordinary circumstances.

Yet, the present circumstances were far from ordinary, and he supposed that he would have to make certain allowances for the sake of the mission. Still, he intended that his "command" would perform the way he wanted it to perform; otherwise, none of them would leave Planetoid 48 alive.

CHAPTER FOURTEEN

▼

THE SCOUTING PARTY

"MYJOR, OI'VE PICKED UP A Constabulary patrol vessel on the sensors."

"'Ow far off is it?"

"'Arf a loight, sir. D'ye fink it's lookin' for us?"

"Oi doot it. We've been jumpin' aboot so much lytely that the Constabulary canna know where we are. It's prob'ly a sector patrol vessel. Still, keep an oi on it, and notifoy me if it starts movin' oor wy."

"Aye, sir."

Doctor Mubutu Weyerhauser listened in on this conversation intently and was thankful that he had neglected to discard his vidcom. Standard procedure for the JUR was a communications black-out during a given mission, unless some unforeseen situation required fresh orders. Once the pirated MOME had been made operational, the black-out came into effect; only the team leader could break it for non-emergency reasons.

The astrophysicist now entertained new hope. The news that a Constabulary ship was in the neighborhood represented a potential rescue mission, if it was truly responding to the distress signal the escaping crew members of the *Astarte* had sent out once they were clear of Planetoid 48. That it also represented an opportunity – even a slim one – to contact it and effect a *bona fide* rescue was worth a bit of risk. The trick was to find a working vidscreen. He turned to the Bithan XO, who had also been listening to the conversation intently.

"A new hope, Mr. Tas. If we can contact that ship, they can prevent this madness once and for all."

"Are you right, Professor. But, means this that must leave we this area and seek out the Communications bay."

"How far away is it?"

"All the way to the uppermost deck, am I afraid. Do not know I if are still looking your comrades – pardon me, your *former* comrades – for us."

"We'll have to chance it. Lead on."

"Shall do we what about Mr. Zam and Mr. O'Grady?"

The Doctor scowled. As far as he was concerned, those two hotheads had abandoned them to go "Reemie-hunting" – a fool's errand if ever there was one – and they were on their own. It was imperative that a functioning vidscreen be found quickly, and he had said as much. He shook his head to relay that notion to the Bithan. Then he regarded the two remaining crew members: the traumatized man, Mr. Corbo, and Stewardess Hernandez.

"We'll have to leave them here," the academic said sadly. "They'll just slow us down."

"No!" the woman protested. "That's cruel! We'll be unprotected. Please, Mr. Tas. We won't slow you down."

"Have to agree I with her, Professor. Cannot leave we them here unprotected."

"Very well. But make sure you keep up."

"We're all going to *die*!" Corbo moaned.

The foursome began to backtrack the way they had come, twisting and turning through the ruins of the lower decks. Their only consolation was that the further up they climbed, the less they had to do so in a stooped position. Even though Dr. Weyerhauser had implied that Corbo and Hernandez would be left behind if they didn't keep up, more than once he halted until they had caught up. Corbo especially was a worrisome problem, since there were no able-bodied persons to carry him along, and he was constantly lagging behind.

They passed the point where the bodies of their late co-worker and the JUR member still lay and averted their eyes. The sight elicited even louder moaning from Corbo.

The astrophysicist thought they might lose Corbo altogether when they reached the bulkhead lying across the companionway. Crawling up it was decidedly more difficult than crawling down, and they kept slipping and sliding backwards. Hernandez uttered more than one unladylike expression as, on her third attempt to negotiate the slippery metal, she collided with a motionless Corbo. He was sitting on the deck with his head in his hands.

"Come on, Ivan," she entreated. "You can't stay here."

"We're all going to *die*!" he responded.

She stared at him for a moment, then shook her head in disgust.

"No, not all of us. Just *you*. The rest of us are going to escape. You can just sit there and wait until the terrorists find you. I don't care any more."

With that, she clambered up the bulkhead in one quick motion, aided by a sudden adrenaline rush. Behind her, Corbo blinked in confusion. The very real possibility that he might be abandoned to an awful fate slowly sank in, and he moved his mouth wordlessly. The retreating backs of his companions filled him with terror. In a panic, he pushed himself forward and crept up the bulkhead in fits and starts; and eventually, he traversed the distance and rushed past the others. The Doctor smiled slyly at Hernandez.

"A bit of reverse psychology?"

"Yeah," she mumbled and followed after Corbo.

As the party approached the mid-section of the MOME sphere, the Bithan suggested an alternative route to the Communications bay just in case there were more terrorists lurking about. The decision almost proved to be disastrous. They were close to the companionway leading to the next deck on the alternative route when they heard shouting, followed by gunfire and more screaming, ending in complete silence. Tas motioned them into a maintenance compartment just before footsteps sounded on the companionway. He kept the hatch cracked a few millimeters so that he and Dr. Weyerhauser could peek out.

Three JUR members rushed by, cursing as they went. The astrophysicist recognized two of them: Cutty and Jingles. He frowned. Their presence here boded ill for anyone not a member of the cell; it meant that the Major was very serious about apprehending him and the other escapees and wasn't sparing anybody in the search.

"Suppose you has happened what?" the XO whispered.

"I suspect it has to do with Zam and O'Grady. We've got to proceed with extreme caution from here on."

They waited a few moments until they were absolutely sure that no more terrorists were in the vicinity and quietly slipped out of the maintenance compartment. Slowly, they made their way up the companionway. At the top, Dr. Weyerhauser's worst suspicions were confirmed. Three blood-covered bodies sprawled on the deck, and two of them were Zam and O'Grady; the third was a JUR man the astrophysicist recognized but whose name he couldn't remember.

"Preserve Hashin us!" Tas invoked the name of the chief deity in the Bithan pantheon. "Is this monstrous, Professor!"

"I knew this would happen. I tried to warn them, but they wouldn't listen. They were too full of revenge to listen." He stared down the passageway in an effort to detect any telltale signs of other JUR members. "Well, we can't do anything for them. We've got to keep moving. Which way, Mr. Tas?"

*   *   *

On Captain Halvarson's mark, all launch-bay hatches of the *Steadfast* were opened and all warships launched. The fighters came out first, by squadrons, followed by the support vessels; lastly came the troop carriers (minus the troops) and the shuttle craft. The launch had all the earmarks of a full-scale attack against a major target – except that there was no attack. All ships deployed in the direction of the Rhea Silvia system. When they had reached a point ten thousand kilometers from the patrol vessel, they began a series of maneuvers which simulated attacks on an imaginary target; each maneuver involved a specific combination of fighter, support, and troop ships, and the various groupings executed specific flight patterns according to scenarios devised by the High Command on New Switzerland.

In short, the combat crew of the *Steadfast* were "in training" in Deep Space away from the normal shipping lanes. The Captain had decided to kill two birds with one stone; he would provide Warden Rodriguez with his diversion and give his people some practice for the real assault to come, if and when the Warden deemed it necessary. He hoped that all of this activity would draw the JUR's attention away from a shuttle craft which was now splitting off from the main group and following a course perpendicular to the line between the *Steadfast* and Planetoid 48. If it didn't, Rodriguez was on his own.

Life aboard that shuttle had gotten off to a rocky start, and it was getting rockier by the nanosecond. When the Warden went in search of his "command," he found it either in the chow line or sitting at a table eating. No small amount of audible grumbling greeted his announcement that they were to gather up their combat gear and report to the shuttle launch bay in one kilosecond. Sgt. Running Deer had to issue threats of a transfer to the brig in order to get his recalcitrant troops moving; he himself wasn't too happy about this sudden change in plans but confined his ire to a grim expression and a curt salute.

On the positive side, Rodriguez quickly gathered up Lt. Ralfo and Sgt. Utumi, both of whom were delighted to go into action. That delight was destined to be short-lived.

A shuttle craft was designed to carry one pilot and six passengers to wherever the passengers wanted to go. It was not designed to carry a platoon of troopers (plus their gear) – even a short-staffed platoon like Gamma. Currently, Gamma numbered thirteen (one of the corporals and a private were on sick call). Added to the mix were the Warden, the Pluj, and the Capellan, and they were not pleased to be jammed into a small space with a less than enthusiastic crew. Ordinarily, Ralfo might have been excited being surrounded by males upon whom she could work her charms; but the tight quarters – and the intensified body odors they provoked – served to dampen her kind's pheromone production. Besides, she found herself inexplicably pressed against the lone human female in the team who kept glowering at her. The one individual who was decidedly ill at ease was, of course, Utumi; the average Alkon warrior stood at one-and-three-quarters meters, and this warrior was finding no head room at all but had to endure the ride in a semi-crouch. Besides, he thought all humans stank; breathing normally was out of the question as far as he was concerned.

The shuttle headed for the center of the central spiral. The plan was to travel five thousand kilometers at maximum velocity, swing into a wide arc to circle back, and come at Planetoid 48 on its far side. Hopefully, the JUR would be keeping a sharp eye on the "maneuvers" in front of them and not pay any attention to the smaller vessel.

If he had stopped to think it all out, Rodriguez would have spotted any number of flaws in the plan, all of which were possibly fatal to the entire mission. At the Academy, during his senior year, all of the members of his class had had a chance to be "Team Leader" on a particularly complex and hazardous exercise. On his turn, he had spent some time reviewing his options when the voice of Master Fresh rang in his head demanding to know why he hadn't begun the exercise yet. The cadet replied that he was attempting to choose the correct procedure whereupon the Aldebaranian caustically remarked, "The 'correct procedure,' lack-wit, is that which results in the fewest casualties. Why is this so difficult to understand?" Rodriguez had then chosen the option which met his mentor's parameters. The choice had resulted in only one casualty when the exercise was completed and in class honors for him.

That had been a hypothetical situation. This was the real thing, and there didn't seem to be any option which would result in less than a dozen casualties – and that was just on *his* side! Quite possibly, they would all die. And Captain Halvarson would be free to pursue his own strategy – resulting in more deaths.

In the midst of his pensiveness, the voice of Corporal Chen burst out angrily:

"Whichever of you fraggers got his fraggin' hand on my ass had better bort, or he'll pull back a fraggin' stump!"

"Sorry, Corporal, nobody meant nothin' by it," an anonymous human voice responded. "It's just we got no room to move around on this fraggin' bucket."

"Free *my*…ass is," Ralfo piped up, "if interested anyone is."

"At ease, you fraggers!" Sgt. Running Deer barked. Addressing the Pluj, he said: "Beggin' your pardon, ma'am, but it ain't wise to encourage this pile of *braka* bait."[37]

"You I thank, Sergeant. That I shall remember."

"We need some cheerin' up around here," the same anonymous voice declared. "Who's got a tune?"

To the Warden's great surprise, one of the troopers responded with the first line of an ancient Dunian nonsense song requiring an active – and perverse – imagination. He hadn't heard "Ninety-Nine Bottles of Beer on the Wall" since childhood!

At maximum velocity, the shuttle still required fifty kiloseconds to circle around and approach Planetoid 48. Long before then, "Ninety-Nine Bottles" had expanded to "Two-Hundred-Ninety-Seven Bottles" before petering out through a combination of weariness and lack of imagination. There followed a long, tense silence. Then, surprisingly, Ralfo allowed that the current situation called to mind a rather embarrassing incident which had occurred when she was a child. In spite of themselves, Gamma Platoon laughed at the story. This prompted Running Deer to relate an embarrassing incident of his own, except that it involved a botched sexual encounter. Soon, everyone had a story to share, allaying the tension. Only Rodriguez and Utumi elected not to participate in this impromptu camaraderie. The Warden could have shared any number of embarrassments from his past; but, now that he was a Warden, he felt he had to maintain a solemn demeanor in public. He did laugh – quietly – at the others' stories. The Capellan also had his share of embarrassments, but he was damned if he'd speak of them to humans; he had his reputation to think of, and that of all Alkonu everywhere. Instead, he attempted to meditate.

Eventually, Lt. O-da, the shuttle pilot, informed Rodriguez that the far side of the runaway was dead ahead and that he was not detecting any activity on the part of the JUR. The Warden thanked him and called for attention.

"Listen up, people! You'll be happy to know that we'll be landing soon, and we can all get out of this bucket." The announcement provoked a round of cheers which Sgt. Running Deer quickly stifled. "But, first, you need to know a few things about Planetoid 48. One, it still has an atmosphere, but it's a thin one. You'll be required to use a breath mask at all times. Two, as you might imagine, this world is bitterly cold. Wear your cold-weather gear at all times. Three, the gravity is lighter than what most of you are used to, so adjust your movements accordingly. And four, this world may or may not have been inhabited at one time. If it was, there may be artifacts scattered

---

37 A *braka* is a carnivorous game animal on New Switzerland, prized for its long, curved set of four horns. It is, however, a reticent creature and must be enticed into the open by setting out a wounded or sick "bait" animal upon which it can prey – CMT.

about. All artifacts are to be reported to either me or Lt. Ralfo. *Absolutely no 'souvenir-hunting' will be tolerated!* Do I make myself clear?"

"Aye, sir," Running Deer acknowledged for the group. "Anyone found with an artifact on his or her person will get his or her ass kicked."

"Thank you, Sergeant. Any questions?"

"I got one, sir," the trooper who had groped Corporal Chen piped up. "How soon can we get off this tub? The corporal has given me a piston as big as a tree, but I doubt she's goin' to let me do the riggers with her."

That remark netted the speaker a hearty laugh from his male compatriots and an elbow in the ribs from the corporal.

"Well, we can't have Chen damaging government property, can we?" the Warden replied with a smirk. He peered at the shuttle's vidscreen which currently displayed a view of Planetoid 48 and its environs. "I should judge about a kilo." To Running Deer: "Sergeant, establish a bivouac area centered about the shuttle as soon as we land."

"Aye, sir. Standard security?"

"Right – until further notice."

The shuttle touched down ten seconds shy of a kilosecond, to the half-muted cheers of the whole platoon. There might have been a stampede toward the outer hatch if not for Running Deer's imposing himself between it and his troopers. Amidst a bit of grumbling, he forced them to exit in single file, making sure that each and every one had his/her breath mask in place. As soon as they hit the ground, the platoon quickly donned their cold-weather gear. Rodriguez, Ralfo, and Utumi were the last to leave. But before the Warden exited, the shuttle pilot caught his attention.

"What is it, Leftenant?"

"What my orders, sir?"

"Do you have urgent business elsewhere?"

"No, sir. I just asking."

"We may have to leave in a hurry. Until further notice, you're on stand-by alert. Stay aboard the shuttle."

"Aye, sir."

Outside, the Warden donned his own breath mask and cold-weather gear, then scanned the area. He was sure that, once, this world had been full of life – plants, animals, perhaps sentient (or, at the very least, semi-sentient) creatures. Now, sunless, its atmosphere slowly dissipating into space, Planetoid 48 was nearly as barren as Dunia's moon. What vegetation remained was brown and brittle; it crumbled to powder with the slightest touch. The few trees left were stunted and leafless, and Rodriguez believed he could knock them all down with a sharp blow. If there had been fields and gardens and orchards here, they had long gone to dust – and, along with them, any fauna.

About a kilometer away rose a range of hills. They too looked weathered and beaten down. Further on, say, five kilometers, he saw the peaks of mountains. And beyond the mountains were the JUR.

Sgt. Running Deer was busily overseeing the unloading and setting up of the life-domes. In olden days, soldiers in the field lived in tents made of canvas. Such constructions were vulnerable to the vicissitudes of Nature – rain, snow, wind, heat, and the like – and they failed almost as often as they served. The life-domes, manufactured by a company in the Murchison empire, were able to withstand most of what Nature had to offer and some of what sentient life-forms had to offer. They consisted of five-millimeter-thick polyethylene envelopes stretched over titanium-steel support rods to form hemispheres two meters in diameter; each could accommodate two troopers plus all of their gear with no loss of comfort. Each dome contained a heating unit which attached to the base of the center pole. A snap-on flap served as entrance.

Nine of the life-domes were erected around the shuttle. By Constabulary regulations, the officer-in-charge had one to himself; his dome also acted as a "command post" and "conference center." The regulations also stated that the genders were to be segregated, and so Lt. Ralfo shared a dome with Cpl. Chen, an arrangement the latter found distasteful. The two sergeants also shared a dome, and neither of them was at all pleased. The remaining eleven troopers drew lots (their ID tags) to determine who would be the lucky one to occupy a dome by himself. Running Deer paired up the "unlucky" ones himself.

During the set-up, Rodriguez spied one seeming anomaly: Ralfo in standard uniform. She was not wearing any of the cold-weather gear issued her, gear which saved the rest of the unit from instant frostbite (and worse). He was not too surprised. Pluj was a cold world – though not as cold as Planetoid 48 – and its inhabitants had evolved to survive in its climate without artificial aids. When he lived on that planet, he had had to bundle up securely before stepping outside, and he had been as conspicuous a sight as if he had had two heads. Ralfo was in her true element here.

The set-up took two-and-a-half kiloseconds to accomplish, and the troopers would have gotten in their domes immediately but for a signal from the Warden to Sgt. Running Deer. The non-com ordered the platoon to fall in and listen to what their officer had to say.

"It's been a long day," Rodriguez said conciliatorily, "and I know you're all tired. When you've eaten, get some rest. We'll be moving out when the *Astarte* has been located. Sgt. Running Deer, post your guards. Sgt. Utumi, break out the probe and prepare it for launch. That is all."

Running Deer dismissed all but two of his platoon and set those two on a circular orbit of the bivouac area, one walking clockwise, the other counter-clockwise.

The Capellan strode over to the shuttle storage compartment – now almost empty with the extraction of the life-domes – pulled out a black, metallic sphere a meter in diameter, and placed it gently on the ground. The probe was in essence a flying vidcom, except that it possessed four cameras, each set equidistantly around the circumference for a one-hundred-degree coverage. Coverage could be tracked by a hand-held vidcom which also served as a remote-control pilot. The device's electronics were solar-powered while a miniature ionic engine provided motive power. Utumi switched the probe on and ran it through a series of tests to ensure that all functions were operational. Then he powered up the engine. With a low-level hum, the probe lifted straight up and hovered at about two meters off the ground. He nodded to Rodriguez.

"Very good, Sergeant. Maintain the probe at its current height and at its maximum velocity until it reaches the opposite side of the planetoid."

The Alkon warrior entered the desired parameters on the keypad of his remote control and pressed the "launch" button. The probe shot away at fifty meters per second toward the mountains the Warden had viewed earlier. Due to the lack of illumination on Planetoid 48, Utumi switched to the high-resolution setting of the cameras' visual system. The images he received were still barely discernable.

Rodriguez quick-marched to his "command post," anxious to get inside and shed his cold-weather gear. When he stepped inside, he discovered Ralfo lounging on an inflatable mattress. She grinned hugely at his appearance.

"What's to eat?" he asked disingenuously.

Ralfo examined the array of white paperboard packages she had obtained from the shuttle's food-storage cabinets. Inside, separated into four equal-sized portions – allegedly the four basic food groups – were multi-colored globs of textured vegetable protein to which had been added artificial flavors and scientifically-measured doses of vitamins and minerals. Stamped on the packages were the designations (in Standard) of what the contents were supposed to be. Since her race's digestive system was nearly akin to that of humans, she had chosen human comestibles; from the brief expression of disgust on her face, however, she was still not happy with her selections, but she had had to choose either those or some designed for other races.

"You may find some value with these, Lixu. I will be dining lightly, however."

The Warden picked up the collection, one by one, scanned the designations, and wrinkled his nose.

"I heartily agree with you, Anafu. Deep Space rations leave a lot to be desired." He heaved a sigh. "I miss your father's cooking."

"And I. He is a wizard with food."

Males on Pluj did all the cooking, both at home and in the public sphere. In a role-reversal society, this task was part of their chief responsibility, i.e. keeping up the home. The more skillful were allowed to be employed as chefs in restaurants or government dining rooms, but it was always understood that employment outside of the home should not interfere with their domestic duties. Even the mate of the planet's Chief Administratrix was not exempt from this precept; when he was not engaged in household chores, Ralfo's father taught in a cooking school (owned and operated by a woman, of course), and he had not necessarily obtained this position because of marital connections.

Rodriguez had always enjoyed his visits to the Ralfo residence because "Uncle Ceptu" went out of his way to put a sumptuous feast on the table when Dunia's ambassador and his family came calling. Ten-course affairs they were, each course rivaling the others for excellence; and the master chef knew how to whet the appetite and to instill a sense of anticipation for the next course. The Warden admittedly had made a pig of himself at each affair, though it was sometimes a struggle to eat everything placed before him. To his credit, "Uncle Ceptu" waved off all praise, labeling his culinary creations as "simple fare."

"Does he still make *hufok*?" Rodriguez was asking.

"Yes, but not as often as he used to, not after you went to Warden Academy."

Hufok was a Pluj pastry, actually a layered cake in which each layer contained entirely different ingredients. In effect, one was served a multi-course dessert. As might be expected, *hufok* required great skill to create, and few Pluj males could master the techniques or devote the time involved as well as the male Ralfo. The first time Rodriguez took a bite from the top layer – *hufok* was properly eaten layer by layer so that the consumer could experience successively higher levels of taste delight – he had been hooked, and it became his favorite dessert. "Uncle Ceptu" always made sure a fresh *hufok* was available when the Rodriguezes came calling. Even after young Lixu had left to attend University, he received by special delivery a large slice of the pastry to enjoy while "cracking the books." Sometimes, he had even shared it with close acquaintances.

"When this mission is completed, I'm going to put in for a furlough so that I can visit Pluj and renew old friendships."

"*Mutofu* [wonderful], Lixu!' Ralfo squealed. "We shall take a furlough together." She rose to her feet, sauntered toward him, and wrapped her arms around his waist. "We can do one more thing to make it a special occasion."

"What's that?"

She peered into his eyes solemnly and stroked his cheek with an index finger.

"We can become a mated pair."

He regarded her with disbelief.

"Are you serious?"

"Yes, my lovely Lixu, I am. Dearest, will you marry me?"

Even in matters of the heart, the females of Pluj always took the initiative. There had seldom been an instance when an i-Pluj had proposed marriage since the days when role-reversal became the norm; a Pluj usually "popped the question," and it was left to the male to accept or to decline. Rodriguez was aware of this custom; but, never having been personally involved in such matters, he had tended to slough over the implications. Now, however, he was being proposed to, and he was at a loss for words!

"Anafu, I – I do love you. But, as a rule, Wardens don't marry. The obligations of married life would interfere with our prime mission."

"But, there are no regulations against it?"

"No."

"We are both of us soldiers, and we can keep professional and married life separate." She stood on tiptoe and kissed him passionately. "Oh, Lixu, I love you so much. Please, *please*, say 'yes.'"

"I – I've got to think this over. It's a huge step for any man to take – and especially for a Warden. You understand."

"I do." A mischievous twinkle appeared in her eyes. "And, while you are thinking, do me a favor."

"And that is?"

"Demonstrate to me human sexual techniques."

Now he kissed her passionately.

"Yes, ma'am," he whispered.

*　　　*　　　*

"Who's there? Oh, it's you, Sarge."

"Of course, it's me. Were you expecting someone else, Quinn? The JUR maybe?"

"Nah, it's as quiet as a Ru'uhaad lizard around here."

"Quiet? You ain't been fraggin' payin' attention then, trooper."

"Huh?"

"I made the fraggin' mistake of bivouackin' next to our officers. And, for the past fifteen K's, I've had to listen to 'em do the fraggin' riggers."

"Yeah?"

"Yeah. I done the riggers any number of times, but I can tell you it's fraggin' embarrassing to listen to others do 'em – especially when you don't expect one of 'em to be doin' 'em."

"How's that, Sarge?"

"We all know the Pluj will fuck anything with a fraggin' piston – anywhere, anytime, anyhow. But, I always thought a fraggin' Warden took a vow of chastity or something. Not this one! And he moans and groans like crazy!"

"No shit?"

"Green across, trooper. Well, I'm goin' to check on Smitty. Stay alert from now on."

*   *   *

"Rodri-go," the voice of Sgt. Utumi called softly (or as softly as a Capellan can speak) through the "wall" of the "command post," "I contact with the *Astarte* have make."

Inside the life-dome, the Warden came awake immediately. His training at the Academy had included the ability to sleep on one level and to be alert on another. One could not say that he had been "half-asleep," since each mental level was capable of operating independently; therefore, he could be both asleep and alert simultaneously. In the present circumstance, he had "programmed" his alert level to awaken him on receiving certain keywords, e.g. "*Astarte*," "JUR," or "Planetoid 48."

He came awake to find himself entangled with Lt. Ralfo. They were facing each other; Anafu's left leg was draped over his right hip, and both of her arms were wrapped around his shoulders. His right arm was resting on her waist, while the left one served as a cradle for her head. Both were completely naked, a state which pleased him immensely and which would have pleased her immensely as well if she had been awake to notice it. How they happened to have fallen asleep at the same time was anybody's guess. All he remembered was making love nonstop to this fabulous creature in various human positions and subconsciously listening to her gasps of delight and moans of pleasure. It had been a most rewarding interlude – on several levels – and he looked forward to others.

Unfortunately, duty called at this moment, and he was obliged to answer. Slowly then, he disengaged himself from Anafu's embrace, taking care not to awaken her. At one point, she stirred, murmured "Ah, Lixu!" and drifted back to sleep. He quickly pulled on his trousers, padded over to the flap of the dome, drew it back, and peered at the Alkon warrior. The latter pointedly ignored his state of dishabille.

"How far away is she, Sergeant?" he came right to the point.

"I it 400 kilometers from here should judge to be. I the probe one kilometer from the ship did set down."

"Excellent, Sergeant. Get some sleep now. We'll move out in ten K's."

The Warden finished dressing, donned his cold-weather gear, and stepped out into Planetoid 48's thin atmosphere. He strode over to the shuttle and opened an external panel to reveal a built-in monitoring station. The essential equipment was a fifty-centimeter-square vidscreen and the remote control; there was also an audio component which enabled the observer to listen to any sounds in the vicinity in which the probe was located. He activated the probe's transmitter. An image formed on the vidscreen after two seconds, revealing the environment where the *Astarte* was supposed to be. He saw nothing but rocks, grayish in color, jagged, and large, and surmised that he was looking at a mountain scene. The other three cameras confirmed that conclusion. The rearward one pointed at a desolate valley while the lateral pair showed a long line of steep rock walls.

He removed the remote control from its cradle and tapped in a command. The image on the vidscreen shifted as the probe was elevated. Now he maneuvered the probe to port, then to starboard, in order to get a more complete view of the site. Approximately half a kilometer to the starboard of the probe's position, he spotted an anomaly and immediately magnified it. It was indeed what was left of the *Astarte*'s MOME sphere, wedged into a crevice between two outcroppings. Furthermore, he spied no human activity nearby which told him that the probe had not been detected – yet. Whatever the JUR was up to, they were too absorbed to place any guards outside, and that carelessness would prove to be their undoing. He returned the probe to the ground and switched it off.

He sought out Sgt. Running Deer and found him snoring in the life-dome originally assigned to the single trooper. Why the non-com had chosen to sack out here instead of in his assigned dome was a minor mystery, but Rodriguez had no interest in solving it. It was time to get Gamma Platoon moving! He shook Running Deer's shoulder gently at first and, when he received no response, more vigorously. The Dunian came awake, blinked several times to focus his vision, and peered at the Warden questioningly.

"The *Astarte* has been located, Sergeant. Get your people assembled."

"Aye, sir," the other mumbled and clambered to his feet.

One-and-a-half kiloseconds later, the platoon was at parade rest near the shuttle. None of them seemed too happy to be roused out of a sound sleep, but it was hard to determine for certain since the breath masks covered half the face. If the hard looks in a dozen pairs of eyes were any sign, however, Rodriguez didn't need to see the full face. Not that their discomfit would have made any difference – they were not a tour group out to see the sights.

"Our primary mission," the Warden declared, "is to locate and apprehend Dr. Mubutu Weyerhauser. Secondarily, we will be on the look-out for any survivors from the *Astarte* and escort them to safety. At all times, we'll avoid any confrontation with the JUR, if at all possible. Once we achieve our mission, I'll send for the cavalry and let them deal with the Indians." He winced and turned to Running Deer. "Sorry, Sergeant, that didn't come out as I wanted it to." The non-com shrugged. "We'll proceed to the target site in two groups. Sgt. Running Deer and I will take a squad and set up a picket line. The shuttle will return here and pick up the rest of you. Once there, Sgt. Utumi will scout out the best approach to the *Astarte*. Any questions?"

There were none – spoken aloud, that is. The Warden nodded to Running Deer, who barked an order. Six troopers wheeled and boarded the shuttle, followed by the sergeant. Rodriguez turned to Ralfo.

"Anafu, while you're waiting for the shuttle to return, strike the bivouac, ready to load up. We won't be coming back here."

"Aye, sir." She paused briefly, then switched to Pluj. "Our Lady watch over you, Lixu."

"And you as well," he responded similarly and hopped aboard the shuttle.

As a precaution, he instructed Lt. O-da to fly low over the surface of the planetoid in order to avoid detection. Though the probe had not registered any *external* activity around the *Astarte*, there was always the possibility that the JUR had sensing devices to warn them of any incoming "traffic." Flying at a low altitude would serve to negate the sensing devices. In addition, he ordered all lighting, inside and out, shut off; the Uhaad was reduced to piloting only by his instruments.

Nor was this the Warden's first flight in the dark, but it was his first as a passenger. One of his training exercises at the Academy had been to pilot a craft similar to the present one under similar circumstances. The exercise had taken place on Xix, one of the moons of the Aldebaranians' home world, the only one to have an atmosphere. That Xix was also the sole penal colony for the Central Spiral Collective may have had something to do with its choice as a training ground. In the first place, the moon was as desolate as Mars and contained nearly the same type of topological features, which made it a natural obstacle course and a deterrent to escape. In the second place, it was prone to frequent moonquakes, thus providing an additional hazard to safe navigation. As tests went, flying over Xix was a cadet's nightmare come true and tended to separate the chaff from the wheat (so to speak).

Cadet Rodriguez nearly did not complete the exercise, he remembered with a shudder. Two kilometers from the end point, a moonquake occurred and created a sudden fluctuation in air pressure; his craft bucked sharply to port and toward a rock outcropping he would ordinarily have missed by a comfortable margin. It took all of his skills and concentration to regain some control and to avoid being dashed to pieces. As it happened, the craft collected a "souvenir" in the form of a five-centimeter score along its entire starboard hull. The future Warden also collected a "souvenir": he had fouled his trousers during the struggle and had had to endure snickers from his fellow trainees and a deep frown from the instructor.

While he didn't expect anything of that nature on Planetoid 48, there were hazards nevertheless. One, he was in uncharted territory and, two, he was heading into a veritable lion's den. It behooved him then to employ as much stealth as he could. A chance encounter with the JUR might prove fatal as they had a reputation for never surrendering, even if the odds were against them, making them all the more dangerous.

The journey to the probe's location took only half the time it took the probe. Lt. O-da made a soft landing about one hundred meters from the sphere, whereupon Sgt. Running Deer ordered his squad outside to establish a picket line. Rodriguez stored the probe aboard the shuttle and sent it back to pick up the other squad.

The mountain before him looked even more formidable in reality than the image sent back by the probe had suggested. A bit of climbing awaited the platoon. He was thankful he had decided to include a Capellan scout on this mission; Sgt. Utumi was highly qualified to locate the easiest and/or shortest way up to the *Astarte*. Nevertheless, the climb would be difficult, and the Warden was not going to delude himself otherwise.

A sudden movement high above the mountain caught his eye. He peered into the sky, squinting, and shook his head in anxiety.

"Sergeant, your binoculars, please."

The non-com obeyed, then gazed upwards himself.

"What is it, sir?"

The Warden focused the binoculars and scanned the area of his concern. He shook his head again and wordlessly handed the binoculars back to Running Deer. The non-com made his own scan.

"Damn!" he growled. "That's a fraggin' Reemie ship, by the looks of it. Where the frag did it come from?"

"I couldn't say. But I'm less concerned about where it came from and more about where it's going. Get your people under cover!"

CHAPTER FIFTEEN

▼

ASSAULT ON THE *ASTARTE*

"Freedom 4 to Myjor Tshambe."

"Tshambe 'ere. What is it?"

"Sir, this my be noffin', but ship's sensors detected a sloight movement on the planetide's surface, at the byse o' the moontain where the *Astarte* is."

"Anyfing specific?"

"Na, sir. The movement was too short in durytion."

"Circle back and go to a lower elevytion. Oi want to know what's oot there."

"Aye, sir. Freedom 4 oot."

"Tshambe to Lt. Kurabao"

"Kurabao 'ere, sir."

"Leftenant, are ye done wif yere current assoignment?"

"Aye, sir. Any further orders?"

"Aye. Tyke yere people ootsoide and see if there's anybody cloimbin' up to the *Astarte*."

"'Oo'd be doin' that?"

"Oi dinna know. But there's a Constabulary patrol vessel 'arf a loight awy. Thy've spent the last several kilos on maneuvers. Noo, that could be legitimate – or it could be a diversion. Check oot the moontain and report back."

"Aye, sir. Kurabao oot."

*   *   *

"Mr. Tas, did you hear that?"

"Yes, Professor."

"Then it's imperative that we get to that Communications bay quickly."

"Have to go we not far – the next passageway, in fact."

The escapees moved stealthily forward, keen to hear any telltale sounds which might be the approach of a JUR search party. Doctor Weyerhauser was especially alert and prepared to bolt at the first sign of his former comrades. His life was forfeit, he knew, and he had nothing to lose in attempting to keep the Remans at bay. What would happen to his present companions fell into the realm of a shrewd guess; since the Major had given no heed whatsoever to the safety of the crew of the cruise ship since their escape, they were not likely to see their homes again. Their only hope – and it was a slim one at best – was to send a distress call to that Constabulary ship out there and then to lay low until rescue arrived.

At the junction of the passageways, the Bithan peeked around the corner in both directions, happily saw no one in sight, and signaled to the others to proceed. The cross-passageway ran to only fifty meters in the direction the XO was heading. A single hatch lay ahead, marked "Communications" in bold lettering. The party reached it in a few quick steps; Tas opened it and winced as the mechanism made too much noise for his liking.

Inside, signs of a struggle were evident in the form of a bullet-riddled corpse on the deck near the central vidscreen. The bulkhead on the other side of the dead man showed scoring by bullets which had missed their mark. The astrophysicist and the Bithan both shook their heads in sadness. Stewardess Hernandez buried her head in the former's shoulder and wept softly; he put his arm around her in a half-hearted attempt to console her. Corbo merely stared blankly at the scene, his face a mask of stone.

"D'ya think he got a message off before he…?"

"Is it unknown. Would have to check I the log. Would like to think I that did he."

"Well, we can't dwell on that if we hope to avoid his fate. Is the vidscreen operable?"

"Seems to be it." Tas sat down before the console, and he entered his personal activation code. The vidscreen came alive with a greenish glow; the Bitha's fingers flew across the console as the words "Activation code confirmed" appeared, followed by "New message?" More commands called up the log. "Ah," he crowed, "shows the log that was sent a partial message."

Now he entered the emergency code which would – with luck – be picked up by any Constabulary ship within five light-years of the sender. It may have seemed like forever before a response to the distress call was received, but it was actually only a few seconds. The blank screen gave way to the image of an

Ekath or Okath in a Constabulary uniform. Tas's and Doctor Weyerhauser's faces brightened immensely.

"I bees Lt. H'rum of the *CSS Steadfast*. What bees your emergency?"

"Thank the gods!" the Bitha whispered. Aloud: "Is this the *Astarte*. Require we assistance immediately!"

At the mention of the name of the ship, the Communications officer's eyes went wide with surprise.

"You bees the *Astarte?*" she whispered. "I must inform my Captain."

The vidscreen blanked out and remained so for what seemed to be another eon but again was only a few seconds. Then the granite face of Captain Olaf Halvarson winked into existence. He looked at Tas quizzically.

"I'm Captain Halvarson. Identify yourself, please."

"Am I Commander Tas Omaro, Executive Officer of the cruise ship *Astarte*. Were highjacked we."

"Yes, we're aware of that. Where are you now? And what is your situation?"

"Crash-landed JUR terrorists part of the cruise ship on" – he glanced to one side — "is called what this world, Professor?"

There was a murmur in the background.

"Thank you." To Captain Halvarson: "Crash-landed we on Planetoid 48. Escaped captivity is what left of the crew, but could be discovered we any moment. Must hurry you!"

While Tas related the peril to the *Astarte*, the Captain's eyes also widened in surprise. He turned to speak to someone off-screen, nodded at a presumed response, and regarded the Bithan again.

"Well, Commander Tas, this is an amazing co-incidence. It just so happens that we've been tracking Planetoid 48 because it's been reported to be the scene of terrorist activity. Therefore, I can assure you that help is already on the way. In fact, a Constabulary unit should already be there. All you need to do is to sit tight."

"Are grateful we, Captain Halvarson."

"Just how many are there of you left?"

"Regret to say I that are there only two others of the crew. And is Doctor Weyerhauser with us."

"*Who?!?*" Halvarson roared, a look of consternation etched deeply on his face. "Did you say, 'Weyerhauser'?"

Now the astrophysicist moved into view and gazed at the *Steadfast's* skipper somberly. A myriad of emotions raced through his mind. By identifying himself, he increased his chances of being apprehended, tried for a host of crimes, and imprisoned for life. Yet, he had to get away from his former comrades because they were all raving lunatics, and he wanted nothing more to do with them. The Constabulary meant safety even if it also meant a loss of freedom, but he had no other options available to him at the moment.

"I am Dr. Mubutu Weyerhauser. I used to be a member of the JUR. I have…defected."

"Doctor, I'm obliged to inform you that our Warden has a warrant for your arrest."

"No doubt. I'm prepared to surrender myself to him and co-operate anyway I can."

"Glad to hear that. Warden Rodriguez should be on Planetoid 48 even as we speak. As I told Commander Tas, sit tight, and we'll send a rescue party ASAP. *Steadfast* out."

The vidscreen went blank again. The Doctor faced the XO.

"An amazing co-incidence indeed, as Captain Halvarson said. I suggest we hide again until the rescue party arrives."

"Were we where before?"

"Yes, that seems to be the best option. I–"

"'Old it roight there!" a voice issued from the hatch.

Four pairs of eyes swiveled around to take in the sight of a hulk of a man wearing the yellow armband of the JUR with its image of a falcon.[38] Dr. Weyerhauser vaguely recognized him but did not know his name. Whoever the fellow was, he represented the academic's worst fears, and the threat was backed up by an automatic rifle pointed in his direction.

"Well, well, well, if it ayn't the escypees." He eyed the Doctor with glee. "Ah, Doctor, the Myjor will want to 'ave a wee chat wif ee."

"I'm sure. What's going to happen to these others?"

"Oi wouldna concern mesilf wif them. Thy'll be well tyken care of." He waggled his weapon. "Noo, let's go."

The astrophysicist took the lead and marched slowly toward the hatch, all the while scowling fiercely at the Reman. Tas followed, and Hernandez and Corbo trailed behind. The latter hung his head down and shuffled his feet. Abruptly, he fell to his knees and held his head in his hands.

"We're all going to die!" he moaned. "*We're all going to die!*"

The terrorist stared at him uncomprehendingly.

"'Ay, what's wrong wif 'im?"

"Had he a mental break-down, thanks to you," the Bithan responded bitterly. "Will be he never the same again."

---

38 The JUR chose this Dunian bird of prey because of its reputation for swiftness, single-mindedness of purpose, and especially viciousness of attack. Whenever the terrorists staged an operation, they always left a representation of the falcon as a "calling card" – CMT.

"Sick in the'ead, ay? Well, Oi ayn't got toime to deal wif 'im. Leave 'im."

Tas muttered something in his own language and continued toward the hatch. The terrorist turned his attention away from Corbo, and that cost him. The *Astarte* officer rose to his feet, pulled a pistol from a pocket of his trousers, and shot their would-be captor twice at point-blank range. The latter grunted in pain and collapsed to the deck. The others regarded Corbo with shock.

"Did get you where that pistol?" the Bithan demanded.

"From that fellow Zam and O'Grady shot. I thought we'd need it. I was right."

"Then pretended to be you mentally ill?"

"Oh, I went bonkers all right. But I snapped out of it when Hernandez here threatened to leave me behind." He smiled at her, and she grimaced in return. "Funny how the mind works, huh?"

"I'd say so," Dr. Weyerhauser agreed. "If you're well enough to travel under your own steam, I suggest we get out of here. That gunfire is bound to bring others."

"Too true. Shall return we to the life-boat launch deck."

Tas now took the lead, exited the Communications bay, and turned in the direction from which they had originally come. The Doctor and Hernandez quickly fell in behind him. None of them noticed that, before exiting himself, Corbo kicked the JUR man in the head.

*   *   *

Rodriguez crouched behind a convenient boulder and peered at the Reman ship cruising overhead. He watched it every meter of its flight until it disappeared over the horizon. He still didn't move until he was absolutely sure that the craft was not circling back. Only then did he stand up, pulled his breath-mask away, and whistled. At the two-note signal, Sgt. Running Deer and his squad popped up from behind whatever cover they had been able to find. The non-com trotted over to the Warden.

"D'ya think they spotted us, sir?"

"Hard to say. But, I don't intend to take any chances. Let's assume they did and contacted their people on the ground." He searched the slope of the mountain beneath the *Astarte*. It looked to be a rigorous climb at that point but doable. "Send two of the squad a hundred meters up that slope as pickets. As soon as Sgt. Utumi arrives, I'll have him scout the entire area."

"Aye, sir."

The Warden leaned back against his boulder and resumed his sky-watching. He had had no illusions that this would be an easy mission, but he had hoped that he could have made it to the *Astarte* before the trouble began. Now, it appeared to be a fight every step of the way.

In due time, the shuttle returned with Lt. Ralfo, Sgt. Utumi, and Cpl. Chen and her squad. Rodriguez updated them on the situation, then ordered both squads to take positions fifty meters up the slope. He charged the Capellan to seek out a quick path to the *Astarte*.

"What are your orders for me, sir?" Ralfo asked softly.

He regarded her for a moment, pondering an answer.

"As I recall, you used to go mountain-climbing on Pluj. You even tried to get me involved."

"And a futile effort it was, Lixu. You had no desire for it."

"No, I didn't. Anyway, Sgt. Utumi might take offense, but I want you to follow him – discreetly – and watch his back."

"Who will watch *my* back?" she asked half-seriously.

"Why, all of Gamma Platoon, of course. I won't, because I'm off to pick flowers."

Ralfo giggled insanely, threw her arms around his neck, and kissed him juicily. She then pivoted and carried out her orders.

Incredibly, Pluj possessed only one mountain range. It had been formed when the planet came into being, slightly more than nearly two hundred thousand teraseconds ago; and due to the low level of geological activity, it had changed very little over the eons. Equally incredibly, this range formed a ring around the planet at its equator, giving rise to the *nom de vive*, the "belted world." This ring had, in its early days, served not only as a geological barrier but also as a cultural, linguistic, and social one. The sentient beings in each hemisphere had always claimed that their opposite numbers had been the "offshoot" – and therefore the "inferior" – race. These claims had resulted in several major conflicts and may have produced more had it not been for the plague which wiped out most of the male population. The female populations on both sides of the divide decided that the belligerent acts of the past had all been the males' fault and that *they* could unite the planet in a lasting peace. Hemispheric pride still existed on Pluj, but now it manifested itself in non-aggressive activities, such as athletic contests and artistic competitions. While most of these events involved females, some males had managed to "invade" the latter sphere.

The "Belt of Pluj" (as the mountain range is sometimes called) was as rugged as the Himalayas on Dunia, and there were no easy peaks to scale. They were all equally difficult to climb, and *officially* no one had ever claimed to have scaled all of them. The best mountaineers (of whom Anafu Ralfo was one) laid claim to no more than half of them, but that failure never deterred anyone from attempting to succeed where others had failed (and often died).

Ralfo peered up at the mountain range before her and grinned. This grouping was no higher than the least grouping on her world, and she would have considered it a "cakewalk" (to use an ancient Dunian expression she had learned from the Rodriguezes) were it not for the fact that Reman terrorists lurked on its heights, perhaps waiting in ambush. The sentient challenge presented a far greater danger than the mountain. She checked her sidearm to assure herself that it had a full clip and began her ascent.

She had already noted which way Sgt. Utumi had gone and approved of his choice. Obviously, the Capellan was no stranger to climbing mountains himself, for he was steadily blazing a trail up the slope which was both efficient and strategic. All she had to do was to follow his lead, and she did so with much aplomb and alacrity. She had thoughtfully brought along a piece of red chalk; and with it, she marked an "R" on the rocks every five meters. When Utumi slowed down – which was rarely – so did she; when he resumed after sorting through his options, she picked up the pace. And always, she maintained a twenty-meter gap behind him.

Five hundred meters up the slope, Ralfo squeezed between two jagged outcroppings and halted abruptly. Utumi was nowhere to be seen! She crouched low and scanned her surroundings in confusion. She was positive he had come this way; this section of the mountain was quite rugged and barely navigable, and the narrow opening through which she had just passed was the only viable path. So, where was he?

She continued to scan, then decided to shift her vantage point in order to get a better view. As she stood up, something nudged her arm. Instinctively, she whirled about and assumed a martial-arts stance, not an easy thing to do given the limited space in which she found herself. The tall, imposing figure before her offered no threatening posture, however, but his yellow eyes gleamed in self-satisfaction. Ralfo visibly relaxed but glared at the Alkon warrior furiously.

"What you here to do, Leftenant?" the Capellan asked quietly.

"Me as back-up Warden Rodriguez sent, Sergeant."

"He so little of my skills did think?"

"Sure he is that capable you are. But an unknown danger we face, and special precautions we must take."

"Mayhap." His yellow eyes now gleamed in amusement. "You did think that you an Alkon warrior unnoticed could track?"

"You I was not tracking," she sniffed. "Your lead I merely followed."

"If you to follow to wish, then to come. We this mountain together will take."

The sergeant pushed off and continued his climb, oblivious to Ralfo's presence. The Pluj scrambled after him at a distance of only five meters. After a zigzag course for another hundred meters, he halted, pressed against a nearby outcropping, and motioned Ralfo to take cover. She eased up next to him.

"What the problem is?"

"I three Oo-mans to see, thirty meters in that direction." He pointed to a ridge off to their left. "They in ambush to wait." He stroked his left cheek in contempt. "They clumsy fools to be."

"A plan you have?"

"Aye. I up there will go and them kill."

"By yourself?"

Utumi stared at her, his yellow eyes gleaming in indignation.

"I an Alkon warrior to be, aye?" he replied simply and was off in stalking mode.

"You Our Lady preserve, Utumi" she whispered and began to follow again, this time more slowly.

Ten meters from the spot of the presumed ambush, she saw the Capellan halt and search from side to side, supposedly scouting out a path. Then he scrambled off to his right and disappeared behind a boulder. Ralfo tracked the movement and expected to see him come back into view again. When he did not after twenty seconds, she became worried and eased her way to the point where he had diverged. A sudden movement to her left caught her attention; she swiveled around, focused, and gasped in amazement. Utumi had backtracked and was now inching his way beneath the ridge where the presumed ambushers were waiting.

The warrior maneuvered slowly but doggedly toward the far end of the ridge. When he had reached it, he crawled upwards and disappeared from view again. Long moments passed without a sign of him anywhere. Ralfo began worrying again and eased up the slope a few more meters. She was in plain view of anyone who might be on the ridge, and she half-expected shots to be fired at her. None were, and she continued to inch up. At one point, she thought she heard a scream; but the sound was muffled and of short duration, and she chalked it up to imagination.

Abruptly, a figure stood up on the ridge. Ralfo froze in place. The figure unexpectedly waved to her, and now she recognized it to be Utumi. She murmured a prayer of thanks to her Goddess and moved toward his position. Another movement, this time to her right and further up the slope, caught her eye. She spied another human, and he was raising an automatic rifle to bear on the Capellan. The latter was apparently unaware of his presence. Ralfo had no time to call out a warning, even if she could have; in order to call out loud enough for Utumi to hear her, she would have had to remove her breath-mask which would have defeated the effort at once. She had only one option. She drew her sidearm, took a quick but careful aim, and snapped off three rounds. The human jerked spasmodically as two of the rounds found their target. He fell backwards and did not move again.

She now joined the sergeant on the ridge and scowled at what she saw there. He was calmly wiping blood off the stilettos which every Alkon warrior carried in scabbards on their forearms. She looked past him and learned that he had been true to his word. One body slumped on the ground two meters away, a trickle of blood oozing out of its throat; a few meters away, another heap lay on the ground. That was all she could see, but she had to assume the third would-be ambusher had met a similar fate.

"Excellent work, Sergeant," she forced herself to say.

"I careless did be," he responded and stroked his right cheek as a sign of embarrassment. "I that fourth Oo-man did not see. I you to thank, Leftenant. You indeed my back did watch."

"The same for me you would have done." She peered up the slope. The *Astarte* loomed before her approximately six hundred meters away. "More ambushers there are?"

"Nay. The way now clear to be. You the others may signal."

*   *   *

The first to arrive at the *Astarte*'s final resting place was Pvt. Quinn, who had been assigned as point man (and been told to stay alert). His reaction to the wrecked ship was one of wonder, and he shook his head at the enormity of it all. He was followed ten seconds later by Sgt. Running Deer and the rest of his squad. Immediately, the non-com posted sentries. They were all greeted by a very relaxed Lt. Ralfo, who was leaning leisurely against a nearby boulder, and the ever-impassive Sgt. Utumi, who stood ram-rod stiff next to her. As the squad passed the pair, they eyed the Pluj wishfully and the Capellan with ill-disguised contempt. Ralfo grinned hugely at each and every one, while Utumi ignored them studiously.

Thirty seconds later, Rodriguez, Cpl. Chen, and her squad arrived, and the greeting "ritual" repeated itself. The Warden stared up at the wreckage and wondered what madness drove people to this kind of destruction. He recalled his classes in psychology at the Academy in which the instructors not only examined the nature of Evil, its roots, and methods of detecting its presence, but also instilled in the cadets a measure of cosmopolitanism so that they might be immune from similar impulses. Education, they said repeatedly, was the only answer to Evil; nothing was ever gained by repaying evil with more evil. As he examined the *Astarte* more closely, he realized – from a strictly objective point of view – that the Remans had done a thoroughly professional job of it. They had separated the MOME sphere from the rest of the cruise ship, tugged it to Planetoid 48, and removed the MOME as expeditiously as possible. The sphere itself – and any possible surviving crew – had been left to an uncertain fate. He faced his "scouting" party.

"Any trouble finding the trail you did have, Lixu?" the Pluj inquired with a sparkle in her eye.

"Only where you two seemed to have encountered an…'obstacle.'"

"No obstacle it was. It all in stride Sgt. Utumi and I took."

Rodriguez smiled in spite of himself. Pluj were noted, among other things, for their talent for understatement; no matter what the situation – be it political, social, economic, cultural, or martial – a Pluj who had been in the thick of it always managed to downplay her part in it to one degree or another. He remembered Anafu's mother explaining how she had averted a political crisis by getting the opposing parties to sit down, hold hands, and sing an old folk song (wherein she had sung the first stanza). She had described the incident as a "silly little *tete-a-tete*" and her role as a "mere referee." And Anafu herself often responded to praise by saying what she had done was "nothing to speak of."

"Perhaps for you it wasn't, but I'm not sure about the rest of the platoon." He now regarded the Capellan. "Sergeant, you probably did the right thing, but the idea of Alkon warriors killing humans still rankles many of my kind. I suggest you keep a safe distance between yourself and the others."

"I usually to do," the Capellan replied stolidly. "Except for you, Rodri-go, I most Oo-mans distasteful to find."

"I may say that 'most Oo-mans' find the three of us distasteful as well, but for different reasons. We don't fit into 'normal' society."

"A horrible thing that to say is, Lixu," the Pluj protested. "But too true." She brightened abruptly as all of her kind were able to do when the mood became too somber for comfort. "Nevertheless, anything the three of us can conquer."

The remark brought deep smiles from both of her male companions, each in his own fashion.

Sgt. Running Deer approached then after having set his pickets and awaited further orders. The Warden pulled a schematic of the *Astarte*'s MOME sphere out of his waist pouch, spread it against a nearby (somewhat) flat surface, and studied it briefly. He pointed out the locations of the airlocks and directed the sergeant to take Cpl. Chen and reconnoiter. He and Ralfo went on their own little fact-finding expedition which consisted mainly of keeping a sharp eye on the sky in case the Reman ship returned.

After their walk-about, Running Deer and Chen were waiting for them.

The latter reported that one of the airlocks were completely inaccessible because it was on that part of the sphere which had taken the brunt of the crash-landing. The other one was functional but, because of the angle of the crash, required that the platoon crawl in on all fours. Rodriguez nodded by way of accepting the report and sent the non-coms to assemble their squads.

Gamma Platoon fell in haphazardly. On a rugged mountainside, there was little opportunity to line up in a proper military fashion, and the troopers lined up as best they could, regarding the Warden expectantly.

"I can't emphasize strongly enough," he began, "the necessity of taking every precaution you've ever learned. You've been trained to board ships in Deep Space under varying circumstances, and I doubt that any of you has come up against the present circumstance. I know I haven't. So, watch yourselves – and each other. Also, I can't emphasize enough the necessity of keeping calm and collected. No one – and I mean *absolutely* no one – is to shoot first and ask questions later. Return fire if you're fired upon, but don't fire at every moving thing. Any questions?"

Again, there were none spoken aloud. Rodriguez signaled to Running Deer; the non-com sent out his point man (Quinn again), waited a decent interval, and took the lead of the first squad. The Warden and Ralfo fell in behind them, followed by Chen and her squad. By mutual agreement, Utumi acted as rear guard.

Running Deer had not been exaggerating about the narrow access. There was only half a meter between the *Astarte*'s hull and the rock face. In order to gain entry into the airlock, one had to crouch down before the opening, brace one's back against the rock face, and insert one's legs into the opening. Once so positioned, one had to slide down the rock face until one was sitting down, then wiggle one's body until it was completely inside, flat on one's back. This maneuvering would have been painstakingly slow if one had had no encumbrances upon him/her. But, these were Constabulary troopers in full combat gear – which meant that one had to remove one's gear and weapons, gain entry, and have the next person push his/her equipment after him/her, *ad infinitum.*

The entire operation required five kiloseconds to complete, and there was considerable grumbling throughout. Still, the only real problem encountered arose when the last person's turn came. The Capellan was very reluctant to make the effort. In the first place, the average Alkon warrior stood one-and-three-quarters-meters high – almost half a meter taller than the average human. If squeezing through that narrow opening was difficult for the human (and the Pluj) components of the unit, imagine what it would be like for a Capellan! In the second place, most warriors had a dread of entering caves; for them, it was akin to entering a tomb where spirits of the dead might lurk. Urban-born

Capellans were slowly but surely overcoming that particular superstition, but the rural-born were still gripped by it. And, though technically speaking, an airlock was not a cave, because of the manner in which this airlock was situated, entering it was reminiscent of entering a cave in the mind of Sgt. Utumi. It took Rodriguez a good deal of coaxing and cajoling to get the sergeant inside; and every few seconds, the latter would mutter a new prayer to one or another of the many Capellan gods.

When all of the platoon had re-assembled inside, the Warden took stock of the location, consulting frequently with his schematic. They were in an emergency exit, and it lead to a starboard cargo bay. From there, they could either work their way toward the lifeboat launch platform or toward the next level up. In either case, the way would be difficult due to the damage suffered here.

Rodriguez dispatched Cpl. Chen and her squad to the launch platform to see if any of the lifeboats had been used by survivors. He posted Sgt. Running Deer's squad at the companionway leading to the next level; there they would wait until Chen reported back.

The silence inside the sphere was eerie. Ordinarily, a cruise ship was a beehive of activity around the clock in all sections. Throughout, maintenance personnel conducted inspections of the structure and equipment continuously, making repairs where needed; cargo handlers received, stowed, and/or distributed supplies to all parts of the ship; and the technicians kept a watchful eye on the functioning of the electronics and especially of the MOME. The command staff received, filed, and/or acted upon reports from all sections and made entries to the log as required by the Central Spiral Collective's bureaucracy.[39] Every second, someone – or more properly, many someones – were on the move from one point to another.

No such hustle-and-bustle existed now, and the only sounds which could be heard were the creaking and squealing, the groaning and moaning, the grinding and scraping of metal shifting and settling. They were inhuman sounds, and they sent a chill up and down Rodriguez's spine much like the scraping of fingernails across a chalkboard did. For all intents and purposes, the *Astarte* was dead.

Chen returned one-and-a-half kiloseconds later to report that a number of lifeboats were missing. She also reported that one of the launch-bay doors had a red smear on it and "looked like blood."

"Quite possibly, then," Rodriguez mused, "some of the crew are floating

---

39   In this particular instance, the CSC's Commission for Interstellar Trade had jurisdiction and, like its sister Commissions, expected strict observance of its regulations by all who operated a commercial enterprise in Deep Space, regardless of its nature – CMT.

around in Deep Space. As soon as we return to the *Steadfast*, I'll have Captain Halvarson search for them. Good work, Corporal. Sgt. Running Deer!"

"Sir?"

"We won't be needing cold-weather gear from here on. Have your people strip down to their fatigues and prepare to move out."

"You heard the man!" the non-com barked. "Strip to your fatigues! Quinn! Where the frag is Quinn?"

"Excuse me, Sergeant," the Warden put in. "Are you planning on putting Quinn on point again?"

"Yes, sir. He's my best man." The sergeant eyed his officer with concern. "Do you want someone else on point?"

"If it's all the same to you, I'd like to put Utumi on point. He *is* a scout, after all. Also, if we run into any of the JUR, they might think twice about tangling with an Alkon warrior, and that'll give us an edge."

"All right. You're the boss. Get ready to move out, you fraggers!"

Rodriguez motioned to the Capellan to join him.

"Time to earn your pay, Utumi-go. Go up to the next level and check out what's ahead of us."

"Aye, sir," the other responded, his yellow eyes gleaming with anticipation.

As graceful as a cat, the warrior pivoted, broke into a trot, and bounded up the companionway three stairs at a time. The Warden turned to Ralfo.

"Stay with Chen's squad and act as rearguard. I'll be with Running Deer."

"Over you Our Lady watch, Lixu."

"And you, Anafu. Sergeant! Move 'em out!"

The advance squad was split into two teams. One team, behind Rodriguez, hugged the bulkhead on one side of the companionway – and the passageway on the next level – while the other team, behind Running Deer, hugged the opposite bulkhead. They moved at a snail's pace, one cautious step at a time; if they came to a hatch, they halted and listened carefully for any telltale signs of sentient life within the compartment. Mostly, however, all they heard was the incessant creaking and squealing, the groaning and moaning, and the grinding and scraping of shifting and settling metal — and their own heartbeats.

Halfway down the passageway (which, as luck would have it, was the same exact route Dr. Mubutu Weyerhauser and his party had taken), the Warden spotted his scout quickly but stealthily returning from his foray. He halted the squad.

"I three Oo-mans and one Listu[40] have spy. The Listu and two of the Oo-mans the uniform of the *Astarte* to wear, but the third Oo-man a civilian to be. They this way to come."

"Ah, maybe we'll get some useful information from them. Good work, Sergeant. Running Deer, come with me."

The pair walked briskly down the passageway and turned into a cross-passageway. Fifty meters from that point, the party of escapees approached from the opposite direction. Upon spotting the Constabulary personnel, the quartet halted abruptly and actually took a couple of steps backward out of sheer reflex before they recognized the oncomers.

"Look, Professor!" the Bithan exclaimed. "Is it the Constabulary! Are to rescue they us here!"

"Thank God!" the astrophysicist murmured. "Our luck is changing."

Rodriguez and Running Deer closed the gap. The latter drew his sidearm as a matter of precaution. The former reached into his tunic, produced his badge, and held it up high.

"I'm Warden Rodriguez, assigned to the *CSS Steadfast*. Who are you?"

"Am I Tas Omaro, Executive Officer of the *Astarte*, with the two remaining crew left alive." He gestured at them. "Is this Stewardess Hernandez and Lt. Corbo."

"And this other gentleman? Is he a passenger?"

"No, is this Professor Weyerhauser."

Rodriguez peered at the tall Reman with some surprise. Even though he had been searching for the man with orders to place him under arrest, he had not expected to find him this easily and under these circumstances.

"Professor Mubutu Weyerhauser? Lately of the University of New Nairobi?" The other grimaced and nodded. "I've been looking for you."

"I know. We've been in contact with your Captain Halvarson. He told us you were on your way here."

The Warden turned to Running Deer.

"Bring Lt. Ralfo up here."

"Aye, sir," the non-com said, pivoted, and trotted back the way he had come.

While he waited for Ralfo to join him, Rodriguez took a statement from Tas. He held off questioning the Reman until he could be positively identified. The Bithan spoke at length about what had occurred since the attack on the *Astarte*; several times in his narrative, his voice faltered and tears came into

---

40   This is the Capellan term for the inhabitants of Bi. Though Capella and Bi are essentially militaristic societies (and allies in the War of the Eight Suns), neither had a great opinion of the other. The Capellans regard the Bithans as weaklings, while the Bithans consider the Capellans as barbarians – CMT.

his eyes. Near the end of his tale of woe, the Warden became aware of Ralfo at his side. She was trying not to cry herself.

"Thank you, Mr. Tas. You can rest assured that those responsible will be suitably punished. Anafu, the tall gentleman claims to be Dr. Mubutu Weyerhauser. Can you verify?"

The Pluj brightened and gazed at the astrophysicist. The latter gave her a tight little smile.

"Yes, Lixu, Dr. Weyerhauser he is. How you are, Professor?"

"I'm OK – under the circumstances. You look familiar. Have we met?"

"Astrophysics at the Constabulary Academy you taught. Your 'prized pupil' I was."

"Ah, I remember you now – the Pluj with so many questions. I regret that we meet again under these circumstances."

Rodriguez fished out his badge again and held it up.

"Dr. Mubutu Weyerhauser," he declared in his best official tone of voice, "I have a warrant for your arrest. You are wanted for questioning about several matters, not the least of which is the highjacking and subsequent destruction of the cruise ship *Astarte*. You may elect to remain silent, but any statement you do make can be used against you in a court of law."

"But, Warden," the Bithan stepped forward to protest, "is he no longer a terrorist. Has defected he. Has helped to escape he us."

"That may be, Mr. Tas, but I am duty bound to turn him over to the proper authorities. If there are mitigating circumstances, the court may exercise leniency."

"Don't worry about me, Mr. Tas," the Doctor said. "I'm prepared to face justice. Serve your warrant, Warden. I'll tell you anything you want to know. Just get me away from that madman down there."

"And which madman is that, Professor?"

"Major Anton Tshambe. He's the leader of the JUR cell responsible for the atrocities you're investigating. And he's not done yet." He took a deep breath and let it out slowly. "He intends to aim this world at Romulus and destroy it."

"That would support a theory I've heard recently. Well, let's get you and these others back to the *Steadfast*. Mr. Tas, we came in through the emergency hatch near the lifeboat launch bay. Is there another way out?"

Before the XO could reply, the unmistakable sound of automatic-weapons fire issued from the direction of the launch bay. The sound echoed and re-echoed throughout that section of the ship. Both Rodriguez and Running Deer recognized two types of weapons being fired, suggesting that a pitched battle was in progress. The exchange of gunfire was short-lived, however, and the silence which followed disturbed the Warden and the sergeant even more than the fighting itself. Both men regarded each other with concern. Ralfo showed her concern by clutching at Rodriguez's arm. The civilians expressed various degrees of fright. Only Sgt. Utumi, silently standing by all this while, remained impassive.

"Anafu, stay here with the civilians. Running Deer, Utumi, you're with me."

The trio took off at a fast trot, sidearms at the ready. When they reached the top of the companionway leading to the launch bay, the Warden called out for a response from Gamma Platoon. The response came instantly.

"It's all green across, sir," the voice of Cpl. Chen floated up. "A couple of the terrorists touched down unexpectedly and tried to hom us. We hommed them instead."

"Any casualties on our side?" Running Deer inquired.

"Yeah, we took some hits, Sarge. Two dead, three wounded."

"This is not good," the Warden muttered, half to the sergeant, half to no one in particular. "That gunfire is sure to attract the rest of the JUR here."

"Aye, sir. We may have to fight our way out, with the added disadvantage of having to exit the way we came in."

"Set up a perimeter, and see to the wounded. I'll go back for the others. Afterwards, we can assess our situation."

CHAPTER SIXTEEN

▼

RETREAT FROM THE *ASTARTE*

CAPTAIN OLAF HALVARSON OF THE CSC patrol vessel *Steadfast* was toying with a helping of mashed potatoes in the officers' mess. First, he plumped up the mound, forming a conical structure; then he squashed the apex of the "cone" until he had created a crater with high "walls." Next, he elevated the "walls" so as to transform the whole into a deep pit, and finally, he swirled his fork though the mass and returned the potatoes to their original amorphous pile (albeit with a flattened surface).

Obviously, his heart was not in the consumption of this, or any other, part of his lunch. He had too much on his mind, not the least of which was the pretense of being on maneuvers while actually keeping his eye on Planetoid 48. The rogue was closing in on the Rhea Silvia system and, at its present velocity, would penetrate it in approximately one megasecond. The trouble was that it was not limited to its present velocity; having been jury-rigged with an MOME, it could be inside the star system in a matter of kiloseconds. Halvarson's only consolation was that an MOME required a hundred (or more) kiloseconds to re-energize itself, depending upon the length of its previous warp-out. The *Steadfast* was playing a waiting game, a game it might not be able to win.

The Captain's other major concern was the progress of the advance party he had sent to the planetoid. It hadn't been his idea to send that party – he had wanted to stage an all-out assault – but he had been over-ridden by the wishes of his resident Warden, who was under orders to apprehend a particular individual reportedly on the runaway. He was now biding his time until the

242 | By Charlton Clayes and C. Malcolm Trowbridge, PhD.

Warden reported back and cleared the way for the assault. If the Warden were delayed in finding his man and the MOME was fully re-energized, the *Steadfast* would have to re-deploy closer to Rhea Silvia and begin the search all over again.

Damn Rodriguez! the Captain swore. *Why hadn't he minded his own business? Oh, right, he* was *minding his business. But, he was interfering with my business while he was at it.*

He pushed his tray away and stared at the overhead. The food was cold by now, and he hadn't been that hungry in the first place. He could go for a few laps in the pool right now – preferably with Lt. Commander von Lichtenberg. Too bad Felicia was on duty at the moment. He sighed heavily and traced imaginary patterns in the overhead.

The beeping of his personal vidcom brought him quickly out of his reverie. He activated it and peered at the neutral face of Commander Krishnamurthy.

"Yes, Tomiko?"

"Sir, Warden Rodriguez has broken radio silence and is waiting to speak with you."

"Finally! I'll be right down."

His pace was somewhere between a brisk walk and a trot, and he made record time in reaching the Bridge. The XO immediately vacated the Captain's chair and resumed her own seat. She gave him a tight little smile and received one in return. Halvarson opened the channel to the Warden's vidcom. The latter regarded him with his usual grim expression.

"I have good news, Captain. I found my man sooner than I expected. In fact, he was looking for *me*."

"Yes, he managed to contact the *Steadfast* earlier, and I told him you were on the planetoid."

"Excellent. We're presently inside what's left of the *Astarte*, but we'll be vacating shortly. We've suffered a few casualties, and that will slow us down a bit. Give us, oh, five kilos, and then you may commence your own operation."

"Thank you, Warden," Halvarson responded with the barest hint of sarcasm in his voice. "I'll see you when you return to the ship."

Insolent pup! he grumbled. *As if I needed* your *permission to run my ship.*

He pressed the button on his console marked "Conference," then entered the codes for the offices of Commanders Rux and Mbaku. The images of the combat brigade commanders appeared on a split screen. Both looked appropriately grim.

"Gentlemen, our young Warden has given us the 'all clear.' Deploy your forces as we've planned."

The Bithan and the Romulan nodded and wordlessly switched off. The Captain ordered the Display to be activated.

The Constabulary's standard operating procedure was to deploy sufficient forces to overwhelm whatever opposition it might encounter. The Central Spiral Collective, for the purposes of defense, had been divided into ten sectors, and each sector was patrolled by a fleet of ships, five hundred in all. At each level of command, these ships were assigned particular regions of Deep Space, according to an assessment of criminal activity in each sector. Assessments, of necessity, were reviewed on a regular basis and assignments were re-ordered when and where justified. For the most part, fleet, task force, and ship commanders had a certain amount of leeway in the deployment of their individual forces based upon the exigencies of a given situation. If they required additional forces, all they need do was to request them from their immediate superiors; ordinarily, few requests were ever refused which boosted the Constabulary's reputation for being able to meet any threat anywhere.

In the present instance, the battle plan was to utilize two squadrons of attack craft and only two light cruisers from the support squadron. The thinking was that, since the JUR seldom operated in Deep Space, they would have only transport-style ships at their disposal; therefore, "sufficient forces" meant the minimum number of attack ships to encircle the opposition. On the other hand, the number of JUR operatives on Planetoid 48 was unknown, and the troop brigade commander was taking no chances on being caught under-manned. And, given the past ferocity of Reman terrorists in general, he was ordering out the entire brigade – three companies of troopers and a support company.

On the Bridge and in each brigade operation room, everyone concerned gazed intently as the Display blips representing each ship appeared in formation. The fighter craft formed the standard semi-circle while the cruisers positioned themselves aft of the squadron leaders' ships. Six troop carriers lined up behind the fighters, followed by the light cruisers. Captain Halvarson nervously chewed his lower lip as he watched his forces close in on the target. He hoped he had time to pull this operation off. Otherwise, Romulus was in serious trouble.

*   *   *

Doctor Weyerhauser regarded the bodies of the slain JUR members with a mixture of regret and disdain. Regret because the two dead men turned out to be Cutty and Jingles, the only members of the cell who had shown him any courtesy, and disdain because they had been complicit (as he himself had been) in the most horrendous crimes imaginable. They had been part of a

244 | By Charlton Clayes and C. Malcolm Trowbridge, PhD.

search party looking for him and the survivors of the *Astarte*, but they hadn't expected to run into a fully-armed platoon of Constabulary troopers. The firefight had been brief and fatal. And this would only be the beginning; when the rest of the troopers arrived to flush out the remainder of the terrorists, Planetoid 48 would become a bloodbath. Ironically, he might become the sole surviving member of the cell.

He snorted in derision. Being the last one struck him as very small consolation. His fate was sealed. He would be tried, convicted, and sentenced to life imprisonment for his complicity in crimes against sentience. From a court of law, he would be transported to the star system of the enigmatic Aldebaranians and swallowed up by the penal colony on Xix. No one who ever served a life sentence ever left it alive, and no one ever escaped it. He would never see Remus again. Worse, he would never see Petra again. Would she write to him, knowing what evil he had committed? Not likely, and he wouldn't have blamed her in the least. This was the price of his misguided idealism and his naiveté – to lose everything he held dear because he had trusted the wrong people. It was a bitter lesson indeed.

The Warden from the Constabulary ship completed his report to his Captain and signaled him to re-join him. He walked slowly across the launch bay like a man in a daze.

"Can we expect any more of your friends?" Rodriguez asked, gesturing at the dead JUR men.

"I can't say. Cutty and Jingles were part of a group sent out by Major Tshambe to look for me and the *Astarte* people. How many he assigned is unknown. I do know that six of the group (including these two) are dead. Mr. Tas's people killed four of them on the upper levels."

"And where might this Major and the rest of the cell be located?"

"This whole world is honeycombed with caves and tunnels. My...'friends,' as you so quaintly put it, are scattered throughout them."

"And the MOME?"

"It's in one of the largest caves, deep inside the planetoid."

The Warden nodded sagely.

"Thank you, Professor. Now, if you'll excuse me, I have to check on our wounded."

Rodriguez walked briskly to a makeshift triage area opposite the companionway. The two dead troopers lay a few meters apart from the wounded, covered by their own bedrolls. He gave them a cursory glance and shook his head sadly. Sgt. Running Deer was regarding the wounded with a minimal amount of concern.

"What's the situation here, Sergeant?"

"Quinn here was only grazed by a bullet." He gave the private a look of mock-scorn. "He'll live – if he's careful."

"You told me to be alert, Sarge," Quinn grinned, "and I was. When the shootin' started, I danced around and dodged every one o' them fraggin' bullets. Well, almost every one."

"And the others?"

"One stomach wound and one leg wound. I don't give the stomach wound much of a chance of survival if we don't get him treated right away."

"Didn't any in your platoon receive first-aid training?"

"Aye, sir," the non-com replied grimly. "The one with the stomach wound."

The Warden grunted.

"Happily, I received combat first-aid training at the Academy. Where's the first-aid kit?"

Running Deer gestured at a light-blue knapsack, thirty centimeters long by twenty wide, near the trooper with the stomach wound. The knapsack had been embroidered with a red caduceus underneath the dark-blue insignia of the Constabulary.

Rodriguez now moved into the triage area, bent down over the stomach wound, and examined it with appropriate detachment. The bullet had punctured the lower part of the stomach, just above the intestinal tract, and was causing the victim considerable pain. He groaned and whimpered incessantly. Blood oozed from the wound in a steady stream. The Warden opened the first-aid kit and rummaged through it; he removed several large gauze pads, a roll of adhesive tape, and an alcohol wipe. From a small pouch on his belt, he produced two clear plastic ampoules, one containing a grayish liquid and the other a clear liquid. With his thumbnail, he punctured the ampoule with the grayish substance and quickly held it under the wounded trooper's nose. As soon as the liquid inside was exposed to air, it turned gaseous; as the victim breathed the vapor, it acted upon his nervous system and numbed it. This substance, called "anesthol" by humans, was developed by the Aldebaranians (who called it something else, but not in public) and issued only to Wardens. True to form, its manufacture was a guarded secret.

Once the trooper's pain had been neutralized, Rodriguez went to work on the wound itself. He ripped open the man's tunic and used one of the gauze pads to soak up the excess blood. Then he swabbed the wound with the alcohol wipe to disinfect it. Next, he pressed a second pad against the wound and directed the sergeant to hold it firmly in place while he measured out several long strips of tape. He then taped the pad securely to the wound. Finally, he broke open the ampoule with the clear liquid, opened the trooper's mouth, and trickled the substance into it. This was a powerful antibiotic and was reputed to work against all harmful bacteria, most viruses, and several toxins. It was another marvel of Aldebaranian medical science – termed "anti-tox" by humans – and was another well-guarded secret.

After seeing that the stomach wound was resting quietly, the Warden moved on to the leg wound. The injury did not appear to be serious; the trooper had caught a bullet in the thigh, resulting in a bit of bleeding and no other symptoms. Rodriguez fashioned a makeshift tourniquet out of a section of the trooper's trousers, wrapped it tightly around the upper thigh, and secured it with a sailor's knot. He then slapped a gauze pad over the wound, taped it up, and administered another ampoule of the clear liquid.

"That's about all I can do at the moment," he remarked to Running Deer. "As soon as the assault force gets here, we'll evacuate the wounded first and hand them over to the medical team."

"What about me, sir?" Quinn whined. "I'm injured too."

The Warden regarded the sad sack with a mixture of amusement and annoyance. The latter stared back with puppy-dog eyes. Wordlessly, Rodriguez fished in the first-aid kit, extracted an adhesive bandage, and tossed it to the trooper.

"Consider yourself treated, Quinn. Put that on and re-join your comrades."

"Oh, *frag!*" the other moaned.

"And be quick about it, fragger!" the sergeant added. "Or I'll put you on fraggin' point again."

"Oh, *frag!*"

"How soon will the assault force be here, sir?" Running Deer inquired.

"I'd say it'll take them less than half the time it took us." He checked his chrono. "Say, twenty K's."

"They can't get here any too soon. I feel itchy, knowin' there's a pack of Reemie terrorists crawling around."

"That makes two of us, Sergeant. I suggest you find some busywork for the platoon. It'll keep them occupied and alert."

"Aye, sir."

The Warden now took advantage of the temporary lull to take stock of the situation. He mentally created two columns, one marked "plus" and the other "minus." Into the "plus" column, he listed first the arrest of the wanted fugitive, Dr. Mubutu Weyerhauser. Secondly came the astrophysicist's complete co-operation in providing information concerning his former comrades. Thirdly were the deaths of several terrorists – recommendation: a special citation for Sgt. Utumi for his part in averting an ambush and preventing Gamma Platoon from suffering severe losses. Fourthly was the rescue of some of the *Astarte*'s crew. In the "minus" column, he listed at the top their own casualties

– two dead, two major wounded, one minor wounded. That was followed by the approximate number of JUR operatives still on the loose. A quick analysis of his tabulations suggested that the batch of misfits which made up Gamma Platoon had acquitted themselves reasonably well, considering what they were up against. He wasn't too pleased about the loss of life – on either side, for that matter – but, in these circumstances, one had to expect it.

He didn't have to wonder what Master Fresh would have made of his first "command." From personal experience, he knew that his mentor would (1) extract a highly detailed report of all decisions made, all actions taken, and all accomplishments achieved, (2) follow through with a point-by-point critique of said report, and (3) provide "suggestions" for improving one's behavior during any subsequent exercises. And, all the while, Master Fresh would fix him with a steely glare and poke him in the chest repeatedly. He would then dismiss him summarily so that he might lick his wounds and meditate upon what a lack-wit he was for thinking he was Warden material.

A lesser being might have given up the fight long ago, but Lixu Rodriguez had very much wanted to be a Warden. And so, he had persevered and endured the humiliation and worked hard to succeed in his goal. And he had graduated at the top of his class. And, wonder of wonders! he had spied, out of the corner of his eye, his mentor actually smiling broadly when the oldster thought no one was looking.

When this mission was concluded, he'd critique it himself in the same fashion as his mentor might have. He'd follow the same routine, ask the same questions, make the same observations, and draw the same conclusions as Master Fresh had done so many times before. He'd be as hard on himself as any Aldebaranian, and he'd feel as smug about it as they did.

Having seen to the wounded, the Warden turned his mind to further interrogation of Dr. Weyerhauser. At the moment, the latter was engaged in conversation with Lt. Ralfo; and, from the smiling and laughing which accompanied the talk, he guessed that they were reminiscing about their days at the Constabulary Academy. One would never have believed that the Reman was a wanted fugitive from his current behavior; rather, one would have believed that he was simply renewing his acquaintance with an old friend.

But Rodriguez knew the mindset of the Pluj better than any human did, and he was not surprised by the scene before him. Anafu's people were as guileless as small children, adapting themselves to each situation as it came, without judgment or prejudice; any emotional baggage which may have been attached to the parties involved was quickly forgotten if the new circumstances did not re-enforce it in any significant fashion. Mubutu Weyerhauser may have been a mass murderer, wanted by all the law enforcement agencies in the central spiral; but to Anafu, he was only her former instructor, and nothing else mattered. She was not even concerned that he would soon be tried for his complicity in a long list of crimes against sentience.

He strolled over to the chatting couple and waited calmly as the conversation wound down. Ralfo regarded him gleefully.

"Lixu, you did know that an interest in Pluj cosmology Dr. Weyerhauser has?"

"No, I didn't know that."

"True it is. He says that – but him of it I will allow to speak."

The Warden turned to the astrophysicist and gazed at him expectantly (and somewhat bemusedly). The latter pursed his lips.

"Actually, I have an interest in *everybody's* cosmology. As a hobby, I've been collecting the myths and legends of a number of cultures, human and alien. The details vary, as you might imagine, but the basic structure is extraordinarily similar throughout. Some god or another is either bored or lonely, so it decides to create something to pass the time (which, of course, doesn't exist in a static Universe). This god starts out with the 'basics' of stars and planets and moons and sets them all whirling about. Then, it gets a bit more creative and moves from the inorganic to the organic, selecting a few planets at random and populating them with living things. With each new creation, it needs new challenges to its powers and thus fashions ever more complex organisms until finally it hits upon sentient beings whom it can converse with and/or manipulate. Occasionally, the god finds flaws in its creations (which is a contradiction in terms, don't you know?), destroys the flawed 'product,' and starts again with a new design.

"Interaction with a sentient being is a given as well, and interaction can take many forms. Sometimes the god appears before its creation in a recognizable form, i.e. the creation's form; sometimes it appears in a symbolic form, e.g. a bright light or a 'vision.' Appearances presage a warning, a prophecy, an instruction, or a compliment; those who claim to speak for the gods get to decide which it is. Having sex with a god represents the next-to-the-highest praise of oneself, while having the god's offspring is the highest.

"I've gathered enough data to write a multi-volume examination of this subject." He peered off into the distance wistfully. "I reckon I'll have the time to write it as I while away the rest of my life on Xix."

"But a pawn you were, Professor," Ralfo protested. "Used you were. Lixu, nothing there is we can do?"

The Warden rubbed his jaw. Right now, he was torn between his duty to uphold the law and sympathy for someone who apparently had fallen in with the wrong crowd but who was willing to make amends.

"Officially, I am bound to take you into custody, Professor, and deliver you to New Switzerland. On the other hand, I can also note in my report that you co-operated in the apprehension of a JUR cell and the prevention of an act of genocide. That'll be a mitigating circumstance and may help to reduce your sentence. More than that is out of my hands."

"Thank you for that, Warden, but even a reduced sentence will hardly erase what I've been a party to." He furled his brow. "Speaking of cosmological data, though, there's some to be gathered on this world."

"Really? This world was inhabited once?"

"Yes. I've discovered a stone henge on the other side of this mountain range, presumably dating from the days before this planetoid got knocked out of its orbit. I've also come across the remains of a humanoid species in one of the caves where the indigenous population retreated when they could no longer survive on the surface – not that it did them any good in the end. And, most significantly, I've found this." He pulled the metallic plaque he had found at the henge out of his coat pocket and gave it to Rodriguez. "I found a similar piece in one of the caves. It had only one symbol on it" – he paused for dramatic effect – "the mark of the Wayfarers."

"The Wayfarers!" the Warden exclaimed. "My God! They were *here*?"

The Wayfarers: that ancient, unknown race of beings who had criss-crossed the Galaxy and left behind tantalizing "souvenirs" of their passing. The Wayfarers: the root cause of many a myth and legend throughout the central spiral, including Dunia. The Wayfarers: a will o' the wisp, as elusive as the wind and as substantial as a shadow.

Rodriguez had heard all of the tales from childhood on and been caught between belief and disbelief. He had even visited the Galactic Museum of Natural History on New Switzerland and seen the meager display of artifacts purportedly attributed to the influence of those legendary creatures, and he still could not make up his mind as to their existence. Now, he had the opportunity to investigate another potential site of Wayfarer presence and the possibility – a *slim* possibility, to be sure – of ascertaining the truth of the legends. More, he had the *obligation* to do so.

Assembly Act #33, passed by the Grand Assembly of the Central Spiral Collective in the year A.C. 24, stated quite specifically that "all personnel of the Central Spiral Collective of whichever commission, agency, bureau, office, or capacity in which they may be employed are hereby directed to investigate any and all reports, conversations, or rumors pertaining to the nature, whereabouts, or identity of the race of beings popularly known as the 'Wayfarers'... Further, all said personnel are hereby directed to gather, obtain, or seize by all legal means any and all devices, artifacts, material goods, cultural property, and other substantive evidence pertaining to the existence of the said race of beings... It is the purpose and aim of this body to gain as much knowledge of these enigmatic creatures as it is possible in order to give form to legend and to acknowledge our common galactic heritage."

The Act created a clearinghouse, the Office for the Search for Ancestral Beings (OSAB), to implement the directives of the Assembly, and it had hit the ground running. Attached to the CSC's Commission for Cultural Affairs, its agents set up a network of investigators, informants, and spies to track down the rumors and to ferret out the material evidence. With such a broad mandate, at times these agents did not act entirely within the law; and the OSAB received its fair share of criticism (and several lawsuits) concerning their methods which included "rough treatment" and "illegal confiscation of private property." Such counteractions only served to attest to the efficiency and thoroughness of OSAB operatives (if not their politeness), and the results they produced encouraged the CSC to downplay the rough stuff.

The visible part of these results resided in the Galactic Museum for all to see. The *invisible* part resided in a vast collection of computerized files concerning every investigation conducted and its outcome; these files were accessed by the general public on a need-to-know basis, and much red tape was involved, to the eternal chagrin of the press and scholarly researchers.

Wardens were not immune from Act #33. In point of fact, due to the nature of their office, they were perhaps in as good a position as any OSAB agent to discover the nature, whereabouts, and identity of the Wayfarers. Their special training by the equally mysterious Aldebaranians opened them up to see things others might miss; and their omnipresence throughout the Collective put them in places where few others dared to go. Even while engaged in law enforcement, they were nevertheless also obliged, as personnel of the Collective, to be alert for signs of that ancient race.

Now Warden (L1) Lixu Rodriguez found himself sitting on top of a sign, and he knew his duty.

"This puts a new wrinkle in our situation. Originally, I had planned to evacuate Planetoid 48 as soon as I'd found you. I see now that I'm going to have to test the limits of your co-operation even further, Professor."

"I've already agreed to co-operate fully. What do you want me to do?"

"Simply, we need you to guide us through these caves and tunnels until we find those artifacts and remains and secure them."

The astrophysicist stared at him incredulously.

"You can't be serious! There are nearly two dozen homicidal maniacs down there. You wouldn't stand a chance."

"I didn't say it would be easy. I'm well aware of the risks involved. But, if it'll make you feel any better, we'll wait until the assault force from the *Steadfast* arrives."

"Yes, it would make me feel better, though I'm not completely mollified."

"Thank you. To start with something relatively safe while we're waiting, we'll go outside and have a look at this henge of yours. I want to make a visual record of the site and take some samples for the archaeology people on New Switzerland to play with."[41]

"What do you intend to do with the *Astarte* people?"

"They can stay aboard the shuttle until it's safe to transfer them to one of the troop carriers." He flashed a quick and insincere smile. "You can break the news to them."

Rodriguez sought out Sgt. Running Deer. The non-com was checking the positions of his troopers at the bottom of the companionway and offering words of encouragement. Gamma Platoon did not seem particularly encouraged, however, given their recent experience.

"Sergeant, I'm going to take Chen and her squad outside to investigate an archaeological site Doctor Weyerhauser has discovered. This will keep at least some of the platoon occupied while we're waiting for the *Steadfast*."

"Aye, sir. Corporal Chen! Front and center!"

The Romulan trotted over and came to attention. She appeared as nervous as everyone else.

"Corporal," the Warden said casually, "the Professor and I are going to explore an archaeological site on the other side of this mountain range. You and your squad will provide security. In particular, I want you personally to keep an eye on the Professor. I've placed him under protective custody, and I don't want anything to happen to him."

"Aye, sir. I'll guard 'im like he was my own brother."

"Fine. Get your squad over to the airlock and help the *Astarte* people. They'll be put aboard the shuttle, out of harm's way."

The Warden then searched for Lt. Ralfo and found her sitting on the second step from the top of the companionway in a meditative mode. Pluj did not meditate very often (except on religious holidays); they were usually filled with an ebullient self-confidence and therefore had little need for morale-boosting exercises. Why Ralfo was meditating at this time was a mystery, and Rodriguez debated whether he should ask her. He supposed she would tell him sooner or later. He cleared his throat loudly and intentionally. Instantly, her eyes popped open, and she gave him a big grin.

"I would like to make love to you right now, Lixu."

"I'd be all for it myself – if we weren't on duty." She frowned. "And

---

41 Reference is made specifically to the Institute for Exo-Archaeology, a private organization which contracts with the CSC to explore and analyze ancient sites. Currently, its teams are engaged in thirty-four digs on eleven planets – CMT.

duty dictates that I have to leave you for a while." He explained what he was planning to do, and her frown deepened. "As soon as we get back to the *Steadfast*, well..." Her smile returned. "Keep thinking good thoughts, Anafu."

"I always do. Our Lady watch over you."

The exiting of the *Astarte* was not as arduous a task as the entering, for two reasons. One was the smaller number of bodies doing the exiting. Rodriguez had debated whether to take Sgt. Utumi with him but decided that the Capellan's abhorrence of narrow spaces would slow things down unnecessarily and that he would be more useful keeping a watch out for more JUR people who might be wandering around the ruined cruise ship. The second was that most of the exiters knew what to expect and made the process more efficient. The only slow-down was in getting the tall Dr. Weyerhauser through the narrow opening; the *Astarte* people took the effort in stride.

Once in the clear and with a well- marked trail down the mountainside, the going proceeded quickly. There was an awkward moment when the party reached the point where the would-be ambushers had had the tables turned on them; Stewardess Hernandez wanted to faint at the sight of slashed throats, and Mr. Corbo wanted to kick the bodies repeatedly. Only a sharp order from the Warden – echoed by the Bithan – got them moving again.

At the base of the mountain, Rodriguez bundled everyone aboard the shuttle and got them strapped in. He directed the astrophysicist to give the pilot directions to the henge, then instructed the Uhaad to stay as low to the ground as he could in order to avoid detection by the JUR ship cruising overhead. The trip to the henge was convoluted since the shuttle had to weave around clefts and outcroppings the entire way; there was a more direct approach, but it was also more exposed to enemy eyes. In due time, the Doctor indicated the spot where the henge stood, and the shuttle was set down fifty meters from it.

Exploring ancient ruins was a commonplace for Lixu Rodriguez. During his childhood on Dunia, he had gone on one archaeological adventure after another with his grandfather; Spencer Rodriguez had been an amateur archaeologist in his spare time and took the boy along whenever possible. The youth had soon learned all the techniques of locating artifacts, digging them up, and cataloging them by watching the older man very carefully. By the time young Lixu reached adulthood and ready to enter the University, he had visited every known site in the Southern Hemisphere and had been in on the discovery of some of them. Visiting a new site stirred his blood nearly as much as being a Warden.

As he approached the henge, he struggled to retain an outward calm, although the sight filled him with a great excitement. Briefly, he scanned the henge and nodded knowingly; he'd seen this sort of thing before in old photographs of Dunia's Northern Hemisphere. The details were different, of course, but the overall layout represented a religious calendar marking the times of major astronomical events in conjunction with rituals and observances. A careful study of this henge would reveal the length of the "year" the former inhabitants had marked off, possibly the seasons (if any) which had taken place, which times of the year the rituals and observances were held, and, if one were very lucky, the ranking of the rituals and observances. Rodriguez wished he could be a part of any future investigation, but his Wardenship took priority. Still, he'd record the site thoroughly, gather up any loose artifacts, file a report with the proper authorities, and make some recommendations based upon his personal experiences in the field.

But, first things first. He called Cpl. Chen to his side. The woman seemed to be as fascinated by the henge as he was; she found it hard to take her eyes off of it. He'd have to get her opinion of it when he had the chance.

"Deploy your squad about the perimeter, Corporal. If they spot that JUR ship – or anyone who isn't wearing Constabulary gear – they are to give a holler immediately. Then return here and keep close to the Professor."

"Aye, sir. And d'ya want me to help you with the lock-on?"

The Warden noted the gleam of eagerness in her eye and in the tone of her voice and recognized them as his own so many years ago.

"Certainly, Chen. The more searchers, the better. But be careful not to touch anything before I have a chance to record it."

"Aye, sir."

"As soon as Chen returns," he told Dr. Weyerhauser, "I'm going to video the site from all angles. If you can remember exactly where you found that artifact, we might be able to re-construct the scene." He smiled conspiratorially. "And no one has to know it's a re-construction, eh?"

"Roight ye are, guv," the other responded in Reman fashion.

While he waited, Rodriguez studied the corner symbols on the square of metal the Doctor had given him. And, to his utter surprise, he recognized the one in the lower-left-hand corner. It was very similar to a character in the Aldebaranian alphabet; that character was an equivalent to a "ch" in their language and, in olden times, represented the sky. While at the Academy, he had taken an interest in the language of his mentor and had acquired a rudimentary vocabulary. But, though he was able to read it a little bit, speaking it coherently was quite beyond him (or any human, for that matter) due to the differences between Aldebaranian and human vocal structures. Master Fresh had been surprised at his interest in a language he could not speak but never discouraged him from learning it.

The fact that this particular symbol was connected to Planetoid 48 meant that there was a possible link between the Wayfarers and the Aldebaranians. The Community had always denied that they were descended from those mysterious, galaxy-traveling beings, but they had left open the question of their having been visited by them. Did the Wayfarers "drop by" and teach the Community civilized behavior? And did the "pupils" adapt Wayfarer language to their own? It was an intriguing thought, one which the CSC's Commission for Cultural Affairs would mull over a good long time once he had made his report.

Chen returned shortly, and the three of them began strolling about the henge's outer ring, videoing as they went and keeping a sharp eye out for more artifacts. As luck would have it, the corporal made the first discovery – a crudely-fashioned metal bracelet engraved with miniature representations of unidentifiable animals – wedged under one of the crimson-colored stones. She was beside herself with glee and danced around her find like a child at its birthday party. The Warden videoed it *in situ*, then pocketed it along with the square.

The inner ring produced no artifacts but there was some evidence of a ritual sacrifice. What appeared to be blood was smeared on the central monolith. The stain was a dark amber in color. Rodriguez's breath caught in his throat; the blood of the Aldebaranians was also a dark amber.

As he was finishing his videoing, the Reman called out to him in alarm.

"Warden, listen to this!" He held up his vidcom, still in the "receive" mode. "I don't like the sound of it."

"— ye up to full pooer yet?"

"Aye, Myjor, we are."

"Excellent. Let's 'ave one last jump, ay?"

"Who is that?" the Warden asked.

"That's Major Tshambe. When he made me a prisoner with the *Astarte* crew, he forgot to confiscate my vidcom. I've kept it open all this time. That's how we were able to keep one step ahead of him."

"That was very resourceful of you, Professor. He mentioned something about 'one last jump.' Does that mean what I think it does?"

In answer to the question, the ground began to quiver, gently at first but increasing in intensity with each passing second. In the space of five seconds, the ground was shaking visibly.

"Good Lord!" the astrophysicist exclaimed. "They're firing up the MOME again!"

"This is not good. Chen! Get everyone back to the shuttle! *On the double!*" He grabbed the sleeve of the Doctor's parka. "Let's move, Professor! We haven't got a second to spare!"

CHAPTER SEVENTEEN

▼

LOST IN SPACE

LEGEND HAS IT THAT THOMAS Edison Murchison I, inventor of the oscillating-matrix engine which bore his name, was born to be a tinkerer.

His father had been a tinkerer, and *his* father before him had been a tinkerer. Grandfather Murchison even claimed that there had been a tinkerer in the family going back twenty-plus generations. It was thus only a matter of time until a Murchison was given the name of the greatest tinkerer of all time – Thomas Alva Edison.

The family pre-occupation weighed heavily on the young man, but he was up to the challenge. He took a degree in electronic engineering and, when that field provided little satisfaction, turned to nucleonics. The idea of tinkering with the powerful and mysterious forces of the Universe stoked his imagination, and he dreamed of harnessing them for the greater good of humankind. His close acquaintances warned him that he was playing with fire and that the forces of the Universe were better off left alone. Far from being discouraged, however, Thomas Edison Murchison was more determined than ever to succeed where others dared not to go. He had, after all, a family tradition to uphold.

At the time Murchison was beginning his career in nucleonics, the United Dunian Government had sent out the first exploratory ships into Deep Space in order to locate suitable, habitable worlds for Dunia's excess population. Those ships were ion-drive craft, theoretically capable of obtaining velocities near the speed of light; their major draw-back was Einstein's old time-dilation factor, i.e. the closer one approached the speed of light, the slower Time passed. What would seem like months to the crew of an ion-drive ship would actually be centuries to those back on the home world. Efficient though such a drive was, it was not practical in terms of space travel. And so, while he taught nucleonics in a classroom by day, Murchison bent his tinkerer's mind to a solution by night; and for that, he turned to another of Einstein's dictums – the creation of gravity wells.

As all school children knew, gravity wells were produced by strong gravity fields, e.g. those surrounding planets and stars. The strength of the field determines the depth of the well. When a well is created, space is contracted, and points on the event horizon of the well come closer together. A Deep Space vessel employing an auxiliary ion-drive may then travel from one point to another in far less time than would otherwise be possible.

Murchison studied the physics of gravity wells, becoming an expert on them. He performed the mathematics needed to create one and, from the theoretical model, designed an actual prototype of what would eventually be known as an "oscillating-matrix engine." And, when he first tested the model, it blew up in his face. Subsequent tests also failed, and Murchison was forced to re-think his idea.

Legend has it that the solution to this new problem came to him in a dream. He dreamed (he claimed) that he was walking in a woods and enjoying the scenery when he came upon two bears who had discovered a berry bush at the same time. Both bears were very hungry, and each wanted the berries for itself. They fought over the right to the berries until they had inflicted mortal wounds on each other and died. Murchison interpreted this dream as a conflict between two opposing forces. He then concluded that one could not create a gravity well inside of an existing one of equal or greater strength.

He followed through by conducting his next test in Deep Space, far from any interfering natural gravity wells. The test was a resounding success; and, in the months which followed, he constructed ever larger models until he was confident enough to take the machine to his corporate sponsors. And, according to a hoary old cliché, the rest was history.

One other caveat Murchison discovered in the process: loose objects in the vicinity of an artificially-generated gravity well tended to be flung away like so much flotsam.

*   *   *

"Captain! Sensors here! We've lost Planetoid 48 – again!"

"Damn!" The New Swiss pounded his chair with such force that the sound caused the normally implacable Commander Krishnamurthy to jump.

"We were too late, Tomiko. The bastards warped out before we could get to them."

"What now, Olaf?" the XO inquired.

"Well, the first thing we do is to contact our assault group and determine their status."

He entered a code into his vidcom which would connect him to Commander Mbaku in the command craft. The face which appeared was appropriately worried, and anxiety radiated from its eyes.

"Enrique, what's your status?" the Captain demanded.

"Not good, sir. Another fifty seconds or so, and we would've had them." He swallowed compulsively and licked dry lips. "I – I've lost the lead squadron. They got caught in the warp field. God knows where they are now. I've got sensors and communications at maximum range, and the other squadrons are making a physical search of Deep Space."

"Keep one squadron out there searching. The rest of you get back to the *Steadfast* ASAP."

"Aye, sir."

Krishnamurthy eyed the Captain with concern. His teeth were clenched tight and threatened to crack under the pressure of his jaw.

"What's the plan, Olaf?"

"The JUR are a single-minded bunch. They carry on until they've achieved their mission or they're all dead. My guess is that they're going to get as close to Romulus as they can before abandoning the runaway. As soon as Mbaku returns, I'm going to try to be there waiting for them." He got to his feet. "I'll be in my office, working up a plan of attack."

*   *   *

The *Steadfast*'s shuttle had just barely lifted off the surface of Planetoid 48 when the pirated MOME kicked in. At a distance of two kilometers, it was not far enough away to avoid being sucked into the gravity well which formed about the rogue world. To an external observer, the tiny craft suddenly disappeared; but, to those inside it, the stars disappeared. Both of those perspectives were correct, and neither was. It was all a matter of relativity.

Theoretically, the larger the MOME, the greater the gravity well. A typical cruise ship engine measured a half a kilometer in diameter and was capable of achieving a maximum of just over twenty-five light-years in a single warp-out. Constabulary ships, on the other hand, which possessed an engine twice that diameter could warp-out for fifty light-years at a time. And the huge Relay Stations with a five-kilometer diameter could send a ship across

Deep Space one hundred and fifty light-years at a time. The depth of the gravity wells created by each of them extended to proportional distances.

Except that no one knew just exactly what those distances were, and no one cared to know, if truth be told. In order to take an accurate measurement, one would have to be physically *inside* a well; and that was a risk no one was willing to take, since the physics which governed gravity wells was still little understood. Depending upon the size of the well, a ship caught in it could easily be torn apart, or it and its contents could be crushed into a super-dense mass.

Only two known incidents of a Deep Space ship having been sucked into a gravity well and surviving the experience were on record. In both cases, the crews had been relatively inexperienced (the reason they had had the mishap in the first place), and their accounts of the incidents were largely incoherent. Rumors of other, unreported incidents filtered across the spaceways, but they shed no more light on the matter than the reported ones.

The shuttle had two mitigating factors in its favor. The first was an Uhaad pilot. Uhaads, it had been discovered shortly after first contact had been made with that species, possessed brains differently wired than most other species; this differentiation allowed them to retain spatial orientation no matter what the situation. For this reason, they made the best pilots in Deep Space where anything could – and often did – happen.

The second was a Warden, a highly-trained individual, physically and psychologically, who had the capacity to cope with any given situation, thanks to his Aldebaranian mentors. And the fact of the matter was that, though the general population of the central spiral – including the Constabulary itself – was ignorant of the dynamics of gravity wells, Wardens were not, because their enigmatic trainers had long ago taken the risk of exploring wells inside and out, documented their experiences in great detail, and passed the knowledge on to their pupils, the future Wardens. Further, with their own version of the Constabulary's VR helmets, the Aldebaranians created a program which, based upon their experiences, simulated a journey inside a well.

Rodriguez had run this program twice in his last year at the Academy and knew well what to expect. He had hoped, of course, to have avoided this scenario altogether – if not for his own sake, then for that of his shipmates who hadn't a clue as to what was happening to them – but the activation of the MOME had taken him by surprise, and there hadn't been enough time to get safely away from the planetoid.

When the gravity well came into being, the shuttle was pulled into it and sent spinning around the circumference of what for all practical purposes was a "cosmic whirlpool." Lt. O-da strained to maintain control, and his efforts just barely kept the shuttle oriented in an upright position. The passengers (save two) yielded to panic and cried out in terror; their distress was multiplied by their being flung about the cabin like so many rag dolls. Only the Warden and Dr. Weyerhauser had the presence of mind to grab something to hang onto, the former because of his training, the latter because of his knowledge of astrophysical phenomena. The shuttle's vidscreen displayed an absolute blackness which did nothing for anyone's peace of mind but which did not surprise the two exceptions one bit. It was common knowledge among travelers in Deep Space that this was part and parcel of an MOME-field, that it skewed the fabric of space into an all-encompassing blankness; but, in their panic, the passengers had momentarily forgotten this fact.

As soon as Rodriguez had oriented himself, he began to shout orders to both the pilot and the passengers. O-da puzzled over the orders given to him, because he doubted they would help matters; but military man that he was, he carried out the orders and bent to the task. To his amazement (and relief), he discovered that the Warden's commands did much to tame the wild beast he was riding and that the descent to the bottom of the well was a little less rough.

Orders to the passengers were received with varying degrees of success. The troopers of Gamma Platoon struggled to overcome their initial panic and find something to hold onto; only because they too had been trained to follow orders did they, one by one, cease to fly about the cabin. They were further encouraged by Cpl. Chen's barking in their ears. The civilians from the *Astarte* were another matter altogether, since they were beyond the pale of this experience, and they had done the most screaming. To her credit, Chen ordered her people to grab any civilian who chanced to come their way and hold onto them for dear life. In due time, the deed was done, and relative calm prevailed in the shuttle, broken by an occasional obscenity from one trooper or another.

The Warden heaved a large sigh of relief at having restored some semblance of order. If he hadn't been trained to react as he did, there would have been utter chaos aboard the shuttle until such time as the MOME shut down and the gravity well collapsed. He eyed each individual with concern and attempted to infuse a little self-confidence in him/her.

"Is everyone all right?" he asked perfunctorily. "Any injuries?"

"I got a bloody nose, sir," one of the troopers responded. "I banged it against the fraggin' bulkhead while we was flyin' around."

"You'll live, I expect. Anyone else?"

"Beggin' yer pardon, sir," Chen piped up, "but what's the fraggin' cyke?"

"We were caught out in the open during a warp-out, and we were dragged into a gravity well."

That casual assessment provoked not a few murmurs of alarm and despair. The corporal silenced them with a few choice vulgar comments.

"So, how do we launch?" she inquired.

"We don't, at least not until the JUR shuts down the MOME."

"Can't we just fly out?"

"We could, if we had a more powerful engine. These shuttles aren't designed for heavy-duty tasks."

More and louder murmurs of alarm and despair filled the air. Chen had to yell more vociferously and vulgarly.

"How long do we have to ground?"

"I can't be very specific. But, because the terrorists are amateurs when it comes to operating an MOME, they have had to limit themselves to minimum warp-out each time they jump – ten light-years – and so they have to operate the MOME for a set period of time. Mr. Tas, can you confirm that assessment?"

The Bithan shifted around to face the group. He had grabbed the first handy object he could, one of the shuttle's seats, and was hugging it with all his might. Despite his presumed greater knowledge of MOME's and gravity wells, he expressed as much fear from his current situation as any of the military contingent.

"Yes, can I, Warden. Has – *had* the *Astarte* the basic model. Required it five hundred seconds to achieve maximum strength and five kiloseconds of steady power output to maintain a ten-light-year gravity well."

"*Five kiloseconds?*" someone yelped and was promptly admonished by Cpl. Chen.

"Thank you, Mr. Tas. I'd hazard to guess that one of those kilos has already elapsed. So, we've only got four more to go."

The Warden's attempt at levity elicited much moaning and groaning, and Chen threatened to toss the lot of them out the airlock.

"Beggin' yer pardon again, sir," she observed, "but we don't find that one fraggin' bit green across."

"Just hang in there, Chen, and we'll–"

"*Sir!*" O-da exclaimed. "Something just passing by us!"

Rodriguez whipped around and stared at the Uhaad. The latter had his gaze fixed on the vidscreen. His dark skin had paled considerably. The Warden carefully picked his way forward and examined the monitor. It remained as black as ever.

"What did you see, Leftenant?"

"I not knowing, sir. One second, it there, and the next, it gone."

"Did it have a shape?"

"Hard to tell. I having the impression that, whatever it, what I seeing only part of a larger object."

Rodriguez's mind called up the memories he had of the two exercises with gravity wells. He remembered all too well that first experience. The Aldebaranian instructor in charge had created a well, and instantly, all the stars had disappeared. He had been gripped by a wave of loneliness, of emptiness. Had it not been for his prior training, he might have succumbed to sheer terror. Instead, he had steadied his mind and focused on the wonder of it all. When he sat in for the second exercise, he knew what to expect and adjusted to the situation rapidly. This exercise had an added element: other objects. While the physics of being inside a gravity well stated that one could not observe objects in real space, only eternal blackness, one could observe other objects in hyperspace (albeit on a different visual level). And, during that exercise, he had been required to identify accurately and in detail everything he saw. There had been a variety of objects to identify, from machine parts to spaceships; one was expected to score one hundred per cent, even if one had to repeat the exercise.

"I should hazard to guess," he said at last, "that we are not alone here."

"Not alone?" the voice of Dr. Weyerhauser wafted over his shoulder. "What do you mean?"

"I mean, Professor, that someone – or something – else got caught in the well with us. Who or what it is won't be known until we have a better look at it – if possible."

"Are we in any danger?"

"From collision, yes. Beyond that, I can't say."

Three heads bent over the vidscreen. Three pairs of eyes peered intently into the blackness it revealed. No one made a sound, except that of breathing. Then:

"There, sir!" O-da whispered, pointing at the monitor. "There it again!"

Against the ebon background, an object slightly less dark and shimmering with a ghostly glow hoved into view. It possessed straight lines, suggesting an artificial origin, but no complete shape was yet discernible. The thing drifted out of view in a second's time, and the watchers were left with the blackness again. Moments later, the object – or a different one – came into view; and this time, a shape was evident – an isosceles triangle. It was slowly spinning about an invisible axis which permitted the observers to catch a very brief glimpse of a superstructure.

"Lord of All!" O-da muttered. "That looking like one of our fighter craft."

"You may be right, Leftenant," the Warden mused. "Captain Halvarson must have dispatched the assault force, and one or more of the lead ships was close enough to Planetoid 48 to get sucked into this gravity well along with us."

"They look like they're out of control, just as we almost were," the Doctor observed.

"They probably are. Ships getting caught in gravity wells are a rare instance, and few pilots have the experience to teach others how to handle a ship so caught."

"But, *you* knowing, sir."

"My training goes far beyond the mundane, Leftenant. You'll never know what I know."

There followed an awkward silence, and the watchers bent toward the monitor to follow the slowly rotating fighter with an eye to a possible collision.

Abruptly, the scene changed, and the stars became visible again as the MOME was shut down and the gravity well collapsed. Planetoid 48 lay off the shuttle's star board bow, on course toward its destiny. Additionally, four other objects lay off the shuttle's port side about a hundred kilometers further away from the rogue – the vanguard of the *Steadfast*'s assault force. None of the squadron was in a recognizable formation but occupied random points in space after having been jumbled by the vortex of the well.

"There you are, Leftenant," the Warden stated matter-of-factly. "Our 'well-mates' have been identified."

"Aye, sir. And they not looking any worse for their experience – except, maybe, their pride wounding."

"Understandable under the circumstances. Raise them, will you? I have a task for them."

O-da punched in the *Steadfast*'s ship-to-ship code for fighters, and the vidscreen's starry image was replaced by a very confused pilot. She was a Bithan, sporting the red crest of that world's highest caste.

"Identify, please," she asked in a tremulous tone.

"Leftenant – Tor, isn't it? This is Warden Rodriguez."

"Oh, thank the gods![42] Have had we a frightful experience."

"I know. Your squadron and we were sucked into a gravity well when Planetoid 48 warped out."

"Sent Captain Halvarson us to intercept the rogue. Had hoped we to reach it before had charged up the terrorists the MOME again." A brief expression of disgust passed across her face, and she muttered: "Failed we."

"It's still early in the game, Tor. But, I have a job for you which may wipe

---

42   The inhabitants of Bi are as polytheistic as the Capellans – with one notable difference. Each of the six castes has its own specific god, and there are four general gods worshipped by all Bithans. As might be expected, these gods are militant in nature – CMT.

away your failure. The terrorists have a ship in orbit around the planetoid. I want your squadron to neutralize it so that none of the JUR has a chance of escape."

"Aye, sir. Is that what call you Hoomans a 'piece of candy.' By the way, sir, can tell you us are we where in the seven hells?"

"Not a problem, Leftenant. I've got the CSC's foremost astrophysicist with me – Dr. Mubutu Weyerhauser – who will provide you with some co-ordinates, as spacers say, 'double mome.'"

"Weyerhauser? Is he the terrorist that seek we."

"Dr. Weyerhauser has renounced his allegiance to the JUR and is now in protective custody. Professor, can you provide Lt. Tor with our location?"

"I'm way ahead of you, Warden. Scan eleven degrees negative from your present orientation, Leftenant, and you'll spot a familiar 'landmark.'"

All five pilots swiveled their external cameras toward the designated area of Deep Space. Audible gasps issued from five throats when they realized what the "landmark" was. Half a light-year away hung a greenish-yellow star with two of its four planets sharing an orbit. It was Rhea Silvia.

*   *   *

Sgt. Running Deer was having difficulty finding enough "busywork" for his squad to do. The most immediate thing he had been able to think of was to dispose of the dead bodies in the area. There were four of them – two of his troopers and two JUR members. The former he had secured in their sleeping bags and placed by the airlock for eventual evacuation; the latter he had dragged off to the farthest corner of the launch bay and covered with a tarp found in a supply locker. His only consolation was that he hadn't all that many bodies to keep busy. With Cpl. Chen's squad outside providing security for Warden Rodriguez's project and the losses from the brief firefight with the terrorists, his available manpower numbered only six, counting himself and the wounded.

Quinn, an inveterate scrounger, was put on scavenging duty in order to ferret out anything of worth, e.g. food and water, so that the unit could keep their own supplies in reserve. He was still gone, and Running Deer was beginning to worry – not about his being set upon by the JUR, but about his "zeeing off" somewhere – because Pvt. Quinn was also an inveterate slacker. The remaining troopers had been posted to the bottom of the companionway to guard against any potential assault by the terrorists. If the latter came in force, how long would two men last?

No, make that three men and one woman.

The Capellan scout was still squatting motionlessly at the *top* of the companionway, ever alert for danger, though he had not been formally assigned to that post. Admittedly, Sgt. Utumi could hold his own against any attack. The Dunian still had the image of the three dead terrorists outside firmly in his memory; the Alkon warrior had dispatched them singlehandedly even though they were lying in ambush for the platoon. If it came to a fight, he could almost feel sorry for the JUR, because they'd have the Devil's own time of it in a run-in with a Capellan. Still, Capellans were not invulnerable. They could – and occasionally did – die if the opposing force were large enough.

Then there was the "second-in-command" of this mission, and he hadn't a clue about how to deal with her. All he knew about Pluj was that they were notorious "sexers" – anyone, anywhere, any time, any way – and that human males found them irresistible. Running Deer had caught himself fantasizing about Lt. Ralfo and had had to force himself to think of something else. Not that she would ever "do the riggers" with the likes of him or anyone else aboard the *Steadfast* – she seemed to be quite enamored of the ship's Warden. Of Pluj combat ability, he also had no clue. Presumably, they could fight, since they were given the same training as any other trooper; but no stories of their prowess seem to have crept along the grapevine. Consequently, he did not know if he could trust her in a dust-up. Lt. Anafu Ralfo would just have to prove herself "momey!"

And, speaking of the leftenant, where was she? After Rodriguez and Chen's squad had departed, apparently she too had gone off somewhere. He supposed he'd have to locate her, if only for the sake of keeping track of all the mission's personnel. He wasn't planning on playing nursemaid to a Pluj – officer or no – because he'd never hear the end of it from one end of the central spiral to the other.

The sergeant did not have to search long for Ralfo, however. He found her also at the top of the companionway, keeping her own watch for terrorists. He approached the pair gingerly. The Pluj gave him a large smile, while the Capellan eyed him dourly.

"Ah, Sergeant, in order all is?"

"Yes, ma'am. We're ready to evacuate as soon as the assault force arrives."

"Excellent. The possibility of scouting the upper decks Sgt. Utumi and I were discussing."

The human scowled.

"Is that wise? We don't know the strength of the enemy. We've already had one surprise today."

"Far we will not travel – just far enough the 'lay of the land' to determine. Besides, us something to do it will give."

"All right. You're the boss – ma'am."

Ralfo studied Running Deer's face a moment.

"You it does bother, Sergeant, that the 'boss' I am?"

The Dunian swallowed hard.

"It's not my place to question my officers, ma'am," he replied diplomatically. "I just follow orders."

"On you overly I will not impose. Only one I will give: your people up here post while away Sgt. Utumi and I are."

"Aye, ma'am. And good luck!"

Ralfo and Utumi began to walk stealthily down the passageway, each hugging opposing bulkheads. By unspoken agreement, Utumi maintained a position two meters ahead of Ralfo. They covered the distance to the first cross-passageway in short order and without incidence. At the junction, each peered around the corner in opposite directions and spied no signs of JUR activity. Cautiously, they crossed the intersection and proceeded toward the next cross-passageway. A meter before they reached that point, the Capellan halted, held up his hand to stop his companion, and sniffed the air. She joined him on his side of the passageway.

"What you do detect, Sergeant?"

"Oo-mans recently here have be. They a distinct odor to have."

"That also I have noticed. But not all that unpleasant the odor of some humans is."

The warrior pursed his lips, and his yellow eyes gleamed with bemusement.

"Mayhap you among those our Warden to count?"

"I do."

"It well to be. I to believe that he pleased with your scent as well to be. All warriors an excellent female at their side to require."

"And an 'excellent female' I am?"

"Of the Perru[43] I little knowledge to have. But thus far, I this one worthy to find."

"You heartily I thank, Sergeant. Now, cautiously we must proceed."

They inched their way toward the intersection and peered around the corner. Utumi's nose had not failed him. Four members of the JUR were creeping down the cross-passageway toward the junction themselves, and they appeared to be extremely nervous, stopping at each hatch and pressing an ear to it. Inexplicably, they did not bother to open any hatch and investigate the compartment beyond, a tactic which the circumstances might have dictated.

The Capellan quickly drew both of his razor-sharp stilettos from their

---

43   The name given the Pluj in the Alkon language – CMT.

forearm scabbards and held them in the ready. Ralfo unholstered her service pistol and poised herself for action.

The first terrorist to enter the intersection spotted an incongruous object out of the corner of his eye, turned his head to investigate, and looked directly into a pair of yellow eyes gleaming with malice. He gasped in shock and froze. It was a natural reaction – and a fatal one. Without hesitation, Utumi brought up one of his blades and rammed it into the man's throat; for good measure, he gave the stiletto a sharp twist. The Reman dropped to the deck, drowning in his own blood.

The second terrorist raised his assault rifle to cut down the intruders, but he was much too slow in his reaction. The Alkon warrior was already executing his next maneuver which consisted simply of hurling his second blade and burying it deeply inside the man's brain. The latter dropped without a sound.

Meanwhile, Ralfo, using the dying first terrorist as cover, jumped into the intersection and fired three rounds at the third terrorist. One of the rounds caught him in the chest; he staggered against the bulkhead, rebounded, and staggered forward. The Pluj fired twice more, and her target fell dead next to the JUR man with a stiletto in his head. The fourth terrorist, believing that retreat was the better part of valor, turned and ran. He did not run far. Ralfo took careful aim, squeezed off two rounds, and dropped him before he had traveled ten meters.

Utumi wiped his first blade clean on the uniform of his first victim. He then moved over to the second one, placed his boot on the corpse's chest, pulled the stiletto viciously out of its skull, and wiped it clean in a similar fashion. He gazed serenely on the carnage he and the Pluj had wrought and rubbed all six fingers against his left cheek, the Capellan sign for utter contempt.

"The JUR a reputation for ruthlessness to have," he muttered, "but it against weaker opponents to occur to seem. Against a greater force, they craven to be."

"Of the prowess of an Alkon warrior I have heard," Ralfo said in a low tone, "but, until now, I believed that only exaggerations they were."

Utumi merely cocked his head to the left, his kind's equivalent of a shrug.

"We on to continue?"

"Lucky here we were. The next time, maybe not. The platoon we shall re-join and for the assault force wait."

The return trip was made in greater silence than the outward one. Each of them concentrated on listening for other sounds of JUR activity. When they reached their own outpost, Running Deer regarded them with anxiety.

"I heard shots down there. What happened?"

"A slight altercation," Ralfo replied with customary Pluj modesty. "Some of the JUR we encountered and them defeated."

"You took an awful chance – ma'am."

"A good team Sgt. Utumi and I make. No problems we had. How here you are holding up?"

"I got some bad news, I'm afraid. My trooper with the stomach wound died about fifty seconds ago – too much internal hemorrhaging. I put him with the others."

"Regretful that is, Sergeant. Sorry I am."

"Thank you, ma'am. I'll sure be happy to get off this fraggin' rock."

"And also I."

Utumi volunteered to resume sentry duty, and so Ralfo told the two troopers on the companionway to get some rest. Running Deer put Quinn on sentry duty as soon as the latter returned from his scavenging. The trooper made no secret of the fact that he wasn't at all pleased to be working along side of "that person."

Ralfo wandered off by herself to meditate on the day's events so far. She soon discovered that the day's events couldn't hold her attention for very long; her mind kept returning to thoughts of Rodriguez and how he was faring outside. She wanted very much to cuddle up with him and feel him inside her. She had never met a human male so desirable, so delicious, so satisfying as he was; and, despite her mother's cautionary advice that human males operated by a very different set of mores, she wanted to bed this one as often as she could. As soon as this mission was concluded, she intended to propose marriage again to Lixu at the first opportunity. Undoubtedly, he would resist the idea again, citing his duties as a Warden; but, she knew that he wanted her as much as she wanted him and that he knew she knew. All she had to do was to increase the output of pheromones all Pluj emitted, and he was hers forever.

It has been argued, from the time of the first encounter between Dunians and the inhabitants of the Pluj system that this biochemical interaction was the basis of the eventual partnership of the two species against the Alliance for Free Space during the War of the Eight Suns. Human males tended to be aggressive, socially and sexually, and they found their equal in the Pluj. While co-habitation between the two was still in the nascent stage, each found the other attractive enough to engage in frequent sexual gymnastics. And encounters between two natural sexual predators resulted in a great many stories being spread around to the point where they became "urban legends." Those few couples who took their relationships to the final stage of life-long commitment had to cope with the differing mores every step of the way.

Neither could afford to jump into marriage without first giving the matter a great deal of thought and seeking counsel from friends, family, and trusted third parties, because the need to dominate had to be tempered by the need to compromise. Both human males and Pluj had always had the upper hand in their respective societies; and, if either attempted to behave as usual, the relationship was doomed to fail.

Anafu Ralfo knew all this. From the time that she had first expressed an interest in Lixu Rodriguez to the present day, her mother (who was well aware of the consequences of misguided sexual attraction) never failed to counsel her child to think the matter through thoroughly. And Anafu had, and she still wanted Lixu.

She must have dozed off, because the next thing she was aware of was someone shaking her shoulder. For an instant, she was transported back to her home where, when she was a child, he mother had marched into her bedroom exactly at dawn each day and shaken her awake so that she would not be late for her classes. It had always been a struggle – between her and her desire to sleep late, between her and her insistent parent, and between her and the never-ending routine of preparing for the vicissitudes of the new day – and, more often than not, she had found herself on the short end of the stick. She popped one eye open, half-expecting to see her mother with her perpetual mirthless smile, and was momentarily disoriented to see the concerned expression on the face of Sgt. Running Deer. Reality rushed into her consciousness, and she came fully awake.

"Wrong what is, Sergeant?"

"Something's happening, ma'am – something terrible."

It had begun as a barely perceptible vibration, accompanied by a barely discernible hum. Vibration and hum permeated throughout the launch bay; and, as both intensified in frequency and volume, the effects became more visible. It was as if a giant hand had seized the ship and was shaking it vigorously.

Running Deer sat down on the deck when he could no longer stand on his feet. Ralfo looked around and noted that everyone else was also sitting down. She did not attempt to remain standing.

"It is what I think it is?"

"Yes, ma'am. I've been through more warp-outs than I care to think about, and this is what it feels like. What I don't understand is *why* it's happening. This ship is wrecked – she's not going anywhere."

"No, she is not, but Planetoid 48 is."

"Beggin' yer pardon, ma'am, but that's crazy! A whole world?"

"Theoretically possible it is, if a powerful enough MOME you have. And a small world this is. This must be how the planetoid the *Steadfast* 'lost.'"

The non-com shook his head in disbelief.

"You're sayin' that the JUR *hijacked* a whole fraggin' planet? But why?"

"On our way here Warden Rodriguez explained that this world into Romulus the JUR was planning to ram."

The sergeant's eyes went wide.

"That's even crazier!"

"A better explanation you have, Sergeant?"

"Um, no, ma'am, but—"

He was cut off by the screams of one of his troopers who had been completely unhinged by the intensity of the vibrations and the volume of the humming. He was writhing about on the deck with his hands over his ears. His comrades averted their eyes and concentrated on their own survival of this ordeal. Running Deer shook his head sadly. The distressed man was the wounded trooper.

As quickly as the disturbance had begun, it died away, and the sudden silence in its wake seemed just as nerve-wracking. Both Ralfo and Running Deer gained their feet and went to assess the situation in their respective areas of concern – the sergeant to his troopers (especially the remaining wounded one), the lieutenant to the sentry outpost.

The Pluj soon learned that Utumi was taking the disturbance as badly as the humans. He crouched on the deck, rocked back and forth, and murmured in Alkono. Although she did not understand one word of his language, she guessed that he was praying to one or more of his gods for deliverance; in his position, she would have done the same and beseeched her Goddess for protection from evil. Seeing the Capellan so locked up in his prayers put the same idea in *her* head. And that idea quickly brought to mind something she had temporarily forgotten, something which now filled her with horror.

Those inside the *Astarte* might have been rattled by the effects the operation of the MOME had produced, but at least they were safe from harm. What, however, of those *outside* on the surface of the runaway? They were in the open and subject to the same fate as all loose objects were during a warp-out. Had they all been flung into space, to die a horrible death by pressurization?

For the first time in her short life, Anafu Ralfo knew fear. If it were possible for a Pluj to be paler than they normally were, she was now. Her heart began beating rapidly, and her breath came in short gasps. The man she loved with all her soul was out there. Had he been taken cruelly away from her? Was she to lose all happiness in this life forever? Quickly, she kneeled and cupped her hands before her face. In her own tongue, she whispered:

"Oh, Holy Mother who art Our Protectoress, blessed by Thy Name. Thy daughter humbly beseeches Thee to lay Thy Blessed Hand upon him who has her heart, to protect him from all harm (and also those in his company), to bring him safely back to her so that our love will grow and bear fruit and glorify Thee forever and ever. Holy Mother, hear Thy daughter's plea. *Ajah!*"

When she had finished praying, she started weeping.

CHAPTER EIGHTEEN

▼

A CHANGE OF PLANS

THE *STEADFAST* WARPED BACK INTO "normal" space, a quarter of a light-year from Romulus. Five seconds later, Blue Zone reported the same to Captain Halvarson, who then asked the obvious question.

"I bees scanning, sir," Sensors senior officer, Lt. Commander G'lun (an Ekath) responded. Then: "Sensors shows Planetoid 48 0.84 gigameters from our position, bearing 14.08 degrees (relative)."

"Give me the Display, Mr. G'lun."

"Aye, sir."

The air in the holographic-display area shimmered briefly as the computer powered up. Multi-colored dots began appearing, first in the center of the display, then in succeeding rings, as the relevant data was fed in. The zone officer selected the minimum detection range of ten light-years so as not to clutter up the Display with unnecessary images; therefore, the star field which came into view was sparsely populated with the nearby Rhea Silvia holding center stage. Secondarily was the runaway, and it was steadily creeping toward its proposed target. The only object between the two was the Constabulary ship.

"How far from zero-point is the rogue?" the Captain inquired.

"It deviates only by 0.6 degrees, sir."

"I'm not surprised. Dr. Weyerhauser has lived up to his reputation as an expert astrophysicist. He proved to be a valuable asset for the JUR." He turned to Commander Krishnamurthy. "Tomiko, call up our weapons inventory. We may need everything we've got to stop that thing."

"Aye, sir." She paused, then looked at him with deep concern. "What about our people there?"

Halvarson gazed off into the distance. At the Academy, he and his fellow cadets had been told time and again that there would be times when they were obliged to make difficult decisions, decisions in which many lives hung in the balance. And, the instructors had added, whatever decisions were made, one had to live with for the rest of his/her life [if (s)he survived him/herself]. Until now, Olaf Halvarson had had a relatively easy time of it during his career, pursuing pirates, freebooters, smugglers, and the like and dealing with them summarily. Now, for the first time in his life, he had to make a difficult decision involving more than half of his combat forces. He took a deep breath and let it out slowly.

"Commander, you and I both know that some sacrifices have to be made for the sake of the mission. The mission here is to protect Romulus and its four billion inhabitants. If some of our own are lost, then so be it."

"I don't envy you at all, Olaf," she murmured and laid a hand gently on his arm.

"I don't envy me either, Tomiko. Now, let's have that inventory."

"*Sir!*" Lt. Commander G'lun broke in. "Sensors bees registering four – no, makes that five – vessels heading our way. Sir, they bees our missing squadron – and the Warden's shuttle."

"Well, that's certainly good news. Mr. G'lun, inform Commander Mbaku that his lost sheep are returning home."

"'Lost sheep,' sir? But, they bees vessels, not animals."

"Never mind, Commander. Just inform Mbaku."

"Aye, sir."

"Ekath!" Krishnamurthy muttered. "They make fine officers, but they're too damned literal-minded."

"Grin and bear it, Tomiko," he chided her with a grin. His expression quickly became solemn. "At least, we won't have to worry about sacrificing anyone, will we?"

*   *   *

The four fighter craft approached the *Steadfast* in a modified "X" formation, the lead ship a kilometer ahead of the others. Between it and the three others nestled the shuttle. At two kilometers from the patrol vessel, the fighter craft broke formation and headed for the cylinder which joined the spherical parts of the ship; and, as they did so, four hangar-bay doors gaped open to receive them.

The shuttle veered off towards the shuttle bay. Another door opened and swallowed it up. As soon as the smaller ship had been secured, Rodriguez popped the hatch and strode briskly toward the ramp leading to the upper levels. On the fly, he instructed Cpl. Chen and her squad to re-supply themselves and to grab a few kilos of rest before going back to Planetoid 48 to rescue their comrades. With his four civilians in tow, the Warden commandeered a shuttle car large enough to accommodate all of them and drove the vehicle to the command level at its top velocity. More than once, pedestrians had to leap out of the way to avoid being run over; and, more than once, said near-victims silently cursed the driver, both for his recklessness and for his station in life. If the driver was aware of the consternation he was causing, he did not show it but drove on relentlessly.

Rodriguez slammed the shuttle car to a halt just outside the Bridge, nearly spilling his passengers to the deck, and strode purposefully toward the Gold Zone, an expression of tight-lipped determination masking his face. Commander Krishnamurthy spotted him first and murmured something to the Captain. Halvarson swiveled around and regarded the black-clad figure with wariness.

"Ah, Leftenant," he said in an even voice, "good to see you again. Was your mission a success?"

"Partially." The Warden then launched into a detailed account of what had transpired on Planetoid 48. He concluded: "But, I rather suspect you already know how well it went."

"I had some inkling, yes. When the runaway disappeared again, I knew that nothing good would come of it. And I was right." He glanced at the civilians. "Hmmm, I recognize Mr. Tas from the *Astarte*. And two of his crew. And Dr. Weyerhauser, of course." He signaled to the two security guards at the entrance to the Bridge. Both walked briskly over and awaited further orders. "Take this man to the brig and post a guard there. He's a wanted terrorist."

The security detail stepped forward to take the academic into custody. The latter looked at the Warden with shock and concern. Rodriguez held up his hand to stop the guards in their tracks.

"Belay that order, troopers."

The guards stared in surprise at the Warden, then looked at the Captain in confusion.

"Excuse me?" Halvarson growled.

"This man is under my protection, and *I'll* decide what's to be done with him."

A deep frown came over the Captain's face and quickly turned into a scowl. He was not accustomed to having his orders countermanded on his own ship, and he was damned if he'd let this still-wet-behind-the-ears upstart dictate to him in front of his own people.

"And just what do *you* plan to do with him?"

"Frankly, that doesn't concern you, Captain. But, for the sake of good relations, I'll tell you that he and I are returning to Planetoid 48, first to rescue the rest of my team, and second to recover some valuable artifacts I'm obliged to obtain. I'll require a troop carrier and another two platoons for this purpose."

"You will, huh? Well, I'll take it under advisement."

"You will give me what I ask for. May I remind you that all law-enforcement agencies and personnel are required to assist a Warden in the performance of his/her duties when asked?"[44]

Krishnamurthy placed her hand on Halvarson's arm.

"He's got you there, sir. You know as well as I do what the penalty is for non-compliance – relief of duty and demotion of one rank."

"What about Planetoid 48?" the New Swiss grumbled. "Another warp-out, and it'll be right on top of Romulus."

"If it jumps, stay with it. I should be on it before the MOME is fully charged – *if there are no delays*. Once I complete the rest of my mission, you may do as you please. Now, do I get what I asked for?"

"Damn your impudence, Rodriguez!" the Captain rasped. "All right. I'll clear it with Commander Rux."

"Thank you. Now, if you'll excuse me, I have to report in."

The Warden stepped over to the niche wherein resided the *aaxyboxr*. He regarded the creature with resignation, took a deep breath, let it out quickly, and placed his hand firmly on the gray mass. As before, he stiffened and blanched at the contact.

*　　*　　*

— *Greetings, fellow sentient. We are the* aaxyboxr. *How may we assist?*

— *Greetings to the* aaxyboxr. *I am sentient Rodriguez. I wish to send a message.*

— *State the message.*

— *"To Lt. Commander Ruba at Constabulary Headquarters from Warden (L1) Rodriguez aboard the* Steadfast. *I have successfully apprehended the fugitive, Dr. Mubutu Weyerhauser, and placed him under protective custody. The reasons for this action will follow later. I am returning to Planetoid 48 in order to retrieve*

44 The relevant language can be found in Article five ("Law Enforcement"), Section Five ("Powers of Wardens"), paragraph three ("Requests for assistance") in the Treaty of Aldebaran – CMT.

artifacts pertaining to the Wayfarers which Dr. Weyerhauser has discovered." End of message.
— *It is sent.*
— *Thank you. The peace of Kum'halla be with the* aaxyboxr.
— *The peace of Kum'halla be with sentient Rodriguez.*

*   *   *

On the return trip to Planetoid 48, the Warden was exceptionally reserved. The recent unpleasantness with Captain Halvarson was playing on his mind, and he was uncomfortable with having to dress down someone older and more experienced than he. On the other hand, the circumstances had warranted that he "pull rank." At the Academy, he had been taught that there was a time for firmness and a time for diplomacy; the trick was to determine which approach was the best given the facts of the moment. Master Fresh was continuously drumming that point into his head, and the instructors devised ever newer and more complex scenarios to test the cadets.

To be sure, tension between Wardens and ordinary Constabulary personnel always existed just below the surface. The cause was the differing missions of the two forces. Wardens, having been given the power of arrest and detainment, single-mindedly pursued their quarries at all costs; ordinary Constabulary personnel, having been given the task of law enforcement, therefore tended to be just as single-minded. One might have supposed that both of these forces had common cause; but, more often than not, they conducted their individual duties with different methodologies, and these methodologies worked at cross purposes. This was partly due to the type of training each force received. Wardens, by reason of their purpose in life, looked upon themselves as a sort of priesthood guarding the common morality against all manner of evil and eschewing all the profane elements of society (including a trooper's way of life). Constabulary personnel, however, underwent standard military training which had existed since the formation of the Universe, and they looked askance at anyone who regarded them as "inferior."

When all was said and done, then, the principal cause for the tension was the mind-set of the two. The Constabulary regarded Wardens as aloof, uncaring, cold-blooded, and utterly alien; "conventional wisdom" had it that the black-clad clan could read minds and thus knew everyone's secret thoughts. Wardens regarded the Constabulary as a necessary evil and a tool to be used as expediently as possible; and, if that included perpetuating the notion that they had powers beyond the norm, then so be it.

Whether it was in Olaf Halvarson's nature to be contradictory or he was simply attempting to gain the advantage in a difficult situation, Rodriguez couldn't have said. Obviously, there was a personality conflict at work here, and perhaps an element of inevitability to it all. But the Warden hadn't the time or the inclination to sort it out; the JUR were too close to accomplishing their goal of smashing Romulus to pieces and allegedly "freeing" Remus from "tyranny." They had to be stopped – he, Lixu Rodriguez, had to stop them – by any and all means at hand, and no amount of diplomacy seemed to be called for in these circumstances. Let Captain Halvarson have his opinions and his objections if he so wanted to indulge in the same. But he had best stay out of the Warden's way!

He glanced over at Dr. Weyerhauser, sitting in a seat where normally a Constabulary trooper would have been. Troop carriers normally transported three platoons of combat forces and one of support forces. As only two of the former and none of the latter were aboard this vessel, there were extra available seats, and they were taken up by Cpl. Chen's squad and the Doctor.

The corporal and the astrophysicist seemed to be engaged in a very amiable conversation. Chen was a bright person (for a trooper, Rodriguez thought), and she had apparently found something in common with the Reman. So much the better, as the diversion prevented any anxieties from cropping up. The Warden had enough to worry about without having to nursemaid a guilt-ridden turncoat. He turned his thoughts toward the mission, but they didn't stay there long.

The coziness between Dr. Weyerhauser and Cpl. Chen reminded him of his growing relationship with Anafu Ralfo, and the rescue mission took on an urgency he couldn't hold back. He now knew that he loved her – had probably always loved her – on an emotional level as well as a physical one. It wasn't just because she was a Pluj working her wiles upon any male she happened to take a fancy to; it was also because he had gotten to know her on an intellectual level during the years he had spent on her world. She'd always been fun to be with, and they'd had the most marvelous conversations (even while she was trying to seduce him!). If ever there were a woman for him, then Anafu Ralfo was the one.

Their love was impossible, of course. Too many obstacles stood in the way of a healthy relationship.

He was a Warden, and he had taken a solemn oath to serve and protect the Central Spiral Collective and all sentient life therein. He was expected to serve from the moment he graduated from the Academy until he retired from the Service, and any lapse on his part risked disaster to all those about him. He could no more put his duty on hold than he could order a river to flow backwards.

There was no hard and fast rule forbidding a romantic relationship (of whatever structure), and some Wardens – especially those in the upper echelons – had taken mates. Those mates always understood that the relationship took a back seat to duty, no matter the outcome. As a rule, however, most Wardens refrained from such entanglements on the grounds that the nature of their duty allowed them no time to take mates and raise families; any relationships they might indulge in were usually non-committal, and the partners recognized them as such. The common but erroneous public perception was that Wardens were celibate, and this perception re-enforced the notion that they were aloof, cold-hearted, and dispassionate creatures.

Still, Lixu Rodriguez could not deny the fact that he loved Anafu Ralfo with a passion he should not be entertaining. And the sooner he got to Planetoid 48 and rescued her, the sooner they could discuss their future life.

So, why was this damned troop carrier taking so long to reach the runaway?

He peered at the vidscreen. Even though the image was steadily enlarging, it seemed like a snail's pace to him. Troop carriers were not as speedy as fighter craft or even as fast as the lighter shuttles, and all he could do was to stare at the screen and grind his teeth.

He was vaguely aware of someone settling into the seat next to his, and he turned his head slightly to gaze into the serene face of Cpl. Chen. She wore a thoughtful expression.

"It won't be long now, just a few clicks, sir," she remarked. "I'm sure Sgt. Running Deer has hit the red zone, wonderin' where we are."

"It can't have been more than fifteen kilos since we left the *Astarte*. Yet, it seems like fifteen *megs*."

"Aye. I even miss that fraggin' slacker, Quinn."

She fell silent, and Rodriguez regarded her for a moment. She *showed* no signs of anxiety, despite her words, but seemed to possess a sense of wonder he hadn't seen before. Briefly, he wondered why she was a member of Gamma Platoon in the first place. He had scanned her service record – had scanned the records of everyone in the platoon, even that of Running Deer – and noted that she had a "reputation" for questioning orders. All soldiers, in every place and in every time, always questioned the orders of their officers whenever they thought those orders were nonsensical – in private – but obeyed the orders rather than risk severe punishment and hoped to survive long enough to complain formally. Still, there was nothing in Chen's record concerning disciplinary action. Was she then in Gamma Platoon merely for being a gadfly? And, of so, whom had she annoyed so much that (s)he would relegate her to the "misfit squad?"

"You and the Professor seem to have hit it off," he said by way of making conversation. "Doesn't it bother you that he's a wanted terrorist?"

"He ain't no more'n a fraggin' terrorist than you are – sir," she retorted. "'Sides, you told me to orbit 'im, and that's what I'm doin'."

"It didn't appear to me like casual conversation. You two were enjoying each other's company."

Chen made a happy face, like a child would when receiving an unexpected present.

"He was tellin' me 'bout his work at the University, 'specially 'bout some o' the 'lunkheads' – as he put it – he had to teach. Then he wanted to know what interested me, and I told 'im I'd like to comp archaeology if I ever got the chance. He said the University had a special scholarship program for veterans if they wanted to get an ejacation after their tour of duty was up. That got me to scopin' for sure!" She frowned now. "The Professor said he woulda sponsored me if he wasn't in the red zone right now. Does that sound like a 'terrorist' to you, sir?"

"He isn't a terrorist, Corporal, as the word is generally defined. I'm convinced of that now, and you're right to question other people's opinion of him. Mubutu Weyerhauser had the bad luck of falling in with the wrong crowd, and now he'll pay the price for his poor judgment. If it's any consolation, he's punishing himself more than any court of law will ever do."

The non-com looked at him squarely, an expression of disapproval twisting her face askew.

"It ain't no fraggin' consolation at all – sir," she grumbled. "He don't deserve what they're gonna do to 'im."

"Probably not. But neither you nor I are in a position to do much about it." She expressed surprise. "Does that shock you, Chen? My report will include a plea for clemency based on his co-operation in the present matter; but, in the end, I have to serve the law like anybody else. It's a soldier's lot, eh?"

"Aye, sir. The more's the pity."

Rodriguez glanced at the vidscreen again.

"We're coming up on Planetoid 48 – finally. Go aft and tell the assault teams to prepare for the drop."

As soon as Chen departed, the Warden advised the pilot as to where he should land. As the gap between the carrier and the rogue closed, he spotted the JUR vessel five kilometers off to port, drifting uselessly in space, having been "neutralized" by the *Steadfast*'s fighter craft. A well-placed missile had sheared off the cesium-ion drive and left the ship without motive capability. Later, when the main threat posed by the terrorists had been eliminated, the crew would be collected and detained. Their leader, Major Tshambe, was now effectively trapped.

*   *   *

The reunion was joyful but constrained – with one exception. The exception was Quinn, who whooped it up uproariously when he spotted the first of his missing team-mates (Cpl. Chen) wriggling through the half-hidden airlock. He would have seized her and given her a bear hug, but she quietly informed him that she would break both of his arms if he tried it. Quinn was reduced to dancing around and slapping the returnees on the back.

To Rodriguez's great surprise, Sgt. Running Deer greeted him with a huge smile and an outstretched hand and told him that he was welcome to take back command of "this fraggin' rabble."

Sgt. Utumi saluted the Warden in the Alkon fashion, treating him like a brother-in-arms. Rodriguez returned the gesture.

On the other hand, Lt. Ralfo was the epitome of restraint, but her eyes spoke of a desperate need to be held tightly by her man and smothered with kisses. Under the circumstances, she might have behaved as Quinn had attempted to do with Chen, but she recognized the need for decorum at this moment. Later perhaps...

The Warden gathered together his "senior staff," i.e. Ralfo, Utumi, Running Deer, and Chen, and they all updated each other on recent developments. The Pluj did not disguise her horror upon learning of the shuttle's being caught in a vortex during the previous warp-out. Neither did Rodriguez disguise his dismay when he learned of her and Utumi's encounter with members of the JUR, and he cautioned both of them about taking unnecessary chances. After the brief exchange, he signaled to the commanding officers of the extra platoons to join him. Those officers approached him warily, and he sensed that they would rather be somewhere else *and* under someone else's command. Both of them were Senior Lieutenants, and they saluted him perfunctorily. He returned the salute in an exaggerated fashion to let them know that he didn't care what they thought about their present assignment and that he wasn't going to tolerate any insubordination.

One of the platoon CO's was a human, and Rodriguez vaguely recalled that he was a Dunian from AD #13. He had quite definite Polynesian facial features. The other was an Uhaad, and the Warden eyed him curiously. Uhaad were not known for their military prowess – they were mostly silica miners on their desert world – and he wondered what had prompted this individual to join the Constabulary.

"Gentlemen," he began pleasantly, "have you been briefed on your mission here?"

"Aye – sir," the Dunian replied testily. "We're to root out the JUR with all deliberate speed."

"Holds not being barred," the Uhaad added.

"Exactly so. You'll begin by scouring the *Astarte* and making sure that all JUR presence aboard her is removed. Once that has been accomplished, contact me and I'll give you further orders. Is that understood?"

Both SL's nodded in acquiescence.

"I'm assigning Sgt. Utumi to you. He'll alert you to any threats which may arise and advise you how to deal with them."

At the mention of the Capellan's name, the two platoon CO's now regarded the warrior for the first time. The latter glared back at them stoically; the only hint of emotion was a slight gleam of amusement in his yellow eyes. If it were possible for the Constabulary men to blanch, they would have; it was patently clear that neither of them had had any dealings with Alkonu and that neither of them wanted to have any.

"He'll give...advice, sir?"

"Of course. That's why we have scout units in the first place, yes? How you deploy your troops is entirely up to you, but I strongly urge you to listen to what Sgt. Utumi has to say. Your lives may depend upon it."

"Aye, sir."

"Very good, gentlemen. Move your troops out."

The SL's returned to their respective platoons and began issuing orders. The Warden held Utumi back for a moment.

"Keep an eye on those two, and see that they behave themselves."

The Capellan puckered his lips, and his eyes gleamed more brightly.

"Aye, Rodri-go. I like a mother to them shall be."

Rodriguez now focused his attention on Ralfo, who was standing off to one side. She regarded him with unabashed joy; the perpetual twinkle in her eye was less mischievous and more rapturous. She drew close to him and placed her hand against his chest (the Pluj gesture reserved for lovers).

"I prayed to Our Lady for your safe return, Lixu," she murmured. "And She answered my prayers."

"You were never far from my thoughts either, Anafu."

"I wish that we were in a more private place. I need you so much."

"And I you. But, we'll have to wait until we return to the *Steadfast*. We should join the rest of the platoon now."

Gamma Platoon was still laughing and joking around and swapping "war stories." Even Sgt. Running Deer had relaxed a bit and was participating wholeheartedly in the reunion; in particular, he was needling Chen about her "R-and-R" while he was facing death moment by moment. The corporal gave as good as she got by countering that she had gone face-to-face with "cosmic mysteries." Interestingly, she remained close to Dr. Weyerhauser, who was listening intently to the revelry but not actively participating. At the Warden's approach, however, the platoon quieted down and looked at him expectantly.

"I'm glad to see you all in such a happy mood," he remarked wryly. "So, are you ready to go back to work?" No one spoke. "I thought so. Well, I've got an easy assignment for you. What we were doing before that last warp-out, we're going to finish – which is to say, we're going treasure hunting. You'll be running interference for the Professor and me. How's that sound?" Still, no one spoke. "Uh-huh. All right, gather up your gear. We're moving out."

"You heard the man, people!" Running Deer barked. "On the double!" To the Warden: "Isn't Sgt. Utumi coming with us, sir?"

"No. He'll be scouting for the other platoons I brought with me and tracking down the JUR for them."

"Huh! I could almost pity the fraggin' Reemies. Those fraggers are going to be in the red zone, double-mome."

Once outside the ruined cruise ship, Rodriguez loaded the platoon aboard a troop carrier and gave the pilot the co-ordinates of the henge. With the JUR ship neutralized, they did not have to hug the base of the mountains but could fly out in the open on a more direct course; consequently, the second trip took less time than the first. At the approach to the henge, everyone crowded around the vidscreen to get – for some of them – their first glimpse of the site. Reactions were mixed, as might be expected, ranging from mild interest to boredom. Most of the latter came from Quinn, who loudly expressed his disdain for "dead things." Chen gave him a sharp jab in the ribs with her elbow.

The Warden directed the pilot to land the carrier fifty meters from the site in order to maximize the search area. Running Deer ordered the platoon out and established a perimeter. Dr. Weyerhauser and his bodyguard followed them and immediately began a more methodical search for artifacts than had been conducted in the first foray; they walked around the henge in a spiral pattern, carefully eyeing the ground for anything, large or small, which looked artificial. Occasionally, one or the other would pick something up, examine it, and either toss it aside or place it in a specimen bag. The discards far outnumbered the retained items.

Meanwhile, Rodriguez brought out his vidcam and picked up where he had left off before. He criss-crossed the site, attempting to catch all aspects of the henge from different angles. Then he took close-ups of all the major objects, especially those with markings on them. He hoped the video record would make the CSC's archaeologists happy in lieu of being able to visit the rogue world personally.

Ralfo, having nothing particular to do, tagged along behind the astrophysicist and Chen, but she did not search the ground with them, preferring merely to observe what they were doing. Frequently, she cast wistful glances at her lover.

The quietude which surrounded the henge might have gone on forever. But, in the larger cosmic scheme of things, there was bound to be disruptions. In this case, the disruption was the sound of an assault rifle being fired. Instinctively, Cpl. Chen seized her charge and bundled him behind one of the obelisks; the astrophysicist did exactly what she told him to do.

"Take cover!" Running Deer roared and found a convenient boulder to duck behind. Frantically, he scanned the area to determine the direction from which the gunfire was coming. "Report!"

One by one, the platoon sounded off, making their presence known by name. Rodriguez and Ralfo crouched down and joined the sergeant.

"Is everyone accounted for?" the Warden inquired.

"Haven't heard from two of 'em yet, sir. Quinn, Smith!" he yelled. "Where the frag are ya?"

"Over here, Sarge," Quinn replied hoarsely. "I'm in the green zone, but – but Smitty took one in the chest. I think he's dead."

"Damn!" Running Deer muttered.

"Lixu," Ralfo spoke up, "the shooters I see." She pointed to a rise thirty meters away. "Three of them there are."

"Hooray for Pluj eyesight. I would've had difficulty spotting them, and I've had the benefit of Aldebaranian training." He looked around and located the Doctor. "Professor, any idea where those goons might have come from?"

"I certainly do. There's a tunnel further up the slope which leads to the network of caverns I mentioned before. I discovered it by accident when I was exploring – between times I was giving information to Major Tshambe. That's how I came across this henge in the first place."

"I see. So, if we want to find artifacts in the caves, we're going to have to take out those three up there. Sergeant, who's your best marksman?"

"Believe it or not, sir, it's Quinn. He can shoot the eyes off a fly, one at a time."

"Quinn!" the Warden shouted. "Over here!"

In a low crouch, the trooper zigged and zagged from his previous position to that of Rodriguez. The latter was surprised to note that he had been crying but said nothing about it.

"D'ya see that outcropping over there?" He pointed toward a three-boulder collection off to the left of the henge and approximately twenty meters up the slope. Quinn nodded. "Make for it. We'll lay down cover fire for you. When you get there, pick your targets as you can."

"Aye, sir," the trooper rasped. "I'll hom them fraggers, sir. Smitty was my best buddy."

"Sergeant, return to the troop carrier and have the pilot fly over and harass those goons."

"Aye, sir."

The Warden then gave the order to open fire on the JUR position. He had little expectation that any of the platoon would actually inflict any casualties on the enemy, but perhaps someone would get lucky. Quinn had the best chance on that score once he was in position.

"Corporal, loan me your sidearm."

"Aye, sir. But, ain't that against yer code, to shoot a person?"

"We're forbidden to take a life, but there's nothing to prevent us from shooting *at* a person."

Fire was steady if scattered until Rodriguez determined that Quinn had reached the outcropping and called a ceasefire. The next move was up to Running Deer. That move was not long in coming. Out of the corner of his eye, the Warden saw the carrier rise up into the sky and swing around in a wide arc toward the JUR position. He was counting on it to draw fire from the opposition and give Quinn his opportunity.

The terrorists followed their "cue" and began shooting at the vessel. What they hoped to accomplish against a machine constructed to withstand the rigors of Deep Space was anyone's guess. Perhaps they thought *they* might get lucky. Their bullets merely bounced harmlessly off the carrier's armored hull. The pilot flew over the outcropping, then swung around to make another pass. The JUR people held their fire until it was right over them.

In the lull, a single shot rang out. Sgt. Running Deer, via his vidcom, immediately informed Rodriguez that one of the terrorists had fallen to the ground. A second and a third shot quickly followed. Running Deer reported a second casualty. From her position, Lt. Ralfo spotted the third man scrambling back up the slope toward the tunnel from which he and his comrades had emerged; Running Deer confirmed the sighting and directed the pilot to follow the fleeing man. That individual did not flee far, however; Quinn brought him down before he had gone twenty meters.

With the threat to the mission removed, the Warden contemplated his next move. He wanted to enter the tunnel complex and investigate what Dr. Weyerhauser had told him. But, if the tunnel were full of JUR members, he'd have no chance of investigating safely. His forces, never a full complement to begin with, had suffered casualties, and they would be facing a desperate and ruthless foe. His best tactic was to contact the two platoons inside the *Astarte* and have them move up their timetable, an action which carried its own risks since the platoon leaders were not familiar with the layout and the JUR were.

He contacted the carrier and directed the pilot, first, to drop off Sgt. Running Deer and, second, to set up a relay point so that he could communicate with the platoon leaders. He then motioned to the Doctor to join him.

"Do you have any idea why those three men should be in that particular tunnel?"

"None" was the worried reply. "Perhaps they were aware of the Constabulary presence in the *Astarte* and were looking for an escape route."

"But we destroyed their ship."

"If I know Major Tshambe, he'll have a contingency plan."

"Have you heard anything from him over your vidcom?"

The astrophysicist reached into his coat pocket, frowned, and searched other pockets without apparent success.

"I seem to have lost my vidcom," he announced. "It must've fallen out of my pocket when we were being bounced around in the vortex. What now, Warden?"

"First, we wait until the carrier acquires a suitable position to put me in contact with the two platoons. Then, you'll give them directions out of the *Astarte* and into the tunnels. That should distract the JUR enough to allow me to do what I came here to do."

The wait seemed interminable. Rodriguez occupied himself by completing his video scan of the henge. Ralfo accompanied him in silence but kept a sharp eye out for other intruders. Dr. Weyerhauser and Cpl. Chen resumed their search for artifacts.

Presently, the carrier signaled the Warden, and he had the pilot establish a link with the platoon leaders. The SL's reported that they had covered a third of the ruined cruise ship and had encountered only one lone terrorist prowling about. That individual had fired at them randomly, resulting in one minor casualty, and then run "like ten Capellans were after him." Rodriguez asked to speak to Sgt. Utumi, who linked into a conference call via his own vidcom.

"Sergeant, what's your assessment so far?"

"It my opinion to be, Rodri-go, that the Chemku[45] the *Astarte* have abandon. We no longer them here will find."

"Thank you, Sergeant. Gentlemen," he addressed the SL's, "it's time to widen the search into the tunnel network on this world. Professor Weyerhauser will provide you with directions." He handed his vidcom to the academic. The latter spoke tersely but precisely and returned the vidcom to the Warden. "Very well, gentlemen, you have your orders. Move out."

"There shouldn't be too many left in the cell, Warden. We started out with two dozen men. Since then, they've suffered about a fifty percent loss."

"Then, if we enter the tunnel system from here, we might catch them in a pincer move, even while we look for more artifacts."

---

45 The Capellan term for Remans. Their term for Romulans is similar – "Chimku." Both terms reflect, not racial traits, since all humans look alike to Alkon eyes, but to occupational traits – CMT.

"Nothing personal, Warden," the Doctor said, grimacing, "but do you have sufficient numbers here? The Major is as cagy as they come."

"Sgt. Running Deer, are your people up to the task?"

"We'll do what's necessary, sir," the non-com replied grimly. "After today, Gamma Platoon won't be the laughing stock of the *Steadfast*."

"Well said, Sergeant. All right, people, follow me. Lt. Ralfo, you and Quinn have the point."

"Aye, sir," the Pluj responded with a wicked grin on her face. "Before us, nothing will stand."

She bounded off toward the outcropping against which Pvt. Quinn was lounging lackadaisically, signaled to him to follow her, and began scrambling up the mountain like a child on a grand adventure. Rodriguez set out at a brisk pace himself with the rest of the platoon close behind. Fortunately for all of them, Planetoid 48 was a small world and therefore possessed a lighter gravity; otherwise, they might have exhausted themselves before they had gotten halfway up the slope. It was still rough going, however, as they had to pick their way around stray boulders and outcroppings and avoid (or try to avoid) any missteps which would turn an ankle or break a leg.

At the top of the slope and before the tunnel entrance, Rodriguez halted the group and peered into the darkness in order to spot any potential danger before actually encountering it. All seemed quiet, but he knew that was an illusion. Extreme caution was the watchword from here on.

"Stay close together, everyone," he admonished. "Professor, this is your turf. Lead the way."

CHAPTER NINETEEN

▼

HIDE-AND-SEEK

SR. LT. KANAKA WAS EXTREMELY frustrated.

His mission, as explained to him by Commander Rux, was to assist Warden Rodriguez in the securing of Planetoid 48. And the Warden had given him specific orders to "cleanse" the hijacked cruise ship *Astarte* of all Reman terrorists, a task he had looked forward to with great relish. He had lost a brother to the JUR's predations, and he wanted to settle accounts.

There were, however, no Remans on the *Astarte* with whom to settle accounts. He and his platoon and Sr. Lt. E-ma's platoon had been scouring the ship, deck by deck, compartment by compartment, for the better part of ten kiloseconds, and only one terrorist had been seen and that one had turned tail and run. There were corpses all over the place – mostly civilians – but no live bodies to "cleanse" and provide his team with "war trophies."

His frustration was multiplied by the fact that he was required to take orders from an individual ten years his junior. He'd been in the Constabulary for close to six standard years and, until now, all of his superior officers had been in service as long as, if not longer than, he had been. Now, he was taking orders from a "fuzz face," just out of his Academy, who had no combat experience whatsoever. And the fact that the "fuzz face" was a Warden who could operate as he pleased did not endear Sr. Lt. Kanaka either; as far as *he* was concerned, the "fuzz face" could take a vacation on the planet Amazon!

And, if *that* weren't bad enough, he was forced to work with a Capellan for whom he also had no use. Sr. Lt. Kanaka had lost a great-uncle in the Great War, one of many casualties in the ill-famed expedition to Planetoid Delta, and he still saw Capellans as the enemy. That they had been incorporated into the Constabulary galled him no end. And this particular Capellan galled him to infinity. For one thing, he did not disguise his contempt for humans very well; for another, he behaved as if *he* were in charge of his and E-ma's platoons, making "suggestions" one after another and expecting them to be acted upon post haste!

Finally, there was E-ma the Uhaad, a mica miner who had no business wearing a Constabulary uniform. He didn't even know how to salute properly! And he had the annoying habit of tapping his teeth with a fingernail whenever he was undecided – which was most of the time.

How could a seasoned campaigner like himself work under these circumstances? It was enough to want to resign his commission and forgo a pension.

Sr. Lt. Kanaka was extremely frustrated indeed!

While he was grousing about his lot in life, Sgt Utumi slithered up behind him and stood silently for a moment, observing him, before announcing his presence with a clearing of his throat – a signal of attention-getting in human culture, but a warning of danger in Capellan. However Lt. Kanaka interpreted the gesture, it came so suddenly that he actually gasped loudly, paled, and whirled around in fright. The sergeant may or may not have been playing a joke on his nominal superior officer, but he did take pleasure in unsettling any human he chanced to meet.

"Damn it to Hell, Sergeant!" the lieutenant bawled as soon as his heartbeat returned to normal. "Don't sneak up like that! I might have shot you!"

Utumi pursed his lips briefly. This fool would have been dead long before he had a chance to draw his weapon. Why, there would have been plenty of time to choose a suitable death for one so unalert as this human. He glared stoically at the Dunian and waited for him to calm down.

"What do you want anyway? Have you got anything to report?"

"I my latest foray to report," came the unemotional reply. "The next deck clear to be. We may advance."

"Very well. We seem to be making remarkable progress. Do you think there are any JUR left aboard the *Astarte*?"

"I my doubts to have. If they wise to be, they at the earliest opportunity should have evacuate."

"Remans aren't noted for their intelligence, Sergeant. They're all a bunch of farmers. Well, let's proceed to the next deck, shall we?"

Sr. Lt. Kanaka marched off, happy to be doing something and happy to have wrested control of the situation from the Capellan, however briefly that might be. Secretly, he hoped to run into some of the terrorists. Perhaps the sergeant would become a "casualty."

* * *

"Well, 'ave ye foond anyone yet?"

"Na one, Myjor. Just some bodies 'ere and there."

Major Tshambe frowned deeply as he peered about the cave where he had set up his command post. A dozen pairs of eyes stared back at him, eyes filled with concern and not a little anxiety. If the reports he'd received were accurate, he was looking at all which remained of his cell; most of them were sympathetic technicians, incorporated into the JUR to operate the MOME they had highjacked, and they all had had only a rudimentary training in the use of a weapon. The bulk of his combat-ready people was now missing in action and presumed dead.

"Damnytion!" he swore. "'Oo would 'ave fought a single Constabulary patrol could do so much damage?"

"Oi examined two of oor people. Thy were killed wif a stiletto."

"A stiletto?" The Major knitted his brow. "Are ye positive, man?"

"Aye. That means thy've got Capellans wif 'em."

"Damnytion!" Tshambe swore again. "One Capellan is worf a 'ole platoon o' troopers. Can we escype frough the *Astarte?*"

"Na, sir. Oi 'eard vices up there, and thy were speakin' Standard."

"Huh! Oi dinna loike wanderin' frough these tunnels wifoot knowin' where Oi am, but it looks loike we dinna 'ave na chice. Batumbo, is the foinal program set up?"

One of the technicians stepped forward, licking dry lips. Perspiration beaded his forehead.

"Aye, Myjor. As soon as the MOME is fully re-charged, the automatic sequence will commence. There'll be a foive-second warp-oot which will put Planetoid 48 wifin a 'undred thoosand kilometers of Romulus." He attempted a smile, then fell back into a neutral expression. "Since this world is travelin' at approximately one kilometer per second, it will intercept Romulus in two standard dys."

"Excellent. Whatever 'appens to us will be worf the cost. The damned Rommies willna know what 'it 'em until it's too lyte! All roight, tyke only what ye can easily carry, plus yere weapon, and 'ead for the tunnel leadin' to the opposite soide o' these moontains."

* * *

Lixu Rodriguez, his grandfather always said, was a natural spelunker. There wasn't a cave or a tunnel he encountered that he didn't want to explore right away. More often than not, he had to be restrained or else no one would see him for the rest of the day.

In administrative district #17 on Dunia, where the Rodriguezes originated, the central feature was the towering Andes Mountains, and they possessed lots of caves and tunnels, some simple constructs, some complex systems of galleries, grottoes, and subterranean streams. Though the Rodriguezes lived in the Administrative capital of Lima and thus were city-bred, they always vacationed in the mountains during the summer, and young Lixu indulged himself the whole time. Sometimes, he would be accompanied by his father or his grandfather or both (but never his mother who confessed to suffering from claustrophobia); more often, he would go off on his own, wandering through Subterranea at a leisurely pace, exploring each cave and tunnel in minute fashion, and absorbing the ambience of a silent world punctuated only by the dripping of water or the rush of the wind or occasionally the low muttering of some disturbed wild thing (which he never encountered). He dreamed he was on a different world and was the first human to explore it. And the tales he would tell when he finally returned home rivaled those of real-life explorers.

The last time Rodriguez had been in a tunnel was the last month of summer before the family re-located to Pluj upon his father's appointment as Dunia's envoy to that frigid world, when he was just eleven years old. There were caves and tunnels on Pluj, of course, but they were frozen affairs, possessing an uninteresting sameness, unconducive to serious exploration. Caves and tunnels also abounded on the Aldebaranian home world, but obviously he had had no time to get away from the rigorous training schedule and check them out. (And what would Master Fresh-Bloom-in-the-Face-as-the-Day-Begins have thought of his little hobby?)

Now, for the first time in twelve years, Warden (L1) Lixu Rodriguez found himself in a tunnel on an alien world, and he was beside himself with excitement. Outwardly, he maintained the somber, cool-headed image Wardens always tried to project; inwardly, however, he was the child again, eager to explore and impatient with those who would hold him back.

He stood just inside the entrance to the tunnel and waited until his eyes adjusted to the darkness. Then, in an action which surprised his companions, he removed one of his gloves and brushed the rock face with his fingertips. This was a ritual taught to him by his grandfather from whom all he had learned everything he knew about spelunking; the old man had declared that each cave and tunnel had its own "personality" and that one determined that personality by touching the rock. Whether it was true or not, the child was not about to contradict the man and so adopted the ritual faithfully.

The rock here was fine-grained and smooth to the touch, meaning it was basaltic in nature. From experience, Rodriguez deduced that the tunnel's "personality" took on the nature of a sensitive person, given to anxiety and self-doubt. He nodded knowingly. If Doctor Weyerhauser was correct and this world had once been inhabited by sentient beings, then the loss of their life-giving sun would most assuredly have filled them with anxiety and self-doubt, which feelings had been magnified by the surrounding material.

Moreover, the rock was covered with flat surfaces punctuated by sharp edges. This told the amateur spelunker that the tunnel had not been formed by natural processes but hewn by sentient beings, and they had been in a hurry to burrow into the interior of the mountain in order to escape the freezing cold outside. Now that his eyes had adjusted, he noted that the tunnel was not uni-dimensional; lumpy projections abounded on both walls. The burrowers had not been too concerned with creating a perfect structure.

Whoever those burrowers had been, they had been short-statured. The distance from roof to floor was only a meter-and-three-quarters, and most of the company – especially the astrophysicist – had to crouch in order to maneuver their way along the tunnel. Only Cpl. Chen did not have to worry about cracking her head on the low-lying roof.

The group, following the Doctor's lead, began a slow march into the interior of the mountain. The amateur spelunker reasoned that they were descending at an eight-degree decline. The further one penetrated the mountain, the warmer one became – relatively speaking. The temperature difference between the surface of Planetoid 48 and its bowels couldn't have been more than 3-4 degrees; no one here was likely to strip down to avoid overheating. Only Lt. Ralfo, dressed in just her field uniform, seemed comfortable.

Rodriguez estimated that they had traveled a hundred meters before coming to the first cave off this tunnel. He halted, flashed his lamp inside, and saw nothing. He stepped inside and shone the light back and forth, up and down. The cave was completely empty. What he had hoped to find, he was not prepared to say at this time, though the others in the party all gave him questioning looks. He shrugged his shoulders and moved to exit the cave.

In that moment, the lamp illuminated something not natural to caves in general, something on the wall near the entrance: a pictograph.

The Warden panned the light back and forth and discovered that the rock art was the left-hand one in a series of six, irregularly spaced from each other. And, at the far end of the series was a most familiar symbol – an inverted "T" with a small circle on the right-hand side of the vertical stem, halfway up.

The mark of the Wayfarers.

His heart beat faster now, and his breath caught in his throat at the momentous discovery. He played the light over each pictograph in the series, inscribing it into his brain, and realized that the series described a brief narrative of events as interpreted by the artist. He now became aware of Ralfo at his side; she too was staring in wonder at the artwork. Doctor Weyerhauser and Cpl. Chen joined them, but how they were reacting was unknowable.

"These pictures you can interpret, Lixu?"

"I can make a stab at reading them. Look at the one on the right." He shone the lamp on a group of six stick figures in a kneeling position, facing the Wayfarers' symbol. "The exo-anthropologists have determined that primitive peoples who encountered the Wayfarers tended to worship them as gods. This drawing is yet more proof of that theory; the former inhabitants of Planetoid 48 are bowing down before their gods.

"Now, you have to read these pictographs from right to left. Otherwise, they make no sense. The second one is somewhat confusing, and I don't know what to make of it." The representation depicted another group of six figures (or perhaps the same six) in two staggered rows of three each; above the upper-most row was a circle with lines emanating from it. "The only thing that looks familiar is the circle with the lines; it's obviously the sun which this world once orbited.

"The next two 'scenes' have to be read together, I think." The third pictograph showed the stick figures in a horizontal position. Above them was a triangle facing to the left; from the triangle, two arrows pointed at the stick figures. In the fourth panel, a second triangle appeared, facing the first one; arrows from the second were pointed at the first. "From the legends," Rodriguez explained, "gathered from several different cultures in the central spiral, the exo-anthropologists have conjectured a 'war in heaven,' meaning the Wayfarers were divided into two factions. Why they were has been the subject of endless speculation. But the fact remains that wherever the factions interfaced, horrendous warfare occurred, involving weapons of mass destruction. You see here that there was 'collateral damage' done to the indigenous life forms on this world as a result.

"We now come to the heart of the matter in number five." The drawing showed a group of stick figures with "arms" raised high. Above them, the circle with lines emanating from it had re-appeared, but it was smaller than the circle in the first representation. "We can surmise that the 'war in heaven' resulted in Planetoid 48 being knocked out of its orbit and sent spinning away from its sun. The people are understandably alarmed.

"Finally, the end comes." The last pictograph contained more stick figures, some kneeling, others lying horizontally. "Whoever drew these had the presence of mind to make a record of what befell his people, even if he didn't understand why it happened."

"Them Our Lady preserve," Ralfo whispered.

"Gor!" Chen croaked. "A whole world – *hommed*! What a fraggin' red zone this is!"

"Warden," the Doctor spoke quietly, "I'll take you to the remains of some of those unfortunate creatures. They're not too far from here."

"Right. As soon as I video these pictographs, we'll be on our way."

*   *   *

"Lt. E-ma, have you completed your sweep yet?" Lt. Kanaka asked in a bored tone.

Having had the "benefit" of Sgt. Utumi's leading the way and using his unique skills to sniff out (figuratively and literally) the enemy's forces, his platoon had searched its half of the *Astarte* in record time and found no JUR personnel lurking about. Deck after deck, the platoon had verified the Capellan's assessment of the situation and was in danger only of becoming blasé about their mission. The constant glares from their scout and the constant stroking of his left cheek kept them on their toes, however, more out of spite for him than out of concern for their own safety. When they had finally been given the "all clear" on the final deck, they dared to relax their guard – though the scout remained alert – and bantered with each other.

"I having two more decks to search, Lt. Kanaka," came the reedy thin voice of the Uhaad officer. "We not seeing any terrorists at all."

"As I suspected. Those bastards have cleared out and are holed up God-knows-where. When you've completed your search, rejoin me, and we'll find out what our Warden's pleasure is next."

"Aye. We finishing in five kilos."

Kanaka observed Utumi regarding him coolly, was properly annoyed by the unwarranted scrutiny, and walked away, ostensibly to check out his platoon. Happily for him, he did not notice the Capellan rub his cheek with all six fingers.

The five kiloseconds passed with all the deliberateness of a lava flow on a low-gravity world. Some of the Constabulary troopers had actually dozed off and were roused by a swift kick in the ribs by one sergeant or another. They were then ordered to hastily designated guard duty posts. This example served to keep everyone else awake. Eventually, E-ma showed up and reported that his half of the ship was clear of terrorists. Kanaka nodded and switched on his vidcom.

"Lt. Kanaka reporting to Warden Rodriguez."

"Rodriguez here, Leftenant."

"Sir, we've searched the *Astarte* top to bottom and have observed negative JUR activity."

"Very good. That means they're in the tunnel complex inside this mountain. That'll be your next assignment."

"You want us to go into unfamiliar territory without reconnoitering it first?" the SL inquired without bothering to disguise his disbelief. "That's insane – sir!"

"Relax, Kanaka. I didn't intend that you should walk in blindly. I have a specific location for you to secure – the cave where the *Astarte*'s highjacked MOME is secreted. Dr. Weyerhauser will provide directions to that spot from where you are. Professor?"

Kanaka listened to the astrophysicist's detailed directions with only half of his mind. The other half was grumbling over having to take orders from both a Warden *and* an alien *and* a civilian. It was just too irregular! And so, when Rodriguez asked him to repeat what he had just been told, he stumbled over half of it. The Warden's tone of voice registered disdain.

"Sgt. Utumi, did you understand the procedure?"

"Aye, Rodri-go," the warrior replied, ignoring the grimace on the lieutenant's face. "It straightforward to be."

"Take the point then and find that MOME. Then shut it down any way you can – safely, that is."

The Capellan turned on his heel and wordlessly began the long trek into the tunnel complex. Kanaka shook his head in disgust but nevertheless barked orders to both platoons to fall in and move out. He and E-ma took the center post.

*   *   *

Rodriguez bent over the skeletal remains of the long-deceased inhabitants of Planetoid 48, a male, a female, and their child, all huddled together in death as they had been in life. He examined each body carefully, because there was something vaguely familiar about these humanoids, though he couldn't quite put his finger on it just yet. When he concluded his examination, he videoed the bodies, taking shots from all angles and at near and far distances. He hoped there would be time to remove the remains and turn them over to the exo-anthropologists on New Switzerland; but, if there weren't, at least the eggheads would have a pictorial record to study.

Next, he played the lamp around other parts of the cave. If there were bodies here, it stood to reason that there were also personal belongings, artifacts which would provide clues to the life-styles of these unfortunate beings. A bit of pottery, a utensil, even a child's toy – any material object could prove to be valuable.

There! A meter away from the trio laid a ladle-like instrument. And, there! Next to the "ladle" was a definite pot.

The Warden videoed both of them *in situ* before he touched either one. The "ladle" seemed to have been carved from a tree branch; its handle still possessed tiny knots, and signs of twigs having been hacked off were in evidence. The pot looked for all the world to have been fashioned from ordinary clay, but the experts could determine its composition better than he. Around the midsection ran a faded-red series of triangles, every other one inverted; each triangle was spaced five centimeters from its neighbors, and every sixth figure contained a single blue dot in its center. Rodriguez added both items to his collection bag.

Now the lamp highlighted a group of symbols on the rear wall of the cave. The Warden stared at it in amazement, then rummaged through his collection bag. He pulled out the plaque the astrophysicist had given him. The symbols engraved on it matched exactly those on the wall, except that the latter were larger. And he spotted a second grouping underneath the first grouping on the wall. What was really amazing was that he recognized some of the symbols in the second group. He touched each one of those in a reverent manner.

"I can't believe what I'm seeing here," he announced to the others – Dr. Weyerhauser, Cpl. Chen, and Lt. Ralfo — who had crowded into the cave with him. "I've seen some of these ideographs on Aldebaran. They're part of the ancient language of the Community before it created an alphabet."

"But what are they doing here?" the Doctor asked. "Planetoid 48 originated deeper inside the central spiral, close to where it joins with the main body of the Galaxy. Aldebaran is only seventy-five light-years from where we are now."

"The only logical explanation is that these creatures were the primitive ancestors of the Aldebaranians." He peered at the skeletons again. "And that's why these remains looked so familiar to me. They have the same body structure but are smaller in stature. I saw enough Aldebaranians in five years to know."

"But, Lixu," Ralfo murmured, "how the Aldebaranians to their present world came?"

"That, my dear, is the K 64,000 question. There's a theory floating about concerning trans-migration, but it's quite far-fetched. In any event, it's important to secure these remains and artifacts and let the scientists puzzle over them. Corporal, I want one of your troopers assigned to haul everything in this cave back to the carrier." Chen nodded in acquiescence and returned to the tunnel. "Professor, have you seen anything else that might be of interest?"

"Sorry, Warden, but no. I poked around here and there just to get away from Major Tshambe, but I didn't have all that much time to myself. I'm sure there's more though."

"Uh-huh. Let's press on then."

* * *

"Captain Halvarson," the Sensors officer reported, "Planetoid 48 has changed positions again."

The Captain had been updating the ship's log when this announcement broke his train of thought. He straightened up and peered into the Display; he had to blink his eyes a couple of times in order to focus on the area he wanted to see. It was true, he realized. The runaway was no longer a half a light-year from the Rhea Silvia system but closer to a light-*minute* away. Instantly, he contacted Commander Quintus Ling, *Steadfast's* Chief Engineer (and reputedly the oldest member of the crew). The Oriental face regarded him with a Mona-Lisa smile.

"What'll it be now, *boyo?*" Commander Ling was the only person on board who had the effrontery to speak to the Ship's Master disrespectfully, and he claimed that his advanced age entitled him to do so. "Another little jaunt?"

"You got it, Quint. Planetoid 48 just moved again. It's now a light-minute from Rhea Silvia. I want to be *half* a light-minute from it."

"Is that all?" the ancient asked in a mock-surprised tone. "And would ye be wantin' me to recharge the Old Lady[46] while I'm at it?"

"Later, perhaps. Right now, I want that warp-out – and I want you to handle it personally."

"Roight ye are, guv!" Ling intoned and threw up a comic salute.

Halvarson's next action was to announce an immediate warp-out. The crew had fifty seconds to prepare themselves.

The familiar gut-wrenching sensation occurred right on schedule and caught more than a few individuals less than prepared. They found themselves flat on the deck wherever they were and in various awkward positions. Happily, the warp-out was of short duration, lasting no longer than five seconds, and the hapless individuals recovered quickly.

The Captain stared at his vidscreen and selected a sequence of viewing angles. One after another, the scenes appeared: Rhea Silvia to starboard, Romulus to port, and Planetoid 48 aft. Ling was right on the money – as usual. Halvarson was now aware of Commander Krishnamurthy sliding into her chair.

---

46   Romulans' and Remans' affectionate term for their star – perhaps the only thing they can agree on – CMT.

"Ah, I'm glad you're here, Tomiko. I've got a little problem for that analytic brain of yours to solve." The XO raised an eyebrow questioningly. "But, first things first."

He punched the silver button on his console. The face of an Ekath appeared on his screen.

"Aye, sir?"

"Leftenant, bring the ship fifty degrees about, facing Planetoid 48."

Next, he called up the Black Zone and faced a Bitha female who sported a blue crest. She wore the rank of Lt. Commander and was the Zone's CO.

"Aye, sir?"

"Commander Mun, do we have a full complement of long-range missiles?"

"Do we, sir."

"And are all fighter craft fully armed?"

Mun consulted her charts.

"All loaded and primed, sir."

He turned to Krishnamurthy with grim determination etched across his face. She regarded him coolly.

"What do you have in mind, Olaf?"

"A big risk, that's what. We need to nudge the planetoid away from its present course so that it will pass by this system harmlessly."

"'Nudge' it? And how do you propose to nudge it?"

"I'm going to fire missiles at it – all I've got, if I have to – and hope that the fire power is sufficient to deflect that rock."

"You're serious!"

"I am. And I want you to determine where to concentrate the bombardment to accomplish the job. Can you do it?"

"That shouldn't be too difficult to calculate." Now she frowned. "But what about our people there?"

"If I warn them in advance and they take cover, they shouldn't be in any danger. But, I need to take action soon. Otherwise, nothing will prevent a major calamity."

"God! I hope you know what you're doing."

"So do I, Tomiko, so do I."

*　　　*　　　*

Gamma Platoon was not caught off guard as they had been the first time they experienced a warp-out of Planetoid 48. This time, they realized what was going to happen the second the vibrations began. Everyone lay down on the floor of the tunnel they were in and relaxed. They did have one mitigating factor in their favor: since they were *inside* the runaway, they were not in danger of being shaken off the surface and sent flying into Deep Space. They rode out the warp-out in comparative peace.

All except Rodriguez, who never could get rid of the butterflies in his stomach whenever an MOME was activated. For the duration, he closed his eyes, gritted his teeth, and tried to meditate.

He remembered the time Master Fresh had summoned him to his private quarters – his first visit there, but not his last – for a private consultation. He had stood before his mentor, his mind full of consternation because Master Fresh had never divulged the reason for the visit – but then he *never* gave a reason for anything he did. And Master Fresh had studied him in silence for what seemed like a megasecond before finally speaking.

"Describe to me, pupil, what you experience during what you humans call 'warp-out.'"

Rodriguez's consternation turned to shock at both the question and its abruptness. How had the Master found out about that? And why did he want to know? He began to stammer as he searched for the proper words – a difficult task since he barely understood his problem himself.

"Speak, lack-wit! Have you no tongue?"

"It's hard to describe, Master, at least in terms which you would understand."

"And what causes you to believe I would not understand?"

"I can describe the phenomenon in *human* terms, but not in Aldebaranian terms."

"Then speak however you can, pupil. You may be surprised to learn what I am able to understand."

And so Warden-to-be Rodriguez spoke in halting speech about what effects an MOME had on him: the butterflies in the stomach, the migraine in the head, the shaking from head to foot, his body parts threatening to fly off in different directions — and the sense of relief when the ordeal passed. When he had finished his recitation, Master Fresh studied him silently once again, then abruptly dismissed him. The consternation returned. On the other hand, his mentor never raised the issue of his weakness again.

What would his mentor say if he knew that his lack-wit of a pupil still hadn't conquered this weakness?

That weakness, surprisingly, lasted only five seconds. Ordinarily, maximum warp-outs required a hundred seconds of activation, and an expert could fine-tune the duration to accomplish a jump to within half a light-minute. For some unfathomable reason which the experts could not provide, an MOME could not be coaxed to go beyond the one hundred seconds; some as-yet-undiscovered law of physics dictated against it, no matter how much the designers and manufacturers upgraded the product. The Warden, who had been expecting something longer than five seconds, could not believe his good fortune at the quick departure of the butterflies; in a perverse sort of way, he felt...cheated.

"A short jump," Doctor Weyerhauser stated the obvious.

"Exactly."

"I didn't think any of the Major's so-called 'experts' could fine-tune a warp-out that much."

"You won't hear me complaining, Professor. The less time I spend flat on my back, the more time I have to pursue my mission. Let's go. I want–"

What Rodriguez wanted was lost to eternity as he was interrupted by the sound of a gunshot. Within the confines of the tunnel system, the shot echoed and re-echoed several times before dying away. The platoon hit the deck instantly, weapons at the ready, but no further gunshots were forthcoming. Sgt. Running Deer jumped to his feet.

"Who the frag fired that shot?" he bellowed.

"I did, Sergeant," Ralfo confessed. "A JUR member I saw and instinctively reacted."

"The JUR – in this area?" Rodriguez queried. "Is that possible?"

"It is, if they're looking for an escape route," the astrophysicist responded. "There are two platoons of Constabulary troopers between them and their first choice."

"Hmmm. Did you hit him, Leftenant?"

"No, sir. Cleanly he escaped."

"He'll warn his comrades then. Sergeant, Alert Level Three."[47]

"Aye, sir. D'ya want me to send some troopers after that fragger?"

"I do *not* – not until I call up some re-enforcements." He activated his vidcom and tapped in a code. The sour face of Lt. Kanaka appeared; he seemed to be particularly annoyed at this moment. "Where are you, Leftenant?"

"Um, we're about one hundred meters from our target. We should access it in approximately three hundred seconds."

"Any signs of trouble?"

"No, sir. The *Astarte* looks deserted. All we've seen are bodies and wreckage."

"Good. I've got a change in orders for you." The SL frowned even deeper. "Deploy just one of your platoons to the cave to carry out your original

---

47 There are only three levels of alert status in the Constabulary. Level One signifies "proceed with caution – possible danger"; Level Two means "proceed with great caution – probable danger"; and Level Three indicates "proceed with extreme caution – imminent danger" – CMT.

mission. Take the other platoon and close in on our position; Dr. Weyerhauser will provide directions. We've got a chance to catch the JUR between us."

"That's certainly good news. Do you have a preference in platoons?"

"No. I'll leave that to your judgment. Oh, and send Sgt. Utumi with your choice. He'll run interference for you."

"Very good, sir."

To Sgt. Running Deer, the Warden said: "Find a reasonably defensible spot around here and position your people. Lt. Kanaka is going to 'beat the bushes,' so to speak, and drive the JUR into our waiting arms."

The non-com grinned hugely.

"We'll give 'em a warm welcome, sir."

"Permission them to join, sir," Ralfo requested.

"Permission granted, Leftenant." He stroked her cheek in the Pluj fashion. "The Lady watch over you."

*   *   *

The Reman ran through the tunnel system at breakneck speed, careening against the walls every few steps. He didn't think he was being followed, but he wasn't about to take any chances. Too many of his comrades had already died on this god-forsaken rock, and he didn't wish to be the next on the list. At last, he reached the main party – what was left of it. Major Tshambe waited expectantly, a grimness on his face and in his eyes. The soldier pulled up in front of him and took several deep breaths before attempting to speak.

"Oi tyke it ye sawr the enemy," the leader stated matter-of-factly.

"Aye, Myjor. And Oi was spotted too. One o' the fraggers took a shot at me!"

"Do ye fink thy're in pursuit?"

"Oi dinna know. Oi didna stop to foind oot."

"Na matter. Everyfing is going according to plan."

"But, sir, we're trapped!"

"Buck up, *boyo*! Didna ye fink Oi 'ad a back-up plan? There's a smaller tunnel that branches off this one na far fum 'ere. It'll tyke us aroond those Constabulary barstards, and we'll come oot close to the shuttle Oi foughtfully brought along. We'll be off this rock before thy realoize thy've been fragged." He smiled crookedly, and a wicked gleam filled his eyes. "And then, p'r'aps, thy'll foind the little surproise Oi left 'em."

CHAPTER TWENTY

▼

CAT-AND-MOUSE

THE ASSEMBLAGE IN CONFERENCE ROOM A was as grim as it could be. If any of the individuals had had a pleasant thought before entering, (s)he checked it at the hatch and put on a "proper" expression. Interestingly, Captain Halvarson was already seated at the head of the table rather than making his usual grand entrance, and the senior officers took their own chairs without formality and waited expectantly.

"Ladies and gentlemen," the Captain announced, "we are now at a crucial point in our mission. What happens in the next few kilos will determine the success or failure of that mission." A brief smile. "You'll excuse the melodrama, but I'm quite serious. I have given Commander Krishnamurthy a problem to solve concerning what we ought to do next. She will now present her solution."

The XO rose and strode over to the vidscreen. She tapped several buttons on the control panel, and the screen coalesced to show a grainy image of two male Dunians standing at a medium-length table whose borders were surrounded by wide, raised rails. On the table, a number of colored spheroids, five centimeters in diameter, lay in scattered positions. The two Dunians held long, narrow wooden rods which were tipped in a cloth-like material.

"Before I present my solution," Krishnamurthy said, "I want to explain the principles behind it. To do that, I'm going to introduce you to the ancient Dunian game of 'billiards.' The object of the game is to send all of the multi-colored balls into pockets located around the perimeter of the 'billiard table.' The players strike the white ball – called the 'cue ball' – with the 'cue sticks' in their hands, and the cue ball will in turn strike another ball at which the players are aiming. Actually, this is basic geometry: striking a ball at a certain point will force it on a path at a certain angle. The skill in the game is to determine that point which will knock a ball into a pocket. The players play in rotation, and a player may continue to play without interruption so long as he can knock balls into pockets."

She touched another button. The image on the screen began to move, albeit in a very jerky manner. At times, the image froze and/or skipped, but the audience was able to see enough of the game to understand its principles. After a hundred seconds or so, the XO tapped another button, and the images disappeared.

"I apologize for the quality of the graphics. What you've been looking at is a video recording made nearly four hundred years ago on Dunia. The technology was obviously quite primitive.

"What I propose now is that we play our own game of 'billiards.' Instead of a 'cue ball' and a 'cue stick,' however, we'll use our missiles to strike our 'target ball' directly." She called up another image, a sketch of a sphere in black-and-white. A series of dashes advanced toward the sphere, struck it at a pre-determined point on its circumference, and sent it off on a pre-determined path. "We'll program the missiles to hit Planetoid 48 at a certain point on its surface and continue the barrage for as long as it takes to deflect it from its current path."

The gasps of shock rippled around the conference table loud enough to equal a shout from a single person. The senior staff stared at one another in disbelief, and some of them muttered prayers to whatever gods they believed in. The ever-demonstrative Commander Rux was on his feet in an instant.

"Sir, cannot be you serious! Have not we sufficient missiles to accomplish this – this mad scheme."

"Commander Mun?" Halvarson responded.

The senior Weapons officer stroked her crest in a show of nervousness and looked at Rux with pleading eyes. It was no secret aboard the *Steadfast* that the two of them were having an affair, even though on their world such a liaison would be unthinkable. Blue Crests occupied the bottom rung of the Bithan socio-economic ladder and were regarded with disdain by all other colors. Commander Mun would not, by custom, contradict an upper-level crest under ordinary circumstances and certainly not her paramour.

"Believe I, Captain, that do we have the necessary firepower. But, sir, will leave this action us practically defenseless if were attacked we by hostile forces."

"I'm well aware of that possibility, Commander. Yet, we face a dire situation here, and we must take bold action. Tomiko, where do you propose to strike Planetoid 48?"

The XO entered another coded sequence. On the vidscreen, the previous white sphere re-appeared; a large red dot could be seen in the lower-right-hand quadrant.

"Here, at 38.5 degrees. Concentrated fire at this point should nudge the runaway into a new path that will carry it above the plane of the ecliptic and harmlessly into Deep Space."

Rux shook his head vigorously and glared at his lover.

"Have I great doubts that will work this. Is not Planetoid 48 an asteroid which can be moved easily."

"It's a calculated risk, Araru," the Captain replied softly, "but one I'm prepared to take." He turned to the Green Zone chief, an Uhaad. "Commander I-zu, issue a warning to the Romulan Defense Force and have them clear the shipping lanes in the vicinity of the proposed course change. Then notify HQ of what we're going to do."

"Aye, sir."

"How do you think HQ will react, Olaf?" Krishnamurthy asked after the rest of the staff had departed to prepare their sections for the new maneuvers.

"Oh, they'll rant and rave about the risk we're taking, and someone will suggest that I've overstepped my authority. But, if we succeed, we'll all be heroes."

"And if we don't succeed?"

Halvarson gazed at the overhead meditatively.

"I imagine I'll be relegated to a desk job on Amazon, don't you?"

"It's unthinkable, isn't it?"

"They'll have no choice. I *am* overstepping my authority." He looked at her bemusedly. "Then you'd be in command of the *Steadfast* – at least, temporarily."

"If it's all the same to you, Captain, I'd rather not take command under those circumstances. I want to *earn* that right."

*   *   *

Lt. Kanaka and his platoon had to quick-march in order to keep up with Sgt. Utumi. Since Capellans were taller than most humans, they took a longer stride. But that was not the chief factor in the rush. The sergeant was anxious to re-unite with Warden Rodriguez and Lt. Ralfo – whom he respected more than his present companions – and so he hurried his pace more than usual.

What is his bloody hurry? Kanaka grumbled to himself (not for the first time). *Is he so bloodthirsty that he can't wait to find some more terrorists to kill? I want to kill those bastards myself, but I'm certainly not going to face them without a plan. They don't take prisoners, and they don't surrender, and that's the worst kind of fighter.*

He rounded a bend in the tunnel in which the renegade, Dr. Weyerhauser had indicated would bring them to the Warden's position (if they didn't run into the JUR first!), halted in his tracks, and signaled for his men to hold up.

Utumi was nowhere to be seen!

Damn! Where the hell did that Cappo[48] get to? Did he take a wrong turn? Or did we? Or is he deliberately trying to get us lost? I wouldn't put it past that copper son-of-a-bitch!

He motioned for his senior sergeant to come forward. The latter, a New Swiss, trotted over, looked down the empty tunnel, and frowned as deeply as his officer was doing.

"Where's our 'scout,' sir?" he whispered.

"Your guess is as good as mine, Sergeant. I hope he's up ahead, scouting. Otherwise, we've been abandoned. Did you see any side tunnels on our way?"

"Nay, sir. But then, I wasn't looking for any. What do we do now?"

"I'd like to go back to the *Astarte*, where it's safe. But our damned Warden will have our hides nailed to the bulkhead if we did – assuming, of course, that any of us survive this little outing." He sighed deeply. "I suppose we'll just have to keep moving forward until we see someone we recognize."

"And if we see someone we don't?"

"Shoot first and ask questions later, as some ancient Dunian once said."

*   *   *

Sgt. Utumi slowed his pace when he failed to hear the sound of heavy footsteps behind him and peered back in the direction from which he had come. He saw no troopers. The tunnel was as empty as any hole in the ground.

The Capellan closed his right eye for several long moments, a sign of extreme apprehension. He wasn't so much concerned about the whereabouts of the platoon or what might have happened to it as he was about his own situation. The quietude of his surroundings was too unnatural to his way of

48 A derogatory reference to all Capellans by the less polite segment of Amazonian society, i.e. Romulans, passed along to other humans. It was coined during the War of the Eight Suns when politeness was not a requisite when dealing with one's "enemy" and has endured ever since – CMT.

thinking; it put him in mind of a tomb and of the spirit of a dead man which might be lost and therefore angry and dangerous. His kind avoided tunnels and caves whenever possible for this very reason; and, when they were forced by circumstances to enter one, they wanted as much company as they could obtain.

Now, he was alone in a tunnel, and his kind's superstitious dread kicked in in full force. Even the presence of humans (whom he mostly despised) was preferable to loneliness.

Laggards! he thought furiously. *Why could they not keep up? Humans are all lazy lumps! It's a wonder they ever left their home world to explore the stars. And, for all the evil they've caused, they should* not *have left it!*

Perhaps I should not have been so impetuous. Rodri-go advised me to keep an eye on the platoon and see that they did not cause any trouble. But I was too anxious to go to his rescue and forgot myself. Now, I am alone in this accursed place.

He closed his right eye again for several more long moments, undecided as to his next course of action. Should he return the way he had come and seek out the platoon? Or should he just continue on until he rejoined Sgt. Running Deer's platoon? And what would the Warden say when he learned his trusted scout had abandoned his charges.

He knew what *he* would say: "Irresponsible fool!"

Just then, he heard a sound ahead of him. It was very faint, but it was not natural. He stopped his breathing and concentrated his mind – not an easy task since his heart was beating like a tribal drum. He now entered a meditative state and willed himself to be calm. When he was as calm as he was likely to be in a place like this, he moved slowly forward and listened intently.

The faint and unnatural sound became less faint but no less unnatural. In the stillness of the tunnel, it traveled unhindered, and he recognized it for what it was.

A voice!

A *human* voice!

But whose? According to Dr. Weyerhauser's directions, he could not have reached his comrades so soon. They were at least two more kilometers away. So who was speaking up ahead?

There was only one possibility: the remnants of the JUR cell which had attacked the *Astarte* and stolen its MOME. Having been cut off from any exit near the ruined cruise ship, they were now seeking another way out on the opposite side of the mountain range. Were they aware that a Constabulary unit was also on that side, ready to intercept them when they emerged from the tunnel system? Unless they had reconnoitered beforehand, they were in for a surprise!

On the other hand, the match-up between Rodriguez's force and the terrorists seemed to Utumi, based upon his recent observations, to be wholly favoring the terrorists. The Warden and the Pluj had already proved themselves to be capable warriors; the others, a rag-tag bunch of misfits, had not. The JUR had a reputation for viciousness which made them extremely dangerous. He had heard tales told around a campfire told by veterans of the Great War between the Amazonians and the Alliance in which the Reman units had been more difficult to defeat than Romulan/Dunian/Okath units. Why simple farmers should be so tenacious remained a mystery; perhaps, even then, they were preparing for their rebellion against the Romulans.

As much as he would like to have scored several coups against these Remans, it behooved him to warn his own comrades of the potential threat. But first, he had to slip by the terrorists and get ahead of them.

He removed one of his stilettos from its sheath and cautiously inched his way forward. The more he closed the gap between him and the JUR, the more distinct their voices became. For some reason, they had halted and were now arguing amongst themselves. He approached a bend in the tunnel, became still, and strained his hearing.

"...dinna loike it all, Myjor."

"Ye dinna 'ave to loike it, *boyo*. Ye 'ave to follow orders." A brief silence. "Look, Oi've been in this branch twoice, and Oi didna 'ave any problems. Noo, oor former compytriot, Dr. Woyer'auser would 'ave 'ad the Divil's own toime of it which my be the reason 'e didna notice this branch hissilf."

"Ye're sure this branch will tyke us through to the ither soide?"

"Absolutely. Noo, 'oo's forst?"

"Oi'll go forst, Myjor. Oi'm the biggest 'ere."

"Good lad. Off ye go then."

Utumi peeked around the bend and observed one of the yellow-uniformed individuals squeeze sideways through a half-meter-wide crack in the tunnel wall. When he had disappeared from view, he shouted an encouragement to his comrades.

"Ye willna believe it, but this tunnel is woider furver on. Come on, lads!"

Thus encouraged, the remainder of the terrorists eased themselves through the crack and left the main branch silent once again. The Capellan now rounded the bend, approached the crack stealthily, and peered into it. He closed his right eye again. This branch was even more confining than the one he was in, and he certainly had no desire to enter it. In such confinement, he could easily have dispatched all of the enemy one by one; they all would have died quietly and quickly, and those in the forefront would never learn the fate of those in the rear until that fate caught up to them. But he would not enter for any reason, not even for easy prey. He would leave them to the Constabulary troopers.

Now that there were no more obstacles between him and Rodriguez's group, he could pick up the pace and deliver a warning. If all went well, the platoon could re-group and achieve the pincer move the Warden hoped for.

*   *   *

Rodriguez activated his vidcam, pressed the "play" button, and fast-reversed the images to the point where the ancient symbols had been recorded. He wanted to study them further while he waited for the JUR to show up; he hoped to make an attempt to decipher some of them and, perhaps by so doing, to learn a little of the history of the Aldebaranians. The Community, an ancient race, knew much, but they shared little with outsiders. Any information he could glean could go a long way in understanding their motives for whatever they did.

The War of the Eight Suns, thirty-five years ago, had devolved into a stalemate, a war of attrition. Neither the Amazonian Federation nor the Alliance for Free Space had had a clear advantage by which to force the opposition to the negotiating table. On the other hand, given the passions of the day, neither side was very much interested in negotiation; both desired an unconditional surrender, and both fought savagely in order to obtain it. That neither side could achieve it made the conflict all the more horrendous as death and destruction rained down on military and civilian targets alike.

The problem – if that was the correct word to use in an unwinnable war – was that each side had had a tactical advantage which tended to cancel each other out. The Federation relied on its fleet of MOME-equipped ships to place its troops wherever they needed to be almost instantly; the Alliance seldom had ample warning to prepare a defense against Romulan/Reman militiamen and their allies dropping out of nowhere when they least expected them. The Alliance, for its part, relied on the Capellans, the most highly-trained, highly-organized, and highly-efficient fighting force the Galaxy had ever seen in its long history. A handful of Alkon warriors could slice through an enemy unit with great ease without suffering very many casualties of their own; fierce as Romulan/Reman militiamen were, they were seldom a match for a race which had been bred to fight to the death.

The Great War had plodded on for five years after the establishment of the Amazonian Federation. Then the Aldebaranians intervened.

No one either in the Federation or the Alliance or in those few worlds which chose to be neutral parties had the least idea that such a race existed. Rumors abounded, of course, of intelligent activity deeper into the central spiral, but none had been confirmed. Those ship's captains who ventured near Aldebaran could not recollect any intelligent activity, and not a few of them denied ever having entered the star system. It was as if a collective amnesia had gripped anyone who showed the least curiosity. Thus, when the Community did decide to make their existence known, they were a complete and utter surprise to all concerned; and, as it happened, they were immediately feared and loathed by all concerned.

With the threat of their power-dampener behind them, the Aldebaranians effectively made it impossible to wage war anymore, and so all parties agreed – reluctantly – to the peace terms "recommended" to them. The peace held, despite a great deal of grumbling over the high-handed methods used to achieve it; but, once the machinery was in place, the Aldebaranians "retired" to their own world, never to bother or to be bothered by, "lesser mortals" again. Despite repeated efforts to engage them in economic or cultural exchanges, the Community refused them all. The veil of silence descended once more.

Except in one particular.

The Aldebaranians insisted upon training the law enforcement officers, i.e. the Wardens, personally. Candidates came and went – and some few were chosen for training – but all were sworn to secrecy concerning what they had seen and heard on the Aldebaranian home world. No one – least of all the selectees themselves – was quite sure of the consequences of breaking their oath of silence; but, given the formidable powers of that enigmatic race, no one – least of all the selectees themselves – was bold enough to put the matter to the test. Thus, for thirty-five years, the membership, human and alien, of the Central Spiral Collective, enjoyed a fruitful, if uneasy, peace.

Warden (L1) Lixu Rodriguez was one of many charged to maintain that peace, and he endeavored to carry out his assignments to the best of his ability. Now, however, he held in his hand what appeared to be the means to lift the veil of silence between the Community and the rest of the Collective and to learn something – if only a *little* something – about his former mentors. Despite his training, he knew only a fraction more about them than did the general populace, and he had the same sense of curiosity that all humans possessed and the same sense of acting on that curiosity.

He paused the recording at the point where all of the symbols were depicted *in situ* and studied them, individually and collectively, all the while wracking his brain to recall the meanings of the symbols he remembered from his studies at the Academy.

The second symbol from the right in the top row – a backwards English "E" – was similar to the Aldebaranian word for "life" in one context and for "giver of life" in another. By extrapolation then, the first symbol might refer to "arrival" or "appearance" or "advent." Thus, the Wayfarers had arrived on Planetoid 48 and introduced life to it (although how that had been accomplished remained a mystery). In light of other creation myths throughout the Galaxy, this made perfect sense.

The third, fourth, fifth, and sixth symbols of the top row were all unfamiliar to him, but he presumed they elaborated upon the creation myth of this world. The next familiar symbol was the second one to the right in the bottom row – a circle with three dots inside it forming an isosceles triangle. Its meaning in Aldebaranian was "rejection" or "shunning," and it made no sense in the present context. Who rejected or shunned whom? And why? Only those other, unfamiliar symbols might provide a clue, but they were not part of his "vocabulary."

As he pondered the conundrum, he became aware of another person beside him. The latter regarded him dispassionately.

"Yes, Professor?"

"Warden Rodriguez, I'd like to thank you formally for all you're doing for me."

Rodriguez looked at him in a puzzled fashion.

"I've executed a warrant for your arrest. I can count the number of people who have thanked me for that on…no hands."

"But, you've placed me under protective custody, and you've indicated that you'll make statements in your official report in my favor. You didn't have to do any of that."

"No, I didn't. We Wardens have a reputation for being hard-nosed when it comes to doing our job, and often we are. But, you should know that our training also includes courses on psychology and sociology, and so we're charged to examine our cases from those perspectives. In the present instance, I've concluded that you're not the criminal type – politically naïve, perhaps, but not criminal. And the fact that you're willing to testify against your former comrades speaks well of you."

"What kind of a sentence do you think I'll get?"

"Frankly, Professor, that's not my concern. You're likely to receive a reduced sentence, but I won't guess what that might be."

"Well, I'll still thank you." He sighed heavily. "I just hope Petra understands how 'politically naïve' I was."

The Warden grimaced. He had nearly forgotten the tragic discovery he and Anafu had made in New Nairobi until now. The astrophysicist's passing remark now created a dilemma in his mind. Should he tell Dr. Weyerhauser about the incident? Or should he let the man find out later from others? The Reman had just thanked him for allegedly doing him a favor; if he broke distressing news, the fellow might retract his sentiments. Not that Wardens were expected to seek reward for their services – it wouldn't do to tarnish their perceived image as hard-as-granite law-enforcement officials – but secretly, every Warden hoped that all sentient beings would come to appreciate what (s)he did to maintain peace and order in the Collective.

Yet, honesty was still the best policy. And it was the Second Principle of the Enlightenment, that quasi-religious precept the Aldebaranians had insisted upon instilling in their trainees day and night. If he, Lixu Rodriguez, were an honest person, then he ought to inform the Doctor of the facts that he possessed and let the consequences develop as they would.

"Um, Professor, there's something I've been meaning to tell you about your lady friend. With all the rush of events lately, I haven't had a chance to tell you."

"What?" the other exclaimed. "What's happened to Petra?"

"Lt. Ralfo and I sought her out a few days ago in order to question her about you. When we arrived at her apartment, we found her in the bedroom – *dead*. She'd been…murdered."

The Reman's face went ashen at the news, and he actually staggered backwards a step or two. Not unexpectedly, he moved his mouth but could not speak.

"*Murdered?*" he rasped finally. "Who could have done such a thing? And why?"

"Her neck had been snapped. It's the trademark of JUR assassins."

Dr. Weyerhauser stared off in the direction of Major Tshambe's base of operations. His face now became a mask of rage.

"Those *bastards!*" he growled. "There was no need to kill her. She didn't know a thing about my…*extra-curricular* activities."

"The JUR doesn't believe any non-Reman is 'innocent.' They eliminate perceived threats as surely as real ones."

"My…poor…Petra. She – and I – had such plans for the future. Now–"

His shoulders sagged, and his head dropped to his chest. Rodriguez felt powerless to comfort him, as he had never been in this situation before. All he could do was to mumble some empty, hollow words.

"They'll be punished, Professor. You have my word on that."

The astrophysicist jerked his head up. Anger flashed from his eyes.

"Punished? How? There's no death penalty anymore. Your precious Aldebaranians saw to that!"

"Personally, I can't think of a worse punishment than spending the rest of my life inside a lifeless moon."

"So you say. Well, I guess I'll find out soon enough. Excuse me."

The Doctor walked away but did not return to his previous location, with

Gamma Platoon. Instead, he plopped down on the cave's floor several meters from its entrance, lowered his head, and sobbed quietly. The Warden signaled for Chen's attention. She joined him and regarded him intently.

"Keep a close watch on the Professor, Corporal. He's just received some bad news, and he may try to do something foolish."

*   *   *

"Sir, I think you had better look at this."

Lt. E-ma stared at his human sergeant in consternation. He'd been in a state of consternation since Lt. Kanaka's platoon had gone off chasing the JUR and he had been relegated to finding the hijacked MOME. He was beginning to regret his decision to forsake working the family business and following in the footsteps of countless generations of E-mas and instead to seek out adventure in the wider Universe. He wasn't cut out to be a soldier – no decent Uhaad was – and his so-called "comrades" let him know that in various subtle and not-so-subtle ways. Now, he had been assigned another make-work project, the latest in a long list which highlighted his so-called "military career."

He supposed, however, that looking for an errant MOME was much safer than the alternative: chasing after terrorists. He didn't envy Lt. Kanaka, even though the Dunian was a bit of a prig and a snob. There was no guarantee that Kanaka would come away with a whole skin – or any skin at all, for that matter.

Finding the MOME had been relatively easy. The renegade astrophysicist, Dr. Weyerhauser, had given good directions, and it had been child's play to maneuver through the winding and twisted complex of tunnels and arrive at the lower-level cave in which the giant engine had been secreted. The hard part was in the "pulling the plug" (his human sergeant had said) on the thing and rendering it useless. E-ma had no expertise in that area. Happily, his other sergeant, G'lut, had in his spare time read up on MOME's and thus had a working familiarity with their operation. After studying the control panels for half a kilosecond, then tracing some of the wiring, the Ekath returned with a worried look in his eyes (and Ekath always looked worried!).

"What worrying you, Sergeant?" E-ma asked in a whispery voice.

"The circuitry bees not correct. It haves beed re-configured, and I thinks there bees a danger."

The lieutenant followed the non-com to one of the control panels, and the latter opened it up to expose the array of circuit boards inside. To the Uhaad's untrained eye, it appeared to be a collection of children's cards albeit with unfamiliar symbols.

Legacy of the Wayfarers | 311

"Observes, Leftenant. This circuit" – Sgt. G'lut pointed to a yellow line – "does not belong here. It bees re-routing energy away from other systems and feeding the power couplings. If I cannot disengage it, power will build up and create an overload."

"What will resulting?"

G'lut regarded his officer with the same dispassion all Ekath show toward alien species.

"It will explode," he said simply.

The Uhaad's eyes went wide with sudden fright. He didn't have to possess the three degrees – nucleonic, quantum mechanics, and power generation – that all operators of MOME's were required to have in order to realize what would occur should one of those colossi were to go out of control. A supernova would be a minor event by comparison. To date, only a few MOME's had ever erupted (and there had been any number of near-mishaps); but it seemed that another one was on its way. And it was no consolation that Lt. E-ma would not survive to witness the extent of the destruction.

"Positives?" he asked tremulously.

"Aye, sir."

"You must disengaging it. You doing?"

"Nay, sir." The Ekath pointed to a series of six green lines running parallel to the yellow one. "This array bees what the Yumans call a 'booby-trap.' If I attempts to neutralize the yellow line, the energy flow will be shunted through the green lines. They bees connected to devices maked from ekathite and will detonate them instantly. And those explosions will de-stabilize the MOME."

E-ma's head began to ache, and his vision blurred. He was sure he was caught up in a nightmare from which he could not awaken. Why, oh why, did he ever leave Ru'uhaad?

"How soon?"

"I bees uncertain, sir. I haves not finded a timer yet – if one exists."

The Uhaad released a long, low moan.

They were doomed!

*   *   *

Quinn was the first to hear footsteps approaching rapidly toward Gamma Platoon's position, and he jumped to the inevitable conclusion. He raised his assault rifle and sighted down its barrel. He tightened his finger on the trigger and waited with bated breath. The footsteps became louder.

Then a copper-colored body came into view, and Quinn gasped with surprise.

"Me not to shoot, Oo-man!" Sgt. Utumi grumbled. "I not the enemy to be!"

"Sorry, Sergeant," the trooper murmured. "We're all a little on edge."

"All the more reason more alert to be. Where Warden Rodri to be?"

"About twenty meters further back. What's goin' on where you came from?"

The Capellan ignored the question and pushed past Quinn, who scowled fiercely. The warrior greeted Lt. Ralfo and Sgt. Running Deer in the most perfunctory manner and continued on. He would have walked past the cave where Rodriguez was studying the proto-Aldebaranian-language glyphs had he not noticed the gleam of the Warden's lamp. He pulled up quickly, pivoted, and entered the cave.

Upon spying the glyphs on the wall, his eyes went wide with fright, and his lips moved in silent prayer. Like all of his race, he held the so-called "invisible world" in awe and superstition. At the top were the "Great Ones," a polytheistic array of gods and their consorts who (it was claimed) had visited Capella millennia ago, taken up residence in various outstanding natural formations, and worked their "influence" from afar. There were also the usual groups of "spirits," good and evil, which had to be propitiated at select times. Those Capellans who dwelt in cities were slightly less superstitious than their rural brethren; but, since old ideas die hard, the urban dwellers did not go out of their way to offend the denizens of the "invisible world." Even with contact with other races and the advent of off-world travel, the necessary rituals were practiced to one degree or another. Sgt. Utumi was not unaffected by what he was seeing.

And what he was seeing was not unfamiliar to him. Some of the proto-glyphs – though not necessarily the same ones that Warden Rodriguez recognized – he had seen before on his own world; they had been carved long ago on rocks near the dwelling places of the "Great Ones," and they signified warning to mortals that trespassers would be dealt with severely. Insofar as he knew, Planetoid 48 was not a dwelling place of Great Power, but the glyphs were "incontrovertible" proof that Great Power had once visited this world. He whispered a few more prayers, then waited patiently until the Warden acknowledged his presence.

His wait was not long. Having wracked his brain for understanding, Rodriguez decided to put the task aside for a while and return to it when he was refreshed. He turned to exit the cave and nearly bumped into the silent figure next to him. Momentarily startled, he retreated a step.

"Sergeant, why didn't you speak up when you entered?"

"You...pre-occupied did be. I you to disturb did not want."

"This" – the Warden gestured at the wall – "could've waited. It's been waiting for 20,000 years. A few more megs wouldn't have mattered." He looked past the warrior. "Where's Lt. Kanaka?"

"He…shortly will come. I here did hurry because I intelligence for you to have."

Tersely but precisely, the Capellan reported on the JUR plan to exit the mountain via a different tunnel and the possibility of being taken unawares. Rodriguez rubbed his jaw in alarm and stared off into the distance as if to peer through solid rock and spy the terrorists. He came to a quick decision.

"Sgt. Running Deer! Gather up your people. We're evacuating the tunnel."

Ralfo trotted up to him and regarded him questioningly. He repeated what Utumi had told him. She frowned.

"Off this world how they would get, Lixu? Destroyed their ship was."

The Warden did not answer immediately but turned to Dr. Weyerhauser.

"Professor, how many ships did the JUR bring here?"

"One, plus part of the *Astarte*. Why do you ask?"

"They had no others?"

"Not as far as I knew. On the other hand, they kept me under wraps until we were well into Deep Space. What's the problem?"

"Sgt. Utumi has reported that the remnants of your cell – excuse me, your *former* cell – are escaping through a previously unknown tunnel. They may have another ship secreted somewhere, as a contingency measure. Or" – his face became a mask of deep concern – "they may attempt to hijack *our* ship. Whatever the case, we've got to intercept them."

"Sir," Cpl. Chen spoke up, "I'd like to give a clear channel that we're badly undermanned. If we encounter those fraggers, they'll launch us into the red zone."

"Thank you for your concern, Corporal, but we have little choice in the matter. If we're to survive at all, we have to risk a fight." He thumbed his vidcom on and punched in a code. "Kanaka! Where the devil are you?"

The Dunian's face appeared on the tiny screen, and it looked annoyed.

"About five hundred meters from your position – sir. We should be there in, oh, half a kilo."

"You've got a quarter of a kilo, Leftenant. We're evacuating the tunnels."

The annoyance deepened.

"Aye, sir. Double-time it is."

"That should even the odds, eh, Chen?"

"Aye, sir. But we better mome and lock on to a good defensible position."

"Move out then. I have to contact Lt. E-ma."

Gamma Platoon moved out without another word spoken. Only Utumi remained behind. The Warden regarded him with a raised eyebrow.

"I for Kanaka shall wait," the Capellan said simply.

Rodriguez returned to his vidcom and contacted the Uhaad officer. He was taken aback when the lieutenant's face appeared. He had never seen anyone so frightened as this person was, and he knew in his gut that even worse news was forthcoming.

"Report," he said quietly.

E-ma moved his mouth, but no words came out. He merely stared at the Warden's image, wide-eyed.

'Lt. E-ma! Snap out of it, man!"

Still no response came from the Uhaad. Abruptly, the vidcom's screen panned away from the petrified officer, and Rodriguez peered at an Ekath.

"Sir, I bees Sgt. G'lut. I haves examined the MOME personally and finded it to be – how you Yumans says – 'booby-trapped.' Power bees building up, and the MOME will become overloaded. I cannot intervene, because intervention will de-stabilize the MOME."

Rodriguez did not have to be drawn a picture to understand the implications of what G'lut was saying. He knew enough about MOME's to realize that everything within several square light-years of Planetoid 48 would be instantly obliterated when the engine blew. He also realized that this must have been the JUR's purpose all along; they hadn't intended to create massive geophysical damage by a near-collision of worlds as originally theorized but rather to destroy utterly a hated foe once and for all, regardless of the cost. It was a monstrous plan on the face of it, and there seemed to be no means to counter it.

"How soon will it explode, Sergeant?"

"I cannot say, sir. I does not know how long the overloading process haves beed taking place."

"Then haste is called for. It's clear that Lt. E-ma is…incapacitated. I'm placing you in command of the platoon. Get everyone out and as far away from this world as you can."

"Aye, sir!"

The Warden's mind raced through his available options, and he was dismayed to learn that he had few of those. It was imperative, of course, that he get his own group off the rogue. There would be no time, therefore, to prevent the JUR cell from escaping. Once he returned to the surface, he had to contact the *Steadfast* and warn Halvarson of the danger he faced. Then perhaps he could explore possible solutions to prevent the destruction of half a star system.

He spent two last seconds gazing reverently at the petroglyphs on the wall of the cave. Here was the most important archaeological find in half a gigasecond, and it was doomed to obliteration. True, he now had a visual recording of everything (plus a few artifacts), but recordings were a poor substitute for the real thing; the context of the remains of the indigenous life-forms and their artifacts would be forever lost, and the researchers would be left with only fuzzy speculations.

It's a damned shame, he thought bitterly. *Damn the JUR!*
And where the devil is Kanaka?

*   *   *

Captain Halvarson had the view in the Display magnified to the maximum extent in order to focus on the area of Deep Space within a radius of one light-year from the *Steadfast*. In this view, only one major object was visible: Planetoid 48. Twenty-six smaller blips massed near the large one; they represented the entire fighter brigade on standby to add their own firepower to the upcoming assault, should it prove necessary. Halvarson judged that all was in order and opened a channel to Commander Mbuku aboard one of the heavy cruisers.

"Are you set on your end, Enrique?"

"Aye, sir. We're itching for action."

"Let's hope it won't come to that. Halvarson out." He next contacted Communications. "Lt. Zuf, any word from the landing party?"

"Nay, sir," the orange-crested Bithan responded. "Is the signal being interfered with. Is it puzzling."

"I should say so. Well, we can't wait any longer. They'll just have to ride it out." He punched the button for Armaments. "Commander Mun, have the missiles been re-programmed?"

"Aye, sir. Have just finished we entering the co-ordinates supplied by Commander Krishnamurthy."

"Excellent. Stand by."

Now he faced his XO, who gazed at him steadily. She had a look of eager anticipation in her eye.

"What's your recommendation, Tomiko? All at once, or in bursts?"

"In bursts, I think, Olaf. Five seconds apart. That way, none of the missiles will detonate against one another instead of the target."

"Did you catch that, Commander Mun?"

"Aye, sir. Will launch we the missiles one at a time, five seconds apart."

"On my mark then." The Captain stared at the Display again. The scene remained unchanged. The stage was set. *"Mark!"*

CHAPTER TWENTY-ONE

▼

A DESPERATE GAMBLE

DURING THE WAR OF THE Eight Suns, the Alliance for Free Space had had a slight advantage in weaponry. The core of the Alliance was the planet Ekaxan, a natural chemical laboratory where all manner of formulations could be produced almost overnight for any purpose whatsoever; the Ekath had exported many of these substances to any and all buyers, and the exports had been their chief source of revenues. During the War, the Ekath naturally put their collective minds to the task of creating a powerful explosive which (they hoped) would be so devastating that the Amazonian Federation could not hope to survive a sustained attack. After much experimentation and testing, they produced what they believed to be the desired article, thereafter dubbed "ekathite."

Ekathite was indeed a powerful explosive, and it rivaled a thermonuclear device in its destructive potential. A single missile with a payload of five kilograms could vaporize any ship the Amazonians set against the Alliance. If not for the Murchison Oscillating Matrix Engine, the Federation might have lost its entire fleet; only the ability to pop in and out of "normal" space at will kept the Amazonians' war effort afloat. The same amount could do the same to any city below the classification of a metropolis. Happily, however, the Ekath used their "super-weapon" judiciously and targeted only military installations and ships. Their High Command saw no advantage in obliterating whole populations; such needless destruction, they reasoned, would only strengthen the Enemy's resolve rather than weaken it.

When the Aldebaranians brought the War to a screeching halt and set up the Central Spiral Collective, they sought a proper place for ekathite. They could have banned its use outright, but any prohibition would have been difficult, if not impossible, to enforce. Therefore, they designated only a small number of uses for the explosive, subject to the issuance of special (and expensive) licenses. More importantly, only the armed forces of the CSC Constabulary were authorized to carry ekathite-enhanced weaponry, and violations invoked severe penalties.[49] At once, the Ekath had a new source of revenue with which to repair its exhausted economy, and a "super-weapon" was given into "safe" hands.

The theory that ekathite-enhanced missiles ought to be able to move small bodies in space (if not obliterate them entirely) was a sound one, but it had never been applied pragmatically.

That was about to change.

The *Steadfast*'s Black Zone CO, Lt. Commander Mun, delivered her missiles with great precision upon the target. One by one, they impacted Planetoid 48 where Commander Krishnamurthy had deemed the most effective site in facilitating her plan. One by one, detonations of titanic proportions shook that world and threatened to break it apart. The runaway did not break apart, however, because it was much too large to sustain that sort of damage; it did lose some mass to Deep Space as the assault gouged out huge amounts of material and created large geysers which escaped that world's low gravitational pull.

On the *Steadfast*'s Bridge, all eyes were glued to the giant vidscreen opposite the Captain's chair. The screen took a feed from the command vessel of the assault force, now in synchronous orbit around the rogue and provided a most graphic demonstration of the actual capability of a Constabulary patrol vessel, a demonstration not seen since the close of the War of the Eight Suns. The effects of that capability on the Bridge crew were varied, according to one's race/experience/psychological make-up, but no one was unaffected. The militaristic Bitha were generally pleased by this display of might, while the Ekath were surprised by the massive nature of the assault. Humans were grim, and Uhaad were horrified. Inexplicably, the Okath shook their heads sadly.

Captain Halvarson watched the devastation intently, searching for confirmation that The Plan was succeeding and that Planetoid 48 had indeed been "nudged" into a different trajectory. Next to him, the author of The Plan sat wide-eyed with wonder as she witnessed the multiple fiery blossoms she had set in motion. Two tongues licked two pairs of dry lips. Two foreheads

49 Cf. Article Five ("Law Enforcement"), Section Three ("Table of Personnel and Equipment"), paragraph nine ("Special Weaponry") of the Treaty of Aldebaran – CMT.

were dotted with perspiration. Two hearts beat rapidly, and two sets of lungs inhaled/exhaled audibly.

Barely able to tear his eyes away from the awful spectacle, Halvarson gazed into the Display to learn if the dot which represented Planetoid 48 was moving in a new direction. It did not seem so to him, but there could have been several reasons for his inability, not the least of which was the dripping of perspiration into his eyes. He wiped away the sweat and fumbled for the Blue Zone button. His vidscreen lit up to reveal Lt. Commander G'lun staring upward, enraptured by what he was viewing on the giant screen.

"Commander G'lun! Report!"

The startled Okath snapped his head toward his own vidscreen and peered at it as if it were a new thing. Slowly, he recognized his Captain.

"Ah, uh, Captain," he mumbled. "What bees your desire?"

"I desire to know if Planetoid 48 has changed course."

"I will check, sir." He looked away to consult his computer terminal. Presently: "Aye, sir. Planetoid 48 haves shifted one-half degree from its previous course."

"*One-half degree?* Is that all?"

"Aye, sir."

"In which direction?"

"Its new course will take it above the plane of the Rhea Silvia system."

"Thank you, Commander." Halvarson turned to Krishnamurthy with a big grin on his face. "You did it, Tomiko! You actually pulled it off!"

The Romulan smiled sweetly.

"Did you ever doubt I could?"

"Once or twice, I did. But, I'm convinced now."

"So, what's our next move, Olaf?"

"Now, we find out how our people on that world are faring."

"If," the XO muttered to herself, "they are faring at all."

*   *   *

Rodriguez picked himself up off the ground and brushed the dirt off his cold-weather gear. He surveyed the area outside of the tunnel from which Gamma Platoon had just emerged and discovered – not surprisingly – that everyone else had been bowled over as well.

The platoon had no sooner returned to the surface of Planetoid 48 when the tremors began. At first, they represented a simple quivering of the ground; but, as the seconds passed, they became stronger. No one could explain why they were occurring, because they were completely different from the tremors which the hijacked MOME had produced when it initiated a warp-out. In any event, a warp-out was out of the question as there was no sentient being in a position to initiate one. All were too busy evacuating the runaway. These tremors were more like those produced by detonating explosives. But how was that possible?

"Is everyone all right?" the Warden inquired.

"No serious injuries I have, Lixu," Lt. Ralfo responded. "On a rock my hand I scraped, but I will live."

"No one badly hurt here, sir," Sgt. Running Deer reported. "What the frag hit us?"

"I have no idea, Sergeant. But, we can ponder the question later. Right now, we have to get off this rock – fast! – as soon as Lt. Kanaka links up with us."

As if on cue, the missing platoon (plus Sgt. Utumi) tumbled out of the tunnel and approached Gamma Platoon shakily. Rodriguez greeted the Capellan warmly but regarded the Dunian with ill-disguised displeasure.

"About time, Leftenant. We're on a deadline, so to speak."

He rattled off a brief version of the situation and watched with satisfaction the color drain out of Kanaka's face. The latter stared in horror over his shoulder.

"How soon?" he whispered.

"Unknown. Are you ready to leave?"

"Aye, sir," came the weak reply.

"Fine. Let's–"

"Sir!" Quinn called out. "Look!"

The trooper was pointing up at the sky, and the Warden tracked his motion. High above them, a spacecraft was rapidly ascending and speeding away from Planetoid 48. In a matter of seconds, it had disappeared from view.

"I reckon that was the fraggin' JUR leavin'," Quinn observed. "They did have another ship in reserve."

"Obviously," Rodriguez retorted. "Well, we'll worry about them later. Into the carrier, people!"

The two platoons made a mad dash toward the waiting craft. They had to pick their way through a scattering of fresh rubble created by the successively more powerful tremors. The silence of their picking was punctuated by not a few curses. After what seemed like megaseconds, they reached the carrier and scrambled aboard. The Warden was the last to board; and, before he did, he took one last look at the rogue and shook his head sadly.

All that valuable archaeological material, and it's going to be destroyed. What a waste!

As soon as the carrier was off-world, Rodriguez contacted the other troop carrier. Sgt. G'lut responded to the call and assured the Warden that the remainder of the expedition was safely away and on its way back to the *Steadfast*. He also reported that Lt. E-ma was still in a state of shock and had had to be sedated. Rodriguez nodded by way of understanding and signed off.

"All in all," the Warden remarked off-handedly, "I'd say that Gamma Platoon acquitted itself the whole while." He paused for dramatic effect. "Even Quinn. I'm going to recommend all of you for a citation when we return to the *Steadfast*."

"Thank you, sir," Running Deer murmured. He grunted. "Imagine: someone in Gamma Platoon getting a citation! I just hope it don't go to their fraggin' heads!"

Rodriguez returned to the troop section and took a seat next to Ralfo and Dr. Weyerhauser. The latter appeared especially morose, and the former tried her best to console him. The astrophysicist heaved a huge sigh.

"More deaths on my account," he muttered. "Will there be no end to it?"

"What you do mean, Professor?"

"When that MOME blows, it'll vaporize Romulus and Remus and snuff out Rhea Silvia. Billions will die."

"Lixu," Ralfo exclaimed, "true this is?"

"I'm afraid so, Anafu. A destabilized MOME releases more energy than five super-novas. It would have to be at least five light-years away from inhabited space to be rendered harmless."

"What then we can do?"

"I'm forming an idea, but it assumes a colossal risk. I'll explain when we return to the *Steadfast*. Right now, I'm exhausted, and I need a nap."

*   *   *

As soon as the troop carriers docked, the Warden made straight to the Bridge. Ralfo tagged along since, technically speaking, she was still assigned to him. The Doctor also accompanied them since, technically speaking, he was still under protective custody, and he didn't think it was wise for an accused "terrorist" to be wandering about on a Constabulary ship alone. Rodriguez took no particular notice of either one; his mind was awhirl with the possible reactions from Captain Halvarson to the proposal he was going to make. Mentally, he rehearsed all possible responses to those reactions.

The Bridge crew was, generally speaking, in a jubilant mood. They had just succeeded beyond their wildest dreams in pulling off what had once seemed to be an impossible task. But, as Sensors had reported, and as everyone could observe in the Display, Planetoid 48 was shifting away from its original trajectory and heading out into Deep Space. The most pleased of the crew were, of course, the Captain and the XO, both of whom had taken a large gamble in depleting the ship's offensive capacity in order to accomplish what they set out to do.

Rodriguez thought it would be a damned shame to dispel this mood, but dispel it he must. The stakes were too high. Besides, he was hardly "Cn. Fash" as it was. As he approached the Gold Zone, Halvarson and Krishnamurthy both broke out in uncharacteristic grins.

"Warden," the Captain boomed magnanimously, "glad to see you back safe and sound."

"It's good to be back safe and sound under the circumstances. Can you explain the series of perturbations we experienced on Planetoid 48? They were rather unnerving."

Halvarson did explain, giving proper credit to Krishnamurthy and embellishing a bit on the actions of the crew. The Warden nodded in agreement.

"Under other circumstances, I might've endorsed that plan wholeheartedly." Halvarson beamed even more. "Unfortunately, I've got some rather distressing news which changes the circumstances." Tersely, he related the actions taken by the JUR to overload the MOME and cause it to become unstabilized and the "booby trap" in place to prevent anyone from countering the overloading. As he had expected, the jubilant expressions on the faces on the Command personnel quickly disappeared, to be replaced by ones of sheer horror. "It's imperative, then," he concluded, "that we act quickly."

"How – how much time do we have?" Halvarson asked.

"I can't say. I would hazard to guess that the JUR would have given themselves plenty of time to put a safe distance between them and Planetoid 48. Would you concur, Professor?"

The astrophysicist was stirred out his own reverie, a reverie which was decidedly far from jubilation. He was concerned about his own role in this impending tragedy, about how he had been tricked by the JUR, about the senseless murders of innocent people – including a lady dear to him – and about the sort of "legacy" he would leave behind. Just now, he felt quite uncomfortable in his present surroundings.

"Eh? Oh, yes, I do. I could give you a short lecture – from an astrophysicist's point of view – of what you could expect. But, as the Warden says, time is of the essence."

"So, Warden, do you have a plan?" the XO asked softly.

Rodriguez took a deep breath and let it out slowly. The moment he dreaded had arrived, and he could not afford to re-think his position. He fixed the Captain and the XO with as firm an expression as he could muster and prayed for strength.

"Planetoid 48 must be moved further away from the Rhea Silvia system so that it can explode harmlessly. And there's only one way to move a body in space over a long distance quickly."

Halvarson's and Krishnamurthy's eyes went wide with disbelief. He looked at her, and she shook her head.

"You can't be serious!" the Captain yelped. "No one has ever warped out a natural body. It can't be done!"

"If no one has ever done it," the Warden countered, "then no one knows definitively if it can be done or not. The JUR used an MOME to turn Planetoid 48 into a large 'spaceship.' There's no reason to believe we can't use the *Steadfast* as a 'relay station.'"

"But the time factor..."

"That's why we must act quickly."

"And you expect me to go along with this scheme?"

"I do."

Halvarson regarded his XO again as if to learn what his response should be. She spread her hands in a gesture of helplessness. The Captain grimaced and set his jaw.

"This is a foolhardy idea, *Leftenant*, and I'm not about to risk my ship on some dangerous experiment."

"Not even if a Warden requests it?"

"Frankly, I've had enough of your shenanigans, Rodriguez, and I intend to report you to your superiors. Now, kindly leave the Bridge!"

Rodriguez set his own jaw and stared at his adversary for all of three seconds. Then, in a very quiet voice which no one but those in the immediate vicinity could hear, he uttered:

"I can't say that your reaction was unexpected, but I will say that it is unacceptable. You leave me no choice in this matter."

He reached into his tunic, withdrew his "badge," and held it up before Halvarson. Even in the dim illumination of the Bridge, the golden disc gleamed like a miniature sun, and both of the Constabulary officers squinted at the brightness of it. Both of them swallowed compulsively.

"Captain Halvarson," the Warden intoned formally, "I, Warden (L1) Lixu Rodriguez, hereby invoke Article Five, Section Five, paragraph four of the Charter of the Central Spiral Collective. You will comply."

The Charter of the Central Spiral Collective was based largely on the Treaty of Aldebaran with only minor alterations. Each point of the Treaty had been bitterly contested by one or another of the warring parties, but the enigmatic race which forcefully intervened in the Great War had been most determined to maintain the upper hand. (It goes without saying that, since no one could operate any engine of war until the Aldebaranians released their dampening field, maintaining the upper hand was all too easy for them.) With great reluctance, the parties had to concede most of the points and sign the Treaty. When it came time to ratify the Charter (with the Aldebaranians in the background keenly looking on), the bitter debate was renewed. The future members of the Central Spiral Collective wrung a few concessions out of the "master race" but had to acquiesce in the granting of enormous power to the Collective in order to deal with all possible contingencies. More than wanting to avoid antagonizing the "masters," they simply wanted to get on with the business of life.

The very last Article to be adopted, however, was Article Five ("Law Enforcement"), because it gave tremendous power to the newly-formed Constabulary. And the last Section of that Article to be accepted was Section Five ("Powers of the Wardens") for the same reason. The principal hold-up was paragraph four which outraged everyone at the negotiating table, perhaps the only thing both the Federation and the Alliance ever agreed upon. Paragraph four stated: "In the event of a dire emergency, a Warden shall have the authority to assume total command of any and all forces at his/her disposal without having to obtain permission from any other authority, and (s)he will retain that command until said emergency is concluded. Pending an inquiry presided over by the Chief Constable, or his/her assigns, a Warden shall be held blameless for any action (s)he may take to deal with said emergency." The Charter might have failed altogether because of this paragraph if the Aldebaranians had not stepped forward and issued a "gentle reminder" (their words) of the consequences of stubbornness.

Captain Halvarson's jaw dropped, and he stared at the disc dumbfoundedly. His face registered total shock. Krishnamurthy's face went pale. Ralfo's eyes went wide with wonder, while the Doctor kept a neutral expression.

"I can't believe what I'm hearing," the New Swiss said at last. "That paragraph has only been enforced once, and by someone of a higher rank than yours."[50]

"Rank is not a factor, Captain. The paragraph says 'any Warden,' and this" – he waggled his disc – "is my authority. Since you refuse to comply, I'm relieving you of command." He signaled to the sentries at the entrance to the Bridge. The pair approached warily. "I'm placing Captain Halvarson under house arrest. Please escort him to his quarters and post a guard there."

The sentries fell into instant confusion, and neither moved for a long

---

50 In point of fact, it was the Chief of the Warden Service himself who had assumed temporary rule over Eka-xan in the early days of the Collective in order to remove the safe havens for pirates on that world – CMT.

moment. Rodriguez's face hardened further, and he practically pushed his badge in their faces.

"Unless you two would care to spend the rest of your tour of duty in the brig, you'll do as I tell you."

The sentries turned to Halvarson, their expressions running from helplessness to resignation, and one of them gestured to the Captain to comply with the order. The latter scowled fiercely.

"Damn you, Rodriguez! I'll see you broken for this!"

"Perhaps," the Warden replied calmly, "but, at the moment, you are dismissed." Now he addressed the XO: "Commander, unless you're of the same mind as the Captain, I'm naming you as Acting Captain of the *Steadfast*."

Krishnamurthy regarded the Warden with a mixture of disgust and resignation. She faced Halvarson to plead silently with him.

"Tomiko, don't give in to him. Help me fight him."

"I'm...sorry, Olaf. He has the right, under the Charter, and I'm obliged to obey – as you are."

"You really *did* want my command, didn't you?" Halvarson spat out. "Well, enjoy it while you can."

Rodriguez signaled to the sentries, and they led the ramrod-stiff ex-Captain of the *Steadfast* away. The tension on the Bridge was thick enough to slice. The Acting Captain, with all the disdain she could muster, saluted Rodriguez.

"What are your orders – sir?"

The Warden returned the salute with the barest of smiles on his lips.

"I want you to maneuver the ship close to Planetoid 48 and match its velocity. Then, I want you to initiate a warp-out – maximum power – and maintain it until further notice. I'm going to find quarters for Dr. Weyerhauser. I'll return shortly."

"Aye, sir. I hear and obey."

Rodriguez ignored the obvious sarcasm and exited the Bridge with Ralfo and their "prisoner" in tow.

*   *   *

The pupil stands before his mentor, at attention. He knows why he is here, and it matters not to him. He had made what he felt was the correct decision – the only decision possible – and he can live with it, even if others look askance.

Master Fresh-Bloom-in-the-Face-as-the-Day-Begins regards his pupil a moment or two dispassionately. He re-reads quickly the analyses of the exercise before him, particularly the final, uncharacteristic statement of the instructor-in-

charge. A very tiny smile flickers across his lips; and, before anyone can discern it, sternness returns to his expression.

"You have employed a most unorthodox method in performing this exercise, pupil."

"Yes, Master."

"There were other methods you could have employed."

"Very true, Master, but none of those – in my estimation – could have brought the particular situation to a satisfactory conclusion."

"In your *estimation? Do you now presume to understand more than your instructor?"*

"No, Master! What I meant was–"

"Never mind. I know what you meant. And you should know that your instructor was quite impressed by your initiative. In fact, he has suggested that your method be incorporated into the curriculum. I am inclined to agree with him."

"I am gratified, Master – and humbled – by your praise."

"I doubt that you have been humbled, lack-wit, but I shall not make a point of it. Now, return to your quarters and meditate on the consequences of your performance."

The pupil departs in a smart fashion. Another very tiny smile plays across his mentor's lips.

*   *   *

As soon as he had squared away Dr. Weyerhauser, Rodriguez returned to the Bridge and made straight for the niche in the bulkhead which housed the *aaxyboxr*. He regarded it with trepidation for half a second, then gripped it firmly. As before, the contact sent a shock throughout his nervous system, and his body stiffened.

*   *   *

— *Greetings, fellow sentient. We are the* aaxyboxr. *How may we assist?*

— *Greetings to the* aaxyboxr. *I am sentient Rodriguez. I wish to send a message.*

— *State the message.*

— *"To Lt. Commander Ruba at Constabulary Headquarters from Warden (L1) Rodriguez aboard the* Steadfast. *I have taken the fugitive, Dr. Mubutu Weyerhauser, into custody and will transfer him shortly. His compatriots now pose a new threat to the peace of the Collective, and I am taking steps to counter this threat. In so doing, I have invoked Article Five, Section Five, paragraph four. A detailed report will follow in due time." End of message.*

— *It is sent.*

— *Thank you. The peace of Kum'halla be with the* aaxyboxr.

— *The peace of Kum'halla be with sentient Rodriguez.*

*   *   *

The Warden released his grip on the gray mass and took a deep breath to steady himself. He turned to speak to Acting Captain Krishnamurthy and received a shock. Large numbers of the ship's crew were entering the Bridge and milling about. From the designations on their uniforms, it appeared that all zones were represented; there were also contingents from the troop and flight brigades. Most of the personnel were talking amongst themselves, but they were casting ominous glances at Rodriguez. With the exception of the Chief Engineer and the Chief Medical Officer, all of the senior staff were present, and their subordinates gathered about them like chicks around their hens. Rodriguez did not like the looks of this at all; these people ought to be at their posts preparing for the warp-out he had requested. He motioned to Krishnamurthy.

"What's going on here, Commander?"

"I would hazard to guess that the word has gotten around about Captain Halvarson being relieved of command and that the crew wants to know why. You may have a mutiny on your hands – sir."

Mutiny!

The Warden's mind flashed back to his history classes at the University and particularly to the seminar conducted by Professor I.M. Hensley, the acknowledged expert on the development of the Amazonian Federation. Since humankind had ventured out into Deep Space and begun to colonize the stars, there had been only one mutiny of record during that entire period. The Reman members of the Federation's militias had refused to take up arms at the outbreak of the War of the Eight Suns on the grounds that Romulan imperialism was at the heart of the hostility between humans and aliens, and they wanted no part of it. The mutiny was brief, having been brutally suppressed, but the resentment lived on. Surprisingly, however, the Remans comported themselves with honor during the War. One possible explanation for this anomaly – also given by Prof. Hensley – was that the Remans wanted the military training afforded them so that they could use it someday against the Romulans. After the formation of the Central Spiral Collective and the Constabulary, no such actions ever occurred again.

The Warden hoped he could extend that record.

"I don't need a mutiny just now, Commander. I suggest you get them back to work."

"Perhaps *you* ought to speak to them, sir. This *is* your show."

He regarded her for a moment. She was on the verge of insubordination herself, and she knew that he knew and probably didn't care if he did or not. He shook his head.

"They're more likely to listen to you than to me. If you please."

"Very well, sir, but be prepared for the worst." She faced the growing crowd. *My first command,* she mused, *and I have to deal with a potential mutiny right off. What a malfy dock this is!* "Will someone please tell me why you are here and not at your duty stations?"

No one stirred for a long moment, each person waiting for someone else to take the initiative. Then, Lt. Commander von Lichtenberg, head of Silver Zone, stepped forward. Krishnamurthy gazed at her with no small amount of cynicism.

Why am I not surprised? The Captain's lover, ready to defend her man's honor. Well, she's in the red zone for sure.

"I've – *we've* heard that Captain Halvarson has been relieved of his command," the tall woman answered tremulously. "*We* want to know why."

"The Captain was in violation of the Charter of the Central Spiral Collective," was the flat reply.

"How so?"

"He refused to co-operate with a Warden in an emergency situation. The Warden therefore invoked Article Five, Section Five, paragraph four which gives him complete authority to take command. Look, I don't like this any more than you do. But, the Charter is the Charter, and we all took an oath to uphold it."

"What the frag's the 'emergency,' Commander," someone from the flight brigade piped up. "We succeeded in diverting Planetoid 48 and avoiding a calamity."

Murmurs of agreement rippled through the assembly. Tersely, Krishnamurthy explained that the emergency was not over because of the new information about the threat it represented. Instantly, the would-be mutineers registered shock, and murmurs of a different sort spread amongst their ranks.

"Is this true?" von Lichtenberg demanded.

"Believe it, people," a voice at the entrance to the Bridge sounded. "I've got the trooper who investigated the jury-rig right here."

All eyes, including those of Rodriguez and Krishnamurthy, focused on the new speaker. The former was surprised to see Sgts. Running Deer and G'lut pushing their way through the milling crowd. And they were not alone. Lt. Ralfo and Sgt. Utumi were hard on their heels. And behind them were his former "command," Gamma Platoon, all still in combat gear. The assembly quickly gave way to the newcomers, though Rodriguez suspected they were more in awe of the gleam of determination in the Capellan's yellow eyes than they were of the Dunian's remarks. Gamma Platoon surrounded the Warden and the Acting Captain (who was more than a little alarmed at this new development) and faced the group defiantly.

"Explain, Sergeant," Krishnamurthy asked breathlessly.

"This is Sgt. G'lut of Lt. E-ma's platoon," Running Deer replied, pushing the Ekath forward. "He's one of the few non-professionals aboard the *Steadfast* who understands MOME technology. And he's seen what the JUR did to the MOME they stole from the *Astarte*. Tell 'em, G'lut."

The non-com swallowed hard at being thrust into the limelight. Even though he and a few others of his kind completely supported the principles of the Central Spiral Collective, few others trusted his kind completely.

"It bees true," he stammered. "I examined the circuitry and noted the alterations the Remans maked. They setted the engine to overload and thus to explode. And, further, they maked sure that any attempts to undo what they doed would hasten the process."

The murmuring began anew as this information sank in. It was hard to doubt the word of an Ekath. Obnoxious as his kind were (most of the time), they did not mince words but spoke as forthrightly as they could, especially in matters of science and technology.

"I would like to impress upon you," Rodriguez now spoke up, "the urgency of the present situation. I regret having to relieve Captain Halvarson of his command, but he chose caution over urgency. We need to take action – and soon."

"And is what that action – sir?" Commander Rux sneered.

"We're going to warp Planetoid 48 out and as far away from here as possible. It's a desperate gamble, I know, but we haven't got many options at the moment." He paused briefly. "If there are any of you who refuse to co-operate, return to your quarters and stay there until the emergency is over."

Not a few of the crew eyed each other questioningly, and not a few – including Commander Rux – who started to turn toward the entrance to the Bridge, thought better of it, and remained where they were, albeit with hard expressions on their faces.

"If there are no further questions," Krishnamurthy said crisply, "I'd appreciate it if you all returned to your posts."

"One last thing, Commander," von Lichtenberg stood her ground, "who's in charge here – you or...*him*?"

"*I* am, Commander. Make no mistake about that. I'm co-operating with the Warden, as the Charter demands, but *I'm* the Captain until the emergency is over. Now, return to your post."

The New Swiss glared at her for a couple of seconds. Then her resolve evaporated. She saluted smartly, pivoted, and marched off toward the Helmsman's chair. Their "leader" having yielded to the "New Order," the remainder of the crew went its separate ways. Only Gamma Platoon remained.

"Sorry about getting here so late, sir," Sgt. Running Deer apologized to Rodriguez. "Sgt. G'lut needed a little…persuading to make a quick report."

"He threatened me!" the Ekath protested. "He sayed he would throw me out the airlock unless I speaked."

"Now, now, G'lut," the Dunian soothed. "You should know that us humans don't speak as precisely as your kind does. You simply misinterpreted what I said."

"I misinterpreted nothing. I–"

"Never mind, Sergeant," the Warden cut in. "What's done is done. And I for one appreciate your contribution."

"I thanks you, sir. I will return to my quarters now."

"Are you ready on your end, Captain?" Rodriguez asked Krishnamurthy, placing a slight emphasis on the word "Captain."

"As ready as I'll ever be, sir."

"Fine. Proceed as planned. I'll be in my own quarters as well."

The Plan was simple – in theory, at least. The *Steadfast* was to be maneuvered into a position parallel to the trajectory of the runaway and five hundred meters from its surface. The ship's MOME then would be activated at maximum power and create an artificial gravity well deep enough to allow a passing body to "avoid" the maximum of ten light-years of Deep Space. There were several unknowns involved in the procedure, any one of which could result in a failure to translate theory into practicality and destroy the ship. In the first place, no moving MOME had ever been used to warp out another moving body; that action had always been performed by a stationary MOME in orbit about a star system, i.e. a Relay Station. If anyone had suggested the idea, that idea had never been recorded in professional journals. The danger, in theory, was that the gravity well could not be maintained for any length of time.

In the second place, no MOME had ever attempted to shift a body larger than five kilometers in diameter. The conventional wisdom was that a gigantic engine, say, five or more kilometers in diameter, with a power ratio to handle such a huge load, was required to do the job successfully. And, even after two centuries of development, such a behemoth had not been created; a MOME, being highly unstable, apparently had a size limitation beyond which it would not function as expected. And a malfunctioning MOME was instant death and destruction.

Which meant, ultimately, that the *Steadfast's* MOME would have to operate beyond its optimum capacity, both in terms of power and length of time. If the MOME shut down before Planetoid 48 could be moved a safe distance away from Rhea Silvia – and remained stable — then one was back to square one with no other options at hand. A risky business indeed!

All this – and more – trickled through Acting Captain Krishnamurthy's brain like acid. She was in a most unenviable position, and she knew it. She had had a choice between obeying a lawful (if odious) order from a Warden and following Olaf Halvarson off the Bridge under house arrest. She knew better than to cross a Warden, even an untested L1 like Rodriguez, in the performance of his duty; Wardens were better trained than ordinary policemen, and they had the backing of the *real* power in the central spiral. She was not about to jeopardize her career on a point of law, if she could possibly help it.

I'll do exactly what the Warden tells me to do, she mused grimly. *And, when the inevitable inquiry takes place, I'll be first –no, make that* second *– in line to rake him over the coals. He'll wish he was stationed on Amazon before Olaf and I are through with him.*

She stepped over to the Helm, where Lt. Commander von Lichtenberg was still grousing, and directed the woman to maneuver the ship into a course parallel to that of Planetoid 48. At the Captain's station, she then called up Chief Engineer Ling. The old man appeared on her vidcom with his usual expression of annoyance.

"And what would ye be wantin' now, Missy?" He called all of the females aboard ship "Missy" – never by their true names or ranks – and no amount of complaining on the Captain's part had dissuaded him. Quintus Ling was Quintus Ling, the best in his business throughout the Constabulary, and that was all there was to it. "A cruise through the Wall?"

"Nothing simple like that, Quintus," she replied smoothly. "I'm going to warp-out, and I want a sustained output – say a hundred and fifty seconds – in power. Can you handle that?"

"*A hundred-and-fifty second warp-out?!?*" the Chief Engineer yelped. "What in Heaven's name for? D'ye want to ruin me poor babe?"

Krishnamurthy quickly explained the mission, and Ling's eyes bugged out.

"Ye're daft, Missy, if ye think that'll work."

"I'd've thought it would be child's play for you, my dear," she retorted with tongue in cheek. "But, if you can't do it, I'll find someone else."

"*Bloody hell!!*" he thundered. "No one touches me poor babe on a job like this. I'll be after doin' this meself, I'm thinkin,' thank you very much."

With that, the screen went blank. The Acting Captain smiled to herself.

She then activated the PA system, issued the standard warning of an impending warp-out, and sat motionless, counting the seconds quietly to herself, while all around her was a beehive of activity.

The lights dimmed as the MOME was switched on. An imperceptible humming followed, increasing in intensity as the huge engine generated a fantastic amount of energy. Immediately following came the vibration which traveled through every part of the *Steadfast*'s structure, also increasing in intensity. Of necessity, MOME-enhanced vessels had to be exceptionally thick-hulled in order to withstand the tremendous stress put upon them; otherwise, they would literally fly apart within a few kiloseconds.

Presently, both humming and vibrating leveled off as the maximum power output was achieved. That was the "easy" part. The hard part was to maintain that level for longer than the recommended time; the harder part was to sit through the ordeal and hope for the best while the MOME created the gravity well. For, once activated, the MOME became, for all intents and purposes, an independent force until the computer's programming ran its course; the engine could be shut down in an emergency, but the procedure required painstakingly slow stages to accomplish lest the devilish machine become destabilized.

Krishnamurthy dispatched one of the shuttlecraft to a point a thousand kilometers off the stern. It would provide an objective view of Deep Space that the *Steadfast* could not while the MOME was operating. On the large vidscreen on the Bridge, Planetoid 48 had disappeared from the standpoint of those aboard as Einstein's relativistic ideas worked themselves out on a practical level. The gravity well was, of course, non-visible as well because it was only an abstraction, without shape or substance. Theoretically, the rogue should be skimming across the event horizon of the well even as the *Steadfast* remained in a fixed position relative to it. But, since both ship and runaway were in a state of "in-between space" and thus beyond subjective vision, biological and electronic, the reality of the matter would be the business of the remote viewing post.

The Acting Captain's vidscreen blinked on, and the worried face of Quintus Ling appeared. For the first time since she had met him, he was not his usual devil-may-care self. She could relate, however, as she was feeling more than a little concerned about the fate of the ship herself.

"How much longer, Missy?" the Chief Engineer pleaded, his voice nearly drowned out by the humming and vibrating. "Me poor babe is after cryin' its heart out."

"I can't say, Quintus. Until I'm assured that Planetoid 48 is positioned to do no harm, I have to maintain this power level."

"Sure, an' it's a cruel thing ye're doin' too."

Sorry, Quintus, she thought as he disconnected. *It's damned if you do and damned if you don't.*

The seconds ticked off, and the 100-second mark came and went. Mentally, Krishnamurthy agonized. An ordinary warp-out took no longer than fifty seconds, even for maximum range, and the *Steadfast* was now in unfamiliar territory. So long as Chief Engineer Ling did not report that the MOME was overloading, however, she had to keep it operating. So long as the shuttlecraft did not report that Planetoid 48 was more than five light-years away from Rhea Silvia, she had to endure the fearful and panicky expressions now registering on the Bridge crew (and undoubtedly on the rest of the crew below decks). She snorted suddenly. Olaf Halvarson was comfortable in his quarters, not missing anything!

The 125-second mark approached. Krishnamurthy's heart beat like a kettledrum, and her breath came in short gasps. She felt streams of perspiration running down her cheeks.

"Captain," the voice of the shuttlecraft pilot rasped, startling her, "Planetoid 48 is being pulled down into the gravity well. She's not moving forward."

"That's not good, Leftenant, not good at all. How far away is it from Rhea Silvia?"

"About 4.8 light-years, ma'am."

Damn! Not far enough. But, it'll have to do. If the rogue sinks to the bottom of the well, it'll pull the Steadfast in with it, and we'll all be done for.

"Thank you, Leftenant," she acknowledged. "Return to the ship." She opened the channel to Engineering without hesitation. "Quintus, shut it down – *now!*"

"Aye, Captain! Oh, me poor babe!"

Krishnamurthy contacted Silver Zone and barked: "Helm, as soon as the MOME is down, bring us hard about fifty degrees and head back to Rhea Silvia!"

"Aye, ma'am," the New Swiss responded, her eyes wide with surprise.

The Acting Captain leaned back in her chair and took several deep breaths.

God, what an ordeal! Rodriguez's gamble paid off, but I hope I never have to go through this experience again. Being Captain just isn't worth the risk.

CHAPTER TWENTY-TWO

▼

THE CHASE RENEWED

"Anafu, do you think your mother would consent to performing the joining ritual for us?"

She gazed at him with a mixture of rapture and surprise.

"You are accepting my proposal of marriage?"

"I am, as soon as this mission is over."

"Mother will be *overjoyed*! She always believed that we were right for each other. We will be so happy together." She now gazed down and saw that he was erect again. She stroked his shaft the full length with her index finger. "Now, my darling Lixu, you must fuck me in the human fashion."

"Yes, ma'am. Get off me and lie down."

Ralfo raised herself up from the straddling position she had assumed when they first got into bed and rolled over on her back. Rodriguez rolled over on his side and looked at her with a merry gleam in his eyes. She grinned back. He bent over and kissed her lips. Their tongues met and performed a slow, liquid massage. With a free hand, he sought out a breast and caressed it gently. She began purring like a cat.

Now, he blazed a trail with his lips across her cheeks and chin and down her neck. At the hollow of her throat, he pressed his tongue against her and elicited a short "Ah!" The manual massage of her breast was replaced by the stroking of its nipple lightly with a finger. The nipple hardened and thrust upward. The kisses continued downward.

His lips reached the plump mound he had been massaging, and he began to pepper it with short kisses. Around and around he went, spiraling in toward the peak of the mound, until at last he arrived at the hardened nipple. Playfully, he stroked the nipple with his tongue and elicited another, longer "Ah!" from her. Now, he ran the length of his tongue across the nipple; she shuddered with pleasure and ruffled his hair. He pursed his lips and wrapped them around the nipple; very slowly, he sucked the nipple and released it. He shifted slightly and performed the same ritual with her other breast. All the while, the fires of desire built up inside both of them. She thrust her hips against him and away again in a slow rhythm and was pleased to feel his stiffened member pressing against her thigh.

His lips left her breasts and continued the trail down the center of her body. When they reached her navel, on an impulse, he pushed his tongue into it and wiggled it briefly. The gesture surprised her, but she giggled with delight nevertheless. His lips moved on until they reached the thatch of her pubic mound; here, they detoured down the outside of one thigh and returned up the inside. They crossed the mound and journeyed down and up the other thigh. She panted now in anticipation of what she knew would surely come next. He did not disappoint her. He lifted one leg into the bent position, the better to expose her nether lips, bent down, and kissed those lips gently, first jointly, then individually, first lightly, then passionately. She shuddered again with fierce pleasure and pushed his head deeper into her crotch.

Now he played his tongue across her sweet lips sensuously and elicited a series of short "Ah's!" He pushed the upright leg slightly to one side and opened her crevice; into it went his tongue, as far as it would go. He massaged the crevice from side to side, went deeper into it, and found her clitoris. He massaged her there with the tip of his tongue and brought her to a climax. She moaned and shuddered violently.

"Ah, Lixu!" she rasped. "My sweet, sweet, Lixu! I want all of you!"

"And all of me you shall get," he murmured.

He rose up and maneuvered himself between her legs. She spread wide to accommodate him. He positioned himself to enter her and was pleasantly surprised when she reached down, gently grasped his throbbing manhood, and pushed the head of it against her wet crevice. He thrust forward and sank his shaft into her as far as it would go.

"Put your legs around me, sweetheart, and hold me tight."

She complied at once, and he began the rhythmic pumping in long, slow strokes so as to elicit the maximum amount of pleasure for both of them. In a matter of seconds, they were caught up in a furious passion, grunting and groaning with increased frequency. Climax came to both explosively. As he ejaculated, her body lifted several centimeters off the bed with enough force to push his body up as well. Then they lay still for a while, panting and sweating, her legs still locked around him and his manhood still inside her.

"That was *marvelous*, Lixu!" she breathed. "You must take me that way again."

"It *was* marvelous, Anafu, and I will – as soon as I catch my breath."

He withdrew from her, and she unlocked her leg grip. He rolled over to lie next to her and began massaging her pubic lips with an index finger. She gripped his shaft and stroked it gently.

They were about to initiate their third session of love-making when a voice over the vidscreen interrupted them. Rodriguez reluctantly got out of bed to respond to it. He peered with annoyance at the face of Lt. Tombu.

"Yes?"

"Ye're wanted on the Bridge, sir. We've just shut doon the MOME."

"Very well. I'll be there in a kilo." He switched off and regarded Ralfo, who assumed a most provocative pose. "Duty calls, sweetheart. Let's go hear what our dear Acting Captain has to say."

The Pluj jumped out of bed and planted a wet kiss on his mouth. Then she donned her uniform (which took all of ten seconds). The Warden found his own uniform and took his time putting it on.

Exactly a kilosecond later, both of them strolled onto the Bridge and headed for Gold Zone. Krishnamurthy sat there drumming her fingers impatiently and eyed them with no little disgust. She assumed that they had been "doing the riggers" while she had been sweating buckets wondering if the ship would hold together while she strained the MOME to capacity and beyond. She may have secretly been thrilled over having the opportunity to command a Constabulary patrol vessel – a privilege denied her by the dictates of the interfering Aldebaranians – she was nevertheless nonplussed by the method by which she had assumed command. She knew all too well that her command was only temporary. Warden Rodriguez had done her no favor with his high-handedness, and it had been better if he had taken a different tack. As the pair approached, she put on her "happy face."

"Were you successful, Captain?" the Warden inquired.

Only partially, sir. The MOME was in danger of overloading, so I shut it down at the last possible second. However, we did manage to displace Planetoid 48 by 4.8 light-years."

Rodriguez rubbed his jaw. Did he detect a note of defiance in her response? No matter: partial success was better than no success, and he was not about to quibble. That would come later, during the obligatory inquiry when he would have to justify his actions to his superiors.

"Very good, Captain. Not the ideal outcome, of course, but we'll avoid any severe repercussions. You'll excuse me now. I must report to HQ."

He stepped over to the niche housing the *aaxyboxr*, took a deep breath, and made contact with the creature.

*　　　*　　　*

— *Greetings, fellow sentient. We are the* aaxyboxr. *How may we assist?*

— *Greetings to the* aaxyboxr. *I am sentient Rodriguez. I wish to send a message.*

— *State the message.*

— *"To Commander Ruba at Constabulary Headquarters from Warden (L1) Rodriguez aboard the* Steadfast. *Planetoid 48 has been diverted from its potentially destructive course by an unprecedented warp-out procedure. Due to modifications of the MOME hijacked from the* Astarte *by the JUR, it is in imminent danger of explosion. Its present position is"* [he rattled off a string of numbers] *"4.8 light-years from the Rhea Silvia system, and all standard warnings to navigation should be posted. I also request permission to pursue the remnants of the JUR unit responsible for this threat and bring the matter to a close."* End of message.

— *It is sent.*

— *Thank you. The peace of Kum'halla be with the* aaxyboxr.

— *The peace of Kum'halla be with sentient Rodriguez.*

*　　　*　　　*

Once he recovered from the ordeal of contact, he rejoined Krishnamurthy and Ralfo. The former was doing her best to ignore the latter, while the latter was being herself. Ralfo smiled broadly at her lover.

"'Mission accomplished,' as you humans would say?"

"Not yet, Leftenant. We still have to deliver Dr. Weyerhauser to the proper authorities."

"Even after all he has done?"

"Even after. The law is the law." To the Acting Captain, he said: "And, speaking of which, the emergency here is over. You may restore Captain Halvarson to his command."

"Aye, sir, at once."

Rodriguez then strolled over to the Blue Zone, wearing his by-now-familiar expression of grim determination. Lt. Commander Tuva stiffened in her chair.

"Commander, you were monitoring all traffic in the vicinity before the last warp-out, were you not?"

"Aye, sir. Oi myde note of everyfing. Oi can ply back the record, if ye wish."

"Please do."

The Reman entered a code on her console. Instantly, the image of the current view of Deep Space in the Display vanished and was replaced by a new image, an image of where the *Steadfast* had been several kiloseconds before. Conspicuous was the large blip which represented Planetoid 48. Abruptly, three smaller blips separated themselves from the larger one; two of the small blips, bearing the identifying coloring of Constabulary vessels, moved in parallel toward the center of the Display, while the third (marked as a Romulan freighter) arced off at an oblique angle. The Warden asked for a freeze of the image.

"Extrapolate the trajectory of that third vessel, Commander. Where was it headed?"

"If thy 'eld to their course, thy would 'ave myde stryght for Remus, sir."

"And did they think they'd be safe there, after what they had done?"

"Sir?"

"Sorry. I was just thinking out loud. Good work, Commander."

The Warden strolled back to Gold Zone and failed to notice the look of wonder on Tuva's face. Ralfo waited until he drew near, then pointed to the *aaxyboxr*.

"It is summoning you, Lixu."

"Hmmm. That was quick. They must've been waiting for my report."

He made contact with the hive-creature again but released himself only a few seconds later. The message had been brief and to the point: "Escort prisoner to New Switzerland. Request being considered."

As he turned away from the niche, he observed Captain Halvarson marching onto the Bridge and wearing the same expression he had on when he left under house arrest. He resigned himself to an unpleasant confrontation.

"Don't expect me to thank you for giving me back my command, Rodriguez."

"We Wardens never expect to be thanked for doing our jobs. It comes with the territory. In time, you'll come to appreciate the action taken here today."

"Would you please hold your breath while you're waiting?" Halvarson grumbled. "I find your actions both unconscionable and reprehensible. And I still intend to file charges against you."

"That is your prerogative, Captain. You'll be pleased to hear that I'll be leaving the *Steadfast* shortly. I'm taking Dr. Weyerhauser to New Switzerland for processing. You probably won't see me again until the mandatory inquiry concerning my actions is held."

"You'll excuse me if I don't give you a banner send-off. Now, get off the Bridge – *Leftenant!*"

*   *   *

Warden (L3) Dmitri Worthington stood at his office window, staring at the scene below — and frowning.

It was High Summer on New Switzerland, and the current temperature had just edged past thirty-five degrees. It was only mid-morning; before the day ended, the temperature was expected to rise at least ten more degrees. The planet was as close to its primary [*Tau Ceti 2 on Dunian star charts – CC*] as Venus was to Old Sol; only the fact that it had an atmosphere and plenty of liquid water mitigated what would otherwise have been an intolerable environment. The New Swiss sweltered during High Summer, but they did not bake as Uhaads did on their world. Thanks to its lack of axial inclination, New Switzerland possessed only two "seasons" – High Summer and Low Summer. And its elliptical orbit provided some relief from the heat; Low Summer averaged only twenty-five degrees, rarely going above thirty-five. New Swiss generally took their vacations during the "cooler" season and stayed indoors as much as possible the rest of the year.

Warden Worthington, a short, stocky, completely bald figure with steely gray eyes and a penchant to huff a lot, was not frowning because of the temperature. (Since he occupied an air-cooled office, he had no reason to feel discomfited.) He frowned because he had a tough decision to make, one which required him to choose between following the letter of the law and seizing an opportunity to hand the vicious Reman Army of Liberation a serious defeat. Worthington was Chief of Intelligence of the Warden Service, and it was his job to locate and ferret out all those bent on criminal activity. As such, he took his job seriously and was often considered single-minded in his duty. Now, however, he was of two minds and faced a dilemma of major proportions.

The dilemma had been dropped into his lap by the other occupant in his office, Warden (L1) Lixu Rodriguez, now standing at the "at ease" position in front of his desk and staring off into the distance (the typical stance of all Wardens in the presence of their superiors). Warden Rodriguez had proposed to pursue and apprehend the cell of the JUR responsible for the highjacking and destruction of the cruise ship *Astarte* and for the attempt to destroy part of the Rhea Silvia star system along with several billion of its inhabitants. Furthermore, Warden Rodriguez proposed to enlist the aid of one Dr. Mubutu Weyerhauser, a member of the JUR and a suspect in several recent criminal acts, in the apprehension of the said JUR cell. His intelligence might also lead the Service to other cells. Yet, according to the laws of the Central Spiral Collective, Dr. Weyerhauser should be in detention, awaiting trial for his alleged crimes.

Shto dyelat [what to do]? Worthington asked himself in his mother's tongue for the fourth time in the past kilosecond.

He turned from the window and regarded the younger man for a long moment. Rodriguez held his gaze with a stoical expression.

The intelligence chief could scarcely believe that this Warden – barely out of the Academy – could create a firestorm within the Service. The Service was used to firestorms, to be sure; it seemed that every decision it made created one, at least in the eyes of non-Service personnel and civilians. It had mostly to do with the perception – not entirely without foundation – that Wardens were the hand-picked agents of the despised Aldebaranians sent out far and wide to keep all the other races in line. The idea of an elite security force grated on most sentient beings, having experienced one at one time or another in their individual histories. For humans, it had been an organization known as the "KGB"; for Okath, it had been the Ekath "Red Sleeves," a particularly nasty bunch which provided the incentive for the former's migrating *en masse* to another world; and for city-bred Capellans, it had been (and still was) their "country cousins" who hired out as mercenaries to anyone promising loot. Even as benign a race as the Uhaad had had its war-like period, the excesses of which prompted them to follow (more or less) a pacifist path.

However rightly or wrongly the public perception, Wardens had acquired a certain reputation, and no amount of denials or positive-spin literature could dispel it. Worthington and his kind – from the Director down to the Academy cadets – walked alone in this Universe, shunned by one and all.

And now, here was a new problem. By this time tomorrow, the scuttlebutt would be all over Collective officialdom: a Warden had dared to invoke Article Five, Section Five, paragraph four, place a Constabulary patrol vessel Captain under house arrest, and seize command of his ship. Moreover, this same individual wanted him to violate the laws of the Collective and the protocols of the Service, all in one fell swoop. Warden (L3) Dimitri Worthington would rather have meandered through the Wall in the Rhea Silvia system without instruments than make a decision which could cost him his career.

"Well, Rodriguez," the Chief of Intelligence spoke at last in a deceptively soft voice, "you've put me in a difficult position."

"Aye, sir, but I feel this is the correct course to take."

"Do ye now? The old 'ends-justify-the-means' notion with which I'm sure you're familiar?" The younger man did not respond; the question was a rhetorical one and required no response. "The arguments you've presented are quite convincing, and someone else might be inclined to follow through on them. However, I am not 'someone else'; I must obey the law." A brief smile played across his lips. "That sentiment might sound strange coming from one in my position – Kum'halla knows I've bent a few rules now and then – but we're talking about the very foundation of the Collective here, and we can't take any precipitous action and risk calamitous consequences. Do you understand, Rodriguez?"

"Aye, sir, I do. Nevertheless, I stand behind my recommendations."

"You've got guts, boy, is all I can say. Well, for once, I'm going to play the bureaucratic game and kick this problem upstairs to the Director himself. Whatever decision he makes, that *will* be what you'll be bound by. Is *that* clear?"

"Aye, sir – perfectly."

"Excellent. You're dismissed."

Rodriguez came to attention, saluted his superior smartly, pivoted, and quick-marched out of the office. Warden Worthington sighed heavily and switched on his vidscreen.

*　　*　　*

Rodriguez strode into Conference Room 4 in the Collective's Secretariat on Remus rather full of himself, though he took care not to display his feelings outwardly. Ever mindful of the need to show detachment from the mundane things of this Universe, he maintained the customary neutral face of the Warden Service.

The Secretariat in the Reman capital city of New Lagos was, like its Romulan counterpart in New Nairobi, the tallest structure in the metropolitan area. And, because New Lagos was smaller than New Nairobi – thanks to the difference in economic underpinnings between the two worlds – the Collective outpost seemed to loom even more over the landscape. This perception was re-enforced by the fact that, unlike its Romulan counterpart, the building was located in the central city instead of the outskirts; it stood, in fact, next to the Reman government building, appearing for all the world like the king next to its queen on a chessboard. The reason for the difference in location had to be patently clear to anyone who understood the history of the development of the Twins; the Romulans despised the interference of the Central Spiral Collective and so relegated its planetary headquarters to the fringe of society, while the Remans welcomed the protection of the Collective against the predations of its sister world and gave its planetary HQ a prominent place in society.

Rodriguez was on Remus and not still on New Switzerland as a result of his persuasive arguments concerning what was now being called the "Planetoid 48 Affair." Chief of Intelligence Worthington had kicked the problem raised by the young Warden up to *his* superior, the Director of the Warden Service, Tak Hiroshi; that worthy had pondered the implications of the various arguments, pro and con, and then consulted with the Speaker of the Grand Assembly of the Central Spiral Collective. The Speaker was not about to jeopardize her relationship with the Speaker Emeritus, Spencer Rodriguez, by quashing his grandson's plan of action and so issued a favorable ruling. ("We can't let those JUR bastards get away with this," were her exact words. "Do whatever is necessary to send them all to Xix.") Warden (L3) Worthington then recalled Rodriguez back to his office and told him his plan had official approval and that he had *carte blanche* to carry it out. The young Warden could scarcely believe his ears but nevertheless refrained from dancing with joy until he had returned to his quarters.

As soon as he entered the conference room a half a megasecond later, all those already there rose to their feet and stood at attention. He smiled broadly and waved them back to their seats. He gazed about and studied briefly the familiar faces which regarded him with something close to reverence.

Part of The Plan was to re-unite old comrades-in-arms. And, since he did have *carte blanche*, he used his authority to effect a number of transfers to his "command." Present then were Lt. Anafu Ralfo (now wearing Rodriguez's Service ring as a form of "betrothal"), Sgt. Utumi, Sgt. Running Deer, Cpl. Chen, and the rest of Gamma Platoon. ("Why break up a winning team?" he had asked rhetorically.) All of them were wearing civilian clothing so as not to attract undue attention. A military unit in full regalia inside a government building might provoke gossip which could be overheard by unfriendly ears. A group of "civilians," on the other hand, might just be either sightseeing or petitioning the Collective for one thing or another.

Dr. Mubutu Weyerhauser was also present. Temporarily on parole, he was acting as a "consultant"; he had also stood for Rodriguez's arguments, not because of military protocol but because of genuine respect for the Warden (and, perhaps, because of a show of thanks for keeping him out of prison).

"Friends and colleagues," the Warden began softly, "we are together again." Quinn thumped the table in a show of "solidarity" which netted him a deep frown from Running Deer. "We are going to finish what we started on Planetoid 48."

"I assume you have a plan, sir," the Dunian sergeant stated the obvious.

"Indeed I do. And it's not without its risks; I won't deny it. But, we've taken a lot of risks lately, so what's one more, eh?

"Phase One: Dr. Weyerhauser will attempt to make contact with his former cell and set up a meeting. This is risk #1. If his Major Tshambe has briefed the network on recent events, the JUR just may shoot him on sight."

"Perhaps, and perhaps not," the astrophysicist commented with a mirthless smile. "Major Tshambe may allow the meeting to take place, if only to have the 'privilege' of shooting me personally."

"Ain't no fragger goin' to hom you, Professor," Chen declared vehemently and placed a hand on his arm. "He'll hafta cinter *me* first!"

"And will you be my shadow, Corporal?" he responded, patting her hand.

"To Amazon and back."

"The Professor will be wearing a tracking device," Rodriguez continued, secretly amused by the unlikely camaraderie between scholar and soldier, "if and when Phase Two kicks in. We'll be able to follow him, no matter where he goes. As soon as he arrives at the meeting place, Phase Three begins. Gamma Platoon will deploy to cover all possible escape routes. That's risk #2: since we won't be able to reconnoiter the meeting place in advance, we may not net all of the cell."

"I'll put Quinn on the highest point available," Running Deer said. "He'll cover more ground that way."

"Right, Sarge," the trooper grinned hugely. "I'll pick 'em off, one by one."

The Warden chuckled in spite of himself. They were up against one of the most ruthless organizations in the central spiral, but Quinn was making a game of it! Perhaps his self-confidence would rub off on the others. Otherwise, they were in for a very rough time.

"Very good, Sergeant," he allowed. "Now, once that's done, we begin Phase Four. And I'll be blunt about this; it will entail risk #3, the biggest risk of all. Lt. Ralfo, Sgt. Utumi, and I will approach the meeting place and announce that everyone there is under arrest. I'm gambling that the JUR will attempt to escape."

"There few to escape will be," the Capellan murmured, his yellow eyes gleaming with anticipation. "Lt Ralfo and I 'target practice' will enjoy!"

"I will wager, Sergeant," the Pluj said sweetly, "that more 'target practice' than you I will have."

Utumi puckered his lips in the manner of his kind to affect a smile, and his eyes gleamed even brighter.

"An Alkon warrior a wager never to refuse. Three megaseconds' pay, mayhap?"

"Done!" Ralfo cried gleefully.

"Hey, you two!" Quinn exclaimed. "I want in on this too."

Ralfo and Utumi regarded each other questioningly. The former tapped her forehead, the Pluj gesture of acquiescence, while the latter cocked his head to the left, his kind's equivalent of a shrug. Rodriguez observed this little tableau with no little wonder and recalled an ancient line of Dunian poetry he had once heard at the University – "Fools rush in where angels fear to tread." Everyone in this room might die during this operation, but some of them would go down laughing!

"Any questions?" he asked. "Suggestions?"

"I have one suggestion, sir," Running Deer piped up. Rodriguez motioned for him to continue. "Silencers for our weapons. The enemy won't be able to pinpoint our positions if they can't hear our gunfire."

"Good point, Sergeant. Consider it done. Anyone else?"

He was answered by silence, and he dismissed Gamma Platoon and Sgt. Utumi. They filed out of the conference room in a jaunty manner, joking with each other. The Warden turned to Dr. Weyerhauser.

"Lunch time, Professor. Can you recommend a good restaurant?"

"As a matter of fact, I can. And it isn't far from here. We can walk there easily."

The layout of New Lagos was similar to that of New Nairobi – not surprising, since the original settlers of the Twins had come from the same social class and therefore had had the same ideas about building community. The chief difference between the two capitals then was their size; because of the nature of the natural resources of Romulus and Remus – mineral wealth for the one, fertile soil for the other – the former could afford more elaborate construction projects. Otherwise, one saw government buildings at the center surrounded by concentric rings of increasingly lesser status and lastly by residential areas also graded by class.

The streets here also formed "wheels" with "spokes," and they were equally crowded with both pedestrians and motorized traffic. The presence of "Proceed" and "Wait" signals at each intersection testified to the fact that urban life had changed very little in three-hundred-plus years; the Founders had no more cared for chaos than did their ancestors, and they melded old ideas with modern ones in the erection of this city.

The restaurant in question was three streets from the Civic Center. It was all chrome and glass, a single story establishment surrounded by multi-story office complexes; and, from the looks of the clientele inside, it appeared to cater strictly to the denizens of the business community and the government bureaucracy. Rodriguez briefly wondered how Weyerhauser could have afforded such a place on an educator's salary but was willing to accept the latter's assessment of the quality of the fare and the service.

The moment the trio entered, all heads turned in their direction. Both the clientele and the staff stopped whatever they had been doing – almost in mid-stride – and literally gawked at the newcomers. Rodriguez knew the reaction well. A Warden in public always attracted attention, no matter where (s)he was or what (s)he was doing. And many of the persons here evinced the nervousness others did in the presence of a member of the Service. Likewise, a Pluj always attracted considerable attention – albeit for the opposite reason – regardless of the circumstances. Human males ogled, and human females wrinkled their noses in disgust; and aliens of both genders expressed either boredom or mild interest.

Despite the initial reaction to their entrance, they did not have to wait long for service. Immediately, a portly fellow, wearing a name tag which identified him as the *maitre d'*, literally trotted over to see to their needs. He wore the standard-issue smile and presented the standard-issue effusiveness that all in his profession had affected for millennia.

"Sirs, madam," he puffed, "welcome to our humble establishment. A table for three? Right this way, please." He led them off to their right and halted before a table near the front window. "Our best location, sirs and madam. Please be seated. I'll have the wine steward and the waiter serve you in short order."

"No wine, if it's all the same to you," the Warden advised. "We're still on duty. Just coffee for me and the gentleman, mint tea for the lady."

"Very good, sir."

The *maitre d'* rushed away, and Rodriguez shook his head in amazement. He then regarded the astrophysicist with curiosity.

"How could you possibly afford this place on your salary? Do you have a secret trust fund?"

"I can't afford it," the other replied with a chuckle. "Actually, I've never been in here. I just know a lot of people who dine here regularly, and they've all praised the place to the sky."

"Lucky for you, then, that we Wardens have unlimited credit."

They sat in silence, interrupted only by a wait person – a young blonde human female who smiled warmly at the men and presented a neutral face to the Pluj – with their coffee and mint tea and by a middle-aged, balding human male who set menus in front of them. Both hurried away to see to other customers' needs.

Abruptly, Ralfo gripped Rodriguez's arm. He stared at her with concern.

"Lixu," she whispered in Pluj, "see who just came in."

The Warden pivoted slowly in his chair in order to seem to act casually, and immediately his face registered surprise. Gone were the long, shaggy, graying hair – replaced by a neatly trimmed and groomed head of gray – the rumpled, thread-worn, blue business suit – replaced by an expensive-looking gray tweed suit – and the black and maroon sandals – replaced by a shiny pair of black oxfords. But the face remained the same, and the Warden recognized it instantly; it belonged to his erstwhile informant in Old Town on Romulus, the one who called himself the "Professor."

The latter examined the diners with his usual owlish expression as if looking for someone in particular, his eyes sweeping the restaurant in a professional manner. When they focused in Rodriguez's direction, they quickly turned away.

"What is he doing *here*?" the Warden asked rhetorically. "I wouldn't have thought he could afford this place any more than you could, Professor."

"Who are you talking about?" When Rodriguez nodded in the newcomer's direction, the academic turned around; he gasped sharply, and his jaw dropped. "My God! What's *he* doing here?"

"Him you know, Professor?"

"Indeed I do. He's a former colleague of mine at the University. He taught political science. He was dismissed two years ago for taking money in exchange for passing grades. The whole school was in an uproar. How do *you* know him?"

"He's a professional informant these days," the Warden replied. "We, uh, did some business with him recently, on Romulus. Apparently, the information business pays better than I had believed. Wait here. I'll get to the bottom of this."

He rose and carefully and slowly wended his way toward his quarry. The grim expression he wore elicited a few worried looks from the other patrons. The "Professor," by now, had begun to move back toward the entrance and was studiously avoiding any further eye contact with his former "client." The Warden caught up with him just as he was half-way out the door and clapped him on the shoulder. The informant gazed at him with fright.

"What's your hurry, 'Professor'? Won't you join Lt. Ralfo and me for a cup of coffee – on me, of course?"

"Uh, I'd rather not. I just remembered an important engagement elsewhere."

"But, I insist." His grip tightened, and he steered the man toward his table. "After all, we haven't seen each other for ever so long."

The Warden halted the informant before his table, roughly pushed him into the lone empty chair, and took his own seat. Ralfo eyed the man as a cat might a mouse, while Dr. Weyerhauser registered awe. The "Professor" squirmed a bit, then put on his best professional manner. He looked at the astrophysicist.

"Weyerhauser, isn't it? The word is out that you're a wanted man and there's a reward for information leading to your arrest."

"You're a little late for that. I'm in this Warden's protective custody." He regarded the other pensively. "My God, Brooks, what's happened to you?"

"It's a long story, chum. But, I'm guessing 'this Warden' has other matters on his mind than pleasant reminiscing."

"You can say that again, "Professor,'" Rodriguez responded testily, "and the first thing I'd like to know is why you're on Remus instead of in your usual haunts."

"I travel a good deal, Warden. One never knows where one can obtain useful information. I'd even go to Eka-xan itself if I thought it would be worth my while." He rubbed his jaw. "As to your question, I'm working my contacts here for anything that might convert into carats on Romulus."

"How enterprising of you. Now, I'm looking for some information which I will make it worth your while to provide me."

"And that is?"

"We're trying to locate a fellow named Tshambe, who recently returned to Remus. Can you tell us anything about him?"

The "Professor" rubbed his jaw again and stared off into the distance.

"Tshambe – Tshambe," he mused. "A rough character, I've heard – someone you wouldn't want to cross. They say he might be part of the JUR."

"'They say' correctly. Anything else?"

"No-o-o. I try not to be too curious about the JUR. It's bad for business, don't you know?"

"As I said, I'll make it worth your while."

"How much?"

Rodriguez reached into his pocket and pulled out the same roll of banknotes the informant had seen at their first encounter. The latter surreptitiously licked his lips. The Warden peeled off two 100-carat notes and slid them across the table. The "Professor" eyed them hungrily, all the while debating with himself as to the advisability of entering into this "contract."

"That's an 'upfront,'" Rodriguez slipped into spacer's slang. "There'll be three more when you provide me with a location."

"Five C's are hard to turn down, and I'd be crazy to do so. I'd also be crazy to risk getting involved with the JUR. It reminds me of Amati's world,[51] wouldn't you say?"

"I would say so. What's it going to be then?"

"I'll take the contract. *But* – and it's nothing personal, mind you – I don't ever want to see you again."

"I'll try not to lose any sleep over our parting. How do we make contact?"

The "Professor" pulled a notepad and a stub of a pencil from his jacket

---

51 Amati's world in the Forutran star system [*Wolf 459 on Dunian star charts – CC*] was the scene of a minor skirmish between Dunian militiamen and Alkon warriors. Since the latter had the reputation for never taking prisoners, the former had the choice of being massacred or committing suicide. The Dunians chose the latter; their CO set down a full account in his personal diary, even while his men calmly blew their brains out – CMT.

pocket and scribbled some numbers on it. He handed the note to the Warden.

"Call that number every day at noon. If someone answers, you ask for 'Fred.' 'Fred' will ask your name; you'll say 'Peter Pan.' If 'Fred' has anything to report, he'll say, 'Fine weather we're having"; if not, he'll say, "Terrible weather we're having.' Continue to call until you get what you want or you give up in frustration."

He scooped up the K 200, stood up, and strode briskly out of the restaurant. Rodriguez smirked and waved at the retreating figure.

"Warden," Dr. Weyerhauser asked, "why are you dealing with Brooks? All I have to do is call *my* contact and request a meeting."

"And I want you to do just that, Professor. But, on the very real possibility that your Major Tshambe has been debriefed by his superiors and that they have spread the word that you're no longer 'reliable,' I need an alternate source of information. There's also the very real possibility that you've been targeted for termination."

"When I make contact, I'll insist on being debriefed as well. That should buy us some time." He stared up at the ceiling. "If they do kill me, so what? I've got nothing to live for. It'll be better than life imprisonment on Xix." He fixed the Warden with a steely look. "I want one favor from you, Rodriguez."

"And that is?"

"I intend to kill Major Tshambe for what he did to Petra. Give me that opportunity."

"You know I can't do that."

"You've already broken the rules by paroling me. You'll find a way to break them again."

*   *   *

"'Ello?"

"'Stargazer' here. I want to report in."

"Do ye noo? We lost track of ee, Doctor."

"The Constabulary caught me, but I told them nothing of consequence."

"That's na what Myjor Tshambe finks. 'E sys ye're na to be trusted."

"It's all been a big misunderstanding. I'm still loyal to The Cause. Bring me in, and I'll explain everything."

"Well, we'd loike to talk wif ee, that's for sure. Are ye in New Lagos noo?"

"Yes. I'm staying at the Hotel Remus."

"All roight. Be at the corner of Fifth Street and New Lagos Boulevard tomorrow at the third hoor. We'll send some'un to pick ee up."

"I'll be there."

"And, Doctor, na tricks, or ye're a dead man!"

"Understood."

*   *   *

Warden (L1) Lixu Rodriguez dials the number given him. The vidcom (with video disabled) rings several times before someone answers. A baritone voice is heard.

"'Ello?"

"Is Fred there?"

"This is Fred. 'Oo are you?"

"I'm…'Peter Pan.'"

"Ah, 'ow are ye, Peter?"

"I'm fine. How are you?"

"Oi'm well, fanks." A brief pause. "Foine weavver we're 'avin,' eh?"

"Yes, it is. What's the forecast?"

There follows a detailed set of directions to a farmhouse in the southern hemisphere of Remus, approximately five hundred kilometers southwest of New Lagos. Then the connection breaks off.

Rodriguez turns to Lt. Anafu Ralfo and Doctor Mubutu Weyerhauser and smiles broadly.

"I really didn't expect this information so soon. I think the 'Professor' was being too modest by half about his abilities. In any event, Phase Two begins now."

CHAPTER TWENTY-THREE

▼

THE ENEMY ENGAGED

RHEA SILVIA WAS QUICKLY ASCENDING into the western sky. To those humans who were more accustomed to watching sunrise in the east, a Reman sunrise proved to be a most disconcerting phenomenon. One had to learn to re-orient oneself or risk a nervous break-down.

As far as anyone knew, Romulus and Remus were the only planets in the central spiral (and perhaps the entire galaxy) to share an orbit and thus to possess opposing axial rotations. When, during the formation of the star system, the primary spat out molten masses which became its planets, two of those masses – nearly equal in size and in geophysical construction – behaved similarly to two side-by-side billiard balls which had been struck by the cue ball at the same time. This phenomenon was not lost on the first settlers; the first generation on Remus had to adapt quickly and did so – as long as they remained on their world. Whenever subsequent generations chanced to travel off-world, they found themselves in the same dilemma the Founders did.

Dr. Mubutu Weyerhauser, having been born on Remus, found the sunrise quite "normal," and he watched it as he dressed for his "appointment" with his erstwhile confederates. Foremost in his mind was the fear that he would never see Rhea Silvia rise again after today. His erstwhile confederates were likely to charge him with "treason," summarily execute him, and dump his body in some public place as a warning to all Remans what would happen to anyone who wasn't a "loyal" citizen. They had used him from the beginning, taking advantage of his naiveté and idealism to draw him into their nefarious schemes. They had turned him into a seditionist, a saboteur, a kidnapper, and a mass murderer in one fell swoop; worse, they had prostituted his expertise in astrophysics in order to perpetrate those horrendous crimes. But, the most unforgivable sin they had committed was the assassination of the one person in all of the central spiral who meant more to him than Life itself. He could have turned a blind eye to all the rest, but this one act cried out for vengeance – and he would avenge Petra if it was the last thing he ever did.

He finished dressing and sat down to calm himself. He also spent the time in rehearsing his "report" to the JUR and devising answers to all the possible questions put to him. There would be many of these, he knew, meant to trip him up and reveal him as a police spy. A slip-up on his part would also doom Warden Rodriguez's plan to capture or kill his interrogators in short order.

A soft rap at the door of his room at the Hotel Remus interrupted his reverie. He swiftly stepped over to it and cracked it open. He recognized Rodriguez (though the latter was now in civilian clothing) and let him in.

"Why the civilian clothes, Warden?"

"A simple precaution. I had to assume that the hotel would be under surveillance by the JUR once they knew where you were. If I had been in uniform, their suspicions would've been raised instantly."

"Yes. They can be quite paranoid. So, why are you here?"

In response, the Warden opened the flat box he was carrying and pulled out a brightly-colored shirt. He unfolded it and held it up for the astrophysicist's inspection.

"A 'present' for you, Professor. Wear this shirt instead of the one you've got on."

"What's wrong with the one I'm wearing?"

"It hasn't got any buttons which function as a tracking device or as a micro-vidcom."

The Doctor took the shirt from Rodriguez and gaped at it in an attempt to discern its "special features." He examined it from different angles and even held it up to the light. Finally, he shook his head in frustration.

"Which buttons are the special ones?"

"Our tech people didn't say, and I didn't ask. I only know that they're on the shirt." He regarded the academic briefly in silence, then: "It's better that you don't know either. Otherwise, you might inadvertently call attention to them and ruin the plan."

"You're right, of course. Well, I'd better change. It's close to the third hour."

"Once you put that shirt on – so I'm told – your body heat will activate the special buttons. They'll continue to function as long as you wear the shirt. I'll leave you now, but we'll be tracking you every step of the way. Good luck, Professor."

"Thank you, Warden – for everything."

Once Rodriguez had departed, the Doctor stripped off his own shirt and donned the new one. It didn't feel any different from all the other shirts he had ever worn; it was just as soft and silky and did not abrade his skin. Moreover, it created a warm sensation on his skin and helped to relax him. He wondered idly if that was part of the technology of Constabulary laboratories or merely a psychological state on his part.

He checked his chromo again and realized he had but fifteen minutes to reach the intersection of Fifth Street and New Lagos Boulevard.

The city of New Lagos, unlike New Nairobi, was nowhere near the original settlement. That place was several hundred kilometers to the east and had been constructed on a flat plain. When the settlers discovered how fertile the soil was, they decided not to waste a valuable resource by building a city in the middle of a potential plantation. The search for a suitable site for the capital, however, was protracted because most of Remus consisted of flat, fertile plains; the few mountain ranges which existed defied the technology of the time to carve a city out of solid rock. Eventually, explorers came upon a solitary hill which overlooked a plain like a sentry on duty. The new Remans were overjoyed; they would build their capital in the same fashion as their namesakes had done in ancient times on Dunia.

In many respects, New Lagos resembled New Nairobi on Romulus. The government buildings occupied the apex of the hill; other structures – commercial, recreational, cultural, and educational – surrounded the center like acolytes, and the residential areas fanned out beyond them. The streets, laid out in concentric circles, were actually terraces dug into the slope of the hill; the "spokes" of the "wheels" were gentle inclines, although they were all a pedestrian could do to navigate them. Streets were given numerical designations for no other reason than the Founders could not settle on any proper names to give them. The criss-crossing "spokes" were called "boulevards" only because they were wider than the streets; boulevards had proper names, but those reflected geography rather than personal affectation. Buildings on the terraced streets were constructed on the edges of the terraces in order to prevent vehicles from spilling over.

Only the size of the city differed from its Romulan counterpart because, whereas the latter tended to sprawl outwardly in additional rings, the former ended at the base of the hill, beyond which the plantations stretched in all directions. Everywhere else on the planet, small villages were scattered about, providing homes and commercial and non-commercial amenities for the people who worked the plantations. The original settlement was one such, except that it also housed a museum and memorial park in honor of the Founders.

The Hotel Remus stood at the corner of Third Street and New Lagos Boulevard, two terraces up from the designated rendezvous point. The "sidewalks" between terraces were in reality long, wide staircases on either side of the boulevards. Native Remans took these walkways in stride, climbing up or down much like a collection of mountain goats. One could differentiate them from off-worlders fairly easily; the latter tended to stop and catch their breath after navigating a flight of stairs (and those from lower-gravity worlds had an especially difficult time of it!).

Despite his New Swiss heritage, Dr. Weyerhauser was quite used to the geography. He ambled down to Fifth Street in a casual manner and paid little attention (as all Remans did) to the huffing and puffing of the tourist trade. No sooner had he arrived at the specified corner than a privately-owned vehicle which had been parked across the street came to life, shot through the intersection – just as the blue "Proceed" traffic light turned to the orange "Wait" light – and screeched to a halt in front of the astrophysicist. Two persons occupied the front seat: a rail-thin woman (the driver) with a large overbite and stringy brown hair; and an equally thin man with a crooked nose and a bald pate. The man leaned out the window and motioned for the Doctor to get in, scowling all the while. The Doctor did not recognize the woman, but he had seen the man once or twice before at political rallies. He was rumored to be an "enforcer" of JUR rules, and his presence here did not bode well for Dr. Weyerhauser's chances of survival.

The astrophysicist squeezed into the back seat, and instantly the woman floored the accelerator and tore down Fifth Street in an easterly direction. Whatever else she might have been, she was a skilled operator, deftly maneuvering her vehicle in and out of traffic, and never once eased up on the accelerator. At the intersection of Fifth Street and New Abidjan Boulevard, she turned left just as the traffic light turned orange, narrowly missed colliding with a vehicle proceeding from a stopped position, and roared down the decline toward the city limits. Dr. Weyerhauser's heart beat increased at the thought of being crushed to death in a multi-vehicle collision. Within a few seconds, they were out of the business district and whizzing through a residential area. The nature of her surroundings fazed the driver not in the least; she continued her mad dash as though she were on a speedway, vying for the winner's cup. Just as rapidly as she had traversed the central city, she crossed the city limits into open country. And still she did not ease up on the accelerator.

During this time, neither the man nor the woman spoke to their passenger or to each other. The Doctor recognized the cold-shoulder treatment when he saw it. When the members of the JUR were not carrying out their murderous missions, they generally bantered with each other as most humans did. That these two were maintaining a rigid silence was yet another signal of personal danger to him, and he knew better than to attempt any bantering of his own. He fervently prayed that Warden Rodriguez was keeping a close watch on him as he had promised.

*   *   *

High above the speeding ground car, a black, meter-wide sphere cruises silently through the upper atmosphere of Remus. It is a standard Constabulary probe, now doubling as a relay station as it receives transmissions from the micro-devices passing as "shirt buttons" and directs them to a shuttlecraft higher up in altitude.

In the shuttlecraft, the man in the black uniform studies his vidscreen grimly. He is worried about the lack of audio transmissions from below; either the microphone is malfunctioning or no one has yet engaged in conversation. As for any visual transmissions, he is disappointed that his cat's paw is not moving around in his seat and allowing him a more panoramic view of the countryside. If he cannot recognize any landmarks, he will have to rely solely on the tracking radar.

He forces himself to relax by uttering a well-used mantra taught to him by his mentor. Next to him, his second-in-command smiles and squeezes his hand. He gazes fondly at her and squeezes back. The sight of her does more for his equipoise than any mantra.

Unfortunately, equipoise will soon be overcome by the deadly business at hand.

*   *   *

It has been said many times that Remus is one huge farm. Generally speaking, this is a true statement. Yet, the structure of Reman agriculture is quite complex, and one learns quickly that it does not compare with a Dunian structure in the least bit.

As soon as the original pioneers had settled in and decided how to take advantage of their natural resources, the entire planet was divided into districts of one thousand hectares each. In the center of each district stood a village which consisted of several small businesses and social centers to service the workforce and a hundred or so domiciles to house it. The districts were properly called "plantations," and they and their villages assumed the same nomenclature, e.g. "Smithson Plantation." The earliest plantations were named after the original settlers, while subsequent ones adopted a name generally agreed upon by the villagers themselves. Each plantation was subdivided into four parts. One part was planted with the primary crop; another with a secondary crop; the third with clover; and the last was left fallow. Reman agriculture thus operated in four stages; each growing season – three per year – the activity in each subdivision rotated so as to keep the land fertile in perpetuity.

The village was run by a council consisting of ten individuals selected by the villagers to serve for two years on a staggered basis. At each election, five vacancies were filled, and no council member could serve consecutive terms; eventually, all the villagers took a turn at governance. At each council session – one for each growing season – the members drew lots to determine who would serve as chairperson for that session. The council established ordinances for good conduct and functioning of the village, and it also organized the villagers into work brigades, assigning each person to a specific task. If any disputes arose of a criminal or civil nature, the council chairperson acted as judge and the villagers in a committee-of-the-whole served as the jury.

Curiously, the one thing a village council did not do was to determine which crop (primary or secondary) to plant. That decision was made in the halls of power in New Lagos, specifically the Ministry of Agriculture. For, the plain fact of the matter was that Reman plantations were organized to produce food on a quota system; each district was assigned a primary and a secondary crop to grow and was obliged to produce X measures of each crop each growing season. The central government then distributed the output according to a complex formula; the lion's share was exported off-world to feed a growing population in the Central Spiral Collective. With the revenues from agriculture, the Remans were able to purchase manufactured goods in any amount they desired.[52]

The highway on which the JUR vehicle was roaring down skirted the Hashimoto Plantation on the right and the Moreno Plantation on the left. The primary crop of the former was potatoes, a staple favored only by humans and Pluj; all other races found it either tasteless or poisonous. The primary of the latter was carrots which only the Pluj considered poisonous; all others considered them intoxicating. (Only the Ekath shunned human foodstuffs altogether for cultural/political reasons.) As far as the eye could see, the produce bloomed in ruler-straight rows. Occasionally, one could see workers

---

52 Dr. Tomas Bashaong has likened the Reman set-up as a "feudal" system where the workers are the "serfs" and the Reman High Council in New Lagos is the "lord of the manor." Cf. his essay, "The Feudal System of Remus," *Amazonian Review*, vol. 41, no. 2 (Armstrong 152 A.R.). This might be true were it not for the fact that the Remans deliberately chose to establish a particular way of life. It has worked for them for over three centuries – CMT.

in the field inspecting the bounty in order to determine its readiness for harvesting.

Presently, the vehicle approached the turn-off which led to the Village of Hashimoto. The driver slowed down ever so slightly and made the turn with screeching tires. A kilometer further on, the village came into view, first half of the residences, then the business district, followed by the second half of residences. It had been said, and it was true, that, when one has seen one Reman village, one has seen them all. Each village had been laid out according to a generic plan, and no variations had been permitted; if a villager in one part of the planet ever had the desire to move to another part of the planet (rarely), (s)he would immediately feel right at home.

The driver slowed down to a relative crawl briefly in order to avoid running over an elderly villager crossing the road. For a split second, Dr. Weyerhauser envisioned his personal "body count" increasing! As a rule, the JUR never harmed a farmer intentionally – unless said farmer was discovered (subjectively speaking) to be a "traitor" or a "collaborator."

At the far end of the village, the vehicle turned off the main road and onto a narrow lane covered with pea gravel and lined on both sides with oaks, poplars, and maples in no particular order. The trees were the only anomalous growths on an otherwise pre-planned world. At the end of the lane stood four buildings in a circular clearing, three of which were larger than the fourth. Those three held the tools of agricultural life, and there the villagers started their work day. The remaining building, opposite the three, was a simple one-story A-frame and served as the residence of the plantation manager, an appointee of the village council who served for pleasure.

The driver passed half a dozen other automobiles and halted in front of the manager's residence, and she and her companion piled out and began walking toward the building. Neither checked to see if their passenger was following behind; it was just assumed that he would be. And, for his part, the astrophysicist hesitated for only a second before forcing himself to get out of the car and fall into line with his erstwhile confederates. He prayed that the tracking device on his shirt was still functioning and that Warden Rodriguez was even now zeroing in on his position. Otherwise, he hadn't the proverbial prospector's chance in the Wall of surviving this encounter. He took several deep breaths to slow his suddenly rapid heart beat.

The JUR pair entered the house, and the Doctor was only two steps behind them. He found himself in the living room in the midst of a dozen people seated on various pieces of furniture, all eyeing him intently. He was not in the least surprised to spy Major Tshambe among this assembly; he was surprised, however, to see the man smiling broadly at him. This was not a good sign; the Major never smiled at anyone unless he had something nasty in mind for that person.

"Well, well," Tshambe hooted, "oor lost little sheep 'as returned to the fold. 'Oo good to see ee agyn, Doctor."

Before responding, the academic quickly scanned the faces of the other members of this "welcoming committee." One of them looked familiar; he thought he had seen that person conferring with the Major before the cell had set off on their mission. The man was called "Toshimuto" and had the rank of "Captain" in the JUR; what else he was was indeterminate. The others were total strangers. All of them wore neutral faces, and he idly wondered if this was the "jury" in his "trial." He faced Tshambe with grim determination.

"Good to see you too, Major," he lied. "I've had a rough time of it since I last saw you."

"'Ave ye noo? Well, that's whoy ye're 'ere – to be debriefed. Tyke a seat, and we'll begin."

The Doctor looked about and actually saw a vacant chair. It didn't appear to be the most comfortable piece of furniture he'd ever seen; but then, he wasn't here to be comfortable – just the opposite, in fact. He seated himself, shifted his weight a bit in order to minimize the discomfort of the chair, and regarded his adversary with feigned nonchalance.

"Noo, Doctor, tell us what 'appened to ee since we last spoke."

"First of all, I'd like to go on record to protest the treatment you accorded me by putting me in with those crew members of the *Astarte*. When they found out who I was, they were ready to kill me. I had to talk fast in order to save my skin."

"It looks loike ye were successful." The JUR leader squinted at him fiercely. "But, see 'ere, Doctor, what Oi did was for your own good. Some of the fellows didna trust ee, and *thy* wanted me to kill ee before ye jeopardoized the mission. Oi 'ad to put ee oot o' 'arm's wy."

"I...see. All right, that seems logical. Anyway, I made up a tale that I had had a falling out with you and that you made me a prisoner too. That seemed to mollify them."

"Uh-huh. Tell us aboot the escype."

"Um, well, the crew was planning to overpower the guards you'd placed at the hatch and then make their way to the Communications bay where they'd contact the Constabulary. Naturally, they didn't confide in me; and, when I did learn what they were up to, they threatened to kill me if I alerted the guards to the plot.

"By the way, much as I hate to criticize my comrades, those two guards were drunk. They'd found several bottles of liquor and were swigging the stuff like it was Founders' Day. That's why it was child's play for a bunch of unarmed amateurs to take them by surprise."

"Um, if that's the cyse, thy pyde for their folly. Continue."

"The crew members made good their escape and took me along so that I wouldn't give an alarm. Eventually, we ran into a Constabulary patrol which was reconnoitering Planetoid 48. The crew pointed me out as a JUR 'terrorist,' and the officer in charge placed me under arrest. I was closely guarded thereafter all the way back to New Switzerland."

"But, thy freed ee?"

"I was wanted for questioning about the highjacking of the *Astarte*. I told them I had been taken against my will and forced to co-operate. I think – I hope – they believed me."

"A pretty story that, Doctor. These gentlemen 'ere noo 'ave some further questions to ask ee, just to clarifoy a few matters. 'Oo want to go forst?"

*   *   *

The troop carrier comes in low and uses the trees lining the lane as a screen against any JUR sentries. It is barely fifteen meters above the ground, and its passage is barely a whisper above the gentle breeze which wafts across the giant potato patch. Fifty meters from the tree line, it sets down as gently as its pilot is able to do so (although its weight still crushes many potatoes).

The troopers of Gamma Platoon clamber out the carrier's hatch, led by Cpl. Chen, and set up a perimeter. They are quickly followed by the "command" personnel. Sgt. Running Deer makes a final check of each trooper's equipment and assures Warden Rodriguez that everyone is as prepared as can be. With Rodriguez and Lt. Ralfo in the lead, the unit picks its way at a low crouch through the potato plants and covers the distance to the trees in short order. Running Deer and Sgt. Utumi act as flanks.

The platoon creeps stealthily the last ten meters, and each individual takes cover behind a tree, awaiting his/her order to deploy. The Warden scans the clearing where the target building stands, searching for the best available vantage points. He signals both sergeants to join him.

"What do you think of this lay-out?" he asks the Capellan.

"There not much cover to be," the warrior replies matter-of-factly. "The enemy from the rear of the dwelling could escape."

"I agree," Running Deer adds. "I can put Quinn on the roof of one of those outbuildings and the rest of the platoon at scattered points around the front and sides. But the rear presents a problem."

"Utumi-go," Rodriguez murmurs, "you're the best scout we have. Could you make your way around the building?"

"Aye, but it time will take."

"Go then. Signal when you're in place." A shadow of a smile plays across his lips. *"Anafu, go with him. You two seem to work well together."*

"You I thank, Lixu. A formidable barrier the sergeant and I will make."

"I'm sure. Move out then. Running Deer, deploy your people."

∗   ∗   ∗

Dr. Weyerhauser was perspiring heavily now, under the fierce interrogation from the JUR "jury." Each of them fired a question at him in machine-gun fashion; as soon as he had answered one, the next one followed rapidly. Sometimes, an interrogator asked a question relating to his personal expertise/experience; other times, the individual re-phrased a previous question. It was becoming obvious to him that they were hoping to trip him up and "prove" that he was a "traitor to The Cause." And he was sure that they would, sooner or later. He had told so many half-truths that he had lost count; worse, he had had, at one point, to claim a "faulty" memory and retract a statement when he realized that it was an out-and-out lie.

All the while, Major Tshambe eyed him closely and smirked. He was clearly enjoying this little drama, watching his victim squirm under the press of questions, and waiting for the right moment to pounce on him. The Major did not offer a single question himself – he was leaving that to the "experts" – but he would pronounce the fate of the "prisoner" in due time.

The astrophysicist had to persevere, however, and give Warden Rodriguez time to get his team into position to assault the building. After that, it didn't matter what he said.

"What is your relytionship wif the Warden Service, Doctor?"

The question was totally unexpected, simply because it had nothing to do with previous inquiries, and it took him aback. He gaped at the inquisitor whom he had previously identified as "Toshimuto," a large jowly man with black beads for eyes and a penchant for wearing mismatched clothing, and tried to wrap his mind around the query.

"Wh – what? I don't understand."

"Ye've been seen talkin' wif a Warden. What did ye tell 'im?"

"Oh, *him.*" The Doctor thought quickly. "He was the one who arrested me on Planetoid 48. He read me my rights and asked if I understood them. I didn't expect to speak to him again, but for some reason he sat in on my interrogation back on New Switzerland."

"Come noo, Doctor, refresh your memory a wee bit. We've been watchin' ee ever since ye contacted us. One of oor aygents saw a person enter your 'otel room shortly before we picked ee up. This person was followed after 'e left ye, and it didna tyke 'im long to lose oor aygent. 'E struck us as a fraggin' golder.[53] So, 'oo was 'e?"

"Um, he claimed to be an employee of the hotel. He delivered some laundry I'd sent out."

"Oi dinna fink so, *boyo*. Your story smacks o' phoniness frough and frough." Toshimuto leaned forward, a feral look on his face. Through clenched teeth, he said: "Ye've been co-operytin' wif the auforities, 'aven't ye? What did ye tell 'em?"

The astrophysicist leaned back in his chair, stared up at the ceiling, and heaved a long sigh. He had run out of half-truths, and his inquisitors weren't believing anything he had told them. He hoped he had stalled them long enough for the Warden to ready his assault. In any event, he knew his number was up – time to tell the truth and be done with it. He met Tshambe's gaze and smiled.

"I told them everything they wanted to know – and then some. The whole rotten business. And I made prominent mention of your name, Major. I should imagine there's an arrest warrant on its way to be executed."

The reaction to this confession was immediate – and predictable. Half of the assembly was on its collective feet, staring wildly in all directions and seeking the best avenue of escape. The other half remained stiffly seated and scowled deeply at its erstwhile member; some of them had drawn pistols and were pointing them at him. The Major was the only one exhibiting an air of relaxation. He continued to regard the academic with a smirk.

"Well," he said presently, "noo we're getting' sum'eres. Is the Constabulary comin' to your rescue then?"

"Perhaps – if you don't shoot me in the next five hundred seconds."

"Oh, ye'll certainly be shot, Doctor, na doot aboot that – and soon. But, forst, tell me whoy ye turned trytor."

"You *used* me, you bastard! You took advantage of my adherence to the cause of liberty for Remus and involved me in one heinous act after another." A snarl played across his lips. "But, the worst thing you did was to murder my lady friend, Petra. There was no need to do that; she didn't know anything about my involvement with the JUR. But you killed her anyway, just for the sheer pleasure of it. You like to kill people, don't you, Major?"

"Oi do what needs to be done, Doctor, and Oi dinna worry aboot the consequences."

"Well, one of the 'consequences' is that I'm going to kill you, if it's the last thing I do."

---

53 "Golder" is Amazonian slang for a Warden. The term refers to the metal used to fashion a Warden's badge – CMT.

"Are ye noo? Oi dinna—"

"Myjor!" exclaimed the woman driver who was standing at the front window and surveying the yard. "There's sum'un comin' up the droive. Gor! It's a golder! And 'e's all alone."

Those who had been milling around the room now rushed to the window and craned their necks to see what she had seen. The Warden was strolling toward the house as if he hadn't a care in the world, least of all for a concern for performing his official duties. The group at the window was joined by the remainder of the assembly, and all began to babble excitedly.

"It's a clean shot," one of them murmured. "'E's myde 'imsilf an easy target."

"Calm doon, ye fools!" Tshambe barked. "Do ye fink 'e's really alone? Use your 'eads!"

"So, what'll we do, Myjor?"

"Quoiet! I'm finkin'."

"YOU IN THE HOUSE!" a voice boomed suddenly. "THIS IS WARDEN RODRIGUEZ SPEAKING. YOU ARE ALL UNDER ARREST, ON SUSPICION OF HIGHJACKING, SABOTAGE, KIDNAPPING, HOMICIDE, AND ACTS OF TERRORISM AND SEDITION. COME OUT WITH YOUR HANDS OVER YOUR HEADS."

The voice shocked everyone in the room, not so much by the contents of the message as by its origin. It seemed to emanate from Dr. Weyerhauser. The JUR members were not as shocked, however, as the academic himself; he could swear that it was his *shirt* speaking. Apparently, Rodriguez hadn't informed him of *all* of its "special features"!

"Well, Major," he sneered as soon as he had collected his wits, "it looks like the game is over."

"Dinna be too sure aboot that. We've got ee as an 'ostage. Wardens are sworn to protect loife, aye? Toby, cover the good Doctor."

One of the men at the window detached himself, drew his weapon, and padded over to stand behind Dr. Weyerhauser. The latter glanced briefly at him, then at the Major, displeasure etched sharply across his face.

"Noo, let's go and 'ave a wee chat wif the Warden, shall we?"

Toby seized the Doctor by the shoulder, roughly yanked him out of his chair, and pushed him toward the door. With Tshambe right behind them, they exited the house and walked slowly toward Rodriguez's position. To demonstrate the JUR's intent in this situation, Toby place the barrel of his pistol against his captive's head. The astrophysicist flinched when he felt the cold steel touch him.

The Warden watched the trio approach him with an air of nonchalance.

His arms were folded across his chest, and his face was neutral. Mentally, however, he was recalling the last time he had been in a hostage situation.

That last time had been a field exercise at the Academy, but he was expected to treat it as the real thing and act accordingly. Classroom theory was one thing, but the exercise was quite another, especially when the instructor was monitoring each action closely. Each member of the class had actually participated in two field exercises, the first as a "hostage," and the second as a "negotiator." It had been Rodriguez's turn to be "negotiator," and he was understandably nervous; no one would suffer any physical harm, of course, but a misstep anywhere in the exercise meant failing the course and, quite possibly, dismissal from the Academy. The Aldebaranians were not noted for giving cadets a second chance where life-and-death situations were concerned.

The "hostage taker" had adlibbed at every opportunity, challenging the "negotiator" to make the correct response. At one point, Rodriguez had misspoken himself, and the "hostage taker" had seized on the miscue as an excuse to increase his "demands," The "negotiator" had had to spend a minute or two to regain control of the situation and negotiate a successful conclusion, but he had sweated buckets (mentally speaking) the whole time.

He had sweated more buckets afterward as Master Fresh reviewed his performance. The questions were surprisingly perfunctory, and his mentor had not once uttered a criticism of his handling of the exercise. He had, on the other hand, offered his usual caution about hasty actions and dismissed his pupil with a casual wave of the hand. Rodriguez had counted himself fortunate to escape with only that and later conducted his own review of the exercise per the previous "suggestion" of Master Fresh. Self-examination was instilled into each cadet from the very beginning of his/her training, and this cadet knew what he should do the next time he encountered a hostage-taking.

The first thing he did in the current situation was to assess the physical scene, i.e. the number of "players," their weaponry, their body postures, their facial expressions, etc., etc. and from those data formulate the correct responses. Later, he would add in tones of voice, vocabulary, and gestures. He noted that Dr. Weyerhauser was not as upset over being a hostage as an ordinary person might in the same circumstances; he concluded that the Doctor was confident that he would be rescued. Now, he glanced surreptitiously at the JUR man with the weapon at the astrophysicist's head; that one appeared to be resolute in what he was doing, and Rodriguez suspected he would pull the trigger at the least provocation. He began tapping one of the buttons on his tunic in a nervous fashion but halted after four seconds.

The other JUR man was a surprise. He was smiling like a Cheshire cat, not the usual behavior for a hostage-taker. Apparently, he was supremely confident that he would get his own way in this matter, no matter what the "negotiator" said or did. Whatever was said, or did, then, had to be directed toward this individual, and he had to be manipulated as quickly as possible. The Warden now put on *his* best smile.

"Major Tshambe, I presume?"

"Aye. Ye've 'eard o' me, then?"

"Dr. Weyerhauser has described you to a 'T'."

"'As 'e noo? And did 'e tell ee what Oi'm capable of?"

"Not in so many words. But, given the JUR's general reputation, I wouldn't be surprised by what you're capable of. The real question is, are you aware of what *I'm* capable of?"

"Given the reputytion of the Warden Service, aye. But, Oi dinna care, one wy or t'uvver."

"What do you hope to gain here?"

"Syfe passage for me and moy people, of course. If we dinna get it, Oi blow the good Doctor's brines oot. It's as simple as that."

"But you lose your hostage – and your advantage – and open yourself to retaliation."

"Na fum ee, Oi'm finkin'. Ye 'ave to protect the 'ostage fum any 'arm. It's the law."

"I have options in the manner by which I carry out the law, some of which will leave you in a bad position."

"Will thy noo? See 'ere, Warden, enough o' this small talk. Do Oi get me syfe passage, or do Oi shoot this turncoat?"

"Neither, I'm afraid. Surrender, or suffer the consequences."

Tshambe regarded Rodriguez with a mixture of disbelief and resignation, then turned to his confederate and nodded. Toby grinned wickedly and cocked the hammer of his pistol. Dr. Weyerhauser gasped audibly and stiffened. The Major gave the Warden a crooked smile. The latter raised an eyebrow and began tapping – apparently nervously – one of the buttons on his tunic. The tapping lasted no more than two seconds.

Two more seconds passed. Toby suddenly grunted, his eyes widened in surprise, and his head jerked backward. His pistol fell harmlessly to the ground, while he himself collapsed in a heap. Blood gushed from a bullet hole in his forehead.

Rodriguez looked at Tshambe sternly and drew his own pistol. The JUR man exhibited great consternation.

"The next bullet belongs to you, Major, if you don't surrender immediately."

"Ye took a loife," the other murmured. "It's not allooed."

"Take a life to save a life. It's allowed. As simple as that."

"Gor! Ye'll na foind me so easy to tyke doon."

Tshambe unexpectedly moved laterally and placed himself behind Dr. Weyerhauser. He gave the man a hard shove; off-balance, the astrophysicist stumbled forward and collided with the Warden. Both of them tumbled to the ground. The Major then wheeled and made a mad dash toward the house. As soon as he untangled himself from the Doctor, Rodriguez sat up, aimed his sidearm, and snapped off a somasol-tipped flechette. By this time, however, the target was out of range, and the flechette fell harmlessly to the ground.

"Shoot, ye barstards!" Tshambe bellowed as he bounded onto the porch. "Kill the fraggers!"

Rodriguez searched for the nearest cover and found it in the form of a nearby harvesting machine. He jumped to his feet, yanked the Doctor to his, and shoved him toward the implement.

"The Major is getting away!" the academic protested. You've got to stop him!"

"He's not going anywhere. You just keep your head down."

Instantly, a hail of gunfire erupted from the windows, and bullets sprayed the yard. Miraculously, both men ducked behind the harvester without a scratch. The gunfire continued unabatedly. Rodriguez peered cautiously around the machine and sized up the situation; then he tapped on his tunic button a few more times. Dr. Weyerhauser stared at him incredulously. The Warden gave him a tight little smile.

"My tunic has 'special' buttons too, Professor," he said by way of explanation. "I've just transmitted a coded message to Sgt. Running Deer." He paused briefly. "I sent another message thirty seconds ago, which resulted in Trooper Quinn's taking out the man with the gun to your head."

"Clever. Risky, but clever. Now what?"

"You'll see."

As if on cue, a new round of gunfire (muted) erupted, this time from the trees surrounding the house. Gamma Platoon had joined the fray!

CHAPTER TWENTY-FOUR

▼

WINS AND LOSSES

IN TERMS OF SHEER MANPOWER, Gamma Platoon was outnumbered. It had already been understaffed before the mission started, and it had suffered a few casualties on Planetoid 48. Its present complement – not counting Warden Rodriguez, Lt. Ralfo, and Sgt. Utumi – now stood at six; therefore, when the order was given to open fire, that fire was sporadic, coming as it did from widely scattered points. What the unit lacked in numbers, however, was compensated for by a renewed *esprit de corps*. It, like other Gamma Platoons on other Constabulary patrol vessels, had been the last assignment for foul-ups before discharge, and as such it was the laughing stock of the CSS *Steadfast*. With the routing of the JUR from the runaway and the prevention of a major catastrophe, the platoon had found new pride, in themselves, in each other, and in the unit as a whole.

Therefore, when they opened fire, they did so with a will, making every shot count and inflicting maximum damage on the enemy. The chief targets were the windows of the house; and, after the first ten seconds of fire, none of the windows was intact. How many casualties they had inflicted on the JUR remained to be seen, but that did not concern the troopers at the moment. They had their orders, and they carried out those orders with great professionalism.

Rodriguez was well aware of the mismatch in numbers. Via the video link on Dr. Weyerhauser's shirt which had transmitted a continuous image of the wearer's environs, he had determined the strength of the foe and planned accordingly. The Plan was to lay siege to the house until either the foe admitted the hopelessness of its position and surrendered (unlikely) or it attempted to escape at which time it would be cut down to a man. Gamma Platoon may have been outmanned, but it had superior firepower – and plenty of ammunition! – and could lay siege for as long as the Warden cared to.

After fifty seconds of firepower, Rodriguez ordered a ceasefire, then waited for a response from the JUR. Their return fire had been sporadic, hampered as they were by (1) the withering assault by the platoon, (2) a lack of defined targets at which to shoot, and (3) a small number of defensible positions from which to shoot. He would give them one more chance to surrender. Presently, the front door flung open, and a figure appeared in the doorframe, arms held high. It was the woman driver who had delivered the Doctor to her cohorts with reckless abandon.

"Dinna shoot! Dinna shoot!" she shouted. "Oi surrender!"

Rodriguez raised himself cautiously to check the woman out. She seemed to be unarmed. Nevertheless, he trained his pistol on her. He then exposed himself just high enough for her to see him and waved his arm.

"Over here then. Keep your hands where I can see them."

The woman stepped off the porch and took a few steps toward the harvester. A pair of shots issued from one of the windows and struck her in the back. She crumpled to the ground and lay still. In response, from his vantage point on the roof of one of the storage sheds, Quinn fired a volley of gunshots at the window and elicited a scream from within.

"The bastards!" Dr. Weyerhauser rasped. "They don't allow anyone to surrender."

"They'll pay for their perfidy, Professor. I promise you that."

The Warden signaled for the platoon to resume fire. Again, a hail of bullets struck the building. This time, there was no return fire by the JUR. After another fifty seconds, he ordered a halt to the assault. An eerie silence lay over the scene like a shroud, and no movement inside the house could be detected. He whipped out his vidcom and contacted Sgt. Running Deer.

"Sergeant, move your people in – *cautiously* – but keep Quinn where he is."

Abruptly, the astrophysicist gripped his arm. He faced the Reman and was startled to see wild-eyed panic written all over the man's face.

"They're not in the house anymore!" the Doctor exclaimed. "They've escaped out the back way!"

"We don't know that for sure. If they had gone out the back way, they would've run into Ralfo and Utumi, and we would've heard a commotion from that quarter."

The Doctor shook his head vehemently.

"No, they're getting away! I can't let the Major escape! I have to kill him!"

Before the Warden could stop him, the academic bolted from the harvester and loped toward the house. Inexplicably, no shots issued from the building to cut him down in mid-stride. As he approached the porch, a lone figure could be seen erupting from the line of trees; on a dead run, Cpl. Chen also headed for the porch without any regard for her own safety. Rodriguez cursed himself softly and followed after the Doctor.

*   *   *

Dr. Weyerhauser burst through the front door and scanned the room which not long ago had been his "interrogation center." The first things he noticed were the three corpses near the front and side windows. In the back of his mind, he was gratified that Gamma Platoon had scored against the enemy, even if only on a small scale. After that, he noticed a smoldering fire in the middle of the room. He looked at it wonderingly, then remembered a lecture by a JUR leader shortly after his recruitment; he had been cautioned not to leave behind any incriminating evidence at the scene of an action which could potentially lead to the identification and arrest of any of the membership. The smoldering fire told him that Major Tshambe, true to form, was burning his bridges behind him – in this case, literally.

Gunshots emanating from the rear of the building confirmed his suspicions that the remainder of the interrogation team had indeed attempted to escape and, yes, had run into Lt. Ralfo and Sgt. Utumi. He grimaced and walked quickly in that direction.

"Major?" he called out in a surprisingly calm voice. "Are you there? It's...'Stargazer.' I want to talk to you."

As he passed from the living room into the dining room, Captain Toshimuto emerged from the kitchen, pistol in hand. He was bleeding from his left shoulder.

"Ah, Doctor, ye've come back, 'ave ye? How unfortunate for ye. We've myde a decision concernin' ee."

He raised his pistol and was about to pull the trigger when Cpl. Chen entered the building in the least stealthy manner she could pull off. She trotted into the dining room, assault rifle at the ready. Worry etched deep lines into her face, but they disappeared when she spotted the Doctor. The smile quickly faded away when she spied the JUR man.

"The cavalry to the rescue, eh, Doctor? Two for the pryce o' one."

Toshimuto swung his weapon toward the greater threat. Dr. Weyerhauser reacted instinctively.

"Chen, look out!"

He gave her a hard shove, sending her staggering to one side a couple of steps. But his action now put him directly in the line of fire of Toshimuto's pistol. The latter fired two quick shots, both of which slammed into the astrophysicist's chest. He grunted and slumped to the floor. Blood smeared his brand-new shirt.

"That's 'ow we deal wif trytors, *boyo*. And this is 'ow we deal wif oppressors."

He brought his weapon to bear on the corporal. Chen, momentarily stunned by the attack on her beloved professor, shook off her paralysis and allowed her military training kick in. She twisted to one side as Toshimuto fired his pistol, and the bullets passed by harmlessly. Now she raised her weapon and with a feral expression pulled the trigger. A stream of heavy-duty cartridges tore into the JUR man's body, pushing him backwards against the far wall. Chen emptied the rifle's magazine but continued to pull the trigger in a futile effort to pour more bullets into the hated foe.

"Chen!" Warden Rodriguez called out behind her. "Stop! He's dead."

Rationality returned to the trooper, and she threw her weapon to the floor. She knelt before the Doctor, cradled his head and shoulders in her arms, and wept openly and loudly.

"Chen, is that you?" came the weak voice from the mortally wounded man. "Are you all right?"

"Oh, Professor, Professor, *why*?" she sobbed. "I was s'posed to protect *you*, not the other way around."

"I couldn't let another person die. I had too many on my conscience."

He coughed briefly, and dark red blood trickled out of his mouth.

"I don't want you to die…Mubutu. I – I *love* you."

"It's better this way, my dear. I won't have to spend the rest of my life on Xix, thinking about what I've done. This is a more fitting punishment for my crimes." He gazed into her tear-stained face. "I just hope Petra can forgive me."

He let out a long, rasping breath, and another trickle of blood oozed out. His eyes glazed over, and he became still. Chen rocked back and forth with his head in her arms and cried even more loudly.

The Warden looked away in embarrassment and frustration. He was sure he could have prevented this tragedy if only he had been thinking properly. Master Fresh would be very disappointed by his failure.

* * *

In a group of three small trees behind the house, Lt. Anafu Ralfo shifted her body for what must have been the dozenth time in order to prevent muscle cramping. She had been crouching behind a tree a scant meter in diameter and six meters from the rear entrance of the building for the past half kilosecond, waiting for – *hoping* for – something to happen. The sheer boredom of waiting had caused her mind to wander toward other, more pleasant thoughts; though this laxity in alertness might prove fatal, she could not help herself. No Pluj could. She looked forward to the end of this mission at which time she and Lixu Rodriguez would request a furlough, journey to Pluj, and start preparing for their nuptials. She knew that her parents – especially her mother – would throw themselves into the nuptial planning.

Wedding ceremonies on Pluj tended to be simple affairs, a consequence of the shift in the social order centuries before. Males had preferred long, elaborate rites, the better to impress their friends and neighbors, to establish/ improve their status in society, and to inform the females just who was the dominant force. When the plague which killed off much of the male population had run its course and left a power vacuum to be quickly filled by the females, the many changes in the way things got done on Pluj included marriage and property rights (which generally went hand-in-hand). Rather than a long, drawn-out affair, weddings consisted of a gathering of the happy couple and a select group of their closest friends as witnesses before the local civil magistrate; said magistrate then extracted promises of love, honor, and fidelity from both parties, pronounced them woman and husband, and sent them on their merry way.

Elaborate affairs occurred *after* the marriage rites. All sentient beings loved parties, and the Pluj were no exception; only the details differed from culture to culture. On Pluj, celebrations lasted three days. On the first day, the parents of the woman opened their home to one and all for a staggering feast; on the second day, the parents of the man did likewise; and on the third day, the happy couple chose a public venue which had some special meaning to them to stage yet another staggering feast. The Pluj partied from dawn to dusk – and beyond in many cases; guests came and went as they willed (often several times) and turned the event into a biological kaleidoscope.

Ralfo's wedding ceremony/celebration would be more elaborate than the norm for three reasons. First, her mother was Chief Administratrix; therefore, all of Pluj officialdom was likely to show up in order to see and be seen, and Anafu's marriage would take on the trappings of an affair-of-state to be mentioned in the annals as a Significant Event. And the imprint of the State would be made by the Administratrix herself because she would be performing the ceremony as magistrate. Second, Ralfo was marrying an off-worlder, a human to be exact; and that was sure to cause a stir since Pluj may have had sexual encounters with any number of off-world lovers but seldom encouraged any of them to "join the family." The fact that the groom was a human mitigated any real concern because (1) Pluj-human political relations were quite cordial because (2) Pluj and humans were biologically compatible and therefore could beget children. And third, she was marrying a Warden, a member of that mysterious law-enforcement elite who elicited so much awe and fear and enmity throughout the Central Spiral Collective. A Warden in the family (so to speak) might be politically beneficial to Pluj and enhance its position in the Collective.

Lt. Anafu Ralfo was beside herself with anticipation. The thought of having Lixu between her legs on a long-term basis sent a delicious thrill up her spine and made her giddy, and she had to force herself to focus on the business at hand.

Her companion, two meters away behind an equally small-diametered tree, also found his mind pre-occupied with other matters, none of which had anything to do with fending off boredom while waiting for something to happen. Sgt. Running Deer had seen fit to issue him a sidearm – "in case you need it," he had been told – and now he was examining it with all the contempt a Capellan could muster up.

Alkon warriors formed the Scout Division of the Constabulary, because few humans felt comfortable serving with them in a combat situation. And until there was a change in cultural attitudes, there they would remain. Nevertheless, all Constabulary personnel – regardless of their assignments – were required to qualify with standard Constabulary weaponry, particularly the Mu-18 assault rifle and the Mu-2 automatic pistol.[54] The Capellan complement, keen of eye, qualified easily enough, but none of them cared for the humans' weapons; they believed that firearms were not the proper tools for the True Warrior, that the test in battle came with hand-to-hand combat, and that killing one's enemy from afar was a mark of cowardice. Happily, Scouts were not issued firearms as a matter of course since they were not considered to be "combat troops," and the Capellans were mollified.

Utumi eyed his Mu-2 and hissed in resignation. He would not use it, he decided, unless he had nothing else at hand with which to fight (and an Alkon warrior could always find something at hand). He had his stilettos, his sling, and his garrote for close quarters and his bow and spear for assault situations. These had served him well before, and they would continue to serve until he could no longer wield them, i.e. when he was dead.

He shifted his weight slightly. He too was beginning to feel his muscles

---

54   Both weapons are manufactured by a wholly-owned subsidiary of the Murchison Group. Its founders married into the family and signed over the controlling interest of the company as part of the nuptials – CMT.

cramping, and he prayed to the Great Ones of Alko that the enemy would appear soon so that he could leap out at it and strike it down.

It is an extremely moot point whether the gods answer mortal prayers. Some say they just sit back and amuse themselves over the ridiculous antics of those mortals. In the present situation, the Great Ones of Alko may have performed one of their divine functions. The sound of sporadic gunfire at the front of the house, followed by faint screams snapped both the Capellan and the Pluj out of their respective pre-occupations; both tensed and focused on the door before them, waiting – *hoping* – for someone to open it and attempt an escape.

There was a brief lull, then more sporadic gunfire and more screams. Finally, after another lull, the moment Ralfo and Utumi had waited for arrived. The door burst wide open, and several figures streamed through it. Though the proper tactic would have been to wait until all of the enemy's forces were clearly visible, Sgt. Utumi's patience had run out. He moved away from the tree and shouted:

"To surrender, Oo-mans, or to die!"

"Gor!" one of the JUR men rasped. "Thy've brought a Capellan wif 'em!"

"And a Pluj!" Ralfo piped up. "Your weapons throw down, and surrender!"

"*Fuck ee, bitch!*" another voice roared, and its owner fired aimlessly into the trees.

The Constabulary contingent returned fire without hesitation (although the pistol felt awkward in Utumi's hand), and three of the terrorists dropped to the ground.

"Split up!" an authoritative voice commanded. "'Ead for whatever cover ye can foind. Move it, ye barstards!"

The remainder of the group (save one) followed their orders and split up into two smaller groups of four persons each; one headed for the village further down the line, and the other bolted for the potato field in the opposite direction.

"Sergeant, which group you do want?"

"We for re-enforcements should wait, Ralfo-go."

"But they will escape."

"Nay. No Oo-man from me can escape. I one at fifty meters can smell. But you few tracking skills to have. I your pardon for to be so blunt to beg, but it true to be."

"Well, I am going to try. One group you take; and, when with them you have dealt, backtrack and me assist. Agreed?"

The Capellan stroked his nose in the fashion of his kind to express doubt.

The Pluj had proved herself in battle, he admitted, and was a formidable warrior. But, he had been there to provide a back-up. What she was capable of on her own, he could not say. Mayhap she would measure up, mayhap not. If not, and if she were injured or slain, Rodri-go would surely question his judgment in allowing her to go off unattended. He had come to respect the Warden as a great leader and did not wish to lose his trust.

But Ralfo was his superior officer, and she was determined to pursue the quarry. What to do?

"Very well, Leftenant," he responded formally. "I short work of one group will make and you as quickly as possible will re-join."

"Which group you are taking?"

"I to think that those their way across the field to make the easiest to track. They less cover to have."

"Excellent. Carry on, Sergeant."

Ralfo was off like a shot in hot pursuit of the JUR people heading for the village. In a matter of seconds, she had disappeared from view, leaving the Capellan to stroke his nose again. He cocked his head to the left, pivoted, and trotted after his own quarry. As he had surmised, it was easy to follow; humans had a very distinctive body odor, not very pleasant most of the time, and it lingered long in the air. Only a person without a sense of smell would fail to detect it.

Unerringly, he followed the scent and soon spotted the four terrorists running as if all of the Great Ones were dogging their heels and bedeviling them with huge gouts of fire. He puckered his lips. At the pace they were maintaining, they would soon be exhausted and thus become easy prey. Under other circumstances, he might have waited until the prey actually halted before pouncing on it; he might have made some sport of it before dispatching it. But, he had not the luxury of time. He must deal with these fools rapidly and return to lend Lt. Ralfo a hand before she got into trouble. He maintained his own pace until he was less than twenty meters away. So bent on escape, none of the quartet was aware that they were being followed or that they would shortly fail in their attempt.

Even while on the run, Utumi unloosed his sling from his uniform's belt, opened a pouch hanging from the same belt, and withdrew a steel ball bearing. On Alko, he would have gathered up a handful of rocks of a suitable size to use in the sling; but, since joining the Constabulary, he had discovered better weapons in the ball bearings the engineers utilized in their machines. He slipped the ball into the sling, whirled it over his head four times, and let fly. The missile struck one of his targets at the back of its head, fragmenting the skull and driving pieces of bone into the brain. The JUR man fell without a sound; he was dead before he hit the ground.

The thud of the body of his comrade alerted the nearest terrorist to him, and he looked over his shoulder to see what had caused it. His eyes went wide with surprise, then fright, and he cried out in terror even as he reached into his pocket for his pistol. The Capellan was ready for him, however; even while his first victim was breathing his last, he was loading his sling again. He whirled, let fly, and caught the second man on his temple. The latter dropped with a grunt.

The remaining two fugitives reacted to their confederate's cry of terror predictably – with drawn weapons. It was doubtful, though, that they had ever encountered an Alkon warrior in full combat mode; if they had – and survived the encounter – they might have chosen a different tactic, e.g. abject surrender. But such was their credo that they did not consider that option and so paid for their folly with their lives. Having two targets before him of equal strength, Utumi tossed aside his slower weapon and drew his faster ones, i.e. his stilettos. He threw one after another in ambidextrous fashion with deadly accuracy, and both targets went down without having had a chance to fire a shot.

The sergeant examined each body quickly but carefully for any signs of life. Only his second victim exhibited a pulse beat, and it was weak. He activated his vidcom, tapped out a code, and was greeted by the concerned face of Sgt. Running Deer.

"Utumi! Where are you?"

"I in the field behind you to be. I four terrorists have down. One still alive to be" – here, he puckered his lips slightly – "but he medical attention to require."

"OK, I'll get the medoc over there ASAP. Where's Lt. Ralfo?"

"She…other terrorists to pursue. I to her assistance to go."

Whereas before he had been trotting, now he broke into a full gallop back the way he had come. Time was of the essence. He believed the Pluj was out of her league in her endeavor to capture four individuals at once, and she was too valuable an ally to fall victim to her self-exaggerated capability. In half the time it had taken him to down his own quarry, he returned to his original starting point and was passing it when he was halted by the sound of Warden Rodriguez's voice. The latter, after having consoled Cpl. Chen, had been examining Utumi's and Ralfo's first scores and found one still breathing. He almost missed the Capellan but for the heavy tread of footsteps through the underbrush. Utumi was making no attempt at stealth!

"Sergeant! Report!"

The warrior drew up, took a deep breath, and exhaled noisily.

"Rodri-go, I – I to Ralfo-go's aid to go. I to believe she in grave danger to be."

"And why did you let her go off on her own? That's against all the laws of tactics."

"I to know, and I...to apologize. But Lt. Ralfo headstrong to be, and she us to split up did order."

"I see. Well, this is no time for recriminations. Let's get after her and hope we're not too late."

*   *   *

Why, oh, why didn't I listen to Sgt. Utumi? He was right. I don't have the tracking skills he does.

Lt. Ralfo was berating herself for the sixth time since she began pursuing the fleeing terrorists. It seemed like a grand game to her at the time, playing cat-and-mouse; but now she wondered what had possessed her to run off as wildly as she had. Who was now the cat, and who the mouse?

The Constabulary teaches us combat troops few tracking skills. That's what the Capellans are for. And, even Wardens have been trained to track fugitives. Maybe this should change.

She surveyed her surroundings. She was now at the edge of the village of Hashimoto proper, looking down a row of private dwellings. The sameness of the layout of each plot boggled her mind. Didn't Remans have any imagination? On Pluj, no one would ever think of copying her neighbor's designs; at least one difference was noteworthy in order to make a personal statement about the occupant. And most Pluj seldom stopped at one difference but attempted to achieve as many as possible without ending up with a monstrosity on their hands. In essence, home-building had become a contest for the most innovative designs, though few were conscious of this fact.

Monotonous they might be, but these Remans structures still harbored any number of hiding places where a potential ambusher lurked, ready to leap out and overwhelm a pursuer. All she had been able to do up to this point was to travel in the same general direction as her quarry, her only clue some trampled grass. The JUR people could have split up for all she knew and hole up in separate buildings.

She approached the first home with extreme caution, looking this way and that, with her sidearm at the ready. Were the terrorists now peering out a window and waiting for her to pass by in order to catch her in a pincer move? She examined all the windows of this house, upstairs as well as downstairs, but failed to see anything but a reflection of the external environment. Briefly, she considered the bold move of walking up to the back door and knocking on it to gain someone's attention and to interrogate that someone. There were four major problems with that approach. One, whoever lived here might not be at home, and so she would be wasting her time while the terrorists put distance between her and them. Two, whoever lived here might not be willing to answer the knock out of fear of being arrested for complicity, and she would again be wasting time. Three, whoever lived here might be sympathetic to the JUR cause (and she was sure many Remans did support them in some fashion – wasn't Dr. Weyerhauser a case in point?), and so she might be lulled into a trap. And four, whoever answered the door might well be the terrorists themselves, ready to shoot her the moment the door opened. No, she wasn't going to take that approach if she could possibly help it.

But, maybe a quick peek through one of the windows…

No! That was even more foolish.

I could use Sgt. Utumi's sense of smell right now. He could sniff out humans just as a Dunian canine could and go unerringly to where they were hiding.

Feeling even more frustrated than before, she proceeded to the next house, scanning for any sign of movement, either outside or inside, but was disappointed. Out of the corner of her eye, she discerned some activity in the next lot. She froze and attempted to keep a low profile while she investigated the activity. On the surface, it appeared to be a farmer's wife (in traditional Reman costume of a plain, ankle-length dress buttoned down the front and a large face-concealing bonnet) hanging her wash on a clothesline. It seemed innocent enough, but that could be a deception, a front to throw her off her guard and set her up for an ambush. What to do?

Ralfo decided to skirt this house at a safer distance, all the while keeping an eye on the housewife for any change in behavior of a threatening sort. None came, and she continued on. As she approached the fourth building in the row, a nagging suspicion entered her head. There had been something out of context about that housewife after all – but what? She looked back. The housewife had disappeared. Yet, she could have sworn that the woman had been wearing boots! Now, Ralfo reversed course and crept back to the suspect house.

Without warning, something struck her between the shoulder blades, causing great pain. She whirled about just in time to see a Reman male in the JUR uniform emerge from behind a bush with a brick in his hand. Another brick lay at her feet. She sublimated the pain in her back and aimed her pistol at the terrorist.

"In the name of the Constabulary, you I order to surrender."

"Na bloody loikely, ye Pluj bitch!" the man replied.

Someone grabbed her from behind, swung her around, and rammed a fist against her jaw. Instinctively, she shifted her weight which softened the blow, but the force was still sufficient to stagger her backwards. In the process, her pistol slipped out of her hand and fell to the ground. She faced her new attackers, three in all, and one was still wearing the garb of the "housewife." All of them were brandishing firearms.

"Do we get rid of 'er noo, Myjor?" one of them asked the man in the housewife's clothes.

"Aye, but dinna use your guns. We dinna want to alert anyone to oor whereaboots." Major Tshambe actually chuckled. "Fists only for this one, Oi'm finkin'."

It may be fairly said that Pluj were no strangers to physical attack, although they tended to minimize the chance of it wherever and whenever possible. Where and when it was unavoidable, they had one simple option: counter-attack. It may have been an exercise in futility, leading to the same inevitable conclusion, but Pluj believed in going down fighting and inflicting as much damage on the assailants as possible.

Ralfo steeled herself, let loose a banshee-like yell, and literally leaped up at the trio in front of her. The action took the JUR by surprise (as it was supposed to do), and they hesitated. That hesitation was all she needed in order to inflict maximum damage. As she rose into the air, she swung her left leg outward and struck one of the terrorists square in the face. He fell backwards, cursing, his nose bleeding profusely. When she reached the apex of her leap, she twisted twenty-five degrees and kicked at a second man. The blow caught him on the temple, and he dropped like a rock. Her counter-attack ended there, however. Major Tshambe recovered from the surprise move, quickly picked up the brick lying on the ground, and flung it at the now-descending figure. The missile slammed against the back of her head; she crumpled to the ground unconscious.

"Myjor," one of his underlings announced, "Oi see two Constabulary toipes approachin'. Gor! It's the golder and the Capellan!"

"We canna wyste any more toime then. Forget the Pluj bitch and mome it!"

*　　　*　　　*

"You that scream did hear, Rodri-go? It like an attacking *aa* did sound."

"That, Sergeant, was the cry of an attacking *Pluj*. Which means Lt. Ralfo is in a hand-to-hand-combat mode. We'd better pick up the pace."

Rodriguez and Utumi had just rounded the storage sheds and were about to cross the thirty-plus meters which separated the manager's farm from the outskirts of the Village of Hashimoto proper when they heard Ralfo's war cry. On the move, the Warden had informed Sgt. Running Deer of the dead and wounded JUR members at the back of the house and of his intent to pursue the remaining enemy forces. Though he wanted to pick up the pace, that was easier said than done. The space between the farm and the village was not entirely open; Remans had learned to utilize every square meter of ground for growing food. What space was not devoted to their assigned crops was turned into truck gardens for growing produce and herbs for local consumption. The Constabulary duo thus had to step over row after row of small green plants with variously-configured leafage and were prevented from moving on a dead run. The Capellan had the easier time of it, however, because of his race's greater height, and he had to slow down occasionally to allow his human companion to catch up.

After what seemed like ages, both arrived at the house on the edge of the village. Utumi examined the ground minutely and judged that several boot-clad individuals had recently come this way and one set of tracks – smaller than the others – had to be that of Lt. Ralfo. He then broke into a trot in the direction of the footprints. The Warden pushed himself to keep from falling behind.

Even at a distance of forty meters, the warrior had spotted the crumpled-up form of the Pluj. All of his senses went to full alert, and he unsheathed one of his stilettos; but he did not detect any other sentient beings in the vicinity. As he approached the still figure, he berated himself again. This was his fault; he should have disobeyed her order and accompanied her. Instead of her suffering an attack on her person, her would-be attackers would instead have been lying there, either dead or wounded. He knelt down and touched a fingertip to her neck. Vaguely, he was aware of the Warden at his back.

For Lixu Rodriguez, the sight of his betrothed was not merely tragic but *devastating* as well. She was bleeding profusely from a head wound. He knelt beside her, tears trickling down his cheeks, and brushed one of her cheeks with his fingertips. Her flesh was still warm to the touch, and he gave thanks to Kum'halla that she was still alive.

"I no pulse did feel, Rodri-go. I – I truly sorry to be."

"She's not dead, Utumi-go. Pluj have different pulse points, even though they're first cousins to humans. Check behind her ear."

The Capellan did so and cocked his head to the right, his kind's expression of surprise.

"Aye, there a pulse to be, but it weak to be."

"Call the medoc and get her over here on the double. I'm going to search for the people responsible for this."

"I with you should go."

"You stay here and watch over Ralfo. That's an order, Sergeant."

Utumi hissed in resignation.

Rodriguez wiped away the tears and stood up. On an impulse, he bent down again, retrieved Ralfo's service pistol, and tucked it into his belt. Then he was off, grim determination in both his face and in his eyes.

He supposed that the Capellan was the better tracker since the skills involved were drummed into each male child almost as soon as it learned to walk. Still, he was not exactly a rank amateur in that department. Tracking a fugitive through all types of terrain had been part of the curriculum at the Academy, and the Aldebaranians put the cadets through their paces just as rigorously as they did with any other aspect of the training. The instructors learned early on that this Dunian had an edge over his classmates. Having grown up in Dunia's Administrative District #17, he had had plenty of opportunity to engage in tracking activities, following in the footsteps (as it were) of countless generations of his ancestors; and each summer, his father and grandfather would take him camping and pose a scenario in which he was expected to practice different survival skills. As it happened, he enjoyed these little exercises as much as exploring caves and took great pride in successfully completing them.

He had had to conceal his pride while at the Academy, of course. The Aldebaranians always cautioned against overconfidence and smugness. On more than one occasion, Master Fresh had given him a sharp rebuke on this score, not so much with words as with a certain facial expression or gesture. Despite this, Cadet Rodriguez acquired a reputation for being the best tracker in the history of the Academy; and, in his final year, the instructors called upon him to conduct exercises with the younger cadets.

The trail he was now following was ridiculously easy, almost an insult to his skills. The fugitives had made no attempt to conceal themselves but, rather, to escape the area in the shortest time possible. Where vegetation grew, it had been recklessly trampled down; where bare ground lay, it revealed clear sets of footprints. The terrorists were headed toward the opposite end of the village – a sensible move inasmuch as the community's shuttle launch-pad was located there. Therefore, tracking the JUR was as much a race against time as it was a pursuit of justice, and the Warden had to win it if he hoped to avenge the injuries done to his fiancé.

In this regard, he abandoned his respect for whatever edible vegetation might be growing here and there and trampled it with the same recklessness his quarry was exhibiting. If a few dozen potatoes were instantly mashed, what of it? Someone might not get his daily starch for one meal, but (s)he was not likely to starve to death.

A third of a kilosecond later, he approached the launch-pad and went into a stealth mode. He crouched down and slinked up to a tree at the edge of the tarmac; when he peeked around, he immediately spotted the JUR people. One of them – Major Tshambe – seemed to be arguing vehemently with one of the villagers. Rodriguez was too far away to hear distinctly anything being said, but the wild gesticulations provided all the meaning one might need.

Presently, the villager slapped something into the hand of the terrorist leader and walked away in obvious disgust. The latter and his three cohorts walked briskly toward one of the parked shuttles. The Warden had to act quickly and decisively; they were all easy targets and with luck, he could take them all down before they had a chance to enter the aircraft. They were all out of range of his own non-lethal pistol and so he pulled Ralfo's pistol from his belt, took careful aim at the Major, and began to squeeze the trigger.

(WHAT DO YOU, PUPIL?)

The "voice" in his head came so suddenly and so forcefully that Rodriguez gasped in shock and dropped the pistol. He fell back against the tree, wide-eyed, and tried to identify the voice. Understanding was not long in coming.

"M-m-master Fresh?" he whispered.

(AND WHO ELSE WOULD I BE, LACK-WIT? I HAVE ASKED YOU A QUESTION. I DEMAND AN ANSWER.)

"I – I am attempting to apprehend suspects in acts of terrorism, Master."

('APPREHEND'? DID I NOT SEE A WEAPON IN YOUR HAND? AND WAS NOT THAT WEAPON A *LETHAL* ONE? IS THIS YOUR DEFINTION OF 'APPREHEND'?)

"They – they have committed heinous crimes, Master. They must be dealt with severely."

(AND SO YOU HAVE ASSUMED THE DUTIES OF JUDGE, JURY, AND EXECUTIONER. AS I RECALL, YOUR TRAINING DID NOT INCLUDE THESE DUTIES. THE POWER OF ARREST IS YOURS, YOUNG WARDEN, AND NO OTHER. NOW TELL ME: WHAT IS THE FIRST PRINCIPLE OF THE ENLIGHTENMENT?)

Rodriguez swallowed hard. He knew a reprimand when he heard one, having heard more than a few from his mentor. And he knew he deserved one.

"The First Principle, Master, is the Sanctity of All Life. We must not take sentient life needlessly."

(IS THEN THE ENLIGHTENMENT A LIE?)

"No, Master! The Enlightenment is the way to right thinking."

(SO HOW DO YOU CORRELATE ITS PRINCIPLES WITH YOUR ACTIONS?)

"I – I cannot, Master. I have…erred – grievously. I beg forgiveness."

(I HAVE NOT THE POWER TO FORGIVE, PUPIL. YOU MUST LEARN TO FORGIVE YOURSELF. THE PEACE OF KUM'HALLA BE WITH YOU.)

"The peace of Kum'halla be with you as well, Master."

The slight discomfort Rodriguez had experienced when Master Fresh's "voice" first came into his head disappeared as quickly as it had appeared. He was now aware of perspiration trickling down his face. He took several deep breaths to calm himself.

He felt ashamed. He had come very close to violating his oath of office and destroying his career because of a fit of pique. Seeing the injuries done to Anafu had produced a wellspring of murderous rage, and he had had no other thought than to execute those responsible without any regard for the law which he was sworn to uphold. Master Fresh was letting him off easy, he believed, but he knew that he had a long way to go before he could forgive himself.

He turned his attention to the launch-pad. The JUR people were nowhere to be seen, and one of the shuttles was missing. In the brief time he had been "communicating" with his mentor, the opportunity to end this mission here and now had slipped away. Dejectedly, he picked himself up and began walking back to the farmyard.

The chase was still on.

CHAPTER TWENTY-FIVE

▼

MISSION ACCOMPLISHED

WHEN THE WARDEN RETURNED TO the farm manager's house, he discovered that a Constabulary medical-evacuation shuttle was already on the premises and that its personnel were either treating the wounds of the injured or placing the dead in body bags. Of the former, there were only three: two JUR members and Lt. Ralfo. Rodriguez first sought out Sgt. Running Deer and found him lounging on the porch of the house along with most of Gamma Platoon; the non-com was in an uncharacteristic jovial mood, laughing and exchanging "war stories." The only one not participating in the banter was Cpl. Chen, who sat by herself, still overwrought by the death of Dr. Weyerhauser. At the Warden's approach, Running Deer jumped to his feet and assumed a more serious demeanor.

"How many casualties did we suffer, Sergeant?"

"Just three, sir – if you count the Professor."

"Three? Who's the third?"

The Dunian grimaced.

"Quinn scraped his knee sliding off the roof of the storage shed. I'm sure he'll want a Red Palm[55] for it."

"He'll get one. And I'm putting all of you in for commendations."

"Thank you, sir. The platoon will appreciate being recognized for something other than red zoning."

"They've earned it. This was a tough mission."

---

55 A medal awarded to military personnel injured in the line of duty. Shaped like a human hand, it is fashioned from brass and fired to give it a crimson color – CMT.

"Aye." The non-com hesitated a moment, then faced his troopers. "Gamma Platoon! Fall in!"

The troopers were startled by the unexpected order but hastily scrambled to their feet nevertheless and came to attention. Running Deer about-faced.

"Platoon – present...*arms!*"

He and the rest threw up their best salute. Rodriguez was taken aback by this remarkable display. Given the enmity that most Constabulary personnel exhibited toward the members of the Warden Service, a gesture of respect was the last thing he ever hoped for from anyone in the ranks. He was momentarily at a loss for words.

"Platoon – order...*arms!*" the sergeant commanded. "May I say, sir, on behalf of Gamma Platoon, that it's been a...privilege to serve with you?"

Rodriguez's surprise grew, but he completed the ritual and saluted back.

"Thank you, Sergeant. It's been a...pleasure to serve with *you*."

"Like most troopers, I didn't have much use for Wardens. Always thought they were a stuck-up bunch of fraggers." The Warden raised an eyebrow. "I'm – *we're*, the platoon and I, are beginning to think there might be some real troopers in your bunch – if they're anything like you. You gave us our dignity back when no one else would. You made us proud to be soldiers again. We'd – we'd like to continue serving with you – if possible, sir."

"I'm afraid that's not up to me. But, for what's it worth, if I ever need back-up again, I'll request re-assignment for you and the others. Now, if you'll excuse me, I'd like to check on Lt. Ralfo."

"Aye, sir. Um, with your permission, one of us will visit her every day whenever you can't do it."

"That's very kind of you, Sergeant. Anafu would appreciate that."

He saluted the platoon again and walked briskly away.

The medical officer in charge was a New Swiss. Like all of her ethnicity, she towered over most sentient beings in the Collective, Capellans being the only exceptions; and, like all of her ethnicity, she exercised authority as easily and as efficiently as if it were her right. Here, she "commanded" a team of four doctors, each of whom represented a specific specialty and evaluated the wounded and the dying much like an assembly-line-oriented manufacture, assisted by eight nurses. Upon arriving at the scene of carnage, the team had automatically set up a triage and begun examining each body as it was brought to them. In the present instance, they hadn't had all that much to do since there were only four injuries to treat; for the most part, they had directed the Constabulary troopers where to stack the corpses.

Rodriguez approached the MOIC in the same fashion as he did other Constabulary officers. The MOIC – whose name tag identified her as "Major Keller" – regarded him just as coolly.

"Greetings, Major," he said in a neutral voice. "Not much work for you this time, eh?"

"Considering that we're dealing with the JUR, I'd be surprised otherwise." She shook her head in disgust. "What a shoot-out this was!"

"You have no idea. What's the prognosis on Lt. Ralfo?"

"She took quite a blow to the head. Pluj aren't known for their rugged physiology. My initial prognosis is that she slipped into a coma in order to ameliorate the trauma. I won't know for sure until I get her back to Base and make a more thorough examination."

The Warden's heart sank. His dear Anafu – in a coma! From what little he knew of that medical condition, she might recover in a kilosecond or a megasecond or a gigasecond, or she might not recover at all. And, if she did recover, how might her traumatic experience affect her psyche? Admittedly, he knew little about Pluj psychology. She might return to normal – or what passed for "normal" for her kind, or she might become a stranger to him, rejecting his love and their hopes for a life together. He fought to hold back the tears; it would not do to appear as weak as other humans in the face of tragedy – especially in the presence of a Constabulary officer.

"How about the injured Remans? Can I talk to them?"

"The one with the gunshot wound is in critical condition. I've sedated him, but I'm not optimistic about his chances for recovery. The one with the head injury is still unconscious. Sorry, Warden, you won't be able to interrogate either one just yet."

Was that a smirk which passed across Major Keller's face for the space of a microsecond? Rodriguez wouldn't have put it past her. The medical profession was one of only two groups of beings (the other was the ecclesiastic establishment) which could legitimately refuse to accede to a Warden's request for co-operation, and this doctor knew it. Well, there were other ways of gaining information. He shrugged and asked to see Lt. Ralfo.

The Pluj was already in the medvac, strapped to a gurney. (Subconsciously, Constabulary personnel were accorded preferential treatment.) The Warden swallowed hard when he gazed upon her paler-than-normal face. Take away that head wound, and she might have seemed like a small child fast asleep. What was taking place inside her brain? Was her body busy with the healing process? Was it finding the task overwhelming? Was Anafu fighting the fight of her life to overcome the trauma she had experienced? Was she now struggling her way back to the world of the living?

He touched her cheek lightly with his fingertips. It hadn't been so long ago that he had seen the mischievous grin on her face, listened to her elfin laughter, and smelled the delicious aroma of her body. Was that to be no more? Had he lost her forever? Now the tears did come, and he did not hold them back. For the space of a quarter of a kilosecond, he gave his emotions free reign.

Damn the JUR! he swore. *Damn them to Hell!*

He would obey the Principles of the Enlightenment, but he would also have his vengeance. Silently, he promised Anafu that her attackers would pay for their sadism.

He clambered out of the medvac and noted that Keller and her team were finishing up their "paperwork" before returning to the Constabulary hospital in New Lagos. She regarded him as coolly as before.

"Who will notify the next of kin for her?" she asked matter-of-factly.

"I will. I'm a close friend of the family" – that elicited a raised eyebrow from the New Swiss – "and her mother will appreciate hearing the news from me rather than from some faceless bureaucrat."

"Good fortune to you, Warden."

"Thank you, Major."

He wheeled and rejoined Sgt. Running Deer. The non-com had returned to his unaccustomed camaraderie with the rest of the platoon but turned serious again at the Warden's approach.

"Sergeant, I'm going into the village to interrogate one of the locals. I'll take Chen with me."

"Aye, sir. Are you sure you don't want the rest of us?"

"Chen is all I need for this job. Meanwhile, you get the platoon back to the shuttle. Then contact Air Traffic Control in New Lagos and ask if they've got a track on a shuttle leaving this vicinity."

"Aye, sir."

Rodriguez strolled over to Chen, still moping. Her face was as rigid as stone, and her eyes were red from prolonged crying. She was staring off into space, seeing nothing. But, as the Warden pulled up in front of her, her military training kicked in; she jumped to her feet and came to attention.

"I'm sorry about the Professor, Corporal. He proved himself to be a hero in the end. I'll put that in my report."

"Thank you, sir," she murmured.

"I've got a job for you. Some of the JUR – including this Major Tshambe the Professor wanted to kill – escaped. I'm going to question the manager of the village's shuttle launch-pad, and I need you to help persuade him to co-operate."

Chen's face hardened.

"I'll be *very* persuasive, sir."

"Good. Let's go."

It may be fairly said that Wardens did not require assistance in persuading people to talk. They had their own powers of persuasion, and usually those powers were sufficient to wring information out of even the most recalcitrant of "interviewees." Those powers derived not from any actual ability but from the perception on the part of the general populace of what that ability was. The conventional wisdom was that Wardens could read minds and therefore determine whether or not a person was telling the truth. Needless to say, the Service neither confirmed nor denied the rumors but employed them to best advantage.

What Rodriguez was attempting to do was to snap Corporal Chen out of her black mood and return her to some semblance of functionality. By giving her a task which could be perceived as revenge for the murder of Dr. Weyerhauser, he had made a good start. It remained to be seen if he could keep her focused.

The walk down the main street of the Village of Hashimoto produced predictable reactions – re-enforced by the awe Wardens provoked in ordinary mortals. The few inhabitants who were on the street halted to stare at the Constabulary duo in silence, pained expressions on their faces. They knew that the only reason the law enforcers were here was to seek out the JUR; and they resented the presence because they were powerless to prevent it. The Warden took note but maintained his pace. He also observed a number of faces peeping out of windows, dark expressions upon them all, and lips which formed bitter words. Whether they were relieved that he paid them no attention was a moot point.

Presently, Rodriguez and Chen arrived at the launch-pad office. The former pounded on the door authoritatively. After the space of a few seconds, it opened slightly, and a single suspicion-filled eye peered out. The Warden flashed his badge at the eye for good measure, and the eye blinked nervously.

"I'm Warden (L1) Rodriguez," he announced sternly, "and I wish to speak to you."

"What aboot?" a husky voice asked.

Chen stepped forward and gave the door a hard shove. It swung open, and the sound of a body thudding to the floor followed. She stepped inside and glared at the prone figure, now with fright written on his face.

"We'll quest here, fragger!" she growled. "All you have to do is be a beamer!"

"Sy, ye canna just barge in loike this. Oi've got roights, ye know."

Chen bent down, seized the fellow by his coveralls, and yanked him to his feet. Rodriguez blinked in surprise; he hadn't thought this slight woman would have had the strength to manhandle anyone. Perhaps she was full of adrenaline!

"And where d'ya think you'll lock on to a green-zone slammer, fragger?" she responded, pushing her face into his and staring daggers at him. "My

Warden here has got the roberts to do what needs to be done. I'm giving you a clear channel to sync, double-mome. Copy?"

"That's enough, Corporal," the Warden interrupted. "You're frightening the poor man. I'm sure he'll be happy to co-operate." He narrowed his eyes. "Won't you?"

The manager swallowed compulsively but nodded in acquiescence.

"Fine. First question: a shuttle departed from here two kilos ago. Four men were aboard. Who were they?"

"Um, some o' the locals. Thy went to New Lagos for supploies."

"Those 'farmers' were wearing JUR uniforms. Would you care to re-phrase your answer?"

The Reman became tight-lipped, but perspiration began to form on his forehead. Rodriguez turned to his companion.

"Cpl. Chen, this…gentleman is not being very co-operative after all. What do you suggest we do?"

The non-com slipped her service knife from its sheath and held it up before her. What little light there was in the room glinted off the shiny blade. She grinned wickedly. The manager shrank back a step.

"Let me unball the fragger, sir. He'll sing soprano from now on, but he'll sing."

"Why, Corporal, you know I detest physical violence. I have a better method." He regarded the Reman coolly. "I'll use a mind probe on you, my friend. I'll rip the information I want out of your mind; and the more you resist, the more pain you'll feel."

"Na! Na! Ye canna do that!" the other screeched. "It's – it's…in'uman!"

The Warden merely opened his eyes wide, a gesture meant to suggest that he was initiating a mind probe. It was a colossal bluff on his part. He could no more explore a person's mind than he could raise the Secretariat from its foundations by the power of thought alone. He was counting on the reputation Wardens had acquired in order to intimidate the Reman sufficiently and cause him to talk freely and at length. The latter's face turned ashen, and his breath came in short gasps. If he were experiencing any discomfort from the "mind probe," it was purely psychosomatic in origin, precisely the effect Rodriguez had hoped for.

"All roight!" the manager whined. "Oi'll tell ee anyfing ye want to know! Just sty oot o' me 'ead!"

"See, Chen, physical violence wasn't necessary, was it? Start talking, you."

The Reman admitted that the four individuals in question were indeed members of the JUR and that they had wanted a shuttle to return to New Lagos. He had argued against the request on the grounds that compliance would bring the authorities down upon the Village of Hashimoto. Not everyone here was sympathetic to the JUR. The leader of the group, who had identified himself as "Major Tshambe," threatened him with retaliatory measures for being a "collaborytor" if he didn't hand over the operating code for a shuttle. He had made one last protest but surrendered the code in the end. To the question of where exactly in New Lagos the group might be headed, the manager was vague. He knew of a "safe house" on Katanga Boulevard on the outskirts of the capital; he didn't know the street number, only that it was between Sixth and Seventh Streets. Then he fell silent.

"Now, that wasn't so difficult, was it?" the Warden smiled insincerely.

"Fuck ee, ye barstard!" the Reman murmured.

"Corporal, call Sgt. Running Deer and have him pick us up – and our "friend" here. We've got a date in New Lagos."

"Whoy me? Oi co-operyted, aye?"

"Yes, but it wouldn't do to let you get anywhere near a vidcom and send out a warning to anyone, would it?"

*   *   *

In the long history of sentience in the Milky Way Galaxy (and most likely in other galaxies), each rising culture has gone through a period – sometimes brief, more often lengthy – of social stratification. Classes of people were not necessarily ordered in the same fashion from one culture to another or from one era to another, but they were most assuredly ordered by the strictest of regulations – either by law or by custom – to insure that no one strayed beyond his/her bounds and therefore violated the mores of his/her society. However a culture was ordered, the class at the top of the heap generally oversaw the regulating and hired others to enforce the rules. Histories have been replete with the methods employed in such regulating, ranging from social ostracism to brutal suppression.

One of the major consequences of social stratification was the urban-rural divide. Cities have historically been the centers of economic wealth, political power, and cultural regulation; the villages and hamlets have been the homes of the poor, the powerless, and the regulated. The classes at the top of the social order tended to build their homes in the cities (or very close to them) in order to display their wealth, power, and regulatory ability more efficiently, although in some societies they also maintained country estates as a further show of high status. Always, however, they possessed the best land and left the dregs to the lower classes huddled in their small huts/cottages. With wealth, power, and regulatory authority came ostentation; that is to say, the upper classes surrounded themselves with all manner of luxury goods, the best food and drink, the most modern transport, and the largest and most elaborately decorated domiciles. Even the most casual observer could deduce the social class of any given individual simply by examining the exterior of his/her residence and its location in the city.

Homo sapiens sapiens has been no exception to the rule of social stratification or the urban-rural divide. Even in those supposedly "egalitarian" societies, someone was always at the top and someone else was at the bottom. The former was an urbanite and the latter a ruralite; the sole difference was that it was easier to move up the ladder through education, training, and/or innate skill. In some societies, however, certain segments of the population actually *chose* to remain poor, powerless, and regulated. Either because of religious scruples or a disdain for ostentation or a desire to preserve the environment in a pristine state, these simple folk rejected the concept of social stratification entirely, lived unostentatiously, and regulated themselves. They were often divided, marginalized, and/or ignored, but it mattered little to them.

When *homo sapiens sapiens* went to the stars, it took some of its social baggage along as well. Thanks to the "Six Weeks' Party" on Dunia, humans had finally learned to live with each other and form a more or less egalitarian community. But not completely. The old ways were hard to shed and still popped up now and then and here and there.

Remus was one such "now and then" and "here and there." The city folk lived ostentatiously (relatively speaking) while the country folk chose to live simply. The divide was evident in the houses each group selected for itself; the former built somewhat larger and more elaborate dwellings, and the latter smaller and unpretentious ones. The closer one moved toward the center of power, i.e. the capital of New Lagos, the less subtle were the differences in social class.

The vicinity of Katanga Boulevard between Sixth and Seventh Streets was a case in point. In another time and another place, the residents might have been labeled "middle-class" – neither rich nor poor, neither powerful nor powerless, neither more or less regulated. In a supposedly classless society, they would have been considered..."comfortable."

At the intersection of Katanga Boulevard and Sixth Street, a robot street sweeper moved slowly and methodically in one direction and then another one. Pedestrians paid little attention to it, for it was a common sight in a community which prided itself (as New Lagos did) on keeping its environs clean and tidy. Those pedestrians might have been shocked to learn that this particular street sweeper possessed "special equipment" quite unrelated to its primary function.

The "special equipment" was an ultra-sensitive listening device which, when aimed at a given building, could eavesdrop on any and all conversations of those inside. Warden Rodriguez had contacted the New Lagos Ministry of Public Safety prior to departing from the Village of Hashimoto and made an emergency request, under his special authority, for the device to be installed and deployed by the time he and his team arrived at the city. The Ministry hemmed and hawed for a few seconds – resenting the heavy hand of the Warden Service – until Rodriguez flashed his badge, and that was the end of the matter. He had been assured that the "snoop phone" would be in place within the space of three kiloseconds. In the Warden's unspoken opinion, that wasn't soon enough, but he had other concerns on his mind to argue the point.

While waiting for the "snoop phone," he directed the troop carrier's pilot to circle the neighborhood in order to spot any physical activity which might provide a clue as to the whereabouts of the fugitives. The carrier's powerful vidcom detected nothing out of the ordinary, only the normal street and sidewalk traffic. Yet, the Warden kept Chen at the monitor for no other reason than to keep her occupied. When he was informed of the arrival of the specially-equipped street sweeper, he re-assigned her to the "snoop phone's" audio pick-up.

As the street sweeper rumbled on in its slow and methodical fashion, Rodriguez fidgeted in his seat, waiting impatiently for the telltale sounds of fugitives conversing with each other. And, all the while, he tried not to think about Anafu Ralfo lying in a hospital bed, between life and death. He had had many anxious moments at the Academy as he waited for Master Fresh to pass judgment on his recent performances and decision-making. But all of those sessions together could not compare, in terms of intensity, with what he was experiencing now. He needed something to occupy himself with even more than Chen did.

Abruptly, the non-com jerked upright in her seat, turned up the volume of her headphones, and narrowed her eyes in concentration.

"Sir!" she called out. "I think I've got something!"

Rodriguez was out of his chair in an instant and covered the distance in two giant strides. Chen handed him the headphones, and he too concentrated on the pick-up.

"...until dark,'" an authoritative voice was saying. "Then Maxie will pick us up in 'is delivery van."

"We dinna loike this fraggin' wytin', Myjor," another voice whined. "Each second we're 'oled up 'ere brings that fraggin' golder closer to us."

"It canna be 'elped. If we leave..."

The transmission faded away as the street sweeper moved out of range. Rodriguez grinned mirthlessly.

"We've got them, Corporal. Which house are they in?"

Chen studied the visual pick-up a moment, then pointed at the image.

"That brick house, sir, on the north side of Second Street, third from the corner."

"Good work, Corporal." She nodded in acquiescence of the praise. The Warden pivoted. "Sgt. Running Deer!"

"Sir!"

"Get the platoon ready to go. We're going down!"

"Aye, sir! All right, you miserable excuses for troopers, you heard the man. Mome it!"

The Warden directed the pilot to land the carrier in the middle of the street in front of the targeted building. The sight of a rapidly descending Constabulary craft was enough to alarm all the civilians in the vicinity. Those who lived in the neighborhood immediately retreated indoors. Passersby ran in all directions to avoid being squashed. The few land vehicles present screeched to a halt, made U-turns, and sped back the way they had come (one roared through the intersection against the signal and collided with a cross-bound vehicle). The carrier landed in a completely deserted street, its warning lights flashing blue.[56]

Gamma Platoon spilled out of the carrier, weapons at the ready, and assumed the standard assault mode. Sgt. Running Deer barked orders, deploying his meager force in as strategic a fashion as he could; the troopers fanned out to cover all sides of the house. The front door flew open, and a middle-aged man raced out with hands held up high. The sound of breaking glass accompanied him, followed by gunshots. The man pitched forward and fell to the ground. The platoon returned fire even as they ducked for whatever cover was available. One trooper was not as quick as he should have been; he took a bullet in the chest and died instantly.

As the Warden's suggestion, Cpl. Chen seized a grenade launcher. As soon as she had found suitable cover (a tree), she loaded it with a somazol grenade and peeked around. Sporadic gunfire continued to come from the house while steady fire entered it. Chen aimed the launcher and sent a grenade flying through the broken window. In her mind's eye, she "saw" the grenade fall to the floor, split open, and discharge its contents – the unconsciousness-rendering somazol in its gaseous form. At once, the gunfire from the building ceased. Running Deer ordered the platoon to close in.

---

56 Humans have historically associated the color red as a symbol of danger. This has not been the case with alien races whose optical apparatus is different. In an early session of the CSC's Grand Assembly, the color blue as a danger symbol was agreed upon as it had been determined to be visible equally by all the races in the Collective. Needless to say, this arbitrary decision – like much else in the "new order" – required a long while to take hold – CMT.

390 | By Charlton Clayes and C. Malcolm Trowbridge, PhD.

The troopers moved in slowly, not out of fear of being shot at but of allowing the somazol to dissipate and avoiding its effects themselves. Rodriguez was right behind them, his own weapon thrust out before him. Abruptly, off to his right, he heard Quinn cry out and alert the others that two of the fugitives had exited out the back door. Gunshots came in rapid succession, then silence. The Warden and Running Deer loped toward the scene of battle and discovered Quinn on the ground gripping his left leg, now oozing blood. A JUR man lay six meters away, lying in a pool of blood.

"The – other one – went – that way," Quinn gasped out and pointed in the direction of the city center. "The – one I shot – called him – 'Major.'" He winced in pain. "That fragger – shot *me*!"

Rodriguez peered off into the distance and spotted a figure on a dead run. The figure was wearing a JUR uniform.

"Take charge here, Sergeant," he said quietly. "I'm going after that... 'fragger.'"

"Wait up, sir. I'll get someone to go with you."

"Don't bother. I won't waste another second. This one belongs to me, and to me alone."

"Very well. Good luck, sir."

I don't need luck, Running Deer, he thought savagely. *Just stamina.*

His training at the Academy had taught him many things concerning the pursuit of suspects and fugitives. The principles had been pounded into his head as much as any other instruction by the unrelenting Aldebaranians. But, Cadet Rodriguez had formulated some principles of his own based upon his observations and experiences during his childhood in the mountains of Administrative District #17. First and foremost, always maintain a pace which will both keep the target in sight and avoid tiring oneself out. Secondly, allow the target to tire *himself* out. And, thirdly, immobilize the target immediately in order to avoid last-second treachery.

In the present instance, Principle #1 was easy to apply. Thanks to New Lagos' being built on a hillside, one could look up and down and view much of the city at a distance, and that view included anyone who was out and about. The Warden watched his target dashing up Katanga Boulevard as fast as he could. At the pace *he* was maintaining, he'd tire himself out in short order. For his part, Rodriguez assumed a fast trot. Even though the target was keeping a large distance between them, he was always in sight.

Two streets from Sixth Street, the target elected to cross the intersection against the traffic flow. The foolhardy action produced much screeching of brakes and honking of horns – and no little cursing from irate motorists – and the target nearly was struck twice in the process. Worse luck for him, his rash interface with heavy traffic sufficed to close the gap between pursuer and pursued. Consequently, it spurred the pursued to greater effort. Meanwhile, the pursuer held to his own pace.

Instead of continuing up the hill, the target abruptly turned left and ran down the cross street, all the while examining each house he passed. At one point, he slowed to catch his breath, then went up to the door of the house in front of him and pounded on it furiously. Presently, the door opened to reveal a middle-aged woman with apprehension and shock etched across her face. The Warden was too far away to hear what was being said, but the gesticulations employed – threatening by the target, negative by the homeowner – told him all he needed to know. After two deciseconds, the charade ended when the woman slammed the door in the target's face. The latter scanned Katanga Boulevard and spotted Rodriguez gaining ground. He broke into a dead run again and headed toward the next boulevard.

At this next intersection, the target resumed his upward path but went only one street before turning right and seeking out another house. What he hoped to accomplish, the Warden neither knew nor cared. With a steady pace and controlled breathing, he was keeping the target in sight, and that was all that mattered. It would not be long, at the target's pace, before he was run to ground.

At this second unannounced stop, the target encountered a young man who was even less friendly than the middle-aged woman. In fact, he dared to gesticulate threateningly himself, even though he must have realized with whom he was dealing and the reputation of the JUR. The target gave up the effort and moved on. But, he was beginning to flag as his energy reserves dwindled; and, by the time he returned to Katanga Boulevard, he was running only half as fast as when he had started out. The Warden smiled to himself as the gap between them shrank.

Again, the target chose to cross the intersection against the traffic in a desperate attempt to escape his tormentor, and this time the attempt nearly was fatal. One vehicle whose driver could not stop in time to avoid a collision brushed up against the running man and pushed him aside. The impact sent the target spinning and into the path of another vehicle. This time, the driver did stop in time to avoid serious injury. Amidst a shower of honking and cursing, the target managed to reach the far side of the intersection, but he was limping slightly. The Warden slowed his pace accordingly, from a fast trot to a slow trot. The target would soon be his, and so he could conserve his energy for the "kill."

The target continued down this cross-street toward the next intersection where he came to a complete halt. He had run out of breath, and the pain of his injury was increasing. He wanted to sit down and rest, but he didn't dare. He gazed down the street and spied the black-uniformed figure crossing

Katanga Boulevard. He cursed silently, reached into a pocket, and pulled out a pistol.

Rodriguez, coming up fast, recognized danger when he saw it – but not entirely to him. This particular area happened to be moderately populated with pedestrians; and many of them appeared to be off-worlders, either touring New Lagos or engaged in some private business. If the target started shooting in his direction, any number of innocents could be killed or wounded. He could not allow that to happen, as it would violate the First Principle. And, as yet, he was still too far away to use his own sidearm effectively. He raced through all available options and selected the only one which would prevent mass injuries, even if it meant risking his own life.

The idea was simple enough: he would change directions and draw the target's fire away from the innocents. The risk was also clear enough: he would have to cross over to the opposite side of the street, against traffic, and confront the target at a different angle. He had to plan this very, very carefully.

He assessed the situation and, when he spied a small gap in the traffic flow, made his move. It was like running through a maze, turning this way and that, avoiding vehicles with only a split-second's warning, and taking advantage of any and all openings of whatever size, all the while keeping one eye on the target and observing its reaction to his stratagem. Fortunately, this game of "dodge-'em" was not a new experience for him. At the Academy, the cadets underwent an exercise every ten days which consisted of running through a gauntlet of moving obstacles in order to hone one's reaction times. None of the exercises had been repeated; always, there were new configurations so that no one could anticipate an obstacle and thus defeat the purpose of the exercise. Cadet Rodriguez had suffered his share of bumps and bruises before graduation, but he managed to pass with flying colors. Now, he was being put to the real test.

He cleared the last obstacle, leaped onto the opposite curb, and scanned for signs of the target. The latter, confused by the seemingly insane maneuver, had not bothered to remain at the scene to puzzle it out but had instead used the respite to catch his breath and continue his escape. He had turned away from the uphill climb and was now hobbling down the cross-street, still searching for particular addresses. The Warden did not follow after the target but instead climbed the hill to the next cross-street and established a parallel course. If the target thought he had caught a lucky break, he was in for a big surprise.

Meanwhile, the target repeated his entreaty at a third address and was rebuffed yet again. By now, he was absolutely furious and swore that those who had refused to assist him would pay dearly once he had reported back to the JUR Directorate and put together a new task force. At least, he had lost his pursuer for the moment and did not have to run. His injury was still affecting his movement. At the next intersection, he turned and began the upward climb again. He was five meters from the next cross-street when he heard a solemn voice behind him.

"Major Tshambe, I presume?"

The JUR leader whirled about in surprise just as Warden Rodriguez stepped out from behind a bush. Hastily, he reached into his pocket for his pistol, but his adversary was close enough to neutralize the threat. Rodriguez lunged forward, knocked the pistol out of Tshambe's hand with a sharp blow to the wrist, and drew his own weapon.

"Gor, how the frag did ye manage to catch up wif me?" the Major snarled.

"You set yourself a pattern, and I anticipated your next move." He smiled broadly. "Checkmate."

"Dinna be too sure, Warden. Oi've still got some tricks up me sleeve."

"Ah, but you won't have the chance to use them."

He aimed his pistol at Tshambe. The latter's eyes went wide with shock. Rodriguez pulled the trigger and sent a somazol-tipped flechette into the man's neck. The Major clutched at it, but the drug was already acting upon him. He stared at the Warden with quickly glazing eyes.

"Damn ee to 'ell!" he whispered and slid to the sidewalk into unconsciousness.

Rodriguez stared at the unconscious man with no little contempt.

"That was for Anafu, you son-of-a-bitch!"

*   *   *

In the three-hundred-plus years since humans ventured into Deep Space, medical technology advanced by leaps and bounds, financed chiefly by the wealth generated from the colonies. Many procedures – which, in pre-ENO days, might have been called "science fiction" – were now commonplace and routine; the majority of humankind enjoyed good health and long lives, free of most diseases and disorders which formerly had killed untold millions. Whether one considered DNA scans to ascertain a disposition toward specific diseases and disorders or extra-cellular matrixes to regenerate human tissue or cryosurgery to freeze and destroy tumors or nanotechnology to repair injuries on the molecular level, there was very little medical science could not do (short of granting immortality). Even the role of doctor and nurse was in jeopardy as robotic machines handled the delicate work of rooting out the problem; humans only monitored the procedures and input suggestions for greater efficiency. No one had yet discovered a way to dispense with the human element altogether; and, truth be told, no one wanted to, as the human-patient bond was considered sacrosanct.

Warden (L1) Lixu Rodriguez observed the handling of one such patient with no little anxiety. Lt. Anafu Ralfo, currently in a coma and unable to contribute to her own recovery (at least on the conscious level), was hooked up to as many machines as necessary in order to keep her alive and her organs functioning. She looked so still, he thought, that she might be more dead than alive. Pluj were, by reason of their environment, pallid creatures, but Anafu was ghostly white as if all of her blood had been drained from her body. Or perhaps, he tried to convince himself, he was simply letting his imagination run away with him. One sure thing he did know: he was absolutely helpless to do anything for her beyond holding her hand and murmuring reassuring words (and hoping they would reach into her subconscious). He was forced to rely on the machines and their human overseers to work on bringing her out of the coma and to full functionality again.

He was not alone in his voluntary sentry duty. Sgt. Utumi stood at his side as silent and as somber as all of his kind was when they were not on their home world. He had requested of the Warden to be here and received immediate leave to do so. Of all of Gamma Platoon, only he had had close contact with the Pluj officer, had fought the enemy side by side with her, and had pronounced her a "mighty warrior." According to the Alkon Code, it was his right and duty to stand guard over her, to protect her from all attacks, and to intercede with the Great Ones on her behalf. Rodriguez was well aware of the warrior's code and had no qualms about the Capellan's being there. Besides, he could use some company himself; it made the time pass less painfully.

He glanced at Utumi surreptitiously. The other was moving his mouth, though no words could be heard. He had to assume that the sergeant was praying to one or more of the two dozen deities most of his race recognized and worshipped slavishly. He had never been all that religious himself, having been brought up by a very liberal family, but he had no reason to disallow others their beliefs if they freely chose to observe them.

"I the Great One of the Yellow Mountain have beseech," the Alkonu announced abruptly. "I Him did beg that He over Ralfo-go to watch. I to believe that He so will do."

"Someone will watch over her," the Warden murmured. "Kum'halla, your Great Ones, Anafu's Lady, Gamma Platoon, and me, for as long as it takes. I intend to be right here when she returns to the world of the living."

"I also here shall be, when duty to allow."

"Thank you for your support, Utumi-go. Would you mind if I have a moment alone with her?"

"I to understand. I outside will wait."

The Capellan saluted, first the patient, then the watcher, and marched out of the ward. Rodriguez regarded the still form again and marshaled his thoughts. There was so much he wanted – *needed* – to say; but visiting hours were limited in these circumstances, and he had to choose a few of the more cogent things on his mind. He stroked her hand tenderly.

"I can't stay for very long, my love," he spoke in Pluj. "But I'll be back as soon as I can. I've already contacted your mother, and she'll catch the next transport from Pluj to Remus. She may already be in transit. I'm not sure if I'll see her when she arrives – I hope so – because I have to give an account of myself for the colossal gamble I took in commandeering the *Steadfast*.

"And speaking of the *Steadfast*, Gamma Platoon chipped in to buy you several bouquets of flowers from Pluj and to have them shipped fresh. If – *when* you open your eyes, you'll see the biggest display outside of a florist's shop! The Platoon also sends its regards and hope you have a speedy recovery. Even Quinn choked up, and you know what a grumbler Quinn is!" He paused to choose his next words carefully. "I have never known what true loneliness was until now, and I can't imagine life without you. I love you more than Life itself, Anafu, and I will wait forever for you to come back to me." He bent down and kissed her hand. "The peace of Kum'halla be with you, dearest."

He took a deep breath and began singing a Pluj lullaby.

APPENDIX A

▼

(The following essay is the second in a series written for the Journal of the
Romulan Historical Society *[vol.74, no.2 (Gagarin 149 A.R.)] by Dr. C.
Malcolm Trowbridge, Chair of the Department of History of the University
of New Nairobi, commemorating the fiftieth anniversary of the Convention of
Aldebaran. It is entitled "The Role of Miscegenation in the Settling of Romulus
and Remus" – CC.)*

I had intended to discuss the origins of the conflict between humans and the
Ekath during the settling of Romulus and Remus, but I shall defer that essay
to a later date.

As you know, there has arisen a fierce debate over the role miscegenation
has played in the expansion of humankind's horizons into the wider Galaxy.
It began as a chance remark during a session of the Board of Governors of
Romulus, evolved into a difference of opinion between political factions
on the Board, spilled over into the House of Delegates,[57] became a clarion
call amongst the general population, and eventually seeped into the halls of
academia. Personally, I viewed the entire affair as trivial on the face of it. I
could not see what difference our genetic heritage made when it came to who
we are; we are all human, and everything else is mere detail, in my estimation.
(Of course, the Remans might have difficulty understanding that point, but
that is another matter altogether.) Nevertheless, I now find myself drawn –
against my better judgment, mind you – into this debate. Hence, this essay.

I daresay that there is not one person reading these words who is a so-
called "pure-blood" (whatever that means). I certainly am not one, and I make
no bones about it. In fact, I am rather proud of my mixed heritage. In any

---

57 The lower chamber of the legislature of Romulus. The Board of Governors is the upper
chamber – CC.

event, I cannot change what I am, nor can anyone else change him/herself. This "fact of life" is what makes the current debate so futile. Still, I will put in my two points' worth.

One of the interesting, albeit controversial, consequences of Dunia's so-called "Six-Weeks' Party" — the devastating nuclear exchange which rendered the entire Northern Hemisphere uninhabitable – was the complete miscegenation of the human race. Before then, mixed marriage/cross-breeding as both a philosophy and a practice had been limited to those progressive (and brave) individuals who saw no stigma in it. Always, throughout humankind's checkered history, the concept/actuality had been *officially* discouraged on the grounds that it provoked civil disorder. *Unofficially*, however, the reason for opposition was that it violated the tenets of "racial purity."

If one seeks the origins of "racial purity," one will have to go back to the era of pre-history before Dunia's ENO. As *homo sapiens* spread out across the planet, it split into various ethnic groups; as these groups became less nomadic and more territorial, the idea arose that unchecked interbreeding, one grouping with another, would ultimately lead to genetic "deterioration." Specifically, miscegenation was viewed as the strengthening of one gene pool at the expense of another. Therefore, groupings which claimed to be "racially superior" not only discouraged the practice but also outlawed it; and, in some parts of Dunia, the powers-that-be were not above using physical force – up to and including murder – to enforce their views.

It was not until two centuries before the end of the pre-ENO era that the "stigma" of miscegenation was loosened. Thanks to great strides in communications and transportation, the disparate segments of humanity came closer together and realized that they had more in common than they had previously believed. The door was open to a new paradigm, and our ancestors embraced it, tentatively at first, then wholeheartedly. To be sure, isolated pockets of Dunians resisted the trend, but their numbers were shrinking.

The "Six-Weeks' Party" struck the final blow upon the concept of "racial purity." The nuclear exchange between the old nation-states of the United States of America and the People's Republic of China created an upheaval of monumental proportions, not only geophysically and geopolitically but also geoculturally. Hundreds of thousands of refugees from the North fled southward toward those areas which had been largely unscathed by the conflict. They traveled by any means available – automobile, train, airplane, boat, or foot (some even found animals to ride!) – but, however they traveled, they had just one common goal: escape from radioactive fall-out.

The peoples of the Southern Hemisphere had viewed the conflict as either just desserts for the horrors Northerners had visited upon the South over the centuries or cause for alarm for fear of being dragged into a war which had no bearing on their individual or collective lives. But, as the refugees entered their territories, a new fear possessed them – the fear of radioactive contamination and a slow and horrible death. The Southerners put aside their own differences in order to meet a common threat and created a new governmental entity – the United Dunian Government – to deal with it. By reason of its easier accessibility by all concerned, the African metropolis of Nairobi was selected as the seat of the new entity. (In time, Swahili became the common language.) A quickly-selected constitutional assembly drew up a comprehensive charter, and elections for a parliament and a president followed immediately. The first order of business on the parliament's agenda was the refugee problem which, in southern eyes, was escalating.

The "Northern Solution" was swift – and drastic. Each nation-state in the South contributed to a special military unit, consisting of ground, air, and naval forces, which formed the basis of the later-named United Dunian Armed Forces. This unit closed the borders on land, patrolled the airways and sea lanes, and detained as many refugees as it could find. Special internment camps were erected, and the refugees were quarantined there under heavy guard. Any refugee who attempted to escape was summarily shot. Teams of medical personnel performed thorough physical and psychological examinations on all detainees, regardless of gender, age, or national origin. Those given a clean bill of health were issued a certificate of acceptance and allowed to continue their migration; the rest were remanded to the camps and re-tested periodically. Many became *permanent* residents. Certificate holders were required to carry their papers at all times and to present them on demand; failure to do so was punishable by a return to the camps for a period of five years.

The new immigrants faced the same challenges that countless millions before them faced: jobs, housing, and discrimination. The UDG had limited resources to devote toward settling the great influx of new citizens; a special placement bureau was set up to assist them, but the bureaucratic machinery creaked along at a snail's pace. Those newcomers who had special skills/ expertise in a wide range of occupations which the UDG sorely needed had an easier time of it and were quickly assimilated. The majority, however, had to make do as they could, and most ended up in government-sponsored work brigades where they performed menial tasks at subsistent wages. On the bright side, they were permitted to take educational courses in order to qualify for higher-paying jobs, and many succeeded in improving their lot in life.

What the Northerners could not obtain readily were mates from their own ethnic/racial groupings. In the first place, they were now the new minorities, and their choices were limited; and, in the second place, old traditions/attitudes were hard to break, and many were relegated to lives of bachelorhood and/or celibacy. Eventually, as the newcomers and especially their children assimilated into their new homes, the barriers were broken down, and Northerners and Southerners freely intermarried. The process of miscegenation has continued even to this day so that now we have achieved a new, amalgamated human race.

That is the historical background to the present state of affairs. Mixed marriage is now the norm, rather than the exception, and one must search far and wide to find a human being who wonders what the fuss was all about.

As to the debate which is currently raging, I call attention to the treatise published last month in this publication by the illustrious Dr. Tomas Bashaong, who argued that miscegenation has played only a minor role in human exploration of Deep Space and the subsequent colonization of suitable worlds in other star systems.[58]

Dr. Bashaong's two main arguments are Inevitability and Predictability. Of the two, the first requires a lengthier rebuttal.

The argument from Inevitability says that we humans would have explored Deep Space and colonized other planets even if miscegenation had never occurred. The Murchison family is given as an example. So far as anyone knows, all of the Murchisons (and their in-laws) stem from the same ethnic grouping; and rumor has it that no one in the family is allowed to marry outside of that grouping on pain of disinheritance. (Since the Fourth Murchison, the "black sheep" of the family, obvious did so, one may assume that none of his family's wealth passed into his hands – not that he needed it after he became the first Chief Constable of the Constabulary.) Whatever the motivation has been to keep the bloodline "pure," according to the argument, one must agree that the Murchisons have accomplished a great deal since the First Murchison gave humankind the MOME.

Inevitability further states that, in a given gene pool, there will always be a certain number of inventors, scientists, engineers, educators, and explorers. They will come to the fore when the proper circumstances present themselves. One may recall the hoary old question here: do events make the man, or does the man make the events? Inevitability clearly suggests the former. There is also an element of fate at work in this attitude, i.e. nothing occurs except that it is foreordained. When the circumstances are right, what will be will be, and no amount of human tampering will change it.

If one accepts this argument – and I do not – then one must believe that humankind is a collection of lab rats which are manipulated and

---

58   Cf. Dr. Tomas Bashaong, "Miscegenation: Help or Hindrance?," *Journal of the Romulan Historical Society*, vol. 74, no. 1 (Glenn 149 A.R.) — CC

conditioned until they make the "correct" choices and are rewarded for their "proper" behavior. Such a view belittles our species and diminishes our accomplishments.

Having said that, I must also say that Dr. Bashaong is absolutely right – as far as he goes. Humankind would inevitably have gone to the stars and spread its seed to other worlds. We are a plucky lot and a curious one; we want to know what is on the other side of the mountain and to settle there if it is better than where we are. Nothing in our long history has deterred us when we were determined to explore and to colonize, and that determination has propelled us far, far from our Home World and set us in a dominant position in the wider Universe.

But the argument from Inevitability does not go far enough, and neither does it explain what actually happened a century and a half ago. It is widely known that the original settlers of Romulus and Remus were chosen by lot. What is not so widely known is that the lottery was not as random as one might have thought. In a random selection, one will get all types, from common laborers to prize-winning scientists. This never happened. The selections were made from very small groups of people representing various skills and occupations; only the top five percent in each skill/occupation group ever made the lists, and the "winners" were chosen from those abbreviated lists.

So, what part did miscegenation play in this bogus "lottery"?

Social scientists on Dunia have for centuries toyed with the idea that each ethnic group possessed specific "qualities" which made that group "unique." While there have been no statistical analyses to back up this claim, the general populace has been led to believe, by sheer punditry, that such ethnic-specific qualities in fact exist. For instance, Caucasian peoples are said to be industrious (positive quality) and aggressive (negative quality). Mongoloid peoples are said to be philosophic (positive quality) and non-assertive (negative quality). And Negroid peoples are said to be athletic (positive quality) and servile (negative quality). Obviously, through observation, many members of these groups display the qualities arbitrarily assigned to them; but inductive reasoning will not work here, because there are too many biological variables at work.

We must therefore restrict ourselves to the individual and his/her genetic make-up.

Life qualities, it has been demonstrated time and again, derive from one's genetic code, passed down from one generation to the next for countless centuries. For example, if a gene or combination of genes predisposes a person toward science or art or medicine, it is highly likely that that gene or combination of genes will show up in every generation, *regardless of an individual's ethnic grouping*. Such predisposition can be, and has been, investigated via exhaustive genetic tests, long periods of observation, and extensive interviews. The facts speak for themselves.

Now, what happens when the genetic code from a given ethnic grouping is combined with that of a different grouping, i.e. via miscegenation?

Immediately, the gene pool widens as new combinations of genes occur. The resultant offspring acquires new predispositions toward life qualities (s)he would never have gained had his/her parents practiced endogamy exclusively. The newly hybridized individuals now are open to learning extra skills beyond those to which (s)he would otherwise have been limited. (Obviously, the converse might occur in that new *negative* qualities would re-enforce old ones and produce a criminal/psychopathic individual.) The more miscegenation occurs, the greater the gene pool becomes and the more skills potentially acquired. This too can be, and has been, investigated scientifically.

When Dunia was ready to send its children into Deep Space in order to colonize the new worlds of Romulus and Remus (and eventually others), the selectors had all of these data concerning life qualities at their fingertips, and so they "rigged" the lotteries to insure that only persons from highly miscegenated families would be sent out first. There would be time enough to send out "lesser mortals" who desired to escape the miseries of the Home World, but the selectors wanted them to wait until the "greater mortals" had prepared a place for them in which to thrive.

Further, once the original reports from the exploration team were thoroughly analyzed and the project managers understood what natural resources were available to potential settlers, the "lotteries" were fine-tuned again so that only certain special skills/occupations went to a specific planet. Thus, engineers, metallurgists, miners, manufacturers, etc, were on the "Romulus" list while agronomists, animal husbandry men, botanists, biologists, etc. made the "Remus" list.

In short, if Inevitability played any part in this enterprise, it was that nothing was left to chance. The entire operation was planned down to the last detail.

This process, I may add, continues to this day, and it has become more or less routine. Since miscegenation now seems to be the rule rather than the exception, the human race is thriving as it has never done when it was in the grip of "racial purity."

As for the argument from Predictability, the claim is made that humans were destined to explore Deep Space regardless of their biological make-up. Dr. Bashaong rightly points to the drive by humans in the pre-ENO era to explore the Home World from the depths of the oceans to the highest fringes of the atmosphere. And, of course, he says that, before the "Six-Weeks' Party" overtook our ancestors, they were dabbling in the exploration of the Solar System. He shall get no argument from me in that regard.

However, as an historian, I shy away from the metaphysical concept of "destiny." My studies tell me that nothing is "pre-destined" or "pre-ordained" or "foreseen" or any other phrase one cares to use. For me, cause-and-effect is the reason for most of human history; that is to say, a given event was caused by a particular set of human actions/non-actions, and that event spawns a new set of actions/non-actions. Human history is thus like a chain reaction in slow motion; if one of the variables changes, history takes a different path than it otherwise might have taken. Co-incidence, *not* pre-destination, is the key here.

Permit me to relate two examples which will back up what I have said in this essay. The first is well-known, and the second is strictly personal.

On the first settlement ship to Romulus was one Dr. Perry Bashaong, Dr. Tomas Bashaong's six-times-great-grandfather. Dr. Bashaong may or may not forgive me for dragging his illustrious ancestor into this fray, but perhaps he will understand why I chose to do so. Perry Bashaong, soon to become Romulus' first Colonial Governor, was a fourth-generation miscegenated person who held degrees in physics and chemical engineering; he was the ideal person to develop the mineral wealth of this planet. He came by his intellectual skills from his various ancestors, among whom were chemists and mathematicians. Over the course of four generations, the genetic codes of these ancestors combined and re-combined to produce an offspring who could master multiple disciplines. Further miscegenation in the Bashaong bloodline produced other remarkable offspring, including the present possessor of the family name whose talents run to mathematics and civil engineering.

Neither Inevitability nor Predictability played any part in the Bashaong family's many accomplishments. They came about only through unconscious acts of cross-breeding, i.e. co-incidence. I fear that Dr. Bashaong is short-changing his own ancestors when he promotes his theory.

My own family is not so illustrious, I must admit. Both of my parents were monoculturists; they were products of strict endogamous pairing. In point of fact, my father had been engaged to a woman in his own ethnic grouping when he met my mother. He was an archaeologist working on a dig on the North Island of New Zealand[59] at the time, and she was a native New Zealander employed as a librarian in the public library in the North Island city of Hamilton. They met purely by chance, fell in love, and moved my father to break off his engagement in order to marry my mother. I did not

---

59   The eastern half of the United Dunian Government's Administrative District #10 – CC.

know my parents very well, as they both died tragically when I was a child. But, I have done some genealogical research to learn more about them, and I am convinced that I have inherited my interest in history from their combined genetic codes. Had they not met and procreated, I should not be here to write these words. Some other "C. Malcolm Trowbridge" would be walking about, doing who-knows-what with his life!

We humans are remarkable creatures. We have explored, colonized, and developed our own planet (and, admittedly, ruined it in the process); and we have taken a giant step into the wider Universe to explore, colonize, and develop other planets. (Hopefully, we will not ruin *them*!) But, I will argue that Inevitability and Predictability were not the major actors in this drama. The fact that we improved ourselves through miscegenation – the combining and re-combining of diverse genetic codes – has made all the difference; predispositions toward various advanced skills have accomplished in a relatively short space of time what our monoculturist ancestors would have required many more generations to accomplish. No one could have foreseen this, but it is a special talent of humans to re-create ourselves whenever the need arises.

The pre-ENO Dunian philosopher, Henri Frederic Amiel, once wrote: "The universe is but a kaleidoscope which turns within the mind of the so-called thinking being, who is himself a curiosity without a cause, an accident conscious of the great accident around him, and who amuses himself with it so long as the phenomenon of his vision lasts."

Thus has it ever been.

Appendix B

▼

TABLE OF ORGANIZATION
of the
CENTRAL SPIRAL COLLECTIVE CONSTABULARY

A. General Organization
   1. Speaker of the Central Spiral Collective's Grand Assembly, who oversees
   2. The Commission for Law Enforcement (five civilians), which oversees
   3. The Chief Constable of the CSC Constabulary, who oversees
   4. The Deputy Chief Constable for Operations, who oversees
   5. The Admirals of the Fleets (10 in all), who oversee
   6. The Commodores of the Task Forces (5 in each Fleet), who oversee
   7. The Captains of the Patrol Vessels (10 in each Task Force), who oversee
   8. The Commanders of the Brigades (3 in each Patrol Vessel)

B. Patrol Vessel Organization
   1. Troop Brigade
      a. Each troop brigade consists of 4 companies (3 combat, 1 support), each of which is commanded by a Lt. Commander.
      b. Each company consists of 4 platoons, each of which is commanded by a Sr. Lieutenant.
      c. Each platoon consists of 1 Jr. Lieutenant, 1 Sr. Sergeant, 2 Jr. Sergeants, 4 Corporals, 8 Sr. Privates, and 8 Jr. Privates.

2. Fighter Brigade
   a. Each fighter brigade consists of 6 squadrons (5 combat, 1 support), each of which is commanded by a Lt. Commander.
   b. Each combat squadron consists of 4 fighter craft, each of which is piloted by either a Sr. Lieutenant or a qualified Jr. Lieutenant.
   c. Each support squadron consists of 2 heavy cruisers and 4 light cruisers, each of which is piloted by either a Sr. Lieutenant or a qualified Jr. Lieutenant.
3. Operational Brigade
   a. Each operational brigade consists of 10 sections, each of which is commanded by a Lt. Commander (except for Gold Section).
   b. The ten sections are Gold (Command), Silver (Helm), Red (Astrogation), Green (Communications), Blue (Sensors), Violet (Environment/Life Support), Black (Armaments), Yellow (Maintenance), Orange (Technical Services), and Brown (Stores)

C. Designation of Rank
   1. Chief Constable = five platinum starbursts
   2. Deputy Chief Constable = four platinum starbursts
   3. Admiral of the Fleet = three platinum starbursts
   4. Commodore = two platinum starbursts
   5. Captain of Patrol Vessel = 1 platinum starburst
   6. Commander = four diamonds
   7. Lt. Commander = three diamonds
   8. Sr. Lieutenant = two diamonds
   9. Jr. Lieutenant = one diamond
   10. Sr. Sergeant = four stripes (colored according to Zone)
   11. Jr. Sergeant = three stripes
   12. Corporal = two stripes
   13. Sr. Private = one stripe
   14. Jr. Private = no stripe